Betty Roberts was born in Wyoming County, West Virginia, graduated high school at Matoaka High, followed by graduation from the University of Virginia School of Nursing in Charlottesville, Virginia. Betty had an active career as a nurse, working in the delivery room or as a General Supervisor, with the last eight years of her nursing career spent in long term care. Betty also attended the University of Alabama in Huntsville and in Tuscaloosa, concentrating on her first love, writing. After retiring, Betty studied oil painting and with seven children and numerous grands and greats, she has no problem getting rid of her paintings. Betty spends her time writing, painting and enjoying her large family. Her other works: *Leaning into the Wind: The Wilderness of Widowhood* (under the name of Betty Bryant), *Midnight Chronicles: A Love Story* by Betty Roberts, *Cave-In* a short story published in the Scribbler, University of Alabama in Huntsville Magazine (under the name of Betty Osborne) and her latest book *Still Climbing* published under the name Betty Roberts.

Dedicated to Mom and Dad,
to mountaineers, wherever they live,
and to our servicemen who continue the battle for freedom.

Betty Roberts

IN THE SHADOW OF THE BRIDGE

AUSTIN MACAULEY PUBLISHERS™

LONDON * CAMBRIDGE * NEW YORK * SHARJAH

Ordering Information
Quantity sales: Special discounts are available on quantity purchases by corporations, associations, and others. For details, contact the publisher at the address below.

Publisher's Cataloging-in-Publication data
Roberts, Betty
In the Shadow of the Bridge

ISBN 9781685622954 (Paperback)
ISBN 9781685622961 (Hardback)
ISBN 9781685622978 (ePub e-book)

Library of Congress Control Number: 2023903650

www.austinmacauley.com/us

First Published 2023
Austin Macauley Publishers LLC
40 Wall Street, 33rd Floor, Suite 3302
New York, NY 10005
USA

mail-usa@austinmacauley.com
+1 (646) 5125767

Although this novel is based on facts, some events, characters, and places are fictional. Quotes from *The Bluefield Daily Telegraph*, and the railroad photographs were taken by Alyssa B. Weisner and are acknowledged with grateful appreciation.

Table of Contents

Thus, I set Pen to Paper with delight
And quickly had my thoughts in black and white,
For having now my method by the end,
Still as I pull'd, it came; and so I penn'd
It down; until it came at last to be
For length and breadth, the bigness which you see.

From: *The Pilgrim's Progress*
By John Bunyan, in *The Author's Apologue*

One

Developing a sense of direction in the Appalachians is difficult, for rivers run downhill but also northward, and the sun is high in the sky when you first see it, never an early sunrise like at the ocean or on the plains: light moves over the mountains and slides down into the valleys already bright.

The mountains lie northeast to southwest, not an orderly north to south, but in a pattern all their own, overlapping, meeting in deep V-shaped coves. On Flattop Mountain, the winter snows and seasonal rains gather force as they drop from over 3,500 feet to only a few hundred feet above sea level at the Ohio river.

Coon creek flows out of the southern slopes to join Gooney Otter Creek which runs down the northwestern side of Herndon mountain; together they flow through a narrow, Y-shaped cove, between deep-slashed hills, and with many twists and turns, becomes Barker's Creek, which joins Slab Fork river, forms the head waters of the Guyandotte; the cold, clear water flows north to the Ohio, west to the Mississippi, and finally south to the Gulf of Mexico.

The railroad crosses the cove on a high 17-foot span black steel bridge that is 738 feet long, and 121 feet high, crossing over the creek, the road, and the houses. Coville lies 1900 feet above sea level, yet the thousands of feet of mountains looming above the camp make it feel like it is at the bottom of the world. Cove village. Coville. Population, at the beginning of this year, 1941, one hundred and sixty-five.

Coville's mark of distinction is undisputedly the high railroad bridge spanning the break between the mountains, an engineering feat the residents view with pride, even when the cinders filter through the sleepers and fall on their houses, turning their laundry gray, and dirtying their hair.

When Faith Henley married William Phillips before the Justice of the Peace in Tazewell, Virginia, it was their second trip to the county courthouse, the first having ended unpropitiously two weeks earlier. Faith, dressed in a baby blue lace dress, and only five-feet-two, had looked underage; their marriage application was denied. William, suffering from a carbuncle on his left buttock, was too gentlemanly to explain his predicament. He was relieved at the delay: his pain was such that consummation of the marriage would have been difficult.

The week after the first trip to Tazewell, William did not contact Faith, being busy with black salve and hot soaks. The second week was spent convincing her he wanted to marry her, provided her mother would accompany them to the judge as a witness to save a second embarrassment. William refused to be accused of 'robbing the cradle' a second time.

William had been offered a job on the Virginian Railroad stringing the high voltage wiring to carry the electricity for the new electric engines. The pay was better than the Norfolk and Western, and he would be foreman, with his own crew and motor car. He talked it over with Faith, explaining they would need to move from Virginia to Wyoming County, West Virginia. Wyoming County, secluded in the high mountains, wrapped in deep primordial forests, isolated, with poor roads, and a population largely of coal miners, is at the end of the world.

"Is there a school for children?" she had asked. "You know we plan to have children."

"Oh, yeah!" William had replied, "It's not that isolated!"

Faith's answer was Biblical: "Whither thou goest, I will go, and where thou lodgest, I will lodge."

Thus, William and Faith became mountaineers, and William was as dedicated to the Virginian Railroad as Faith was to her God.

It was New Year's Eve. El placed the double-barreled shotgun firmly against her shoulder. Daddy stood behind her to catch her when the gun kicked. It will knock you down, he said, and if it is not firm, it will make a bad bruise. She pointed the old gun to the skyline where black mountains blotted out the rising moon, aimed above the high bridge with one eye to the sight and the other squinched up. She would shoot both barrels, one for the old year going out. the other for the new one coming in, tradition and thrift dictating the number. It would be a great year, Daddy said, and Mother, shivering without a coat, only her apron wrapped around her arms, agreed. Daddy always said it would be a great year, that was also tradition.

This was the first time El had been allowed to stay up until after midnight to see the old year out and the new one in. She expected to see a clearly marked difference as one year left and the other began, perhaps a change in the air, or the sounds of the night, but one faded into the other, imperceptibly running together, one second indistinguishable from the next. She was concentrating on holding the big gun just so, firmly against her old brown coat, the barrel aimed beyond the high black railroad bridge, and Daddy, his railroad watch in his hand—the watch accurate to the minute because the trains ran by his time—yelled NOW! And she pulled the trigger.

The roar of the first shot scared her and she fell against Daddy's rough Mackinaw, raking her cheek as he grabbed the gun. She had been better prepared for the second shot. El never forgot that the new year began with a disappointment. New Year's Eve had always been special, a bright glitter of time reserved for adults only. Now it was here and she was let down. It was her first inkling that growing up might not be all pleasure as she had presumed. It was New Year's Day, 1941.

She turned to Daddy. "Is that all?"

Daddy, understanding, drew her back into his arms in a rare, quick hug. Mother rushed for the door, calling them to come in, she had hot apple cider ready. They closed the door, pushed the rolled rug against it to stop the cold draft that swept along the polished hall floor, and rejoined the party.

During the first three years of their marriage, Faith and William furnished their house on the mountain in a little camp called Monte Carlo, with a solid mahogany bed, a mohair sofa, and a large, coal-burning kitchen range that warmed the whole house as well as did the cooking.

The house was isolated from others, deep into hardwood trees, with hickory and oak furnishing food for countless gray squirrels; Faith could stand on her front porch and bag dinner with one shot from her 22 rifle.

Like a mother bird, Faith feathered her nest with down-filled pillows, handmade quilts, and washable rag rugs to catch the ever-lasting black mud at the door. She had decided on three children, and William had agreed, saying, "You're the one has to do the hard part, whatever you say."

Faith talked on, democratically deciding that if she named the girls, William could name the boys. William thought all the talking was premature as they were just now in the process of making babies, and they had at least nine months to figure out names, but Faith continued: At least five years between, she had no intention of having a baby every year, wearing herself down like the mountain women, growing worn out before her time." Whatever you say", was William's reply. Indeed, it was his standard reply as Faith arranged their lives, leaving William to concentrate on his ever-demanding responsibilities on the railroad.

Faith, perhaps overly zealous at times, gave each of their daughters a Biblical name, believing it would influence the direction of their lives. William professed that religion was for women, children, and old men, and he was neither. He gave each child a common, love-inspired name, a name free from the burden of religion and more fitting for a small, helpless child.

The firstborn was christened Martha Jane, Martha for that woman so close to Jesus, the worker most admired and emulated by Faith, and Jane to honor William's mother. Faith managed to call her 'Martha' for several months, but William began and ended his conversations calling her his "sweet baby Jane." The baby responded by showing him favoritism when he was home, all the while becoming a replica of her mother, a miniature Faith, same heavy dark hair, same heart-shaped face and wide gray eyes—even at an early age she had the same serious, proud head-holding, looking level at the world and finding it good. Jane carried on a conversation like an adult, never having heard baby-talk, and she sang in church with a clear, sweet voice with perfect pitch. It was customary to ask her to entertain guests and it followed naturally that a piano would be purchased specifically for 'Baby Jane'.

When daughter number two was born, it was into an adult household of three. Faith was determined that biblical names should prevail; this child would be a constant reminder to William that he was risking eternal reprobation by refusing to accompany her to church. The baby was long in coming, stubborn and independent even before birth. Rachel Elizabeth was a long title for such a scrawny child, but Faith thought William would have trouble shortening it. She had planned to name her Mary, thinking Martha and Mary a nice precedent, but when the baby was so long overdue, she changed the name to Rachel, the last two weeks of her confinement seeming like seven years and requiring the patience of the biblical Rachel.

From birth, Rachel would lie in the oak crib nearly asleep and would suddenly jerk awake, crying, shaking uncontrollably. The more Faith tried to hold her, the worse it would get until, finally, she would put her back into her crib to cry it out. Doc Steelman said it might be Saint Vitus' dance, he had seen it before though never in one so young, a disease of the nervous system with involuntary muscular contractions, and an irritable, cantankerous disposition. Her lungs seemed weak from all the crying, causing her to have pneumonia every winter, but Daddy said, no, it was just the damn coal dust they could never get away from, and burning coal to heat the house, the smoke…whatever the cause, the sitting up at night usually fell to William, Faith being worn out with caring for her all day. Oddly enough, Rachel slept very well in her Daddy's arms.

Rachel loved to hear her mother talk about her baby years. It was her favorite story. "Tell about the old woman," she'd beg, "tell about the coffee."

"Well," Faith would begin, "you were just a month old when I took you down to Pineville to the well-baby clinic, looked like you were having fits. Now, an old woman from the mountains brought her grandbaby to the clinic and she sat, watching you, for some time. Then she told me to put some strong coffee in some cream and feed it to you with a spoon. I told the doctor about it but he just snorted!"

"After I got you home, I thought, now what would it hurt to try it? So, I tried it and it worked! Doc Steelman said it was the cream, that my milk wasn't good, but I think it was the coffee, settled your nerves somehow."

Mother would pause, remembering, then pick up the tale again. "Anyway, when we went back for your six-month checkup, you were as healthy as any baby, and at one year old, you won the award for being the healthiest baby there!"

"She was so pretty then," Jane said, "but look at her now!" and Mother said, "Jane, that's not nice!" and Bun, from her seat on Mother's lap, would say, "Pretty as me?"

Mother—predictably—would squeeze Bun and reply, "No, of course not, Honey Bun. No one is as pretty as you!"

"Not Shirley?" Bun would persist, and Mother would say, "Not even Shirley."

The story-telling would move on: Tell about El swinging on the electrical wires coming into the house, how she climbed out the window to the porch roof and called out to Mother, "Look at me, Mother!"

And Mother, in the backyard hanging clothes on the clothesline, calmly called back: "Rachel, come down here and I'll give you a cookie," and while Rachel climbed back through the bedroom window, Mother stood in the backyard thanking the Lord her baby hadn't been electrocuted. They didn't spank her; afraid the St. Vitus' Dance would return.

Tell about her climbing on top of the kitchen cabinet, pulling out the drawers to make a ladder, found sitting not a foot from the ceiling and her not yet two years old. Tell about Rachel climbing trees, or walking the top railing of the neighbor's fence and her not three, or about her running to the telegraph office over two miles away at five. Mother would sum up the stories with a quick hug, and "You'll be the death of me yet, Rachel Elizabeth!"

William had chosen the shorter Rachel over the longer Elizabeth, but it took the birth of the third daughter to shorten Rachel to a less-biblical-sounding name. When little Naomi Louise—Naomi for the unselfish mother-in-law in the book of Ruth, and Louise for Faith's own mother—began to talk, she couldn't form her "R's" well, thus Rachel came out a long slur, followed by a clear, ringing "L". Daddy, delighted, adopted it as his own, and Rachel, "ewe-lamb of God", became forever El, daughter of the devil, or at least of ole Jimmy Dickens, placed on earth to test the endurance of Faith.

Naomi Louise was an exceptionally pretty child, God perhaps compensating the parents for the errors made with the second daughter. She was red-haired, as red as the moustache William grew in spite of his coal-black hair, red in contrast to the midnight darkness of Faith and Jane, red in contrast to the muddy-water brown of Rachel's. Red, prompting old 'milkman' jokes to which Mother replied with a narrowing of her lips and a cold silence. No one ever joked about the little red-haired baby but once to Mother, and, anyway, the only redheaded man around was old man Kerrigan who ran the telegraph office for the railroad in Herndon.

Naomi Louise had skin as white as milk, and eyes as blue as the morning-glories that opened at dawn. She was born on the day she was due, between lunch and dinner while Doc Steelman was making a routine call, saving him an extra drive up to Coville from Mullins where his office was located. She slept right through her first night, allowing everyone, including Aunt Bea, who had come to take care of Mother, a good night's sleep. Naomi became Aunt Bea's pet before she had her first bath, but not just Aunt Bea: everybody loved her.

She had a disposition of sweetness and a happy smile; she would play contentedly in her crib until someone picked her up, which was frequent, for she was delicious to hold. She was soft and sweet-smelling, good enough to eat, resembling one of Mother's rolls made for Sunday dinner, a puffy white pastry covered with powdered sugar—a perfect little sugar-bun, a tasty little honey bun. Immediately, William shortened it to, simply, Bun. It suited her. It was a short, sweet, softly rounded name for a short, sweet, softly rounded baby.

Faith's three daughters were Martha, Rachel, and Naomi; William's girls were Jane, El and Bun. Although it was William who 'called the shots' as Mr. Gillespie, manager of the company store said, it was Faith who—faithfully—carried them out.

For two years, Jane had begged for a New Year's Eve party but Mother had said not until you are seventeen. This year, when she begged, Daddy said, "Oh, why not, probably won't have one next year, with the war and all," and Mother had given in.

"Well, just a small one, just the kids from Coville, not the whole county!"

Uncle Charlie and Aunt Bea came, of course, because they always spent holidays, not having kids of their own, and the Plovers, Mother and Daddy's best friends since before Jane was born, their children, Jimmy, Jr. who wore his heart on his sleeve over Jane, and Nancy Sue, who was El's best friend. Ben and Mary Beth, Jane's friends, were invited, and Will because he was just home from University, Hollie and Emmett because they were 'family', Mr. and Mrs. Collins, from next door, because it wouldn't be neighborly to have a party right in their face and after all, they were the teachers in the town.

More adults than youth, Jane said, and next year she wanted a party all her own, just her friends. El said Jane was selfish, Mother said, "We'll see," and Daddy just snapped his newspaper like he does when he's irritated.

The second El fired the old gun, Jane started playing "Auld Lang Syne", and Mother passed around the apple cider; Uncle Charlie and Daddy already had theirs in tall glasses, and Uncle Charlie sang louder than anyone.

Ben was standing next to Jane at the piano, and he kept trying to look down her sweater, all the time feeling across Mary Beth's bottom. El, from her place on the sofa beside Daddy, could see it all. Ben sat down on the piano bench with Jane and started rubbing Mary Beth's leg, and Mary Beth didn't move away like a nice girl should. El had heard Mother talk about Mary Beth, worrying about her, she could get into trouble so easy, Mother said, being raised like she was and with all those brothers, and Jane must be especially careful to set a good example for Mary Beth.

Last year, El had been sent to bed at ten o'clock, but she remembered waking up when Jane played the traditional air; this year she was enjoying being a part of the celebration.

The Plovers were getting ready to leave, Nancy Sue staying to spend the night. Ben and Will were arguing over who would walk Mary Beth home, settled it by deciding they both would, and Jane would go with them since they had to come right back by the Phillips' house to their own, next door. The four left in a flash of cold air from the front door.

"Does Mary Beth like Ben?" asked Nancy Sue.

"No, they are just friends," said Mother.

"He put his hand up her leg," said El, and Nancy Sue nodded in agreement.

"Rachel! It's not nice to talk about Mary Beth like that!" said Mother.

"I wasn't talking about Mary Beth," said El. "I was talking about Ben."

"You don't know what you're talking about," said Mother weakly.

El watched as Daddy ran an oiled rag through the old gun barrel—it had been his father's—and wrapped it in a worn-out sheet. He was saving it for his son, if he ever had one, he always added. In the meantime, El was his boy, her being a tomboy and all. She saw Mother's warning looks and knew she and Nancy Sue were being sent to bed.

Tomorrow she would show Edgar the bruise on her shoulder. She heard Ben telling Jane good night at the gate and sat up in bed to look out her window. Will was not with them; she lay back on her pillow and wondered why not. Much later she heard the creak of the Gillespie's iron gate. Will was home. It sure had taken him a long time to say good night to Mary Beth.

New Year's Day, 1941, Wednesday. The rain that began early on Tuesday continued intermittently, but the temperature was slowly rising. There wouldn't be snow today or tomorrow either, and on Friday the Phillips family would drive to Virginia to visit Grandmother Phillips. School had been out for two and a half weeks without one spit of snow, nothing but rain, rain every day, a gray drizzling mist, too wet to play outside. On the few days without rain it had been too cold to go out. Why couldn't the rain and cold come together? El had her sled by the back door, it having been brought down from the attic with the Christmas decorations, waiting for the first snow of the season. All the rain had caused rock slides on the railroad tracks, taking Daddy out to work in the middle of the night more than once.

El lay on the edge of the double bed. Nancy Sue and Bun slept spread-eagled beside her, their heads sharing a pillow, Nancy's blonde curls and Bun's red ones intermingled. The house was still and cold; Daddy had not stirred the fire—she would have heard him shaking the grate. Everyone seemed to be sleeping late after the party the night before. She thought about the party, remembered the thrill of shooting the gun and tried to move her arm. It had been a long time since she had seen Edgar; he and Joe had left for their Grandma's on the eighteenth. Edgar probably got his bike for Christmas—his grandma was very good to the boys—and, having no mother, they went to Logan for all the holidays.

Christmas had been a disappointment for El. She had wanted a bike so badly as did every kid in the fifth and sixth grade. There wasn't a bike in the camp, but they had seen them in the store in Mullins, and in the movies. El thought she would get one—she had begged and begged, but on Christmas morning she found a bright red scooter under the tree. It was safer, Daddy had said; less expensive, Jane had added; and Mother hadn't said anything.

No one understood that she had outgrown a scooter; Bun could ride it in the spring. She had no intention of using it—a scooter was baby stuff and she'd die before she let Edgar see her on it! Maybe a bike for her birthday, or maybe Edgar would let her ride his, if he got one.

She couldn't be sure Edgar liked her; sometimes he acted like it, other times he ignored her. He was older than the other boys in her room, older than all the sixth-grade boys and she thought it was so romantic, the reason he was behind in school. Edgar was four years old and Joe was two when their mother left them. Just up and left while their father was at work. Mr. Mitchell was so afraid the state would take the boys away from him that he made them hide while he was at work in the coal mines. Edgar took care of Joe until he was six years old and they started school the same year. Because Edgar was already eight, Mr. Collins promoted Edgar to the second grade, leaving Joe in first grade, and now Edgar was doing fifth and sixth grade work every day so that next year he could start Herndon Jr. High School in the seventh, finally catching up with boys his age. Edgar was so smart, much smarter than most fourteen-year-olds—everybody said so—and he was by far the best looking, blond hair and blue eyes, while Joe's hair was coal black, and his eyes were brown. Edgar was tall—taller than El—and really fast: he was the only boy in the camp who could outrun her.

Maybe he did like her, he had come over to tell her goodbye before he left for Logan, staying long enough to listen to the radio, squatting beside the Philco on his heels. She thought back to that day. The family was seated for dinner when he knocked on the back door, and Mother had asked him to join them for dinner. El knew she would just die if he accepted, but he had refused. He started to tell her he was leaving when Daddy put his hand up for silence. The news was on and nobody talked when the news was on, not even company. Edgar knew not to interrupt.

...explosion in the mine directly below the streets of this southern West Virginia coal capital, killing seven men and injuring another five. This is the sixth major mining disaster this winter in the nation, and the second in West Virginia...

"Where?" cried Mother.
"Listen!" commanded Daddy.

...occurred two miles inside the No.4 mine of the Raleigh Coal & Coke Company, which has three mines operating on the outskirts of the city...

"Beckley," said Edgar, "it's at Beckley No. 4."

...as is customary after a disaster, all mines will be closed tomorrow. This is the first serious accident this company has had in forty years. There were 70 men working inside when the blast occurred. All but twelve were in an unaffected area. The rescue team brought the bodies out on coal cars through entrance #3 which is only a short....

"It's a slope mine," said Edgar.
"You're right," said Daddy, looking at him from under his brows. "How did you know?"
"Pa worked there a while, few years back."

U.S. Bureau of Mines termed 1940 the blackest year in more than a decade, from the standpoint of lives lost. In five previous disasters a total of 267 men have been killed this year, and now, with this accident, there have been 274 deaths…

"My God!" exclaimed Daddy.
"Bud, the children…" said Mother.

…another tragic reminder to those who are preventing the enactment of the Neely-Keller mine inspection bill, that more innocent blood…

"Turn it into politics, you bastards."
"Bud!"

…will not be released until after notification of kin. A crowd of about two hundred gathered at the entrance to No. 4, and about the same at No. 3 for the man-trip to come out with the dead. There was no hysteria, and only two screams were heard as the first ambulance started up the road to Beckley…

"I told you, Beckley", said Edgar. He waved awkwardly at El as he left. "See ya," he said and jammed his cap on his head even before he got out of the dining room.

El remembered sitting so still, afraid someone would surmise how she felt and tease her; she didn't want to call attention to herself so she ate the cold spinach she had left on her plate. Mother looked at her, but it was Jane who spoke.

"Why, El, you ate your spinach! Ain't love grand!"

"She said 'ain't', Mother. Jane said 'ain't'."

"It's going to be a sad Christmas for those families," was all Mother said. She never corrected Jane like she did her.

They would have a big breakfast because Daddy was home. Later, they would take down the lights from around the porch, pack away the candles that had burned in the front windows. The dried popcorn and cranberry strings from the tree would go over the clothesline post for the many brown sparrows and the black and white ladder-backed woodpeckers.

The glass ornaments would be wrapped carefully in quilting cotton 'til next year. Daddy would carry the dead hemlock outside, leaving a trail of fine flat needles on the patterned living room rug and on the polished hardwood floor of the hall. The dry pine branches would be removed from the piano and from the gilt-trimmed mirror in the hall. The wax choir boys, in their red robes, would be taken from the octagonal table, packed in a box lined with excelsior; Bun would kiss them goodbye before the lid was tied down with a discarded red ribbon. Christmas was wonderful, with presents, bright lights, turkey, fruit cake and gingerbread men: packing Christmas away was sad.

Thursday was spent cleaning house and packing for their trip to Virginia. Daddy had three days off—he had stayed on call all through the holidays— and Charlie Wolfe was in charge of the line gang. Daddy would not report back to work until Monday, unless, of course, there was an emergency.

The family gathered for the evening meal and it was unusually quiet. Mother tried to revive the holiday euphoria, to a lesser degree, with cheerful talk, but Daddy seemed preoccupied.

"What did you like best about Christmas, Bun?" she asked.

"Santa Cause," Bun responded quickly, bringing a light chuckle from all.

"Me too," said El.

"*You liked Santa Claus?*" said Jane, knowing her disappointment over the bike.

"Sure, young Santa—you know, in the play," said El.

"Oh, you would!"

The church had presented a play by members of the Sunday school and Edgar had played the part of a young Santa, coming to the rescue of an Old Santa, played by Mr. Gillespie, his belly being just right for the role. The two Santa's distributed brown paper bags holding candy, nuts and a Florida tangerine, goodie bags prepared by the Ladies Missionary Society, no small task for there were one hundred and thirty-five children in the Sunday school. The church served both Coville and Herndon and was built on the main highway halfway between the two towns.

"What did you like best, Daddy?" asked El.

"Oh, I don't know," said Daddy thoughtfully. "There is so much to study about just now."

They waited, knowing Daddy would continue when he had it sorted out.

"I guess the best Christmas present came several days before Christmas."

"What was that, Bud?" asked Mother, trying to recall a special treat.

"The President's plan for aid to Great Britain," he said.

"Oh, that!" exclaimed Jane. "That doesn't count! We mean here—at home, our Christmas!"

"Well, Jane, you see," said Daddy slowly, "in the long run, that decision probably means our Christmases will stay just like they are—and that's a mighty good present."

"I don't understand," said El.

"I do," said Jane with a superior air. "He means the 'pay in kind' proposal that President Roosevelt presented in his speech. I don't think that counts, Daddy", and she reproached him with the tone of her voice.

"Well, how about your Mother's oyster dressing—does that count?" He reached across the table and roughed up Ellie's hair, "We liked that, didn't we, El!" They laughed, remembering how El and Daddy had stolen the crisp, browned oysters out of the mixing bowl almost as fast as Mother could fry them, leaving barely enough to flavor the turkey dressing.

"Next year I'm going to make chestnut dressing, the way my mother used to make it, and you two can fry your own oysters!" said Mother.

"Mama," said Bun, "what did you like?"

Now Mother was thoughtful. "Well, there were several special moments. After you were all in bed, your Daddy and I sneaked up the stairs just to look in on you…I felt very fortunate, the three of you, my pretty girls…" She didn't tell them that she and Bud were making sure they were all asleep before putting Santa's gifts under the tree. They knew Jane didn't believe in Santa, but there was Bun, only five years old, and they didn't know about El—she acted like she thought there was a Santa, but she would be twelve soon…they just didn't know.

"And then there was the lighting of the Yuletide Tree in Washington, his words…I have them here, somewhere; I think they bear repeating, if you'd like…"

"We'd like, wouldn't we, girls," said Daddy, sensing that Faith wanted to read them.

"I was asleep," said Bun. "I didn't hear the presents' words."

"That's right, Honey Bun," said Daddy, "you slept right through it."

Mother pushed her chair back and went to her desk in the living room, returning with a clipping from the *Bluefield Daily Telegraph*. "What I saved," said Mother, "was an article quoting several people. Maybe you'll understand why I kept it if I read it all. We're so fortunate to live in a land like ours."

El twisted in her chair; Bun supported her head on her chairback, struggling to keep her eyes open. Jane folded her napkin neatly, placed it beside her plate, and Daddy moved his chair back, crossed one leg over the other and began filling his Briarwood pipe. Mother began to read:

By the Associated Press from Berlin, the words from Hitler's Deputy, Rudolf Hess, came through the night and into the German homes.

Almighty God, you gave us our Fuehrer… now give the power to him…
Goering: May next Christmas be one of peace …and victory.

El wondered who Goering was but didn't ask; it would prolong the reading and she found it boring. Bun's head was against the back of her chair, her eyes were closed. Bun was asleep.

"Now this is what our President said when he turned on the Yuletide tree lights," said Mother.

"President Roosevelt: "It cannot be a 'Merry' Christmas, but for most of us it can be a 'Happy' Christmas, if by happiness we mean we have done with doubts, that we have set our hearts against fear, that we still believe in the golden rule of all mankind, that we intend to live more purely in the spirit of Christ and that by our works as well as by our words, we will strive forward in faith, and in hope and in love." "Declaring it to be "Unintelligent" to be defeatist," Mr. Roosevelt added: "Crisis may beget crisis, but the progress underneath does not wholly halt—it does go forward. Mankind is all one—and what happens in distant lands tomorrow will leave its mark on the happiness of our Christmas's to come."

Mother concluded the reading and there was silence around the table. Daddy cleared his throat. "I guess that was what I was trying to get across," he said, "We've had a good holiday. It may never be the same."

Bun was asleep. She had missed the 'present' again. Daddy gathered her up in his arms and started up the stairs.

"Mother," said El softly, "are we going to be in the war?"

"I hope not, Ellie, I certainly hope not." She rose from the table. "Help Jane with the dishes now, and hurry up to bed. We'll be getting up early in the morning."

Two

William and Faith had been born in Virginia. Their great-grandfathers had fought the Indians and the English while the Scotch-Irish population had grown and prospered. Grandfather's farm had wide open spaces, valleys, and gently rolling hills, sweet-flowing rivers, livestock and game grazing in proximity, a land of gentle breezes and clean air, a fact that Mother always commented on.

Daddy drove on their long trips, with Mother beside him and the three girls in the back seat of the "Tin Lizzie", an old Model A Ford.

Grandmother's house was large and rambling; the girls were free to explore the house, barn and sheds, the fields and woodlands with minimum supervision. There were cousins to play with and Aunt Maude even washed the dishes, saying it wasn't fair to ask the little ones to do it when there were so many to wash.

There was an unexpected air of excitement on this trip: Daddy was talking about buying a new car. He and Uncle Cameron left early on Saturday morning and didn't return until almost dark; when they came back it was not in the Tin Lizzie, but in a shiny-new, 1940 four-door sedan, a gray, chrome-trimmed Ford, a "real bargain" Uncle Cameron said, for it was a "demonstrator" and only he had driven it.

"Can we afford it?" Daddy asked Mother. "Cameron can fix it up for us, if you think we can swing it."

"How much?" asked Mother.

"It's a Demonstrator, only a few miles on it, practically new," said Uncle Cameron, moving his cigar from one side of his mouth to the other.

"How much?" Mother asked again.

"Five hundred, and the Tin Lizzie," said Daddy.

"That much!" cried Mother.

"We need new tires," said Daddy, "and we'll have to overhaul the Tin Lizzie before spring to keep her going."

"Yes, and she needs washing, too," said Mother sarcastically. "How many miles?"

"Now, Faith," said Uncle Cameron, "that doesn't matter!"

"Oh, yes it does!" Mother cut in quickly. "Tires are five, maybe six dollars, Bud can do his own overhaul, that won't cost much, and besides, it's not like it is a *new* car, Cameron!"

"Well, practically new, Faith!"

"But not *new*, new!"

"For cryin' out loud, Faith!" said Daddy. "Do we, or don't we!"

"Four hundred and fifty—and the Tin Lizzie," said Mother.

"He won't make anything on the car at that, Faith," said Daddy.

"And why should he? He's your brother! You certainly do enough for him! And, besides, if you take this one off his hands, he will get another—a really new one—make it a demonstrator, or whatever you call it!"

"Okay, okay, okay!" Uncle Cameron handed Daddy the keys. "It's all yours. Send me a check when you get home."

The girls could hardly believe it. A brand-new car, never mind the miles Uncle Cameron had put on it, what a Christmas! For the first time, El forgot her longing for a bike.

They left Virginia immediately after breakfast, Uncle Cameron coming to see them off, still glowing with the special pride a good salesman has in his product, taking his pocket handkerchief out to shine the headlights and polish the chrome." Now, Billy, you call me if you have any trouble, any trouble at all, and I'll make it right."

"You bet I will, much as I paid for this thing!" said Daddy.

The girls piled into the back seat. The upholstery was gray, soft and warm, feeling like old Marsha's fur coat; the seats were seamed with large covered buttons to hold it smooth. El laid her cheek against the tufted back and breathed in the newness. Aunt Maude had loaded the trunk with Virginia beauties from her own trees, held in the cellar until William came home. The fresh scent of the car blended with the smell of apples, mixed with the pungent spices of a Virginia country ham, wrapped in brown paper and placed on the floor boards in the back seat, Aunt Maude's Christmas present to her favorite brother.

"Best git goin'," Uncle Cameron said. "They's weather moving in, mought git right bad afore you git home."

Mother and Aunt Maude hugged again, promising to write; Aunt Maude had Jane roll down her window and she handed one more bundle for the back seat. "Might need this," she said. El knew it would be fried egg and biscuit sandwiches, wrapped in brown paper by Aunt Maude while everyone else was getting ready to leave. They would taste good, about noon, when they stopped on Brushy Mountain to eat; that and an apple, and the silver-cold mountain water would have to do until they reached home. There were no eating places along the way.

Jane sat behind Mother and Ellie sat behind Daddy with Bun in between, leaning first on one and then the other. They were not out of town before Bun hollered potty, but Daddy made her wait until they were past the houses and out in the country. He pulled over, opened both doors to shield her from view by the Sunday morning traffic. Once out of the car, Bun couldn't go; she squatted on her heels, screwing up her face for all the world like she was trying to pee.

"Come on, Bun, we've got to go."

"Just a minute," said Bun. They sat in silence, helping her concentrate.

"Oh, for heaven's sakes," said Jane. "Why didn't you go before we left Aunt Maude's!"

"Didn't hafta," Bun said. Mother reached down, picked Bun up, pulled her panties up and sat her on her lap.

"Close the door, Jane. She can use her potty later." Bun began to cry. Jane and El brought out their borrowed books and began to read. El thought the best part of the trip to Virginia was the many books they borrowed from Aunt Maude. Aunt Maude was a school teacher, like Mr. Collins: school teachers always had books.

By the time they reached Wytheville, it was raining steadily, a cold drizzle that seeped into everything, a soft hum on the roof, sounding loud in the silence of the car.

"Don't this motor purr?" asked Daddy. Later he commented, "Reminds me of sleeping under a tin roof."

"Makes me sleepy," answered Mother.

"Go ahead, take a nap."

"No, I'll sleep tonight."

"I may not, if this keeps up."

"Why does it have to rain all the time?" complained El.

"It doesn't," answered Daddy.

"Seems like it," insisted El.

"Almanac says West Virginia has about a hundred and forty rainy days a year," said Daddy. "That's on average."

"That's not even half the time," agreed Mother.

"That's two sunny days for every rainy day," Daddy said.

"Doesn't seem like it," insisted El.

"We pay more attention to bad days, because they interfere more in what we want to do," said Mother. "But when we look back, it's the good things we remember."

"Yes," agreed Daddy, "and we remember them as being better than they were!"

"Like sleeping under a tin roof!" Mother said, laughing.

Jane and El read, Bun slept on. Mother and Daddy talked sporadically. "If this keeps up, we're in for trouble."

"It will be much worse in the mountains—I just hope you aren't called out."

"The storm is traveling a good deal faster than we are."

"Temperature seems to be dropping, too."

"Easy to tell we're driving north."

"Yep."

As they started up Big Walker Mountain, the wind began to rise, buffeting the car, making it difficult for Daddy to hold it in the road. The trees were bare, but the dead leaves swirled across the road, picked up from their winter beds in the ditches. As they crossed the Appalachian trail and entered Jefferson National Forest, the wind-driven rain, more sleet than water, crackled against the window and the car rocked with the force.

"We're in for a snow storm," said Mother, seriously concerned as she watched the changing conditions. El secretly hoped it would snow; at home, her sled was waiting by the back door.

"Cameron said there was a bad one coming; he usually knows."

They crossed Brushy Mountain through sleet and fog that obscured the dense forest on either side of the road, and reached Rocky Gap where the cold water ran from an iron pipe pushed horizontally into the rock. This was their usual stopping place; they would eat the fried eggs on biscuits, drink the icy water, run through the woods, find a rhododendron bush for an outdoor toilet, using the large waxy leaves for paper, and return to the car knowing they were halfway home. But today the sleet continued, and Daddy pushed on, hoping to make Bluefield before it began to snow. They ate in the car, with nothing to drink.

On top of East River Mountain, they crossed the Virginia-West Virginia state line, and at four thousand feet, the sleet had changed to snow. It was sticking to the rocks, outlining the bushes and tree branches. In the sheltered curves it began to accumulate, but on the outward rims the wind swept it away.

"We don't have chains," Daddy commented, thinking aloud.

"Where are they!" cried Mother.

"Let 'em go with the Tin Lizzie. Wouldn't fit these tires anyway. We'll get some in Bluefield."

El watched the snow-covered patches of the road; she wanted to say, IF they reached Bluefield, but she kept quiet, trying to help Daddy by not talking. He seemed glued to his place behind the wheel: he had not moved his head or his hands for miles. And he was very quiet. So was Mother.

From the top of the mountain, travelers could usually look down into the valley, for the road jutted outwardly, projecting over the rim, leaving an unobstructed view of the river winding through the pastures below. El thought about the many times they had stopped at the lookout, at the carpet of blue flowers covering the fields from which the city took its name. Chicory, Mother said. Daddy did not stop today, nor could they see the town. There wasn't a glimmer of the shining river below: they were looking into turbulent clouds that roiled and tumbled, stretching outward as far as they could see. Halfway down the mountain they came out of the clouds, the snow disappeared, and there was only icy rain.

Jane put her book away and watched the winding, dizzy descent. "We won't need chains after all," she said, relieved that the snow was gone.

"It's Herndon Mountain I'm worried about," said Daddy.

"Is it higher, Daddy?" asked El. "Not higher, but rougher, and farther north," he said, "And later, and darker," he added softly to himself.

"Will we make it?"

"Of course, we will!" said Mother stoutly. "Don't we always?"

"We've got to," said Daddy grimly.

31

In Bluefield they found a filling station, the lights burning brightly in the early afternoon. The rain continued in a steady drizzle. Daddy bought chains for the rear tires and added one more box to the floor of the backseat, not wanting to put them on unless necessary for fear of ruining the new tires.

Mother bought grape sodas for El and Bun, threatening them with the end of the world if they spilled it on the brand new car that had to last at least through her lifetime, if not through theirs, because with the price they had paid and with the war going like it was, they would never have another one as long as she lived. Mother and Jane had Coca-Colas, and Daddy went inside the grimy station for hot coffee in a thermos-bottle cup, drinking two large cups so hot it was steaming while he drank it.

When the soft drinks were finished, Mother took them to the dirty restroom, holding Bun over the seat, watching while El squatted over it, careful, don't touch anything, you'll get germs on you, and Bun got away while Mother used the toilet, running into the station and calling to Daddy, "Didn't get any Germans on me, Daddy, didn't get any Germans on me!" El, embarrassed, went to the car without her.

They left Bluefield somewhat rested and, as if to ease the trip, the rain slacked too. Only heavy, dark clouds remained, seeming to follow them as Daddy tried to make up lost time. When they drove through Princeton, Mother's spirits seemed to brighten. She tried to interest him in the landscape but he kept his attention on the road, pushing the new car on straight stretches, easing into the curves, swinging as little as possible.

"Look how neat and clean these streets are," Mother said as they entered the town. "There's the courthouse—it looks like the state capital, doesn't it."

"Not as pretty," said El, remembering the one time she had seen the West Virginia capital, in Charleston. The gold dome of the state capital reflected in the Kanawha River like a rare painting.

"This is a pretty town," Mother said, almost to herself. The winding road led through Kegley, and downward. Suddenly the mountains opened into a wide valley with a small lake in its center. They reached a fork in the road, where State Road 10 turned toward Matoaka, and Route 19 continued to Beckley.

"That's the way to Beckley," said El, "where the mine blew up before Christmas, right?"

"Yes," answered Mother. "That was bad, really bad." But El was thinking about Edgar; tomorrow school would start and she would see him. She didn't reply.

There were rich bottom lands surrounding the lake and on both sides of the road, following the natural valley made by the Bluestone River. Only an occasional house was sighted, large, two-storied white houses, built for large farm families with strong sons to tend the land.

"Even the towns through here are pretty," said Jane. "Spanishburg, Lake Shawnee, Matoaka—"

"What's wrong with Coville?" interrupted El crossly.

But Jane and Mother ignored her, listening instead to what Daddy was saying: "That's old Red Kerrigan's place. It used to be a schoolhouse and he rebuilt it. I've heard it's a showplace inside."

"And he drives from here to Herndon every day?" asked Mother incredulously.

"It's not so far, not when you get used to it," Daddy said. "Course, if the weather is bad, he has to stay over, but that's not often."

"Would you mind a drive like this?" asked Mother.

"No, not if it would get you and the girls out of the coal camp. There's miners drive all the way from Princeton, I've heard, but I don't know that for a fact."

El felt a growing fear move through her; was Mother considering leaving Coville? She might never see Edgar again!

"I couldn't get to work fast enough from here if there was trouble," said Daddy and El relaxed a little. Still, she watched Mother, almost knowing she was not fully convinced. Mother would not give up so easily if she set her mind to it.

They were climbing again, leaving the fertile valley below. The storm moved in suddenly after the lull, and Ellie thought it had let up just to give Mother a good look at the pleasant valley with the gentle river of blue water. It was only three o'clock but it was getting dark. In Matoaka the street lights were burning by the drug store, a yellow spot in the fog and rain. At the train station there was no one in sight, and the parking lot beside the Baptist Church was empty; being a Sunday, the A&P grocery store was closed. It was an eerie ghost town, with silent, deserted streets.

As they climbed to Arista, the storm engulfed them again, breaking apart over their heads as they ascended Herndon Mountain. They were inside the clouds and thunder vibrated around them, roll after roll, rocking the car with its force, raising the hair on their arms with the electricity, running up their spines, crackling in their hair. With each loud noise, Bun, curled between El and Jane in the back seat, stirred restlessly in her sleep. El held her tighter, patting her gently and Jane leaned forward, her arms on the back of Mother's seat, watching each turn in the road.

"Can you see where you're going?" Jane asked Daddy.

"Yep," he answered, then, trying to ease the tension, added, "It's like driving through cold potato soup!"

"Ugh!" said Jane.

"I'd like to have a good bowl of potato soup now," he continued, "hot or cold."

"You should have eaten two biscuits," Mother chided.

"We'll eat soon", Daddy said. "We'll be home soon."

As if to contradict his reassuring statement, the rain began to freeze as they climbed higher and higher. It lumped against the windshield wiper blades, accumulating between the half-moons cleared with each swipe, sticking on the hood and fenders. As they left Arista the hard-surfaced road ended and they were on an unpaved stretch all the way to the top of the mountain, to the Wyoming county line. Mercer county had not placed this section of the highway on a high priority for funds.

They had not passed a car since leaving Matoaka. The low slush of the tires on the graveled road, the thick snow falling heavily, the whump of the windshield wipers, the silence in the car—all made them feel isolated and afraid. Daddy spoke their fear aloud.

"If we slid off this mountain, they wouldn't find us 'til spring."

"Hush, Bud. You'll frighten the girls."

"We're already frightened," said Jane as they felt the car slip on the curve.

"Look down there, see if the siding at Hiawatha is full."

As Jane leaned back to look out the window, the car slipped again. "I said, look, not jump!" yelled Daddy.

"Sorry," said Jane. She and Mother tried to spot the railroad far below, but the snow was too thick. "Can't see a thing," said Jane.

Daddy had slowed the car to a crawl, hugging the inside lane close to the mountain and sounding his horn each time they rounded a curve. The road was becoming more hazardous with each mile as the packed dirt surface began to hold the snow without melting. The windshield began to freeze under the wiper blades, and a thin film of ice covered the glass, like looking through water.

"We'd never have made it in our old car, Faith," said Daddy solemnly.

"No," she agreed. "Wouldn't have had the power."

"Or the traction, on those old tires."

"What are we going to name this car?" asked El.

"Talk about that later," Daddy said grimly. "I should have put those chains on in Matoaka."

Bun stirred, stretching her legs across Jane.

"Potty, Ellie" said Bun. "I've got to go potty."

"Not now," whispered El. "But I've got to!" and Bun began to cry. "Want up there, mama, want up there with you!"

"No, Bun, not now, wait 'til we get to the top—Daddy's going to stop at the top and put the chains on, just a few minutes."

"Be a sweet little lady, now," coaxed Daddy, "help Daddy out, Honey Bun."

Just before the mountain leveled off there were two curves, both deeper than average, with poor grading, sloping to the outer rim, away from the mountain. Daddy crept around the first one, hugging the inside lane. As he approached the second one, he swore softly. The side of the mountain had given way: a rock slide covered the inside lane, forcing him to the outer edge. The surface was covered with ice where the water had dripped across the road, and the wind, howling with gale force around the mountain tip, had swept the road free of snow.

Daddy held the accelerator down with a steady pressure, staying as near the rock slide and as far from the edge as possible, but the car began to slide, sliding sideways at an angle. It held for the space of a breath, then slid again. He held the gas pedal down, not touching the brakes, but the slow backward slide did not stop: the wheels had a mind of their own, skating over the ice, lightly turning with nothing to grab. The car drifted to the edge of the packed dirt surface, easy, almost gently, sliding toward the edge of the mountain, heading for the valley far below. There were no rails; the trees were several feet below the road's edge: There was nothing to stop them.

"Don't move, don't anyone move," hissed Daddy between his teeth. Mother closed her eyes, her mouth working in prayer.

Slowly, gently, barely touching the pedal, Daddy began to brake. The right back wheel went off the packed surface into the soft dirt at the edge, digging into the loose, narrow strip of earth that remained. The sliding stopped as the car swung at right angles across the road and both rear wheels dug into the loose gravel on the crumbling edge. Carefully, he pulled the emergency hand brake and took the car out of gear.

"Now, girls, we are in a tough spot. We could go down the mountain. We won't go far, and we won't get hurt—we'll hit a tree before we get to the bottom." He took a deep breath. Mother opened her eyes.

"Trouble is, I won't have any way to get us back on the road before morning."

"Now, don't anybody move—don't even breathe", he continued. "I've got to get out and get a rock behind those wheels."

He eased the door open carefully and the icy wind swept into the warm car, freezing them, bringing home the terrible realization that they could freeze to death before they were found if they went over the edge. Daddy stepped one foot out, lifted his weight from the seat, knowing that any movement could crumble the road beneath the car.

"Put your foot on the brake, Faith."

"Bud, I—I can't. I'm afraid I can't hold it."

"Damn it, Faith! Do what I tell you! You've got to! I've got to scotch those wheels! Put your foot right here and push—push hard!"

Mother held the brake, reaching her foot across, not moving from her side of the car, pushing until the veins stood out on the side of her neck and her glasses slipped on her nose. Daddy closed the door gently, reducing the cold wind. He found two large rocks and placed one behind each of the rear wheels.

"Girls," Mother whispered, "whatever you do, don't move."

El realized the danger was acute. She gripped Bun's hand and whispered softly to her. "You can have one of my dolls when we get home if you don't move an inch."

"Which one?" Bun whispered back.

Did it hurt to die? El had never thought much about dying; she tried to imagine what it would feel like. She wouldn't want to hurt; she wouldn't want Bun to hurt either. She had heard that if you freeze to death, you went to sleep first. That would be better than hitting a tree and getting hurt. She thought of Bun, pictured her asleep, little red curls in tight coils, chubby fingers together like when she said her prayers, but she didn't like to think about her little sister dead. It would be easier to think about Jane dying; with Jane gone she would be the oldest and wouldn't be bossed around so much. Jane looked pretty when she was asleep, her hair got loose and spread out like Edgar Allen Poe's raven, black against her pillow like a raven's wing and her face wouldn't be frowning—she'd look like the pictures of Snow White, waiting for her Prince to wake her with a kiss. Trouble was, Jane was so picky, she'd probably sleep a thousand years before a Prince came along who would suit her!

El concentrated, and tried to picture herself dead, but it was impossible: she had never seen herself asleep.

She could see the side of Mother's face. Her eyes were closed, her lips were moving. Maybe she should pray too: *Lord, forgive my sins, especially for being so mean to Judith and Mr. Reeves, and for being so fussy with Bun and hateful to Jane.*

The chains rattled as Daddy worked them carefully around the back wheels. He came to the door and spoke to Faith. "We're going to be all right now, but you'll have to help me."

"What do you want me to do?" asked Mother.

"Move over here and take the wheel. You'll have to pull forward a foot or two so I can hook the chains."

"Bud, I don't think I can—what if we start sliding again—you'll be behind the car!"

"Damn it, Faith, that's nonsense! You'll have to do it!" He didn't wait for an answer, but closed the door. Mother moved cautiously to the driver's seat.

"You can do it, Mom," whispered Jane and El thought it sounded so strange, Jane calling her 'Mom', like she had grown up suddenly.

"Sure, you can," said El, but she didn't risk calling her Mother 'Mom', like Jane did. She and Bun crossed their fingers and squeezed their eyes shut. El began to shiver, as much from the suspense as from the cold; she felt the car begin to inch forward, the tires spinning, throwing mud on Daddy's good tweed overcoat, gradually burning the ice away for a few feet, finally resting on the chains.

Once the chains were in place and the huge rocks again behind the wheels, Mother moved back to her seat, Daddy took the driver's place. Holding one wheel on the edge of the road in the loose gravel, the car slowly rounded the final curve and topped Herndon Mountain.

There were no tracks on the downward trail; only the next curve was visible through the snow, then the next. Daddy was using the lowest gear to hold the car back instead of the brake, inching his way around and down, around and down, corkscrewing into white nothingness with no end in sight, foot by foot into breathless silence. The lights on the falling snow shone only a few feet ahead, occasionally touching the dark north side of a tree trunk or a wet spot on the clay bank where the snow had blown away.

As the road leveled off, Garwood railroad bridge loomed black out of the white haze, and a deep sigh of relief went through the car as they all exhaled.

"We made it," breathed Daddy.

"I knew we would," said Mother.

"Oh, you did, did you! Why were you praying so hard back there? Weren't you asking for 'divine deliverance' up on the mountain?"

"Of course not!" said Mother stoutly. "I was merely thanking Him in advance!"

"Thy will be done," said Daddy sarcastically.

"It wouldn't hurt you to try a little prayer, once in a while!" replied Mother. As they approached the road into their camp, a snow plow came toward them, followed closely by a flatbed truck where two men stood, throwing cinders in a wide arc across the road.

"Ain't that the way? Now that we don't need them. A day late and a dollar short."

"That sounded like Mr. Gillespie," said Mother, but her lips were still tight with aggravation.

When they reached home, they found the house warm and comfortable. Thank goodness for Hollie, bless her little heart, wasn't she sweet to come out in this storm to tend their furnace. Daddy asked how do we know it was Hollie, might have been Mr. Reeves. But mother said no it was Hollie and they should get right to bed and unload the car in the morning, but Daddy said, no the apples might freeze. Besides he might be called out and would need the car. You take care of the girls, I'll take care of the car.

Just before she drifted off to sleep, El heard the hall telephone ring. Daddy was being called out to work, probably to work all night clearing the ice from the tunnels, maintaining the catenary system so the trains could go through, more than likely work all day tomorrow if this storm continues to rage. She remembered her prayer on the mountain and added a line, *" Lord, please keep my Daddy safe and not too cold tonight."*

The holidays were over. Tomorrow school would resume. And Edgar would be home.

"Spirit of America" Artist Zula Larson

Three

Monday morning dawned dark and cloudy; the mountain tops obscured by snow falling steadily. It had snowed all night, heavy wet flakes accumulating on trees and fences, covering the deeply-rutted road in front of the house. El looked out of her bedroom window, her room being on the front of the house, and cried in dismay: school would be cancelled. No one would be out in this unless they had to. It was eerily quiet, the snow blanketing even the sound of the wind, and inside the house no one was stirring. She couldn't see where Daddy parked the car and was unable to tell if he had made it home or was still out. It was cold in her room, freezing her bare feet as she slipped out of bed to go to the bathroom. Bun slept soundly beside her, Jane's door was still closed, but Mother's was open, and the bed was empty. Leaving the bathroom, she tiptoed down the stairs, coming into the kitchen just as Mother opened the back door.

"Ellie! Go back and get your robe! You'll catch cold!" Mother stood at the furnace door, feeding small sticks of kindling into a sparse blaze.

"Daddy's still out?" Ellie asked.

"Yes, and school has been cancelled—you can go back to bed until the house warms up, if you'd like. No use you getting up this early."

El went to her room and put on her warm blue chenille robe and her socks. Bitterly disappointed, she returned to the kitchen. Maybe, since there was no school, Edgar and Joe could come over later and they could play games or— but Mother stopped her planning with a shake of her head.

"The roads are closed, El. This is one of the worst snow storms we've had for years. I'm afraid your friends won't make it back from Logan today. You might as well forget about that."

"If it stops can I go out to ride my sled?" she asked.

"Not much chance of that," Mother said. "You'll have to find something else to do today. You and Bun can have the old catalogue now. I just got the new one."

El and Bun would cut out men, women and children from the catalogue, playing with them like paper dolls, complete with clothing, beds, rugs, and a regular household, all spread out on the steps between the downstairs and upstairs, requiring anyone going up or down to step over their "houses". Jane was the only one who fussed.

El knew early that her family was different from the others in the camp, thinking it likely due to the fact that Mother was from Virginia. She thought Mother brought manners and customs somewhat more refined, a bit more particular, than her neighbors, or was it just that Mother tried harder?

Daddy said that his fortune was made when he married Mother, not because her family had money—they were poor as beavers without a pond—but because of her thrift and industry which rode side by side with an ambition to build a better tomorrow. Thrift and ambition, complementing each other, the sum total of Mother's being, or, as she put it, just doing the best you can with what you've got. She would be remembered as standing a good deal taller than her five-foot-two. Daddy would put it thusly: Chin out, shoulders back, look 'em in the eye, and give 'em Hell! Which is what Mother usually did.

Those in the coal camp, already dependent on the coal company, depended upon Faith, their only decision being when to call Mrs. Phillips, and that they did easily. If it ever bothered her, no one knew it. Day or night she answered their call, never refusing to go, never needing to be thanked twice. She was as "good as ary Angel," Mr. Gillespie said, but even that did not fully depict the warmth and love, the special regard in which she was held by the people in the town. El knew there was not another woman in the entire state of West Virginia who could walk through the camp picking up cow-piles and putting them in an old coal bucket without causing ridicule or laughter. When Mother did this, it set an example of thrift and wisdom: hers was the only yard in town where flowers bloomed from April to October; hers the only garden that flourished in cinders and ashes, providing food for her family and food to share with her neighbors.

While Faith's kingdom was the coal camp of Coville, Daddy's was the Virginian Railroad, as William spent all of his days and many of his nights working. There were some who might not even have recognized him except he was the only man in town who wore sixteen-inch, laced up boots with his pants firmly tucked in, a necessity for climbing the high poles to reach the high-voltage wiring. William's dedication to the railroad was well-matched by Faith's dedication to the town.

As Ellie stood at her window facing the high black bridge, she saw Mr. Gillespie standing in snow nearly to his knees, trying to open the iron gate to his yard. The Gillespie's occupied the other two-storied house in the town due to his position as manager, and only clerk, in the company store. He gave up and returned to the house, likely figuring he wouldn't have any customers in this weather anyway. Mr. Gillespie wore dress pants and a long-sleeved dress shirt to work as fitted his position, with a long, white, bibbed apron that came well below his knees and had strings that went around his large abdomen, a bib with strings that tied behind his chunky neck. The bib had a pocket that held a pad of tickets upon which he wrote the bill of goods for his customers, a pad with a carbon paper. He tore off the top copy, repositioned the carbon, ready for the next customer. The carbon left black streaks on the top of the apron, the more streaks, the more customers so it was easy for Ellie to tell when it had been a busy day at the company store by looking at Mr. Gillespie's apron. When Mrs. Gillespie hung her wash on the line each Monday, there would be six white aprons and El could smell the Clorox when the wind blew. He was a friendly man to everyone, regardless of color, which was more than could be said of Mr. Reeves, the camp caretaker, the only other coal company employee. Mr. Gillespie spoke in clichés', and had a handy saying for everything as though someone else had already said it better than he could.

Mildred Gillespie was as opposite from her husband, Rayford, as she could possibly be, and Rayford explained it by saying, "Opposites attract, likes repel." Whereas he was large and robust, Mildred was small-boned and delicate with an air of grayness about her—gray-brown hair, gray skin, no make-up, store-bought dresses that hung straight down, no belt, but she did use talcum powder, rose, or lavender, as though her clothes were packed in a chest and came out of storage when she put them on. Her hair was smoothed back into a tight little wad at the back of her head and held there with invisible hairpins so it looked like it stayed there all on its own. She kept a neat, clean house, although lately it was daughter Judith who did most of the work, leaving Mildred with time to sit, holding her hands in her lap, just perched there with nothing in her lap. El wondered what she thought about, sitting so quiet and still. Mother never sat idle, always busy, something in her hands, sewing, crocheting, snapping beans, or shelling peas, but Mildred just sat.

Wilford, the oldest of the two Gillespie boys, graduated from Herndon High school at the top of his class and was now a freshman at the University in Morgantown. A tall, stalwart boy much like his father, he had played basketball in high school but exchanged it for football at college, using his big, strong hands to advantage as he made a name for himself carrying the ball. He also exchanged the name, Wilford, for the shorter, more updated, Will. Mildred didn't approve, but said nothing, while Rayford said, "To each his own." Wilford—Will—would be the first boy from Coville to graduate from college, and he was coming back to Wyoming county when he received his engineering degree. He would stand in the road in front of his house, a big, tall mountaineer with brown hair and dark brown eyes, and jerk his thumb toward the high steel bridge behind him and say with the confidence of a winner, "I'm going to build bridges like that one someday—only for cars, not trains!" Everyone was sure he would.

The second Gillespie son was named Thomas Dunn Gillespie, after Thomas Dunn English, first mayor of Logan and a relative of Mildred's on her mother's side. Thomas Dunn English was famous as the author of the ballad of Ben Bolt. It was under the elms in Logan that English wrote the famous lines: *Don't you remember Sweet Alice, Ben Bolt, Sweet Alice, whose hair was so brown, who wept with delight when you gave her a smile, And trembled with fear at your frown?*

When Thomas was in fourth grade, he wrote about the origin of his name, with his mother's help, for a homework assignment. For weeks after that he was called "Sweet Alice" until his fists made a change—not back to Thomas as before, but to "Ben Bolt." Mildred never again was allowed to help him with homework, but he had learned an important lesson: his fists were valuable tools which he would learn to use to his advantage. By the time he reached sixth grade the "Bolt" had been dropped, and he became forever "Ben", accepted by everyone, except Mildred who preferred Thomas. Because of his fists, people around the town were comparing him to another Logan citizen, Jack Dempsey. Ben, like Dempsey, was a close fighter, grappling with the other boys, rolling on the cindered dirt, punching with the style of Dempsey himself, short hooks and jabs, until the other boys gave up, including big brother Will who would much rather play ball than fight. By the time he went to Herndon, most of the girls would gladly be his 'sweet Alice,' including Jane, who was one of his first conquests.

Judith Gillespie, older than El and younger than Jane, had few friends. The only time she had been close to being friendly with El was when they invented the telephone—a string with a tin can on each end which they pulled between their bedroom windows. They had found lots to talk about, then, but it didn't last long. Judith returned to her housework and El returned to her books.

On the other side of the Phillips' house lived Thomas Jefferson Collins, principal of the elementary school, teacher for the fifth and sixth grades, and his wife, Sarah Jo, teacher for the first and second grades. Mr. Collins was a well-read man, with a University education, although it was whispered that he did not graduate, hence his position in a small elementary school in Wyoming-God-forsaken-West Virginia, which was Sarah Jo's name for their camp. He was dark complexioned, swarthy, mother said, only that made him sound dashing and Mr. Collins was anything but dashing with his dark hair combed straight back from a high forehead: he might have been good-looking except for his nose. That feature of his face stood out large and crooked, making his profile look like the Indian on the buffalo nickel, only without the feathers. El, from her seat by the window—fifth graders sat by the window, sixth graders by the wall—often thought about how Mr. Collins would look with long turkey feathers stuck in his hair, another one hanging down, like on the coin. Judith said he looked more like his namesake, Thomas Jefferson and she got out the history book to prove it, but Judith was in the sixth grade and had a crush on Mr. Collins—yes, Mr. Collins, No, Mr. Collins—until El got tired of it and accused her of being afraid she was not going to be promoted if she didn't butter up her teacher.

It was bad, living next door to your teacher; Mr. Collins told Mother every single little thing El did. She had to work even if she didn't feel like it, or he would talk to Mother over the fence, and then Mother would put a hand on her head, ask if she were feeling bad. If she said yes, she couldn't go out to play. If she said no, she got a switching for not doing her school work. She couldn't win. There was one good thing about living next door to another bookworm: she got all the new books as soon as Mr. Collins was through with them—she had even read *Gone with The Wind* before Jane got it! Mr. Collins wasn't at all stingy.

Mr. T.J. Collins looked younger than his wife. Sometimes, in the summer when the windows were open, you could hear Sarah Jo calling, "T.J. do come here…T.J. bring me…T.J., T.J.…"but everyone else called him Mr. Collins, even Mother and Daddy. He looked younger than his wife because Sarah Jo had white hair and lines on her face that powder wouldn't cover, and she said it was from teaching first and second grades for so long. El thought it might have something to do with the cough syrup bottle she kept in her desk drawer at school. After lunch Mrs. Collins always took a sip, then sat down for a nap while one of the older girls came from Mr. Collins' room to read the little children a story.

As if that were not enough rest, Sarah Jo always went to bed early, usually right after supper, taking along the newest book from the Guild, or maybe the newest magazine, *The Saturday Evening Post*, or *McCall's* or perhaps just the paper. El knew: when you lived practically in their faces, with only the side yard between, and the windows open all the time, you couldn't help but know that Mrs. Collins was almost always asleep before dark: she snored.

There was one good thing about the space between the Phillips house and the Collins. There was a giant willow tree growing half in one yard, half in the other. It was easy to climb, just up the fence and step into the branches, and in the spring, when the titmouse leaves came out along the slender wands, it was impossible to see anyone up the tree unless you were standing directly beneath it and looking straight up. It was a perfect place to read, and the higher you climbed the cooler it got. Like everything else about the Collins, that willow had a disadvantage too; it provided perfect switches all year long—and Mother knew just how to use them!

On the other side of the Collins' lived Grandma Gillespie, the store manager's mother. She lived alone, near him but not with him and it was rumored she got her rent free. It was also rumored that Mildred refused to let her live with them and once Mr. Gillespie, talking about Mildred, said "still water runs deep", and that set tongues wagging for days. El thought one thing was certain, Mildred was still most of the time, you could see that without half looking. Grandma came from the old country when she was a girl and crossing the water was the experience of her life, nothing coming after that except Indian fighting, having babies, and hard work.

When it grew dark Grandma went in, took off her glasses with their attached hearing aid, put her teeth in a china cup and went to bed: she didn't believe in socializing after dark.

On down the road, beside Grandma Gillespie, lived the Whites. Emmett, a miner, who worked at Alpoca on the day shift, and Hollie, his wife, had lived in Coville for five years.

Hollie was born in Wyoming county, up the holler from Herndon; her Pa was killed in the mines before Hollie was born and she had never known what he looked like there being no pictures. Her Ma had stayed on at the homeplace, looking after her own Mother-God-Bless-her, until she died, living off the land with a little savings that dwindled over the years. When Hollie was born, there had been little to give her. Thus, when Emmett came along, Hollie's Ma had latched on to him, recognizing an opportunity for her pretty young daughter. Hollie was fifteen and in the tenth grade at Herndon High School. Emmett had a regular job in the mines, worked regular as many a man, more regular than some, was single, no debts, didn't drink more than average, and besides, he weren't bad lookin'. It didn't matter that he had quit school at fourteen to work in the mines, lying about his age, no one really cared. Ma had told Hollie she could git that man with a little trying, because Emmett didn't peer to be the kinda man would leave a gal in trouble, especially a little gal as purty as Hollie. With Ma suggesting, and making ample opportunity, Hollie didn't finish tenth grade because she started showing and the wedding date was set before the last day of school.

Emmett had money for a house of their own, and with not even a shack to be had in Herndon, they had moved to Coville. Hollie's Ma died before the baby was born, almost like she had known she was going to die. They had buried her beside her own mother and let the land go to seed; it was too far up the holler for Emmett, too far from his job, and besides, Hollie liked living in a real town and having neighbors, going to visit and keeping house like a real woman. No one had farmed the land for years and brush filled in the path, making it hard to find the cabin. Emmett took her once a year to clean off the graves and to put wild flowers in the mason jar buried at the headstone. In between, the place belonged to the squirrels and birds, to the possum, the coon and the bobcat, to wasp nests and wild honey bees in the orchard grass, to the honeysuckle and the briars. It was no longer home to Hollie; there was nothing there for her.

When Hollie started labor, she walked up the road to Faith. She hadn't known it was labor pains when her back had started hurting in the middle of the night; she hadn't said anything to Emmett, him needing to go to work, and she wasn't sure when the baby was due because she and Emmett had been bedding for quite a spell before she stopped falling off the roof every month.

It was different with Faith, with her education; she had marked the calendar and knew exactly when Bun was expected, and Bun had arrived right on time with little bother to anyone. Faith often said she didn't know why Hollie's mother had let her get in the family way before she was married, but, since it had happened, she was there when Hollie needed her. Bun was two months old when Hollie walked up the road to Faith, thinking she might just stay there until Emmett got home from work: she stayed four weeks.

Faith asked few questions, just sat Hollie down beside her, put her hand on Hollie's abdomen, and watched the clock. When she felt her abdomen grow hard and push out every five minutes, she went to the hall telephone and called Doc Steelman. He got there in time to help Faith tie the cord, the birthing having gone without a problem. Hollie, being young and strong, and having watched animals on the farm, had no trouble at all; she had taken hold of the pull sheet wrapped around the bed post and pushed her baby into the world like she was made for having babies.

Mother had sent El to Mrs. Gillespie's house and she had to stay the night, sleeping with Judith, and she hadn't slept well with all the changed smells and strange sounds of the night.

Doc Steelman wouldn't let Hollie out of bed for three weeks, then she could hardly stay up. All in all, it was nearly four weeks before El got her bed back, but she didn't have to stay at the Gillespie's. She moved in with Jane, but Jane fussed. Yet Jane would do almost anything for Hollie, treating her more like a sister than a neighbor or a friend, she loved her so. There was no one in the whole camp, or Herndon either, as pretty as Hollie.

Hollie had skin like Mother's prized Dahlia, creamy with a tingle of pale pink beneath the surface, like a blush thinking about coming, and not a freckle or a wrinkle anywhere. She had sky-blue Irish eyes with a light behind them coming on bright when she smiled, which was often. Emmett said she even smiled in her sleep for he lay watching her before he got out of bed: he got up early to go to work in the mines and left Hollie and Shirley laying in the big bed. Sometimes Shirley would go to sleep nursing and Hollie would go to sleep too, leaving the baby at her pink-nippled breast all night, and that made it hard, later, when Shirley was almost five years old and Hollie wanted to go to work in the company store. Shirley wouldn't let anyone take care of her except Mother.

Emmett called them his big doll and his little doll, and they both smelled like Ivory soap because they both washed their hair with Ivory flakes in the big zinc tub on the kitchen floor. Shirley's hair was almost as blond as Hollie's and had its own way of curling, being trained by Mother right from birth. Shirley's curls were as long as Bun's and her already two months old. It was almost like they were twins, right from the start, being born so close together and Mother taking care of them both until Hollie could get out of bed. Jane, ten years old and already grown up thought she was in heaven, having two babies to play with, and since Shirley was the youngest she would take her, allowing El to look after Bun, sitting in the middle of the bed, her legs spread wide with Bun between them so she couldn't roll off, both arms wrapped tightly around her. Jane would take Mother's rocker and hold Shirley until she got hungry or until Mother came upstairs and took her.

It was a good four weeks. Mother taught Hollie to sew, making skirts and blouses out of flowered feed sacks saved by Mr. Gillespie, blouses that needed no buttons or buttonholes, just elastic around the neck and sleeves, and skirts gathered around her small waist on a band. When Shirley got bigger, she made Shirley dresses from the scraps so they could look alike. Then Emmett called them his dolls, "How's my big doll? And how's my little doll?"

Coming in from work he'd set his round miner's pail, with the water compartment under the sandwich tray, on the table and gather them both in his arms, "How's my big doll, how's my little doll?" Nobody in the camp was as happy as Emmett with his pretty girls. Mother liked to ask them up to dinner because they were so happy and fun-filled, so loved and loving, and Daddy liked them to come, saying Hollie was like a spring day and it in the dead of winter when he said it.

Emmett would wash up pretty good, getting his face fairly clean except for the black rings around his eyes but all miners had that, a black ring that didn't wash off. Emmett was a tall mountaineer, but he had worked inside the mines so long he was somewhat stooped from compensating for the low coal seams, from bending over the shovel, from crawling on his knees to get to the face of the coal, inside, where the work was harder but the pay was better. Emmett would call the two little girls funny names when he came to dinner. "How's my buckaroos?" he'd say, or "How's my ding-bats?" or call them "double-trouble", and say how like they were to be no kin. Mother would perpetuate the illusion by dressing them alike, or in the same colors, rolling their hair over her fingers into long curls, making two hairbows instead of one—when Bun got a new hair ribbon Shirley got one too. When they came to the company store, Mr. Gillespie would give them suckers alike, and he'd shake his head over them, saying, "Like as two peas in a pod," he'd say, "Like as two peas in a pod."

Before Christmas, with the trouble in England, the mines started working six days a week, sometimes seven, and the miners had more money to spend. Hollie was hired to help out in the company store: she handled all the script and kept the cards for Mr. Gillespie. Mother was keeping Shirley nearly every day now, so Hollie could work, make a little money for herself. Emmett said any money she made, she could keep, no wife of his had to work, and by God he didn't aim for it to last very long! Shirley was always at Bun's anyway, so it wasn't an imposition. The two spent hours playing dolls, and dress-up: neither was happy without the other.

By late afternoon, the snow had stopped; everything was buried in a thick coating of white, now beginning to freeze on the top as the temperature dropped. Daddy had not been home since going out to work on the night they returned from Virginia. El begged Mother constantly to let her go out, but Mother was unmoved by her pleas. "With your history of bad colds and pneumonia?"

"Well, at least let me go out to get the coal, so you don't have to," El said, over and over. But Mother refused. "Daddy will be here soon; he will take care of it." Mother would stand in the hall with the telephone to her ear by the hour, listening to the exchanges between the control tower and the train engineers. Sometimes she was able to hear it when Bud called to ask clearance for his motorcar; then she knew he would be on his way home soon, and she would be certain to have a hot meal ready on the back of the big cook stove.

There was no sign of life at the Mitchell house across the street; the boys were still in Logan with their Grandmother. They had potato soup for supper, one of El's favorite meals, and Jane didn't like it, and Bun played with hers. Still tired from their trip, Mother sent them all to bed early, but it was already dark, and only five o'clock; El took two of the new books loaned by Aunt Maude to bed with her, two in case she finished one before she got sleepy.

Hours later, she heard Daddy talking in the kitchen. Mother had waited up to get a hot meal on the table for him. Relieved to know her Daddy was safe, she put her light out, scrunched down in the warm bed beside the soft body of her baby sister, and went to sleep, dreaming, as she did frequently, of flying with Charles Lindbergh, skimming just above the angry waves of the ocean, and the lights in the distance were on the coast of England: they were going to fight the Germans, and the battle would be won in the air.

Mother and Charles Augustus Lindbergh were born in the same year, and on the same day, albeit different months, Lindbergh on Feb. 4, 1902, and Mother on August 4, 1902. Lindbergh didn't know this remarkable fact, but to Mother it was of major significance. The year Lindbergh started flying school, 1922, was the year Mother and Daddy were married, a very important year for both of them. Lindbergh's early flying was an example of his bravery, with no instructions, taking off on his own, and it was the year 1923, the year Mother and Daddy took off for the wild untamed parts of West Virginia called Wyoming County. In 1924, Lindbergh's father, a Congressman representing the sixth district of Minnesota, passed away, and in that same year her Grandfather Henley died. Charles, now a national hero, joined the Army Flying Cadets and graduated in 1925, one of the hardest, most meaningful things he had ever done. In 1925, Mother gave birth to her first child, one of the hardest and most meaningful things she had ever done. The year Lindbergh flew across the ocean alone, in a single-winged airplane, was the year Daddy was promoted foreman on the Virginian Railroad—and the year Mother started compiling her list of coincidences. Lindbergh returned to the United States to a reception never before equaled in the history of the nation.

President Calvin Coolidge greeted him with a warm handshake and an overly-long speech:

"My Fellow-Countrymen:
It was in America that the modern art of flying heavier-than-air machines was developed...
On a morning just three weeks ago yesterday, this wholesome, earnest, fearless, courageous product of America rose into the air at Long island in a monoplane christened "The Spirit of St. Louis"...he was alone...

thirty-three hours and thirty minutes later, in the evening of the second day, he landed at his destination…this young man has returned…and as President of the United States, I bestow the Distinguished Flying Cross, as a symbol of appreciation for what he is and what he has done, upon Charles A. Lindbergh."

Lindbergh, as a boy, spent many hours with his maternal grandfather, a Detroit dentist and scientist, and learned early to appreciate language as a clear-cut science. His reply to the long-winded speech by the President was typical of his manner of thinking and speaking:

"On the evening of May 21, I arrived at LeBourget, France. I was in Paris for one week, in Belgium for one day and was in England for several days. Everywhere I went, at every meeting I attended, I was requested to bring a message home to you. Always the message was the same.
You have seen, the message was, 'the affection of the people of France for the people of America demonstrated to you. When you return to America take back that message to the people of the United States from the people of France and of Europe.'

The brevity of his speech, after the length of President Coolidge's message shocked the throngs of people gathered for the celebration. They stood in silence, uncertain what to do. Is he finished? Is that all he's going to say? Then the cheering began, and it has not ended to this day…

In July Charles Lindbergh started flying a series of trips from state to state, and on August the fourth—Mother's birthday—he landed in Wheeling, West Virginia.

It was a hard drive, from Mullins to Wheeling, but she and Daddy had just purchased a Model A Ford. Daddy knew he was going to be the new foreman, his income would increase, and he would be on salary—besides, it was Mother's birthday!

They left the day before, with baby Jane asleep on the back seat and a room arranged in a widow's boarding house. By the time Lindbergh touched down they were part of the thousands waving, crying hysterically, cheering him as their hero, and, finally praying for him as he was escorted off the field to spend the night in their very own state, before taking off the next morning for Cincinnati, Ohio.

The boyishness of the tall aviator, the charm and personality that reached across the crowds and made them feel close to him—as Mother talked about Lindbergh, El felt she knew him herself, knew the drive, the longing to fly, to get as high as she could go, her feet free from the clutch of gravity, a kindred spirit. He was the same as their forefathers, at one with grandparents and parents who cleared the land and fought the Indians and shot the bears: he was a pioneer. West Virginians understood pioneers: that was the most noble calling of all.

Mother continued to compile her list of similarities. In 1928 Charles presented *the Spirit of St. Louis* to the Smithsonian in Washington, and in 1929 he married Anne Morrow, daughter of the Ambassador to Mexico. In 1930 Charles Augustus Lindbergh, Jr. was born—and so was Rachel Elizabeth Phillips.

In February of 1934, President Franklin Delano Roosevelt cancelled all airmail contracts due to irregularities. This angered Lindbergh and he wrote letters to the President protesting his action. A personal war between the hero and the President began.

The young son of Charles and Anne was taken and held for ransom; it was four years before the killer was caught, and Charles and Anne, sorrowed by the loss of their son and persecuted by the never-tiring newsmen in the United States, moved to England. The year—1935, the year Bun was born.

Charles, Anne and their children returned to the U.S. in 1939; that was the year Daddy took Mother and the girls to the New York World's Fair, and Mother brought home a picture of the *Spirit of St. Louis* as a souvenir; she hung it in the dining room and it became one of her most cherished possessions. The painting, hung over the Philco, occupied a prime spot in the dining room, and El would gaze at it during most meals, getting lost in her imaginary flights, especially if the news was boring. She would soar into the painting, it was so real she could hear the hum of the motor, feel the vibration as she skimmed dangerously near the turbulent water. The painting hung over the cathedral-like Philco with its speaker shaped like a stained-glass window, the radio an alter before which the family worshiped nightly, picking words out of the static like choosing crumbs at communion: thus she was reared to worship the trinity of Roosevelt, Lindbergh and the radio as equal to God, the Father, and the Holy Ghost.

Unknown to her parents, El intended to fly. She would be another Amelia Earhart Putnam, but she wouldn't disappear over the Pacific; she would fly over the Atlantic and see Europe, Africa, India, as Charles and Anne had done. She would fly. Her feet weren't made to stay on the ground; she had scaled every high place available ever since she was born, every high place except one: **she had yet to go up on the bridge.**

Four

On Tuesday morning the girls awoke to a white wonderland. The snow had stopped, skies were light blue and cloudless, the wind moving gently without disturbing the thick white blanket of frozen snow covering everything. It was a perfect day for sledding, and, fortunately, due to so many county roads still unplowed, school had remained closed.

El and Bun had been given one chore for the day, and when it was done, they could play. They had to wrap the apples brought back from Virginia for storage, each one individually wrapped in newspaper squares, placed in boxes and put on pantry shelves, way back under the stairs where it was cool and dark. They would have fresh apples until spring and the pantry would smell like apples each time the door was opened.

By ten o'clock El and Bun were cross and fighting. Bun would not work, she was tired, she wasn't doing it right and El had to do it over, and why couldn't Jane help? But Jane was changing sheets on the beds upstairs.

Bun would pick up an apple and put it back, deciding not to do that one. "Oh, for heaven's sake, Bun! We have to do them all!"

"El?"

"What!"

"It's stopped snowing."

"I know that! If you'll help me, I'll pull you on my sled if Mother will let us go out!" Jane came downstairs, her duties done for the day. "I'll let you ride my sled if you'll help us, Jane," said El.

"Not on your life!" replied Jane. "I'm through with my chore, you do your own. Besides, I don't want to go out—it's too messy."

Mother came to the kitchen from another spell of listening on the phone. "Did you hear Daddy?" asked Jane.

"No, but he will probably be in on time today, looks like the snow is starting to melt."

"Can we go out?" pleaded El, "it's going to all be gone before I get to try my sled!"

"Please, Mother?" said Bun, "Pretty please with sugar on top?"

"It's too cold, girls. You'll be sick."

"No, I won't, honest, I'll wear my snowsuit—"

"Now, that's enough—"

"I can get the coal while I'm out, Daddy won't have to do it, and take out the ashes—I'll shovel the walk, too."

"Me too," begged Bun, "and El said she'd pull me on the sled—please Mother?"

"What about the apples?"

"We can finish them tonight!" Mother went to the back porch thermometer. It was beginning to warm up, the sun was out, didn't seem to be much wind…"

"Well, for a little while. Put on extra socks," she added.

"Whoopee!" shouted the girls, running upstairs. They found their snowsuits, tucked in their dresses, crossed the suspenders across the back, put a sweater on under the short jacket, grabbed toboggan and gloves, and ran back down the stairs to the back porch where their boots sat by the furnace. They went out into a changed world.

Gone was the black mud, the unpainted fence railings, and the bare tree branches. The snow lay white and clean over everything. Even the car tracks were gone, covered by the morning accumulation. Bun ran circles and figure-eights in the yard while El shoveled the snow from the brick walk and scattered ashes over it to prevent falls on the ice. She brought in three buckets of coal, enough to last through the night. At last she was free to bring out the sled, pulling it to the road she called to Bun, "Come on, I'll give you the first ride!" Daddy had oiled the runners before he had stored it, and now it looked almost new.

There had been no sign of the Mitchell boys while she was working; now she put Bun on the sled and started running up the road, Bun squealing in delight. By the time she got to the schoolyard fence Edgar and Joe had caught up with her, throwing caps and jackets on, not even owning boots or gloves.

Joe grabbed a handful of snow, making it into a snowball, and threatened to throw it at Bun. "Don't you dare!" said El. "You want to throw snowballs, pick on someone your own size!" Joe backed down. "I'm going to get Billy'n'Bob," he shouted, and ran down the road.

Edgar walked beside El. "Want me to pull her?" he asked.

"You want to?"

"Sure, I'm stronger."

"Get your bike?"

"Nah. You?"

"No."

"Grandma said it cost too much."

"We got a new car."

"A car! Wow!"

"I'd rather have had a bike." El suddenly realized: if her parents had enough money for a new car, they had enough for a bike. So why didn't they want her to have one? She didn't tell Edgar about the scooter—he'd think she was a baby.

Within an hour, pants, gloves, and feet were wet. Bun started crying to go home just as she and Edgar got easy with each other and started having a really good time. She knew Mother would make her stay in if she went home.

"Tell you what," said Edgar, "Let me keep your sled and you'll have to come back out to get it."

El quickly agreed and led the shaking Bun home. Mother had her coat and boots on, "I figured you'd be ready to come in by now," she said. "I was coming to get you."

"I'm not ready to come in," said El. Mother felt her pants, wet to the knees, and then her hands. "Yes, you are," said Mother, "You've been out long enough."

"But I left my sled—!"

"Edgar will bring it in," said Mother. "But I told him I'd come back!" El protested.

"You are wet and cold. You'll be sick! Don't you think you can trust Edgar?" said Mother. "Go change your clothes right now!"

There was no use arguing with Mother; when she got that emphatic, nothing she said would change her mind. Maybe Edgar would come in when he brought the sled in. He had looked so handsome, his cheeks red from the cold, his blonde hair curling out from under his blue cap—he had even pulled her on the sled after she let him go down the slope by the schoolyard a few times. She and Edgar were having a really good time until Joe and Billy'n'Bob came, and then Bun started fussing—oh, well, she was cold, and the hot cocoa Mother made for them did taste good.

It started snowing again before three o'clock, and the temperature began to drop. Daddy was still out. El argued with Jane and picked at Bun because Mother was at the phone again, listening to the railroad traffic. Jane heated up the potato soup and Mother baked cornbread; when she heard Daddy report in, she would slice the Virginia ham and open a jar of canned greens. It was after four o'clock when she heard Daddy's voice on the line, talking to the power director in Narrows. "Bert, all breakers closed—we're ready to roll." She knew Daddy had the wires energized and was asking for clearance on the track for his motor car. He would be home within the hour.

They gathered around the supper table and listened to the six o'clock news. President Roosevelt had delivered his annual message to Congress and that was nearly all that was discussed. Roosevelt had talked about his Lend-Lease program, which El didn't understand and found boring. When she tried to ask Daddy about the railroad trouble, he shushed her; when she tried to tell him about sledding, Mother said, "not now, Rachel." She didn't try again. She knew something important was going on. They sat quietly, gathered close beside the Philco, listening intently. Perhaps her parents had a premonition that this was a message of historical import, but for El it was just another long presidential speech. He had just been re-elected for another four years: why was he still making speeches?

Mr. Collins answered El's questions in the next few days as he presented a comparison of the lives of President Roosevelt and Winston Churchill to the fifth and sixth grades. Mr. Collins, a voracious reader, expected much from his students, and El had no choice but to listen.

Winston Leonard Spencer Churchill was born in 1874 at Oxfordshire, England, a flat island country drained by the Tames, locally called the river Isis. His father was Lord Randolph Henry Spencer Churchill, a descendent of the first Duke of Marlborough; his mother was Jeanette Jerome, daughter of an American businessman from New York. With the blood of both English-speaking peoples in his veins, he entered the world prematurely and seemed to stay ahead the remainder of his days.

Winston lost his first election, went to South Africa where he won fame by rescuing an ambushed train and escaping from a Boer prison camp. In 1900 he returned a hero, and won the election at Oldham. He was a successful politician at the age of twenty-six.

While Winston was still a schoolboy at Harrow, in the old country near the Thames River, another boy was born in the new country on the banks of the Hudson river. Had his parents followed tradition his name would have been Issac, but it was a new country and traditions were easily broken. Jacobus Roosevelt came from pioneer stock, the grandson of a Dutchman who settled in New Amsterdam in 1644. Jacobus begat Issac who begat James, and James built a house near the Hudson River. James fathered Issac who married an Aspinwall daughter and built a house near his father. Now Issac named his son James, who married Rebecca Howland and to this union was born James Roosevelt who bought five hundred acres nearer the Hudson and builded a new homestead, the original having been destroyed by fire.

The first Mrs. Roosevelt died, and James Roosevelt, being now past fifty, in his prime, and needing a warming companion, married Sara Delano, a young, good-humored neighboring lass of Flemish origin. The only child of James Roosevelt and Sara Delano was born on January 30, 1882; Sara had her way, and called her son Franklin Delano, after her favorite uncle. As he was being christened, his fourth cousin, Theodore Roosevelt, was beginning his political career in the New York State Assembly.

Franklin was brought up in the country with French and German governesses; each year they spent the summer abroad. At the age of Five, Franklin was given two puppies and required to take care of them himself; at seven he was given a pony for the same purpose, that being to teach him responsibility. At fourteen he had shot and stuffed a wide collection of bird specimens, acquiring a name for himself as a natural history buff, and his father presented him with a life membership in the Natural History Museum in New York. About this time, he was given a 21-foot knock-about in which he cruised the bay and coast of Maine. As a young man he hunted and fished, played polo and tennis, and the new game of golf.

Franklin was enrolled in Groton but would have preferred Annapolis, having developed a love for the sea, and he moved from the study of natural history to naval history and navigation. The Spanish-American War in 1898 brought forth the desire to enter the military, and had he not come down with the measles, he would have slipped away and joined the navy.

In 1900, when twenty-six-year-old Winston was representing Oldham, and laying the basis for his fortune by giving lectures in England and the United States, Franklin was eighteen years old and entering Harvard university. His cousin, Colonel Theodore Roosevelt, Governor of New York, was the Republican candidate for Vice-President, with McKinley as President. In 1901, President McKinley was assassinated, and Theodore became President of the United States.

In 1904 Winston joined the Liberal party and attacked Joseph Chamberlain, acquiring a reputation as a radical, and Franklin graduated from Harvard. His cousin, Theodore, was reelected to a second term as President.

The year 1910 was fruitful for both men: Franklin began his political career as a delegate to the Democratic convention and was nominated for the traditionally Republican seat in the 26th district. In his acceptance speech he set the tone for future campaigns:

As you know, I accept the nomination with absolute independence. I am pledged to no man: I am influenced by no specific interests, and so shall I remain…

Elected with votes to spare, FDR decided to make legislating a full-time occupation and rented a house on State Street, contrary to the usual practice of senators who returned to their homes in midweek. This was the year that Sir Winston Churchill became home secretary and quickly was involved in a wave of industrial revolutions. He called upon the military to settle a Welsh miner's strike, and promptly became unpopular with his radical followers.

In 1911 Churchill transferred to the Admiralty, and his first duty was to create a naval war staff. The next year Roosevelt suffered from Typhoid fever and, unable to campaign for reelection to the state legislature himself, took out a full-page advertisement—the first of its kind—and was voted in with more than seventeen hundred votes to spare. In 1913, while Winston was still in the Admiralty, Franklin realized his ambition to be a Navy man also: he took office as Assistant Secretary of the Navy, and he leased the "little white house" in Washington. He was thirty-one.

Roosevelt discovered that most sailors were from interior states, from the wheat fields of the mid-west, and the coal fields of West Virginia. He instituted the 'Swimming Cup', attained by the ship with the largest percentage of men fulfilling the swimming requirements. He stopped the practice of recruiting from the prisons, men being sentenced to the navy for punishment instead of going to jail, and began the search for desirable men, building the service into an acceptable, if not elite, society, encouraging pride, skill, and dedication. In 1913, Roosevelt insisted the work of building the collapsed docks at Pearl Harbor, in Hawaii be completed. After finding the volcanic foundations of the islands unsuitable for the usual construction methods, he successfully instituted the floating caisson method. And halfway around the world, Winston ordered a "test of naval mobilization," and after the review he ordered them to remain mobilized.

War was no surprise to either man when it was declared on April 6, 1917.

Roosevelt was summoned to the White House and ordered to "divide his men" with the Army, precipitating a trip to Europe to inspect the American Bases. At a dinner, Roosevelt and Churchill met briefly for the first time, but there was no opportunity for them to talk. Winston was impressed by Franklin's vitality and his tall, magnificently youthful appearance. Franklin crossed the channel on a British destroyer and motored to Paris, then to Rome, but he came down with influenza, developed pneumonia, and missed action for the rest of the war. While Roosevelt was making plans for the United States to enter the League of Nations in 1919, Churchill was assuming the duties of Secretary of War and handling the difficult duties of demobilization.

In 1921 Franklin fell ill; He had helped extinguish a small forest fire, made a two-mile run across the island with his children, swam in the icy waters of the Bay of Fundy, sat for a time in his bathing suit, reading his mail. The next morning, he had symptoms of a cold, and his legs felt peculiar: it was Infantile Paralysis—poliomyelitis: He was paralyzed from the hips down. He remained crippled in defiance of all experts and the best of care, but he was forced to give up some of his duties. He was thirty-nine years old, and forced to—almost—retire.

The next year, Winston was struck by an attack of appendicitis and prostrated, appearing in a wheelchair in public only two days before election, now without a seat, without a party and without an appendix. Ironically, Roosevelt had been nominated for Vice President in 1920 and had lost his election, too. Both men had reached, simultaneously, an interlude in their careers, a time for evaluation, for writing and speaking, and for Churchill, for painting. Franklin spent his days at Warm Springs, Georgia, in therapy; Winston wrote *The World Crisis.*

In 1924, Churchill returned to parliament; in 1928 Franklin was elected Governor of New York, and in 1929 the British government fell, and Wall Street crashed.

Franklin now had five children, one named James, after his father; Winston had one son, named Randolph, after his father.

Mr. Collins ended his history lesson with the two men as compatriots, working together to "save the world," as he put it. El rushed home, full of questions, most of which either her Mother or Father could answer because they had grown up following these men as they moved into leadership roles in their respective countries.

Going down the road, past Hollie and Emmett's house, lived the Wooten's, whose ancestors are said to come from the old country even before the revolution, coming into the area when Washington came to claim lands along the Kanawha river, and their great, great grandpappy had been a foot soldier under General Washington. He had deserted and was taken in by the Indians after being mauled by a bear, then later claimed land of his own. How he lost that land through gambling was another story, often told by the boys, story-telling being a major way of entertainment for the younger population of Coville. The sons relished the stories and handed them down with the guns and knives from one generation to the next.

The Wooten's were given to large families, predominantly males, and Mama Wooten had five boys and only one daughter. Three of the boys were grown and gone. Then came Mary Beth, who was in high school and a year ahead of Jane, followed by two more boys. Mary Beth was built like Mama Wooten with wide hip bones, stout legs, and thick ankles; she did her mouse-brown hair up in rags at night, trying to imitate Jane's naturally curled black hair, but every morning the dew made the curls come straggling down her back. She and Jane were good friends and walked up the road to catch the school bus and sat on the bus together. Mary Beth was a good sport and didn't mind the teasing she was given. Jane thought it dumb always to be the recipient of practical jokes pulled by her brothers and by the older boys. Mary Beth secretly enjoyed the attention and responded as expected, squealing and running, when they put frogs or wooly worms down her back. Generally, the jokes were harmless and Mary Beth did not try to maintain decorum; she was not gifted with dignity as was Jane.

El liked to have the two younger Wooten boys on her team when they played ball in the triangle in front of her house. The two twin boys were in the fifth and sixth grade: they hit hard, ran fast, and cursed loudly if tagged out, having learned their special vocabulary from their older brothers at an early age. Like the other men in the camp, except Daddy, Papa Wooten was a miner; he rode to work with Emmett, bought his bottle in Mullins each Saturday night, emptying it early on Sunday evening. When it was empty, he went to bed again, this time taking Mama Wooten with him and the boys could stay out late on Sunday nights, there being no one to call them in. Mary Beth went to Epworth League meetings with Jane on Sunday nights.

The Wooten twins were called Billy and Bob; they were spoken of together, running the two names together, BillynBob, like E.E. Cummings' eddieandbill, so a stranger would have thought it was one boy, not two, or one real boy and his shadow, or like the Siamese twins, Chang and Eng. Like all Wooten boys, Billy n Bob were sturdy Scotchmen, and they learned early how to make a penny or two helping out in the camp, hauling coal or splitting kindlin, scattering ashes in the mud-filled ruts in the road. When Will went off to college and Ben started playing basketball, BillynBob took care of the fire for Grandma Gillespie and were paid with suckers from the company store.

Mama Wooten had picked the last house in the row, the small, cindered yard backing up to the creek and handy for the boys to swim in instead of bathing in the zinc tub, and from their house the road led straight up the mountain to the railroad tracks, coming out at the very end of the high black bridge, right in front of the old mine entrance, a real handy place for the boys to sneak off to for a cigarette. The road is almost impassable for cars, but it is the easiest for walking, if climbing straight up can be called easy.

BillynBob had two real good friends, although they played with everyone, even girls like El and Judith, and they were the Mitchells, Edgar and Joe. Same age, same school, and since the Mitchell boys had no mother, Mama Wooten took them in like her own. Edgar and Billy were in the sixth grade while Bob and Joe were in the fifth. Edgar was fourteen, BillynBob were twelve, while Joe was only ten. It wasn't that Bob was dumb, failing a grade, but that he was just shy, and that had been in first grade, but he'd been held back each year, teachers believing it wouldn't be good for twins to be in the same room all the time: they had to be separated so they could 'develop' as individuals, to which Mother had said, "Hogwash!" which was as near as she ever came to cussing. "Hogwash!" El liked the sound of it, but she had learned the hard way not to repeat it in front of Mother!

The Mitchell boys are special in the camp, being on their own, no mother, and their Daddy working all the time. Mr. Mitchell was held in high regard in the camp because of his job. He worked in the mine at night until the boys were old enough to go to school. At that time, he switched to day hours at Winding Gulf mine, working as a roof-pin setter, a job that is dangerous, requiring skill and an intuitive sense of how the rock lays—not just the visible layer, but those above it, out of sight. Mr. Mitchell is good at his job and has earned the respect of the other miners for his innate ability: there has not been an accident or a cave-in since Mr. Mitchell took over marking the spots to insert the long steel rods into the ceiling.

On Saturday's Mr. Mitchell fills a washtub with near-boiling water and washes the boys; next he adds a cake of lye soap and scrubs their overalls and shirts on a board and in the summer, hangs them over the fence. In winter they are draped over a wire strung near the ceiling in the kitchen. Edgar does the cooking and Joe washes the dishes, but almost every day someone sends the family a 'little something', not charity, just neighborly.

El liked to take something over, Mother seemed to have an extra pie, or a cake left over, and Edgar said Mother was the best cook in town, and he ought to know, he had eaten everybody's cooking.

Most of the time Edgar was serious, not all fun-loving like Joe. El thought it was because he had been handed the responsibility for his younger brother at such a young age. Maybe Joe's mother had been a Gypsy, like they said, but who was Edgar's mother? With his blonde hair and blue eyes, he didn't look like his Pa at all, except he was tall and quiet, like Mr. Mitchell. Mr. Mitchell wasn't unfriendly, it was just his way, to sit alone on his porch, smoking a pipe, watching the ball games, never playing, rarely coming over to their porch, even when most of the neighbors were there. El thought he looked lonesome, kinda sad, and she would beg Mother to let her take a 'little something' over, maybe then he would smile.

Edgar was quiet, like his Pa, but there was one big difference. Whenever Edgar got the chance, he had his nose stuck in a book, like El and Mr. Collins. Jane would bring library books home from the high school, and El would read them before they were due back. El would sneak them to Edgar without Jane knowing, and later, she'd say, "Well, how was it?"

Edgar would say," It's okay," and ask for another book, never a good discussion. And his light blue eyes looked right through you, softening only when he smiled.

El's grades began to improve when she started competing with Edgar to get his attention, but he never seemed to mind when she scored a point or two higher in spelling or reading—he got her back in arithmetic or history. They had one major difference in their natures; El loved to give oral book reports while Edgar read the same books and never gave a book report at all. Let them read the books themselves, he'd say, if they want to know what they're about, let them read.

The Mitchell's house was straight across the road in front of the Phillips'. Beside them lived an elderly, retired couple, the Belchers. Mr. Belcher had been manager of the company store until he retired, and now the primary focus of his life seemed to be criticism of the way Mr. Gillespie ran the store. Mrs. Belcher, although a good many years older, was a good friend of Mother's, always helping out with whatever Mother was doing, canning, quilting, coming over to sit on the porch to string beans or shell peas.

They had no children, but in the evenings, weather permitting, they sat on their front porch in identical rockers—well-padded with feed sack covered cushions—sipping sweet tea, watching the ballgames, cheering when someone hit a good one. There were two pots of petunias on the steps to their porch, and when they were ready to retire, they poured the left-over tea into the petunias. There have never before or since been such pots of petunias.

The Belchers looked alike, a little dumpy, slightly stooped, moving slowly about their small house. They had three pictures on the walls of their 'front' room, a large one of Jesus kneeling in the garden beside a large rock—El asked, if it's a garden why is there such a big rock in it? Mrs. Belcher couldn't explain. The other two pictures were just the heads of men, one of President Franklin Delano Roosevelt, the other was President John L. Lewis, one, the President of the United States, the other, President of the United Mine Workers of America. To the Belchers they were equal.

The Belchers never went anywhere, called each other 'dear', like they didn't have any other name, and they patted, patted each other, patted El on the head, like she was a dog, and El told Mother, one day she was going to bark when they did that, and Mother said don't you dare, I won't have you hurting those two dear souls, Rachel, you hear me? She never did, but she wanted to. Just once.

The house beside the Belcher's was empty. It was built nearly beneath the high railroad bridge and was used for storage by Mr. Reeves, the company caretaker. Mr. Reeves kept lumber, nails, plumbing parts—all the supplies needed to maintain the houses, all stored in the one building. The door was padlocked, the windows were boarded up—no use asking for trouble, and the youth in town spent many hours speculating on exactly what Old Reeves had stored there, and why did he lock it up so carefully. The fence around the house was new and had a good front gate, and a stile built by Mother and Daddy out of railroad crossties Daddy's men had hauled in for him. The yard was being used nearly year round for a garden. Exactly what the arrangement was between Mother and Old Reeves, El didn't know, and it remained their private agreement, but when the garden came in, fresh produce was sent his way on a regular basis—a mess of greens, a bag of white potatoes, a few ears of sweet corn, whatever was in season, for Mother's garden produced seemingly in proportion to the sharing, like the five loaves and two fishes, never running out when passed around. This was a good house to use for storage, because nobody wanted to live that near under the bridge.

Across the road, on the other side of the triangle, and beside Coon creek, began another row of houses. On this side of the triangle each house was accessed by a wooden bridge built across a concrete retaining wall that kept Coon creek in its banks with steps up and down, in case of high water, which always happened in the spring when the snow began to melt. That first house in the row, almost directly under the bridge, was the only other empty house in the camp. Some call it hainted, and the spook makes two regular appearances each year: on March twenty-ninth and October the thirty-first.

It was on March twenty-ninth when a flat car let loose a load of poles that was heading for the mines. The poles, about six feet in length but as big around as a half-growed boy, had dropped from the flatcar as it made the curve of the bridge, gone through the roof of that house like so many sticks of firewood throwed on a hearth. Some said it kilt the widow-lady living there, pierced her like an arrow while she was alayin' in the bed; some said she warn't in the bed at all, it jest scared her to death. Others said she was already dead and buried when that car turned over, that the logs jest hit where she had laid for a long time and if she hadn't already been dead, they woulda kilt her fer sure!

Either way, on March twenty-ninth you can hear her moan if you get close enough, if you dare to cross the footbridge over Coon creek and listen. On Halloween, October thirty-first, she just naturally comes around with all the other spooks and goblins and such, not wanting to be left out of the fun.

The old lady was called Granny Hall. On some nights, even if it's not March or October, you can hear her moan, if you are under the bridge at night. It gives Coville a nice distinction, having its own spook that stays around the same place, not running off like other ghosts and goblins. Daddy says the reason she is always right there is because it is the wind in the guy wires up on the bridge—the wires don't move off or run away so the sound is always there, only changing as the wind changes, and he ought to know, because he is the only person in the world who climbs those poles on the bridge, always doing it himself because it is so dangerous and he doesn't want his men to get hurt, and Mother says what about you getting hurt, and Daddy says, oh, well, he knows how to handle those hot wires, done it all his life. Anyway, Daddy says, the wind blows on the bridge all the time and plays those wires like a harp, a ghost harp, Mr. Reeves says, and Daddy says no, like a harp from heaven, all depends on how you look at it.

Oddly, the sound is only heard after the 9:30 freight train has gone free-wheeling it downhill, and the quiet behind it is shattered by a wild, keening sound, a humming ending with an eerie suddenness, cut off like a hand put over a mouth, choking back a frightening scream. Some said it was a mountain cat, not Granny Hall. Last fall, it was whispered, a cat had taken a small boy from colored town, back when the trees were bare and you could walk in leaves as deep as your knees and not make a sound, the leaves being damp from the fog and mist that lay over the valley. It was then the big cats would prowl, and the one that lived at the north end of the bridge would howl.

El had asked Daddy, "Which is it, Granny Hall or the mountain cat?"

Daddy had replied with a laugh, "Which do you think, little'un?"

But Mother cut in, "Don't frighten her, Bud. It's the electricity, Ellie, the current generated by the 9:30 freight returns to the substation up at Clark's Gap."

But Daddy, if he wasn't too tired would grin and say, "Are you sure about that Mother? I've seen cats as big as a colt and twice as fast in these mountains. Don't you go in the woods alone, Ellie, 'specially at night. It ain't safe."

"Isn't", Mother would correct, automatically. "Isn't safe."

On Saturday morning Mother gave El and Bun the sad news; they were going to remain in bed, but they could get up later in the afternoon. She was going to Mullins for groceries; they couldn't go. Jane was going to stay with them, and whatever she said was law, no matter how they felt about it. If they "were good, she'd bring them a treat. Remember, now, Jane is boss."

It was a fate worse than having tonsillitis, worse than the fiery red nose drops which Doc Steelman had sent by Daddy to be instilled every four hours. El knew Jane would be mean to them while Mother was gone, probably make her get up and wash dishes or something. From her bedroom window, she watched Mother leave, driving the new gray Ford. She slumped down on her pillow, waiting to see what Jane would do in her new role as Boss. She hadn't long to wait, for Jane came upstairs immediately, loaded down with a tray and other items.

"See what I've got!" she called, and El and Bun sat up in bed.

"What have you got?"

"Good chicken soup, made it myself, and crackers and butter and hot cocoa. If you eat it all, I've got a surprise for you!" Suspiciously, El asked, "What's the surprise?"

"You'll have to eat it all before I tell you," said Jane. "If you're not well enough to eat, you're not well enough for a surprise!"

It didn't take long for the two girls to empty the blue china bowls but the cocoa was dangerously hot. When the last cracker was gone, they called to Jane, "We're ready for our surprise!" They heard whispers downstairs and knew they had company.

In a few minutes, Jane, Hollie and Shirley came into their room. Bun and Shirley jumped up and down, hugging each other and squealing their pleasure. It had been days since they had seen each other. Shirley looked lovely, wearing a red coat with white fur around the hood and bottom, a Christmas present from Mr. Gillespie, who said Shirley looked more like the "Little Colonel " than Shirley Temple did. Shirley did resemble the famous movie star, both having blonde curls, but Shirley White's hair was much longer, and her face more petite, a tiny pearl-colored miniature of Hollie's, so small and perfect it could easily be encircled with two hands. Shirley was jumping up and down on the bed, squealing, "You not sick anymore? You not sick anymore?" and Bun, jumping with her, chanting, "No, no, no, no" …until she began to cough.

"Here, you two!" Hollie got a hand on each one and pulled them down on the bed. "You'll lose your chicken soup if you keep that up!"

"Not on me!" cried El, moving up on the bed.

"See what we have," said Jane. She laid three summer catalogues on the bed, one for each of them, two from Montgomery Wards and one from Sears. She laid a pair of small, blunted scissors on each catalogue. "Go to it!" she said with a big smile.

"Paper dolls!" The three girls grabbed for their treasure and settled back, turning pages to find the perfect model for the family they would cut out.

"They'll be busy for hours," said Jane, "let's go to my room."

El had to help Bun and Shirley cut out their dolls because they were always chopping off an arm or leg, but it wasn't long before they had an entire family cut out for each of them. El continued to cut out dresses, hats, shoes, gowns and robes for each doll, making small tabs at the shoulders to hold the clothing on each paper doll. She added Mirrors, furniture, dishes, a complete household of goods, and they set up housekeeping in opposite corners of the bed.

When Mother returned from Mullins, she found three happy little girls who had been no trouble at all. They were allowed to come downstairs to see what Mother had brought.

"Oranges weren't but 29 cents for ten." Mother said.

"They are 49 cents a dozen at the company store", said Hollie.

"And look! Strawberries!"

"Strawberries in January?" El and Bun dived in.

"I got them for my sick girls, but don't eat them now! I'll make strawberry shortcake for supper,' said Mother quickly."

"What about your girl that took care of your sick girls?" asked Jane.

"You, too," Mother said quickly, then went on with her conversation with Hollie. "Eggs were awfully high—I paid 35 cents a dozen for these."

"They are 75 cents up at the store here" said Hollie, "and coffee is 29 cents a pound. I see you only paid 19 cents for this. No wonder we can't get ahead; we do all our shopping at the company store."

"Don't you get a discount?" asked Mother. "I worked at the A&P before I married Bud, and I got a discount for anything I bought, plus day-old bread was free to employees." Mother continued putting groceries away and the last two items she pulled out of the brown paper sack was two boxes of animal crackers, the beloved cookies shaped like elephants, tigers, and bears. Shirley and Bun fell on them ecstatically and Mother apologized for not bringing a box for El; the box that had gone to Shirley really had been meant for her. A quiet look of understanding passed between Mother and El, and Mother handed El the newspaper she had picked up in Herndon.

El unrolled the paper and spread it on the dining room table:

LEADERS RUSH AID-TO-BRITIAN BILL FOLLOWING FDR'S CALL FOR SPEED; WHEELER BLOCK PREPARES TO FIGHT. NAZIS, SOVIETS SIGN TREATIES.

"Mother?" said El, puzzled, "I thought Russia was on England's side."

"What? Let me see that!" Mother took the paper from Ellie's hands and read the headlines. Slowly she sat down on the kitchen stool. Softly, with tears in her eyes, she said, "Dear Father in Heaven, what will England do now?"

When Daddy didn't eat supper with the family, the meal would be light. Tonight, Mother made fried apple pies with cream, and by five o'clock the chores were done: El had carried the ashes out and the coal in, Jane had washed the few dishes. It was already dark outside. The single light burning over the door to the company store couldn't be seen from the living room windows due to a heavy white fog. The trees were eerily white, the road and fences blended into the mist, ghostly lines in an ethereal world. The top third of the bridge supports and the bridge itself were obscured—the lower legs stretched upward into the mist like black iron ladders into the streets of heaven. El looked out the windows, hoping to catch a glimpse of the Mitchell boys across the road, but even their lights were blotted out by the dense fog.

She wandered through the house and at the slightest noise Mother said, hush, Daddy is sleeping and if you wake him, I'll give you a spanking you'll never forget. The Daily Telegraph was at Daddy's place at the table, beside his plate and coffee cup, ready for him to eat whenever he woke up. The front page gave the text of President Roosevelt's radio address the night before. She recalled his deep, resounding voice as he intoned his national policy. He had a slow-paced delivery, his voice rising at times almost to a shout, a powerful man who spoke so dramatically that even she was awed into listening. But reading his long speech was boring; she turned to the funnies and found Dagwood and Blondie.

There was a knock on the back door and Mother answered it. El listened attentively. "Do you think I could see your paper, Mrs. Phillips?"

"Why, of course, Edgar! What are you doing, out on a night like this?"

"It's not so bad—not as cold as last night, just foggy." Edgar took his shoes off on the back porch and left them by the furnace to dry. El met him in the kitchen.

"You have the paper, don't you, El?"

"I was just reading the President's speech," said El. "That's what I wanted to see," said Edgar. Mother looked at her queerly but didn't say a word as El led Edgar into the dining room. She had folded it quickly when she heard Edgar's voice, not wanting him to know she was reading the comics—that didn't seem very grown up. They leaned over the paper, side by side, El looking at Edgar, but Edgar looking at the speech by the President. He seemed sincere when he started reading it.

Just as our national policy in internal affairs has been based upon a decent respect for the rights and dignity of all of our fellowmen within our gates, so our national policy in foreign affairs has been based on a descent respect for all nations, large and small. And the justice of morality must and will win in the end.

Our national policy is this:

First, by an impressive expression of the public will and without regard to partisanship, we are committed to all-inclusive national defense.

Second, by an impressive expression of the public will and without regard to partisanship, we are committed to the full support of those resolute peoples, everywhere, who are resisting aggression and are keeping war away from our Hemisphere. By this support, we express our determination that the democratic cause shall prevail, and we strengthen the defense and security of our nation.

Third, we know that enduring peace cannot be bought at the cost of other people's freedom.

In the recent national election there was no substantial difference between the two great parties in respect to that national policy...I also ask this congress for the authority and for funds sufficient to manufacture additional munitions and war supplies of many kinds to be turned over to those nations which are now in actual war with aggressor nations…

"Listen to this, El!" Edgar reread the last paragraph. "He's going to have us building planes and guns and tanks and everything, and then turn them over to England or somebody, and then what are we going to do? We won't have a Chinaman's chance of beating the Germans then!"

"But we won't be fighting the Germans ourselves," said El. "We won't have to get into it at all, just give them weapons."

"Yes, we will!" said Edgar. "Just you wait and see! Pa says we will, if Roosevelt keeps on the way he's going. He says once we put our money into it, we're in it!"

"But we haven't put our money is," said El, then she added hesitantly, "Have we?"

"What do you think Lease-Lend is all about?"

El thought she had better stay quiet; she didn't really understand Lease-Lend, something about pay-in-kind, Jane had said, but she didn't want Edgar to know she didn't understand it. She turned back to the paper, more interested in being beside him than in what the President had said. Edgar was so smart, he understood all about this war. She was just glad he wasn't old enough to go into the service. As if he read her mind, Edgar spoke.

"I just hope it lasts long enough for me to get in it! Here, read this. This explains it."

Our most useful and immediate role is to act as an arsenal for them as well as for ourselves. They do not need manpower. They need billions of dollars' worth of the weapons of defense… we shall send you, in ever increasing numbers, ships, planes, tanks, guns. This is our purpose and our pledge.

"See, what did I tell you! He's going to send our planes over there." Said Edgar. "won't be anything left to fly by the time I'm old enough to get a license!"

"Oh, so that's it!" Jane stood in the doorway; neither El nor Edgar knew she was there. "All you care about is getting to fly—not the war at all!"

"Jane, that's not nice!" said Mother from the kitchen.

"Maybe it's not, but it's the truth, isn't it, Edgar!"

Edgar didn't reply. Jane had him figured out and he didn't deny it.

"Would you save this for me, El? I'm collecting the President's speeches."

"I'll save it for you," said Jane, "after I get through with it. I will need it for my history paper." Edgar started for the door.

Jane, a little nicer, said, "I've got the last one, too. You can have it after I get my paper done." She was disappointed that Edgar wouldn't argue with her. Jane, too, was tired of staying in the house, nothing to do—couldn't even play the piano when Daddy was sleeping.

"I'm doing my paper on the Lend-Lease bill," she added.

Edgar slipped his feet into warm shoes and left.

"I didn't know you had a history paper to do," El said to Jane.

"Do you think I tell you everything?" Jane said sarcastically.

"Tain't funny, McGee," El muttered under her breath.

"Girls, keep it down. Daddy is sleeping but from the looks of this weather, he may have to go back out tonight. We need to let him rest."

El did not sleep well: she kept waking up with Bun crowding her, and each time she tried to move her little sister over her skin felt hotter and hotter. About four o'clock in the morning the phone rang. As the light went on in the hall, she got out of bed and went to the top of the stairs. Daddy stood at the hall phone in his robe, and he was saying, "All right, Bert, yes, yes, we're on it, we'll get right up there."

"What is it, Daddy?" El asked as he came back upstairs. Daddy put a hand on her shoulder and said, "I've got a line down, Honey. You go back to bed— Ellie! Wait a minute!" He put his hand on her forehead. "

"Have you got a fever?"

"It's not me, it's Bun. She's awfully hot. That's what I got up to tell you."

"You go back to bed, honey. I'll call your mother."

Daddy left as soon as he dressed. He had thirty minutes from the time of the call to notify his men and report in. When Mother needed the car, she would dress quickly and drive him to Herndon, drop him at his motor barn, then go to the homes of each of the crew. She didn't have to get out of the car, but would pull up in front of the house and blow the horn three quick toots, an arranged signal that the men knew meant they had to report in to work ASAP. When the children were little, she took them with her, wrapped up in a big quilt and they would go back to sleep while she made the rounds. Now, with Jane at home, Mother no longer took the younger girls along, but left them sleeping in their own beds.

This time, before going to the car, she gave El and Bun aspirin and a dose of the fire-hot red nose drops prescribed by Doc Steelman. She tucked them in, spoke to Jane through her door, and left with Daddy.

It was nearly five a.m. but black as midnight. El went back to sleep and dreamed about Edgar. They were flying over the ocean in a small, single-winged plane that looked remarkedly like the one hanging on the dining room wall—*The Spirit of St Louis*. It was strange how much Edgar looked like Lindbergh, with the same blonde hair and direct blue eyes, same shy smile and inner confidence. Lindbergh had always been Mother's hero, and Edgar was hers. She hadn't known he wanted to fly until last night; now they had another thing in common, something else she could talk about to him that nobody else knew about. She was sitting on the porch in the swing with Clark Gable and was so hot, and Edgar was perched on the porch railing, holding her fan away from her and wouldn't give it back, holding it out and saying come and get it, come and get it, but if she tried, she knew he would kiss her and Mother said nice girls don't let boys kiss them but she was so hot, and this dress is too hot, she'd just take it off but she couldn't move, too much effort, to heavy, too tired, she would just sleep…

"El, Ellie!" Bun was shaking her arm. "Wanna drink, Ellie, want a drink, El." El tried to get up but she felt so tired and hot. "Mother! Mother-r-r-r-r!"

Mother and Jane came in together. "Well, you sleepy heads! Are you ready to get up? It's almost noon!"

"Wanna drink, Mama", said Bun, and she and Ellie both began to cry. Their throats hurt, their ears hurt, their fever was up and they felt too bad to pretend they were well.

The next three days were a blur of waking, medicine, hot lemonade, tea with honey, and one evening Daddy came in with Smith Brothers cough drops, cherry flavored. Another evening he came home with lime suckers sent by Old Red Karrigan. El tried to read to Bun but her throat hurt too badly. Jane came and sat on the bed and read Bun's Bible stories to her, over and over. They heard Shirley downstairs but she couldn't come upstairs to visit, might 'catch' what El and Bun had.

On Friday, their names were in the paper as being "confined" to their home due to illness; El clipped it out and pinned it on her wall, along with pictures of Clark Gable, the Lone Ranger, and Errol Flynn from the cover of Life magazine. There were three thousand cases of flu in Logan, out of a population of nineteen thousand, and Mother worried about El and Bun—was it flu or just a relapse of the tonsillitis from playing out in the snow?

El read the newspaper cover to cover and found an announcement about a girl in Logan. Edgar might know her, since he was from Logan and went back there to visit his Grandma.

Logan, W.Va. Jan 9, 1941—School days are ended for Betty Lusk, a bride at thirteen, she revealed today. She told her classmates in the seventh grade that she would become a housewife soon. She and William Smith, lamp keeper for Winding Gulf Coal Co., were married December 26th across the state line in Kentucky. "Too young to get married?" she was asked. "I don't think so," said Betty. "I love him and he loves me and there's no reason why our marriage can't be as happy as other folks who get married."

Smith's father voiced his approval, "I think Betty will make my boy a fine wife. She's honest and stout and a good worker. They'll do jest fine."

El lay in bed and thought about the girl, married at thirteen, less than two years older than she. How would it be, to be married? Maybe to Edgar? Somehow it didn't seem romantic, married so young. Where was all the fun, the dancing, and outings, and parties? Married sounded like cooking and washing dishes and babies. She wondered, did Betty Lusk know how babies were made? Perhaps by the time she was thirteen she would know too. Right now, it was all mysterious, and very improper to ask questions. The subject would be explained to her the day she turned sixteen, Mother said, or perhaps a bit sooner if it appeared she would 'develop' early, like Jane. Jane was developed: she wore a size B bra. El rubbed her hands over her own chest, well-greased with Vicks salve; she was as flat as Bun and twice as skinny, still a child. When would she be a woman?

Churchill was obsessed with a growing anxiety. He argued the seriousness of the threat of Hitler, the need to prevent the Luftwaffe from securing parity with the Royal air force, he compiled accurate information on Germany's rearmament plans—and his warnings were ignored. Meanwhile, Roosevelt was elected President of the United States, using his governorship of New York as a steppingstone, following the pattern set by his cousin, Theodore. The year was 1932. Although Churchill was still excluded from public office, in 1935 he was offered membership on a secret committee on air defense research; his dire warnings of war, like those of Cassandra, fell on deaf ears.

Roosevelt accepted the Presidency of the United States with quiet courage in March of 1933, and set in motion several measures to affect the economic recovery of America, serving up an alphabet stew to replace the long bread lines of the great depression: the AAA, CCC, NIRA, TVA, WPA, SEC, NLRB, FHA. He recognized the government of the Soviet Russia in order to promote trade, and proclaimed,

"This great nation will endure …the only thing we have to fear is fear itself."

In 1936 he was elected to a second term with a magnanimous mandate.

In February, 1938, Hitler assumed command of the entire armed forces of Germany: his favorite topic of conversation was the battles of Napoleon.

On Sunday, March 13th, after German soldiers had secured Vienna, Hitler announced he was affecting the annexation of the Austrian Republic to the German Reich.

Anthony Eden, who had inspired Churchill's confidence, resigned, and Churchill felt the 'dark waters of despair' wash over him. In March of 1939 he pressed for a national government, and the cries of the people of England joined his own as they asked for a joint declaration with France and the U.S.S.R.—but peace prevailed, and Neville Chamberlain, son of Joseph Chamberlain, with whom Churchill had differed in the early days, ignored their cries.

Roosevelt turned from domestic problems to the more urgent demands of foreign policy as he watched the deteriorating conditions in Europe.

September, 1939: GERMANY INVADES POLAND. Roosevelt called a special session to revise the neutrality act, but GREAT BRITIAN DECLARES WAR!

This was the 'quiet before the storm', the 'quiet winter', when all the world knew, and some scurried about with preparations, and some hid their heads in the snow.

Five

The earliest war news that El remembered was when Russia attacked Finland, demanding that Finland release their primary port to the Russians. She was just past nine years old, and the family had gathered around the dining room table, before the cathedral Philco. Daddy was reading the paper and when the announcement came on, he turned pale, and looked at Mother. El thought he was sick; that is why she remembered it. "Russia has attacked Finland," he had said, and she had asked, "Where's Finland?" and Mother didn't answer but she and Daddy clasped hands. She had never seen Daddy even feeling bad.

El was in Mrs. Margaret's fourth grade class, and struggling with long division and how to multiply nine times nine. The war news was as remote to her as the man on the moon, or more so—she had seen the man on the moon, but she had never seen Finland.

She thought about the little Finland's, they probably knew where America was, and she vowed to look it up, but she had received a whole set of The Bobbsey Twins books and was reading them, in order, for the third time. Finland was forgotten.

Finland fought hard, but collapsed in March of 1940.

Norway and Denmark fell in April of 1940. It was Eastertime and the preacher was preoccupied with hanging Jesus on the cross and didn't even mention the war in his sermon like he did now. In May, Holland was invaded: someone took their finger out of the dike because everyone was talking about how the land being flooded was supposed to save Holland but it didn't work because the Germans took over the flood gates.

It was two more weeks before Belgium surrendered. El wondered if Belgium was flooded too, but when she asked Jane, all Jane said was, don't you ever have geography lessons? She did have geography; they were studying Brazil and next week they would talk about the "big ditch," the Panama Canal.

When Holland and Belgium were invaded on May 10, 1940, Churchill was named Prime Minister. He immediately called Roosevelt and asked for a loan of thirty or forty old destroyers which the United States had recently reconstituted, to help bridge the gap between the present emergency and the time—still months away—when Britain's new ships would be ready for sea. Roosevelt, of course, had to seek congressional approval, which would take time.

May 15, 1940. France was invaded by the Germans. Where would the new fashions come from now? Jane moaned over the loss of French fashion pictures, and Mother said, don't give it a thought, all *your* fashions come from the pictures in the Montgomery Ward's catalogue, for Mother just looked at the pictures and sewed whatever Jane wanted, better and cheaper than that in the book: the girls had never owned a store-bought dress.

Great Britain, true to their pact, sent thousands of troops and nearly all of their war machinery into France, trying to stop Hitler, to save the country of their good allies, but the Germans outnumbered and outfought them. France was lost. The withdrawal began on May 29 and continued through June 4, along beaches at Dunkirk, with more than three hundred thousand men, British, French, and Polish, moving troops out of the country by ship and boat. They used all craft available, both large and small, loading at the coast of France, braving bombs and shells from German aircraft, carrying the men across the English channel, and depositing them on the island's shores. Shortly thereafter, Winston Churchill gave a speech that became historic in the next few weeks, a rallying point for his nation, and a battle cry for other countries.

June fourth:
We must be very careful not to assign this deliverance the attributes of a victory. Wars are not won by evacuation.

Then he concluded his address with these heroic words:

...we shall not flag or fail. We shall go on to the end. We shall fight in France, we shall fight in the seas and oceans, we shall fight with growing confidence and growing strength in the air; we shall defend our island, whatever the cost may be. We shall fight on the beaches, we shall fight on the landing grounds, we shall fight in the fields and in the streets, we shall fight in

the hills; we shall never surrender; and even if, which I don't for a moment believe, this island were subjugated and starving, then our Empire beyond the seas, armed and guarded by the British Fleet would carry on the struggle, until, in God's good time, the New World, with all power and might, steps forth to the rescue and the liberation of the Old.

June tenth dawned, and the last straw—save one—was broken: Italy declared war on Britain and France at four forty-five p.m.

Churchill went on the radio and tolled the news:

The news from France is very bad, and I grieve for the gallant French people… What has happened in France makes no difference to our actions and purpose. We have become the sole champion *now in arms to defend the world cause…*

Roosevelt also took to the airwaves that night:

On this tenth day of June, the hand that held the dagger has struck it into the backs of its neighbor.

Thus, the world held its collective breath until, finally, on the fourteenth, the city of Paris fell. The seat of the French government was moved to Tours. On the seventeenth, France collapsed. The Battle of France was over: the Battle of Britain was about to begin.

July 3, 1940. The Royal Navy sank or captured many vessels of the French fleet, for to let them fall into the hands of the Germans could give them supremacy of the seas; that would be disastrous to such a seafaring nation. Now Great Britain truly stood alone.

In September, El had started fifth grade, and Mr. Thomas Jefferson Collins had put a map of the world on the wall and turned the student desks to face it. Every day he had colored, in red, the area occupied by the Nazi army, colored it red for blood lost, for hearts broken and red for the fury of the subjugated people. The British Isles remained white, shining like a diamond on the blue-velvet sea, a jewel of hope on the anguished breast of mankind, a people who had endured the bombardment of death-rain from bombers and fighters of the Luftwaffe, watching as their own young men in the Royal Air Force held the fate of the free world in their hurriedly trained hands. And in September the destroyers on loan from America arrived, the new world coming to the rescue of the old …almost. The destroyers were sent in exchange for naval and air bases on Newfoundland and the West Indies, not yet fully committed.

September also marked the arrival of a new Nazi war horror, the delayed-action bomb. Designed to explode at an uncertain time, this devise added psychological harassment to physical destruction. In October they added incendiary bombs, and lookouts were required on the rooftops of the cities to spot the hundreds of fires that sprang up. These bombs led to the combining of some 1400 local fire brigades into the National Fire Service, becoming a part of the Civil Defense Service. This new group became the fourth limb of the King, in addition to the other three, the Army, Navy, and the Air Service.

The air raids stopped suddenly on November third and the silence was frightening to the British people; when they resumed a change in tactics was evident. The bombs began to fall on Coventry, Birmingham, Bristol, Southampton, and Liverpool, the Industrial Centers and port cities. The British parked old jalopies in their fields to prevent German aircraft from landing, and tethered huge balloons by iron cables to float in the sky, like fat cows grazing in cloud-fields, to force the enemy planes to high altitudes.

In the United States, Roosevelt, campaigning on the second of November for a third term, stated:

Our policy is to give all possible material aid to the nations which still resist aggression across the Atlantic and Pacific oceans.

His opponent, Wendell Willkie, the Republican candidate, said:

All of us—Republicans, Democrats, and Independents—believe in giving aid to the heroic British people. We must make available to them the products of our industry.

Three days after winning the national election, Roosevelt announced that the war goods would be split fifty-fifty, half going to England and Canada, half held in the United States. But Great Britain would soon be out of money, a fact recognized by both Churchill and Roosevelt; as early as November the Treasury Department began working on this problem.

December 8, 1940. Churchill wrote to Roosevelt, a long, wordy letter containing nineteen paragraphs, but reaching his primary point at the end:

If, as I believe, you are convinced, Mr. President, that the defeat of the Nazi and Fascist tyranny is a matter of high consequence to the people of the United States and to the Western Hemisphere, you will regard this letter not as an appeal for aid, but as a statement of minimum action necessary to achieve our common purpose.

Roosevelt, aboard the *Tuscaloosa,* sitting in the Caribbean sun, read and reread the letter, debating not what to do, but how to carry the American people with him in his plan. Treasury attorneys had found a law, written in 1892, under which the Secretary of War could lease Army property if not immediately needed for the welfare of the public. The word "lease" was the key; it would be swallowed with less choking by the isolationist who desired to keep America's wealth of goods in America. Churchill's letter gave him justification to tell the American mothers, once again, that their sons would not be sent to die on foreign soil. Their baby boys would be safe at home in the land of the free and the home of the brave, in the land that stretched from sea to shining sea. He had found a way to delay the truth a few more days, to dupe the public begging to be duped for a few more months. He returned home to prepare the service, to write the obituary that had to be written, just because America's freemen truly would be standing between their loved homes and war's desolation.

Bluefield Daily Telegraph:
December 10: TALK FINANCIAL AID TO BRITIAN

December 11: OFFICIALS GIVEN SECRET DATA ON BRITISH FINANCES

December 15: Editorial: Today Greatest birthday of them All! One hundred and forty-nine years ago today, a handful of sturdy patriots ...incorporated into their Constitution the Bill of Rights...we of this Nation need never fear the plague of totalitarianism if we always keep before us this warning: Liberty is not only a heritage but a fresh conquest for each generation.

December 17th: U.S. MAPS PLANS TO LEASE SUPPLIES TO GREAT BRITAIN.

Roosevelt's words were more elementary:

Now what I'm trying to do is eliminate the dollar sign. That is something brand new in the thoughts of practically everybody in this room—get rid of the silly, foolish old dollar sign.

And again:

Suppose my neighbor's home catches fire and I have a length of garden hose ...I don't say to him, "Neighbor, my hose cost $15.; you have to pay me $15 for it." What is the transaction that goes on? I don't want the $15. I want my hose back after the fire is over.

Incendiary bombs...incendiary bombs...incendiary bombs...
Oh, please, Mr. President, don't tell us too much, don't frighten us...

Frankly and definitely there is danger ahead—danger against which we must prepare. But we well know that we cannot escape danger, or the fear of danger by crawling into bed and pulling the covers over our heads ...our national policy is not directed toward war. Its sole purpose is to keep war away from our country and our people.

...evacuate the troops equally, British, then French, then Polish, along the beaches of France, moving the troops out of danger, British, French, Polish...

Senator Wheeler: ...the Lend-Lease-give program is the New Deal's triple A foreign policy: it will plow under every fourth American boy...

Roosevelt: ...that is not the answer at all, however, to those who talk about plowing under every fourth American child, which I regard as the most untruthful, as the most dastardly, unpatriotic thing that has ever been said. Quote me on that...

And on Christmas Day, the headlines read: **NAZI CHIEF SAYS CHANNEL WILL NOT STOP INVASION.**

Plow our boys under, great opportunity for coal in the coming year, not war, just an arsenal, Lindbergh is a member of the NO FOREIGN WAR committee, Lindy would never sell out America. Oh, yeah? Remember that medal they pinned on him, presented to him by Germany, just a couple of years ago, '38, maybe '39, I'm sure, because he came home right after that, Lindy would tell those bastards to go fly a kite—or a Jenny! Get it? Har-har-har, there's no way he'd not fight, he's no coward—he flew across the ocean while the rest of them sat around with their thumb up their rear, remember?

Holt predicts best year ever for West Virginia and troop trains will roll across the state taking the 201st Infantry of West Virginia National Guard into active duty. They are headed for Fort Benjamin Harrison, where the Guard will replace the 11th Infantry of the U.S. Army. Wonder whar the Army is headed, boys? France? Britain? Hell, no! They're agoin'a kick the pants off them Krauts! Give 'em a lick fer me, boys, give 'em a lick fer me!

But this was Sunday and there was little real news, only a rehash of the President's speech on the sixth of January, his annual message to Congress, the one El and Edgar read together last week, the one in which Roosevelt had concluded with, *"In the future days, which we seek to make secure, we look forward to a world founded upon four essential human freedoms."*

The first is freedom of speech...the second is freedom of every person to worship God in his own way ...the third is freedom from want ...and the fourth is freedom from fear...

With each of the four statements, his last words were, "...everywhere in the world ...everywhere in the world...not just in America, for Charles, or Franklin, or Edgar, or El, but everywhere." El thought it was so noble-sounding and grand. Wouldn't it be wonderful to sit in that great hall of justice; she wanted to see the President, to hear him say words like that! And his conclusion!

This nation has placed its destiny in the hands and hearts of its millions of free men and women and its faith in freedom under the guidance of God. Freedom means the supremacy of human rights everywhere. Our support goes to those who struggle to gain those rights or to keep them. Our strength is in our unity of purpose. To that high concept there can be no end save victory.

His words were so high-minded, so grand. Congress would have to pass the Lease-Lend bill on the first day!

But in front of the Capitol, a mother's crusade—the women in long black coats with fur collars and hats with small black veils and real feathers and long black leather gloves—walked up and down, kneeling upon the sidewalk to pray, carrying flags and signs that read KILL BILL 1776 NOT OUR BOYS. Odd, the number they gave the bill in the House of Representatives—bill number 1776. How did that happen? H.R.1776. Glory, glory halleluiah, and the Star-Spangled Banner in triumph shall wave, O'er the land of the free and the home of the brave!

NAZI, SOVIETS SIGN TREATIES: *this is the last straw!*

Daddy was a true railroader; he lived the work, day and night. He had known no other. If someone asked him about his work, if he liked it or some silly question like that, he would swear a bit as he replied:" this damn hard-drivin', rip-snortin', back-breakin' son of a mother's uncle's job? Hell, NO, I don't like it! Anybody'd be a damn fool to like this cold-killin', bone-chillin', grave-diggin' job!" But he'd been on the railroad since he was big enough to carry water to men laying track, and he wouldn't seriously consider leaving it. Besides, the other choice in this area is coal mining and, as Daddy said, give me a pole as high as the sky before a hole in the ground any day. The only holes in the ground he went in had both ends open!

Unlike Mother and Jane, Daddy couldn't carry a tune in a coal bucket, but his songs didn't need a tune to be entertaining. Sometimes, on a Sunday evening, when he wasn't called out to work, he would put Bun on his foot, swing her up and down, holding her hands, riding a horsey. When the Whites were visiting, he'd take turns, Bun, then Shirley, Bun jumping up and down, me first, me first, and Shirley, dimples deepening, saying okay, okay, me second, me second. When Daddy sang, he usually started with, "Trot a horsey, trot a horsey, in to town, trot a horsey, trot a horsey, throw me down!"—at which the foot would collapse and the little girls would hit the floor. This would be followed by railroad songs, some of them made up on the spot, some of which, he swore, were traditional, born on the railroad and handed down, generation to generation, by word of mouth.

El's favorite was one he sang when they had to get up early, perhaps leaving for a trip to Virginia, or camping down on Barker's creek. He would repeat the single stanza, not always exactly the same:

Rise, bullies, get your four o'clock coffee, Stable boss is up and he's done his work, now it's time to call the commissary clerk, rise bullies, get your four o'clock coffee.

Daddy swore this was a song of the railroad camp cars, where he lived long before he married Mother, and Hollie would cut in with, "You mean you haven't always been married?" And Daddy would say, "Heck no! I was a real ring-tailed roustabout when I was young!" Emmett would laugh with him, shaking his dark head, his teeth flashing, "We sowed our wild oats before these gals latched on to us, right, Bud?"

Mother was in the kitchen slicing lemon pie with meringue an inch high while they took a break from the Rook game that had gone on all afternoon and well past suppertime. El lay on the floor before the hot-water filled radiator, reading the jokes in the *Reader's Digest*; Jane was in her room, her usual place in bad weather, when evening church services and Epworth League were cancelled. Bun and Shirley had come out of their tent—a blanket over a small table in the corner—and the four adults sat around the dining room table for their card game. The radio had had something about the State Nurses and had been turned off. Outside the snow lay a foot deep, gathering the faint light from the sky and reflecting it gallantly, but it was still dark in the shadows of the mountains.

El felt the happy, relaxed mood in the room; all of her favorite people—except Edgar—were there. Laughter ebbed and flowed around her as she read a while and listened a while. Mother was cutting pie in the kitchen, singing, "Swing-lo-o-o-"and Daddy, with Bun on his foot, was singing in the dining room. "Ole Dan tucker was a fine ole man—c-h-a-r-i-o-t—washed his face with a frying pan—c-o-m-i-n-g f-o-r to c-a-r-r-y me home—combed his hair with a wagon wheel—Swing lo, sweet chariot—died with a toothache in his heel!"

The pie was served. Bun and Shirley retreated beneath their tent and El sat Indian-style with her back against the warm radiator. Daddy and Emmett talked. The new passenger station was open in Herndon, a model for future stations, who picked that awful yeller color? Ole Karrigan do that? Nah, that came from the boys at Norfolk. Sure beats that sick orange they used to use on everything. Did ya know the N&W is putting on another run to Radford? The powder plant is almost finished, I hear. The P.D. said the other day there were over eleven thousand men working on that project; said the traffic jam was so bad the men couldn't get to work on time, there's no houses in Radford, people have to live in Princeton or Bluefield and drive down. Looks like Cliff Sanders could get on down there. Hell, he don't want to work! Bud, watch your language, little ears. Well it's true, I offered to put the sorry son of a hound-dog to work, you know what he told me? Said he got dizzy when his feet got off the ground! I told him to go back to his damn gopher hole—sorry, Emmett, I didn't mean no offense—it just made me so mad—that's okay, don't give it a thought, I know what you railroaders think of us miners!"

"All right, whose turn is it to deal?" asked Mother, removing the plates and cups. "Don't you two get into that argument!"

"What do you think of this Senate mess?" Daddy asked Emmett.

"How the hell—sorry, Faith—how did that happen anyway?"

"Well it was like this. It's never happened before, not in the history of our country. It's a first, both the outgoing and the incoming Governor claimed the right to appoint the next Senator. Old Neely took the oath in the middle of the night, secret ceremony, and real fast he appointed Rosier to serve out the remainder of his Senate term. And Governor Holt had named Clarence Martin to succeed Neely! Now it's going to wind up in the U, S. Senate in a big fight—who's going to represent West Virginia in Washington—Rosier, or Martin? Ain't it the dickins?"

El jumped up from her place by the radiator, "But which one is supposed to, Daddy?"

"Rachel, don't interrupt," said Mother, "that's not polite." But Daddy turned to answer her. "That's what we don't know, Ellie. This has never come up in the history of our country. It will go to the Senate; they will make a ruling and it will set a precedent for all states."

"I remember the Senate from our trip to Washington," she said.

"That's good, honey. Now find something to do, you are holding up the game." El turned away. Maybe she could play with Bun and Shirley. She started under the blanket-tent but Bun said, "Go away, Ellie, there's not room!" Bun never wanted to play with her if Shirley was here. She went upstairs to see what Jane was doing, and found her in the bathroom, her hair wrapped in a towel and her face covered with cold cream.

"What are you doing?"

"None of your business, just go away!"

"She's lovely, she's engaged, she uses Ponds!" sang El, making a face. "Mother-r-r-r-!" Make El leave me alone!"

"Rachel? If you can't behave, you can go to bed!"

There was nothing for her to do, nobody wanted her, she might as well take a book and go to bed. She looked in her mirror, picked up the hairbrush and fiddled with her hair but it was no use; she'd never have pretty hair like Jane's. She snapped off the light and went to the window. At least she could see Edgar's house if she couldn't see him. There was a light in their front window; a shadow passed across the window shade, it could have been him, or Joe, or Mr. Mitchell. How she longed for spring and warm weather when they could go out and play, red rover, red rover, send Ellie over! But it was cold and clear.

She looked at the high bridge for the millionth time, the distant moon lay a thin silver line on the high wires, frost shining like a spider web from this distance. She made a resolution: this year she was going to walk across that bridge—if she had to sneak out at midnight to do it!

It would be grand to stand up there and look down at the tops of the houses, look into the trees, almost as good as flying! Mother would kill her, if she knew—but what Mother didn't know wouldn't hurt her! Or, rather, what Mother didn't know wouldn't hurt El!

She could see Mr. Reeves making his nightly rounds, wearing an old Army hat—wonder where he got that, probably from the Salvation Army—she giggled at the thought of Old Mr. Reeves being in the Army—no Army would have a man that old. He had on an old khaki overcoat, buttoned to the chin, his hands in his pockets, and a gun on his arm. Some said he never had any bullets in that gun, Daddy said don't you believe it.

There was smoke coming from the house he used for storage, smoke rising straight up in a thin white line, no wind at all. Guess he didn't want the pipes to freeze up and bust but it smelled like he was burning corn cobs for fuel and she wondered why, when the other house, the ghost house, was so full of good wood. She knew. She had seen him hauling it in, heavy hickory and dry oak logs, hauled it in last fall and he had said, Hey there! What you doin'? You git home to yer Maw, and she had told him, I don't have a "Maw!" but he chased her off and later she told Mother she had sassed him. Mother got after her for not being respectful to Mr. Reeves after all he had done, and El had asked, what did he do? But Mother said, never you mind, you just remember, you are to be respectful to all adults: that's what a proper young lady does.

So, who wants to be a 'proper' young lady? But El was wise enough to keep her mouth shut.

Mr. Reeves lives right next door to the ghost house and she wondered why Granny Hall didn't scare him, but in the daytime, he was always working on the house, opening the door and banging around, like he was doing repairs. Stands to reason he would know if there was anything strange going on, and he's right about not being in any hurry because nobody wants to live so near to being under the bridge, with all the cinders and slack coal falling off the trains when they went overhead, about eight times a day, plus the passenger train, two trips every day, and the freight train at nine-thirty every night, plus the railroad was always returning empties, not on a schedule, just anytime they got enough to make up a train. Sometimes a load of poles goes by, to the mine down at Pineville: they might fall again.

Right square between the spook house and Mr. Reeves' house sits Mr. Reeves' john. It is peculiar in a way, just as Mr. Reeves is peculiar. All the johns in town have a chain on the inside of the door, to be hooked over a nail when occupied; when unoccupied, the door stands open, exposing the bench-style seat with a round hole cut in the middle, and anyone can tell when the john is being used or is empty. But Mr. Reeves, living alone, knows when his john is in use, and, being a carpenter with time on his hands, he has put a neat wooden button on the outside of his john; it is impossible to tell if Mr. Reeves' john is in use or not, a fact which precipitated the trouble that brewed on Halloween night.

El could hear Hollie and Emmett getting ready to leave. Bun was crying, she always cried when she got tired. Shirley didn't; she just climbed up into Emmett's big arms and put her face against his rough neck and went sound asleep, never knowing when they reached their house, never fussing at all. Sometimes Bun was a brat, but Shirley was never cross: Shirley was an angel.

"Why are you sitting in the dark?" asked Mother as she brought Bun up to bed. "Why not?" asked El.

"Don't get smart with me, Rachel." El knew not to pursue it.

"Don't you feel well?" asked Mother.

"I feel fine," El replied shortly.

"Sure you don't have a sore throat again?"

"My throat is just fine!"

Flannel pajamas on, tucked in bed, lights out. El wondered why Mother always thought she was sick if she got fussy; didn't Mother know that sometimes a person could be unhappy or feel blue and not even know why herself? Once she had tried to explain that to Mother, but Mother had said, oh, now, Ellie, you're just having growing pains—you'll be all right. Mother didn't understand. Nobody did.

All the other houses in the camp are occupied by miners and sometimes they didn't stay very long, families moving in and out due to job changes, a man would quit, or get fired for drinking or not showing up for work, or a mine would close and they'd move on, except one, the end of the star point going up the road to the main highway. That house, the one you passed first when entering the camp, that house belonged to Mrs. Margaret Sanders, the third and fourth grade teacher, and her husband Cliff. Now, Cliff was a queer sort of fellow to be married to a school teacher; he didn't stay home much, always looking for something—chasing rainbows, Mother said—because Mrs. Margaret didn't like to be married to a coal miner and there wasn't much else to do in the area if a man didn't have a farm. But Mrs. Margaret didn't like Cliff to come home dirty, she wasn't about to put miner's clothes in her washing machine.

Cliff Sanders had a queer way of speaking, too. No matter what anybody said to him, he'd answer, "Th'hell you say!" If you said, it's going to rain, he'd say, th'hell you say; if you said, it's a pretty day, he'd say, th'hell you say! It was just his way of talking. Mrs. Margaret told him to go find a job, and all he said was, "Th'hell you say!" He hadn't been around lately, so maybe he had found a job, or maybe he was still looking, no one knew.

Mrs. Margaret was a nice-looking woman, big-busted and given to wearing tight sweaters, and she smoked, only woman in the camp to smoke real cigarettes in public. She was younger than Mother but older than Hollie, so didn't have many friends. She painted her fingernails bright red, and they were long and curved at the ends, and when she was angry or wanted the student's attention, she would rake her nails down the blackboard in a horrible screech. Last year, when El was in the fourth grade, Mrs. Margaret brought her nails down the board so hard it scared El and she burst into tears. She made El stand out in the cold hall—each schoolroom was heated by their own coal-burning pot-bellied stove—and El caught cold and missed school for three days. El didn't like Mrs. Margaret after that, but Mrs. Margaret kept calling on her to give book reports. El preferred that Mrs. Margaret go out in the hall and smoke her cigarette with Mr. Collins. They always had a lot to talk about, teacher business, and met in the hall frequently through the day; they couldn't smoke in the classrooms, against the law or something. El thought Sarah Jo should be in on those meetings, but she never was. And at night Mr. Collins liked to 'stretch his legs', and it was generally well known that Sarah Jo went to bed early, and Mr. Collins would walk up the road to Mrs. Margaret's for another teachers meeting. Mrs. Margaret didn't like the noise from the ball games in the triangle, she doesn't like the trains going over head when she is at school, the clack, clack, clackity-clack, or the rattling of the empties that travel faster, going louder down the mountain, faster, lighter, going back to the mines for another load of the soft-blowing coal. In fact, there's not much Mrs. Margaret likes, except being called "Peggy" by Mr. Collins: she sure does like that.

There was a lot of speculating that Mr. Collins had been on his way back from Mrs. Margaret's house the night the boys had gone up Coon Creek. Up colored town, there were about three or four houses nobody went to, usually empty or too close to the bridge, and the negros never came into the camp, seldom lingered below the company store.

One summer night a bunch of white kids decided to go up Coon Creek and look around, sort of visit. They waited until after dark, so they wouldn't get caught, or stopped by parents. Well, they got past the Company store and heard singing. Real nice singing, not at all scary, so they went on.

It's fun hearing Ben talk about it, for he and Will were both in on it. He said they walked on a ways, and the singing got louder, and they could hear clapping, like the colored folks were having a real good time, and he and the kids were real quiet and tiptoed up to the house, meaning to look in the windows, and—all of a sudden—the singing stopped! The clapping stopped! They'd cut off the singing right in the middle of a high note. There warn't a sound. It was so quiet they could hear each other breathing, in fact, that was all they could hear—somebody breathing.

Well, they turned around, aimin' to high-tail it out of there—and there stood Mr. Collins. Right behind them. He never said a word, just stepped over a bit and let them by, Well, they hit out for home as hard as they could go, never looked back. They waited and waited for Mr. Collins to tell their folks and for them to catch it, but he never did, as far as anybody knew. There was a lot of speculation that Mr. Collins had been up to Mrs. Margaret's house that night, but nobody could say anything without telling on themselves. It passed by, but they never went up to colored town again.

Valentine's Day headlines read: WAR MOVES JAR ALL CONTINENTS OF THE WORLD.

In the fine print the paper said the Australian government sees grave situation is in southern Pacific, Yugoslavia is on the verge of accepting Hitler's terms, allowing passage of war materials through their country, and Turkey is ready to fight. There were 600,000 Nazi troops gathered in Rumania, the Dutch were forecasting a blow at the Netherland East Indies, and Japan was increasing their naval units.

On top of all that, a cold wave swept eastward on winter's swift wings and snow blocked most of the roads by Saturday morning. The temperature was hovering around twelve to fourteen degrees, and the sun made little change. But on the lawn, outside the kitchen window, the bluebirds were back, joining the juncos and sparrows at the feeder. Their bright blue wings flashed across the snow, and their reddish-orange breasts stood out when they perched on the clotheslines. El watched them from the window over the kitchen sink and wished she could frolic like the birds; she expressed her feelings to Mother, but her reply was grumpy; she had not gone to sleep until after Daddy got in, sometime after midnight. El got an idea: somebody had to bring in the coal!

"Want me to bring in the coal, Mother? Then Daddy wouldn't have to get out so early this morning."

"Sure you're feeling all right?" asked Mother.

"I feel great!" replied El, not recognizing the sarcasm.

"Well, wrap up real good."

El raced up the stairs, forgetting to be quiet. She threw on her snowsuit and extra socks, slid down the stair rail, and grabbed her boots, hat and gloves from the back porch. She was out of the house in two minutes flat.

Edgar and Joe were throwing snow balls in the triangle and she pushed her luck as she joined them; maybe Mother would give her a few minutes before calling her. The snow was just right, still a little wet and easy to pack into hard balls. The fight was one-sided as both boys began pelting her with snowballs as soon as she appeared. She fought back good-naturedly and for a few minutes the battle made the air white. They soon tired and Edgar tackled her, rolling her in the snow until her suit was covered. El shrieked and tried to get away, loving every minute of the struggle.

Hollie came up the road wearing Emmett's black rubber fishing boots, and carrying Shirley. "Hey," she called, "Want to make a snowman?" The cold air gave Hollie a crisp, clean look, brightening her color, making her lovelier than ever. The boys yelled in agreement, but Ellie said, "I've got to get in the coal."

"What if I ask Faith if you can play a while?" asked Hollie.

"Oh, would you? That would be super!"

Hollie took Shirley to the back door and called to Faith. When Mother came, Hollie sat Shirley inside, talked a few minutes, and came back to the road. "She said it was all right, for a little while."

"Oh, Hollie! I love you! You can talk Mother into anything!"

The four began to roll snow into balls, all over the triangle, up and down the roads, across El's yard and back to the triangle. Before long they had three snow figures lined up, two large ones and one small one. Hollie named them for herself, Emmett and Shirley, but El called them El, Edgar and Joe.

"We'll have to decide," said Hollie," or we won't know what kind of hats to put on them."

Edgar disappeared, returning in a moment with his baseball cap and an old hard hat belonging to Mr. Mitchell. El ran to the back porch and swiped Mother's straw garden hat. Lumps of coal made their faces, and an old broom, a shovel, and one of the boys' baseball bats helped out. Daddy was up and dressed and he came out to see their handiwork.

"Well, what do we have here? Eenny, Meeny, Minny—where's Mo?"

"That's it," cried Hollie. "We just have to make one more!"

"I've got a better idea," said Daddy. "Have you ever made an igloo?"

"Yeah! All right! What a neat idea!" came from the group

"How do we do that?" asked El

"Start by making snow balls, about the size of that one," pointing to the snowmen's midsection. "Bring them around the house."

Daddy had seen the drift of snow in the corner of the house, where the enclosed back porch jutted out making an 'L' with the dining room wall. It would be out of the wind, sheltered by the two walls. He cleared a semicircular arch for the walls. The others brought him the snowballs which he placed like laying bricks, gradually bringing the sides up level with the dining room window sill, packing it tightly. He brought an old stove board from the coalhouse and placed it over the top, piled more snow on, rounding it and packing it firmly. Then he took the shovel and made marks on the outside in squares. When finished, it looked just like the pictures of an Alaskan igloo.

"Get inside, Ellie, and scoop out the extra, make some marks like blocks in there." El crawled in through the cutout door and packed the loose snow on the floor, making blocks like Daddy's on the inside. Edgar, Joe, and Ellie had only a few minutes by themselves before the little girls came, but when they did, there was room for them all. El and Edgar looked at each other in satisfaction, and plotted to use it for a hideout as long as it would last.

"I'll sneak over tonight and pour water on it—it will freeze solid before morning" said Edgar.

"It will probably last until spring!" said El, and Joe said, "Yeah!" They all agreed it was more fun than making snowmen, and they were warm and cozy. Mother spoiled their fun by calling them in for lunch. Just as they left, Edgar turned around and winked at El, right in front of Hollie! El was so thrilled she didn't even mind going inside.

Sunday morning the sun was bright and the roads were clear; there hadn't been a new accumulation of snow since Friday. Daddy felt reasonably certain he wouldn't be called out to work in the next few hours. Faith could take the girls to church, and after dinner he had a surprise for them.

The Lend-Lease bill had been passed by the House of Representatives on February 9th; everyone assumed the senate would push it through rapidly, but the hearings continued day after day, the pros and cons, everybody and his brother being called, Daddy said, just to get in the act—attention-getters. In the meantime, the Aussies had reached Singapore, and Germany was telling Greece to make her peace, their planes flying over the Greeks almost daily. The United States was making plans to increase their air power in the Pacific and fighter planes were to be sent to Hawaii; Japanese troop ships had been sighted heading southward from Formosa and from the mainland of Japan.

Mr. Collins moved the pins he had started placing in the map on the wall, one pin for each time an American troop moved out of the States. The retired military men were meeting regularly, old veterans of the World War, a move sponsored by the American Legion to give the county an emergency force that would be prepared.

El liked going to Sunday School. They divided into classes like school, everyone meeting in the same one-room church, but curtains were hung on wires running near the ceiling. Each grade had their own area, enclosed with the curtains around two or three rows of straight-backed wooden pews.

The girls wore their good coats to church and were allowed to leave their boots at home so their white ankle socks would look nice. Every other day, except Sunday, they had black rings around their legs where the top of the boot rubbed.

The lesson was about David and Goliath, and El got to read first because her teacher, Mrs. Plover, Mother's friend, said she read the best. She stood self-righteously before the class and solemnly intoned: "And David said, what have I now done? Is there not a cause? And he turned from him toward another, and spake after the same manner…and when the words were heard which David spake they rehearsed them before Saul…"

"Very good, Ellie" said Mrs. Plover. "Now what do they mean?" El stood silently. She had read the words, not thought about their meaning. "Sounds like they were going to have a play, they were going to rehearse…" The class burst out laughing. "Now, Ellie, be serious!" El stood there, red-faced, tongue-tied. "Ellie, what do you think is going on here with David?" El looked down at her bible. What Mrs. Plover didn't understand, was, El was being serious. She sat down, embarrassment sealing her throat closed and filling her mouth: she couldn't have spoken if she'd been beaten. Mrs. Plover went on with the explanation herself, then asked another child to read. El didn't hear a word that was said for the remainder of the hour.

The church service began and Preacher Copeland stood before the small congregation with head bowed and eyes closed. El liked to watch him pray. He had a thick fringe of white hair, but the crown of his head was nearly bald; he let one side grow long and combed it over the bald spot. The bald spot didn't show when his head was straight, but when he bowed it in prayer the long piece slipped sideways and exposed his scalp. It was pink. Pink like his cheeks and his hands on the inside, and sometimes, when he'd been crying, his nose was pink, and he cried easily and often, praying and crying each of his lost sheep straight into the arms of Jesus where they would be safe evermore.

El liked Preacher Copeland, he was a lot like Mr. Belcher, old and sweet, hard of hearing and easy of smiling, smelling a lot like Vicks salve even in the summer, and Vicks was a familiar smell to El what with being sick so often in winter, a comforting smell. Preacher Copeland was comforting, except when he was preaching, and then he got short of breath and hollered, winding up fast and running full speed for almost exactly fifteen minutes—El had timed it on Mother's Elgin watch one Sunday when Mother was sitting with her, Mother not knowing what she was doing—then stopping just as suddenly: he preached the wrath of God, hell-fire and immediate incarceration unless forgiveness was granted in time. El wondered how she would know when to ask for forgiveness, did he mean everyone knew when they would die? Knew in advance? In time? Or was she to ask for forgiveness constantly just to be safe? That seemed like an awfully lot of trouble, she'd never get anything else done! She liked it better when he said, "Let not your heart be troubled…" That was the way she saw Jesus. It scared her when Preacher Copeland hit his fist on the podium and thundered, "What Shall Be the End Of Them That Obey NOT the Gospel Of God!"

She thought of Daddy, sitting alone at home, in his undershirt and slippers, reading the paper, his coffee by his hand, happy, resting, enjoying his quiet Sunday mornings—was he doomed and unforgiven? Then she remembered he had a surprise for them after dinner. Preacher Copeland didn't scare her anymore: she just stopped listening.

Bun sat beside her, asleep against her shoulder. Shirley sat on the other side, her head back and her blue eyes wide open, watching the now red-faced preacher. Shirley looked scared to breathe. El leaned toward her and whispered, "It's all right, he's about through." Shirley looked at El with relief and tried to smile. El saw Mother looking at her from her place in the choir and straightened up, but she took Shirley's hand and gave it a hard squeeze. Shirley squeezed back, and then she smiled.

They rushed home and Mother put the Sunday dinner on quickly, having it all ready before church. They were off to see Daddy's surprise, but, said Daddy, we can't stay long, I'll have to get back and check in, never know when some fool engineer will jump his train off the tracks.

They drove up Herndon Mountain, Daddy taking the curves easy, trying to avoid the car sickness that always accompanied this drive. The road scrapers had thrown up a high wall along the edge and in some places, it was too high to see over, and they were driving through a tunnel. Cinders and gravel covered the surface of the road making a gritty sound under the tires, like a dirt road rather than one hard-surfaced.

Mother told them about the plans presently being made in Mercer County." This section of Route 10 is on the list to be paved this spring," she said, "because it is the gateway to Wyoming County. And, Wyoming county is the fastest growing county in the state!"

"Sure hope they finish it before we go to Galax this summer," said Jane.

"Don't count on it," said Daddy sarcastically, "they've been saying that ever since Wyoming paved this side of the mountain!"

They reached the top and pulled to the side of the road, parking in such a way that the dirt road leading on up to the very tip of the mountain was not blocked.

"What time is it?" asked Mother.

"Two-thirty," said Daddy.

"What time did they say they'd be here?"

"Before three," Bert said, "maybe a little later."

"Who is it, Daddy?" asked the girls. "It's a surprise," was all Daddy would say. Mother had thoughtfully brought along a book for each of them. Jane was well into hers. El read to Bun, a story about a wacky duck named Ping who was always missing the boat. Daddy sang a railroad song for a while, letting El read her own, a new one borrowed from Mr. Collins, titled *Forgive Us Our Trespasses*, by Lloyd C. Douglas.

She got to the second page and stopped. Giraffes eat bananas? Do they? She asked Jane, who said, how should I know, and Mother said, we'll look it up when we get home, and then Daddy said, "Listen! I think I hear them coming!" He rolled down his window to listen. There was the sound of a heavy truck winding up the road from the Mercer County side of the mountain.

"They're coming!" El thought she had seldom seen her Daddy so excited; he was acting as young as Edgar or Joe. He got out of the car and walked to the edge of the road, looked down the mountain to the curves below, then returned to the car.

"Now, girls, you are going to see a sight you might not see again in your lifetime. You'll have to stay in the car until I tell you, you don't want to get in the way of these men. And another thing—be very, very quiet, don't want any loud shouting or sudden move, just whisper."

Mother's eyes were twinkling as she asked, "Don't you think I should tell them a little about what they are going to see?"

"Plenty of time for that, after." Said Daddy, still guarding his secret. He walked to the edge of the road again, came back quickly, "There's two of them!" He laughed delightedly.

Bun clamored into the front seat to see better and Jane put her book down. El could feel the excitement radiating from Daddy even though he was standing still.

Two large trucks topped the hill, one behind the other, the type used to haul cattle with canvas around the sides to block the wind and a top to keep the rain out and the cattle in. They couldn't see a thing. Daddy walked to the cab of the lead truck and spoke to the driver. In a few minutes he came back to the car, got in and started the motor.

"We're going to try to follow them; if it gets too rough for the car to make it, we'll hitch a ride in the cab with them."

The girls were on edge, not knowing what to expect, torn between disappointment—who wanted to drive all the way to the very tiptop of Herndon mountain just to see some old cows—and anticipation; Daddy wouldn't drive up here just to see cows either. Or would he?

The trucks ground up the steep narrow road, their wheels dangerously close to the edge, leaving deep ruts which Daddy put the car wheels in, holding them in place. The road led to a fire tower used by forest rangers during fire season and was seldom traveled. The trees grew close by the side of the road and in places it looked more like a path than a road for vehicles.

El looked closely at the canvas-covered back of the truck, trying to get a glimpse of the cargo; they could hear something in the back of the truck, slipping and sliding as the truck took the curves, but there was no bawling or mooing like cows would do. The trucks reached a level spot beneath the high steel fire tower and pulled in side by side. The driver of the first truck got out and came back to their car.

"Bill, you just pull over there on the other side of this clearing. I think your girls can get a good look from there."

"Fine, George, and thank you!" said Daddy.

Although they were bursting with curiosity, the girls remembered what Daddy had said about noise or sudden movement. "Put your coats on," said Mother in a low voice. She eased the door open quietly and stepped out; the girls did the same. Daddy picked Bun up and sat her on the front fender of the car. El quickly claimed the other. "It will be a little while," Daddy said. "If they are rushed, they could get hurt. Now, be real still, and don't talk."

The men untied the canvas at the back of the truck and eased down the tailgate, making a ramp to the ground. A mass of dark brown animals was huddled together, trembling visibly.

"Deer!" Jane breathed softly, "wild deer."

"Shush," said Mother. "Don't move."

The largest of the animals moved toward the ramp as the men stepped out of sight. He moved forward slowly, lifting his head majestically, sniffing the air; he stood directly facing them, his eyes wild and quick, searching the tree-bordered space, examining the steel legs of the fire tower, smelling the sides of the truck and the ramp. They could see the white patch beneath his chin as he lifted his head and the small nubs of horns when he put his head down. His tail was raised and twitching nervously up and down, as were his ears; the muscles of his shoulders and forelegs rippled beneath his heavy dark brown winter coat.

"Buck," Daddy said softly, and the deer immediately shifted his gaze to the car. "He's looking us over," Daddy whispered.

A doe moved apart from the others, approached the ramp, testing it carefully with one foot. She moved slowly halfway down, standing beside the big buck, her eyes on the trees so near. As she reached the ground, a small, spotted fawn tottered down the ramp behind her, following her lead. The doe looked about, her ears flicking as she listened to every sound. She turned towards the car, a sleek, gentle-eyed creature, and looked straight at El. The direct, unguarded look into a wild animal's eyes took El's breath away and she gasped with surprise. The men lowered the second tailgate and the movement startled the doe. She ran swiftly for the cover of the woods, her tiny fawn trotting behind her. Quickly, three more does, heavy with their unborn offspring, dashed down the ramp and escaped to the forest. The buck followed less quickly, still majestically holding his head upright, and in a breath, all six were lost to sight.

The scene was repeated with the second truck, but more rapidly; first a large buck, acting as lookout, then three does and a third younger buck. The three does would soon give birth for their sleek sides bulged under a dark, almost black, winter coat. Their tails flashed white, stiffly erect, as they bounded over the snow and into the woods. In a matter of moments all were hidden in the heavy timber.

With the trucks now empty, the men raised the tailgates and replaced the canvas. Daddy introduced the men to Mother and his girls, thanked the men for letting him know they were going to make the drop, and they were gone also. Mother and El walked to the edge of the trees but all that was left were small half-moons, footprints imprinted in the snow. They stood looking into the trees but there was no sign of the deer. Only the wind moved the dead-looking branches, the only sound that of a few dry, dead leaves clinging to the limbs of the oak trees.

"Only the oaks hold on to their dead leaves all winter," Mother said softly, almost to herself. "I know," El whispered back.

Once back in the car, turned around, and headed back down the narrow, dirt trail, El asked, "Are there wild dogs around here?"

"Why do you ask?" said Mother.

"I just wondered," said El. She could see in her mind's eye the picture of the white doe lying still and cold on the ground, picture it as she had when she first heard about the albino deer—the only one living in Wyoming county, and it had been killed by wild dogs. Now, it seemed more real. They reached the hard-surfaced highway and Mother explained about the deer. "They were brought by the State Game and Fish Commission. They are restocking our county. There will be a total of twenty-five thousand released within the state. We almost let the white-tailed deer be extinguished by allowing the does to be killed."

"How could anyone shoot such a beautiful animal, "exclaimed Jane. "Lots of people hunt them, kill them for food, Honey," said Daddy. "Just a few years ago that was about all people had, that and rabbits."

"How could anyone eat them," Jane insisted.

"Well, now, there's not much better eating than a thick venison steak, 'specially not if your mother cooks them!"

"You would eat them?" Jane said incredulously. "Daddy, how could you!"

"Easy," said Daddy with a grin. But the girls were not joking; they had been impressed with the sight, especially with the tiny spotted, frail-looking fawn. "I wanted to petted him", said Bun.

"No one can pet a deer, honey, they don't let you touch them."

"Why didn't the Buck have horns?" asked El.

"They shed them in the winter," said Mother.

"Where do they put them?" asked El "Why, I don't know," said Mother. "Honestly, El, your questions!"

"Well, I never see any in the woods," insisted El.

"They dissolve," said Daddy, "or the chipmunks and porcupines eat them."

"Ugh," said the girls in unison.

"Those deer can run like the wind, swim across any river, jump higher than my head," said Daddy, "and nothing can hear or smell as good as a deer!"

"Then why are some killed?"

"Accidents happen," said Mother.

"Or they make a mistake," said Daddy. "We always pay for our mistakes."

"Not always, Bud," protested Mother.

"Always," said Daddy. "Maybe deer make mistakes too."

"See what you started," Jane said to El as Mother and Daddy argued.

It was after four o'clock; the pleasant Sunday afternoon was gone. Bun went to sleep on the way home and El sat quietly thinking about what she had seen. Mother and Daddy held hands after their argument, while going down the mountain. She could tell because Daddy held the steering wheel with his left hand at the top so he could make the curves in either direction. It had been a good break in the winter doldrums for all of them. El couldn't wait for school to start in the morning so she could tell Edgar about the deer.

Six

When Monday morning came, El was bitterly disappointed: the influenza outbreak that had closed Logan and Mercer schools had reached Wyoming; the County Health Department reported more than three thousand cases. The students of Coville rejoiced for none of them were seriously ill. The snow was sticking enough for sleighing, the igloo was intact, the sun was shining briefly in the middle of the day, and they were on holiday. El and Edgar found plenty of time to hide in the snow-house and talk. They found innumerable things to talk about as they became better friends. The only thing they fought about was Charles Lindbergh and they tried to steer clear of that subject. It was hard to do because they were always talking about flying and how could anyone talk about flying and not mention Lindy.

By Wednesday it was snowing again and if it wasn't coming down hard it was cloudy and looking like it. The temperatures remained below freezing and on Thursday they were not permitted outside.

Mother allowed the Mitchell boys to come in for an hour. Bun had Shirley to play with and Jane had invited Ben and Mary Beth. When Hollie finished work at the store, she stayed for a while also. After much arguing about partners, Jane and Ben took on Mary Beth and Hollie in a Rook game, the four of them seated around the dining room table, Bun and Shirley playing dolls in their tent in the corner.

El took Edgar and Joe up to her bedroom, her hide-out, under the dresses hanging in her closet. El had 'borrowed' a flashlight from Daddy's supply on the back porch; she often read in bed, under the covers, when she was supposed to have turned her light off. She had recently discovered Edgar Allen Poe, and had his story, *The Tell-Tale Heart* ready to read to the boys. It was pitch dark in the closet and she shielded the flashlight with her hand, illuminating only the page she was reading. Edgar and Joe sat cross-legged, Indian fashion, before her and listened raptly. Ellie read well and dramatically:

True!—nervous—very, very dreadfully nervous I had been and am; but why will you say that I am mad?

She read slowly, emphatically. The closet was dark, warm, and very quiet except for her low-pitched voice.

...But even yet I refrained and kept still. I scarcely breathed. I held the lantern motionless. I tried how steadily I could maintain the ray upon the eye. Meantime the hellish tattoo of the heart increased. It grew quicker and quicker, and louder and louder every instant...I thought the heart must burst...with a loud yell, I threw open the lantern and leaped into the room. He shrieked once—only once...

Joe stood up so suddenly he knocked the dresses off the rack, and grabbing the door handle, he shouted, "Let me out of here—this is boring!"

Edgar and El rolled on the floor, laughing." Boring, my ass," said Edgar, "he was skeered to death!" Edgar loved the story and when it was finished, Joe came back, scooted inside the closet with them.

"Guess what I saw," he said.

"What?" asked El.

"I saw Ben put his hand up Mary Beth's dress."

"Aw, come on, Joe. You're just trying to make up something 'cause you got scared," said Edgar. "You don't have to—we're not going to tell anyone you couldn't take Edgar Allen Poe!"

"Honest Injun, cross my heart," said Joe." I was in the living room, on the sofa, and I saw him, under the table."

Suddenly all three of them had an urgent need to go down to the living room and sit on the sofa. Joe was right. From there they could see all four players' legs, but all four had their hands on top of the table. El was disappointed; she would have loved to know something that Jane didn't know. Were Mary Beth and Ben sweet on each other? She remembered New Year's Eve—but it had been Will that was so long in coming home.

Mother called from the kitchen; it was time for the boys to go home. El was sorry they had come downstairs, for if they hadn't, maybe they could have stayed longer.

On the evening news, station WHIS in Bluefield announced they had joined the National Broadcasting Company, and Daddy said, well good, now we will get some decent news coverage.

And Jimmy Stewart has asked for an A-1 classification; he said he wanted to be treated just like an ordinary soldier. El was devastated. How could anyone treat Jimmy Stewart as ordinary? To make matters worse, on Friday the *Daily Telegraph* carried an account of Lindbergh's speech as he testified before the Senate: Lindy tells Senators America needs arms which would be sent to Britain under the bill ..."

Throughout a barrage of questioning from senators backing the measure, the alert young flier steadfastly clings to his position that: America needs the arms that would be sent to Britain; that American help has not and will not affect the trend of the war; that American assistance has encouraged and is now prolonging the conflict; that a negotiated peace immediately would be the best possible result.

El and Edgar argued loud and long over the speech and neither gave ground, El stoutly defending her hero, Edgar calling him names, and then Edgar refused to play with her, resisting even her invitation to share the igloo. El had not been so unhappy for days.

The railroad strike ballots had been received and Daddy spoke about that situation gravely. The Radford Powder Plant employees signed a petition to get a train on the Virginian Railroad so employees could come from Wyoming County to work on the construction of the big facility. El saw Cliff Sanders Friday evening and hollered at him:

"Hey, Mr. Sanders! How's the new job?"

"Not bad, little'un, not bad!" Mr. Sanders stopped by the gate for a minute. "How have you folks been?"

"Just fine! Daddy took us to see some deer last Sunday."

"Th' hell you say!"

"The Game Commission turned them loose—up on Herndon Mountain."

"Th' hell you say! Now I know where to go huntin' this fall!"

"Aw, Mr. Sanders, you wouldn't kill a deer!" She looked at the big man in the buff-colored coat. "Mr. Sanders, you going to move?"

"Like to, Ellie, but they's no houses down thar. You know, I have to git up at three o'clock in the morning to ketch that dang train!"

"Is it fun?"

"Is what fun—ridin' the train?" El nodded. "Wal, I reckon it ain't all that bad. It's a purty sight, you know, lights winking on and off, all over them hills around Bluefield, kinda like th' stars fell, if you know what I mean, not like here, where the mountain is always dark. And on the train, well it's a jolly-like crew, sorta like the mines, only you can see and it ain't so cold. We play cards, read the paper, they's a feller with a juice-harp, plays some fer us. It ain't all bad."

"That sounds like fun!" exclaimed El, and Cliff Sanders, warmed to his subject by El's interest, continued. "Then by daylight, we're down by New River and they's wild ducks there—mallards, with green heads—puts on a show ever time a train goes by, a real purty sight. They're on the way back to Canada, I reckon." El switched hands with the coal bucket she was holding. "Well, I guess I'd better get in," she said. "I hope you don't move, Mr. Sanders, I'd miss you. Mr. Collins said he wasn't going to let Mrs. Margaret go!"

"Th' hell you say!" Mr. Sanders waved good-bye. Later, when El asked about her husband, she got a cold stare and silence. So, didn't she want the Virginian to put on an extra train so her husband could live at home and work at Radford too? Mrs. Margaret exploded: "You mind your own blamed business, Miss Rachel Phillips, you go sticking your nose in my business one more time you will get it chopped off now you get down to your end of this god-forsaken-coal camp and stay there it's bad enough I have to put up with you brats in school I sure don't plan on it when school is out!"

El looked down at the triangle from her bedroom window; it had started snowing at dark, big, heavy flakes—how could it possibly be true that no two snowflakes were alike when there were this many—covering the dark road, hiding the marks made by their sleds, and the wide bare strips made when rolling the snowmen. Enney, Meeny, and Mighty, stood looking back at her, still holding their broom, shovel and baseball bat, and the snow was sticking to their hats. They still needed to make 'Mo'.

God was making everything look fresh and clean for the new month starting at midnight. It would be the first day of March at twelve o'clock—she had a new concept of time since New Year's Eve—and spring was officially just three weeks away: it had never looked more like winter.

"Well, it came in like a lion, Rachel."

"What came in, Mr. Gillespie?"

"March, in like a lion, out like a lamb, isn't that what they say?"

"They who, Mr. Gillespie?"

The big storekeeper talked on, ignoring her question. "Means we'll have an early spring. Can't come too early for me. Just eggs today?"

"Yes, sir."

"Roads are all blocked. Your mother won't get to Mullins for her weekly shopping this Saturday, will she!" El detected a bit of satisfaction in his voice. "You tell Jane we won't be going to the ballgame tonight; most likely it'll be cancelled anyway."

"Yes sir," said El, but he didn't hear her, just kept on talking.

"You be careful on those slick steps, I haven't got salt on 'em yet, don't want Miz Phillips' eggs broke before she gets 'em!"

"Yes, sir, Mr. Gillespie. Mr. Gillespie?"

"Yes, Rachel?"

"Next time it snows this deep, would you take shorter steps? If I could've stayed in your tracks, I wouldn't have gotten snow down in my boots!" She dodged out of the store quickly.

Mother was going to make snow cream and she wanted to watch. She hit the top step on a slick spot, her feet slipped straight out in front of her and she hit hard on her spine. But she saved the eggs, concentrating on holding them tightly in their brown paper bag as she slid the full length of the high steps, landing at the bottom. She didn't realize her fall had been observed until a strong hand lifted her to her feet. It was Mr. Mitchell, Edgar and Joe's father. He didn't speak at all, just held on to her until she steadied, looking her straight in the face, the way Edgar did, direct and soft-like at the same time, never blinking or looking away, kind of understanding-like. She never had noticed how much Edgar looked like his father until now. She smiled and he let her go, continuing up the steps and into the store. He hadn't said a word.

El plodded knee-deep through the snow, down the road, under the bridge, and home. Noticing how much alike Edgar and his father were just made Joe more of a stand-out, more like a gypsy or an Indian.

Now that she and Edgar had become good friends, she decided she would ask again about their mother. It didn't seem natural for a mother to go off and leave her children, her Mother sure wouldn't do that! Maybe Edgar would tell her more—that is, if Edgar ever got over being mad at her, calling her dumb. He was still angry because she stuck up for Lucky Lindy; he didn't understand how the flier was practically a member of her family, being Mother's hero and all. Oddly, thinking about Charles Lindbergh made her think again about Mr. Mitchell. They both were tall, thin, and light-haired, but it was more than that. He hadn't said a word to her, but he had left her with a good, warm feeling, almost like a friend, almost like she knew him, the same way Mother declared she knew Lindbergh without actually knowing him at all. Gets confusing, thought Ellie, as she ran in the house with the eggs.

Mother was in the kitchen, apron on, snow piled high in an enameled dishpan. When El told her the eggs were still 79 cents, she fussed and fumed; she could have gotten two dozen for that at the A&P in Mullins, highway robbery, no wonder the miners couldn't get ahead, disgraceful, a store that was supposed to look after its men! Jane was upset as well when El delivered Mr. Gillespie's message about the ballgame. This was Herndon's first tournament game, and she would miss it. Mr. Gillespie had promised to take her and Mary Beth when he took Ben—it just wasn't fair! Why couldn't the county clear the roads faster! And Mother couldn't take them because Daddy might be called out and need the car—that wasn't fair either—why couldn't her daddy have a job like other men, and not have to be on call all the time!!

The war news was depressing also. Hitler had taken another country, one El had never heard of: Bulgaria would sign the pact tomorrow. The Japanese had given the French another ultimatum. The Senate was still debating the Lend-Lease bill. The British were still fighting alone, without assistance from anyone. A dark, dark hour.

Between Bun and Shirley, El didn't have a single paper doll with all of its extremities; she wasn't going to play with crippled-up dolls, made her think of all those soldiers getting hurt and killed in the bombings of London. Mother was talking about tomorrow being the first Sunday of Lent. Bun asked, "What's Lent?" El said, "It's that white fuzz that gets on dark clothes when they are washed." Mother heard her. Instead of laughing at her joke, Mother thought El really didn't know, and she had to listen to a spelling lesson and a Sunday school lesson both and it a Saturday!

To make matters worse, Mother was talking about giving up pie and cake for Lent because both she and Jane were too fat. Well, *she wasn't too fat! If anything, she was too* skinny, *and Mother said, well, if she couldn't eat it, she sure wasn't going to bake it!"* El, as usual, when things got too rough, found a book and retreated to her room.

By Sunday the roads were clear and they went to church. The ballgame had been postponed for a week and Jane was happy. Best of all, school would resume on Monday, everyone having been cured of the flu, except the six that died with pneumonia—but none of them lived in Coville.

Monday afternoon El sat at her desk, scribbling on her tablet; she was writing a poem about Brer Rabbit and the Tar Baby, one of her favorite Uncle Remus stories. She thought maybe Bun would like it, or maybe Mrs. Collins' first and second grade class. She felt someone looking over her shoulder but ignored them. After a few more lines, Edgar said, "Hey, that's pretty good! I didn't know you could write poetry!"

"There's a lot you don't know about me," said El with a superior air. "I thought we were mad."

"Aw, come on, El. It's no fun being mad."

When the bell rang, Edgar was waiting for her outside. "Race you!" said El.

"Naw, let's walk. We can talk about your poem. Did you finish it?"

She handed it to him to read. Joe ran by and called to her, "Hey, Ellie, race you!" She ignored him. "Edgar's got a girl, Edgar's got a girl, Edgar's got a g-i-r-l-l-l-!" BillynBob took up the chant, the three of them walking backwards down the black road, laughing and pointing at Edgar and El. The chant changed to, "Ellie's got a feller, Ellie's got a feller!"

"Don't answer," said Edgar. "They'll get tired of pestering us if we don't pay any attention."

"I'll beat them up!" El exclaimed hotly.

Edgar looked level at her. "If they's fightin' to be done, I'll do it. For both of us."

El hesitated, but Edgar kept his gaze steady and his voice calm. He wasn't smiling. "Just do as I say. Ignore them. It won't last long."

As he predicted, the boys soon tired when they failed to get a rise out of either of them and they ran ahead, throwing snowballs at each other. El and Edgar dragged their heels and were the last ones home.

El hadn't noticed how tall Edgar was getting until he walked beside her; he was one of a few boys who were taller than she, and today he seemed nearly as tall as his father. When they reached her house, Edgar opened the gate for her and she walked through like a lady; she couldn't remember doing that before. She had been jumping the fence for years. Mother used to scold if she fell and ruined her dress, but she hadn't done that for years either. They lingered at the gate, talking about the bluebirds at the feeder and the electric wires coming into the house. Edgar was so smart, he knew everything, like which was the male and which the female, and that sparrows would steal their nests if they got half a chance. When Edgar turned toward his house, he said, "Wait for me in the morning," and ran.

Mother was at the back door when El entered the porch and pulled off her boots. "What took you so long? I was getting worried."

"Oh, am I late?" El tried to appear casual, tossing her hair back, like Veronica Lake, but somehow it didn't quite come off the same. Veronica Lake's hair was blonde, very long, and she wore it draped over one eye, while El's hair was dish-water brown and barely covered her ears. But for now, in her heart, she knew she was every bit as pretty as Veronica Lake: she had seen it in Edgar's eyes.

Tuesday and Wednesday the air began to warm, and there was some melting of the heavy snow, just enough to start the spring run-off. Thursday was well above freezing, and the trees had no snow at all on their branches; there were patches where the ground could be seen, where the sun hit on the high slopes in the middle of the day. But Friday night it began to snow again, growing colder as the sun sank behind the hills and the wind sprang up.

On the war front, the Turks had adopted an attitude of watchful waiting while bolstering their defenses against the Germans.

At the State level, a bill making permanent voter registration mandatory was ready for signing, to go into effect next year at the May primary.

It snowed hard all night, Friday, adding six or seven inches to that left on the ground. Sleet and ice made the roads treacherous; cars could not move without chains, and many had to be pulled out of the deep snow banks. It fell steadily for twelve hours, giant flakes that stuck to everything, even the sides of trees and buildings, clinging and building dangerously on the wires carrying current to the homes, as well as those on the railroad; trains were at a standstill. The mines shut down due to damage to the electrical wires.

Daddy went out on Friday night and did not come home until Sunday night. When he came in, gray and exhausted, he dropped the newspapers on the hall table and went up to bed.

Over the weekend El read, *For Whom the Bell Tolls* by Ernest Hemingway, and Mr. Collins had handed her the book, saying," no sticky finger marks on this one, Rachel—it's one I want to keep." The story perfectly suited her cloistered weekend; she went about the house misquoting lines from the book, "It can't snow, it can't be snow, these mountains do not know the names of the months, these mountains do not know it's spring, it can't snow, it can't be snow…" until Jane screamed, "Mother, can't you please make her shut up!" But Jane had played the *Spinning Song,* by Mendelssohn, until El was ready to scream also. However, Jane was justified in being obnoxious—it was her recital song and she had to practice. In desperation, Mother gathered the girls around her. "Let's plan our Easter outfits" she said.

"I want pink," Bun said quickly. "No, honey, not with red hair—how about blue? We'll make pink for Shirley but you will look prettier in blue."

"Prettier than Shirley?" asked Bun. "Yes, prettier than Shirley." Jane wanted navy and white, the military look, you know, it's all the rage, maybe red shoes?"

"What about you, El?" asked Mother, and El said, "BLACK!"

Mother looked at her speculatively, well, if that's what you want, and El felt too disagreeable to change it. She picked up the newspapers and retreated to the living room sofa.

Daily Telegraph headlines:
SENATE APPROVES LEND-LEASE MEASURE BY 60 TO 31 VOTE
17 DAYS OF DEBATE AUTHORIZES AMERICA
THROW ITS PRODUCTS
INTO ENGLAND'S BATTLE

Washington March 8 (AP)—Worn down by three weeks of oratory and dispute, the senate tonight passed the lease-lend bill authorizing President Roosevelt to mobilize industrial America and throw its products into England's battle against Germany.

"Mother, why do they call it Lend-Lease bill one time and then Lease-Lend the next time?"

"I don't know," said Mother. "I guess it doesn't make much difference, it means the same thing"

"They passed it."

"What?"

"The Senate passed the Lend-Lease-Lease-Lend bill."

Mother sat down at the table, silent for a moment, then she bowed her head and closed her eyes, praying. When she raised her head, there were tears in her eyes and tears running down her cheeks. She took off her glasses and wiped them on her apron.

"Girls," she said solemnly, "we are in the war."

The news called the blizzard as bad as the one back in 1888, with some areas getting as much as sixteen inches of snow, but West Virginia was lucky, escaping with only nine or ten inches. The greatest inconvenience for everyone was the "white out" caused by the high winds that blew the snow, making visibility nearly zero. The radio and newspaper offices were bombarded with calls about the brilliant flashes of light that lit up the downtown area of Bluefield, some people thinking the Germans had come and bombs were being dropped. But the officials reassured them: the blue-white flashes were caused by electric motors laboring along under iced electrification wires. El could have told them that: she stood at her bedroom window and watched the light dancing on the wires over the high black railroad bridge, when the trains went up the mountain. When the ice was real heavy on the lines, it was almost as good as the fireworks on the 4th of July.

Glen Rogers had won the Wyoming County title, beating Herndon 48 to 41. They had played the game in spite of the snow. Jane was disappointed at missing it, so upset she went to bed at nine o'clock with El and Bun.

Just before midnight, El heard Mother and Daddy up; he had rested and now was hungry. She slipped down the stairs to see him, the stairs creaked, and Daddy called out, "El?" When she didn't answer, he repeated, "Ellie? I know it's you! Come have a sardine with me!" She ran to the kitchen and he sat her on his knee. They shared a tin of sardines and a pile of saltines—El was the only one who would eat sardines with Daddy, not even Mother would eat them.

As they sat in the warm kitchen, they heard a change in the sounds of the night. "Listen!" commanded Daddy. El stayed very quiet. Mother stopped stirring her tea.

"Rain?" said Mother. "I don't believe it!" She got up and drew back the window curtain. "I don't believe it," she said again. "It is. It is raining."

"Oh, God!" Daddy moved El off his knees and dropped his head into his hand." Oh, God, no!"

"But that's good, isn't it? It will melt the snow!" El was confused.

"No, honey, it's *not* good," said Daddy sorrowfully. "The rain will melt the snow too fast; we'll have floods when all that snow hits the creeks all at one time, and floods mean slides, and slides mean-"

"I know, I know," said El, "and slides mean out to work again, to clean up the mess and clear the—"

"—set up new poles that slide off the road, and take the wire with them, and boulders, and rocks—"

"Bud, please, go back to bed while you can; you'll be called out before morning, if this keeps up."

"Yes, we'd better," he said, and he hugged Ellie tight. "You get to bed, too, little'un."

It rained all night Sunday, all day Monday, and into Monday night. By Tuesday morning the snow was nearly gone, the creeks and rivers were well over their banks, with more water coming down the steep mountainsides, the worst flood in many, many years. At three o'clock on Monday a landslide hit the Virginian tracks at Pepper, Virginia. Daddy took his line gang from the New River division to assist the Norfolk division. The track was blocked for fifteen hours and the Virginian routed the Time Freights over the N & W line.

About six a.m. Daddy came back to the motor barn at Herndon; Mother heard his car go across the railroad bridge and knew he would be home soon, to change clothes and eat, if not to stay. As she cooked hot oatmeal for breakfast, she warned the girls: you are not to go near the creek; you are not to get out of the yard.

"Oh, goody!" laughed El." I don't have to go to school!"

"You know how I meant that, Ellie," said Mother, "and you will be very sorry if you disobey me!" Mother was too worried to take a joke.

El went upstairs to brush her teeth before leaving for school; she was making a special effort to look nice now that Edgar waited for her every morning, and walked home with her every afternoon. Joe and the others had stopped teasing them, it was 'old hat' to them now, just as Edgar had said it would be. She tried to see the creek from the bathroom window, but the willow tree blocked the view. Toothbrush in her mouth, she went into Mother's bedroom and looked out the back window.

The water in the creek was nearly level with the concrete retaining wall; the water was a dark yellow-brown, a mixture of the clay soil and humus from high in the hills above the camp, where there was very little coal dirt exposed. As the creek flowed through Herndon, Bud, and Alpoca, collecting black dust and coal dirt as it went, it would turn black before joining Slab Creek at Tralee. She watched the water swirling around as it came down the hillsides in gullies, boiling through a concrete culvert, nearly touching the wooden bridge over the road.

There were short logs floating and spinning in the water, bobbing along like wooden matches tossed in a commode while being flushed, swirling around, somebody's firewood—probably the whole stack—being carried downstream, a stick at a time. She heard Jane go out the front door to catch the school bus and knew she had a little more time.

The water was fascinating, ever-changing, and she watched it lapping at the edge of the wall in a low spot, not yet running over, just level with the walk. That walk was nearly two feet wide along the top of the wall, and frequently it was used as a way to go from one end of the camp to the other without getting in the heavy black mud. It was a favorite place to play in the summer, perfect for roller skating, and this spring it would be great for trying out the new scooter—no, on second thought, she wouldn't let Edgar see her on that scooter. She would teach Bun to ride it, maybe just show Bun and Shirley how to ride it.

She became aware of an unusual sound, almost like a train in the distance but not the same, either. She listened closely. It was coming from the creek; the water was roaring so loudly she could hear it with the window closed.

El left for school wearing boots and raincoat, even though it wasn't raining now. Never knew what it would be like this afternoon, when school turned out. Edgar met her at the gate and they waded the deep, black mud to the school, removed their galoshes in the hall as usual. The air was warmer, they agreed, and he said she could go fishing with him, soon as the water went down and she said, oh, boy, did you see it this morning? Yes, he had seen it, and it was out of its banks down at BillynBob's house, spread out all over, a regular lake.

They began their spelling test, Mr. Collins standing at the front of the room, calling out the words in a deliberate voice, pausing briefly after each one while they wrote on their tablet: clothes, something one wears; closet, a storage area, collect, to gather, to assemble.

Suddenly Mother was at the door, motioning frantically to Mr. Collins. Everyone turned around to look at Mrs. Phillips, standing at the back of the room.

"Eyes FRONT!" shouted Mr. Collins. "This is a test!"

The teacher walked back to join Mother. El could hear the murmur of their low voices, could feel the urgency in Mother's voice, but could not distinguish the words. Mr. Collins called Edgar to him, and Edgar ran out of the room. A moment later the school bell began to ring, dong, dong, dong, Edgar kept it up dong, dong, dong, the camp signal for an emergency, dong, dong, dong, the call to assemble at the school. Everyone in hearing distance would come. Mr. Collins came back to the class. "Turn in your papers. Rachel, would you collect them, please. I want the sixth-grade boys to come with me. The rest of you, STAY IN YOUR SEATS!"

What has happened? Who is it? Somebody's hurt—who? Is it Bun? It was Mother who came—what's wrong? Where is Bun? There's Bun, in Mrs. Gillespie's arms, and there's Hollie with …where is Shirley? It's Shirley? No, no, no, relief, it's not my little sister, but Shirley's like a sister, thank you, God, Bun is okay, but Shirley? No, no, no… everyone gathered at the windows, nobody stayed in their seats.

Mr. Collins divided the boys into three groups. They were to go house to house in all three directions; it was possible Shirley had wandered away; possible she was still safe. Mr. Gillespie would return to the store and search it; Shirley had spent hours there while Hollie worked, perhaps she had gone to sleep on the flour sacks, she'd done that before. The men would start along the creek banks—but there were only three men in the camp, Mr. Gillespie, Mr. Collins, and Mr. Reeves. A hurried consultation was held, and Mr. Collins came back inside.

"It's been decided to let you all go home. You are to go straight home, stay away from the creek, don't stop anywhere. When you get home, search your house carefully—little Shirley White is missing and it's possible she's hiding somewhere. If you find her, give a yell, and take her to Mrs. Phillip's house, that's where her mother will be. Any questions?"

The children gathered their books, coats and boots quickly and quietly. El ran down the road, spattering mud over her legs and her dress, jumped the fence and burst into the kitchen. Mother stood in the hall at the railroad phone and turned to look at her as she came through the door. El saw the look and realized she had just tracked in more mud than ever before had been on Faith Phillips' kitchen floor. Mother turned back to the phone without saying a word to her.

"Bud? Can you hear me? Where are you? Thank God, you're close! We have an emergency here. We can't find Shirley—we think she may have fallen in the creek! What? We can't find Shirley! We think—what? Yes! There's just Mr. Reeves and Mr. Collins and the boys from school! Yes, yes, all right, yes— and Bud— hurry!"

Mother turned to face El. "Your father is bringing the line gang. He'll find her." El looked down at the mud she had tracked in and back to Mother. "Hollie is in the dining room, Rachel, why don't you stay with her. I'll make some coffee."

Grateful for Mother's unseeing eyes, El went into the dining room to sit beside Hollie at the table. Suddenly she realized that Bun was not there, and wild-eyed, she rushed back to the kitchen. "Mother! Where's Bun?"

Mother turned from the sink and reassured her. "She's with Mrs. Gillespie, Ellie. You can go after her in a little while, but not right now, not until we know—well, in a little while."

El went back to Hollie and took her hands and held them, unable to watch their twisting and turning on the table.

"Emmett said he would bring her up to Faith, he was leaving for work, he said it was too muddy for her to walk, she'd sink out of sight," Hollie turned to look at El and her eyes were frightened, reminding El of the Doe as it stood on the truck ramp and looked at her. "Emmett said she was getting too big for me to carry; said I'd have to put chains on my shoes to keep me from getting stuck in the mud." She slumped against the chair-back. "I thought she was with Faith; I went to work…" She laid her head down on the dining room table, unable to go on.

Mother came in with a wet towel and wiped Hollie's face. "Now, just hold on, we don't know yet, Bud is coming, he's bringing the men, we'll find her, honey."

"Mother, how did you…?"

"Why, I went up to the store for butter, I was going to bake that cake you fussed about—I was so surprised to see Hollie! I didn't know she was working today." Mother pulled Hollie's fair head against her round abdomen. "I didn't know she was coming this morning…"

"She might be with Emmett!" Hollie sat up suddenly. "Oh, God! Faith, she might be with Emmett! Maybe he didn't go to work after all, she might be with him!"

"Wait, wait a minute. I thought of that, and so did Bud. He's sending one of his men to the mine after Emmett, he should be here soon, now. You just hold on; we don't know for sure about anything."

Mother had coffee on the stove in the big camp pot and it began to perk, sounding musical in the stillness as they sat at the table together. El could see the creek from the dining room window, and, as she watched, a log—half-submerged, big end riding lower in the water—floated down the creek, the force of the water slowly twisting it about, turning it round and round; it didn't take long for the log to vanish down the creek, and the log had been bigger than Shirley. Shirley. Little, doll-faced child, delicate, Shirley was such an angel... El jumped up from the table and crying," I've got to wash this mud off!" she ran upstairs. Anything. Anything at all would be better than sitting there, looking at that awful muddy water, or looking at Hollie—and where else could she look?

El put her feet in the tub and turned on the water, rinsing the mud from her feet, legs and socks at the same time. She heard the front door open and turned off the water to listen.

"Faith? I'm just coming on in!"

It was Mrs. Belcher. El recognized her voice. "My goodness! What's all this mud on your kitchen floor! I've never seen such a mess! Hollie, child, I know it's going to be all right, now Faith, where's your mop, I'll just do up your floor." The door again, and Mrs. Belcher was talking to someone on the back porch. Grandma Gillespie. She had come the back way. Then Mrs. Collins, and Mrs. Margaret, they had stayed to bank the fires and lock the doors at the schoolhouse.

Now all the women were here. She wasn't needed to sit with Hollie now, watch her worry and hurt, she could stay upstairs—no! She could go after Bun! She desperately wanted to see her little sister, be close to her, feel her chunky little body, be sure she was safe. She dried her feet, took clean socks from her dresser drawer; she would have to scrub her shoes—but when she reached the kitchen Grandma Gillespie had done them for her. Mother reached her the coat she had thrown on the cabinet.

"You want to go after Bun, don't you," she said, and El nodded. If she spoke the tears would spill over and Hollie would see her crying.

Bun kept asking questions and El didn't know how to answer her. "Why did I have to stay with Mrs. Gis-pee? Where is Shirley? Do you have to go back to school? Is this Saturday? Are we having a party? Did you hear the school bell ring and ring and ring? Why are you hugging me so good, El? You're hurting me!"

"Come on, we'll just let those ol' ladies talk. We'll go upstairs and play house." And El took her precious sister up to their room, spread a quilt on the floor of the closet and told Bun, now this is our house! The voices came faintly from the dining room and now there were people in the living room, too, but if she kept her door shut, she couldn't hear what they were saying—and neither could Bun. They played a long time; Mother brought up peanut butter and jelly sandwiches and milk, hugged them both quietly, and went back down stairs.

A long, long time later, Jane and Mary Beth came in from school, came up to see them for a minute and left. Ben came, opened the door, waved at them and went to join the men.

It was nearly dark when El heard the car stop at the front gate. She saw Daddy at the wheel and Emmett sat beside him. She didn't wait for them to get out of the car but rushed down the stairs to meet him at the door, opened it— and Daddy was coming up the porch steps, something in his arms covered with his brown corduroy jacket. El backed away quickly, but not quickly enough.

It was Shirley. She recognized the yellow dress even though her face was covered with the coat. She knew Shirley was dead.

El turned and ran back upstairs to her room and threw herself face down on the bed.

"El? Daddy's home? El? Ellie, you crying? El?" There was silence. El realized that Bun had opened the bedroom door to go down stairs.

"Peek-a-boo!" she cried, turning over. "Fooled you! See, I'm not crying. Come on, let's read a story!"

The words of the story came automatically, but El was seeing the yellow dress hanging out from under Daddy's coat. It was the one Mother had made for Shirley for the Bible School program, last summer; it had a white lace collar, lace that Mother had made herself, crocheted out of fine white thread, in small loops, around and around, and there were white daisies embroidered on the pocket, the pocket where Shirley had carried her penny for the

116

collection. She could see her, as she had looked the day Mother gave her the dress, so proud, so happy, her dimples deepening and her gold-silk hair in long finger curls, a big yellow bow in her hair, little black patent leather shoes and yellow ankles—dressed just like Bun, except Bun's dress was pale green to go with her shining red hair. They were little princesses and everybody made over them and petted them and she would have been jealous if she had not loved them so much. Shirley had laughed so sweet, just a regular little... Very calmly, without shedding a tear, El said, "Bun, Shirley is dead. She fell in the creek."

Bun thought it over for a moment, then asked, "I can't play with her?"

"No," said El "You can't play with her."

"Tomorrow?"

"No, not tomorrow. Not ever. Not ever again."

Bun was quiet again. "Are you going to finish the story?"

El looked at her solemnly. "In a while, Baby, in a little while."

Something nagged at her mind, something—El put her arms around her little sister and rocked her gently. In a soft voice she began to hum. "Sing the words, El," Bun said softly. El realized that what she was humming was one of Daddy's favorite songs, one often requested by Bun. In a soft, hesitant voice, rocking Bun back and forth, El begin to sing:

I had a little Doggie, who used to sit and beg,
But Doggie tumbled down the stairs and broke his little leg.
Oh, Doggie, I will nurse you, and try to make you well,
And you shall have a collar, and a little, silver bell.

She remembered: The new, just published book Mr. Collins had loaned her, the one she had read over the weekend, Hemmingway's *For Whom the Bell Tolls.* She hadn't understood the book very well, the first time she had read it, and she had kept it hidden until she could read it again. There it was, by John Donne, right in the front:

And therefore never to send to know
For whom the bell tolls; it tolls for thee.

When the school bell rang. That was when she knew. When it rang, and rang and rang, she knew.

Seven

"Rachel? Rachel!"

Mother was calling from the foot of the stairs. El knew the undertakers had come and gone, taking Shirley with them; she knew Mother had bathed Shirley before they came, washing the clay and sand out of her baby-fine yellow hair, wrapping her in Bun's long nightgown and a clean sheet. She knew because Jane had come to get Bun's gown out of her dresser drawer and told her, as if she wanted to hear. Now they were allowed to come downstairs. Everyone was gone except Hollie and Emmett, and Ben, who was in the kitchen talking to Jane.

The whole town had been there but they all went home to get away from looking at Hollie and Emmett. Grief was hard to watch, but the way they were acting made it harder, If Hollie would just scream the way the women did at a mine explosion, or if Emmett would just curse and strike his fist into the door like men did in bad times—but they just sat at the table, staring at their coffee cups, not talking or eating or even looking at each other, like they were afraid of what they would see in each other's eyes, or if they did talk, the words might come out wrong like blame or fault-finding.

Faith tried to fill the silence with 'accidents just happen', said over and over like repeating it would make it mean more. Nobody could have guessed that Shirley would go to the wall. Emmett had let her out at the front gate and she was plenty big enough to come to the front door by herself, once she was on the brick walkway inside the yard. It wasn't muddy there; she had done it a hundred times by herself. The only thing different was the noise from the creek, and the awful water nearly in sight, clear to the top: she must have gone to look and fell in, nobody coulda figured on that. It was just an accident, a terrible, terrible accident, and if Mother had only known…if Emmett had only known …if Hollie had only known …For God's sake, Faith, Stop it! If doesn't help!

119

We can't hide behind IF! Sit down, let Jane and Rachel clear that table, you get off your feet, sit down. Sit down, Faith!

When Daddy shouted at Mother, Emmett roused and looked around like he didn't know where he was, or like he was looking for something.

"Guess we'd best git on home, Hollie," he said.

Hollie hesitated, then stood up. Mother put her arms around her and Hollie just stood there like she didn't even have arms, and then followed Emmett out the door and he didn't touch her and she didn't touch him and neither one looked the other in the face, just walked out, no thank you's to anybody, not to Mother or to Daddy—he's the one found her, caught in the short willows down below the swimming hole, where the water flowed out shallow, being free from the concrete wall, no force or hard powerful surge along there, the water just flowed out natural and gentle, the way creeks should flow.

The line gang had started walking below Herndon, followed the creek right up to Coville, walking in the water in a line, bank to bank, so as not to miss anything, not even a muskrat coulda got past, without one of the railroaders seeing it or coming against it with his boot, and yet it took three times walking over to find her. One of the helpers on Daddy's crew went to the mine to find Emmett, but he was inside and they had to send a special man-trip to get him, and that took a while. Emmett had to change clothes at the bath house and it seemed he didn't believe the man, even though he knew it was one of Daddy's men come for him, kept saying aw, she's jest foolin' her Maw, she's hid somewhere, you know how Shirley loves to tease and play like she's gone, aw she was playin' hidey since 'fore she was walking, you know how little gals are, they learn to tease a man 'fore they're out of diapers, hell her maw is 'bout the biggest tease and cut-up any man ever put up with, the way she romps and plays with Shirley.

Emmett just took his time like he was gittin' paid fer it. Daddy had just pulled her out of the water when Emmett got there, and it was the worst shaking-up a man ever had in his life, you could see the years come over him, he got old just standing there looking at his little girl in that wet yellow dress…for God's sake, Ben, Shut Up! We don't want to hear about it, we don't want to see you cry, you're seventeen years old, a grown man, Ben you stop that sniffin'. Grown men don't cry, Ben Gillespie, and you don't need to have these girls crying, either. Jane, you put that meat away, honey and cover the rest with a cloth, we'll take care of it in the morning. I'm sorry, Ben, you'd better go on home now. El, you take Bun up to bed. You can get your bath in the morning, just go on to bed. Faith? You ready to go up? Faith? Faith, you can't be blaming yourself, come on to bed. I want you to come up with me. You need your rest, and so do I.

But as Daddy walked slowly up the stairs, taking each step like his legs were unsteady, Mother hugged Jane and kissed Ben too, before he went out the door, and then picked Bun up, carried her to bed, tucked her and El both in, holding them close and kissing them on the forehead, and went back down stairs.

El could hear her washing dishes and putting food away, and after a while the aroma of applesauce cake baking came up the stairs, along with more sounds of washing dishes. One thing she couldn't understand: Why was Mother still working? Why wasn't she tired?

The funeral was to be held in the church at two o'clock on Wednesday, no need to put it off. Mother got up early and went down to Hollie's to help her dress. They went to Mullins to pick out a casket. When El and Bun got up, Daddy was in the kitchen making coffee and frying slab bacon. It seemed strange for him to be cooking breakfast.

"Go get your sister," he said as he took the bacon up on a platter, "then, El, you run down to Emmett's, tell him breakfast is ready. I've a feeling he didn't go to Mullins with your mother."

El went upstairs. Jane wasn't in her room, but she found her in the bathroom, washing her hair. "Daddy has breakfast ready," she said, and El was shocked when all Jane said was, "Thank you, Ellie."

She ran down to the White's by the road. The water had gone down, but she couldn't bear the thought of walking on that concrete wall as she usually did. The mud was beginning to dry and she skirted around the holes and the deepest ruts to their front gate. Emmett was sitting on his steps, wearing the same clothes he'd worn the night before, like he'd never had them off. He raised his head as El opened the gate.

"Daddy says breakfast is ready, come and eat."

"No thanks, Ellie. Tell your Daddy thanks."

"Coffee's ready," she said, hesitating to leave. She'd never seen anyone look so sad, not even in the movies. She couldn't look long because she might cry, and she was determined not to do that, especially not where Hollie or Emmett might see her.

Emmett got up and followed her up the road; he, too, avoided the back way. At the house he accepted a cup of coffee and went out on the front porch. The chairs were turned against the wall, the swing still suspended at the ceiling, but Emmett turned a chair around and sat down alone, the brown dead leaves around his feet.

The girls washed up the dishes and El took Bun to get a bath. They could hear the neighbors coming by, speaking to Emmett, bringing food in, everyone assuming lunch would be prepared there before going to the church; all gatherings were held at Faith's house or the school house. Jane helped El and Bun dress in their special dress-up clothes, clothes saved for church or maybe to Mullins on a Saturday night.

By noon, Mother and Hollie were back, and everyone tried to get Hollie to eat, just a bite, now, got to keep up your strength, you didn't touch a bite yesterday, maybe a little cake and milk? But all Hollie said was, my baby sure did like cake and milk. She didn't eat a thing.

Emmett went home to shave and dress, Daddy going with him like a father might have done. He asked about calling family but Emmett said he had no family, and Daddy said what about friends and Emmett smiled, only time he smiled about anything, said, "All my friends are right here."

Mother took Hollie upstairs, Jane and El tagging along. She found a skirt that was too tight for her—she used to wear it a million years ago, keeping it, maybe someday she'd lose weight, and a nice blouse of Janes, with white lace around the neck instead of a collar, made Hollie's face look like an ivory carving, like a cameo brooch of great value. Hollie's eyes were a darker blue now, almost violet with pain, and she held them wide open, maybe afraid of what she would see if she closed them.

Mrs. Gillespie brought over a wool coat, one that would fit Hollie, them both being so thin and all, a wine-colored coat that made Hollie's hair look nearly platinum and her eyes an even deeper violet. She was no longer the pretty young girl-mother, vicariously playing at being grown up: she was a woman thrust into the pain of the world as it is, and more lovely than the girl had ever been.

It was difficult to stop looking at her and all eyes followed her as she moved around the rooms, calm—too calm—and quiet, speaking to each neighbor, thanking them for what they had done. And voices followed her, she's holding up real well, poor thing, you reckon she knows her baby is gone?

how she's staying on her feet I'll never know I heerd she and Emmett sat up all night long that's right neither one let their heads touch a pillow just sat in the kitchen all night If'n I'd aknowed that, I'd have stayed with them for sure but I thought they'd go to bed, hold one another, but no, I heerd they sat up all night...

They gathered at the small church by the side of the road, halfway between Coville and Herndon, a few minutes before two o'clock, wanting to be there when the hearse came from Mullins with Shirley. The men all stood outside the door, the boys running round and round playing tag; the women and girls went in and sat down. It was chilly inside, damp-chill, what with all the snow and rain, hadn't dried out for weeks and hadn't been warm since last fall. The curtains were hanging white and limp along the walls, like for a regular service, but the afternoon sun came through the tall windows blue-clear and harsh, not the mellowed morning sun of ten o'clock, the Sunday school hour, and it came from a different angle.

Mother and Jane sat by Hollie, one on each side like bookends for support, holding her hands, shielding her, and folks stepped up, bowing slightly, saying I'm so sorry, she was a lovely child, such a tragedy, before taking their seats on the other side of the aisle. Jane, Hollie and Mother sat on the second pew with no one on the front row, and behind them sat El with Bun. El felt strange, used to sitting between the two little girls and now only one: the empty space made her feel exposed and lonely.

It was quiet in the church. Outside, the boys called to each other, the men talked. They heard the hearse arrive, heard the gears grind into reverse as it backed up to the door. Daddy and Emmett came down the side aisle and took their seats beside Mother with Daddy on the end. It looked strange for another man to be sitting beside Mother, even if it was only Emmett. Two boys brought standing wreaths and placed them on each side of the pulpit, on the raised platform before the choir seats. One was white gladiolus mixed with large yellow daffodils, the fresh spring-yellow flowers overpowering the white gladiolus until the effect was more yellow than white. The second arrangement was yellow, chrysanthemums interspersed with white baby's breath. El half-closed her eyes, but a yellow haze filtered through her eyelashes, reminding her of the wet yellow dress hanging out below Daddy's jacket.

The undertakers carried the casket wheels to the front of the church, a crisscrossed iron cage with bed casters for wheels, and placed it in front of the pulpit. The pallbearers came down the aisle with the casket, a blue-metal box far too large for such a tiny body. Mr. Gillespie and Mr. Collins carried the front, Mr. Mitchell and—El had to look twice to identify the fourth man. She had never seen Mr. Reeves in a suit with a tie and a white Sunday shirt; he looked so different without his cap pulled down over his eyes. They sat the casket on the wheelbase and took seats in the front pew on the right. Ben and Edgar followed the casket, and after the morticians opened the satin-lined lid, they placed a blanket of small yellow rose buds backed with fine pale-green fern on the closed half of the coffin.

The undertakers came for Hollie and reached for her arm. Jane moved back to the third row, beside Bun as they led Hollie to the opened casket. Mother followed and put her arm around Hollie, holding her tightly, but Hollie was rod-stiff, unbending and silent. She stood before the coffin for a few minutes, then quietly, soundlessly, slipped to the floor.

Doc Steelman was the first one to her, his black bag at his side. He took something from it and soon Hollie was sitting up. El had not known the doctor was there—why had he come? Then she remembered—Shirley was one of his babies, like she was, and Bun, and even Jane.

Hollie stood up, as white and remote as the waxy gladiolus standing erect beside the casket; the doctor and Mother helped her to her seat.

Daddy took Emmett by the arm and led him to view his baby daughter; the two men stood quietly together, heads bowed, then returned to their seats without showing emotion. The undertaker stepped to the third row. Jane got up and reached for Bun's hand. El followed. Jane picked Bun up so she could see and the three girls stood together, looking at their friend.

Mother had selected the sky-blue velvet dress, the one she had made for Christmas, the last one she had made for Shirley. It was hand-smocked across the front with tiny white flowers embroidered where the stitches met, and a white crocheted collar with fuzzy little balls on the ends of the strings that tied the collar in place. El remembered how Shirley had laughed and tickled her own nose with the little white balls of yarn, sitting in church, and in the middle of the Christmas program. Mother often over-estimated the amount of material needed for El's dresses, frequently having enough left over to make Shirley or Bun a dress. El looked down at her own sky-blue velvet dress and knew she would never wear it again.

Shirley's blonde hair lay in long curls on her shoulders, just as she had always worn it, but El knew there was something wrong with the way she looked. She was so white, no rosy cheeks, and her eyes were closed, but there was something more—yes! That was it! Her blue satin hairbow was on the wrong side! Shirley always wore hers on the right side, just as Bun always wore hers on the left, a system worked out by the two little girls so when they put their heads together the bows wouldn't get tangled together. El reached into the casket and took hold of the blue bow. "Rachel!" Mother stood beside her. El jumped. She hadn't realized Mother had come to be with them. "It's on the wrong side, Mother! Shirley wouldn't want it on that side!"

"I'll change it—" but Mother was too late. El had taken the ribbon off and was pinning it on the other side. Her fingers touched the small dead face and she gasped, drawing back quickly: Shirley was hard! She had been prepared for her feeling cold—in books dead people always felt cold—but nobody had told her they were hard as stone! The cold hard feel of Shirley passed through her fingers, her arm, her own body, cold, like the cold flood water, the icy flood water, washing into her own body, cold, drowning her, closing out the sounds in the church and Mother's voice, unaware of Mother's arm around her shoulders, unhearing as Mother whispered that's all right honey, I'll take care of it. She didn't see as Mother placed the bow on the right side as Shirley had worn it, a little cocky, a perky spot of blue among the spun-gold curls, bright as a clipped bluebird wing. El was in shock, cold waves washing over her, and blindly she followed Jane and Bun back to their seats. Cold and hard. No one had told her. She sat numb and cold while all of Coville, half of Herndon, and the men from the mines and Daddy's line gang filed past the coffin, paying their respects to the loved child. The sounds of moaning and crying slowly filled the small church as the people cried for the small girl, cried for the cold, silent parents, cried for themselves. The crying washed over her like water washing over the stones in Barker's creek, cold, deep, touching her on the surface and moving on, leaving water marks etched on her soul for all time.

Preacher Copeland took the pulpit, bowed his head and said "Let us pray, Almighty God we do not know your master plan…"

El listened for the first few seconds, the words seeping like mist through the numbness to register surprise then blur into bewilderment: God planned for Shirley to die? God didn't want that beautiful little girl to live? He had planned for her to die? Then why didn't He just plan for her not to be born at all? Why didn't he interfere when Emmett lay Hollie on the sweet clover in the dry farm-fields above Herndon, him a grown man and her a near-child herself, not yet sixteen and as trusting as a doe not yet conceived, an innocent girl caught between the hot-rutting passion of a male in his prime and the wiles of a mother who knew she was going to die: why didn't God interfere then?

The prayer ended and Bun was tugging on her hand, come on, Ellie, we are 'posed to sing, come on, El. Sing? At a time like this? Who had dreamed up all this program stuff like it was a Sunday school play or a summer revival service to woo the lost sinners into the fold of a conniving God? She jerked her hand away and Bun went alone to join the other children. The children's choir was assembled in a double line, with Mrs. Plover directing instead of Mother, but Jane, head higher than usual, was playing, as usual. The children began to sing: Jesus loves me, this I know, for the Bible tells me so…and as they chanted Yes, Jesus loves me, they really sang out, just as Mother had taught them, singing and smiling…but no one had told them to move together, to close the gap, the vacant place where Shirley had stood. She could see Shirley standing there, beside Bun, her eyes smiling and her tiny mouth moving, laughing, singing—wearing the yellow dress, wet, water-molded to her slight form, floating between the singing children, and she would not go away.

El ducked her head, refused to look, swallowed hard, stared at the floor—she lay on the white-scrubbed wooden floor, a yellow patch of sunlight, and she would not go away. El raised her head and concentrated on the white cross high above the children's heads, but there were windows on either side of the cross and the bare yellow branches of a willow tree lay against the window panes. The pale yellow-green buds were beginning to appear, three warm days and the tree was resurrected, the limbs began to blur into yellow water, muddy yellow water, washing over her, covering her, drowning out the child-thin voices, filling the church with the roar of high-flood waters, and she would not go away.

The children were seated, the water-sound receded, and Preacher Copeland stood, holding his Bible, but he wasn't reading the scriptures: he knew them by heart and recited them while looking up to the ceiling: "I will lift up mine eyes to the hills, from whence cometh my help…" And from whence came the flood waters, the mountains, steep and narrowing to streams in between—El didn't hear the rest of the sermon. She closed her eyes and tried to think of something else, she would think about flying, that always worked, coasting, sky-blue, cloudless…

The people around her rose and sang together: "I come to the garden alone, while the dew is still on the roses, and the voice I hear, falling on my ear, the Son of God discloses. And He walks with me, and He talks with me…"

Was Jesus walking with Shirley now? He already had so many, all the way back to Peter and Paul, and even Judas, because Mrs. Plover said even Judas was in heaven because Jesus forgave him and that made what he did all right. Jesus had so many, couldn't he have left Shirley for a few more years? How would Hollie and Emmett ever walk and talk together again. They hadn't said a word to each other since…just talked around it, like folks do when there's nothing to say. Somehow, El thought, Shirley would rather be walking and talking with Bun.

"He speaks and the sound of His voice is so sweet the birds hush their singing…" The birds had to hush when Jesus spoke? Shirley wouldn't like that, she loved birds…"Preacher Copeland's long sermon on acceptance was ending, and they stood again to sing: "Shall we gather at the river? Where bright angel's feet have trod…" Yes, and one tiny, sweet angel, and the tide wasn't crystal for her, but a swift, muddy, deathly black, river.

The undertakers directed the pallbearers as they brought the casket; Mary Beth, Ben and Edgar carried the flowers. Mother led Hollie to their car and Daddy prodded the dazed Emmett behind them. El and Bun were herded to Mr. Collins' car and there were eight, and Bun had to sit on El's lap. Mrs. Collins looked back and said, I declare, you're a regular little mother to that baby sister aren't you, Rachel, but El didn't answer and Bun kept crying.

They followed the long black hearse up the winding dirt-rock road above Herndon, going up the mountain to the old home place, to lay Shirley beside her grandparents and great-grandparents in a weed-choked family plot with only Hollie left to tend it. The grave was open in the near-frozen ground, on the top of a wind-swept hill, inaccessible to the hearse and cars. The vehicles pulled into the yard around the old log cabin where Hollie was born and the men raised the steel-blue coffin on their shoulders for the climb up the hill. Doc Steelman had replaced Jane at Hollie's side, he and Mother supporting her on the upward climb, while Daddy guided Emmett and the older folks fell in line, the children trailing behind.

When the graveside was reached, Bun wriggled between the grown-ups, searching for Mother. She found her, seated in a metal chair provided by the undertakers. Mother tried to shush Bun's whispered questions, but Bun chattered on and on, her childish voice the only sound, carried on the wind that moved the dead branches and blew cold into their faces.

Preacher Copeland said a few words and then began the Twenty-Third Psalm: "The Lord is my Shepherd; I shall not want…"Why did the Lord say we would not want right when we wanted something so terribly, something we could not possibly have, the worst we'd ever wanted anything?

It was over.

They wouldn't lower the casket while anyone who cared was there; it would be put into the ground later, in stillness and loneliness, with no one to mourn when the dirt was thrown in and clunked on the metal lid with a hollow sound, when the dirt was piled high in a dreaded mound and covered with flowers, a yellow-flowered alter to a God impossible to understand, a God impervious to the pleas and cries of those left behind. What God would plan to take golden-haired children away before the age of six from parents whose lives revolved around that child like planets around the sun? It must have been an accident, as Mother said. Or a mistake, like Daddy said. No one, not even God would plan such pain.

It was true, what Daddy said, about paying for our mistakes. What he didn't say, was, **we also pay for the mistakes of others.**

The world stopped on Tuesday morning when it was discovered that Shirley was missing; after the funeral it started turning again. Many of the neighbors came back to the Phillips' house, to talk in quiet voices and share the food the women had prepared. Mother and Doc Steelman took Hollie up to Jane's room and put her to bed. Doc gave her a sedative so she could sleep and suggested she stay with Faith through the night, to which Emmett agreed, hardly hearing what was said.

Daddy went to the phone the minute he walked in the door. "Bert? This is Bill. I'm home now. Got anything? Good! Say, Bert, call down to Mullins, will you? See if Doc Steelman is needed—he's here at my house. Thanks, Bert."

The men gathered in the living room, leaving the kitchen to the women and children. They talked about the Radford Powder Plant, the first in the nation to be completed under government-owned contracts, the pioneer plant in a group which would eventually cost well over one billion dollars. It was to be dedicated on Friday and would go into full production within eight to ten days, *three months ahead of schedule.*

The Lend-Lease bill that had been signed by the President was a good thing, they all agreed, but we were sure to be in a shooting war by summertime. The N&W was running eight special trains to Radford now, carrying thousands of the twenty-two thousand men who were working there. "When is the Virginian going to put on a train, Bill?" asked the men. "Haven't heard a thing about it", said Daddy. "it would be a long haul from here, have to leave mighty early!"

The five-thirty news came on and Mother turned the radio volume up so the men could hear it in the living room. Roosevelt had signed the bill and he had ordered war supplies shipped to Great Britain. The Nazis were all set to begin a blitz on Greece. Then came the real surprise of the day: the miners have asked for a wage increase of a dollar a day but with no change in hours—a demand that was much less than what was expected! The coal miners and the union leaders met at an eight-state conference to begin negotiations for a two-year contract; the present one would expire on the thirty-first of the month. "That ol' Lewis, he ain't such a bad guy! Naw, he sticks up for us, but he knows this country don't need no strike jest now, he ain't so dumb! Naw, look where he's got us so far—nobody else has done anything for us, not like he has!"

The women washed the dishes and kept the table supplied. They talked about the Bundles for Britain groups in Pineville and Mullins; most of the larger cities had organized sewing groups to knit scarves, gloves and stockings for service men, to sew baby gowns and hospital gowns and surgical garments for the twenty-four hospitals in and around London—and they were getting such an awful beating, wasn't there something they could do? They would ask Faith, when she got Hollie settled, Faith would know who to see about getting a group started in Coville—maybe in Herndon, too, said Mrs. Plover, although she wouldn't have much time until school was out, being busy with teaching and all.

"Didn't Preacher Copeland do a fine job? Sure hate to lose him, he retires in June, you know, don't know when we'll get a new one, especially for a church this small."

Jane came into the kitchen, interrupting the steady talk, anyone seen Mary Beth? No one had, maybe she's upstairs with Faith and Hollie, no, she had looked there. Anyone seen Ben? Ain't he with the men? No, he's not in the house.

And on the news, five hundred American aviators joined the British Air Force. Edgar and El sat on the floor in front of the radio throughout the broadcast. Wow! They couldn't wait to do that! Women aren't allowed in the service! They are too! They are not! Well, by the time I get old enough, they will be, just you wait and see! I'm going to fly one of these days, you'll see! Hey, don't get mad! Tell you what, if you get up early in the morning, you can come up on the railroad tracks and see the eclipse of the moon with me!

"See the what?"

"Eclipse of the moon—it starts at five minutes until six and lasts nearly two hours. Look, here's how it works, see, here's the moon here's the sun, and this is the earth." Edgar took the world globe on its walnut stand from the top of the radio and demonstrated the eclipse.

"What do you say?"

Mother would never let her go up on the railroad, but of course El wanted to, wanted to in the worst possible way. "Can we see the moon now?" she asked.

"Don't think so, it's behind the mountains, but we could go see," said Edgar. They went out on the porch and stood on the front steps, looking at the sky. Two figures moved away from the side of the house toward the backyard.

"Who was that?" whispered El.

"Ben, I think," Edgar whispered back. "Who's that with him?"

"Mary Beth." They looked at each other and grinned. With one mind they stole around the front porch, crouched low, and peeped around the corner. Ben had Mary Beth pinned against the side of the house and was kissing her, his hips flat against her, his hands rubbing over the front of her jacket. They watched, still as possums in a blackberry patch, until Mary Beth pushed him away for breath. El and Edgar flew back to the porch steps and collapsed giggling against each other. "Let's don't tell Joe," whispered Edgar. "He's too young to keep his mouth shut!"

After the company left, the girls went to bed, bundled together in one bed to leave Hollie undisturbed; she had gone to sleep, after the sedation, and Emmett had gone home alone. It was nearly eleven o'clock when the last light went out and the day was done.

El lay awake for a long time, feeling strange and confused. Bun was restless, crowded between the older girls; the only time they all three shared a bed was when they went to Virginia to grandmother's house.

At one-twenty-five the telephone rang and El heard it for she had not yet gotten to sleep. She heard Daddy go down the stairs to answer it, heard him come back up the steps two at a time, the lethargy exhibited earlier now gone. "Get up, Faith, help me round up the men—there's been a bad wreck at Kumis crossing!"

"Kumis Crossing?" Mother said groggily.

"Other side of Blacksburg—it's a bad one, three engines off the track, one man killed, maybe more—hurry up, I need to go!"

Mother dressed quickly and came to the bedroom door as Daddy went out to start the car. "Jane?"

"She's asleep, Mother," said El. "I heard."

Mother came into the room. "You always do, don't you, honey? If you hear Hollie up, wake Jane to get up and stay with her—I don't want her alone tonight. I'll be back as soon as I can."

"I'll hear her, Mother."

"I know you will." Mother went quickly down the stairs and out to the car. El lay awake, following Mother's drive, alone in the gray Ford after she dropped Daddy off at the motor barn, knowing the route as well as Mother; if only she knew how to drive, she could help. Before long Mother returned and came back upstairs, to the girls' room. She sat on the bed beside Ellie. "I didn't see much of you yesterday," she said, brushing Ellie's hair back from her face, "but I want you to know, I appreciated the way you helped me with Bun. I don't know what I'd do without you—without any of my girls..." she began to cry, deep, hard sobs, pent up for two days until she had done what had to be done for everybody, until everybody was looked after. She stood up, groping for her apron before realizing she didn't have one on. El wanted to say something to help her mother, but she didn't know what. She reached the corner of her sheet up to her and Mother took it, wiped her eyes, smiled and hugged El tightly. "Go to sleep, Ellie. You have to get up early for school."

She tried to think about the eclipse of the moon as Edgar had explained it. Maybe, if she tried hard enough, maybe she could keep her mind on that and not on Shirley. Maybe if she thought about going up on the high railroad tracts—maybe even out on the bridge—maybe then the hurting inside would let up, the missing Shirley, the aching for Hollie, the sadness for Emmett, who had gone home alone—maybe if she thought about flying.

Daddy didn't come home until Thursday night, but the girls listened to the evening news with Mother. Prime Minister Churchill said the British Aid Bill constituted a "new magna carta," and that the United States had the "deep and respectful appreciation" of the British people, that it was a "monument of generous and far-seeing statesmanship" on the part of our President and our leaders. His comments almost removed the specter of war from the room, making them feel good about their country and themselves, for they had been in favor of the bill's passage from the start: most West Virginians were.

Mother had spent the day with Hollie, sorting out Shirley's clothes, into give-away, throw-away, and keep, then Hollie had decided to keep it all, as Mother knew she would, it being too soon for decisions like that. She stacked the boxes in the corner of Hollie's bedroom then cleaned up her kitchen, and talked, talked all day long, driving the emptiness away.

Emmett had gone out early in the morning and didn't return until after Mother had gone home. Now, Mother worried, should she go back down there? Was Hollie sitting all alone on the first day after her baby was gone? Was Emmett home with her?

El, knowing better than anyone how tired Mother was, offered to run down to Hollie's, see if Emmett was there, and if not, to bring Hollie back to stay with them another night.

She threw on her coat, and went the back way, trying not to look at the still-high muddy water in the creek. As she came to Hollie's back gate, she saw two people sitting on Grandma Gillespie's coal-house roof, their arms wrapped around each other. Mary Beth and Ben were huddled together like they were glued—or frozen. She pretended she didn't see them and went on to Hollie's back door. Loud voices came from within the house, and El hesitated before she knocked.

Emmett was shouting and Hollie was saying, "No, no, no, no! Not yet! Not now! No, Emmett, no!" Emmett sounded drunk but El couldn't be sure. She didn't know what to do—should she let them know she was there? Mother had said to see if Emmett was home, well, he was home all right. She stood still, shocked by the language she was hearing, words she had never heard spoken aloud, only seen written on the back wall of the schoolhouse.

"You're my fucking wife! You'll do as I tell you, you cheap little whore! You ain't no high-falutin' Phillips girl—you're a damn fucking little bitch and you'll get in that damn bed and sleep in my bed and fuck in my bed and you ain't goin' anywhere! You git out-a that fancy coat and git on yore back, and remember, you used to like it, now be a god-dammed fuckin' wife to me or I'll see you buried too—we're going to have another baby, we're going to git another lil girl, lay still god-damn you, I'll ..."

El was frightened. She ran out of the yard and home as fast as she could. Once in the bright kitchen, her breathing slowed, and she told Mother she had heard Emmett, he was home, and he was shouting. "He seemed awfully mad, Mother," she said. How was she going to explain what she had heard?

She couldn't repeat that kind of language—not to Mother!

Faith was silent for a moment, chewing on her lower lip like she did when she was thinking something over. "I guess that's to be expected. They had to start talking some time. I guess it's natural they'd blame each other, I'm just glad they are getting it out, that's better than holding it all in."

El was still worried. How could she make Mother realize that there was more to it than just 'mad' at each other? Hesitantly, she said, "I heard Emmett say they were going to have another baby." She watched Mother fearfully. But Mother looked relieved. "Why, that's good! There's nothing will take their minds off their grief as quick as another baby! Well, I guess I can quit worrying about them after all!"

Mother shooed them all to bed early, worn out herself. This time she didn't wait up for Daddy, knowing he would be out all night, cleaning up after the big wreck, but El lay awake for a long time, worrying about Hollie.

Would Emmett actually hurt her? What was he doing to her? He had loved her so, before Shirley died, how could he make her scream and cry like that now? What was fucking anyway? Did it hurt that bad? Was fucking and making babies the same thing? She went to sleep vowing to look it up in the dictionary, first thing in the morning.

Friday dawned fair and warmer, the beginning of a beautiful, spring-like weekend, and spirits began to rise with the temperature.

Faith and Hollie started walking each morning, supposedly to help Faith lose weight, but in reality, to get Hollie out of the house and active. Daddy came in before three o'clock and went right to bed, but he asked to be awakened for supper; all he had eaten since Wednesday night was a bowl of 'camp-car special' soup and coffee, obtained at the site of the accident. Faith cooked fried chicken and gravy, mashed potatoes, and, of course, the inevitable greens by which she swore, and the best biscuits in all of Wyoming county. She made banana pudding with vanilla wafers on top, and when Daddy came down in his robe and slippers there was a holiday feeling in the air, the first almost normal family dinner for many days.

As they ate, they listened to the news broadcast; The United Miners and Coal Operators conference had hit a snag of considerable size. John L. Lewis had proposed that the miners keep working while negotiations continued, but the miners were to be paid retrospectively to the expiration date on their contract, which was April 1st.

The miners thought it was the patriotic thing to do, the nation was building for defense, it could not afford a strike, and the UMW was making a significant contribution to the welfare of the country by offering the 'no work stoppage' proposal. But the operators said Lewis was simply making a play for favorable public opinion, and was not offering the contract in good faith. Lewis wanted any benefits worked out to be effective April 1st, regardless of when the contract was signed.

The Operators also rejected the blanket wage increase demand, and the demand for improved working conditions. The negotiations would affect 450,000 workers in the soft coal industry, over eight states in the Appalachian area. The joint conference named a sub-committee to work out details of an agreement.

"They will end up striking," said Daddy. "Those dang miners will have the whole country tied up by the first of the month. You wait and see."

"Oh, Bud, surely not! With the British Aid bill just passed, and with the needs of industry—surely, they won't!" said Mother.

"Tell us about the wreck, Daddy," said El. "What happened? Were there really three engines off the track?"

"Worse than that, honey. A switch split and the three engines, plus ten or eleven full coal cars went off. It was bad, had a fireman killed. One of the section crews was working about five miles from the wreck and he found out it was his brother's train. Well, he found him, all right. His brother was pinned in the cab of one of the engines, and that engine was fifteen feet straight up in the air! That engine was settin' up against a catenary pole and that's all kept it from turning over. The engineer's legs were pinned down, he couldn't move.

Well, some of the men got a blow-torch, cut the man's legs out; his brother got up in there and held his cap over the engineer's face to keep th' sparks from burning him, and they got him out of there. It was bad. The first and second engines just fell over on their side, but that third one, um, um, um..." Daddy shook his head.

"Will the funeral be tomorrow?" asked Mother.

"Two o'clock. I'll go with the gang. He was from Blacksburg, that's where the funeral will be."

"Then I can have the car to go to Mullins?"

"I won't need it."

"I could wait until later, if you think you'll be back before the stores close."

"Oh, please!" cried El and Jane together. "Couldn't we wait and go to the movies? We haven't been since Christmas!"

"There's a good one on, Daddy, you'd like it," said Jane. "*Northwest Mounted Police*, with Gary Cooper, and it's Technicolor and everything."

"You could see the war news," added El.

"Are you ready for your piano recital Sunday?" asked Daddy, trying to look severe.

"You know I am!" said Jane, then realized how little time Daddy had spent at home in the past few weeks. "Tell him how much I've practiced, Mother!" Mother smiled; she knew Daddy wasn't really worried.

"Could we make it home by nine-thirty?" he asked.

"Why nine thirty?" Mother asked.

"Because the President speaks then and I want to hear what he has to say about this mine business. Why don't you and the girls go on, and let them go to the movies while you get your groceries, then we'll all be home early." Daddy settled the plans for Saturday and went back to his newspaper.

On Saturday night Faith and the girls got home just in time to hear President Franklin Delano Roosevelt on the radio:

You will feel the impact of this gigantic effort in your daily lives, you will feel it in a way that will cause you many inconveniences...the arms program must not be obstructed by unnecessary...

"He's talking to the miner's now," said Daddy, "hope they are listening!"

...idea of normalcy and business as usual must be abandoned. There must be no war profiteering... upon the national will to sacrifice and to work depends the output of our industry and our agriculture...upon that will depends the survival of that vital bridge across the ocean— the bridge of ships which carry arms and food for those who are fighting the good fight. ...it must not be obstructed by unnecessary strikes of workers or by short-sighted management or by deliberate sabotage. For unless we win there will be no freedom for either management or labor...

"Give us hell, Franklin, we're probably going to need it!" shouted Daddy.

"Bud! Your language!"

When the President ended his speech, El jumped up and began quoting him, marching around the dining room table, a broom for a gun over her shoulder, Bun following right behind her. "The British people need ships—from America they will get ships! They need planes—from America they will get planes! They need food—from America they will get food! They need tanks and guns and ammunition and supplies of all kinds! From America—and Bun picked up the chant," "...get tanks and guns and nish-shun!"

"Our country is going to be what our people have proclaimed it must be—an arsenal of democracy...our country is going to play its full part!"

"That child is going to be on stage one of these days", observed Mother, "the way she remembers lines."

"No, we are going to fly! Aren't we Bun!" cried Rachel, dropping her broom-gun and jumping on a chair, spreading her arms for wings.

Bun, willing as always, copied her and tried to climb up on the chair. "Goin'a fly!"

"Get your feet off that chair, young lady; right now, it's time for you two to fly upstairs to bed!" Being allowed to stay up for the President's speech had made it far past their bedtime; the two went up to bed willingly.

On an inside page of the Daily Telegraph there had been one small paragraph: "The heavy rains that fell throughout the county on Monday night caused a spring flush-out in the Guyandotte and its tributaries. There being no gauge at the county seat, it is estimated that the water had risen five to eight feet. Swollen waters of the river, blackened by mud and coal dust, washed numerous logs, boards and bottles downstream during the day Tuesday..." And one small girl. But there wasn't even an obituary in the paper.

Eight

March 16th

Britain poured thousands of troops into Greece, and the German army made preparations for an all-out drive. On the seventeenth, the day commemorating Saint Patrick for bringing Christianity to Ireland by killing all the Druids, it rained all day, a slow, icy rain that kept the children in the classroom. Mr. Collins filled the usual recess time by explaining Saint Patrick's Day. They learned that the Druids worshipped the sun, moon and stars and they cut the sacred mistletoe with a sickle made of gold. The Saint had fasted forty days and forty nights, following the tradition of Moses in the wilderness, and the Lord had told Saint Pat he could judge the Irish himself on their day of doom—woe to those who failed to remember his feast day or, to wear his color green! Although El knew she was only one quarter Irish, she decided to not take any chances; she made herself a shamrock, colored it green and pinned it to her collar.

Mr. Collins selected readings from Gulliver's Travels, written by an Irishman by the name of Jonathan Swift, for their literature lesson. Their homework assignment was to memorize a poem by an Irishman, to be presented to the class by the end of the month. Edgar laughed at her for taking St. Patrick's Day so seriously, said she was superstitious, but then he helped her find a poem to memorize.

On Tuesday, the eighteenth, the war news became alarming, and exciting, too, in a dangerous way: U-Boats had been sighted in the Atlantic, headed for the United States. On Wednesday, Winston Churchill confirmed that the Nazi subs were, indeed, operating off the coast of North America.

Mr. Collins had a new marking system for his map tacked on the classroom wall: white tacks were enemy troops on land, blue indicated air raids over the Allies, and now red tacks became submarines moving over the blue map-ocean to America. The tacks seemed to increase daily, but they didn't know anyone fighting in the war. Their town was shielded from the ocean by the high mountains and great distances, their feelings were shielded by ignorance of war.

On the first day of spring, March twentieth, it was colder and cloudier than any day of the week, in nescience of the calendar. The House approved the SEVEN BILLION DOLLAR FUND for war materials and aid to Britain by a vote of 336 to 55. The measure moved to the Senate, and as if in defiance, the Germans loosed their biggest raid yet on London, hitting the heavily populated district and doing immeasurable damage.

Mother decided it was time to take action, and by doing so, brought the war a step closer to Coville. On Friday morning, the ladies of Coville and a few from Herndon met at the Phillips' house and organized their own 'Bundles for Britain' movement. They buzzed industriously all day, making hospital gowns and baby gowns, cutting the material on Faith's dining room table, sewing them on Faith's new electric sewing machine and by hand, making garments to help the Londoners.

Friday night's news was even more discouraging: *The Crown Council of Yugoslavia had conceded to the demands of the Axis powers.*

Another country to color on the map, more tacks to put on the wall. The Nazis stepped up their attacks on the coastal cities of England, increasing the fury of their raids. As if that were not enough, Charles Lindbergh was in the news again, asking the American people to organize and protest the involvement of the United States in this war. Lindbergh said that *by remaining out of the war, the American people could build a military and a commercial position on this continent that would be impregnable.*

El and Edgar threw a softball back and forth in the road after supper, enjoying the new, longer, daylight hours and the warmer days.

"He wants us to protest getting into the war when U-boats are pointing right at us?" said Edgar. "What does he think we are, a bunch of yellow-bellied, lily-livered cowards? I'd be in England right now if I was old enough!" He overthrew the ball and El ran into the triangle to get it. "If I was a hot-shot pilot like him, I'd be right in the middle of it! I wouldn't be sittin' around here— what'th hell's he waiting for?"

"But if he went to England and got shot down, he couldn't help us, could he! He's no coward, he's going to fight for us if the Germans come over here! Don't you see?" said El. "He just doesn't want our country to get hurt. He's seen all those German planes—he was over there, remember? He knows we don't have that many, he wants us to take care of what we've got, and build more for us!"

"You don't know what you're talking about!" yelled Edgar hotly.

"I do too!"

"You do not!"

"I do!"

"You don't! He's a yellow-bellied coward!"

"He is NOT!" And with that, El ran in the house and slammed the door. She would never speak to Edgar Mitchell again as long as she lived!" And she would be a pilot long before he would, even if she was a girl! So, there!

The Mullins rebels were playing the Huntington Pony Express team in the state basketball play-offs, and since spring vacation for the University started on the same day, Will Gillespie came home with the Mullins coach. On Saturday morning he came over to the Philips' house to see everyone, looking older, and taller, more handsome than anyone remembered. On Sunday, he was in church, wearing blue blazer and navy slacks, a white shirt and a pale blue tie that matched his socks. He had a little three-cornered handkerchief sticking out of his breast pocket, precisely placed for maximum effect, and his dark hair waved over his forehead, glistening with sweet-smelling Vitalis. He looked so much older, was so much better looking: all the girls were in a swoon over him, their first contact with *a college man*!

In spite of the cold air, the young people elected to walk home from church, strolling arm in arm up the windy road, laughing and talking, bringing each other up to date on local happenings and the exciting life at a big university. When El asked to join them, Mother forbid it—she would catch her death of cold—but she watched as they paired up, Ben with Mary Beth, Jane with the handsome Will. Jane was clearly pleased, and invited Will to her piano recital in Mullins in the afternoon, but Will declined, saying he needed to spend time with his parents since he had just gotten home.

When it was time for the Epworth League meeting, the same foursome walked back down the road to the little white church for the youth gathering and evening services. As the people came out of church it began to rain; Jane was as mad as a 'little wet hen' because they couldn't walk home. Mr. Gillespie insisted his boys ride home with him. The rain had ruined her day, and she went to her room angry at everyone. It had been a long day, and Jane had been under the strain of her recital, playing at the Masonic Hall in front of dozens of people, and then seeing Will again.

"He's going to be here ten days, you know," called Mother, after Jane stormed upstairs.

"Yes, and I will be in school most of that, too!" Jane shouted from the top of the stairs.

"Does Jane like Will?" asked El.

"She thinks she does," said Mother, "and at that age, it's the same thing."

After supper on Monday evening, Mary Beth and the boys next door came over for a while; being a school night, the curfew time was nine o'clock. Will and Ben were sitting at the dining room table eating pineapple upside down cake, especially baked by Jane for Will because it was his favorite. Jimmy Stewart had joined the army the day before, replacing his monthly salary of $1300 dollars with Uncle Sam's $21.00 stipend. "I'd be pretty happy with the $21.00 a month," said Ben. "'Specially when you don't have to buy your eats out of it."

"Buy a lot of beer and cigarettes, right, little brother?"

"Sure—what more could a feller want?"

"How about a girl?" Mary Beth said softly.

"Wouldn't have to buy that!" said Will, "the uniform would take care of that!" They all laughed loudly and Mother looked disapproving. The subject was dropped and the Rook cards were brought out. El and Bun were sent to bed.

RUSSIA AT WAR IN EVENT OF NAZI ATTACK
FINAL APPROVAL GIVEN FUND BILL BY SENATE

With a vote of 67 to 9, the senate passed the seven-billion-dollar bill
for war supplies.

As El read through the evening paper, Mother asked her if she still needed information on the Senate fight, and El replied that she did.

"There's a short report on it in the paper," Mother said. As El cut it out, she read it. "It's quite a squabble," added Mother.

For two and a half months two distinguished West Virginians have been
camping along the banks of the Potomac, each with some kind of a designation
as Senator in Congress from the sovereign State of West Virginia. Day after
day the Senate shuffles the thing aside and our distinguished citizens wait and
hope. In the meantime, this state is absent in half-measure from the councils
of the great body that holds the strings of our pocketbooks and decides the fate
of the nation as to war policy.

It is understood that the delay is due to the fact that the decision in this
case may establish a precedent, and the Senate is afraid their chickens may
someday come home to roost.

The Japanese Prime Minister, Matsuoka, received a royal welcome from the Nazi high command at Berlin, arriving, it is said, to study the American Lend-Lease plan and its ramifications. The next day, the twenty-eighth, President Roosevelt signed the bill as it was passed by the Congress. Since the President was on his yacht, in the warm Florida waters, his speech before the Democratic dinner was cancelled; his address would be broadcast by radio from the yacht on Saturday night.

Also, on the twenty-eighth, the Senate approved the Mine Inspection bill! The bill asked for greater safety devices, an eight hour day, and no child labor. However, it would be June of 1942 before the new certificates would be issued by a three-man examining board.

The rain that started early in the day as a cold drizzle from dove-gray skies changed to snow before noon. The girls had gone with Mother to Mullins for dress material and groceries; Jane rushed Mother all day, anxious to get home. Will was coming over! She went to G.C. Murphy's while Mother was in the A&P, coming back with a new pair of silk stockings and a bottle of nail polish called candlelight pink.

Mother bought onion sets, cabbage plants and seeds for the garden although it looked more like wintertime than gardening time. When Jane fussed about taking the time to pick out garden seeds, Mother smiled and said, well, you know what Coleridge said, and El asked, who's Coleridge?

"Coleridge is a poet," Mother replied, "and he wrote, 'And Spring comes slowly up this way'…but it does come!"

"I've got to memorize a poem for school," said El, "one by an Irishman. Will you help me?"

"I'd love to! You know how I love poetry. And you can help me plant our garden!"

"Can't we go now?" asked Jane. "I want to bake cookies before Will comes over." She took the bright seed packets from Bun, who was 'helping' Mother choose.

"Make plenty," said Mother. "Hollie and Emmett are coming too."

"Emmett's back?" said El in surprise.

"Yes, he's back," replied Mother. "Where did he go?" asked El.

"That's none of our business, El, and don't you dare ask him, either."

By the time they reached home the temperature had dropped to twenty degrees and it was snowing; never had it looked less like spring.

The young people—Will, Ben, Mary Beth—gathered around the piano with Jane while the older ones took over the dining room table and the Rook cards. Will seemed to be staying close to Mary Beth while Jane was playing and Ben was quiet, almost sullen, not at all his usual, laughing self. The piano was loud. El almost didn't hear the soft pecking on the living room window. She saw Edgar, standing on the porch and motioning for her to come out. Quietly, so no one would notice, she went to the front door and opened it carefully—but the cold air gave her away

"El?" Mother called from the dining room, "Do you have that door open? Is someone at the door?"

El came to the dining room. "It's Edgar," she said. "Can he come in?"

"I don't know," said Mother, studying her cards, "can he?"

"May he come in?" El asked, correcting her grammar as was expected.

"Yes, Edgar may come in," and Mother returned to her card game.

"Want to work on your poem?" asked Edgar, removing his shoes and sticking his cap into one of them; he placed them in the hall, under the wall-hanging telephone.

El grimaced. She would rather do almost anything else, but replied, "Let's sit on the stairs—we won't be bothered there." Taking a seat halfway up the staircase, Edgar whispered, "Know what tonight is?"

After thinking briefly, El answered, "No, what?"

"This is the 29th."

"So? The President speaks tonight, is that what you mean?"

"No! This is the night Granny Hall comes back—she died on the 29th!"

"Have you ever heard her—really, really heard her?"

"I ain't heard her, but Mr. Reeves says she does, says he's heard her."

"You believe everything that old man tells you?"

"I know this—I went over there a while ago and there's a light in that house!" Edgar said triumphantly, his blue eyes sparkling like Mother's glass beads. He was so excited he was almost shaking in his eagerness.

"Joe and me went down to Billynbob's before supper. Joe said he wanted to stay the night, I didn't want to. I came up the road and I saw Mr. Reeves going from his house, out the back way. Thought he was just going to the john, but he passed it up and went in Granny Hall's house. I thought it funny, so I snuck up the front, tried to see in the window but he's hung sacks over them. I heard him coming and had to high-tail it out of there—he didn't see me. You want to sneak over there with me? There's still a light on, you can see it from your porch."

"Let's go look out of my bedroom window!" They ran up the stairs to her room, and leaving the light off, El raised the window shade. There was a clear view of the front of the haunted house. A good inch of new snow lay on the ground but it had stopped snowing; the night was cold and dark, the moon a thin new curve of light resting on the ridge. The house looked ominous and quiet, but, as Edgar had said, there was a light in the back room—it reflected on the snow at the side of the house, a faint, long line glimmering through a half-drawn curtain. They crouched on the floor together, watching in silence.

"El?" It was Bun. She had followed them up the stairs. "Play with me?"

"Not now, Bun. We're busy."

"Why's the light off?" she asked, turning it on.

"Let's go downstairs and play, Bun," said Edgar. "Beat ya!"

Bun took off running and Edgar turned to El. "When everyone's gone, let's sneak over there and see what's going on."

"Mother would kill me," said El, "if she caught me going out, cold as it is."

"Then we won't let her catch us!"

WHIS radio station had changed from 1410 to 1440 on the dial, and it took Daddy a few minutes to locate the station until Edgar told him about the change. The young people joined the others in the dining room for the President's speech. The text of his message was almost lost on El when she noticed the way Mary Beth and Will were making eyes at each other. Didn't Jane see what was going on? What had happened between Mary Beth and Ben?

They were not looking at each other at all, doing just what Hollie and Emmett had been doing for the last two weeks, not touching, finding ways to get around talking to each other, never meeting each other's eyes.

Bun was in her table-quilt tent, asleep on the floor; if Shirley had been there they would have been playing, laughter coming out from under the quilt, joyful and happy. Hollie wasn't happy; Emmett seldom spoke at all, not even to Daddy. She wondered if they had made another baby yet, but Hollie's stomach was as flat as El's. How long did it take to make a baby? She'd be glad when she was sixteen and knew all these things. Now here were Ben and Mary Beth, real close sweethearts just a few days ago, real storybook lovers, and tonight they weren't talking at all. She caught Edgar looking at her and decided she would talk to him about Mary Beth and Ben, and why Will was paying attention to Mary Beth instead of Jane—Will, a college man, and Mary Beth, dumb as a fence post.

Mother sent Edgar home, and El and Bun to bed; shortly afterward, the young people left. El heard Ben goes directly to his house, next door, heard the iron gate squeak and the front door slam, the way Ben always did it. She heard the crunch of snow and giggling as Will and Mary Beth went down the front walk, heard the gate hinges grate, heard their footsteps again as they went up the road—up the road? Quickly, El pulled her window blind up and peeped out. Mary Beth lived down the road, but she and Will were almost to the company store, going toward the school yard! Where were they going? She could see clearly, Will's camel-hair coat, a light tan color, was plainly visible all the way up the road, even in the shadows as they passed under the bridge.

Now she and Edgar would have to wait until they came back, or risk being seen. Maybe they were going to see Granny Hall's house? No, they had passed her house and were out of sight, somewhere beyond the high black railroad bridge.

Hollie and Emmett were leaving. She heard them in the hall, thanking Mother and Daddy for supper and 'a nice evening'. Still kneeling at her window, El watched them walk down the road, walking apart, like they were each alone. El scooted back to her bed; Mother and Daddy would be coming up soon, and sometimes Mother looked in on them before going to her own bed, sometimes pulling the covers over the hot-natured Bun who kicked them off in her sleep. This time, they went to their own room and she heard the sounds from their room like most Saturday nights, unless Daddy was working, a lot of moving around and smothered laughter and whispering; she wondered again what was so funny, what they talked about, late at night, when the children were supposed to be sleeping.

El waited until the light went off, and all was still, then took her shoes in her hand, got her old coat—her mittens and toboggan were tucked in the sleeve—and slipped down the stairs. Just as she reached the fourth step from the bottom it creaked.

"El? Ellie, is that you? What's the matter?" How did Mother know it was her! She would have to wait a little longer. "I'm just getting a drink, Mother," said El.

"There's a glass in the bathroom."

There was nothing to do but return to the bathroom, run the water, and go back to her room. She watched for Edgar but nothing moved. A long time later she saw him standing below her window. She decided to chance it: this time she would skip that fourth step. She slipped out the back door, put her shoes on, and met Edgar at the fence. Remembering the squeaky gate, she climbed over the fence. They went the back way, behind Gillespie's house, along the creek wall, staying low, crossing the footlog to Granny Hall's, slipping into the shadows beside the haunted house.

"Wait! I've got to tell you something!" Edgar stopped. "What is it?"

"I saw—I saw—" she gasped, out of breath, half from running, but half from fear.

"You saw—What!"

"I saw Mary Beth and Will go up the road—I don't know if they are still up there or if they've come back!"

"Oh, so that's who it was! I saw somebody but they were too far away to tell who. Well, if we hear any funny moans or groans, we'll know who it is! Come on, let's see if we can look in the window."

They moved quietly to the window where the light had been earlier, but it was dark now; the sack had been replaced and the light was out.

The night was so still. El couldn't remember ever being out this late, especially not in cold weather, when there was snow on the ground. It was too cold for frogs or crickets, like in the summer; no owl hooted or train whistled. They could hear the crunch of the snow, the sound of their breathing, their own hearts beating. There was no wind and even the trees stood naked and cold.

Edgar stood on tiptoe, looking into the window, but the sack covered it all. Motioning for her to follow him, he stole around the corner to the back porch, crouched on his hands and knees, and went to the door. Silently he tried the door knob—and it turned! He motioned for her to follow him as he stepped into the dark kitchen, leaving the door open for her. El was too scared to move. Edgar was on his own! She would wait for him beside the porch. In a few seconds she saw the flare of a match, then it was extinguished; she heard him moving about, saw another match strike and go out. She wished he would come back; she was getting cold. Why else would she be shaking so hard?

When he did return, she held her breath as he closed the door, afraid Mr. Reeves would be on them with his shotgun. She decided they would have more to be afraid of from the old man than they would from a spook named Granny Hall!

"Wait right here," whispered Edgar." I'll be back in a minute. "She watched as he went back into the house. What was he doing? Why didn't he come back?" Then she heard it. A moan. A soft, low sigh, a whisper of sound, hardly human. She jumped for the porch and Edgar—she wasn't going to stay here by herself—besides, that could be Edgar, trying to scare her! The door creaked as she pushed it open and stepped inside. Someone grabbed her! She started to scream but it was Edgar, holding onto her and saying shush, there's somebody in the front room! They stood still, not daring to move, and heard the sound again, the soft, even sound of someone sleeping, their breath coming heavy and regular with a soft little snore at the end. Edgar pulled her slowly towards the door, eased outside, pulling her with him, and El was too frightened to do more than follow soundlessly. They closed the door gently and slipped off the porch, ran through the yard and into the shadows of the bridge; they threw themselves behind the concrete support, leaning weakly against it, gasping for breath.

"That was Granny Hall!"

"No, it ain't no spook—it's a man."

"How do you know!"

"I seen him! He was sleeping on some sacks."

"But who?" El didn't know whether to be relieved—or disappointed: it was more fun believing it was a ghost.

"I think it was Mr. Reeves," said Edgar.

"But why? Why would he sleep there instead of in his house?"

"Beats me! Shush, somebody's coming!"

They could hear footsteps in the snow, distinct as someone crunched the graveled schoolyard. Edgar and El moved around the concrete bridge footer, staying out of sight, and watched Mary Beth and Will walk right past them without ever knowing it. Mary Beth had Will's camel-haired coat over her own, and Will's soft, gold-colored sweater showed clearly in the reflected light from the snow. Neither one looked cold, but their arms were tight around each other. El and Edgar waited until the sound of footsteps faded into the night and all was still. Then, from high above them, coming from the north end of the bridge, they heard another sound, a low moaning, a faint humming sound, an eerie, ghostly voice in the thin mountain air, and they felt a faint movement of wind upon their faces: Granny Hall was here, after all!

El and Edgar streaked down the road, leaped over the fence and collapsed in the snow beside El's front porch. See ya tomorrow, Edgar gasped, and El slipped around to the back door, took off her shoes, and crept up the stairs, cold and shaking. She undressed in the dark and got into bed beside the warm, cuddly Bun; her teeth were chattering, her hands and feet were like ice, but she had heard Granny Hall. There was no doubt in her mind at all: the elderly spook had come home, found someone sleeping in her house, and went up on the bridge to do her haintin' and visitin'. The really bad part of it was—she didn't dare tell a soul!

On Sunday, March thirtieth, Mr. and Mrs. Gillespie, and Ben drove Will back to the University at Morgantown, leaving before dawn, and no one had an opportunity to tell him good-bye. Jane was cross all day. Mary Beth had stayed home from Sunday school and church, and when Jane went down to find out why, Mary Beth wouldn't come out to talk to her, just sent BillynBob out to the gate to say she wasn't feeling well. Jane came back to the house and started playing the piano, practicing her new music like she had another recital and had to learn it all in one day.

Daddy was home; he and Mother went to bed after dinner for a nap, Bun had gone to sleep at the table. El watched for the Mitchell boys, but they were nowhere in sight; she found a book and curled up on the sofa, but was soon asleep too. When Jane stopped playing the piano, she woke up. Hollie was at the door, taking off her coat, and talking to Jane." …just so lonesome I could die. Sometimes I don't think I can go on, Emmett left again, don't even know where he's gone …Thought maybe you'd cut my hair for me, Jane, or maybe Faith. "

Hollie and Jane went to the kitchen, got a stool and a towel, and Jane started trimming Hollie's fair hair.

"I'd give anything to have hair like yours, Hollie," said El, coming to join them.

"Your hair would be pretty if you'd let it grow a little, Ellie."

"Mother likes it short, 'cause it's so straight. She can't curl it."

"What's wrong with straight hair?" said Hollie.

"Nobody likes straight hair, you know that!"

"Why don't you get Faith to take you down to Mullins and get a perm?"

"Do you think she would?" exclaimed El." Hollie! Will you ask her? She never says no to you!"

"Sure, we'll ask her, won't we, Jane!"

"We can ask, but a permanent isn't going to help Ellie. She's still the ugly duckling in this family!"

"Oh, now! She's not ugly!" said Hollie, "look at her face, how it's shaped, and how big her eyes are!"

"The better to see you with, my dear, and look what big teeth you have— the better to eat you with, my dear! GRRRRRR!" and El tried to bite Hollie on the neck, knocking her off the high stool and landing on the floor with her.

"Oh, Ellie," said Hollie, laughing, "you always make me feel better!"

Mother, Daddy and Bun woke up with all the commotion and came down to the kitchen. Soon they were all laughing and talking, almost like the days before Shirley died, almost a happy time.

Later, after they had eaten and washed dishes, El walked home with Hollie. Mary Beth and Ben were walking up the road, arm in arm, sweethearts again, whispering and talking serious-like together, only waving as they passed El and Hollie, deep into conversation with each other. "Wonder what they find to talk about," said Hollie, almost envious, and El said, "Well, sweethearts always have a lot to talk about", and Hollie said, yes, "yes, I guess so; it's been so long I'd forgot."

There were no lights, and no smoke coming out of the chimney at Hollie's house; Emmett had not come home. Hollie refused the invitation to come back to the Phillips' and El walked back alone. The wind was picking up and clouds moved across the sky, only a little darker than the sky itself. It would snow again before morning. Would spring never come?

"Good morning, Mr. Gillespie!"

"Good morning, Rachel! Come in, come in! That's some April shower, isn't it? You know what they say—April showers bring May flowers! What can I do for you? Your Mother need something?"

"Came by to tell you, you have a phone call, down at my house."

"A phone call? Who'd want me on your phone—something wrong? Something happen to Will?" He came from behind the counter, took off his big white apron and reached for his raincoat, stepped into his galoshes.

"April Fool, Mr. Gillespie!"

"Rachel Phillips!" He stopped, his hand on the doorknob. "You young whipper-snapper! I'll get you! Just you wait 'til next year! Now you get out of here, you get on to school! Ain't no fool like an old fool! But just you wait, next year it'll be my turn!"

El skipped down the long flight of stairs and made it in the school room just as the bell rang, laughing at how she had pulled the April Fool joke. Now, she had to figure out how to get Mr. Collins!

But her teacher looked like he was in a bad mood. There was a scowl on his face and he stood ramrod straight with his arms folded together and stared at each student as they took their seats. The first thing he said when all were in place and quiet, was, clear everything off your desks. "Take out pencil and paper," said Mr. Collins, still stone-faced. He waited until everyone was ready, then walked across the front of the room, staring at each student. A pop quiz. Dread was tangible.

Suddenly he smiled, his big features lighting up, his dark eyes twinkling. "April Fool!" he shouted. The children screamed with relief. No use trying anything on Mr. Collins, he got them first! All of them!

"Now, we'll have the Irish poems," he said, "and that's no joke! Who wants to be first?"

El raised her hand, wanting to get it over with before she got nervous. She stood at the front of the room to recite.

"This is by Thomas Moore and he was born in Dublin, in 1779. The name of it is, *The Bird Let Loose.*

The bird, let loose in eastern skies,
When hast'ning fondly home,
Ne'er stoops to earth her wing, nor flies
Where idle warblers roam.
But high she shoots through air and light,
Above all low delay,
Where nothing earthly bounds her flight,
Nor shadow dims her way."

"Very good, Rachel. Now, who is next?" When all but Edgar had taken their turn, El put her library book away and listened.

Edgar stood straight and tall, shoulders back, head up, looking solemnly at the back wall, as if his poem were written there:

The stolen Child, by William Butler Yeats, born in Sandymount, Dublin, in 1865:

Where dips the rocky highland
Of Sleuth Wood in the lake,
There lies a leafy island
Where flapping herons wake
The drowsy water rats;
There we've hid our faery vats,
Full of berries
And of the reddest stolen cherries.
Come away, O human child!
To waters and the wild
With a faery, hand in hand,
For the world's more full of weeping than you can
Understand.

Oh, Edgar! Why that poem? The hurt lingered inside, heavy, constant, a deep-heart pain without an opiate.

Would Spring never come?

The miners had gone on strike March 31st, at midnight; everyone in Coville was home on April first, except Daddy, who was working on the Railroad, and Emmett, who was—nobody knew where. He hadn't been seen since late

Saturday night, when he had shouted at Hollie that he couldn't stay in this God-forsaken hell-hole in the mountains and he was clearing out. Daddy came home as usual at a quarter 'til four, walked in the door, set his black lunch pail on the kitchen cabinet and the phone rang. He stopped, groaned, and shook his head before going to answer it.

"Yeah, Bert? Yeah, just walked in. What? My God! My God! Oh, God! On my way!" He turned to Mother. "Explosion. A steam engine blew up—there's a good chance it was sabotage. There were three men on that engine—can't even find them."

Mother repacked the lunch box while Daddy changed clothes, preparing to be out all night; the wreck was on the Norfolk Division, but all crews would respond until the trains were moving again. Mother had made a big pot of beef stew for supper and it sat on the back of the coal range, simmering and sending its unparalleled aroma throughout the house. Daddy sat down long enough to eat a large bowlful. "Can you put some of that in my thermos?" he asked, "it sure will hit the spot along about midnight." Mother did so, and he was gone.

El picked up the paper from where Daddy had dropped it on the hall table.

WORK STOPPED AT MIDNIGHT. MINERS OUT ON STRIKE. ROOSEVELT INTERCEDES IN MINE DISPUTE.

Little Chance of Settlement Before Morning. Strike Affects 330,000 Men in Appalachian Area. FDR says uninterrupted operation imperative, cites urgent defense needs.

"Oh, no you don't!" said Mother. "I get that paper first!"

"Who would try to sabotage the railroad, Mother?" asked Jane.

"We don't know if it was sabotage for certain, Jane."

"What's sabotage?" asked El. "Causing the wreck, doing damage to stop the railroad from operating," said Mother. "We do have enemies. There are people right here in our own country who do not want our industry to produce for the war effort."

"But blowing up the railroad?" said Jane. "Isn't that rather drastic?"

"Yes, but possible. You know the Virginian carries an awfully lot of coal—coal the steel mills must have, if they are going to supply the material for

151

weapons and planes." She carried the paper to the living room, to her favorite chair.

"Jane?" El said softly.

"Yes?"

"You don't think anyone will try to hurt Daddy, do you?"

"Oh, of course not, Ellie! He's not a soldier—why would you think that?"

But El felt worried and uneasy. After all, it was her Daddy and his crew of men that kept the trains running around the clock. She would be glad when he was back home.

Statistics for the month of March listed 60,000,000 man-hours lost, compared with the 6,500,000 for the entire year of 1940. The strike situation had clearly accelerated since the defense program had started getting ready for war, but the leaders lacked the firmness needed to keep their own house in order.

On April 2nd, the headlines were even more alarming:

COAL MINERS HALT WORK; CONTRACT TALKS CONTINUE
HARLAN MINE GUARD SHOT! BLOODSHED!

John L. Lewis became President of the United Mine Workers of America in 1920, and in that year the union decided to organize the miners in Mingo County, West Virginia. The operators hired Baldwin-Felts detectives to go into the company-owned houses and evict the miners who dared to join the union.

Open war was declared, less than two years after the boys had returned from fighting in the great World War. The miners were led by "Two-Gun" Sid Hatfield, an old-West type officer; the detectives, their "evictions" done, arrived in Matewan to catch the train. The two groups faced each other and a three-hour battle took place with shooting in the streets, six-guns blazing, no holds barred. The Leader of the Baldwin-Felts agency was killed, the Mayor was shot and killed, six other men died, including two union men. The "Matewan Massacre" was out of control. President Harding sent 500 soldiers to help settle the dispute, but the UMW threatened a major strike unless the soldiers were withdrawn; they were called back but fresh fighting brought them in again, and Governor Cornwell declared martial law.

Thousands of miners camped in tents in the hills all winter, their wives and children with them, and in May the fighting began again. The union miners of

Paint Creek and Cabin Creek organized and marched to Logan. The fighting continued with sniper attacks—and these mountaineers could knock a squirrel out of a hickory-nut tree at forty paces—and the police forbade any assembly except for gospel meetings. In May, the Governor declared Mingo County a state of war, and Hatfield went to Washington to testify before the Senate. Called back to McDowell County, Sid was accused of "shooting up" a small town by the name of Mohawk. He turned himself in at the county courthouse, but as he walked up the broad granite steps, he was gunned down.

The incensed miners marched on Logan, three thousand strong, undeterred by the pleading of "Mother" Mary Harris Jones, who was ninety-one years old at the time. Many of the miners were World War veterans, experienced in military matters, thus the march assumed the style of any military expedition, forming companies, posting sentries, using passwords to screen out spies. They chanted "John Brown's Body" as their marching song—John Brown, leader of the insurrection at Harper's ferry in 1859 to free the slaves. Now it became the theme song for freedom again, freedom from the mines and fourteen-hour days, freedom from poor and dangerous working conditions, freedom from low pay and freedom from control by operators and the company store. Their uniforms were blue denim overalls or old army drabs left from the war, but they all wore red bandana kerchiefs around their necks.

The conflict escalated on both sides through many battles until, on August 31st, the marchers reached the crest of the watershed between the Coal and the Guyandotte rivers. A line was drawn up against them, composed of over twelve hundred police, operators, armed guards, and 'other' volunteers. The "Battle of Blair Mountain" began. Airplanes dropped bombs, physicians and nurses tended the wounded, chaplains prayed for an end to the fighting. The end came upon the arrival of federal troops from Fort Thomas, Kentucky, and a squadron of bombers from Langley Field, Virginia.

Five hundred and forty men were charged with treason, and their trials, through a change of venue, took place in the same courthouse in Jefferson county where John Brown had been tried and convicted, sixty-three years before. This time, unlike John Brown, the miners were acquitted. The operators charged that the United Mine Workers had made war against America! John L. Lewis declared that the miners had no quarrel with the state, only with the hard-nosed operators, who had seized power and used it against helpless miners.

A Senate investigating committee learned that the basic issue was thus: The operators claimed a constitutional right to hire anyone they please, union member, or non-union member, and they refused to hire a union man. The miners claimed a constitutional right to belong to a union, to meet unmolested, and to have freedom of speech. Neither group recognized the presence of another group—that of the American public.

Between 1920, when John L. Lewis took over' and 1929, the UMW membership dwindled from 45,000 paid-up members to less than a thousand. The operators broke their contracts, the miners were unable to make a strike threat stick. HARD TIMES HIT. The stock market crash caused national unemployment and the large miners work force was idle. West Virginians were desperately in need of the National Industrial Recovery Act as it was presented by Franklin Roosevelt. It was not until 1939 that a law was passed preventing children under the age of sixteen from being employed in the mines.

But the strife continues between operators and miners, captive mines prevail, contracts are negotiated and then ignored. And now, April 1941, more violence in the coal fields: a mine guard has been shot.

Daddy came home at the usual quitting time on Thursday, after being out all night and most of the next day at Victoria, the scene of the explosion. After supper, as tired as he was, he sat at the table and read his paper, then talked about the wreck. There were three men killed, the engineer, the fireman, and the brakeman; they didn't find their bodies for two hours—the explosion blew them a half-mile away. It was a strange accident, blew the locomotive to bits but didn't derail a single one of the 150 coal cars in the train. There were two crewmen in the caboose, and they didn't know why they were stopped until they walked up to the head of the train to investigate.

The explosion woke people up for miles around, seared the hillsides on both sides of the tracks, looked like somebody had taken a giant blow-torch to the grass and bushes. The neighborhood boys found rabbits, dead in the underbrush, charred to a crisp.

"Was it sabotage, Bud?" Asked Mother quietly.

"Not sure. Could have been. There were several rails damaged, could have been from the explosion, could have been done before. Hard to say. None of the men had ever seen a steam engine explode like that, but it could have been in the engine, not the tracks. "Daddy shook his head sadly. "And, I ain't never seen men so messed up."

He picked up his paper again, so tired he could hardly hold it. He read the account of the accident again, then turned to the other news:

LEWIS RULES OUT FEDERAL MEDIATION IN COAL DISPUTE
FOUR KILLED IN HARLAN BATTLE

In the fine print, he read: In Harlan, Kentucky every citizen will be sworn in, if necessary, to keep gun toters off the streets. Special deputies are hired for this, the first outbreak of fighting in two years.

"Daddy what does miners in Kentucky have to do with us?" asked Ellie, confused about what a union really was.

"Same union, Honey, and besides, Kentucky and West Virginia are 'bout the same, Sister States, I guess you could call them"

"Don't you recall the big feud across the borders?" said Mother.

"What feud?" asked Jane.

"Jane, you should know that much history!" exclaimed Mother. "The famous Hatfield and McCoy feud!"

"Oh, that! I know about that," and she shrugged her shoulders, immediately uninterested.

"I don't know about it!" said El, "tell me!"

"Well, it began back in the 1800's." Mother said, and Daddy turned back to his paper.

"The Vance clan and the Hatfield clan were joined by marriage," said Mother. Daddy looked up and with a grin, said, "The clans were married?"

"No, Ephraim Hatfield married Nancy Vance!" said Mother. "I may be from Virginia, but I certainly know about the Hatfield-McCoy feud!"

"Tell us, Mother," said El Anything that would put off doing the dishes was worth listening to.

"Well." Mother started her story again, "the two families ruled Logan County. Now the McCoy's lived across Tug River in Pike County, Kentucky, and Abner Vance had helped run the Mingo Indians out of Logan County, a true pioneer"

"Do you mind if I start the dishes? I've got homework," said Jane.

"But I want to hear about the feud," said El, knowing she might get out of dishes if Mother kept talking.

With a nod of acquiescence towards Jane, Mother continued the story. "The McCoys were just as big and powerful as the Hatfields. When the War Between the States broke out, the Hatfields joined the South, and the McCoys joined the North. Anse Hatfield was a big, strong man, a natural leader of men, and he was made a Captain right away in the Confederate Army. He was ordered to shoot two men who had been court-martialed for desertion, and one of the men was his cousin, George Hatfield."

"Now, mountaineers don't shoot their kinfolk, so Big Anse organized his own army, left the Confederacy, and he called his group Logan's Wildcats." And they took out after those Pike County men, Pike county Militia, it was called, and it was headed up by Harmon McCoy, the brother of the head of the McCoy clan.

"Well, the war ended, the boys all came home, put up their guns and went back to making moonshine and working in the mines. Then Ansa's cousin, Floyd, had a fight with Randall McCoy over a pig. The animals ran loose, you know, just anywhere in the woods, and—"

"Wait a minute!" Daddy interrupted. "Now that's not the way it happened at all!"

"They had a trial over it, Bud, a civil trial, and the jury voted in favor of the Hatfields"

"No, no, that wasn't the start of it!" said Daddy shaking his head. "Now, let me tell you what happened. I know for a fact it started over a fiddle. One of the Hatfield boys bought a fiddle off a McCoy for fifty cents and didn't pay up. Old Tolbert McCoy couldn't get his money from Ellison Hatfield so he stabbed him, right in the gut. Then the Hatfields, they strung up some McCoys on a paw-paw tree!"

Daddy stretched his legs out and started unlacing his sixteen-inch boots. "Know who let that tale git spread around?"

"Probably a McCoy!" said Jane from the kitchen; she'd been listening all the time.

"No, it was Elias Hatfield. He was working as a detective on the Virginian railroad, a stranger come into the bar over at Matoaka, told that tale, and Elias was standing there, listening to every word of it and he just walked out and didn't say a word. Now, if'n it weren't true, do ya think a Hatfield would've let it be told?"

"Sometimes you can't depend on those railroad tales," said Mother.

"What do you mean!" exploded Daddy. "Railroad tales are more likely to be the real thing than some of your history books!"

"Oh, come on, Bud! You know how railroad men love to gossip!"

"We do no such thing!" Daddy took out his pipe. "Now let me tell you about—"

"Oh, no you don't! It's time for these girls to get to bed! Besides, you need your rest, too."

"Just one more thing," said Daddy, getting solemn. "Devil Anse Hatfield died over at Island Creek, same year Sid was shot on the courthouse steps, 1921. That about did in the Hatfield clan. Logan County ain't been the same since. That was the year before your Mother and I got married. We sure missed some exciting times around here."

"Kinda looks like it might get exciting again," said Jane coming into the dining room as she dried the big black iron skillet. Oh, goody! The dishes are finished! "If they keep on shooting at the mines, I mean."

"I'm sure glad Coville isn't a real mining town," said El.

"Oh, but it is, Ellie!" said Daddy, raising his head and looking at her directly. "Girls," he said slowly, "these are bad times in the coal fields. I want you to stay close to home, don't go nowhere but straight to school and straight back home. All the men will be home, there's libel to be some drinkin' and ..."

"Now, Bud, you know I'll watch over these girls! You need to get on to bed, you're not thinking, you're too tired," said Mother.

"I'm never too tired to be thinking about my girls," said Daddy. He picked up Bun who had fallen asleep during the feud-telling, and carried her up to bed. Daddy wasn't a kissin' man, but he held her real tender for a moment before laying her down.

The next day, after school, El gathered up all the kids in the camp and related the saga of the Hatfields and the McCoys. They divided into two clans, El playing the leader of the Hatfields because there was more dying to do, and she did a magnificent death scene, so realistic that Bun ran in the house crying and Mother made her come in too. Why couldn't Bun do something on her own? Why did she have to tag around behind her all the time! Why couldn't she go play—no, of course she couldn't find anything to do on her own: Bun had never played by herself in her entire life.

157

Friday morning Mother had a secret-like smile on her face; she waited until Jane left for school, then pulled El to her in a tight hug. "Guess what's happening today?"

"Is it Spring?" asked El, having already been outside to bring in a bucket of coal. She had seen the tiny purple crocuses by the back door. Down by the creek, water cresses had tiny white blooms clustered among the shiny green leaves, the violets had opened their five-petaled blossoms to make a landing field for the bees, and the moss on the tree trunks was green.

"Something else," said Mother. "If I tell you, you must promise you'll do something for me."

"Sure," said El, puzzled.

"Well, Jane is being inducted into the National Honor Society today. It's a surprise to her— they never tell who will be taken in until the assembly. I know that doesn't sound very special to you, but some day, when it's your turn for such an honor, it will."

"What do you want me to do?" asked El, still trying to figure out what this required of her.

"I'm going to the school for the program. I'll take Bun with me. But I don't want you to miss school. I want you to look after yourself for an hour or so, after school."

"Is that all?"

"Now, Rachel, it isn't that easy. You'll be tempted to get into things, or do things that you know I don't want you to—you'll just have to be a grown-up young lady, come in, stay home, no company, and if you get scared you can go over to Mrs. Gillespie's or Mrs. Belcher's, they will both be home."

"I can take care of myself! I won't be scared!"

"All right, but now, Rachel, remember what Daddy was saying, about the miners being home and all. I'm depending on you to use good judgement."

As she walked up the road to school, she fumed to Edgar. Why does Mother always treat her like a baby, didn't she know she was growing up?

"Sounds to me like she knows," said Edgar, "has she ever left you alone before?"

No, not that she could remember, thinking back there had always been Jane, or Hollie, or a neighbor.

"Well?" said Edgar, "what did I tell ya!"

Nine

During the last week of March, the coal mines had produced 11,800,000 tons of coal, operating at 98.3% of capacity. By the first week of April the railroads had moved the coal out, returning the empties to the mines, ready for work to resume. The railroads began to feel the pinch of the miner's strike: The B&O (Baltimore & Ohio) and the NYC (New York Central) had temporarily cut their crews. The N&W (Norfolk & Western), Pocahontas Division, had three hundred idle trainmen. It was no different on the Virginian: the Virginian's business was coal. The freight was going through, but the only coal moving was what had been loaded at the mines before the strike.

The Lend-Lease bill had been promoted and written by law-makers, passed by Congress, and signed by the President: seven billion dollars had been appropriated. All of this was in danger of being lost. The careful planning of the leaders of the nation was being threatened by the strike, being hampered by the leaders of the unions as they refused to aid the defense program, selfishly putting their demands before the needs of the nation and the free world, being hampered by the operators as they looked at profit margins instead of profitable materials for the war effort. Ill feelings began to build, even in the coal field, as the miner's spent their days in idleness, gathering in union halls and at the bath houses and the feed stores, grumbling among themselves.

Rumors of railroad sabotage ran through the coal camps as an engine derailed and overturned on the Winding Gulf line; a box car caught fire and burned on a siding in Matoaka, but a fourteen-year-old boy admitted being in the car, just looking around, prior to the fire.

The southern coalfields rejected the proposed wage agreement, and the steel mills planned to strike on Tuesday.

Palm Sunday dawned warmer and somewhat cloudy; a light dew wet the new grass and left the tree branches shiny, their new growth barely discernible, but winter coats were still needed to go to church.

Preacher Copeland announced his retirement for June first, which was on a Sunday, and it would be his last sermon. There were over one hundred and thirty-two thousand Methodists in the state, he said, and Methodism was the leading denomination in West Virginia, while one out of every four belonged to a church of some kind. There was a brief meeting of the official board following the service and the girls waited for Mother in the car, curious to know why they had called a special meeting.

The clouds were gone by the time they reached home, and at dinner Mother told Daddy about the special meeting: "Preacher Copeland is retiring, Bud, as you know, and today he suggested we apply for a divinity student to come for the summer. He seemed to think we might get one from Wesleyan College. There's a movement underway to appoint Wesleyan College the official institute of higher learning in this Conference, and many of the students need financial help."

"Where is Wesleyan College?" asked Jane, obviously thrilled by the prospect of having a college student as a minister.

"Buckhannon," said Mother.

"Is that far away?"

"Why, I really don't know." Mother hesitated, looking at Daddy for help.

"Too far," said Daddy shortly. "It's way up near Elkins, almost to Fairmont. Roads are bad, take half a day just to get here."

"I think Preacher Copeland was considering letting a student board with him, they talked about it, don't think they've made a decision yet."

"For free?" asked Daddy, "can't see that old coot letting anyone stay for free."

"Now, Bud, that's not kind! He said it would be his way of helping us out of a spot; he doesn't want to see the church go down, not after all the work, and the years, he's put into it, making it grow."

Daddy got up from the table abruptly and went out on the front porch. They could hear him as he unchained the swing from its hooks near the ceiling. He walked around the house to the back porch to get a broom, instead of coming back inside. They could hear him sweeping the dead leaves away from the wall, something that was ordinarily Faith's job. When they joined him on the

160

porch, he said, get a bucket of water and I'll help you clean the floor, but Mother said, no indeedy, my ox is most certainly not in any ditch, time for that on Monday. It was too chilly to stay out for long, but Mother pointed out a robin run-stop-run, run-stop-run on the front lawn. The talk about the ox made El think about Old Bess and she asked Daddy when were they going to Virginia to get their cow.

Daddy, with a wicked grin, said, "oh, probably the first Sunday in June!" He laughed aloud at the dismay on Mother's face, and Jane cried out, "Oh, No!" Daddy went upstairs to take his Sunday afternoon nap, but Mother, her hands on her hips, said, "Sometimes he can be so mean!" She didn't take a nap with him either.

Monday morning was cold and rainy. Mother got sick, threw up and went back to bed. The girls tiptoed around, getting themselves ready for school. El decided that Mother was sick because she was still mad at Daddy, that was why she didn't fix his breakfast. On Tuesday she was sick again but when they got home from school, Mother was at her sewing machine, the material she had purchased Saturday piled everywhere. She had another worry: would the Easter outfits be ready for Easter Sunday?

By Thursday the railroad cars were down by fifty percent, Churchill was giving Russia warnings, the battleship, North Carolina, was commissioned in the Brooklyn Naval Yard and the Easter outfits were finished. After school Mother gathered the three of them into the dining room-turned-sewing room. She helped each one try on their new outfits before calling them complete.

Jane, as the oldest, was first. She had chosen navy blue and white and stood resplendent in a navy suit with white piping and large white buttons; she had new true-red shoes and bag, and a tiny red hat with a wisp of navy veil, and looked like a fashion model. After she added white gloves, Daddy said she looked twenty-one and Jane was thrilled.

Bun was all baby-blue ruffles, ruffles on her panties, ruffles around the hem of her dress, ruffles around the neck and down the front, and even a ruffle on her petticoat. She had tiny black-patent slippers and pale blue anklets with lace around them. A large, blue-satin bow held her bright red curls away from her face. She was a delicious little baby-doll, soliciting hugs and kisses by simply being herself.

Mother had made El's Easter outfit during the day while El was in school, hiding it at night, and when El asked about it, Mother shrugged, and said,

"Well, you wanted black, and I've got this old pair of your Uncle Charlie's pants— he wore out the seat, but the legs are still good—" and El, fearful of the truth, never pressed her further.

When the girls started trying on their outfits, Mother told El to come down in her slip. She had El's outfit piled on her sewing machine and covered with her apron. First, she pulled out a black wool skirt, probably made from the legs of Uncle Charlie's pants—she would never know for certain, and said, "I declare, Ellie, you get taller and skinnier every day! Just a little loose in the waist, I'll fix that." Next she brought out a soft white blouse with little pearl buttons down the front and real lace for a collar. It fit El exactly. From under her apron, she pulled out a black and white houndstooth jacket, a short little suit jacket with a black velvet collar and lapels and black velvet buttons; it, too, was a perfect fit. From a shoebox sitting under her machine, Mother brought out black dress slippers, with an inch heel!

"You'll have to wear hose with these, she said, so you need this." She laid a small white garter belt on the pile. El picked it up in awe; she didn't even know how to put it on.

"And, you'd look funny in a garter belt and no bra," said Mother, laying a tiny white brassiere on top of the shoes. El blushed furiously, at a loss for words. Jane laughed outright. "Why is she going to wear a bra—she doesn't have anything to put in it!"

"Never you mind, Jane. You just tend to your own business! Now, Ellie, lean down a bit." Mother placed a small red corduroy hat on her head. It was designed like those worn by the Army pilots, with a peaked top and a slight crease in it, and on the side was pinned a small gold eagle, its wings outspread.

El was so thrilled she burst into tears, threw her arms around her Mothers neck, saying thank you, thank you Mother, over and over.

Mother had tears in her eyes too, and all she said was, "Careful, now, don't mess up your first suit!" and then she added, "Saturday we're going to Mullins and see about getting you a perm." So, Hollie had talked to Mother for her!

"I've got another surprise," said Mother, "but you will have to help me with it." As El started gathering up her new wardrobe, Mother stopped her. "Wait! I haven't hemmed that skirt yet!"

Daddy, from his place at the table behind his paper, said, "Better watch her, El, she'll be hemming it as you go out the door!"

"I always get it done, don't I?" objected Mother. "Now, Ellie, I need you to go get Hollie."

El grabbed her old dress and streaked out the door, coming back in a few minutes with a bewildered Hollie.

"What is it, Faith? Ellie said you needed me. What's wrong?"

"Nothing's wrong, honey, but I need to talk to you about something." Mother looked at Hollie very seriously. "Hollie, I'm going to need your help this summer, with the garden and the canning and all."

"Of course, Faith, don't I always help you?"

"Well, I can't pay you," said Mother.

"Have I ever expected you to pay me? With all you do for me, have I ever asked you for a dime?"

Mother held up her hand, continuing, "so, I'm paying you now—I've made something for you, but there's one condition." She handed a bundle of clothing to Hollie.

Hollie shook out the material; it was a pale rose-colored dress, the softest percale Mother could find. The sleeves were short bells, the neckline curved gracefully in a sweetheart pattern. Pale shell-colored buttons went down the front to below the waistline, to where the skirt flared out in wide panels that flowed and moved as she held the dress up. "Oh, Faith!" With tears shining in her deep blue eyes, she ran upstairs to put on the dress. When she came back into the room everyone was still, just looking at her. The color was exactly right to bring out a faint blush in her alabaster cheeks; the princess lines made her slender figure look as graceful as a flower on a stem. Her hair caught the glow from the high ceiling light. Daddy put down his paper. Everyone just looked and looked at her. She had never been lovelier.

Hollie turned around slowly, twirling the skirt gently around her white legs. Mother cleared her throat, for some reason sounding choked up. "You'll have to press it a little, the way I had it rolled up."

"Faith, what can I say?"

"I told you, there is a condition."

"Anything!"

"Go to church with us, Sunday. It's Easter."

Hollie was silent. She had not been to church since Shirley died, said she couldn't stand to see where the casket had stood. She looked at Faith and quietly nodded. "I guess I might as well. I have to go sometime."

The girls jumped up to hug her then showed off their own new outfits. Later, they sat quietly while the news broadcast was on.

Prime Minister Churchill warned Russia of Germany's intentions, stating that the Balkan drive pointed in her direction. He pledged that no matter which way Adolf Hitler moved, "we who are armed with the sword of retributive justice shall be on his track..." He also warned the Turkish people against the German army, that they "may at any time turn on her also." He voiced his fear for Libya, painting a dark, dark picture, and for Egypt, too.

It was late when Hollie left, and they had begged her to stay. Emmett was gone, there was no use being all alone, wasn't she frightened? No, she wasn't afraid, and Emmett might come back. She wanted to be there, if he did.

Saturday's trip to Mullins was eventful for the girls. Irving Berlin's movie, *Alexander's Ragtime Band*, starring Tyrone Power, Alice Faye and Don Ameche, was playing at the Wyoming theater. Daddy and Mother went with them to see it and it was a joyous family occasion. The music and dance selections would become favorites for piano concerts by Jane all summer, and, Mother predicted, would be favorites for years. Also, on Saturday night they learned that the Southern Coal Operators had bolted the Appalachian wage Conference and Daddy promised to explain what that meant later, when he wasn't so tired, and when they didn't have all these groceries to put away. What did you do, Faith, buy out the store? Or are you feeding half the families in Coville on this old man's salary? Now, Bud, don't you know we have plenty, we've never gone hungry, have we, no, thank you God, can't you say that a little more reverently? After all, you, know, you are going to church with us tomorrow. Is that so? Yes, that's so, and if you want any dinner, you won't be ugly about it!

Mother sent the girls to bed, and they heard good-natured conversation coming from the kitchen for some time. In the morning there would be Easter baskets beside their beds, baskets filled with colored eggs, jelly beans and chocolate rabbits.

Sunday morning was truly a spring revival. The temperature rose rapidly, almost summer-like, fifteen degrees or so above normal for this time of the year. Jonquils and daffodils waved their golden heads at insects that had emerged overnight. On the steep mountain slopes redbud blossomed, slightly ahead of the white dogwood which was showing only gray-green buds. The sky was as blue as Bun's eyes, as bright as her dress, and the scattered cumulus clouds were fluffy white toys, for effect only, with no serious intention of bringing rain.

Everyone in Coville and Herndon was at church; extra seats were placed along the back and down the aisles. All the ladies wore hats—Mother's was a wide-brimmed black straw with a large red rose—and all the men wore white shirts and ties. Daddy was one of the most uncomfortable men there, Mother having insisted he wear his nice gray suit and a black and gray striped tie, not looking at all like the man who wore riding breeches and sixteen-inch lace-up boots every day of the year.

El felt like a different girl and was told she looked it. She now had short frizzy hair that smelled burned from the electric permanent machine, and she couldn't wash it for a week, might take the curl out. But the fuzzy hair held her new red hat in place and fluffed out around it. She forgot about the severe pain she had gone through to get the new look when she caught Edgar looking at her for the third time.

The children sang special music, the preacher talked longer and louder, the church grew warmer and warmer. The ladies brought out their summer-time fans, the men wiped their red faces with large white handkerchiefs, but finally it was over: Jesus was safely resurrected for another year. Next Sunday the women and children could come as usual, the men could stay home as usual. They stood and sang the" Awakening Chorus," the words ringing out loud and joyful:

> *Awake! Awake! And let your song of praise arise;*
> *Awake! Awake! The earth is full of Glory!*

As they came out of the dim church into the bright April sun, El thought the light was beaming from the skies, the hills were resounding with joy, the earth was joining in the great glad song. Thanks be, the winter is gone, spring has come!

Being such a special holiday brought out the best in people, and today was no exception. The most radiant thing around was Hollie's face. She was beautiful, in her new rose-like dress, and her friends gathered around her, welcoming her back, and folks she hardly knew stepped over to shake her hand, and say so good to see you. Mother asked her to have dinner with them, no sense her going home alone, and while the dinner cooked, they sat out on the porch, first time since Christmas. Mother had helped Bun out of her new dress and into play clothes, but the others stayed dressed up.

Hollie and El walked about the yard, looking at the new growth, the blooming flowers and budding trees, and El felt as grown-up as Hollie. She became aware that someone was watching them from the front porch of the Mitchell house and thought, of course, that it was Edgar—Edgar had spent most of Sunday School staring at her but when they made the turn in the yard and faced the house, she saw it wasn't Edgar at all. Mr. Mitchell stood on his porch, leaning against the post, and anyone with half an eye could tell: he was watching Hollie.

It had been a blessed Easter Sunday, until the evening news came on the radio: there had been an explosion at the new powder plant at Radford. No one had any details. It had happened just shortly before the newscast; it was being investigated. The girls were sent to bed at their usual nine o'clock bedtime. Soon afterwards the telephone rang. Was Daddy being called out to work on this beautiful evening? What could have possibly gone wrong on an evening such as this?"

She went to the top of the stairs. Daddy was saying, "All right, Bert, yes, we'll take care of it, Okay, Bert, Okay, we can do that, all right Bert."

"Daddy?"

"Yes?"

"You going to work?"

"No, not tonight, honey, you go back to bed."

"What's wrong?"

There was silence at the foot of the stairs; Mother was with Daddy, standing by the phone. "We might as well tell her."

"Not tonight, wait until in the morning," said Mother.

"She won't go back to sleep, got to know some time."

El went down the stairs. "What's wrong? Is it Grandmother?"

"It's Mr. Sanders, Ellie. He was in that explosion down at Radford. Your father and I have to go up to Mrs. Margaret's with the message."

El thought about Mr. Cliff Sanders, the way he had looked the last time she had seen him, standing in the road in front of her house, big, broad shoulders bulging out of his dirty, brownish-yellow coat, standing and talking about ducks with green heads, and how the lights in the houses on the high mountains looked like fallen stars, and about the man on the train playing the juice-harp,

166

talking about his new job, down at Radford, and she knew the answer, even before she asked the question.

"Is he dead, Mother?"

"Yes, honey, I'm afraid he is."

Mr. Sanders would've said, "th' hell you say".

The way Mrs. Margaret felt about her husband was well-known about the Camp, for she made no secret of it. She wasn't happy when he worked in the mines and she wasn't happy when he didn't work.

A body would think she'd be real pleased when he went to Radford and got a good-paying job, but no, she still insisted that Cliff Sanders wouldn't amount to anything, he was too do-less, a do-nothing. The way he died proved her right, and gave her license to say it for the remainder of her days.

A high-flyin' crane passed so close to a high-tension wire that it created a "spark-gap": six thousand volts jumped across the space, and *electrocuted the man who was leaning on the crane with his elbow, talking to the operator.* That man was Cliff Sanders. Killed jawing, where he had no business being. Made Mrs. Margaret a very self-righteous widow.

El would miss him; she hadn't wanted him to move away, not even as far as Bluefield, certainly not to heaven. She pondered the question: Would Mr. Sanders go to heaven? He hadn't gone to church, not even at Eastertime or Christmas, but he was a friendly man, always speaking to her like she was as good as a grown-up. Surely there would be something for him to do in heaven. Shirley would like to have him there, somebody she knew, somebody from home.

Mother took Mrs. Margaret to Williamson, the day after the message came, for that was Mr. Sanders' home; the powder plant sent his body, what was left of it, in a polished white oak box for free, and he was buried beside his parents. Being so far from Coville and such a bad trip, the road being so crooked that anyone riding in the back seat got car sick, only Mother and Bun went, and Bun got sick riding in the front seat.

With no funeral, not seeing the casket or anything, it was like Mr. Sanders was still living and just working out of town. Most grown-ups went about their business as usual, but for the children it was unusual. Being without a teacher, the third grade went to Mrs. Collins' room and the fourth grade went to Mr. Collins' room, and the rooms were crowded, and noisy. Mr. Collins seemed to ignore the extra kids, gave them writing work to do, and sat at his desk all day looking off into the past, or into the future: telling which was impossible since he didn't give out clues.

Mrs. Margaret didn't stay in Williamsburg, not really knowing Cliff's parents, and when Mother got her back to her house she and Bun came on home, Mrs. Margaret saying she was so used to being alone, it was just another night like any other. No meal, no neighbors, no preacher, no flowers—Mr. Sanders was Coville's first casualty of the war, said Daddy, a mighty sad ending for a friendly man.

El wondered: was being friendly enough to get into heaven?

Horace Tucker, the only mortician in Mullins, volunteered to lead the newly enlisted soldiers to Huntington; out of sixty-seven men needed from Wyoming to fill the draft quota, only nineteen were actually drafted. The other forty-eight were volunteers.

The Mullins wildlife club offered a bounty of fifty cents for every gray fox pelt brought in, and at night the baying of dogs echoed across the mountains, carrying far in the still-chilly night air. The money would be used to restock the rabbits and quail which the over-abundance of foxes had made scarce.

Along with the increased activity in the woods and the warmer, drier air, the fire season started, with forty-three separate fires spotted in the mountains. Normal visibility is fifteen to twenty miles in the mountains, but due to the smoke and haze, it was reduced to four or five miles. The air smelled of wood fires, reminiscent of camping and fishing along Barker's creek, and trout season opened with a legal limit of fifteen per day, but the season opening day was delayed due to wildfires.

Not all miners were running hounds or fishing for trout. Four were killed in a mine shooting, and twenty-five were injured. The miners tried to reopen the mine at Kent; pickets blocked the road. One thousand, one hundred and sixty-nine miners applied for relief and twelve items, such as beans, corn, flour, potatoes, were stocked as surplus commodities and distributed to the jobless miners.

By Thursday, there were over a hundred forest fires raging in the state, mostly along the West Virginia-Kentucky border. There had been no rain for two weeks; CCC boys, rangers and volunteers battled the fires around the clock as the rainfall for the area averaged less than one-sixth of the norm. On Friday, the few local showers failed to make a difference.

Friday, April eighteenth, the YUGOSLAVIAN ARMY SURRENDERED.

And the heaviest air attack thus far left London to dig out from under the heaviest damage yet. Military officials feared the raid was the prelude to an invasion of the island by the Germans. On the state level, Troopers were sent to protect the citizens as the Union refused to divide the North and South locals. John L. scheduled a meeting with southern operators and pledged there would be no return to work until the entire area signed.

"One for all, all for one", Mr. Gillespie said. But the most disturbing news of all on Friday evening came from their beloved hero, Charles Lindbergh. He had become a member of the America First Committee and it was announced prior to his Chicago speech on Thursday night. The regard in which he was held was clearly demonstrated by the headlines in Friday's paper:

LINDY SAYS WAR LOST ERA START
Asserts Collapse of British Empire Will Be Tragedy to World;
Urges U.S. Guard Materials

Emmett was home. He walked in his house on Friday evening, at suppertime, threw his jacket on the bed, and asked Hollie if supper was ready, like he'd been gone one day instead of twenty. Hollie said he never told where he'd been, or what he'd been doing, but acted like he'd never been gone.

Mother sat at the table with Daddy while he read his paper. "I want to ask them up for dinner on Sunday," she said. "No," said Daddy, "I don't think you should, not this soon."

"She's like my own girl, Bud, I can't ignore the fact that he's back."

"Don't have to rush them, either," said Daddy. Nevertheless, Mother felt she had to see about them, and as the girls washed supper dishes, she walked down the road to the Whites. She was gone for a few minutes and came back obviously upset; she sat down at the table without a word. Daddy looked over his paper at her, frowned, and said, "You can't let well enough alone, can you?"

"She's like my own daughter, Bud. You can understand that, can't you?"

"Sometimes it's better to let daughters alone, let them manage their own business," said Daddy, and went back to his paper.

By Sunday night the high winds were whipping the forest fires into an inferno; there had been no rain for three weeks and one hundred thousand acres in eight states were burning simultaneously. Most of the men were either fighting fires or recuperating from the long hours spent in the forests. Church attendance was poor and an uneasy feeling pervaded the small group of women and children who were there. The acrid smell of desiccated woodland spread through the small wooden church. The blue haze rested just below the ridge, obscuring the tips of the high hills and the sky, a smokey fog blotting out the sun, moving with the wind, sweeping up the valley like smoke up a flue with the damper open.

Mother couldn't tolerate the estrangement from Hollie. She sent El down to ask them to dinner, against Daddy's wishes. When El reached the house, she could hear the arguing before she knocked on the door; timidly, half-hoping they wouldn't hear, she pecked on the door. The voices stopped; there was movement at the window, and she heard Hollie say, "It's Ellie", heard Emmett answer, "Don't open that door." Heard Hollie's reply, "I've got to, Emmett, she ain't never done nothin' to us, there's no cause to treat her like that."

"Mother says you and Emmett come eat with us, she's got a big pot roast and a cake. Says all she has to do is throw in another spud."

"No thanks, Ellie, honey. You tell Faith we've already eaten, but we sure appreciate it." Hollie had a small cut on her cheek and one on her lower lip. One eye was blue around the lid and below it. She made no effort to hide her face from El. Her hair was uncombed and she wore only a pink slip, and she was barefooted. El knew she had gotten her out of bed. In bed in the middle of the afternoon.

El ran back to her house, her lungs filling with the smoke in the air, her eyes filling with tears—but not from the smoke. She burst in the back door, out of breath. "Hollie says they've eaten," she said and then added quickly, "Mother, I think Emmett has beat up Hollie!"

"Rachel!"

"I saw her, Mother, she's got a cut on her mouth and a black eye!"

"Rachel, you know Emmett wouldn't do something like that!"

"I saw her Mother, I heard him say don't open the door, but Hollie did anyway, and I saw her!"

Mother turned to Daddy, her face tense and worried. "Bud, what shall we do?"

"Nothing," said Daddy.

"Nothing! How can you say that!"

"We don't butt in between a man and his wife."

"Bud! What if he hurts her!"

"Emmett wouldn't hurt her, Faith. He wouldn't harm a hair on her head. Rachel is exaggeratin'," and he snapped his paper in irritation.

"No, I'm not, Daddy. I saw her and I know Emmett hit her in the face."

Daddy looked real straight at El and she met his eyes unblinking. He folded his paper and placed it beside his plate at the table, pushed back his chair, and walked heavily out of the room, out the back door, and down the creek towards the White's. There wasn't a sound in the kitchen until he came back, walking just as deliberately, picked up his paper and resumed his reading.

"Well?" said Mother.

"Well what?" asked Daddy.

"Well, *is Hollie all right?"*

"Yes, Hollie is all right."

"And?"

"And what?"

"And, did Emmett hit her?"

"I told you, we don't interfere with a man and his wife."

"You are the limit!" said Mother, in exasperation.

Dinner was eaten in almost total silence. While Jane and El washed the dishes, Mother went down to Hollie's; she had to be sure Hollie didn't need her. When she came back, she went into the living room with Daddy and closed the French doors between the two rooms, so El and Jane couldn't hear their conversation. They talked quietly for a time, but gradually their voices rose in disagreement. Finally, Daddy got up and went out the front door. Mother sat in the near-dark living room, and through the glass doors El could see her crying into her apron.

While Daddy was gone, El cut her homework out of the paper:

West Virginia's Tangled Web—Interest in the contest between Messrs. Rosier and Martin, appointees of the warring Governors, to fill the unexpired Neely term in the United States Senate, has flared up again. These designations were made on Jan. 3, and three months have passed, and the Senate, which is the judge of its own membership, has made no decision in the matter… This contention, the hostilities it is engendering, the sores it is opening and the result that is coming, are the babies of West Virginia's "Divided democracy".

When Daddy came back, he and Mother went upstairs to bed, and it wasn't even all the way dark. Daddy seemed gentler with Mother, perhaps trying to make up for crossing her over Hollie, and they walked up the steps side by side, with Daddy's arm around Mother's shoulders.

El put Bun in the bathtub without being told. Jane went to her room to do homework. El sat at her window, looking at the quiet town. The smoke curled around the catenary poles on the high bridge, and sealed out the sky; the light over the door of the company store burned sulfur-yellow in the haze. Mr. Mitchell sat on his front steps, dressed in black work clothes, looking like he had come out of the mines, but in reality, he had come out of the forest where he'd been fighting fire and was resting up before washing off the carbon-black and mud. The boys were nowhere in sight.

As she sat there, her mind on Hollie, worrying about her safety, she saw Emmett coming up the road, his jacket hooked over his shoulder on one finger, carrying a brown paper bag twisted at the top. He walked past the house and on towards the highway, his head down, looking at the black dust-dry road, moving one foot before the other, slow and heavy, like his heart wasn't in it, like he didn't know where he was going.

El watched until Emmett was out of sight; she felt so sorry for him, but there was nothing she could do. On the other hand, there sat Mr. Mitchell, alone on his porch steps, and he had volunteered his days and half of his nights battling forest fires, to save people's homes. He was a handsome, heroic figure in soot-blackened armor.

On impulse, she went down to the kitchen and cut a large slice of the chocolate cake Mother had baked for their Sunday dinner, wrapped it in waxed paper, and slipped out the back door. She ran across the dirt road to the Mitchell's front steps. Mr. Mitchell raised his head, but he didn't speak. El placed the cake in his hand. "Brought'cha something," she said. Mr. Mitchell took the package, carefully unwrapped it, then looked up and grinned, his white teeth flashing in his smoke-blackened face. El ran quickly out of the yard, not waiting for thanks. Mr. Mitchell didn't say a word, but when El looked back, he was eating the cake like he hadn't had a bite in a 'coon's age.'

On the Saturday before Easter, the southern coal operators had walked out of the Appalachian Wage Conference in a dispute that involved three hundred, twenty-five thousand miners. The operators had stated that they would form their own negotiating group; they had renewed their offer to give the miners an eleven percent increase in wages. They were asking the National Mediation Board to consider a sectional wage difference, but they refused to grant an increase of $1.40 per day.

The Union continued to ask for a flat $7.00 per day for both the north and the south. The present rate was $6.00 in the north, and $5.60 in the south. The southern operators would not consent to eliminating the forty cent differential.

"But, Daddy, why can't they pay all the miners the same? Don't the southern miners work as hard as the northern miners?"

"Sure they do, honey, and that's exactly the position the union is taking. But turn it around. Be a mine owner. Why should a mine owner in the north make a dollar profit on a ton of coal, and the owners in the south make sixty cents on the same amount of coal? You see, it costs the southern operators forty cents more to haul their coal to the shipping point. They want the same amount of money in their pocket, so they cut the miners wages to make up for the extra shipping costs. The miners take the short end of the deal, and if they don't like it, they don't have to work!"

"Doesn't seem fair."

"Fair to who—the operators or the miners?"

On the sixteenth, twenty southern Senators and Representatives planned to ask President Roosevelt to intervene in the dispute. Headed by representative Kee (D. W.Va.) the group felt they had done everything they could possibly do to settle the disagreement.

On the seventeenth, John L. announced he was ready to resume talks…the talking went on and on, all sides agreeing on one primary goal, "the coal must move soon", but disagreeing on how to satisfy the demands of all parties.

Also, on the seventeenth, some of the southern operators and southern miners forgot their differences for a few short hours as they gave a helping hand to a coal company doctor and his nurse:

It was almost midnight when the physician received word that a miner's wife had started labor. The mountain shanty was located in the backwoods, where the American Coal Company had finished timbering, high above operation No. 9, known as the Crane Creek mine. To reach the mountain home by the usual trail meant five miles of hiking straight up. The doctor knew he didn't have that much time. The miners were pressed into service, the operators talked into a motor car, and the race with the stork was on. The doctor and his nurse sped through the mine tunnel, cutting the distance in half and arriving in time to deliver twin boys, saving the lives of both. The tiny twins, and the mother and father came through just fine—but that wasn't so for the miners: A woman had been allowed in the mine and that spelled disaster for the mine! It was just a matter of time before catastrophe fell. Everyone knew it was bad luck for a woman to be in a mine!

Now the thorn in the sides of both miners and operators appeared to be the difference in freight rates, and the northern operators asked FDR to investigate. Roosevelt replied that the Interstate Commerce Commission was looking in to it.

The fires raged on, burning over eight states and the blaze of strikes flared just as hot. The critical coal situation was affecting all areas now. Five blast furnaces in Youngstown, Ohio were shut down: lack of coal. The War Department blamed the union for severe curtailment of defense production.

Finally, on the twenty-ninth, the southern operators accepted President Roosevelt's suggestion that they reopen the mines and continue to negotiate, with the contract retroactive to the date of reopening. The mines would reopen on Wednesday, the thirtieth.

The mines would not open on Wednesday, that would be the last day of a pay period, and payroll clerks would have to make up an entire payroll just for one day. The mines would resume work on Thursday, the first day of May. Aw, hell! Why ruin a weekend? We was goin' fishin', the trout are running, season's open, fires are out, sun's shinin', got a dollar- a- day raise, we'll just wait 'til Monday, nobody starts back to work in the middle of the week!

Ten

Spring is here! The mountains awake, stretch, and burst into white dogwood bloom. The honey bees find the violets, the hummingbirds sip the dew, squirrels squawk from tree to tree, the woodpeckers screech like crows, and the robins peck over the lawn.

The porch swing is down and Mother scrubs the floor with Super Suds; she paints the steps a bright blue and fills the flower boxes with woods dirt and seeds.

After school the boys draw ten-foot circles in the dirt of the road and pile their favorite marbles in the middle, trade taws and share steelies—when using a steelie is agreed upon. The girls bring long jump ropes and spend hours jumping and singing and proving their championships, jumping one hundred, two hundred, four hundred times, down in the meadow where the green grass grows. There sits Ellie sweet as a rose, along comes Edgar and gives her a kiss, how many kisses does she get, one, two, three, one two tie your shoe, three four, shut the door, five six, pick up sticks, seven, eight shut the gate nine, ten, say it again, one, two three, four…

It was just as well that the boys and girls were greeting spring with separate frenzies, for El and Edgar weren't speaking. The cause of their alienation was, as usual, Charles Augustus Lindbergh.

The uproar over Lindbergh's predicament was second only to the coal strike negotiations. After his speech on the seventeenth, before which his membership in the America First Committee was announced, they had held a long and involved discussion about his loyalty to America. Edgar insisted on calling him a coward and a traitor and he upheld Roosevelt's remarks, while El held on to her pride and her affection for the flier. He had been her hero for too many years to just stop now, cold turkey.

It had started in school. Edgar had stood up and read the article about Lindy to the whole class; his gloating expression made El furious. She had been sick and miserable about it; everyone knew her dedication to the heroic flier, and she had run all the way home, jumped the fence like she used to do. Edgar had shouted after her, "It's not my fault! He's a yellow-bellied, sap-sucking, fat-mouthed coward! All I did was read about him!"

She went in the front door quietly, intending to go up to her room, but Mother heard her and came out of the kitchen, drying her hands on her apron. She looked at El with concern.

"Is there something wrong, Rachel?"

"Mother, is Lindbergh really a coward?" she burst out.

"What on earth are you talking about?"

"Why doesn't he want us to help the people in London? Why is he so down on the President? Edgar is mad at me because I take up for him, like he doesn't want me to think anything good about him, and he read that whole speech to the class and they laughed at me!"

"Wait a minute, slow down a bit," laughed Mother, "now, come on in the kitchen, help me with supper. Let's talk about this."

Mother returned to her potato peeling at the sink. El got a glass of milk out of the refrigerator.

"You like Edgar, don't you," she asked El.

"Sure, he's fun, most of the time, but today he wasn't funny at all!"

"Why don't you just give it some time, you'll see. You and I know that Lindy isn't a coward, he doesn't have to prove that to us or to anybody."

"He said I thought Charles Lindbergh was God. It's not that, it's just that I don't understand what he's talking about, not wanting us to help fight the Nazis."

"Rachel, you must not lose faith in Lindbergh, there's a lot of very smart people who think like he does, but time will tell. Just believe in him, believe that he will see it differently when we get into it."

"When we get into it?"

"Yes, when—"

"You think we will be in the war?" El interrupted Mother.

"Your father thinks so, El, and I tend to agree with him."

"I can't see why God would let us get into it," said El." He's not a very good God, letting all this killing and fighting go on."

"Rachel! You mustn't say things like that! You just don't understand!" said Mother sharply. "Now, go change your clothes and help me with supper; we will have a serious talk about this, young lady!"

El walked slowly upstairs. She didn't want to talk about God, anyway. She didn't want to talk about Lindbergh, much as she liked him. She wanted to talk about Edgar, about how to make up with him without being a yellow-bellied coward herself, but Mother didn't understand. She didn't want to give in, but she wanted to be best friends again with Edgar, and she didn't even know how to explain that!

Lindbergh didn't make things better for El, with what he did the next day, not better for El, nor better for America.

Colonel Charles Lindbergh held an America First rally in Manhattan and told a crowd of fifteen thousand that "the United States cannot win the war for England."

Even with a heavy police guard, fighting broke out among the throng outside the meeting hall, and men and women were kicked and beaten. Many were carrying signs denouncing Lindbergh, calling him names.

Lindy said, "pro-Nazis, pro-communist, pro-Fascists, or any other group favoring Un-American theories are certainly not for the America First Committee," he said. "War is not inevitable for this country. Over a million people in this nation are opposed to entering this war. If we are forced into war against the wishes of an overwhelming majority of our people, we will have proved democracy such a failure at home that there will be little use in fighting for it abroad."

"We have been led to war by a minority of our people," he continued. "This minority has power. It has influence. It has a loud voice. But it does not represent the American people...that is why the America First committee has been formed, to give voice to the people who have no newspaper, or radio station at their command, to the people who must do the paying and the fighting, and the dying, if this country enters the war."

"Mother, isn't there a slight chance he is right?"

"I don't know, Ellie, I just don't know."

"No, there's no chance at all," said Daddy. "What he is overlooking, is, WE AIN'T GOING TO BE GIVEN A CHOICE!" When Daddy shouted, everybody paid attention. He continued, a little quieter, but still emphatic. "We won't have a damn thing to say about whether we fight or not!"

"Bud, watch your language."

That was the twenty-third. The day it rained. It began as thunderstorms but gradually developed into a hard, cold downpour, a steady, soaking rain that extinguished the forest fires and cleared the air of smoke. And on that day, Dagwood and Blondie had a baby—a baby girl! A contest would be held to select her name, and El submitted a name: Shirley.

Aviation designer Alexander P. DeSeversky replied to Lindbergh's speech by claiming that before long aircraft would actually fly 25,000 miles and that an air attack against America was a reality in the near future.

El missed Edgar. Who else could she talk to about these amazing new ideas? Mother didn't understand, Jane was too busy for her, Daddy was never home, being tied up now with putting in a new line. Nobody was interested. She cut out the articles from the daily paper and saved them, knowing that Edgar didn't get a paper of his own. Maybe someday Edgar would get over being mad at her, or maybe she would figure out how to resume their friendship.

"I contend," wrote DeSeversky, "that those who deny the practical possibility of an eventual air attack on America are lulling the American people into a false sense of safety as dangerous as the 'Maginot line mentality' that cost France its independence."

What was a Maginot mentality? Edgar would know. She wished she could ask him. "Co. Lindbergh, so well aware of what wishful thinking has done to European nations, should be the last one to join the lullaby."

"Listen, Bun," said El, "listen to this!" And she read aloud again, "Such a craft with a 25,000-mile range seems wholly realistic within five years, and no nation will be immune from direct attack from any part of the world!"

"Five years! By the time I get sixteen! Fly to any country in the world! Bun, wouldn't that be marvelous? Five years!" but Bun was asleep, curled in a tight little ball, her red curls moist around her face and neck, her blanket pulled up around her chin. El pulled the blanket down and opened the window; cool, clean, mountain air filled the room.

On Saturday, FDR was calling Lindy a 'dumb appeaser', classifying him as a "Copperhead."

"What's a copperhead?" asked El, and Jane wise-cracked, "a snake, dummy!"

"Mother! Jane called me a dummy!"

Mother ignored the complaint, as usual, and explained. "A Copperhead is a leader of Northerners whose sympathies were with the South."

"In other words, Ellie, a traitor," said Daddy. "That reminds me, we saw a copperhead—a real one—up at Clark's Gap this morning, right at the tunnel. That sucker was over six feet long!"

"Did you kill it?" asked Jane, with a shudder.

"Elmer did, with a hatchet."

"Wasn't that dangerous? Getting' that close to it?" asked Mother.

"You ain't never seen Elmer throw a hatchet! He cut it in half at ten paces! Why, I once seen him shave the whiskers off a bobcat!"

"Oh, now, Bud, really"

"That's right," maintained Daddy, with a nod of his head.

"Did he kill the Bobcat?" asked El.

"Sure did!" said Daddy with a big grin, "Scared it to death!"

"Now, Bud! If that isn't a railroader's tall tale, I never heard one!"

But Daddy was obviously pleased with the laugh he got.

On the twenty-eighth, Lindy resigned his commission in the Army Air Corps, angered by the President's comments:

My Dear Mr. President:

Your remarks at the White House Press Conference on April 25, involving my reserve commission in the U.S. Army Air Corps have of course disturbed me greatly. I had hoped I might exercise my right as an American citizen to place my viewpoint before the people of my country in time of peace without giving up the privilege of serving my country as an air corps officer in the event of war.

But since you, in your capacity as President of the United States and commander-in-chief of the army, have clearly implied that I am no longer of any use to this country as a reserve officer ...I take this action with regret, for my relationship with the air corps is one of the things that has meant the most to me in life. I place it second only to my right as a citizen to speak freely to my fellow countrymen, and to discuss with them the issues of war and peace which confront our nation in this crisis.

I will continue to serve my country to the best of my ability as a private citizen.

Respectfully,
Charles A. Lindbergh

The next day, the War Department accepted Lindbergh's resignation. The President's secretary, Stephen Early, critically took the flier to task for releasing his resignation to the press before it was received at the White House, but there were those who criticized the President for using his "great office" to interfere with the freedom of speech.

Although local interest centered on the coal strike, and the feud between Lindbergh and the President, the Senate fight also remained in the limelight. A newspaper editorial said the senators were treating the West Virginia contest as a joke, but West Virginians didn't think it was funny! It pained their pride, and having only half-representation in the major decisions needing to be made was unconscionable. And the winner when, and if, one is declared, will draw salary for sitting on his dignified duffer and doing nothing.

Mrs. Gillespie stood at the back fence, her thin face gray with worry, her cotton dress too light to keep out the chill in the early morning air. Mother set her coal bucket down and listened to her neighbor.

"I just don't understand it," she said, "I thought college students were exempt from service. That's one reason Will went into the reserves, so he could finish his education, so he wouldn't be drafted."

"Yesterday's news changed that," said Mother. "I'm not sure what the reserves will have to do, but all the college students will be reclassified when this term ends. That's all they said, just reclassified, not called up."

"I'm so worried I can't sleep. My Will can't go in the service! We have such plans for him, he's so smart—he's on the dean's list, you know—and he has a fine future as an engineer..."

"Mildred," Mother interrupted, "you must not borrow trouble. That doesn't help Will, or you. Remember, God said 'I will be with you, I will not fail or forsake you.' In Joshua, I think, or Hebrews—Preacher Copeland would know, wouldn't he?" and Mother laughed, deprecating her biblical knowledge.

"We're going to miss him, aren't we, Faith? What will we do when he's gone?"

"There you go again! Worry, worry, worry. I declare, you are blue today. Why don't you walk with me this morning? We'll pick dandelion greens—do you good to get out!"

"No, no thank you," Mrs. Gillespie said, "I don't feel up to that, not today."

"I'll go with you, Mother," said El, coming around the corner of the house. Mother laughed. "I'm sure you would, El, but wouldn't that be something? Me letting you stay home from school to pick dandelion greens? Can't you just hear what Mr. Collins would say about that?" Mother was still laughing as she went into the house—and, it looked to El as though Mrs. Gillespie was still crying.

About a mile up the creek, there was a wide place between Gooney Otter Creek and the highway, and it was Mother's own, private— private in that no one else ever visited it —greens patch. In this narrow strip of ground something was always blooming. Mother's dandelion patch had been cultivated over the years by picking the largest leaves and leaving the roots to support the stem. The plants grew so thick it only took a few minutes to pick enough to feed her family, ready to go into a pot with a bit of ham or bacon. Daddy ate the greens with white milk gravy poured over them, like syrup over pancakes. The children ate them if they wanted cake for dessert for Mother's rule was simple: no greens, no cake.

The creek bed furnished watercress greens also, later in the season, and if a fancy sandwich was required, for a wedding or a party, the watercress was just the thing.

But the fun was in the picking, scampering along beside Mother in the first warm days of spring, slipping a foot into the cold, cold stream, finding blue violet faces waiting between the rocks, waiting all winter to be the first flower picked for the teacup on the dining room table. Rabbit tracks and quail tracks could be seen plainly in the sand by the stream, and sometimes turkey tracks were clearly imprinted. El and Bun would race to the old walnut tree with the hole in the trunk, hoping to see a squirrel or woodpecker, but no one was home when they stood on the rocks to peep inside. Going for greens was second only to picking blackberries in the summertime.

At supper, this first day of May, Jane brought up the subject of the draft again. "Volunteers will be accepted during the summer, so they can complete a year of training and return to classes in the fall of 1942. Did you know that was what Will was planning?"

"No," said Mother," I didn't know that, and I doubt his Mother did either, from what she said this morning."

"He told Mary Beth he was going to enlist, not wait to be drafted."

"When did he tell her that?"

"At spring break."

"It will kill his mother if that boy has to go."

"The President bought the first war bond," commented Daddy. "A five-hundred-dollar bond for Mrs. Roosevelt, and stamps for all his grandchildren."

"Are we going to buy stamps, Mother?"

"Yes, indeedy, and war bonds too!"

"Listen to this," said Daddy.

We are engaged in an all-out effort to perpetuate democracy in the new world by aiding embattled democracies in the old world. Distance no longer guarantees safety and defenses which were adequate ten years ago yet are today a 'broken reed'. We add another call—a frank and clear appeal for financial support to pay our arming, to pay for the American existence of later generations.

El listened closely. Now, for the first time, she began to feel that perhaps Lindbergh was wrong, and if so, then Edgar was right in his thinking. How would she make up with him? It had been over two weeks since she had spoken to him about anything. Daddy was still reading the President's words:

...with jobs more plentiful and wages higher, slight sacrifices here, the omission of a few luxuries there, will swell the coffers of our federal treasury...possession of those defense bonds and stamps ...A guarantee of our future security.

The first defense bonds and stamps went on sale on May 2, and by eight o'clock, when Mr. Gillespie unlocked the door, there was a line of residents waiting, everyone wanting to be first. El and Bun held their dimes clutched in their hands and were first in line, with Mother standing proudly behind them, prepared to buy the first bond.

But Mr. Gillespie had the upper hand; before he opened the door, he purchased the first bond for himself, and stamps for Judith, Ben and Will. A crowd collected in front of the small postal window in the company store, and when they learned what he had done, a cry of "foul" went up. Mr. Gillespie just shrugged his big shoulders and wiped his hands on his big apron and said, "That's the way the ball bounces!" and El said, but it isn't fair, and Mr. Gillespie replied, "All's fair in love and war! And this is war!"

Edgar stood on the side of the walk, leaning on the flagpole, as El took her new stamp book to school to show those unable to make a purchase.

"Want to see?" she asked Edgar.

"Sure do!" he took his hands out of his pockets and came to her.

"Hey," he said, "I've missed you."

"I've been right here," she said, smiling shyly.

"Ain't nobody to talk to," he said.

"Sorry I got mad. Guess you're right, too, about Lindbergh, I mean."

"Naw, he ain't a coward, not really. Just got the wrong notion about this war business. Pa says it's because he went to Germany and saw all those planes they had and it skeered him. Now, if he'd been born around here, he'd be used to fightin' and squabbling' all the time, wouldn't worry him none!"

To El's dismay, Lindbergh continued to speak against the war to the American people, and many continued to listen:

I have seen France fall, I see England falling, and now I see America being led into the same morass. I knew in 1939 that England and France were not prepared to wage war successfully and I know that America is not prepared to wage a successful war in Europe.

Lindy told of his pre-war visits to Europe and the lack of preparedness he had found in England, France and Russia. He told of the air strength of Germany, and how he had told Prime Minister Baldwin of England about that strength, and how the minister courteously had changed the subject.

Time and time again, I talked to members of the British government about their military aviation in Europe. They were always courteous, but they were seldom impressed.

"Bud, is our government listening to him now? Or is his warning being ignored again?"

"Ignored? No, I don't think he's being ignored," answered Daddy, absent-mindedly.

"Is he right about our military strength?"

"Probably," said Daddy.

"Are we in danger?"

"Probably," Daddy said again. "But I think Roosevelt knows what is going on. He doesn't need Lindbergh to tell him."

Mother kept the worry lines between her eyes and her mouth made a straight, thin line as she concentrated on her sewing and listened. Roosevelt could be right, but she trusted Lindy's opinion, trusted it almost as much as Daddy's.

On the eighth of May, the Japanese commented on the feud between Roosevelt and Lindbergh, predicting that it would lead to a "feud of States", but, Daddy said with conviction, they didn't know their history very well: the American states had been divided, once, had fought against each other, but that would happen never again, never, never again.

On this same day, the railroads were threatened with government action if their efficiency dropped, and the House passed a measure authorizing seizure of foreign vessels in the ports of the United States.

War, Daddy predicted, was only weeks away, before the snow flies again, he said, before we light our furnace for the winter.

T1936—Germany's area equaled that of France. Annexed Austria.

1937—Added Czechoslovakia in March, Poland in September.

1938—Added Denmark, Belgium, Holland, Luxemburg in April, France in June, Hungary, Rumania in November.

1939—Added Bulgaria in March

1941—Added Yugoslavia in March. In May, Greece defeated, Italy a partner, Spain ready to give up.

Mr. Collins put the list on the blackboard, beside the map which was bright red now, and only Great Britain stood shining white and alone. Stalin was reported as courting favor with the Germans, withdrawing his recognition of three German-occupied countries, Yugoslavia, Belgium and Norway. Only a month ago Yugoslavia and Russia had negotiated a friendly agreement; now there was talk that Russia was planning to join the Axis powers. The Japanese air force made a successful raid on Chungking, and James Roosevelt, the President's son, declared that the United States was already in the war as he left for Cairo, Egypt, as an American observer.

Mother, Mr. Gillespie, and Mr. and Mrs. Plover formed a quartet, with Jane at the piano, and on Mother's Day they sang at the Itman church for the Wyoming County Singing Convention. It was a warm day, and the little church was crowded as singing groups came from every town. Bun fell asleep before Mother and her friends sang. El sat in a crowded pew with Bun's head on her lap, lost in her thoughts. Emmett was back; she had seen him just before dark, Saturday night. Hollie had missed Sunday school and church this morning. She worried that Emmett might hurt Hollie again. She thought back to Sunday, weeks ago, when Daddy had gone down to the Whites and Emmett had left. Later, Daddy had finally told Mother, in the girls' presence, what had happened that day. Daddy had banged on the door, and Emmett had come out on the porch. Daddy had said something real soft to Emmett, turned around and left. Hollie said he sat there, turning his cap round and round in his hands, then got up, put his razor and a small picture of Shirley in the bag, added socks and some shorts, took his coat and walked out, not speaking a word. Now he was back again. Seems like three weeks is about as long as he can leave her alone. Were they in bed again in the middle of the afternoon? Was he hitting her again, like before?

The singing lasted late, and it was dark when they reached home. The evening air was just beginning to cool when they were sent to bed, and Bun had to have three stories read to her before she could fall asleep, what with her long nap during the singing. El told The Three Bears, The Three Little Pigs, and all of E-Pam-Namous, as Aunt Maude used to tell it to her. Bun began to cry when she got to the part about wrapping the puppy-dog in cabbage leaves and cooling, cooling it in the spring. "Don't want the doggie in the water, El, don't want the puppy wet!"

"But that's the way the story goes, Bun!"

"Don't want the doggie drowned!"

Finally, she was asleep. El sat at the window, watching the shadows move under the bridge, listening to the frogs hollering in the creek. Someone moved, over on the Mitchell's porch, separating a dark shadow from the lighter ones. She slipped the screen out of her window and sat on the window sill.

Edgar left his porch and came to stand in the road below her.

"Hey, El, whatcha' doin'?"

"Nothing. What are you doing?"

"Why don't you come on down and let's go watch the frogs croak!"

"I'm supposed to be in bed," she said. Both of them were nearly whispering.

"You're skeered!"

"I'm not!"

"Dare ya!"

Edgar couldn't have planned it better. He knew Ellie could never refuse a dare. El listened to the stillness in the house, looked back at the sleeping Bun—why not? She ducked back through the window and found old shorts and a blouse, stripped off the seersucker nightgown and picked up her shoes. She eased out the window, on to the front porch roof, her bare toes digging into the graveled shingles, her feet sure on the rough surface. At the edge of the roof, she laid flat, swung her legs over the edge and found the corner post. She wrapped her legs around it and slid down to the porch railing, dropped lightly to the soft grass in the yard. She heard Edgar whistle softly as he jumped the fence and was beside her. "Wow!"

"Nothing to it," said El, as if she had climbed out her window every day. She put her shoes on and stood up. "I've had that figured out a long time."

"How are you going to get back in?"

"Same way, no problem. Now, what was that about the frogs?"

They slipped between El's house and the Gillespie's, next door, to the concrete wall containing the creek. The water had receded after the flood and the far bank was all mud-covered weeds with a few scattered cattails not yet in bloom. They sat on the wall and waited for the frogs to resume their racket, having grown silent when Edgar and El had first appeared. They talked in soft whispers, inaudible a few feet away. Edgar told her how the cattails could be eaten, the roots like potatoes, the bloom part as tasty as an ear of corn if roasted—never starve where cattails grow, he said, the Indians used to eat them all the time. The frogs decided there was no harm and resumed their serenade; the air was cool and fresh, smelling of pine and the very earliest blooming honeysuckle as it drifted gently downward from the steep mountain slopes. The peace of the night slipped over them and they sat comfortably together, not needing to talk. In the midst of a particularly rowdy chorus by the small, striped frogs, another sound came to them clearly—someone was walking down the cindered road. They ducked quickly behind the wall and were out of sight.

With only their eyes peering over the wall, they saw Mr. Reeves cross the bridge and head up the road toward the highway, wearing his old army coat in spite of the warm night, his gun over one arm, a fairly large package wrapped in brown paper in the other.

"Wonder where he's going," whispered El.

"Let's follow him and see," said Edgar, moving cautiously along the wall toward the bridge over the road.

"What if he sees us!" cried El in alarm.

"What could he do—shoot us?"

"Worse than that—he could tell Mother!"

As Mr. Reeves moved rapidly toward the main road, they left the shelter of the creek wall and followed along the edge of the road, hugging the fences to keep out of sight. They played Sherlock and Watson, falling naturally into the roles as they had developed them weeks ago, and dropping into their fake English accent.

"Follow me, my dear Watson."

"Aye, Sir, ready when you are!"

Mr. Reeves reached the highway and sat his package down, adjusted his gun, and turned to look back down the road. El and Edgar were crouched in the ditch, half-hidden by morning-glory vines that covered the fences, their flowers closed for the night.

A car came up the highway from the direction of Herndon, and two men stepped out as it stopped beside Mr. Reeves. They took the package, talked briefly, and handed Mr. Reeves a smaller package, which he put into the deep pocket of his old army coat. The car turned into the camp road, backed up and returned in the direction from which it had come. Mr. Reeves started back down the road. They were trapped! He would walk within three feet of them and there was no place to hide!

"Run!" commanded Edgar as he jumped out of the shallow ditch and ran towards the creek, El following on his heels.

"Hey!" shouted Mr. Reeves, "Stop! Stop or I'll shoot!"

But the two fleet-footed kids were out of sight behind the concrete wall, heading down the creek bed towards the Phillips' back gate. They jumped out of the creek and into the coal house in one leap. Mr. Reeves came, walking on top of the wall, walking slowly, studying the creek bed, the back yards, the woodlands on the other side of the creek, walking, stalking, listening. He walked past the coal house without pausing. Once he was out of sight, behind Grandma Gillespie's house, Edgar whispered, "You'd better git in the house quick, he'll double back, come up the road. Quick, now, run!" El did as she was told, ran to her front porch, shimmed up the post, over the roof-edge, and in through her window. She dropped to the floor by the window, gasping for breath, too scared to realize how dangerous her climb could have been.

As her breathing slowed, she peeped over the window sill, the curtains concealing her. Edgar was out of sight, but, as he had predicted, Mr. Reeves was coming up the road, stalking slowly, his gun held in both hands, peering into every yard, walking a few steps, listening, like he was hunting deer. He passed out of sight beneath the high black railroad bridge and was lost in the shadows beyond the company store.

El found her nightgown, changed, hid her shorts and blouse in the back of her closet, and slipped into bed. Bun snuggled against her, and, feeling her little sister's warm body, she realized how cold she was. Gradually, as she began to get warm, the excitement faded, she stopped shaking, and went to sleep.

A heat wave swept across the eastern coast, sending record-breaking temperatures into the state; oldsters scanned the skies for maretail and mackerel clouds, and watched the north for lightening, a sure sign of rain. The city of Bluefield proclaimed that the Chamber of Commerce would serve lemonade on the street corners if temperatures went over ninety, for Bluefield was "Nature's Air-Conditioned City," and it don't git that hot here! On Thursday it reached 88 degrees, but down in the valleys, where the air lay trapped and heat devils danced on the black-cindered road and reflected off the steel bridge, where trees stood still and listless and no cool high breezes blew, the temperature at noon, on the schoolhouse thermometer, registered 105 degrees, and it was in the shade.

Mr. Collins took pity on the children who sat lifeless at their desks, not bothering to swat the flies that landed on their tablets and buzzed around the brown paper lunch bags. He dismissed them at twelve noon. By one o'clock they were wading in the creek, down by BillynBob's house, or sitting on the bank beneath the giant hickory and spruce trees, taking turns in the old tire swing.

Billy told Edgar that Mary Beth was sick most every morning, throwing up so bad she couldn't go to school, and he hoped he didn't catch what she had because he needed to stay in school if he was going to go to Herndon next year. He was tall enough now to play basketball, and he was going to be as good as Will and Ben: if they could do it, so could he! And Edgar said, "I'll be right there with you, ole buddy, I'm going to play too, and when I graduate, I'm going straight in the Army Air Force!"

When El repeated what Billy had said at the supper table, Mother said, "Rachel, you may be excused if you can't make proper conversation at the dinner table." El looked bewildered. "What did I say!"

"Can't talk about getting sick. El, not when we're eating," said Bun.

"See, even little sister knows better than that, El," said Jane. "Mary Beth's just putting on, she doesn't want to stay in school. She can quit, you know, she's over sixteen, that's the law."

"You quitting at sixteen, Jane?"

"I'm already sixteen, Bun, will be seventeen soon, but, no, I'm not quitting. I'm going to college!"

Rudolf Hess, second in line to inherit the Nazi command, dropped from a plane into Scotland! Hess was injured in the parachute drop and was being held by the British. The Nazis are falling apart, the war will end, the leaders have run out on Adolph, the British are winning, the Americans will not have to fight!

No, Adolph is so angry at the defection, he has sent all of his secret submarines to attack America, his planes can fly across the ocean, he has stopped the attack on England and is coming after us!

Rumors flew as the high-ranking German official's defiance of Hitler became known. As Lindbergh said in his April speech, "In time of war, truth is always replaced with propaganda."

On the twentieth, the Axis powers held a special conference, and the topic of conversation was how to deal with the convoys of material being sent to Britain by the United States. Was this an act of aggression on the part of America?

In Philadelphia, the Academy of Music refused permission for Colonel Lindbergh to speak in their hall. The President of the Academy corporation, John Fredrick Lewis, said he refused to accommodate Lindbergh because, "the audiences he attracts are communists and Nazis and enemies of our American

189

form of government." He said that the heads of the America First Committee are not objectionable, they were "isolationists and idealists", but the mobs that come to hear Lindbergh are lovers of Germany and haters of Democracy.

On that same night, in spite of British efforts, the Germans gained mastery of the skies. Their transport planes shuttled back and forth, carrying soldiers, who landed by parachute, and their forces held two main points on the island of Crete.

Marsha was gone. El and Bun walked from one end of the camp to the other, calling, "Here Kitty-Kitty, here, Marsha," at each house, knocking at each door, have you seen our cat? By nightfall, it was clear that Marsha was lost. Mother made sure there was food in her bowl. "Sometimes cats stray," she said, drying Bun's tears, "but they usually show up again in a day or two."

"But she'll get lost," wailed Bun. "It's dark outside."

"Cats can see in the dark, Bun," reminded Daddy, and he carried her up to bed.

"Mother, did Daddy take Marsha away?"

"Of course not, El! What makes you think that!"

"I heard him say he was going to break her neck one of these days," replied El.

"He didn't really mean that, Ellie. He was just tired of all the yowling at night." But El remained suspicious. Never before had Marsha missed a meal!

Mother didn't seem too upset; it was Friday night; the weekend was coming. The house was clean and darkly shining with polished furniture, waxed floors and the shades drawn against the over-powering heat. The groceries had been bought a day early, baskets were ready. Tomorrow they were going camping!

Down between Herndon and Bud, Barker's Creek widened out, spreading over a gravel bed left by some ancient flood, making an ideal wading pool in the summer. Below this area were dark pools of calm, cool water interspersed with swift flowing water, the perfect breeding ground for large speckled trout. An old road bed made a level camping place; the new road, built when Route 10 was paved, straightened out a few curves by being built higher on the face of the mountain.

Along the creek bank the mountains rose sharply, with thickly wooded sides which provided ample firewood for campfires, as well as shade from the hot sun. The spring camp-out with the Plovers was an annual event for Mother and Daddy, beginning even before Jane was born.

Thelma Plover was tall and thin; dry, Daddy said, an old-maid school teacher who just happened to get married. James was a good mechanic, owned one of the two filling stations in Herndon, hard-working and quiet, and a damn-good fishing partner because he kept his mouth shut. Jimmy, Jr. made up for his father by talking most of the time and never saying anything. Nancy Sue, born in the "change of life," was the darling of her parents' eyes and could do no wrong, was prettier than anybody, sweeter than honey, happier than a kitten with a new ball of string. Nancy Sue was a great playmate for El. They ran through the woods, splashed in the water, and ran again.

The adults fished, cooked, and fished some more. By evening everyone was ready to sit around the fire and listen to the whip-poor-will's call bounce off the mountains. Bun was asleep in the tent, El and Nancy Sue sat by the fire, listening to the grown-ups talk. Mr. Plover was saying the price of gasoline was going to go sky-high, if the war didn't end soon, and Daddy said, yes and tires, too, when El noticed that Jimmy Jr. and Jane had moved out of the circle of light.

"Where are you going, Jane?" El called, and they turned back to the campfire. "Can't you keep your mouth shut?" hissed Jane.

"We're going to find that whip-poor-will," said Jimmy, Jr.

"In the dark?" asked Mrs. Plover, sarcastically. "Sure, in the dark. Their eyes shine red when you put the light on them."

"Is that true, Daddy?" Jane moved out of the light again. "Guess she's going to pee," said El.

"Probably going down to the creek to kiss," said Nancy Sue.

"Nah, not Jane."

"I saw them once," said Nancy Sue.

Startled, El looked at her friend. "You did? Jane?"

"At my house, in the kitchen. Before Easter."

"Jane and Jimmy Jr.?" As Nancy Sue nodded, El looked at Jimmy Jr. with new interest. She knew he was crazy about Jane, had been for years, but that Jane might find him interesting—that was a new idea. She inspected his mouth, looking for some indication that he might be good at kissing, but he was staring into the fire, ignoring her as usual, treating her just as he did his little sister.

191

There was a shrill scream, an inhuman, chilling sound, coming from the dark creek bank, followed by another scream, unmistakably the voice of Jane.

"Bobcat!" shouted Daddy, jumping to his feet and rushing toward the sound. Mother moved just as quickly—but not toward the creek—to the back of Plover's pickup truck. She grabbed the loaded shotgun from the truck bed, jerked it upright and pulled the trigger, firing two quick shots one right after the other. The sound of the shots echoed against the mountainsides, reverberating like a dozen, bouncing back and forth, gradually fading away.

El and Nancy Sue sat motionless by the fire, frozen by the shrill, unearthly scream of the cat. They could hear Jane sobbing even before Daddy brought her back into the firelight. Mother took her into her arms and Jane cried like a child.

"That was quick thinking, Faith," Daddy said to Mother. "It was a big cat. He was after the fish leavings we left on the bank."

"Jane interrupted his meal," said Mother.

"Did he hurt you?" El asked Jane as she began to calm down.

"He was going to jump me. He was all crouched down, ready to jump when the gun went off."

"You were lucky, Honey," said Mother. "Don't ever walk out in the woods alone at night. Tell me when you have to go, and I'll go with you."

"You should have a light with you, too", said Daddy. El was glad Jane hadn't been hurt, but she sure would have liked to see that bobcat. And she was sorry, too, about not seeing if Jane and Jimmy, Jr. were going to be kissing. She couldn't imagine Jane kissing any boy; she was much too dignified for that! Nancy Sue must be mistaken.

Bedtime was called for the girls; they rolled into their blankets, lay at the opening to their tent, and watched the sky. The stars looked so high, nearly invisible above the black mountains. The frogs sang in high-pitched voices above the murmur of adult conversation. Once in a while a stick of firewood popped, sending sparks into the air before it fell deeper into the glowing coals. The willows along the stream swayed faintly as the night breeze began to stir, bringing the cooler air down from the mountains. They would have an early breakfast of sweet, fresh-caught brook trout rolled in cornmeal and fried in lard, with thick slices of Irish potatoes and yellow onions, fried in the same black iron skillet over the low campfire. An early morning swim would be their bath, and all day they would play in the musk-smelling woods. No Sunday

School, no Church, no radio or war news, and best of all, no railroad. Run, play, freedom to holler, sing, eat and sleep. A perfect weekend.

On the way home, Daddy stopped in Herndon for his paper. The headlines were printed in inch-high black letters:

H.M.S. HOOD IS BLOWN UP IN NAVAL CLASH OFF ICELAND
German Battleship Bismarck Sinks Pride of the British Navy;
Shot touches Off Powder Magazine in Biggest Battleship in World.
1300 Believed Perished. FDR Fireside Chat Scheduled for
Tuesday Night.

El had first shot at the paper as Daddy helped Mother unload the camping supplies. Jane went to her room immediately, pleading homework.

"Listen to this, Mother," she said, "It's about the Virginian Railroad."

"Wait until your father comes in, Ellie, and you can read it to both of us."

"Read what?" asked Daddy, setting the wooden box of groceries on the table. El read the article tucked in the inner pages.

"Five deeds were recorded transferring land to the Virginian railroad company in compliance of a court order in the office of the County Clerk. The railroad bought an acre of land from Hap Hatfield and Martha Hatfield for $2,800, an amount set by a jury in the April term…"

Daddy whistled in astonishment. "Two thousand, eight hundred for one acre?"

"Also transferred to the railroad were four acres by William and Marcie Hatfield; all of these tracts are located near Guyan and will be used for construction of a new railroad to a region now being developed for mining." El stopped reading. "Are these Hatfields kin to the famous one in the feud?" she asked.

"Probably, honey, they're all related back in those hills. That's not the most important thing about that news, not to me, anyway," said Daddy.

"What do you mean?"

"Well, looks like I'll be working overtime this summer, doesn't it? Be stringin' new wire, up by Cub Creek. Guess it's time, with the way coal demand is increasing these days."

"El, take Bun up to the tub now," said Mother, "and you two be in bed in ten minutes."

"Ten minutes! I can't wash her and myself in ten minutes!"

"Ten minutes," Mother repeated, "by the clock!"

"Wish I was already in college!" said El crossly, throwing the newspaper on the table.

"Don't wish your life away," said Daddy.

"If I was in college, I'd be out of school this week! Will's coming home this Wednesday, did you know?"

"If I were in college," Mother corrected. "Ten minutes!"

At the top of the stairs, Jane took Bun's hand. "Come on, Ellie, I'll help you with Bun." Surprised, El followed Jane into the big bathroom.

"How did you know Will would be home Wednesday?"

"Judith told me, Friday."

"And you went all weekend without mentioning it?"

El shrugged her shoulders, "Didn't think about it."

"Honestly, El! You are the limit!" She scrubbed Bun's face until she yelled, "Let Ellie do it, Jane! You're hurting me!"

"You want Ellie to wash you because she doesn't try to get you clean! Just look at you, Bun, honestly!"

"She's supposed to be dirty. We've been camping," said El

Jane left the bathroom in a huff and El, watching the Big Ben on the wall, dried Bun without further scrubbing. She had less than three minutes for her own bath before Mother came up the stairs. Mother never gave a time limit without following up on it, and, lately, Mother had spells when she was cross with them, so short-tempered.

Eleven

Marsha was back! She strolled around the corner of the house like she'd never been away, right on schedule for supper.

"Look how thin she is!" cried El.

"She looks terrible!" said Jane, taking her from El and cuddling her as she carried her into the house. "Mother! Marsha's back!"

"Well, hello, Marsha," said Mother. "Where have you been—uh, oh!"

"What's wrong? Is something the matter with her?" The girls gathered around the cat, held in Mother's arms.

"Nothing's wrong," said Mother, turning the cat on her back. "Marsha's a mother, that's all. See? She's nursing kittens!"

"Good God! That's all we need, a half a dozen more cats to sit on the back fence and howl!"

"Now, Bud!" said Mother. "Wonder where they are?" said El.

"She'll keep them hidden until they open their eyes," explained Mother. "Get some cream from the refrigerator. We've got to feed her better now, after all, she's eating for four or five."

Tuesday, May 27th, speaking from Washington, the President proclaimed an unlimited national emergency:

Whereas on September 8, 1939, because of the outbreak of war in Europe a proclamation was issued declaring a limited national emergency and directing measures "for the purpose of strengthening our national defense within the limits of peacetime authorizations".

Whereas a suggestion of events makes plain that the objective of the axis...include overthrow throughout the world of existing democratic order...

Whereas indifference on the part of the United States to the increasing menace would be perilous...

Now, therefore, I Franklin D. Roosevelt, President of the United States of America, do proclaim that an unlimited national emergency confronts this country, which requires that its naval, air and civilian defenses be put on the basis of readiness...I call upon our loyal workmen as well as employers to merge their lesser differences...

I call upon loyal state and local leaders...I call upon loyal citizens to place the nations need first in mind and in action...

Will Gillespie arrived home at four o'clock on Wednesday, went in the house and put his college clothes away, placed his books on their shelf: Will had enlisted in the Navy.

He sat beside his grieving Mother, joked with his sister and brother, talked seriously with his father, and went to bed early.

Jane and Mary Beth walked up and down the road in front of the Gillespie house until after dark, gave up and went home. El and Bun went to bed at nine, as usual.

Shortly after nine o'clock, El heard a knock on the Gillespie's front door. She crawled down to the foot of her bed, across Bun, and looked out the side window. The roof of the Gillespie's porch cut off her view and all she could see was legs—Mary Beth's thick piano legs in their white anklets and brown and white saddle oxfords—but she could hear, the voices carrying upward on a fresh spring breeze, a breeze heavy with the sticky-sweet fragrance of honeysuckle in full bloom.

"Is Will home?"

"Well, hello, Mary Beth. Yes, Will got in, but he's gone to bed."

"Mr. Gillespie, I've got to talk to him. Could you call him?"

"Can't it wait 'til morning? He's dead tired—"

"No, no! It can't wait! I've got to see him—please, Mr. Gillespie, will you ask him?"

"Well, I'll see if he wants to get up, just stay right here, Mildred's not well, she's lying down, well, I'll see, just a minute now."

Will came out on the porch. El could see big bone-white feet sticking out from faded pale yellow pajamas. Will leaned against the wall and one pale foot went against the house. "How you doin', Mary Beth?"

"Not too good, Will, not too good."

"What'cha want to see me about? I was dead asleep, have to get up early in the morning. I have to be in Mullins at seven o'clock."

"Will—don't know how to say this—Will, I'm going to have a baby."

Will didn't answer. El nearly pushed the screen out of the window, trying to hear every word. A baby! Mary Beth was pregnant! No wonder she was sick every morning!

"Well, well, Mary Beth, well, well."

"Is that all you can say?"

"What'cha want me to say?"

"Will, it's your baby!"

"Oh, no, you don't! You can't pin that on me, Mary Beth, no way!"

"Will, it is! There ain't no question about that!"

"Oh, yeah? You think I didn't know you been giving it to my little brother, think I didn't know that? Ha! I knew, way back before spring break, I knew! Think I thought I was the first one? Ha! You gotta be crazy!"

"Will! Honest! Ben and I never—I mean we didn't—Will, there ain't been nobody but you!"

"Oh, yeah, I get it! You'er just a po' little innocent country gal and I reckon you think I'll marry you—well, you listen here! I ain't planning on marrying anybody, not yet, and when I do, it won't be a dumb girl like you, don't know enough to keep from getting' knocked up!"

"Will! You said you loved me—"

"For God's sakes, Mary Beth! A guy will say anything to get what he wants! You know that, many brothers as you've got, ain't you ever heard them talk? I thought you knew enough to keep from—good God, Mary Beth!"

"Will, I believed you, and I love you—"

"Ah, come on now, you ain't that dumb, you didn't believe all that shit"

"Will, nobody knows yet, you've got to—"

"Look, Kid, I'm sorry, sorry as hell, but I don't see where I have anything to do with this. I just joined the navy and I leave in the morning, no telling when I'll be back, hell, may not even come back! You'll just have to work this out yourself!"

El sat back from the window as Mary Beth came down the steps; had she looked up, she could have seen El, but her head was down, her feet dragging. As Mary Beth walked down the road, El moved to the front window and watched until she went out of sight beyond Mr. Collins' house.

Poor Mary Beth. What should she do? Should she tell Mother what she'd heard? And have Mother tell her she shouldn't be listening to other folks' conversations, it wasn't polite? She'd get bawled out for eavesdropping, but could she help it if people talked practically under her window?

The air moved through the open window, sweet-smelling, the honeysuckle romantic, and she dreamed about her own wedding, Edgar beside her, Preacher Copeland ready to read the service, standing barefoot at the front of the church his feet strangely like the ones she had seen tonight, her dress as thin as the lace curtains at the window, her flowers, honeysuckle, trailing down from a bouquet, and Jane singing the wedding song, the words very clear:

Oh, the honeysuckle bloom is on the vine,
The bloom is on the vine
And it's sweeter than the wine,
Honey girl, will you be mine.

By morning El wasn't sure what she had heard and what she had dreamed; she decided she wouldn't tell Mother, but she would keep her eyes and ears open—and her mouth shut.

Will left for naval training with three of his college buddies, left early in the dew of the morning, when the honeysuckle smelled the sweetest and the mountain air was the clearest, and while his quiet Mother could stand erect to tell him good-bye. The first of the local boys to go, but then, Will Gillespie is always first. In everything.

Memorial Day dawned bright and hot, but by afternoon there were light, scattered showers to relieve the heat and settle the black dust. The holiday meant no school, and most of the kids gathered on the Phillips' front porch to choose sides for their softball game in the Triangle. It was learned, on the evening news, that twenty-four hundred German sailors were killed when the British sunk the Bismarck, and, they all agreed, that balanced out the loss of the H.M.S. Hood's thirteen hundred sailors. In England, the British ministry opened three cases of machine tools from the United States, and found, in addition to the tools, twenty-four tins of evaporated milk, and a note saying it was for the children, sent without the purchaser's knowledge, by the men who made the tools.

The State Selective Service office estimated that 15,000 young men would be included in the mandatory July first draft registration, those who had reached twenty-one since last October 16, when the first draft registration was held.

May production in the mines hit an all-time high: miners were working hard and long, but the final contract had yet to be signed. On Saturday night, Mother went to Mullins to Eastern Star meeting, and Daddy took the girls to see *Blood and Sand*, with Rita Hayworth, Linda Darnell, and the dark, handsome Tyrone Power, who looked just like Will, only older.

Sunday, June the first, was Preacher Copeland's last day; he would preach his last sermon, lead his last hymn, and, Daddy said, with his wicked grin, take up his last collection! But, no, Daddy wouldn't go with them to watch all of this, it wasn't Easter, it wasn't Christmas. It was a cool summer morning, a beautiful green morning, and the catbirds and robins had started singing at four a.m. When Faith and the girls left for Church, he was going back to bed!

Jane wore a deep red hairband and Bun wore a big blue bow since it was too warm for hats; why couldn't Ellie have something that looked nice also? Mother struggled with a wide white ribbon and scolded as she tried to tie the slippery satin. "Rachel, be still! You're going to make us late!"

Daddy looked up from his paper. "Oh, for gosh sakes! She looks all right! Leave the damn thing off!"

"Bud!"

Daddy pulled his flat, gold railroad watch out, balanced it, studied it briefly, then replaced it in its own little pocket. "You'd better be going; you'll be late for sure."

It was time for the service to start when they reached the crowded church; Sunday School had been omitted, preaching was scheduled for ten o'clock, with dinner 'on the ground' to follow, in honor of Preacher Copeland's retirement. Although the church was full, their regular places were waiting for them, on the front row, beside the Plovers.

Preacher Copeland was dressed in a new white summer suit for the occasion, a gift from his faithful congregation, and the brilliant white made his skin look pinker, his hair whiter than usual, like an angel, fresh-scrubbed and ready to ascend to the right hand of God after a lifetime of duty. The new, student minister, the elderly minister's replacement, sat on the left of the pulpit, awaiting introduction.

This was Preacher Copeland's day. Yet all eyes were on the young man—and he knew it. Theodore Roosevelt McKinney was the son of Jefferson McKinney, the grandson of Lincoln McKinney, the great-grandson of Benjamin Franklin McKinney, and great-great-grandson of Thomas McKinney, a redheaded, freckle-faced, tall, thin Scot who emigrated from Edinburgh, on the banks of the Almond River. Edinburg was the cultural center of Scotland, but also had a long history of wars, stretching back through the centuries. Thomas, upon arrival in America, naturally began looking for a homesite; a few short months later he settled on the banks of the Ohio river and Mary McKinney gave birth to Benjamin McKinney. Benjamin, red-headed, freckled-faced, was possessed with a patriotic love of his native land which he ably demonstrated by fighting, and dying, in the war between the states, on the Union side. The son he left behind was named Lincoln, after his father's commander-in-chief and hero. Lincoln grew as tall and strong as that first Lincoln, a stalwart mountaineer who followed tradition and fought in the Spanish-American war as a member of the second W.Va. Volunteer Infantry. His son, Jefferson, named after the writer of the greatest of all freedom articles, joined the same unit, distinguished himself on the bloody fields of Belgium in the first World War, came home and sired the fifth generation of red-haired, freckled-faced McKinney's. A soldier himself, Jefferson named his son after a man who successfully combined the dual roles of soldier and statesman, Theodore-rough-rider-Roosevelt.

Now, Theodore Roosevelt McKinney, the cause of his father's heartbreak, the last of a long line of fighting men, the disappointingly meek and mild pacifist-minister-to-be, stood before his first congregation at the Herndon Methodist church, and all he could see was the lovely, petite, black-haired girl who walked down the isle of the crowded church, went straight to the piano, and played the prelude like she was in an Edinburg concert hall.

The choir began the call to worship. "Jesus, stand among us, in Thy risen power; Let this time of worship, be a hallowed hour…" and Theodore Roosevelt McKinney forgot to stand until the third line.

Preacher Copeland led the first hymn and the Apostles' creed, as agreed upon, then turned to the student minister.

"We are delighted to have with us, this morning, Theodore McKinney, ministerial student form West Virginia Wesleyan College. He will lead us in our morning prayer."

Theodore—Ted—McKinney stood up, gripped the podium with both hands, bowed his head and said softly, "Let us pray." Lesson number one, public speaking 101: get the attention of your audience before you begin speaking. He paused dramatically before starting his prayer. There was some rustling of song books, some clearing of throats, but gradually the crowded church settled to silence, anticipating the first words of their new boy-minister. As the quiet, hot stillness settled down, a small boy near the front of the church let out an audible poot. Bun giggled, El snickered, as did most of the children and suppressed sounds undulated through the congregation from the front row to the back. Jane, at the piano, turned red; Mother grabbed Bun by the arm, El clamped her hand over her mouth. Theodore Roosevelt McKinney began his first public prayer in confusion and awkwardness: Public Speaking 101 hadn't covered this eventuality.

Later, as Ted and the Preacher sat together at the picnic table for dinner, Ted was still blushing furiously, too embarrassed to talk, and Preacher Copeland could be heard giving him advice: "Never let there be absolute silence, Teddy, my boy, keep 'em moving, singin' or praying. If you don't, they'll do you in every time! Somebody will mess you up, sure as God made little green apples!"

When the girls reached home, El tried to tell Daddy what had happened, but Mother made her hush by sending her to her room to change her new white dress—it had to be saved for graduation next week. El knew Mother couldn't bear to have Daddy think her church, or her preacher, was anything less than perfect.

Mother's group of women were now officially members of the Bundles for Britain sewing club, and the Red Cross had assigned Wyoming County its quota of garments to complete before next winter. Much was required. Twelve sweaters for men, twenty-four for women, and forty-eight for children, material for fifty layettes, forty-eight cotton dresses, forty shirts, and hospital shirts, all by late June. The women agreed, they needed to get started now. Mother volunteered to pick up yarn while in Mullins; they would each begin a sweater at their next meeting.

When Hollie learned Mother was going to Mullins in the middle of the week, she asked if she might go along; she had a chore to do. Mother was delighted to have her. She had seen very little of Hollie during the last few weeks, since Emmett had come back.

The elementary school would be out on Thursday; the children would go back on Friday to pick up their report cards, and school would be out for the summer. The stores all closed at noon on Wednesday, but on Thursday El could watch Bun while she and Hollie shopped.

Mother made out her shopping list, glad bulbs, roses, yarn, twenty yards of gauze, fifteen yards of flannel, material for shorts if on sale, groceries if they had time. Hollie made her list: a headstone for Shirley's grave.

Emmett had gone back to work in the mines, and he had forbidden Hollie to work. She stayed home all day, slept, listened to the radio soap operas and the hill billy music, and moped. Faith tried to get her out, to go walking with her before the sun grew hot, or to pick dandelion greens, but Hollie refused, saying she didn't feel well, or was too busy. Occasionally she would walk up to the garden with Faith but she did that half-heartedly, not like the old Hollie, and Faith would get irritated with her, send her home to take an afternoon nap, something that Faith was doing herself, daily, now that it was so hot.

The family was subjected to a constant stream of worrying about Hollie from Mother, to the point that Daddy said, enough! And after that, Mother tried to keep her worry to herself.

When Mother told Daddy Hollie was going to Mullins with her, to buy a headstone for Shirley's grave, Daddy said, why isn't Emmett taking her? It's his place, not yours, and when Mother brought up Emmett's name to Hollie, Hollie just shrugged her shoulders. Gradually, Faith stopped talking about Emmett at all.

Thursday morning was a perfect June day. Sometimes, in the dead of winter, it is impossible to remember or comprehend the grand and glorious greenness of spring, the new-green on the dark branches of sky-high trees, the lime-green tips on the dark evergreens, the pastel green grass emerging from dried brown brush and weeds, the deeper olive green rhododendron and laurel, the verdant moss and fern spreading over the hills and into the valleys, covering the rotting logs and decaying leaves, covering the scars of winter, but on this June day, the greenness was overwhelming.

Hollie was ready early and came into the kitchen while El and Bun were still eating breakfast; Jane had caught the bus as usual, with one more day of high school before summer break. Hollie sat down at the table with the girls while Mother finished the dishes.

"I'm nearly dead this morning, Faith. I don't know how much more I can take."

"You look tired, honey. We'll not go today, if you don't want to."

"No, no. I want to go. I've been worrying about a marker for my baby's grave, need to get up there before it gets lost in the weeds. Be awful if I couldn't find it, and you know how fast the weeds grow, nobody to tend it, it could be lost before summer is over."

"We'll find a nice one, take it up there soon as it's ready."

"Emmett wants me to, he said so, last night." Hollie started crying, a soft, tired sob breaking her voice. "I declare, Faith I don't know what I'm going to do, he just keeps on and on, and he gits hold of my knees and his thumbs push so hard, I'm black and blue, and he gits to hittin' and hittin' and bangin' and bangin' and I get so dry it hurts awful, but he keeps on and on and—"

Mother interrupted several times, "Hush, now honey, hush, you hush that, you mustn't talk like that—" Mother turned to El. "You take Bun to the car, Ellie, we'll be on in a minute."

Hollie, not noticing that Faith was trying to hush her, continued, more to herself than to Faith, "he's a brute, don't care if he hurts me, all he says is by God you'll have another baby if'n it kills you, and I think he would kill me, if I tried to stop him—"

"Rachel! Now! You two wait in the car!"

"I ain't done nothing to keep from having another baby, don't know why I'm not pregnant now, though Lord knows I don't want one, wouldn't be the same, not like having Shirley back and that's what he thinks, that havin' another one would be like having Shirley back—"

"I'm not through, Mama," cried Bun, watching Hollie fearfully. "Want another biscuit!"

"Hollie, please wait until the girls are in the car! Here, honey, take your biscuit outside—go sit on the steps with Marsha—we'll be along."

"I just want to die! When he's drunk like that, he ain't the same man, Faith, not the man I married at all. He's gone plum off his head, ain't even decent to me."

El took Bun by the hand and led her out the back door. As they left, she looked back and Mother was putting her arms around Hollie like she was a baby, and there were tears running down her face even though her eyes were closed, and her mouth was moving like it did in church when she was praying.

El held Bun's hand until they were seated on the wooden back steps; be better for Bun to eat her biscuit with honey there, wouldn't have to worry about the car getting messed up. Besides, she could still hear what Hollie was saying.

There was a fresh spring breeze moving the willow branches and the air smelled wet and sweet; the mountains were hazy blue along the ridge, misty, as the morning sun pulled the night-dew from the trees. The rhododendron would have pearls of dew on their shiny leaves, and under the trees the grass would still be wet. El's feet yearned to be out of her shoes and walking on the cool spot under the willow. Her heart ached for Hollie, and she thought it wouldn't hurt so bad—she wouldn't want to cry—if she could climb up high in the willow, sit where the breeze blew away the mist, and dried the tears on her own cheeks. A door slammed in the distance. A fat robin sat on the fence and watched for life among the grass blades. Bun was busy, eating her biscuit, and in the house, she could hear Hollie, sobbing her heart out in Faith's arms. Nothing was the same since Shirley died.

On Friday, they picked up their report cards. El had completed the year with straight "O's" for outstanding. On the front of the folded BlueCard was written, "Promoted to the sixth grade." Signed, Thomas Jefferson Collins, Teacher and Principal.

Now that the first U.S. food ship had reached Great Britain, Hitler and Mussolini were discussing the intervention of the United States, and had agreed upon a plan—but nobody knew exactly what the plan was! Within hours it was learned that Germany's ex-Kaiser, Wilhelm II, had died while in exile at Doorn.

FDR had introduced a seizure bill, aimed at ending the strikes, but that power would be used in other situations involving work stoppage of defense preparations. The railroad workers were demanding an increase of wages by thirty to thirty-four cents an hour; the demands involved one million, one hundred and fifty thousand workers, fourteen railway labor organizations, five unions embracing operating personnel, engineers, conductors, firemen, switchmen, and trainmen. The demands of the unions would be presented to the operators—the carriers—on June 10th. They were seeking to provide a minimum wage of seventy cents an hour, and up to a dollar-fifteen for highly skilled workers. The current minimum rate was thirty-six cents, while the skilled mechanics, with training and experience, could earn up to eighty-five cents an hour.

Very, very early Saturday morning, before the break of day, Daddy hitched the trailer behind the gray Ford and they loaded up for the long drive to Virginia: they were going to bring Old Bess home. The old brindle cow would provide fresh milk until late fall, when she dried up. Then she would be taken back to the farm and Aunt Maude. Old Bess was the only cow in the camp, and as such, had many special privileges; she was treated to scraps from many tables, loved to be scratched on the head where her horns had been amputated years ago. El thought the early hour accounted for the sharp chill in the air, but Mother said no, the temperature had dropped into the thirties during the night. The white coat on the hills was frost, even though it looked like snow.

"Blackberry winter," said Daddy, "if we were staying home, I'd have to build a little gnat smoke in the furnace."

El was glad they were going to Virginia, even if only for the weekend. Edgar and Joe were leaving for their grandmother's house in Logan, catching the ten o'clock Greyhound bus this morning. They would be gone two weeks. Two, long, long weeks.

Mother had bought bologna for sixteen cents a pound at the company store, and Mr. Gillespie had sliced it, cutting it thick, like ham. She made sandwiches with the new Vitamin B Enriched white bread, to eat on Brushy Mountain, where the cold mountain water ran out of the old iron pipe in the rock.

They reached grandmothers in time for the six o'clock news, as Daddy had planned. The Federal Mediation Board had urged elimination of the forty-cent differential between northern and southern operators, recommended seven dollars a day for all miners, *plus a ten-day paid vacation!*

The Board requested that the Union and the operators accept their proposal by six p.m. on Monday, June ninth. The government had taken over an airplane factory to end the strike there, and in Europe, it was reported that German troops were massing on Russia's borders.

The family retired early; it had been a long day.

Sunday morning El woke slowly, trying to identify the strange sounds coming through the open window. Instead of Robins singing, she heard a rooster crowing; instead of the train rattling across the bridge, she heard guinea hens cackling. She raised on her elbow, carefully moved Bun's legs off of hers, and eased out of bed. Jane was turned facing the wall and appeared to be sleeping soundly, half-buried in the deep feather bed.

El searched for clean clothes, but the suitcase was not in the room. She put on the shorts and blouse she had worn yesterday, but went without panties; Mother would be angry if she wore the same panties two days in a row, wearing the same panties meant triffliness, and besides, you could get terrible diseases, Mother said, which didn't make any sense at all to El, unless, of course, you wore somebody's panties besides your own. When she had said as much to Mother, all she got in return was," don't get smart with me, young lady, just remember what I tell you!"

It was cool with the early freshness of pine filling the air, but it was not as cold as it had been at home, higher in the mountains. She saw Zane Gray, her cousin, leave his house, just a stone's throw away, watched as he picked up a shovel and disappeared around the corner.

Curious, and lonesome, she followed.

Zane Gray was Aunt Maude's only boy and their house was built a foot or two off the ground, propped up on cinder blocks, not at all like the old, rambling white house of Grandmother's. She found Zane Gray underneath the house where he had dug out a deep hole for a cellar. He had removed the red clay from an area nearly half the size of the house itself. She crawled through the entrance beside the back door and sat down on an upturned cinder block to watch. Zane Gray gave her a cheery smile and continued his rhythmic shoveling of earth.

Zane gray was so romantic, just like the hero's in the Rex Beach books she had discovered in grandmother's library. Even his name was exciting, named after the writer of all those wonderful wild west books, Aunt Maude's favorites, and the only books Daddy ever read. With his shirt off and barefooted, dressed only in the overalls he wore yesterday, overalls stiff with red clay dust and sweat, he looked like someone in a movie. His hair was dark but with the red dust it looked auburn, and he had a faint stubble of dark beard along his chin: Zane Gray was seventeen by several months, a grown man.

After a while he laid the shovel down to rest and squatted beside her on his heels. El was afraid to move, receiving a special thrill from being so intimately close to a boy who was so nearly a man, knowing she could leave, could run like the dickens, knowing she wouldn't, couldn't, because Zane gray was talking about kissing, had she ever been kissed, did she kiss her boyfriend and there is nothing in the world as important as knowing how to kiss when you are eleven going on twelve years old and had never been kissed. Why Nancy

Sue had been kissed already and she was just ten, and Jane had been kissed, even if it was only by Jimmy Plover Jr. Mother said nice girls didn't kiss boys, but now Zane Gray was touching her mouth with his fingertips, and the dry, red dust on his hands tasted like the rocks she used to eat out of the clay bank behind the house in Herndon, where they lived before moving to Coville, and his hands were tender, careful. His eyes smiled and his mouth laughed or was it his eyes laughed and his mouth smiled? Either way, he was too close, she couldn't breathe without inhaling the very air he was exhaling, and when she did the air was filled with the smell of him, his sweat, the red Virginia clay, the cigarettes— he bought Cavalier's in a tin can, a whole hundred at a time and smoked like a man—Zane Gray was more man than boy, more man than she had ever been close to, except for Daddy.

Her shorts were too tight, last year's shorts—Mother had not yet sewed for this summer—and the shirt was too large, it being a hand-me-down from Jane, and it was early on a June morning when the buds were bursting to bloom and the redbirds were mating in the green dogwood trees, and Zane Gray kissed her on the mouth, his mouth dry with the red clay dust at first, but he licked his lips, then hers, and it was better. She kept her mouth closed and her lips hard and tight, not at all like the ones in the movies, and a chilly feeling moved over her bare legs, starting somewhere in her crotch and ending with a shiver up her back; she sat on her hands, gripping the rough cinder block, afraid to move, her body deliciously engaged in strange, exciting feelings, her mind objectively thinking, so this is kissing.

His hands began to move over her legs, rubbing against the stubble. Once, weeks ago, she had swiped Jane's razor and shaved her legs, after a boy at school had whispered, when are you going to start shaving your legs? Now she wished she had kept it up, wished her legs were smooth and round, like Rita Hayworth's had been in *Blood and Sand.*

Zane Gray was already tan to the waist from working out in the sun. He owned his pickup truck and earned gas money working in the hayfields. He went out every night, never saying where, and he rarely talked to anyone. He rarely talked at all, and now his mouth was busy, teaching her how to kiss, "the way it should be done, slow and easy," so she could teach her boyfriend when she got back home. His hand, rubbing her legs, moved higher and higher, touching the hem of her shorts, brushing her inner thigh almost accidently, then slower, more deliberately.

"My hands are cold," he said, as he slipped one between her legs. She couldn't think of anything to say. What if she sounded dumb? In the books, it seemed the girl was always murmuring, now she knew why. It sounded better to murmur than to say uh-huh or something stupid. Zane Gray slid his hand beneath her shorts and touched the soft pubic-fuzz of hair. Startled, he drew back.

"You don't wear panties?"

She jumped to her feet, her skin hot, her face burning with embarrassment. "What's it to you!" she shouted and ran out of the cellar. She could hear him howling with laughter behind her, pictured him rolling on the packed red earth of the cellar floor. She was so ashamed! Not that he had touched her—that had been a new thrill—ashamed because he had found out she didn't have on panties! She could never face him again. She ran for the old pine forest that stretched behind the house, a thick, primeval woodland that had stood for a hundred years, where flat rocks made perfect playhouses, and pale, creamy mushrooms grew, perfect for dishes for elves and fairies who came out of hiding to play with her. Pressed on a flat rock beside a flowing stream of clear, innocent water, she slowed her breathing by counting—one Mississippi, two—Mississippi, three—Mississippi, breathe. Never again, she vowed, would she get caught without her panties. She thought about what had happened, conscious of a strange, warm wetness between her legs; she decided she liked the slow, wet-soft kissing very well, but book writers had never made enough out of rubbing legs.

Old Bess bawled for her calf all the way home. Once there, Daddy tied her to the back fence and filled a zinc washtub with water for her. The old cow's sac was as big as a bushel basket, and El held the flashlight while Mother milked her. She bawled most of the night, long, mournful bellows, and Bun cried with her. "Poor old Bess, let's go back to Ginnia and get her baby, Mama. Why can't she keep her baby?"

The night had been interrupted frequently and the girls didn't awaken until ten o'clock, enjoying their first day out of school, but Mother milked the cow again after Daddy left for work, and by seven she was in her garden that surrounded the house old Mr. Reeves used for storage. She had hoed out the rows and picked the accumulated crop, cherry-red radishes, tender green onions with clear-white bulbs, mustard greens, dark green Bibb lettuce, and a few small, white potatoes carefully scratched from under the plants to go with crisp English peas in little green pods. Mother always carried a knife with her to the garden and cleaned the vegetables there, returning the tops and roots to the soil to enrich it. She gathered up the corners of her apron and made a pouch to carry her treasure back down the road and home.

"Looks like that garden just waited until I turned my back to start growing!" she called to Mrs. Belcher.

"We had rain while you were gone!" Mrs. Belcher responded. "See you got your cow!"

"Hope she didn't disturb you folks last night!"

"Oh, we heard her, all right! But don't worry, it won't last long!"

Mother placed her produce in the sink and turned to hug each of her girls. "I'm so glad to have you home! We're going to have a great summer."

"You're probably the only mother in Wyoming County who's saying that this morning," said Jane. "Everyone else is groaning 'cause their kids are home."

"Now, Jane," Mother said, laughing, "you know that's not so!"

The morning news on station WHIS reported that the Army was going to operate the airplane factory because the strike had not been settled, but the UMW and the coal operators had a new contract! The miner's expressed pleasure on the terms, and the nation as a whole expressed relief that there would not be a work stoppage.

At West Virginia University, seven hundred and seventy-five graduates heard Governor Neely speak, and most of them remembered little of what he said, except, "He who lives by the sword, dies by the sword!"

Jane learned that Benny Goodman was coming to Bluefield, to the National Guard Armory, for a concert and dance, and she would die, just die! If she didn't get to go, to which Mother replied, "You probably won't get to Bluefield, but if you'll help me shell these peas, I might take you to Mullins with me tomorrow."

They took the fresh peas out on the front porch to shell and carefully split the pods, leaving miniature green Indian canoes, just right for fairies and elves. El brought out an enameled wash pan full of water, and Bun floated the pea shells upright on her fairy pond. Before long she was putting roly-polies in the pods to ride. When she put one in the pod, it got along fine, but when she put two in there was trouble every time, the boat turned over and both were drowned.

Mary Beth came to join them, filling her big lap with peas, her big-boned hands moving quickly among them. El studied the girl who sat in the swing beside Jane, her hair rolled up in rags, her face fresh-scrubbed and open. She looked at her abdomen closely, but could see no signs that she was expecting. El wished she knew how long it took to make a baby, how long it took to show. For that matter, she wished she knew how a baby was made!

Mother left the girls to finish the peas, went to the back yard and pulled the lawn mower out from under the back porch. With the rain, the grass was a foot high along the back fence, and Mother began to mow it for a very practical reason: she took the grass clippings and, gathering them into her apron, she fed them to old Bess who was tied to the back fence. El and Bun came to help her.

"When will you turn her loose to graze?" asked El.

"When she stops missing her calf, honey, when she won't wander off searching for it."

"She'll stop missing it?" Asked Bun, thoughtfully, reaching grass through the fence to Bess's wet, slick nose and rough tongue.

"She'll stop missing it in a few days."

"Would you stop missing me, if I went away?"

"No, of course not! But you're not going anywhere!" cried Mother.

Bun, quietly, thoughtfully, said, "Shirley did."

"Want me to mow the yard?" said El quickly, unable to bear the pain on Mother's face. "I can do it, Mother! I'm big enough now!" But Mother had her arms around Bun and was squeezing her hard, her face pressed into Bun's tight curls like she'd never let her go.

El ran into the house, afraid she would cry too, she hadn't cried over Shirley yet, and she wasn't going to now, not when this was the first day of vacation and the sun was shining, the birds were singing, and she could go barefoot in the grass. Not when she could throw herself on the deep sofa in the cool, dark living room and lie there in the half-dark and not think about Shirley. Not remember the golden curls and the white face and the wet yellow dress and not think about the deep hole and the pile of brown-clay dirt, not think, not think. Not think about anything at all except Jane's and Mary Beth's voices coming through the open window, floating on the gentle downdraft that stirred the lace curtains, and the easy creaking of the chains holding the swing, the creaking of the swing, back and forth, back and forth. Suddenly her attention was caught by Jane's voice, raised and alarming.

"Mary Beth, you have to know!"

"I don't, *though," said Mary Beth.*

"How could you not know?"

"Don't be angry, Jane, please, I—I really don't know how it happened, it just did, afore I knowed it. I don't really know."

"But when?"

"Spring break." Jane was silent for a few minutes.

"You're sure, then?"

"I'm sure. I told Will, before he left, I told him."

"What did he say?"

"Said it warn't his—said he couldn't help me. Said he knows it ain't his, had to be Ben's, but I told him, it had to be his'n."

"What did Ben say?"

"I ain't told him yet."

"There's got to be a way to tell," Jane said thoughtfully.

El lay on the couch, hardly breathing. This was grown-up talk, Mary Beth had to be grown up if she was going to have a baby. She might learn the answer to some of her questions. The older girls were concentrating on solving their problem, moving the swing back and forth, back and forth, not saying a word. Then Jane asked, "What are you going to do?"

"I don't know."

"I think you ought to tell Ben."

"And let him know I was with Will first? He'd be awful mad."

"Look, Mary Beth, you're going to have a baby, is that right?"

"No, I mean, yeah, oh Jane, I don't know what I mean!"

"Well, that baby needs a father, and you need a husband. Is that right?"

"Yeah, that much is a fact!"

"And Ben says he loves you, is that right?"

"Well, he says he does, but Will said a guy would say anything to get his way, to get what he wants."

"What else did Will tell you?" asked Jane, sarcastically, but Mary Beth didn't recognize sarcasm and answered honestly.

"He said he was going to enlist, that he'd be fighting in this war and might not ever come back, and he needed someone to think about when he was shooting and killing, maybe git shot himself."

"Mary Beth! And you fell for that line?"

"I didn't know it was a line, I thought he loved me, and Lord knows, I love him! I shoulda' knowed, a girl like me, wouldn't be right for a real smart college boy like Will—oh, Jane! It just happened, afore I knowed what was on his mind!" The anguish in Mary Beth's voice stopped the swing in midair. There was a long silence, then Jane spoke her thoughts aloud.

"Well, whatever he said, it's for sure he didn't love you very much, or he'd have asked you to marry him before he volunteered."

"When I told him, he said he wouldn't marry a girl like me, no matter what, said it would ruin his chances."

"Why, that—that—well, I'll be!" Jane was speechless, trying to adjust her opinion of Will. "Mary Beth, there's got to be some way to figure this out. And you're going to need help. What did your mother say?"

"I ain't told her. She'll kill me."

"Then let's tell my mother—you've got to have some help!"

"No! I mean—not yet! I've got to talk to Ben first, then we'll tell her. Ben might marry me, then I'd never have to tell nobody!"

"You mean you'd marry Ben, knowing you love Will?"

"What would you do?"

The swing began creaking again, agonizingly accompanying the discussion. Finally, Jane said, "And you honestly can't figure out which one it was, got you pregnant?"

"No, it's like I told you. Will wore rubbers, and Ben never got in. I don't know how it happened."

El lay on the sofa, thinking over what she had heard. What did Will having his boots on have to do with anything? And Ben didn't get in what? It didn't make sense to her at all. She heard the swing come to a stop, and realized the girls were coming in the house. What if Jane was coming to play the piano! She rolled over, closed her eyes and pretended she was asleep, just in case, but they went up the stairs to Jane's room. Saved! Quickly she jumped up and went outside; it would never do to let them know she had heard. Mother was showing Bun how to make a chain out of clover, and the little girl was wearing a crown of white clover blooms, and a necklace and bracelet to match.

"Look, Ellie! Look what Mother made me!" The June day had claimed them from their sorrow and fear: it was spring again for Mother and for Bun.

Now that school was out for the summer, there was only one game to play: school. El was the teacher, of course, and Bun was her willing pupil. With

Edgar and Joe gone, El didn't mind spending the time with her little sister, and Mother gave them permission to use the old crayons and tablets left over, promising them new ones in the fall. Bun would start First grade in September, and El started teaching her the ABC's.

Now, as they drove to Mullins, Jane sitting in the front seat with Mother, El and Bun in the back, El resumed the teaching she had begun on the trip to Virginia. "Now, F is next. You make it just like E, only don't finish it, leave off the last arm. See?"

Bun, laughing deliciously, took the short red crayon in her stubby fingers. "Let me, Ellie, Let me!"

In the front seat, Mother and Jane were talking seriously, assuming that El and Bun were preoccupied with their own interests.

"This is what you have to keep in mind, Jane," Mother was saying, "there are millions of tiny sperm in that one drop of fluid, millions and millions, and it only takes one!" Mother shook her head emphatically, and El, looking at Mother's profile, saw her double chins meet, and part, and meet again. Mother seemed to be getting fatter and fatter every day. "That's why it's so important to never, never, let a boy touch you or put his hands on you!"

El and Bun looked at each other, eyes wide, and El put her finger to her lips, asking for silence. Bun nodded.

Mother seemed to have forgotten they were in the car, so intent was she with Jane's question. "Yes, even if a boy didn't go all the way, a girl could get pregnant. If he got that fluid on her leg, say or on his hands, then put his hands on the girl—that's how powerful those little sperm are. They swim right up to the ovaries, to meet the eggs carried by the girl, and when they meet, a baby is made."

El heard and comprehended every word Mother said. Her head sank into her hands; she felt sick to her stomach, her throat closed up and she couldn't breathe. *Zane Gray had touched her with his hand! She could be pregnant!* If he had those squiggly little sperm on his hands, she could be making a baby right now. Not yet twelve years old and her life ruined. She turned sideways in the seat, brought up her knees and doubled over in agony, her stomach turning convulsively.

"What's wrong?" whispered Bun. El hid her face against the soft gray seat; how could she ever face anyone again? With great effort, she took the red crayon from Bun and made a large A, motioned for Bun to make a row of A's across the page. Bun, encouraged as she recognized the letter as one she knew, took the crayon and made a row of scarlet A's across the pure, white page.

El pressed against the car seat, her eyes bulging with unshed tears, Mother might notice, and what would she say? Would her sin come rolling out, confession made to relieve the soul? They were at Alpoca; the coal tipple was looming over her, like a giant praying mantis, its jaws open wide to swallow her with the coal being dumped from the mine cars high up on the hill. The smoke made the sky darken, smelling of yellow sulfur-fumes from the ever-burning slate pile on the side of the mountain, a devil's caldarium. She thought of jumping from the bridge as they crossed the Guyandotte river at Tralee, but realized it might not be high enough, better to wait and jump off the railroad bridge at home. That would be deadly.

Mother continued her lecture to Jane all the way into Mullins, but never addressed the question El was burning to know: how do you know when you are pregnant? How had Mary Beth known? There was a book hidden in Mother's bottom dresser drawer, beneath her good nightgowns. It had pictures of men and women, but without any skin, just bones and blood vessels, like red and blue railroad tracks running all over, and not any details at all about what a man looked like down there; she had never even seen a baby boy without his diaper. She had no information at all on how a man "shall cleave unto his wife and they shall be one flesh." Finally, Jane, God Bless Her, asked the question: "How do you know when you are pregnant?"

Mother was easing the car into the parking lot at the A&P, pulling between a blue car and a red pickup truck; there was almost as large a crowd as on Saturday mornings. What if she forgot to answer Jane's question? But Mother didn't forget. "Why, you stop falling off the roof every month," she said, turning the car engine off and dropping her keys into her over-large purse. "That is what nourishes the baby."

In her anxiety, El forgot she was not supposed to be listening. Mother was getting out of the car. Quickly she spoke up, "What's falling off the roof mean?"

"Rachel Elizabeth! Have you been listening to our conversation? You know that is extremely impolite! I'm sure you know better. Just for that, little lady, you can stay in the car with Bun." She glared at her as only Mother could glare. El turned to Bun for an objection, but Bun was asleep, curled up on the soft seat, with her crayon clutched in her hand, exhausted from her educational efforts.

Miserable, wanting to die, El crawled over the back of the front seat to sit behind the steering wheel. A boy sat in the back of the red pickup truck; after a while, she felt him looking at her. Casually, she rolled the window down and rested her arm on the door. He moved over to her side of the truck and sat on the fender. He gazed at her and she gazed at him. The horror of the whole thing struck her. She was too young to die! She couldn't jump off the bridge, there was so much ahead of her! She would move away, take her baby with her, go to another state, California, maybe, where they were having blackout drills, where the German submarines were swimming up the coast, searching out the cities. She'd be Mrs. Smith, a respectable married lady, Mrs. Rachel Smith.

"What's your name?" asked the boy.

"Mrs. Smith!" said El, caught up in her fantasy, "I mean, Rachel! What's yours?"

"You're married?"

"What's it to you!" she said quickly. From the back seat came Bun's just-awake voice. "Potty, El. Potty."

Relieved at the interruption, El opened the door and helped Bun out of the car. "Come on, Sugar-Bun, we'll go inside."

"She your little girl?"

"Sure!" El answered.

"Why'd you say that, Ellie?" asked Bun.

"Just because," said El, "and don't you tell Mother!"

Mother. Dear God. How long before some little baby would be calling her that? How much time did she have? She would ask Nancy Sue, she was smart, she knew things. When they stopped at the Plover's, on the way home, she'd talk to Nancy Sue about her tragic fate.

From the A&P grocery store, Mother went to the mill outlet fabric store; she bought more gauze, more flannel yard goods.

"What's this for," El asked.

"Diaper material, baby gown material," said Mother.

She knows, thought El, she knows. But, how could she? She turned away, sick at heart, then she remembered. Mary Beth. Maybe Mother was getting the material for her! After all, Jane had said they would talk to her, or maybe it was for the sewing group, the Bundles for Britain Project. That was it. Mother couldn't possibly know about Zane Gray. But, again, as she thought about it, she realized that Mother usually knew everything. Nobody fooled Mother for long.

On the way home, Jane and Mother talked about the material. Relieved, El assumed Jane had told her about Mary Beth. It would make three dozen diapers, and at least eight gowns, with a few small sacques. Would Jane like to help with the embroidering? The little jackets would be perfect to practice her stitches on, and she could use the help, to get them finished in time. Jane, delighted, agreed.

Nancy Sue's house was El's favorite place to play; located halfway between Coville and Herndon, the house was large and rambling, cool in the summer, warm and cozy in the winter. Mrs. Plover was a haphazard housekeeper, preferring reading to cleaning and she let everyone relax and be comfortable.

The railroad ran parallel to the creek behind the house, and the highway ran in front. Across the road were open fields all the way to the edge of the mountain, which rose straight up. In that narrow open space was a fire tower, complete with its own log cabin, quarters for a park ranger. The tower was no longer occupied on a regular schedule, but in times of danger Mr. Plover climbed the iron steps and acted as lookout.

The log cabin had a sturdy oak door with a large, iron lock; an old notice, almost faded beyond reading, was posted on the door: "$500.00 for information leading to the arrest of trespassers." This made it all the more exciting to crawl through the small, high window with the broken glass. The Plover chickens flew through this window also, to nest in the hay stacked in the corner for that purpose. The log house was an ideal playhouse for Nancy Sue and El. They ran off quickly, leaving Bun and Jimmy Jr. behind.

They settled into the hay to talk. Quickly El told Nancy Sue about Zane Gray, about the kissing, about the way he had touched her. Nancy Sue was thrilled and excited. She told Nancy Sue what Mother had said about the swimming sperm, how they were so small it took a microscope to see them, but they were there, millions of them, maybe even billions or trillions, and they traveled to your eggs and made a baby grow.

"But there's something I don't understand, "continued El. "Why don't they come out when you pee?"

"Oh, no, El! It's not the same hole!" cried Nancy Sue. "There's another one, where babies come from. I know, because when I found mine, Mother told me what it was for."

"Are you sure?" said El. Nancy Sue took charge then, pulled her panties down and showed El the tiny opening of her vaginal orifice. El had never examined herself, and now she felt uncomfortable when Nancy Sue acted so freely with her 'private parts', as Mother called it.

"See this little thing? Rub it, feels good!" Nancy Sue said with a laugh. El slipped her own hand into her panties and, properly under the cover of her dress, she obeyed the instructions of the younger girl. She felt a strange sensation pass through her lower body, much like the chills she had experienced when Zane Gray rubbed her legs, and a tightening, convulsive feeling within her belly. The revelation was too special, too profound, too new to share with anyone, not even Nancy Sue.

By bedtime, El was feeling sick and feverish all over, aching and guilty, and all she wanted to do was go to bed. Mother put a hand to her forehead, looked at her tongue, with a spoon-handle inspected her throat, and decided El just wanted to get out of dishes; there was nothing wrong with her.

The family gathered around the radio to listen for the news as John McVane broadcast direct from London; they could hear the bombs dropping, screaming through the air, hear the explosions and the ambulance sirens, the fire alarms howling.

Next came Senator Brewster, (R. Me.) suggesting that Colonel Lindbergh be sent to Berlin as military attaché for aviation. He supported President Roosevelt's foreign policy but criticized his handling of the "Lindbergh affair." As he stated,

No one could be better qualified to divine whether Germany really is building 400 planes a day.

"Up in Maine," the Senator continued, speaking over the radio, "We have been brought up on the sea, and when a ship gets out of sight of land, we recognize the Captain as boss. With breakers ahead and a storm raging, it is not practical to hold a town meeting every time we port the helm or reel a sail... I did not vote for the Captain, but along with one million other Americans, I am still a member of the all-American team. If I am compelled to choose between Roosevelt and Hitler, I choose Roosevelt."

"We will be shooting by the 4th of July," said Daddy, "mark my words."

"With Germany," said Mother, statement, not a question.

"Of course, with Germany," said Daddy, irritated. "Who did you think I was talking about?"

"I was reading an article, the other day, said our danger could come from Italy or Japan just as quickly since Germany was moving troops onto the Russian border."

"Maybe," said Daddy, "but I'd bet on Germany getting us into it on the ocean long before we have to worry about an invasion by land."

"Where does Japan stand in this?" asked El. If she prolonged the discussion, she could postpone getting started on the dishes.

"Japan is a part of the Nazi alliance," said Mother, "a member of the Tripartite Agreement, with Germany and Italy."

"I thought Japan had an Emperor," she said. "Has he joined with Germany?"

"Well, Honey," said Daddy, "right now Japan seems to be having trouble making up her mind who is in charge."

"There are three groups in Japan, El," said Mother. "And all three are powerful. There is the Army, the Navy, and the Civilian government."

"True," agreed Daddy, "but the Civilian section is treading soft, the Army is yelling to fight, and the Navy can't make up its mind!"

"And the Emperor?" asked Jane, as she started cleaning off the table.

"He just goes along with the others, doesn't have much to say about anything," said Daddy.

"I'd have a lot to say, if I were Emperor!" said El." Wouldn't have anyone bossing me around!"

"And you'd never wash dishes, either, would you!" teased Daddy. Jane opened the back door to put scraps into Marsha's bowl.

"Bun! Ellie! Hey, come here! Marsha's brought her kittens out!"

They all rushed out to the back-porch steps. There sat four tiny kittens, two charcoal grays, like their mother, one black and white, and one with gray, black, white, and some yellow markings. Mother reached for it first. "Oh, look!" she cried, "A calico cat!"

Daddy had remained at the table. Now they heard him yell out, "No more cats around this house! No more cats!" How could he say such a cruel thing—he hadn't even seen them.

"Virginian Railroad Bridge" Photographed by Alyssa B. Weisner

Twelve

SURVIVORS SAY U.S. VESSEL TORPEDOED BY NAZI U-BOAT
Officials gravely Concerned
Brazilian Ship Picks Up Eleven Survivors: Thirty-Five Missing

Churchill Faces House Critics: Will Risk Action Declares, Long As He Is
Leader, He Will Continue To Strike Foe. DUCE VIRTUALLY DARES U.S.
MAKE WAR DECLARATION
Mussolini Tells People United States at War In Fact If Not Legally
Assails President Roosevelt in Speech, Declares American
Intervention Will Not Give Britain Victory, But Will Prolong War
Italians To Occupy Greece

"Stands to reason," says Daddy, "with our ships carrying the supplies the British must have, wasn't 'prophetic' at all, just reason. Of course, they are going to shoot at us, torpedo our ships. I'd question their intelligence if they didn't."

"They shouldn't be giving Churchill a rough time of it," said Mother, "He is certainly doing the best he can, under the circumstances."

On Friday the thirteenth, the State Department gave a dramatic account of the sinking of the Robin Moor. A German submarine surfaced and gave the crew thirty minutes to abandon ship, then they torpedoed the ship and left the crew to their fate in open life boats.

Eleven survivors landed, eleven out of forty-six passengers and crew of the American merchant vessel. The Senate, stirred to anger over the incident, approved a bill granting the President the power to seize strike-bound defense plants, and the Air Corps began advertising for high school graduates to enlist.

The news on Saturday stated that the Germans were blaming the United States for the sinking of the Robin Moor—the U.S. had broken the treaty by

220

sending aid to England. Russia was watching as German troops massed on their borders. This was Flag Day. The red, white, and blue waved from staffs along main street in Mullins. Men gathered on street corners to talk of war and strikes and government laws that would stop a man from striking, by god, don't aim to put up with it in this town! We'll work now, but by God, if'n they don't give us vacation with pay, we'll show' em how to strike, won't we, boys? Like to see some of them fine senators down th' hole when the bugdust starts flyin' and the roof starts creakin' and the gas rumbles loud as yer belly!

Daddy went to his Masonic meeting, and Mother took the girls to see *I Wanted Wings*, with Veronica Lake and Ray Miland. El could hardly be contained, the film excited her so; she couldn't wait to tell Edgar all about it. For the first time, she forgot about her personal tragedy and became absorbed in the movie, became the sensational 'blonde bomber', Veronica Lake, and thrilled to the sight of over twenty-five hundred airplanes filling the screen, for the movie was made at Randolph and Kelly fields, with the cooperation of the real Army Air Corps. She couldn't begin to tell Daddy how thrilling it was, how much she wanted to be a part of that highly skilled, high-flying air force. The best she could do was to repeat, over and over, "You've got to see it, Daddy, you've just got to see it!"

"And, when I do, take you with me, right?" Daddy teased her, but El was never more serious in her life when she answered, "Yes Sir!"

On Father's Day, June fifteenth, President Roosevelt froze all German and Italian assets in the nation, and Welles declared that the United States would not be bluffed off the seas by the Germans, to which Daddy declared, "Hell, man, you think they're bluffing?"

The Navy stated that New York's Harbor would be mined, and advised ships to find a navel escort for safe passage. By Tuesday, all German consulates had been closed, news and information services had been banned to Germans. A complete break seemed pending. Italy responded immediately by freezing all U.S. assets.

On another front, the Japanese bombed the safety zone in Chungking, and the American Embassy sent a sharp complaint to Tokyo; a shipment of oil to Japan was blocked. By Wednesday, Berlin expressed a protest against the ban on Nazi consulates, but the good news was, a British vessel had landed thirty-five men from the lost Robin Moor; they had been found near Capetown.

"What do you want for your birthday, Mother?"

"Hey! My birthday comes before Mother's" El interrupted.

"What to get you is no problem," continued Daddy. "You need a haircut!"

"No way!" replied El, as she combed her frizzy curls. "I'm letting it grow, going to let it get as long as Veronica Lake's."

"Ha!" Daddy said with a snort. "Seriously, Mother, wouldn't you like an electric range? They've got a good sale at Montgomery Wards, might be a good idea to get it before we get into war, besides, I'd like you to have it before—"

"Before winter?" Mother interrupted quickly.

"Before winter," Daddy agreed with a grin, and he folded the paper to a picture of a Hotpoint electric cooking stove. "Why don't you go tomorrow and look at this one."

"I'll look at it Friday," promised Mother. "Hollie wants to go on Friday. The tombstone is ready for Shirley's grave. I told her we would go early and take it on up to the cemetery."

"Just make sure you don't lift it," admonished Daddy.

"Don't worry, said Mother," I'll have the girls with me."

Thursday morning, the Navy issued stand-by orders to all reservists who had not been called to active duty. Mrs. Gillespie hadn't been out of the house since Will left home. At the news, she came over to the front porch and sat with Mother in the swing. "Looks like my Will knew what he was talking about, didn't he," she said. "If he hadn't gone on, he'd have to go now."

Mary Beth and Jane, sitting on the steps, exchanged looks. Ben was perched on the porch railing, his feet swinging within inches of the orange and yellow nasturtiums blooming in the flower boxes. He was listening, too, as his mother talked about the naval recruiting campaign. The Navy had increased their roster from eight hundred to twelve or fifteen hundred per month. "The Navy will need that many men when the new warships are commissioned," she said, pride in her voice. "They are adding to the fleet every day, and they have another fleet, too, a…a…"

"Auxiliary fleet, Mother," said Ben, "a back-up fleet, in case it's needed."

"Did you know, the Navy doesn't get a one of the men who are drafted?" Mrs. Gillespie continued. "Not a one."

"I'd no idea," said Mother. "Where do the draftees go?"

"All in the Army," said the thin, tired-faced neighbor. "The Navy is all volunteers, only the best. Doesn't that make us proud?"

"I'm sure it does, Mildred, it surely does." Said Mother.

"Just like my Will, the very best boys are in the navy, right there protecting our shores." She smoothed the brown-gray hair back from her face with a hand that was shaking, looking worn from the lack of sleep. "I'd better git on home, Rayford will be in soon, wanting his supper."

"Stay a while, Mildred," said Mother, "let me make you a glass of tea."

"No, no, don't want to put you to any trouble now, besides, Judith will be looking for me. Coming, Thomas?"

But Ben remained sitting on the porch rail.

Shortly after Mrs. Gillespie went home, Mary Beth and Ben left, strolling up the road towards the company store, hand in hand. El wondered if Mary Beth had told Ben about the baby. Would he claim it and marry her? She wondered again, which one was the father? There had to be a way to tell—the next time she saw Doc Steelman she was going to ask him. No, that might make him suspicious, and she didn't dare say anything about a baby until she knew—until she found out when—well, at least there was one thing she did know! At least she didn't have to wonder who was the father of her baby! That much she did know!

Friday morning, June twentieth, dawned fair and warm; the air lay still, heavily scented with rose and lilac bloom, and Mother predicted early afternoon thundershowers. "Let's be in Mullins by nine," she told Hollie, "and we can be up on the mountain before lunch."

"Let's have a picnic," El suggested, remembering the great, old apple trees around Hollie's old home place. A queer look passed over Mother's face, and she said quickly, "No, we'll eat at home."

They parked in front of the monument company before nine o'clock and when the clerk unlocked the door, Mother let them get out of the car. El and Burl walked among the tombstones, reading the inscriptions, looking for one suitable for Shirley, but they all had dry, prosaic wording carved into the stone: Rest In Peace, Gone But Not Forgotten, Here Lies blank, In Loving Memory, We'll Walk Hand In Hand, Eternal Love, and they found one with a small child on the side, with an inscription that read, Budded on Earth to Bloom in Heaven. Hollie said the one she picked out was inside, and she led them to a dusty, chalk-white workroom. The clerk had seen them coming and had wiped the stone with a wet rag and wrapped it in newspaper, ready to go. They would have to wait to read the words chiseled into it for Shirley.

The next stop was the furniture store. El and Bun were told to wait in the car, they wouldn't be long. Mother, Jane and Hollie went inside.

"Don't you have to go potty, Bun?"

"No."

"Say you do and we'll go inside."

"Potty, El, potty," Bun said agreeably.

"Come on!"

Mother was too busy admiring the electric stoves to worry about them. She was at her best, dickering over the price with an elderly salesman. Bun tried out all the chairs, then found the beds, and El was kept busy getting her off of first one thing and then another, but it was better than sitting in the car. Mother hustled them outside, glancing at the gathering clouds.

"We'll have to hurry if we are going to make it up on the mountain before it rains. I'd hate to get stuck on that dirt road."

As they got in the car, Jane saw Ben Gillespie coming down the street towards them. "Hey, Ben! What're you doing in town?"

Ben threw up a hand in answer, but went on to G.C. Murphy's.

"Well! He sure was in a hurry!" said Jane.

"And so am I, Jane! Please come on," said Mother.

They drove back up the holler to Herndon, turned right, across the railroad tracks and went by the train depot. "Let's stop and see Mr. Kerrigan," said El, thinking of the lime-green suckers in the blue Mason jar.

"If it isn't raining when we come back", said Mother, "we'll stop then."

She passed the depot and continued up the hill. The road was narrow and the ruts were deep, but it was bone-dry. Yellow buttercups and large white daisies with yellow centers bloomed in the fields, and there were patches of Queen Anne's lace, the flowers a creamy white froth with a single blood-red spot in the center to distinguish it from the poison hemlock which had the same lacy, flat-topped flower.

Along the edges of the road yellow wood sorrel bloomed, more plentiful than the red clover. They came to the old log cabin where Hollie was born and parked the car. Mother opened the trunk and Hollie took out the tombstone.

"Let me help you, Hollie," said Jane, but Hollie shook her head. "It's not heavy, it's for my baby."

She led the way to the crest of the hill, through knee-deep timothy and ragweed, along the over-grown path to a small family plot which was nearly obscured. Mother carried her hoe and chopped at the weeds as she walked by, but scarcely made a trail through them. Once at the grave she cleared it of weeds so the grass could grow, threw out the dead flowers, and dug a small trench at the head—the grave faced the sun, feet to the east, head to the west, mountain-style. All of this time, Holly stood hugging the stone to her breast, cradling it like it was her child. She unwrapped it and set it in the place prepared by Mother.

The tombstone was heart-shaped, with a little lamb carved on the bottom, a lamb surrounded by flowers of many kinds and in the center of the heart was engraved the inscription:

SHIRLEY

1935-1941

FORGIVE US

When Hollie placed the heart-shaped marker on Shirley's grave, she threw herself across the small mound and wept like her soul was leaving her body, crying until Mother knelt beside her and took her in her arms, rocking her and crooning softly, there, there, there. Jane dropped down beside them, tears running down her face, and Bun sobbed out loud, "Want to see Shirley, want to see Shirley, El!" El realized that Bun had thought they would see her friend, not just her grave. Everyone cried except El, and all she could think about was how cold and hard the little girl had been, as hard as the stone they now laid upon her grave. She led Bun down the crooked path to the old apple tree, to where the blossoms waved in a strong ground-breeze, and the bees buzzed erratically from white flower to white flower, to beneath the trees where the petals shed, sweet-smelling snow-white flakes, collecting in Bun's red-gold hair. She found last year's bird nest, explaining to Bun that Shirley had flown away to heaven, and Shirley was a real angel now, in heaven, because she had first been an angel on earth, and if Bun would quit crying, she would play with her forever and ever, and Bun dried her tears on the bottom of El's shirt, leaving streaks of dirt where her tears had been.

The storm broke just as they reached the foot of the mountain, and Mother drove directly home. As the rain poured, drowning the dusty weeds, bending the flowers to the earth, whipping the tree branches in the fury of the wind, El thought, the whole world is crying with us.

Lunch was quiet, everyone exhausted by the emotional time at the cemetery. Mother took Bun upstairs with her for a nap, Jane walked Hollie home. El was left alone.

She missed Edgar. He and Joe were due back on Sunday; it seemed like it had been much longer than two weeks. She had a lot to tell him.

On Friday night Germany and Italy ousted the United States consulates, and Finland went on a war footing. Officials began to study gasoline rationing as a means of off-setting the shortage.

The Northern operators and the UMW signed a contract, complete with wage increases and vacations with pay, but the Southern negotiations had yet to be concluded.

As they sat listening to the radio after supper, Mother cut out summer dresses, designing them herself out of sheer organdy or dotted Swiss. Although it was Friday night, all three girls would have a new dress to wear to church on Sunday.

Saturday afternoon Mother was at the sewing machine when the news came: Thirty-three seamen were trapped in a U.S. submarine out on a trial dive. There was very little hope for the recovery of the vessel or rescue of the trapped men, for bits and pieces of the wreckage had floated to the surface. The Navy felt sure the boat had been crushed by the pressure at the four-hundred foot depth. The family felt like they had lost a personal friend, for these were Navy men, and their next-door neighbor was a Navy man.

Lindbergh had addressed a mass meeting in the Hollywood Bowl, again sponsored by the America first Committee, and a miner was killed by a slate fall near Lost River Mountain. There seemed no end to the bad news, for Emmett had left home again, leaving in the middle of the night, without a word to Hollie. She sat at the table with the girls, watching as Mother sewed, helping with the numerous fittings.

There was a knock at the door, and Daddy went to answer it, allowing Mother to continue her sewing. He came back immediately, went into the living room, followed by Mr. Gillespie. "Faith, would you come here?" he called, and Mother arose from her machine and joined them. They could hear Mr. Gillespie as he explained to Mother.

"We've had a terrible shock and I'm concerned about Mildred. Would you come over for a few minutes?"

"Certainly, "Mother said. "Whatever is the trouble?"

"I don't know how she's going to live through this," the big man said, "I'm afraid of what it will do to her."

"What is it, Rayford?" she asked again, "what is the trouble?"

"First it was Will, now it's Ben. Ben has joined the Navy."

When Charles Lindbergh spoke to the crowd at the Hollywood Bowl, he "summarized" the true facts as they appeared to him:

1. *We still are unprepared for the war and it would take years to prepare...*

2. *Even if we fully prepared, we would face the task of crossing an ocean and forcing a landing on a fortified continent...*

3. *We in America have the best defensive position in the world. No foreign power can invade us today...*

"That son-of-a bitch!" said Daddy, and the girls looked at each other and grinned at the language. "He thinks we are a bunch of farmers and shoemakers, thinks we can trade, but don't think we can fight! Huh! He ought to read his history books. We settled this country fightin', we've been fighting ever since!"

Mother was not back from the Gillespie's. Jane made tomato soup and grilled cheese sandwiches and put Mother's on the back of the stove to keep warm.

"I don't see what your Mother sees in this fly-boy, his thinking is not what it's cracked up to be."

"Daddy if we get into the war, will you have to go fight?" asked El, wanting to stop the criticism of Lindy and knowing better than to argue with him.

"Naw, I'm too old, besides, my job is critical. I'll leave the fighting to these hot-shot young pilots, if they've got the nerve." And El knew he was still thinking about Lindbergh.

"I think Emmett has gone into the Army," said Hollie suddenly.

Daddy looked up," What makes you think that," he asked sharply.

"Something he said, while back, about that being the only thing left for him to do."

"Surely he'd tell you, Hollie, before he'd do a thing like that!"

"I don't know, he don't talk to me anymore." She stood up and gathered her things. "Want to walk home with me, El?"

"I'll go with you, Hollie." Said Jane. "It's time for Ellie and Bun to get their bath. Mind you, now, get your ears clean, don't want any dirty girls going to church in the morning!" She sounded just like Mother.

Hollie and Jane left. El bathed Bun, then herself. Tomorrow Edgar would be home from his grandmother's. She had a lot to tell him. He was the main reason she didn't want to leave home, Edgar and Bun. If she went to California, she might never see them again. So far, no one could tell she was pregnant; she examined herself in the bathroom mirror carefully. There was no change in her flat, skinny torso. Not yet, anyway. Poor Mary Beth. First Will ran out on her, now Ben. What would she do? what would her mother do, when she found out? Mary Beth had said her mother would kill her; would she, really?

What would her mother do, when she found out about Zane Gray? It wasn't all Zane Gray's fault, she mused, as she lay in bed. After all, she had liked his kisses. The sin was hers.

Sunday morning was as fresh as a June day could be after the showers of Friday and Saturday. Before they got ready Daddy moved the car around to the front gate so they could use the brick walkway from the porch to the car and stay out of the black mud.

The crowd was nearly as large as that at Preacher Copeland's retirement, everyone turning out to hear the refreshingly new sermons by the student minister—the boy-minister some called him. Jane wore her new dress, a white dotted Swiss with red dots and a red satin ribbon emphasized the shine of her raven's wing black hair. She sat at the piano like she belonged there, as, indeed she did, and played exceptionally well. Mother invited Ted home for dinner, over Daddy's objections, and to Jane's frank delight. She had discovered that Ted sang beautifully; he had a deep baritone voice and knew his music almost as well as he knew his Bible. Ted explained that the college had a male chorus which sang Broadway hits, old favorites, and some show tunes from the newer movies. Ted discovered that Jane had a collection of songs by popular name bands, songs such as those sung by Kate Smith who always introduced her show with Mother's favorite, "When the Moon Comes Over the Mountain." They could hardly finish dinner before going to the piano to try half-a-hundred selections together. Everyone gathered on the front porch to listen to the informal concert. Jane had never enjoyed herself so much, for she had never met anyone who loved to sing, and had the voice, nobody, that is, except

Mother's quartet, and they couldn't be compared to a clean-cut, red-haired college man!

Ted stayed until time for Epworth League and evening services, and walked down the road with Jane, Mary Beth and Ben, moaning because he couldn't walk back with them after church. He would have to hitch-hike to Mullins.

"That suits me just fine," muttered Daddy. "The less I see of that red-headed son-of-a-gun, the better I like it!" Neither Jane nor Ted heard him, but Mother did, and she replied, "Now, Bud, he's a nice boy."

"If you think he's just a boy, you're fooling yourself," Daddy responded.

El and Bun were sitting on the front porch steps. El was teaching Bun the first singing commercial on radio—and Bun finally got the tune and words down pat.

"Listen to this, Daddy, listen to this!" she cried, and Bun began to sing, "Pepsi-Cola hits the spot, twelve full ounces, that's a lot. Twice as much for a nickel too, Pepsi-Cola is the drink for you!" Daddy picked Bun up and hugged her. "I'm telling you, Faith, you'd better keep an eye on that girl. A preacher is still a man, no better, no worse, just a man."

Mother looked thoughtful and the small wrinkle came between her eyes, like it did when she was giving something her full attention.

The two Mitchell boys came down the road with Mr. Mitchell; they had gotten off the bus at the highway. Edgar was home! He threw up his hand in greeting as he passed and El was immediately overcome with shyness. She was very glad to see him; he looked like he had grown a foot taller, was much blonder, much browner than when he left—and much better looking!

Darkness settled slowly between the high hills, and the fireflies began to come out, twinkling in the bridal wreath bushes. Mother and Daddy went in to hear the evening news and El found a jar, filled it half-full of grass and punched holes in the lid. Bun could keep the tiny, glowing insects as she captured them. They ran around the yard catching them, letting them light up in their hands before putting them in the jar. El couldn't be too enthusiastic about what she considered a childish game. She no longer felt like a child. Seeing Edgar come down the road made her feel all goose-bumpy, much as she had with Zane Gray, but it made her sad, too. What would Edgar think of her, if he knew? She ended their lightening bug chase abruptly and took Bun inside. As they joined Mother and Daddy in the dining room, the news broadcast had just started: *Germany had attacked Russia.*

War moved into the narrow valley like the hot wind of summer as the temperature soared. Bluefield prepared to serve lemonade on the street corners, but the mercury there stopped just short of ninety degrees. The Nazis attacked Russia for what they termed a 'border violation' and England vowed to assist Russia while Italy stood by Germany. The battlefront stretched from Norway to the Black Sea, more than fifteen hundred miles.

In Washington, the Senate debated the fate of the bill funding the CCC boys, and newly appointed Joseph Rosier (D.-WVa) made his first speech, which lasted two minutes and it made him "as nervous as a girl." The bill was slashed by ten million dollars; with jobs available in defense plants, and with the numbers of men needed by the armed forces, there was no need for the 'make-work' organization. The WPA would be discontinued when the present projects were completed. The CCC boys would blow up bridges, instead of building them. End of an era.

By the time the girls were awake on Monday morning, the Mitchell boys and the Wooten boys had beat the heat by retreating to the creek. Mother outlined the day's chores before she went to the garden, carrying her coal bucket and shovel to pick up cow piles in the road, transferring Old Bess's manure to enrich the garden soil. Bess now roamed loose in the camp, grazing in the triangle or along the creek, wandering in the woods, returning at the sound of Mother's call in the evening, to be milked by the back gate.

The girls were to clean the house carefully, polish the furniture, wax the hall, shine everything; company was coming after supper. Monday's wash was postponed to Tuesday, Tuesday's ironing moved to Wednesday. Once a year a professional photographer came to take the family pictures. This was the day. Supper was on the table when Daddy came in from work, the girls were bathed, dressed in their best, their ribbons in place.

The photographer was a young man and El and Bun stood silently, stiffly, while he set up his tripod. Jane bustled around, smiling and helpful. He was an attractive, dark-eyed youth, hardly older than Jane, and he quickly explained that this was his last assignment. He had joined the Navy and would leave in the morning for training.

"Do you know Ben Gillespie?" asked Jane.

"Don't believe I do."

"He leaves in the morning, too. He lives next door."

"Well, I'd like to meet him, we're sure to be on the same train. Be nice to know someone before we get to camp."

"I'll take you over, when we are finished with the pictures, and introduce you," said Jane, smiling prettily. El watched as Jane flirted with the young man who was seating her on the sofa, holding her arm like she was injured or something. The calico kitten wandered in and El picked it up, holding it against her distended abdomen. All day she had felt swollen and sore; she thought everyone could see the way her stomach was pooched out in front, showing through her straight, smooth skirt. The kitten felt warm and protective, easing her discomfort and making her feel more relaxed.

"Put the kitten down, Rachel," Mother said, "We're ready to begin."

"But I want to hold it," said El, nearly in tears. "It makes me feel better."

"Oh, for goodness sakes! There's nothing wrong with you, you've been grumbling around for days! Put it down!"

The young photographer turned around quickly, "Oh, don't make her cry!" He said in alarm, knowing there was nothing worse for pictures than a crying child. "Animals really make a nice touch to photographs, please, let her hold it!"

El squeezed between Jane and Bun on the sofa, holding the kitten over her stomach; her hair was still wet and stuck out on the sides in little kinky sprigs and her ribbon was crooked, precariously perched on one side, like a blue-spotted butterfly afraid to light. Bun's curls lay like red satin coils after being wrapped tightly around Mother's finger, and Jane looked the picture of class, as usual. The photographs were made.

Jane and the photographer packed away his equipment and left for the Gillespie's. Daddy took Bun on his knee. El slipped off to bed, feeling like she would surely die before morning. The only thing she wanted was to go to sleep.

Tuesday morning was cloudy and humid; rain lay just over the hill. El was awake when Daddy left for work; she heard Mother, out on the back porch, filling the machine and washtubs to start the laundry, confident that the sun would shine by noon—the weather wouldn't dare rearrange Mother's plans for the day.

El couldn't move, she ached so badly. Is this what it felt like to be pregnant? Was this the 'morning sickness' everyone talked about? If it was, she knew she'd never live long enough to make a baby. Her legs ached so badly she couldn't keep them still; her back hurt, but worse, she had stomach cramps and pains like she'd never had before in her life. She stayed in bed as long as she could, finally had to get up to go to the bathroom.

She sat on the commode and felt a little relief, but there was still pain and a feeling of fullness, no doubt from the pressure within the womb, where the baby was growing. She used the tissue— and there was blood on it! She tried and tried again, but it just kept coming and she knew: she had one of those terrible diseases Mother was always cautioning against. She recalled taking Bun to the toilet at the A&P and remembered: she had failed to cover the seat with paper, the way Mother always insisted. She got off the toilet and curled up on the big window seat, crying like her day of doom had come, her punishment for being a bad girl. Hearing the loud sobbing, Jane got up and walked sleepily to the bathroom.

"What on earth is the matter with you?" she exclaimed, but El cried harder. Jane went to the top of the stairs. "Mother? Mother!"

From the back porch came Mother's answer, "Yes, Jane?"

"Come up here quick! Something's wrong with Ellie!"

Mother came as rapidly as she could, puffing up the stairs, pulling on the polished rail. She took El in her arms. "Why, Rachel, what on earth is the matter?"

"I'm dying, Mother," she sobbed, "I hurt so bad, and I'm bleeding."

"Bleeding? Where are you bleeding?"

"Down—down below!" she wailed.

"On your panties?"

"Yes, and on the p-p-paper!"

And Mother—*Mother laughed! El would never forgive her!*

"My dear, little girl, you're not dying! You've fallen off the roof! You've started your monthly period." Mother held her close. And laughed again. "You'll live through it, we all do. You're just growing up, Ellie." She took a washcloth from the cabinet, showed her how to pin a store-bought pad in place. "It's about time I told you about yourself, honey," said Mother. "I'm truly sorry I haven't prepared you for this. You've started much earlier than I did, or Jane, either, for that matter, and I wasn't expecting it so soon." El wanted to go back to bed and hide under the covers, but Mother, plainly cold-hearted, had different ideas. "No, ma'am! The first thing you learn is to live with it! You get dressed and eat breakfast; I'm going to need help with the laundry!"

El felt like the end of the world, and Mother was worrying about the washing! She dressed and went outside to eat her biscuit.

The clouds had blown away after a brief sprinkle that left the grass sparkling like dew; her joy was as bright and sparking as the new-green grass, aching as painfully as the fire in her belly, for, if she had " fallen off the roof," she couldn't be pregnant! If Zane Gray's sneaky little sperm had found the eggs in her body, they were being washed away by a great crimson flood! And life goes on...

The willow tree swayed in the easy breeze; the last breath of honeysuckle perfume mingled with that of the deep red rose. The ants crawled briskly after a crumb of her bread, handling their burden easily, and over on the Mitchell's porch, Edgar was hanging his denim pants across the porch railing, finished with his weekly wash.

It was a beautiful morning; she picked up two of the kittens and cuddled them in her lap, the warmth of their soft, loud-purring bodies made the pain disappear. And when Edgar joined her on the back steps, she had never been happier: being a woman wasn't all that bad after all.

Later, as she helped Mother with the laundry, she learned about five-day periods and twenty-five day cycles and special hygiene—bathe as you should and no one will know, keep your secret, and now, Ellie, your body is ready to have babies but morally and spiritually ...El didn't hear all of the lesson. She was thinking, *oh, no! not me! No boy will ever again lay a hand on her. Never. Not in a million years!*

Thirteen

Now that two Coville boys were in the navy, the news, Tuesday night, was of deep concern to everyone. The Russian army had captured five thousand Nazi soldiers and three hundred German tanks, but they still had to admit that Brest-Litovsk was lost, while the Germans claimed their Russian Drive was right on schedule. The sympathy of the U.S. was strongly on the Russian side and talk of the Lend-lease aid, or other help, abounded. In other reports, the Japanese were promising to disclose their war policy "soon," but nobody knew what that really meant.

On Thursday, John L. Lewis set the seventh of July as the deadline for signing the contract with the Southern operators. Twelve out of the thirteen associations had acquiesced to the new, two-year agreement, which called for a wage increase of as much as $1.40 per day. Only the Harlan County association held out, refusing to meet the Union terms. At one point they tentatively agreed on a vacation with a token twenty dollars in pay, but the next minute they contended that the contract didn't have a vacation agreement. Working days for the eighty thousand miners in the Southern states were numbered, for if the new contract was not signed before July seventh, the miners would not return to work. The nation, once again, faced a major strike possibility, and only five days remained to reach an agreement; the miners would take Friday, the Fourth of July, as a holiday. There couldn't be a more independent bunch anywhere.

All week Daddy had been stringing new line for the railroad spur into undeveloped mining country, going up above Cub Creek every day. Friday night he talked about the new area. "It's got cherry trees big as oaks, and they are loaded. Must have been planted by the Pilgrims, but there's nobody livin' around there any more, all moved off years ago. That creek has some of the best trout I've ever seen, the cleanest, coldest water, the deepest pools, great for fishing—or swimming either."

"I'd sure like to have some of those cherries," said Mother wistfully. "There's nothing better on a cold winter's night than hot cherry pie."

"Would we have to wait for cold weather?" asked Daddy with a big grin, "Cherry pie is good anytime! We could stay all night, fish, swim."

"No!" Jane laid down her fork emphatically. "I don't want to miss church!"

"Miss church, or miss the preacher?" asked Daddy sarcastically. "If you think I'm going to change the way I live for that red-headed, no-good—"

"Now, Bud," Mother interrupted, "I'm committed to teaching Sunday School, anyway, but why don't we go for the day?"

Daddy sat back, content to glare at Jane. "Want to ask the Plovers?"

"Let's do, and Hollie, too!"

"More the merrier," said Daddy, "anybody but that Irish preacher!"

"He's not Irish. He's Scottish."

"Irish, Scottish, same difference," said Daddy darkly.

The dark red cherries hung in clusters of three, four or five, and could be picked by the handful; their buckets were easily filled. The men fished, the women cooked, the kids swam and played in the deep-forested glens. When it was dusk, they packed up for the drive home. The moon was hanging back a while, and the shadows lengthened. The owls began to call and the whip-poor-wills answered: "Whip poor Will, Who? Poor Will, whip poor will, poor will, Who? Who-who-who? Poor Will, poor will poor will, poor, poor Will."

When they reached home, late as it was, Daddy clamped the cherry-seeder on the edge of the wooden kitchen table and Mother put on the kettle to sterilize the Mason jars.

The girls went to sleep, comfortably lulled by the sounds from the kitchen, the banging of pans, the laughter and occasional bit of song, and finally, the smell of freshly baked cherry pie.

But on the ten p.m. news, the German tanks were advancing northward, rolling deeper and deeper into Russian territory, and the first troop trains were scheduled to roll across the state early Monday morning.

Sunday was hot and muggy, partially cloud-covered, but with temperatures climbing upward to one hundred in parts of the state. The Northern mine workers started their two weeks of vacation with pay, but the Southern mines lay idle, the miners disgruntled and sore. Dinner was brief; Mother and Daddy retired for a nap, worn out with yesterday's cherry picking and late-night canning, and Bun was tucked in for a nap as usual. Jane and Ted sat on the front porch, swinging and talking, talking and swinging—Ted had to kill time between the two services and he had to eat, might as well come home with the Phillips'—and El was left with nothing to do.

The heat pressed down in waves, bounced up from the black-cindered roadbed and came down again, twice as hot. Heat devils danced off the concrete wall around the creek, and the water was so low Mother had forbidden swimming, or even wading, after the report of the season's first death from polio.

She lay dreamily in the thick grass, her head shaded by the blooming day lilies against the side of the house. Last summer, on a Sunday afternoon, the porch had been full of laughing youths, Will and Ben, Mary Beth, Hollie and Emmett, Shirley with Bun. Now only Jane and Ted sat there. Will, Ben and Emmett were gone, Shirley was dead, Hollie and Mary Beth stayed home, each alone. The camp was so still the rasping of grasshoppers seemed an intrusion.

She sat up and reached for the Sunday paper. Dagwood and Blondie had named their baby daughter, "Cookie", no note about who had won the contest. Well, that's as good as "Bun," she thought. The word bomber caught her eye, and sitting cross-legged in the grass, she started reading: Called a B-19, World's largest airplane, cost over three million dollars, a wing-spread of two hundred and twelve feet—why, that was as long as—as—she couldn't visualize what two hundred feet looked like. A hundred and thirty feet long, forty-two feet high. How high was her house? Mother had wall-papered the living room; she remembered the ceiling was twelve feet high, two stories, twenty-four feet—this plane was twice as high as her house! She folded the paper and kept it handy for Edgar, hoping he would come over.

Top speed of two hundred and ten miles per hour. Fantastic! Range, over seven thousand miles—nearly twice as far as Lindbergh had flown. Crew of ten—Edgar as pilot, she'd be co-pilot, Joe could be navigator, if he'd play right without clowning, BillynBob, Bun, Judith, if Mrs. Gillespie would let her come out, still room for three more passengers'! What a plane! Her eyes lifted to the sky, imagining the plane flying higher than the mountain tops—and she saw a break in the clouds: the sun was glinting behind them, leaving bright, white edges. A cloud with a silver lining, a good omen, but, at the moment, the only ones sharing her vision were Jane and Ted McKinney

Sometime later Edgar threw himself down beside her on the cool grass. They lay on their backs, studying the clouds, deciding if they should fly over or under them; the silver-lined ones were gone. She told Edgar about the B-19, and he read the article. "Land at sixty miles an hour—faster than we drive a car," said Edgar, whistling. "Takes eleven thousand gallons of gasoline. No wonder we're going to be rationed soon!"

"Think it will come to that?"

"Sure, and before long, too. Pa says before winter."

"How come your Pa never talks?"

"Why, he does talk!" Edgar said, surprised.

"Not to me, not to anybody 'cept you and Joe."

"Well, he's not the talkin' kind."

"Where did your mother go, Edgar? What really happened?"

Edgar was quiet for a bit, rolled over on his stomach, and put a grass blade between his thumbs, making a whistle. "Tell you, sometime," he said, and blew a long, raucous sound.

"Hey! You'll wake Mother and Daddy!"

Obediently, Edgar dropped the grass blade. He nodded toward the railroad bridge. "Be hot up there, but at least there'd be a breeze."

"I'm going up there some day," said El.

"Been there."

"On the bridge?"

"Yep."

"When?"

"Oh, lots of times! Mostly at night. Can't nobody see you, if you're keerful."

"It's against the law."

"Naw, no harm."

"I've seen the signs: unlawful to trespass, railroad property."

"What they don't know won't hurt 'em."

"You could get hurt."

"Naw, not if you know how."

"Take me."

"What?"

"Take me up on the bridge—I've wanted to go for years and years and years!"

Edgar was silent, thoughtful. Then, "All right, but you've got to do exactly what I tell you."

"Oh, I will! Honest, I will!"

"Promise?"

"Promise, cross my heart, hope to die!"

Edgar laughed. "That's what you might do, if you don't watch out! Okay, tonight, after everyone's asleep. You watch for me, I'll give the signal. We've got to wait until after the 9:20 freight comes, then there's plenty of time before the next one comes along. Got to know the schedule, that's real important, can't get caught up there by surprise, got to plan it."

El was so excited she could hardly eat supper. By eight-thirty she had Bun in the tub and had read several stories. Bun finally went to sleep. She listened to Mother and Daddy getting ready for bed, watched for Jane's light to go out. She exchanged her nightgown for shorts and shirt, put on her winter shoes and laced them tightly as Edgar had instructed, so she could run over the crossties or gravel, depending on the situation. Edgar said Mr Reeves made his last round 'bout nine-thirty, and after that, they were on their own: not a soul to stop them.

The moon, rising late now in the last half of its cycle, cast a faint glow on the bridge, but in the shadows, low in the valley, it was as black as a mine hole without a lamp. The 9:20 freight rumbled by overhead, each car bumping over the one loose rail on the westbound track, de-bump, de-bump, de-bump and a few empties added their lighter, more metallic clack-clack-clack-clackity-clack. Soon it was gone, its lonesome-sounding whistle blowing long and uninterrupted, the signal for approaching a crossing or a station. By the time the red caboose had passed over the bridge, the engine, an EL-3A, specially built by General Electric for the Virginian, would be almost to the passenger station at Herndon. As the sound faded down the valley, El saw Edgar standing in the road. She slipped the screen off the window, crawled down the porch roof, caught the post with her feet, slid down to the porch rail, and dropped lightly on the thick sod of her yard. She waited for Edgar to lead, followed him across the triangle and into the deeper shadows of the bridge.

Her heart was racing audibly; not only was she sneaking out in the middle of the night with a boy—a sin worse than death—but she was going on the railroad bridge, the one area of the camp which was strictly, absolutely forbidden, off-limits even to adults.

What if Mother checked her room? What if Bun woke up, what if—but soon her worries were forgotten. They crossed the footbridge over the creek, slipped by the haunted house, and began to climb straight up the mountain, in the dark, beneath giant hardwood trees and ancient hemlocks, through heavily tangled new-blooming pink and rose and red rhododendron bushes: she couldn't turn back now.

The woods were dark and quiet. She stepped on a pine cone and the crunch sounded louder than a firecracker. It was noticeably cooler under the trees, and gradually her eyes adjusted to the shadows; she began to see the tree trunks, to distinguish the heavier shrubs. She reached out for Edgar and found he was reaching for her; their hands met and she felt secure. An owl hooted over the rise and El jumped. She thought about the bobcat that had frightened Jane and wished she hadn't remembered it.

"Are there bobcats in these woods?" she whispered to Edgar.

"Sure, I guess so," he answered. "You don't have to whisper, nobody can hear us now."

El thought it disrespectful, like talking in church or something. Although unable to express it, she felt solemnity was needed to validate the occasion. The deep night stillness isolated them from the town, from all people; they were alone in a new, unexplored, primordial world, dependent upon each other for survival. She felt very close to Edgar in a new and exciting way; whatever happened, they were in it together.

His hand guided her up the steep slope with a surety born of familiarity, and in a few minutes, breathing hard, they reached the railroad tracks. Edgar leaned over from the waist, his hands on his knees, regaining his breath and El slowed hers in the usual way, breathing through her nose, one-Mississippi, two-Mississippi.

"Now we can talk," said Edgar, and you won't have to worry about bobcats much longer—they won't come out on the bridge—got too much sense."

"Why did we come out on the tracks so far from the bridge?"

"Too steep. Too hard to climb right at the Bridge." Edgar was walking the crossties easily, shortening his steps to hit everyone. El could see the steel rail, shining faintly in the near-moonlight, and chose to walk it, beside him rather than behind. As they walked, he instructed.

"Now, if you get dizzy, just sit down. Don't try to walk on the bridge dizzy, that'd be dumb. And if a train ever catches you on the bridge, lay down, don't run, and whatever you do, keep your head. Lay down between the tracks" he demonstrated by dropping face down on the heavy wood sleepers, his face in the ballast. "And lay on your hands so they don't get chopped off."

El shuddered at the thought of losing her fingers; she could see herself going home with her fingers missing, red blood dripping. "You're sure the train can go over you?"

"Yep," said Edgar, springing to his feet.

"Ever tried it?"

"Nope, and I don't intend to! All it takes is clocking the schedule, and keepin' your ears washed out."

They reached the end of the bridge. El was struck by the size of it! It was so much larger than it looked from below, the tracks were wider, and there was space between them, plenty of room for her to fall through. From the road beneath the bridge, it had looked like a tiny crack between the two tracks. From below the catenary poles looked like short posts. Now, standing beside them, she could see they were as tall as the electric poles in her yard.

"I can't see the other end!" she whispered.

"Of course not. There's a curve in it, and it's got seventeen spans!"

"I'm scared," whispered El.

Protective at once, Edgar reached for her hand. "Don't be—it's great, once you get out in the middle. Come on, I'll hold you."

She tightened her grip on his hand and started out on the rail but Edgar stopped her. "No, it's best to walk on the ties, and set your foot down flat 'cause if it goes between you'll stumble and might go through—or pitch over."

El shuddered at the thought of pitching headlong over the side. Carefully they worked their way to the middle of the bridge, moving a few steps, pausing to let El look around. When she was moving, she refused to look anywhere except where her next step was to be. At the center of the bridge Edgar stopped her. "Careful, now, step over the rail, we're at the lookout."

She did as he instructed and gained the small wooden platform projected outward from the tracks on the side next to the schoolhouse and the company store. She took a deep breath and looked about. It was like being on top of the world! She could see the thin edge of the moon just topping the trees, its light not yet in the valley below. The stars were much closer now, clearer without the mountains overpowering them. She gradually became aware of a faint hum, a constant musical but monotonous tone, and turned to Edgar. "What's that?" she whispered.

"Wind in the wires," he said aloud. She looked again at the tall catenary poles and thought of her father, climbing those poles all year long, every kind of weather, climbing them on top of all the bridges on the Virginian Railroad system. She felt exhilarated, thrilled at being up so high, and realized that her Daddy probably felt the same way, or he wouldn't do it. She looked below and expected to feel dizzy, but found that the amazing height didn't bother her at all. She could see the roof of the schoolhouse—there was a cap, a red cap, lying on the other side. And she could see the roof of the company store; the two-story structure looked so big when she was on the ground but now it looked no larger than her house.

She could see the creek winding around behind the company store, behind the haunted house, disappearing as the bridge blocked her view. She turned, indicating she wanted to see from the other side, see the creek, the road, her house, all of it. Edgar held her arm as she crossed over to the other side and looked down.

Seeing her house was a shock; how small it looked, yet how clearly, she could see every detail, including the white lace curtain hanging out of her window, blowing on the roof of the front porch—a certain give-away. Next time, she would take the time to replace her window screen.

They sat, straddling the crossties, their feet through the spaces between and dangling below the bridge as they inspected the town. The air moved about them, cooler now, sweet-scented and free. There was a light in one of the houses near the end of the camp by the highway, and Edgar, pointing, said, "Mrs. Margaret's. She never left it on afore he died, but now it burns every night, leastways every week end. It must be near ten o'clock. Watch now."

"Watch what?" she whispered.

"You'll see," he said, and added, "you don't have to whisper, can't be heard this fer up."

They sat in silence for a while, but as the moon slowly cleared the trees the beauty of the scene overcame her. She stood up, moved to the small look-out platform and threw her arms wide, spreading them as if she would fly, like a bird spreads its wings. Love for the hills, for the dark, silent trees, for the light of the moon with its reflected sun-glory shining on her face, love for her world, its symmetry and congruency, its fluid loveliness, washed over her in orgasmic waves and she felt a part of it all.

"Oh, Edgar, I wish I could fly!"

241

Edgar answered with male practicality. "Someday I'm going to, just as soon as I'm old enough!" He spread his arms for wings and made the sweeping motions of a plane diving and swooping, walking the rail as graceful as a mountain cat. "I'll have me one of those dive bombers!"

That was not the kind of flying El meant but she couldn't explain her depth of emotion.

Edgar stopped suddenly, reached for her arm and pulled her down to lie flat on the tracks. "Shush!"

Staying low, he moved back to the camp side of the tracks, motioning for her to follow. "Stay down," he whispered. "Look."

Coming down the road from Mrs. Margaret's house was Mr. Collins, striding along briskly but quietly, hands in his pockets. He turned off the road beside the Gillespie's house and walked on the concrete wall bordering the creek to his back gate, disappearing beneath the great willow tree. El sat silent for a time, then asked, "Every night?"

"Nah, every weekend. Pa says he's too old for every night!"

"You told your Pa?"

"Didn't hafta. He seen 'em too."

"Your Pa was up here?"

"Yep."

"With you?"

"Yep, first time. I told him I was coming, he said he'd come with me if'n I was bound to."

El tried to imagine telling her Mother or her Daddy either, that she was going to do something strictly forbidden against the law, and having them give their permission, much less come with her. She gave up. It would never happen. Edgar was saying, "Went huntin' with me, first time, too and fishin'." Like it amounted to the same thing, but El was back to Mr. Collins and Mrs. Margaret.

"And they've been seeing each other ever since he died?"

"Nah, long before that, way last fall, first time I was up here I seen 'em."

She thought about all the times she had seen them in the hall, their smoking breaks, at school. Just looking at them, she should have known. Not that they ever did anything, it was more a matter of how they looked, a reaching out, or something deeper. She tried to feel romantic about it, but she couldn't. She liked—almost loved—Mr. Collins, but she truly despised Mrs. Margaret. Mrs. Margaret didn't fit her idea of a heroine, even if she was a new widow!

Edgar reached for her hand. "We'd best be getting' back," he said, and led the way off the bridge, carefully, watching El's feet to be sure she was hitting the crossties squarely in the center. They slipped down the mountainside through the woods, and ran lightly to her front gate where Edgar held the gate firm to prevent the squeak of the hinges, and walked her to the porch rail.

"Next time," he whispered, "next time we'll go all the way across!" He bent his head quickly and touched her lips with his, whispered, "night!" and ran across the road to disappear into the shadows of his own front porch.

El couldn't decide if he had really kissed her or just thought about it, it was so quick. With a tiny, happy smile she climbed to the porch roof, and through her window. Wouldn't be any harm, teaching Edgar how to kiss, couldn't be anything wrong with that now that she knew all about babies and everything. Next time, she said to herself as she curled up beside the sleeping Bun, next time, Edgar Mitchell, just wait. You just wait and see!

Mother was in the middle of her usual Monday wash when the railroad phone rang. She dried her hands carefully, wiped the soapy water from her arms with her blue-checked apron, and answered it with a look of apprehension and dread: the telephone was always bad news.

"Faith? Hello, Faith? You there, Faith?"

"I'm here, Bud, what is it? What's wrong?"

"Nothing's wrong, now listen! The troop train is coming through in about an hour! They're about to pull out from here. Now you get the kids and the women and get up by the track, wave at those boys!"

"Where are you? Will you be along?"

"I'm stuck behind the train, but we'll follow it, got to get up to Clark's Gap, I thought you might want to be there when they go through and those boys need cheerin' on!" Then Daddy spoke to the dispatcher. "Okay, John, breakers closed and we're ready to roll."

Mother hung up, a worried frown on her face, the corners of her mouth turned down, and her apron in a tight twist. "No trouble," she said to the girls collected by her side. "Daddy wants us to see the troop train go by. El, you round up all the kids, Jane, go over and tell Mrs. Gillespie and Mrs. Belcher, Bun and I will get the Collins' and Hollie as we go by. Hurry up, now, run!"

They gathered on the town side of the tracks, in the wide space at the south end of the bridge. All of the children in the camp and most of the women stood anxiously waiting. Mother stood quietly, listening as Mrs. Gillespie talked: Ben went down to Mullins to talk to the recruiters but he hasn't made up his mind yet, he's not really in the Navy, he might join the Army, might be on this train, but he's still thinking about it. Bun watched her in bewilderment, finally turning to El. "She don't know Ben's gone?" Before El could answer, Mother said, "shush now, you two go on and play, train's coming, train's coming real soon now." And Bun lost interest in Mrs. Gillespie.

The train wouldn't stop on the steep slope, but the grade was so sharp it was slowed to a crawl. There were four coaches, each filled with young men, eighteen or nineteen years old, looking fourteen at the most. They were clean-shaven and their hair was greased down with Vitalis; their shirts were boiled as white as their mothers could get them. They had grins plastered on their faces, grins as stiff as the starched shirts, and they stuck their arms out of the narrow windows of the train and waved at the children gathered by the track, leaning down to shout, "We'll be back! We'll be back soon as we clean out those S.O.B.'s!"

The kids screamed and cheered, the women waved, silent, tears running down the creases in their faces like spring rains down the Guyandotte. As the train ground past, Mrs. Gillespie dropped to the ballast, sitting in the cinders and dirt, rocking and keening like they were already dead. Mother knelt beside her, this mother of two boys already gone, and held the gray-brown head against her large bosom, there-there-ing and patting. The last of the train rattled across the bridge, drowning her sobs. The heat and the smell of sulfur swam around them; oil blotches lay on the sleepers, iridescent circles making small rainbows of color on the gray crossties, and dragonflies hovered over pollen-thick ragweed heads like small airplanes over crowded cities.

Mother always told them, "Never cry unless there's really something to cry about," while Daddy said, "Never cry unless you can't help it—and there's damn few times when a body can't help it!"

The troop trains were a crying time, a time when El truly couldn't help it, but she was not alone. There were no dry eyes as the group trudged back down the steep trail to the camp.

Daddy got home late, having run into trouble at Clark's Gap, and supper was silent and grim. Mother and Jane were cried out, and when El tried to tell him about the troop train, Mother hushed her quickly. As the meal ended, Mother sent her and Bun to bathe for bed.

"But it's not even dark!" protested El.

"Never mind," said Mother," you can read in bed for a while."

El knew Mother wanted them out of the room so she could talk to Daddy, she just didn't know what Mother wanted to talk about.

She ran cool water in the big claw-footed iron tub, gave Bun a lard bucket full of toys, a tin shovel, clothespins for dolls, and quietly sat on the top step to listen. She could hear Jane rattling dishes as she cleared the table, but Mother's voice carried up the staircase as she talked to Daddy, still seated at the dinner table.

"They were drinking, Bud," she said.

"So?"

"I don't think the girls should see them like that."

"It helps the boys, to have the women and children wave when they go by, Faith. What's a little drink or two at a time like that?"

"They should be praying, not drinking, and I don't think the girls should see them drunk."

"Jane," Daddy called, "do you understand why the boys were drinking?"

"Yes, Daddy I understand it," replied Jane, and the sounds from the dishes ceased. "But I agree with Mother, they should be praying, not drinking."

"You would," muttered Daddy, rattling his paper.

"I don't think they should be exposed to that kind of thing needlessly," insisted Mother.

"Faith, Jane is old enough to understand; Ellie and Bun are too young to know what's going on. I want you to get the word out when I call, and I want all of you to be there when those trains come through. The boys need it. That's all there is to it."

When Daddy spoke like that, that was the final word. The pattern was established: Daddy called on the phone, Ellie ran through the camp calling, "Troop Train comin', Troop Train comin,'" and the women and children gathered by the track, believing it their duty to do so, and believing, too, that it would help to bring them home again: they never missed a train coming through."

Green-leaf shade lay over the yard, but in the black-dust road heat waves vibrated upward with a furnace-like blast, and the cinders burned even the toughest feet. The giant willow by the back gate stood still in the breezeless air; horse flies buzzed heavily around Old Bess's water tub and bumble bees drifted timelessly from hollyhock to dahlia, lifting and disappearing in the white sun-sky to some secret hive buried deep on the mountainside, returning again and again. Under the lilac bush El lay undisturbed. Having done her share of the morning's ironing, she was free to travel to the romantic South with beautiful Scarlett and dashing Rhett, a participant to the struggles and pain of an earlier war, unmindful of the new developments in the present one.

The Russian Army had fallen back to form a new front, stubbornly resisting the attacks from Minsk to the Artic coast.

Closer to home, the Southern coal miners would start their projected holiday on Thursday. William Blizzard, UMW vice-president of District 17, said that the mines would stay closed after July 7th if there was no contract. Twelve of the operator's associations are reported to agree on a contract, but the Harlan County field had yet to concur: John L. Lewis still insists that all sign as a group. Southern operators do not recognize the proposed vacation, included in the Northern contract, because an agreement has not been signed. Lewis has taken the stand that no Southern miner will work after the seventh, unless there is a permanent agreement, an agreement along the lines suggested by the National Defense Mediation Board.

The second draft registration became effective, requiring all youths age twenty-one to sign. The Wyoming County unit of the American Red Cross completed one hundred and fifty garments for shipping to the British Isles, and Mother's group had contributed a good portion of that number. And F.D.R. signed the largest bill ever enacted, $10,384,821,624.00. Of that amount, nearly three billion dollars went for twelve thousand aircraft and the equipment needed for them.

Mother came to the lilac bush at suppertime, for El hadn't heard her calling.

"Mama," she said, speaking as she thought Scarlett would, "I'd just love to go to Georgia!"

"I am your Mother, Rachel, not your Mama, and right now you may go to the bathroom and wash your face and hands for supper!"

"Oh, Mother, this is the grandest book! You've got to read it!"

"I did read it, Ellie, when Mr. Collins first gave it to you. How many times have you read it now?"

"Only three or four times, but it gets better every time"

As Mother sat down at the table, she said, "I worry about that girl, she spends too much time reading grown-up books,"

"She's all right," Daddy said mildly.

"But she's growing up, Bud, and I don't want her head filled with a lot of foolish, romantic ideas too young."

"She's still a kid," said Daddy.

"She's started her monthly."

El, about to enter the kitchen, stopped short. Anger and embarrassment struggled for control. Mother had told Daddy about her periods! How could she! She'd never be able to look her Daddy in the face again!

"She spends too much time playing with boys, those Mitchell boys in particular," said Mother. Daddy didn't respond.

"She should play with girls," Mother commented, almost to herself.

"When, did you say?"

"This past month."

"Best keep an eye on her," advised Daddy, "know where she is."

"I always know where she is!" said Mother in a huff.

"Humph!" said Daddy sarcastically, "where is she now?" and Mother called out, "Ellie! Get down here this instant! You are keeping us waiting!" El made a quick entry, slipped into her seat at the table, unable to look at her father. For the first time in her life she was uncomfortable in his presence.

On the evening news, Russia was admitting that the Germans had made gains, and they were asking that the United States rush supplies. As the news ended, thunder rolled across the hills and lightning made the radio crackle; it was turned off immediately for fear a tube would blow out. The lights went off and Mother lit the kerosene lamp, kept for such emergencies. The meal continued by lamp-light until the telephone rang. Lightning had hit a transformer below Tralee. Daddy dressed quickly, laced up his boots, took his slicker and left for work.

The storm broke, filling the stream, making a muddy river of the road, breaking the tall hollyhocks and dahlias to the ground. From her observation post at the dining room window, El watched the sheets of cold rain beat down the flowers and wondered: where do bumble bees go in a storm?

By the third of July Stalin declared:

In spite of the heroic resistance of our army, and in spite of the destruction of the enemy's best forces, he has continued to push forward: ...nevertheless, Hitler's army will be beaten like those of Napoleon and Wilhelm.

One hundred thousand miners in the State of West Virginia started their first vacation, but eighty-two thousand had orders not to return—unless their contract was signed. The operators contended that the agreement written in May did not provide for a vacation, only for a dollar a day increase in pay.

The Japanese, at long last, decided on their future course: they would keep their activity in the German-Russian war a secret, until their action alone disclosed it!

The heat wave was responsible for four deaths, but the storm lowered the temperature by twenty degrees, and on the 3rd, the news reporters were predicting the largest traffic jam in the history of the world for the fourth of July. Thirty million automobiles were predicted to be on the nation's roads over the three-day holiday, and at least thirty thousand of them would be miners, Daddy said, with their pockets full, their tanks full, and never a thought for tomorrow! The nation prepared to celebrate the one-hundred-sixty-fourth anniversary of the signing of the Declaration of Independence.

"Please, Daddy, let's go to Lake Shawnee!"

"Nope."

"Let's go to Barker's Creek, cool off!"

"Dang nigh a cold spell today—whata you mean, cool off?"

"What about the movies?"

"On a Wednesday?"

"What about the parade, down in Mullins?"

"Seen one parade, seen 'em all."

"Oh, shoot!"

"Make your own parade!"

"What did you say?"

"I said, make your own parade, Ellie, but after the President's speech, not before. I want absolute quiet while he's talking, and I don't mean maybe!"

This was to be the first mass celebration of the nation's birthday, arranged by the Office of Civilian Defense. In London, the American flag flew beside the Union Jack. The Crown Princess Martha of Norway and her children, having fled their country when the Nazis overran it, sat beside Mrs. Eleanor Roosevelt for the ceremony. The Marine band played, and all over America and the world, people stood beside their radios, stood at attention with their hand over their hearts as Chief Justice Harlan Stone led the pledge:

I pledge allegiance to the flag of the United
States of America, and to the Republic for which
It stands, one nation, indivisible, with Liberty
And Justice for all.

President Franklin Roosevelt then told the people that the United States could not survive *as a happy and fertile oasis of liberty surrounded by a cruel dictatorship.*

After the President spoke, El brought her gang together and distributed pots and pans, spoons, horns and hastily made paper hats, organizing the first Coville Fourth of July parade. They marched from one end of the camp to the other, following their first official float, Edgar leading Old Bess as she pulled a wagon with Bun, wrapped in a white sheet, and holding aloft a flashlight wrapped in red cellophane, Coville's own Statute of Liberty. Edgar persuaded Old Bess to do his bidding with the aid of a branch from a quaking aspen, and when that failed, a bucket of feed stolen from the back porch.

The parade wound through town, the participants tootin' and bangin' until everyone came out to laugh and maybe cheer, and it ended at the Phillips' front porch where El, as Chief Mischief and Prime Organizer, delivered the address, an editorial, cut out of *The Bluefield Daily Telegraph* by Mother:

The Spirit of '41 is all around us. You can find it in the Army, in the Navy,
and in the offices, factories, stores and farms of the country. There is no
fanfare…no conscious conceit that we are making history. There's simply a
job to be done …and it's being done…with the traditional American energy
and speed. The Spirit of '41 is the Spirit of America and it's getting things
done!

"Aw, come on, Ellie! Enough speech making, let's eat!"

Daddy appeared on cue, carrying a long green watermelon, spread newspapers on the front porch steps and cut half-moon slices for everyone, himself and Mother included.

After dark, when the hot sun had dropped behind the ever-green hills, Daddy stuck three railroad flares in the top fence rail and set them off. They burned for several minutes, giving off sparks of red, yellow and blue-green, a substitute fireworks since fireworks had been prohibited to conserve powder for the defense program. It was a fittin' ending to a fine, fine day.

As Bun and Ellie lay in bed watching the faint twinkle of stars high above the black iron bridge, they expressed satisfaction at the day's activities. Bun had liked being the "Statute of 'ibety" and El had loved giving the speech. They could hear the creaking of the swing, down on the front porch, gently lulling them to sleep. They felt happy and secure, knowing that Mother and Daddy were sitting quietly together on the porch: all was well with their world.

Fourteen

JAPS MAY BLOCK U. S. AID ROUTE

Tokyo—Japan is considering an extension of the limits of her territorial waters which would cut off Russia's Pacific port of Vladivostok, and hamper U.S. shipments to USSR. Newspaper Hoche: If the U.S. sends arms and munitions to the Soviets by virtue of the all-out aid lease-lend law, they must pass through Japanese waters to Vladivostok. This means Germany must apply tripartite tactics. The war would thus be extended to Japanese waters.

Dog days set in with more rain, which pleased the farmers, as folk lore had it that the forty days would be dictated by the weather conditions on the first day. Why forty days, Mother? I'm not sure, Ellie, maybe from the forty days of Lent. No, from the forty days Moses spent in the wilderness. Where did you get that, Bud? I don't know, where do you get your answers? Didn't Jesus stay in the wilderness forty days too? What's that got to do with Dog Days? Just wondering. Anyway, you stay away from the creek, Ellie, 'cause snakes are meaner than ever, their eyes turn milky and they can't see good and they will strike at anything! And look before you walk under trees, they get up in trees too.

So El and Edgar hunted snakes in the creek and the woods, and followed Old Bess over the hills for miles after somebody said snakes followed cow paths. How could you tell if their eyes turned milky if you couldn't find one? Then Daddy said all the snakes were down under the flat gray rocks, not enjoying being fried any more than anybody else.

The southern miners remained on holiday, sitting at home in flat gray houses most of the time, no money to go anywhere on a real trip, just going down to Mullins or over the mountain to Lake Shawnee once to prove they were on vacation, but across the nation three hundred and ninety people died and two hundred of these were the results of automobile accidents.

Rumor had it that a contract was in the last stages, nearly ready for signatures, but few believed it. They stayed at home, drinking moonshine until their eyes turned milky, laying still, in the dark houses, in the cool.

The war crept closer as it was learned that the head coach at Mullins High School, the man named "Coach of the Year" in southern West Virginia, was drafted. Mullins had been conference champions for the first time in history, and now their coach was leaving to fight, and nobody doubted he would be fighting soon, 'fore Christmas, the guess was, 'fore football season ends again. The German and Italian consular officials had been ordered out of the country and had been given passage aboard the liner *America*, now renamed the *West Point*.

By the eighth, the U.S. Navy had landed in Iceland and were positioned to forestall any attempt at seizure by the Germans. The President directed the fleet to maintain an area of security to keep hostile ships away.

Also, on the eighth, finally, the Union and the Southern operators reached a two-year agreement, retroactive to the first of April. The strike was over! Now the miners had money, but vacation was also over. Back pay, plus twenty dollars vacation pay—a fortune to most of them, nearly forty-five dollars per man!

"What's your Pa going to do with all that money?" Asked El.

"Don't know, he ain't said."

"Think you will get a bike?"

"Nah, not before Christmas."

"Wish my Daddy got a bonus! I'd sure ask for a bike for my birthday."

"When's your birthday?"

"Two weeks."

"Whatcha going to get?"

"Don't know, not much, probably a book."

Edgar looked thoughtful. "I'll figure out a surprise," he said shyly, looking beneath his long lashes, "I'll think of something."

They lay side by side in the shade of the house, flat on the thick cool grass, picking out sour-grass to eat, and four-leaf clovers to wish upon. Mary Beth opened the gate and, failing to see them, knocked on the front screen door. Jane answered.

Edgar and El ducked their heads below the porch as Jane and Mary Beth sat down in the swing. "Here, read it," Mary Beth said. There was silence. El couldn't bear the suspense; she raised her head and peered over the porch railing. Jane was reading a letter but El was too far away to see the words.

"Well! This is a surprise!" exclaimed Jane.

"Isn't it wonderful? I've been praying and praying, for something, I didn't know what, exactly but—"

"Mary Beth! You mean you're going to do it?"

"Of course I'm going to do it! Why not?"

"You mean you'd marry Ben, knowing you love Will?"

"That's just it, Jane, I don't love Will, not after the way he's treated me, and after all those things he said, and I'd get a check, not much, but some, and I could give my baby a name—Oh, Jane, I'm so happy I could cry!"

"He'll be home on the eighth, that's just one month from today!"

"And I've got so much to do! Will you help me? I want my wedding to be nice, and Ma's no help, she just said, go cross to Kentucky, but—"

"Indeed you'll not! Come on, let's talk to Mother!"

El couldn't restrain herself; if wedding plans were going to be made, she wanted to be in on it. She climbed over the porch railing with a "see ya" to Edgar and followed the older girls into the house. Mother, Jane and Mary Beth were seated around the dining room table, and El slipped into her usual seat without being noticed. Mary Beth had tears on her cheeks and her eyes were sparkle-bright; she was prettier than she had ever been. Mary Beth had taken to wearing her brother's shirts over her shorts and the bulge in her waistline didn't show. Still, by August she would be looking less than virginal and she couldn't be married in the church.

"We'll have it here," cried Mother. "You can come down the stairs, and we'll put flowers everywhere, maybe stand over in front of the windows, Jane, you'd better start practicing the wedding march—"

El jumped up from the table, and pretending she was holding a bouquet, she marched around the table, "Ta-da, ta-da, tada!"

"Oh, Ellie! You could be my Maid of Honor but you're too young!"

"Who will be?" asked Mother.

"Why, Jane, of course, she's my best friend!"

"But I'll have to play—"

"No, you won't! We can ask Thelma Plover to play and Jane can be your Maid of Honor."

"Ted can do the ceremony, can't he" said Jane.

"I'll need a new dress," Mary Beth said thoughtfully. "I don't have anything that fits."

"We'll make you a new dress, honey, a long one, you leave that up to me. And if Ted can't do the ceremony, we'll ask preacher Copeland."

"And me!" said Bun, standing sleepily beside Mother. She had been awakened by all the commotion.

"Preacher Copeland can marry you, Bun?" joked El.

"Have a new dress," said Bun," I can have a new dress too."

"You can be flower girl," Mother said, picking her up and sitting her on her lap. "And you'll have a new dress, too."

"We'll make a big cake, and punch, and ask everyone—"

"Ellie, you can pour punch, and Hollie can cut the cake, and—"

"What about Judith? After all, she's the groom's sister, 'Bridesmaid,'" said Mary Beth, quickly, "She needs to be included."

"Coville's first wedding!" exclaimed Mother.

"The very first one?" asked Jane. "To the best of my knowledge," said Mother, "Everyone goes to the justice of the peace in Mullins or the church in Herndon, or across the border into Kentucky—"

"That's what Mother wanted me to do," said Mary Beth.

"Don't you worry, honey; you don't have to do that. I'll make you a nice dress, maybe a creamy satin, not white, but almost, and Jane can wear blue, no, mint green for Jane, I think, and Judith pink, El, blue, Hollie yellow…"

"No! not yellow for Hollie!" El interrupted loudly. "Hollie doesn't look good in yellow—"

"Why, of course she does, Ellie! It's one of her best colors, makes her hair look like spun gold, what are you thinking about!" El couldn't explain her feelings. She just didn't want Hollie to wear a yellow dress—not now, not ever! "She could wear blue, like me, we'll be standing side by side, with the cake and punch—"

Mother interrupted, "We can let Hollie decide, give her a say-so."

Supper was almost late, so busy were they in plans. Mary Beth went home, already smiling, like a bride-to-be should. Her baby would have a name.

At the supper table they filled Daddy in on the news. "Don't know how Mildred will take all of this. She hasn't been out of the house since the troop train went by," Mother said.

"Mildred will come through all right," Daddy said "after all she went through as a girl, she'll do all right."

"What did she go through, Daddy?" asked El, not missing the hint that there was more to Mrs. Gillespie than she knew.

"Never you mind, Rachel," Mother said with a quick look at Daddy, "just eat your supper before it gets cold."

July tenth, warm, bright, muggy. Knox was hinting that FDR had given the Navy orders to shoot. FDR was outspoken in his requests for more defense money, more lend-lease funds. Churchill came on the air and predicted that the two countries would join forces in Iceland.

We still propose to retain our army in Iceland, and, as British and the United States forces will have the same objective in view, namely the defense of Iceland, it seems very likely that they will cooperate effectively in resistance to any attempt by Hitler to gain a footing...

Mother had turned her gardening work over to Mr. Reeves. The old man had agreed to do the hoeing for a share of the crop. They seemed an unlikely alliance at first glance, Mother so large and domineering with slightly better than average resources, and Mr. Reeves, so small, used-up appearing and shabby, but they got along admirably. The heat seemed to make Mother ill; she walked up the road early in the mornings, as soon as Daddy left for work, and gave Mr. Reeves his instructions for the day. Later, in the cool of the evenings, she took El with her and gathered whatever was needed for the dinner table, always leaving plenty for Mr. Reeves. Their take was fairly fifty-fifty. Except for the corn. There they differed, and there Mr. Reeves held his ground.

"We'll never use all that!" argued Mother," not if I can a hundred jars!"

"Now, I'll take care of it," Mr. Reeves replied, over and over. "You 'uns eat what you want, can what you will, and leave the rest to me!"

And Mother did. When she had him pull the bean vines, he planted corn. When the cucumbers gave out, he planted corn. When the peas and greens and cabbage were harvested, he planted corn. By the 10th of July nearly all of the garden, except for the tomato patch, was in corn, in one stage or another, and some of it was nearly ready for roasting. The tassels had formed, golden and waving head-high in the summer breeze, the foliage heavy and green, the small torpedo-shaped ears were nearly ready to launch into a kettle-full of boiling water.

About seven a.m., just as Mother was putting on her straw hat, Mr. Reeves appeared at the back door.

"Miz Phillips "he said, when Mother opened the door, "seems we have a bit of a problem."

"Come in, Mr. Reeves, care for some coffee?" She started for the enameled pot sitting on the back of the stove. "What seems to be the trouble?"

"Beg your pardon, Miz Phillips, but there's no time for coffee." He scratched his bald head where his cap had been. "It's like this. Your cow is ruinin' my corn, and my corn could be the runin' of yore cow!"

Mother put on her straw hat and she and the old man went out the back door. El and Bun followed, dripping honey from their biscuits, walking on the grass along the side of the road, the cindered road already too hot to walk on. Edgar and Joe tagged along, and by the time they reached the old house and the garden surrounding it, BillynBob had joined them. Mr. and Mrs. Belcher came out on their porch to see what was going on, and Hollie was on her way up the road to see also.

The yard around the house was enclosed with a strong, high fence, except for the stile at the back. The steps of the stile were built of railroad crossties and were steep, even for humans, impossible for animals. There, in the middle of the corn patch, stood Bess, slowly and methodically chewing her way up one row and down the next.

"Hi!" Shouted Mr. Reeves, "Hi there, you daughter of a swoggle-eyed bamboozler! Out of there!"

Bess turned her head and gazed at him, green corn blades protruding from her mouth, inching upward as she chewed. Mother walked around the yard, to the back stile, and in a conversational tone, the same tone she used to talk to Mr. Reeves, she spoke to the cow.

"Come on, Bess, come on old girl, come on out of there."

Bess turned toward Mother, slowly drew the corn blades inside her mouth and out of sight. Slowly, just as she always did, she started toward Mother, put one front foot on the stile, then one back foot, and, humping her back like a buffalo, the other two feet, walked right up that stile and down the other side, just as easy as any man—or woman.

"Well, I'll be a damned horn-swoggled son of a cross-eyed horse thief!" said Mr. Reeves, slapping his cap on his thigh. Mother took Bess by her collar and led her around the house and down the road. As she passed Mr. Reeves, she said, "Might be a good idea to enclose your corn a little more securely, and I'll thank you to watch your language in front of my girls, Mr. Reeves."

Mr. Reeves stammered and stuttered. The kids laughed. He turned on them, slapping his cap against his leg, flapping his arms like chasing chickens. "Hi! Git outa hyer, you young whipper-snappers. Git outa my sight!"

That day he built a fence across the top of the stile, not leaving room for him or anybody else to get by. Now, the only way to get into the garden was to climb the fence. As the corn ripened, the silks turning brown then drying to black, the kernels filling with sweet milk, Mr. Reeves would come with his five-gallon lard bucket, throw it over the fence, climb over after it, fill it, drop it back over the fence and pick it up again. When the boys saw him coming, they would laugh and holler, poking fun at his baggy pants and at his shirt buttoned up to his neck, even in hot weather. His cap was always on slightly sideways, covering his slick-bald head that was not much larger than a child's. "You kids! I'll git you one of these days, I'll git you!"

On Friday night, a little after six, the hall phone rang. It was Aunt Maude, crying like her heart would break: Zane Gray, her only boy, had enlisted in the Navy. Gone. Didn't so much as talk it over with her, just went into Galax, signed up with the recruiter, brought his truck home, parked it and left with a buddy to get drunk. He would ship out to a training camp in the morning.

Daddy hung up the phone slowly, like hanging up the boy for good. He'll be all right, Daddy had told Aunt Maude, don't worry, he's from good stock, he's smart, he'll be all right, remember, his daddy fought in the World War, can't blame him, it's natural he'd want to go, he'll be all right. Daddy stood by the phone for a long time before coming back to the supper table.

Fifteen minutes later Will Gillespie walked in the front door, brown, strong, slim in blue bell-bottomed trousers and white tee-shirt with his cigarettes rolled in the sleeve. He picked Jane up, swung her around and hugged her, shook hands with Daddy, hugged Mother, Ellie and Bun.

"God! It's good to see all of you!" He accepted a seat at the table. "Heard the news? I'm shipping out when I go back, I'll be on the high blue seas!"

"Where are you going, Will? Which ship, Will?"

"Don't know, exactly, they're keeping it a deep dark secret, but there's rumors it will be the Pacific Ocean. Golden beaches, moonlight, girls, Hey-hey-hey!"

"Goin' to be home long?"

"Three days, just three days. Longer next time. It's a great life, the Navy, but man, do I miss home cooking!" He grinned his same old catchy smile and dug into the banana-coconut layer cake Mother set before him. "Got a promotion, more money. I'll get to finish college if things settle down. Great life!"

After Will left, with Jane walking him to the gate, El asked, "Do you think he knows Ben and Mary Beth are getting married?"

"I'm sure he knows, honey."

"He didn't say anything about it."

"No, and I'm glad you didn't bring it up, either"

"Would you just stay out of it, El? What our neighbors do is none of our business."

"I just wondered, that's all", Why did Daddy have to scold her? She hadn't done anything!

"Well, stop your wondering and get these dishes off the table!"

Honestly! She'd never seen Daddy so cross. Then she remembered. Zane Gray was Daddy's nephew and he was going off to the Navy. Secretly, she was glad! She had been dreading the next trip to Virginia. Now she'd not even see Zane Gray. Oh, maybe years from now, when she was grown up and an airplane pilot She'd have a blue uniform, silver wings on her cap, and her hair would be perfect and she'd wear bright red lipstick, she's toss her hair back, look down her nose at Zane Gray: "Well, you dear boy, I hear you've been in the navy!"

"Rachel! I said get these dishes off the table!"

"Yes, Daddy, right now!"

And on the radio, the announcer was saying, British plans to blast Berlin with planes received from the United States, the worst air raids on London will seem like child's play in comparison. The air base has been established on Iceland, more money has been appropriated for defense, and the miners buried in an Alabama mine explosion have been dug out: all ten were dead.

She took the scraps out to Old Bess's tub and sat on the back steps. The moon was yet below the horizon but it would be full and already was giving some light. Somewhere on the mountain the whip-poor-will began his nightly song, Ship poor Will, ship poor Ben, and now, ship poor Zane. All in the Navy. She didn't know a single soldier, unless Emmett had joined the Army, which she doubted. Still, he'd been gone over three weeks now, past his usual time, she wondered where he was, what he was doing. Hollie didn't say much about him anymore, and now, with the mines working again, she would go back to the company store, helping Mr. Gillespie.

She sat quietly in the shadows on the back steps. Across the road a match flared up and she could see Mr. Mitchell sitting alone on his front porch. Poor Mr. Mitchell. He was always alone. In the Collins' front room, she could see the outline of Mr. Collins' head, bent over a book; he might as well be living alone, the way Sarah Jo went off to bed without him. No, she'd leave Mr. Collins off her 'poor' list, but add Mr. Mitchell. Why hadn't he found another wife? Then for the first time it occurred to her—maybe Edgar and Joe's mother was still living! Mr. Mitchell couldn't remarry if he was still married! She vowed to make Edgar tell her more about his mother—soon. Real soon. Maybe the next time they went up on the bridge.

Senator Wheeler says he sees the United States' patrol of the seas extended; says he wouldn't be surprised if the U.S. Navy undertakes to patrol the sea lanes all the way across the Atlantic! And Daddy says, By God, if that is what it takes!

The railroad officials and the union agree to begin negotiations within two weeks on wage increases. The railroaders are asking for thirty to thirty-four cents increase.

"Why are the miners asking for a dollar and the railroad only asking 30 cents" asked El.

"Because, railroaders have more cents," said Daddy with a wink at Mother, enjoying his play on words." It's true" he continued. "We ain't about to kill the fatted duck or the golden calf, or whatever."

"Aren't you mixing your metaphors or something?" asked Jane.

"Or something," agreed Daddy. "We won't piss around…"

"Bud!"

"Sorry, girls, guess I thought I was talking to the boys!"

"You should be ashamed!" And Mother's mouth stayed in a straight line all through the news. The Germans claimed they had broken through the

Russian lines, but Stalin was saying their lines are intact. Don't know who to believe.

Mary Beth and Will stood out in the road and talked for over an hour; El could see them from the living room window, but she couldn't hear what they were saying. Mary Beth walked slowly away, and Will came to her front door. He was leaving early in the morning and he came to say goodbye.

"Are you glad Mary Beth and Ben are getting married?" she asked as soon as Will was seated.

"Rachel!" Mother said quickly.

"That's okay," Will answered, "I don't mind her asking. Yes, Ellie, I'm glad. Just wish I could find a nice girl of my own." He was looking straight at Jane when he said it.

Jane chose to ignore him, saying, "Wish you could get to know our new preacher, Will. He's in college, too. I think you would like him."

Will looked less and less happy as Jane continued to talk about Ted, and after a few minutes he got up to leave.

"When will you be back, son?" asked Daddy.

"I'm not sure, Sir, probably after Christmas, depends on where we are."

"Well, let us hear from you—Jane, you got his address?"

Jane looked furious, her face turning redder and redder. She answered Daddy shortly. "Yes. Yes, I do, Father."

Father? Jane was mad! She walked Will to the door but returned quickly. "I want you to know, Daddy, I'm not one bit interested in Will Gillespie! Not one bit!" and she ran up the stairs to her room and slammed the door so hard it reverberated through the house.

Daddy laughed and looked at Mother, who, for some reason, refused to laugh or to look at Daddy. Was she mad too? El retreated to the book she was reading before dinner—it was too much for her.

Early the next morning, even before they left for Sunday school, Mr. Gillespie left with Will, driving him to Princeton to catch his bus. Mildred stayed home, didn't even go to church.

With a two-year agreement signed, three thousand miners went back to work on Tuesday morning. Both Churchill and Stalin declared they had inflicted heavy losses against the Germans. Churchill spoke out clearly. "It is time the Germans should be made to suffer in their own homeland...we believe it to be in our power to keep this process going on a steadily rising tide, month after month, year after year, until the Nazi regime is either expatriated by us or, better still, torn to pieces by the German people themselves...Will the bombing attacks of last autumn and winter come back again?...If the storm is to renew itself, London will be ready, London will not wince, London can take it again."

Over the radio, behind the Prime Minister's words, the roar of bombers sounded on a dozen airstrips as a new air offensive left Britain for targets widely scattered over the interior of Germany.

But the newspaper headlines in southern West Virginia concerned Lindbergh:

LINDBERGH NAZI PROPAGANDIST, ICKES DECLARES

Interior Sect. Calls for Hitler's Defeat At All Costs
Internal Dissension Strategy of Fuehrer
New York, July 14(AP) Secretary of Interior Harold L. Ickes asserted tonight that Charles A. Lindbergh's passionate words are to encourage Hitler and to break down the will of his own fellow citizens to resist Hitler and Nazism.

The Secretary continued making remarks against Lindbergh throughout his speech, saying he "didn't have his cue, he didn't want to say the wrong thing, referring to him as 'the Knight of the German Eagle.' "No one has ever heard Lindbergh utter a word of horror at, or even aversion to, the bloody career that the Nazis are following, or a word of pity for the innocent men, women and children deliberately murdered by the Nazis."

"Aw, Hell!" exclaimed Daddy.

"Bud!"

"Well, it makes me sick! What do they want Lindbergh to do, go around moaning and groaning, wiping his nose on his sleeve, crying over every damn battle? The man knows what's going on, he doesn't want our men, women, and children going through the same damn thing! Don't mean he has to act like a damn cry baby over everything, not in public anyway!"

"Why, Bud! I do believe you are taking up for Lindy!"

"No, I'm not defending him. It's just that the Secretary could have made just as good a speech without shootin' down Lindbergh, could have said just as much."

"Then you think Lindbergh is right, Daddy?" asked El fearfully.

"No, I don't! He ain't right! But he does have the right to say whatever he pleases, and so does Ickes, only they can do it without name-calling. Now listen to this, this is a right good point." And Daddy read from his paper:

"Now is the moment," said the Secretary, " for the U.S. to take full advantage of time borrowed from the British and time unexpectedly given by the invasion of Russia, to increase our defenses and aid Britain because such a gift of precious time is not likely to come again." Daddy laid his paper down, stretched out his legs. "How about a little more coffee, Ellie?"

As El jumped to get the coffee, he continued his remarks. "Now Lindbergh has a lot to say, and he's off track, but they're carrying it too far, to say he's bossed by Hitler. A man like Lindbergh don't have no reason to listen to Hitler, he thinks for himself, reasons it out the way he sees it, and tells it like it is—or like he thinks it is!"

Mother was beaming, happier than she had been all day. Daddy was defending her hero instead of tearing him down. Made El happy, too.

But in other parts of the world, the Japanese had closed the Port of Kobe, and officials believed it to be a prelude to a new movement, possibly against the French Indo-China. No foreigners were to be admitted for ten days, and word had it that a large number of reserves had been called into the Japanese army. The Port of Kobe is a choice site for embarkation of Japanese troops to the south. On the seventeenth, the members of the Japanese cabinet resigned and reports stated that the Army and Navy would dominate the new government. These bits of information were overshadowed by the more serious news from the Russian front as the Germans advanced and heavy battles continued.

In the coal fields, operators and miners began talks on the details of the district contracts to cover such items as hospitalization, house rent, and safety committees. Mine fatalities had decreased rapidly with the wearing of hard hats, and hard-toed shoes, and by keeping mine fire bosses.

In Britain, the mysterious Mr. Reginald Britton—a pseudonym used by a BBC announcer—turned a "Victory" stunt into a battle of the air lanes. In a pep talk aimed at German-occupied countries, he suggested the letter, V as a code, a secret signal symbolizing victory. The BBC started playing Beethoven's Fifth (V) Symphony, in which the first notes are three shorts and a long—dot,dot,dot,dash da,da,da,dash, the same as the Morse Code for the letter V, and the German underground began painting the letter V on doors and walls in the dark of night, slipping behind the Nazi soldiers, tapping it out on table tops in cafes. Clocks were mysteriously stopped at 11:05, the shape of a V. Blenheim bombers began flying in a V formation as the British Air Ministry got into the act.

King George and Queen Elizabeth toured factories on official visits and found V's painted on the walls. The German army grew angrier by the day, and replied that the V's stood for the German word, "Viktoria", but the Germans commonly used the word, "sleg" for victory. All the uproar over the symbol proved that the German people listened to BBC, thus the BBC stepped up its broadcasts aimed for the oppressed people.

Also, on the seventeenth, Lindy wrote again to Franklin Roosevelt, continuing to maintain that he had no connection to any foreign government, and he had a right to an apology from Secretary Ikes.

"Mr. President," Lindbergh wrote, "I will willingly open my files to your investigation. I will willingly appear in person to any committee you appoint, and there is no question regarding my activities now or at any time in the past, that I will not be glad to answer."

And the German and Italian Ambassadors head out to sea among a half-thousand other aliens, placed aboard the West Point, sailing toward their worn-torn countries, leaving the land-o-plenty for homelands with shortages and restrictions and regulations on everything.

By the nineteenth the Germans were claiming capture of a Red Division headquarters, destruction of more than two hundred tanks and extensive gains in territory. The United States declared its intention of keeping the sea lanes to Iceland open, and the Islandic parliament in an all-night session approved the occupation of its land.

The Japanese declared their new government was freed from any political ties, and they set about establishing a new foreign policy—but that policy would remain secret for the time being.

On the twentieth, Prime Minister Churchill picked up with interest the sign for Victory being broadcast and painted on everything. He declared a "V for Victory" day and urged the people to go out and under cover of darkness, smear V's on everything, all over Europe, the day set as a special day for an "invisible army of millions" to protest and launch a "fear offensive". Colonel Britton read Churchill's message to millions of BBC listeners: "The V sign is the symbol of the unconquerable will of the occupied territories and a portent of the fate awaiting the Nazi tranny."

The group directing Colonel Britton's campaign firmly believed that his message was heard from the grasslands of Norway to the grottos of Prague.

"Happy birthday to you, happy birthday to you!"

El had wanted to have a party, but Mother pleaded the heat and not feeling up to it; she settled for ice cream and cake, served on the front porch to a few of her favorite people, the time set at two o'clock, after dinner and before supper, as Daddy had said, so we don't have to feed everyone. Edgar, Joe, Hollie, and the family, but Mother said, wouldn't be polite to ask the boys and not include Mr. Mitchell, and what about Judith, and El said, yeah, of course Judith, but Nancy Sue is my best friend, so that includes the Plovers, but no, El said, that's too many with Mother not feeling good. She couldn't explain that she didn't really want Nancy Sue either, not feeling comfortable with her since their last conversation about babies and all. She had avoided talking to her since she started her monthlys. In her heart she believed she had started her periods early as a direct result of touching herself for pleasure, sure that if she did that again she would start her period again. This was her own private conclusion; she'd never dare talk to anyone about it. She remembered the pain and fear with dread; best thing to do was never, never touch her "private parts" again except with a washcloth or towel, and to never, never tell anyone about it. The sweet sensations were buried deep in her mind, along with the loss of Shirley, the horror of death, and the fear of pregnancy. Today she was twelve years old.

Mr. Mitchell wore a light blue sport shirt to her party; his eyes were blue, like Edgar's, blue as the sky. He had washed his blonde hair and combed it wet, no Vitalis, or Brylcreem, and as it dried it loosened into waves, nearly as curly as Edgar's. He stood by the porch rail, easy-like, even if he didn't talk much, and he smiled a lot, especially after Hollie got there, wearing her special rose-colored dress with the shell buttons and bell sleeves. The dress had fit Hollie on Easter Sunday, but now it hung loosely, like it belonged to a different person, a larger person. It still made her hair glow and her skin blush warmer, and she still looked like a slender rose, so fragile she would break with the slightest wind. Within minutes, Mr. Mitchell singled Hollie out and they were

264

walking in the yard, looking at flowers, talking easily, and El wondered what they found to say to each other, forgetting there were but a few years difference in their ages, and they both existed in a state of celibacy since Emmett had gone away. Her interest in Mr. Mitchell and Hollie was short-lived, however, for there were more important matters, like presents to unwrap.

Clothes—shorts, tops and a new dress from Mother and Daddy, books from Jane, and a tiny, badly wrapped package from Bun who stood beside her jumping up and down as El unwrapped it.

"I picked it myself, Ellie, I picked it myself!" Bun squealed in excitement.

When all the papers were removed, El was holding a small tube of Tangee natural lipstick. Her first. With smiles and tears, she hugged her little sister.

"Oh, Mother! May I wear it?"

"You don't think I would have let her buy it if you couldn't wear it, do you?"

Edgar stepped up beside her and said softly, "I'll give you my present later," and she nodded, then ran inside to find a mirror, more interested in using her first make-up for real life—the times she had played dress-up didn't count; they only taught her how to put it on.

Mother had baked her favorite cake, a tall, four-layered chocolate cake with peanut butter icing between each layer and all over the outside. This, with the homemade ice cream which Daddy and Mr. Mitchell took turns cranking, made it a perfectly grand birthday. She was excused from the clean-up and sat in the swing. The calico cat, now officially named Callie, curled up in her lap and she felt like a queen, a very grown-up queen, even if it proved to be a very short reign.

The light in her room had not been out two minutes when El heard gravel thrown on the porch roof. She jumped out of bed and went to the window. Edgar stood in the road in front of her house, his arm drawn back to toss another handful of rock. She removed the screen and leaned out her window.

"Ready for your birthday present?" he called softly.

"Down in a minute!" she whispered. She retreated to her room, changed into old play clothes, found her winter shoes. She scooted down the porch roof, down the post to the rail, and dropped to the grass beside Edgar. "Lead on, Sherlock!"

Edgar led the way through his yard to the old road that led up the mountainside to the railroad tracks. They walked rapidly, pausing only briefly to listen. This road was not as steep as the trail up through the woods, but they could be seen by anyone who happened to be looking. Yet the moon was still behind the hills and most people had turned in; they felt fairly safe as long as Mr. Reeves had made his nightly walk through the camp.

As they quietly moved out on the bridge, El said thoughtfully, "If someone was watching, they'd see our heads, wouldn't they?"

"Yep, if they was lookin' close."

El crouched lower, then Edgar added, "But not many people look up."

"What do you mean, they don't look up?"

"Ain't ya ever noticed? People walk with their heads down, their eyes on the ground, reckon from stoopin' in the mines, only women do it too."

"I don't" said El stoutly.

"You're different," Edgar said in a matter-of-fact manner.

They reached the center of the bridge and dropped down on the small lookout platform, stretched out to study the town below. El gazed about. The excitement was still there, but the fear was gone. She felt comfortable with Edgar and comfortable with being a hundred and twenty-five feet up in the air.

"There's the school bell," she whispered," you can't see it at all from down there."

"There's a man over there," said Edgar, pointing to the company store.

"Who is it?"

"Not sure."

"What's he doing?"

"Peeing, I suppose," said Edgar. El was embarrassed and couldn't think of a good reply, so said nothing. After a minute, Edgar said, "I'm sorry—I forgot you were a girl."

"Wish I weren't," said El

"Why?" Edgar was surprised by her feeling.

"Oh, because," she hedged. She couldn't mention her monthly to him, or how restricted she felt: boys could do as they pleased, whereas girls were watched, corrected, expected, inspected, instructed—she could go on and on.

"I should think you'd like being a girl, don't ever have to go to work in the mines, just stay home and take care of the babies and cook—"

"I'm not having any babies!" The statement erupted from El's lips unbidden.

Edgar didn't know how to respond. He thought all girls wanted to have babies, a house, and a husband to look after them, but, he acknowledged, El sure was different.

The man left the company store, walked under the bridge and started down the road. Edgar knew who it was but decided not to say.

"Who is it?" El asked, not recognizing him.

"Look! There's Mrs. Collins dog!"

"Looks more like a mouse," said El amazed.

"We'd best go," said Edgar, but he didn't move. El was uncertain what they were waiting for, but the night was cool, the moon was high now, round and full, so large it was resting on the next mountain over. She thought, if I stand up and stretch—

"Can I kiss you?" said Edgar suddenly, looking at her shining face.

"Sure, no harm in kissing!" El replied with a wide smile. Edgar leaned over, placed his mouth over hers. He wasn't experienced, like Zane Gray, but he tasted fresh and clean, not like cigarettes; she decided it was much nicer. She wet her lips and kissed him back, slowly, gently, the way Zane Gray had showed her and Edgar drew away first.

"Pa told me and Joe not to kiss girls. Not unless we'd made up our minds to get married. Said that's what it led to. Guess he's right."

Edgar thought about Ben and voiced his thoughts. "Guess that's all Ben can do now, just get married."

"It's not the kissing," said El "Takes more than that."

Edgar sat up and looked at her. "How do you know so much?"

"Heard Mother telling Jane."

"What'd she tell Jane?"

"I can't tell you!" El sat up quickly, embarrassed at the turn in the conversation. "Come on, we'd better go."

"No—wait! Come on, El, you know you can tell me anything! You're the best buddy I've got. I'm your best buddy, too!"

"No, I can't."

"Please, El?" His voice grew urgent. "I've looked in books and there's nothing. Pa won't talk about it, I don't have a mother—come on, if you don't tell me, who will?" He stopped, leaned over and kissed her again, softly, as she had kissed him. Edgar was a fast learner.

El looked at his earnest face. "okay, I'll tell you what I know, only you've got to promise me you'll never tell anyone I told you, never never never. Promise?"

"I promise," he said solemnly.

"And we'll never talk about it again."

"I promise," he repeated.

She took a deep breath. The moon was high now; she could see Edgar good as day. The high wires hummed faintly with electricity and there was a light breeze. In the distance an owl hooted and El counted the hoots, one, two, three, four.

"Tell me," whispered Edgar.

"Well," she said and stopped. The owl hooted again, hoo, hoo, hoo, hoo, hoo. Five times. "That's a great horned owl," she said.

"Don't change the subject!"

"Okay," she said and took a deep breath, "Mother said that boys had sperm and if they got it on a girl they would swim until they found her eggs and that's how babies are made."

Edgar waited. El was quiet. The owl hooted again, and down in the camp, Mrs. Collins' dog howled at the moon.

"That's it?"

"That's it, except the sperm could get on a boys' hands or the girl's legs, or anywhere and if it got on a girl, she could have a baby, and that's why a boy can't put his hands on a girl."

"I see," and now Edgar was quiet. El moved cautiously across the tracks to look down at her house. There had to be more. She knew it, but she didn't want Edgar to learn that she didn't know the rest. When she got sixteen and Mother had "the talk" with her, then she'd understand it all.

Edgar moved to the track beside her. "El, I guess I know why Pa said we shouldn't kiss girls now."

"Why?" whispered El.

"Because, when I kiss you, I want to put my hands on you, too, or at least hold you, but I won't! Honest, if you'll just let me kiss you, I'll never lay a hand on you! Promise! Leastways, not until we're married!"

El felt the warm, fuzzy thrill between her legs again, but shoved it back into her mind. She wouldn't tell Edgar how he made her feel, leaning so close against her, his breath on her face. She tensed beside him, drawing away.

"El?"

"Yes?"

"I mean it. I'll never lay a hand on you, if you'll just let me kiss you." Relieved, El laughed. "I told you, there's no harm in just kissing!" and she laughed again.

"Shush!" Edgar grabbed her arm, pulled her down between the cold steel rails. The man stood at the end of the bridge, silhouetted by the moon. No features showed, only a crushed soft cloth cap and a dark jacket. Edgar grabbed her by the wrist and pulled her after him, across the bridge, up the tracks, to the path in the woods, plunged recklessly down the mountain, through thick-tangled rhododendron bushes, sending pink and red petals down to the leaf-strewn forest floor. When they reached the level land beneath the bridge, they fell against the concrete footer to regain their breath. El collapsed on the ground at Edgar's feet.

"Who was it?" gasped El.

"Don't know," he muttered, "but it wouldn't do for him to make out who you were—might tell your Ma!"

El made a move toward her house, but Edgar held her back. "Wait! Might be watching us! Remember, he can see every move we make, once we get out from under the bridge!"

Eons later they slipped down the creek bed, along the concrete retaining wall, and crossed to the back of El's house, avoiding the moonlit road. They examined the bridge carefully. No one was in sight.

El made a run for her porch and quickly climbed into her window. Bun was sound asleep, but lying on the very edge of the bed. If she had fallen out! Next time, and she knew for a certainty there would be a next time, she would put a pillow in her place. She snuggled against her little sister with a sigh.

It had been a grand birthday. She had liked Edgar's present best of all. She fell asleep with the memory of the high bridge, the cool breeze, and Edgar's gentle kiss drifting through her mind, and there was a smile on her lips—lips still faintly tinged with Tangee natural lipstick.

Fifteen

The next morning, El recalled the dark figure at the end of the bridge. The silhouette had been vaguely familiar, tall with a stoop to the shoulders, and yet she couldn't be certain. She thought about the men in the camp: Mr. Collins was tall, but he wasn't stooped at all. Mr. Mitchell wasn't tall, and his shoulders were rounded from working in low coal. Mr. Gillespie was very tall but he also had an abdomen that couldn't be missed. Daddy wasn't as tall but he was ramrod straight. It was either Emmett—or a total stranger. The feeling of familiarity persisted. She knew Edgar had recognized the man; moreover, he was someone Edgar thought might tattle to her mother. It had to have been Emmett. Yet, here sat Hollie at the kitchen table, helping Mother pin the hem in Mary Beth's wedding dress.

Hollie's face was less a plaster mask today, with color, movement, and life about it; her laugh was back, fresh and easy to come, and once again she was in the middle of things, teasing and picking at Daddy, until he brusquely pushed her away. She had resumed walking in the cool morning with Faith, who seemed to be gaining weight rapidly in spite of the daily exercise. She and Jane primped, trying new hair styles and make-up, keeping the five and dime in business, Daddy said, and had Hollie ever tried turpentine for nail polish remover? Works on boxcars and poles, orta work on fingernails, to which Hollie responded with fresh laughter.

And Bun. Hollie couldn't do enough for her, gave her some of Shirley's dolls, giving them up without the pain showing, saying Shirley would want you to have them, you were my baby's best friend. El watched and admired her constantly, wanting to look like Hollie. Be like Hollie, but so far, all she had going for her was a slim—skinny—figure. Fair Hollie. If Emmett could only see her now!

The President was urging Congress to declare an emergency and keep the draftees in service for another year, stressing to Congress that time was essential. A call went out for every scrap of aluminum, and Mother organized the kids in the camp for a great pots and pans drive.

Edgar took his wagon, El and Joe knocked on doors, begging for anything that could be spared for defense. "Wouldn't you like to think, Mrs. Belcher, that your old teakettle was a part of an airplane wing?"

When it was all collected, a truck came from the county seat and hauled it away. Both Germany and Britain were claiming that the "V" campaign was a success. The coal miners and operators had resumed their talks. Script was declared on "the way out, in the Southern coal fields". Island Creek Coal company had twenty thousand in silver dollars which they were allowing the miners to draw against their wages at the rate of two each day. In Logan, people were calling the American silver dollars "Holden Script," and said it warn't much better. With script out, payroll clerks were issuing cards telling how much a man was worth in wages. The new contracts called for payment in cash or checks, but the clause was not included in all contracts for southern mines. "With friends like that," said Mr. Gillespie, "Who needs enemies?"

The British were rushing troops to Singapore, anticipating an attempt at occupation by the Japanese. "Forewarned is forearmed," said Daddy and Mother said, "You sound like Mr. Gillespie!"

To which Daddy replied, "Humph!"

"Look, Mother," said Jane, interrupting them, "this is what I'd like to do." She handed Mother an article about the USO, which had a breakdown on how a soldier's pay was spent. Out of $21 dollars a month, a dollar went for cigarettes, a dollar for movies, forty cents for cleaning, twenty cents for postage, a dollar for incidentals, eighty cents for travel into town—about four and a half per week, or eighteen dollars per month. "Nothing left for dates or social recreation, which makes the USO very important to all branches of service," read Mother.

"I could help with the entertainment, play the piano, sing, even dance," Jane said, her dark eyes sparkling.

"Drive underway to raise money, each county ..." Mother looked oddly thoughtful. "Don't misunderstand me, Jane, it's not that you aren't talented, or couldn't do it, but I'm not so sure I want my daughter spending her time with a roomful of soldiers and sailors. What do you think, Bud?"

"I said, I don't want Jane helping out in a USO center, Bud. What do you say?" Mother repeated.

"Whatever you say, Mother", replied Daddy, obviously not hearing a word.

"Where is the USO center?" asked El, puzzled.

Mother's face cleared immediately. "Why, you're right, Ellie, there's not one around here, probably not this side of Bluefield!"

"Oh, you don't understand! I didn't mean today! I meant after I graduate! Do you think I'm going to spend the rest of my life in this dirty hole? Why do you think I work so hard in school! And on my music! Don't you understand? I'm getting out of here! OUT! OUT! OUT!"

And Jane ran upstairs to her room, sobbing aloud.

Daddy put down his paper. "What was that all about?" he asked, bewildered. Mother pressed her lips together and shook her head. " I'm not sure," she said, "not sure at all."

El thought she recognized some of the feelings Jane was expressing. It was the way she felt when she thought about flying, or when she was on the bridge looking down. There was a larger world, and there had to be more for her. There had to be more for Jane, too. Perhaps the upcoming wedding was partly responsible for the outburst, or perhaps it was because Jane was seeing Teddy McKinney every weekend now, and Ted talked about his college experiences constantly, making it sound glamorous and exciting to the point that Daddy muttered, "When does that redheaded peckerwood study?"

JAP WARSHIPS REACH INDO-CHINA; U.S. GIVES WARNING

Twelve troop transports were said to be on their way, strategically placed between British bases in Singapore and Hong Kong. FDR was talking plainly and those close to him think he is ready to impose a full embargo on oil.

On the German front, American-made strato-bombers were hitting Nazi ships, flying so high that the first warning was the scream of bombs being dropped. Due to their altitude, the big four-engine bombers, made by Boeing, were covered with frost and ice an inch thick, although it was summer below them. Roosevelt moved to freeze Japanese assets in America as the Japs landed forty thousand troops in Indo-China.

Another trip was made to Virginia, down on Saturday and back on Sunday, to get fresh Alberta peaches for canning: eighty cents a bushel, seventy-five if you picked them yourself. Aunt Maude wasn't the same jolly, plump aunt; Zane Gray had taken that with him when he went into the Navy.

They were on their way back, traveling rapidly through the rolling hills around Wytheville, when a strange warbling sound came from somewhere outside the car.

"What was that!" exclaimed Daddy.

"Blackbirds, Daddy!" said El. They had just passed under a huge oak tree, growing right at the side of the road. She had seen the tree clearly from her place by the window, and the tree was covered with big, black birds—crows or starlings—and hardly had she gotten the words out of her mouth before the trailer began to wobble uncontrollably.

"Oh, oh!" said Daddy. "Blackbirds, hey?" There was a flat on the small trailer he was pulling, a trailer filled with ten bushels of ripe peaches! Having no spare, he took the tire off, patched the tube with a small circle of rubber, and filled the boot with newspapers. They made it home, riding on the *Daily Telegraph*, and the first thing Daddy did was turn on the radio to hear the war news.

Japan had placed a freeze on U.S. and British funds and Franklin had called all Philippine military forces into active duty. The war had heated up as rapidly as the weather: one hundred-degree temperatures stretched from Texas to Atlanta, and in Bluefield it was eighty-eight. The Chamber of Commerce was collecting their lemonade buckets as a heat wave began over most of the nation.

All day Monday, they washed and skinned peaches, filling the wash tubs, buckets and pans. Hollie came early and stayed late to help. Mrs. Belcher and even Sarah Jo came to seed and slice, and went home with a basketful for themselves. El washed fruit jars—her hands were small enough to reach the bottom—and peaches—she could get down to the tubs—until her hands looked like prunes and she had a permanent itch at the back of her neck.

By Tuesday the temperature hit ninety in Bluefield and for the first time since 1934, girls in shorts served eighty-seven gallons of lemonade in one hour, a gallon and a half a minute, as the residents of "Nature's Air-Conditioned City" turned out. Lowell Thomas talked about it on his national news broadcast. Only the New England states found relief from the heat wave that caused deaths all over the nation.

By suppertime, the ten bushels of peaches were either canned in sugar syrup, preserved, or given away. When Daddy came in from work, he rubbed Ellie's head and laughed. "Blackbirds, hey?" he teased.

"Well, the tree was full of them!" she said, "I saw them!"

After supper, complete with peach cobbler for dessert, which nobody but Daddy ate, he sat down with Bun on his knee and began to sing: "Four and twenty blackbirds, baked in a pie…"

"Daddy!" El was tired. She didn't want to be teased. The air lay heavy and thick; the heat of the kitchen and the smell of burned peaches from boiled-over jam nauseated her.

"All right, honey, how 'bout this one?" he said.

> *Work on the railroad, work all day*
> *Eat soda crackers, wind blow 'em away,*
> *Work on the railroad, sleep on the ground,*
> *Eat soda crackers, wind blow 'em 'round.*

Now that he had started, nobody could, or wanted to, shut him up. He threw back his head and roared:

> *Roll out your blankets, sleep on the ground,*
> *Working on railroad, best ever found!*

Bun giggled and squirmed with pleasure. "More, Daddy, more!"

> *Working on the Levee, dollar and a half a day,*
> *Working for my Lulu, give her all my pay,*
> *Don't let yer watch run down, Captain.*
> *Don't let yer watch run down!*

Mother sat at the table resting, wiping her red face on her apron. Every time Daddy started a chorus, she joined him, singing alto; it sounded fine, despite the fact that Daddy never sang it the same way twice. Bun snuggled against him, having a hard time staying awake. Outside, they could hear the thunder getting closer and closer, and the air seemed so thick it was hard to breathe. A faint breeze began to stir the lace curtains in the living room. It would rain soon.

> *Oh, I got a mule and her name is Sal,*
> *Fifteen years on the Erie canal!*

Low bridge, everybody down,
Low bridge, we're comin' ta town,
And if you know your neighbor you'll know yer pal,
If you ever sail on the Erie Canal.

Bun was asleep. Daddy carried her up to bed, and El was glad to follow; she'd never been so tired. The storm broke as she slipped into bed. It rained over an inch and a half in minutes, dropped the temperature twenty degrees, fresh and sweet-smellin' mountain air.

Everyone in Coville was coming to the wedding. Mother frantically counted chairs, planning, planning, but there was simply no way the entire town could be seated in the Phillips' living room. She sat down and wiped her perspiring face, listened anxiously to the noon news and weather report. There seemed to be a possibility of relief soon: a cold front was forming in North Dakota and would be moving eastward. But when? If this heat continued it would be miserable in the house in the afternoon. What about an evening wedding? But Mary Beth and Ben wanted it earlier; he only had Saturday and Sunday and he reported for duty on Monday. She couldn't go with him. Hardly long enough to know they were married, she told them, hardly long enough to count. And only another week to go.

The radio broke into Mother's planning, startling the girls as much by Mother's reaction as to the news. Mother burst into tears. The girls were at a loss as to what to do.

An American Gunboat had been bombed by the Japanese!
The U.S. Embassy in China was in danger and thousands of Japanese were
pouring into Saigon.

Jane went to Mother and put her arms around her, much as she had seen her mother do with countless others, patting and there-there-ing, a miniature Faith. She sent El and Bun out of the house—go, just go!—never mind where, just go outside, you kids have to hang around in here all day?

There was little shade in the yard at twelve o'clock noon; the air waved with the heat, steaming off the moisture from the storm. The mountains were a deep green, fading to an unbroken blue in the distance, only one shade darker than the sky. Moisture in the air made the mountains look blue, Daddy had told them, and there was a lot of wet air today: how come it was also so hot? The heat was so intense even the blue-green flies refused to buzz. El and Bun sat on the thick grass beneath the willow, listlessly pulling the leaves from the long wands that reached the ground. It was the coolest place around, a green tent, and they couldn't be seen by anyone unless they looked really close.

From the open windows of the Collins house El and Bun could hear an angry argument, the words hurled out recklessly, with no thought to who might hear:

"You think I didn't know? Think I had my head up my ass all the time? You're a damn hypocrite Thomas Collins! No thought for anybody but yourself! You and your fat dick your selfish roamin' night-owlin' prowlin' dick, think I didn't know? Now get out of my house get outgetout getoutgetoutgetout!"

The silence, after Sarah Jo's screaming voice, was as frightening to El and Bun as the shouting, but in a few moments Mr. Collins opened the screen door and came out carrying a straight-backed kitchen chair. He brought it straight to the giant willow tree, ducked under the low-hanging branches—and came face to face with El and Bun. There was a long pause while they stared at each other in awkward silence, until Bun, child-like and innocent, spoke up brightly, "Hi, Mr. Collins! You going to read?" Only then did she notice the brand-new book in Mr. Collins' hands. Mr. Collins saw the hungry look on El's face and laughed. "Oh, no, Miss Rachel! I get it first! Then you can read it!"

"What is it, Mr. Collins? What's the name of it?" the ugly screams of Sarah Jo were ignored by all three of them, forgotten in the anticipation of holding a fresh, new-smelling, unhandled book. Mr. Collins held out a copy of Thomas Wolfe's latest book, right off the press, never even opened. It was titled, *You Can't Go Home Again.*

El took the book tenderly in her hands and caressed it, opened it gently and sniffed it like rare perfume, reluctantly handing it back when Mr. Collins held out his hand. "Someday, Miss Ellie, I'm going to get a brand-new book and let you read it first, "he said, "but not this one. Not this one!"

As Mr. Collins propped his chair against the trunk of the ancient tree, El thought it might be safe to go back in the house. Mother was lying down on the sofa in the cool, dark living room, a folded wet washcloth across her eyes. Jane was hemming her own dress for the wedding, taking small careful stitches in the lime-green satin.

"You sure you know how to do that?" asked El, with a worried look toward Mother.

"Shush," said Jane, "she can't do it all, and it's time I learned."

There were nine deaths over the nation from the heat wave, but at night, in the mountains, the katydids had started their rasping crackle: only six weeks until frost. Few would be sorry to see it come after the heat of this summer.

The war between Germany and Russia waxed and waned, reminding Daddy of the way black racers and copperheads fight. When a racer is bitten, he explained, he breaks for a weed which he eats as an antidote for the poison from the copperhead. Then he comes back and crushes the copperhead. Mother commented, rather irrelevantly, on the Japanese calendar, the year 1941 is called *The Year Of The Snake.* The United States accepted the Japanese apology for the bombing of the Tutuila, and the Japanese offered to pay for the damage. Tokyo promised to take measures to prevent another such incident.

The Office of Production Management ordered the nation's silk mills to shut down and stopped the exportation of gasoline and oil to Japan. The ban against producing silk put one hundred and seventy-five people out of work and stopped the manufacture of hosiery altogether. *The American females could not do without silk stockings!*

The very thought was abhorrent. A run on available supplies began in large cities, some women buying as many as thirty pairs. The stores set a limit of six pairs per customer as the smart shoppers tried to lay in reserves; before long the popular sizes and colors were gone. However, the women of Wyoming County stayed calm; there had to be worse things than not having silk stockings! The ladies of Mullins and surrounding towns said they would wear whatever the manufacturers substituted. Almost immediately it was announced that Du Pont was building a big new plant, probably on the Kanawha river, and it had something to do with a new product called Nylon.

The greatest battles in the history of the world raged between Germany and Russia; every movement of their lines was a matter for long, deep discussions and speculations by the adults, and a direct result was another recruiting station, this time in Pineville, to be open twice a month.

The market expanded, production demands were extensive; the nation needed coal and more coal, and the miners tried to meet that demand by whatever means possible, as bituminous coal provided forty-five percent of the energy used in the nation. The Japanese, just as determined, turned to the southern Orient for oil, tin and rubber, ignoring the embargoes imposed by the United States and Britain. Gasoline stations were ordered to close at seven p.m. and not reopen until seven a.m., in the hope that reduced hours would reduce consumption, but motorists lined up before the pumps, lugging big cans and gallon fruit jars, determined to avoid parking their jalopies.

Daddy talked about a possible strike on the railroad as that labor group was polled. The carriers had rejected their demand for a thirty-cent increase in wages. The results of the poll wouldn't be known until next week.

Saturday, August 2nd. The miners received their back pay! Mullins was as crowded as fair grounds on free day as the stores did an impressive business. School was only a month away; shoes, denim pants, flannel shirts, long underwear, jackets, sweaters, boots were bought by the car load by parents relieved at being able to dress their children without having to put it on a ticket at the company store. Miners were spotted in the A&P in Mullins and at Kroger's in Princeton, stocking up on essentials at a saving, but more frequently they were seen spending on treats—watermelon, ice cream, Coca-Cola.

But not all miners bought clothes for their kids and a bottle to carry home: thirty of them had been killed during the month of July, leaving nearly thirty new widows and over a hundred orphans. The increased fatalities were explained by an increase in production, longer hours, tired men pushing beyond their limits, and by the hiring of inexperienced men, men untrained in the ways of the dark tunnels, the ways of powerful explosives and drills, of cutters and loading machines; men who didn't know the way of the rock, the layering of the coal seams, the flow of underground streams, the nature of the land of coal.

On the way into town, El taught Bun the words to the number one hit song, Hut-Sut, and they worked hard to have it down perfectly, planning to sing it for Ted when he came for Sunday dinner. They crowded close to Mother as she picked socks from a bin piled high, long white socks for church, long plaid knee socks, short stripped socks, red, blue, navy, yellow, green socks, enough to last all year. Mother also bought percale, the finest quality for twelve cents a yard, and matched the material with the socks for complete outfits. She would sew ten dresses for each girl, enough for two weeks of school, before school started, and they would have hairbows to match. Home again, they poured over the Sears and Wards catalogues, choosing dresses they liked, and Mother would sew one to look just like the picture. She promised to start sewing for school just as soon as the wedding was over.

Each day of the week now required something special to be done for the big event. The house was shining, waxed and polished with Old English to cover the least scratch on the dark furniture. Mints were made in three colors, Mother having determined the color scheme to correspond with the available flowers in her yard, and Mama Wooten came up to help drop the confection on waxed paper. Hairbows were made to match their dresses, hats being too expensive. Kool-Aid was frozen into cubes to go in the punch bowl, and the cake, a three-tiered coliseum, took an entire day by itself. Faith, with Jane's help, had finished the dresses, Hollie had done the pressing, and they were hung in Jane's closet ready for Saturday. The time had been set at two o'clock, in spite of the heat, for—as Daddy pointed out—it only took ten minutes to tie a man up for life!

Ben arrived late on Friday night, but he stayed at home, talking with Rayford and Mildred, who had consented to come to the wedding, but, Mildred said, that ended her obligation. That was as far as she intended to go. Rayford was willing to bring Mary Beth—and his grandchild—into their house, let her use the boy's room. Mildred fainted at the very suggestion: Will's and Ben's room would stay just as it was until they were home again! She refused to recognize the fact that when Ben returned, he would have a wife and a baby with him! Mildred had yet to speak to her future daughter-in-law, and Mother had advised Mary Beth not to rush her; wait a while. Mildred will come around.

It was somewhat cloudy and cooler on Saturday morning, as if the weather was cooperating, and Mary Beth and Hollie came up to the Phillips' house early. Mary Beth was anxious and nervous, and Hollie, remembering her own wedding, was almost as bad. They helped to set out plates and cups, polished the silver candlesticks again, collected forks from the neighbors. Jane and Sarah Jo arranged flowers for the dining room table and Mother did them over. El and Bun helped Edgar and Joe carry chairs from the Gillespie's house and Mother directed where to place them. She had decided the wedding would be held on the front porch, with chairs for the women, the men standing along the railing, and the children on the grass. She watched the cloudy sky with some anxiety but everyone assumed it would clear before noon: it wouldn't dare rain on Mother's party!

The flower boxes on the porch held bright yellow and orange nasturtiums; along the fence were gold and bronze marigolds, red and orange zinnias, and purple and white asters. By the side of the house, the rose bushes had been stripped bare, furnishing large, bright red roses for the bride's bouquet. The swing was left in place until the last moment, occupied by Preacher Copeland early in the day, and he held long and loud to Daddy. He had baptized Mary Beth and he would do the marrying; he had dipped her in the cold clear water where Gooney Otter Creek flowed into Barker's Creek when she was ten years old, brought her up as one of God's children, his and God's and Ben, too. Ben was one of his converts, strong, too, why that young'un had might near pulled him in when he baptized him! He and God would sanctify their marriage, the beautiful young man going off to sea, wouldn't be back for God knows how long, most likely be a proud father when he got back, now, mind, he didn't approve of getttin' in the family way before marrying but that can't be helped now—For God sakes, Faith don't you need help in the kitchen? I've had about all of that old coot I can take! Daddy? Volunteering to help in the kitchen? He was desperate!

Mary Beth was beautiful. Mother had fashioned her dress to take advantage of her best features, and the full skirt almost hid the reason for the ceremony. The creamy satin gave her brown hair a soft sheen and she left it straight and long, not trying to curl it. Her face was flushed and her eyes were glowing, like it said in the romance books, happiness clearly shining through. She wore a small string of pearls, a gift from Ben, who she had yet to see like they hadn't already had their bad luck. Her flowers, the deepest red roses on Mother's bushes, were looped with satin ribbons and lace, leaving the ends floating free.

Jane's dress was short; Mother said she could use it for church, a long one wouldn't be practical, a pale lime-green that made her white skin and black hair show to best advantage. Ted—present as shepherd of the flock, even if he didn't tie the knot—couldn't stay away from her from the moment she came downstairs, following her room to room like a ruby-throated hummingbird sippin' honey. Pink was a fortunate choice for Judith as it gave her sallow skin a healthy glow. As for Bun, she stole the show, as Mr. Gillespie said, looking like a sugar cake with pink frosting. Mother had stewed and fretted over Bun's dress, saying, redheads don't wear pink, but she had solved the problem by making a wide white lace collar and Bun's red curls spread on the white lace like icing on a cake. Regal. Bun would drop pink rose petals before the bride from a tiny white basket. Bun dimpled and waved, a fist full of pink rose petals, a cherub whom everyone wanted to pick up and hug—which they did.

El's dress was made along the same lines as Jane's and Judith's but on El, the baby blue did nothing for her coloring, and she looked, she said, like a blue toothpick. A grumpy blue toothpick. Her hair had grown out and the perm was gone. Mother and Daddy told her every Friday she needed a haircut, but they didn't understand: Veronica Lake would never consent to bobbing her hair! But, said Mother, bobbed hair was back in style.

When Hollie came downstairs there was an audible gasp among the guests. Mother had made her dress yellow, in spite of El's objections, after Hollie said it didn't matter to her. As usual, Mother was right. Absolutely right. If the rose-tinted dress at Easter made Hollie lovely, this one made her spectacular. The material was soft and flowing, not just "yellow" but a deep sun-gold, light-catching, breath-taking. Her hair waved about her face, caressing her tawny skin turned honey-gold by the summer sun. She was a golden goddess from her crown to her toes, a sun-nymph with a smile that came and went like the sun coming and going, making her surroundings brighten and dim according to her moods. Hollie far outshone the bride.

Ben stood stiffly beside Preacher Copeland in his dress blues until the ceremony began; his stocky, square build was somewhat trimmer in the appealing uniform, but it failed to make him the dashing hero it had made Will. His thick brown hair was cut in the traditional military style, and he looked skinned, raw, unfinished. The Navy had made Will look more of a man; it made Ben look like a fourteen-year-old, a frightened fourteen-year-old, playing at being grown up. Getting married wouldn't change that.

Preacher Copeland stood before the double windows, with Ben at his side. In the house, Thelma Plover began the traditional wedding march. El was the official screen door holder as the wedding party came out to the porch. The neighbors gathered on the sides of the porch, the steps and in the yard, with the older women seated in chairs. Bun scattered her rose petals and Judith walked gingerly through the petals—didn't anyone tell her she could step on them? — followed by Jane, head up, dignified and solemn. Mary Beth, on her father's arm—a sober, suited Papa Wooten—came out to stand before the preacher. Ben moved to take her hand. Thelma played again, and the preacher began: "Dearly Beloved…"

From her privileged place on the porch, El could see almost everyone. Ted was looking at Jane, his feelings drooling over his freckled face; Hollie was standing at the foot of the steps, ready to dash into the house to serve the cake as soon as the service ended, and Mr. Mitchell was standing in the road, one foot placed easily on the fence, his gaze fixed on Hollie. Beside Mr. Mitchell, at a little distance from the other neighbors, stood Mr. and Mrs. Collins, standing together like they never had a cross word; El was surprised, after the screaming accusations she had heard, but there they were, keeping up appearances with the best.

She searched for Mrs. Margaret and found her standing by the porch railing, but her face was turned away from the wedding, and she had the most terrible expression on her face, like—like—yes! She looked exactly like Bun had looked the day she bit into the sour cherry! Her mouth was puckered, and her eyes were glaring, really glaring, and she was staring straight at Mr. Mitchell! Mrs. Margaret was watching Mr. Mitchell watch Hollie!

The minister was asking for the ring, and Mr. Gillespie, as his son's best man, took a thin gold band out of his pin-striped vest pocket. Jane was holding Mary Beth's roses, looking almost like a bride herself. Judith was crying, her uneven sobs the only sound.

Mrs. Plover began to play again, and it was over. As Daddy said, it didn't take long enough for anyone to get overly hot or tired, but the large group was ready for refreshments. El and Hollie were kept busy with cake and punch for some time, but Mother had planned well: The refreshments outlasted the crowd.

"I fully realize that the charge of subterfuge is serious in the extreme," said Charles Lindbergh, speaking in Cleveland at an America First rally.

Mary Beth and Ben honeymooned at the new Pineville Hotel. When his strong young hands moved over her softly rounded belly, she closed her eyes and pictured dark-haired, handsome Will.

"First, Americans were told that a repeal of the arms embargo would be the surest way to keep out of war."

I need you to come home to, after the war, Will had said, need you to dream about, to remember why I am fighting.

"Next we were told that selling arms on a cash and carry basis would mean Victory for the Allies."

Consummated, paid for, cash and carry, on the snow-covered ground behind the school, stolen time on a timeless night last spring.

"It was only last spring that the lend-lease bill was passed, again with the promise that it would keep us out of the war…"

She dreamed of Will but lay with Ben by the coalhouse door.

"…but by that time, we were informed that we had to lend arms to insure victory."

…Lay in his arms, misled by substituting the word sex for love.

The American people were misled by substituting the word 'patrol' for 'convoy'. The hypocrisy and subterfuge that surrounds us comes out in every statement.

"I couldn't help it," sobbed Mary Beth aloud. "He was so sweet and gentle, before I knowed it I told him everything!" She put her head down on the dining room table and cried.

Mother smoothed the stringy brown head and patted, there-there, there-there. "Perhaps it was best," she consoled the upset girl, "at least you have started your marriage on an honest footing and that's very important."

"Wait a minute," sobbed Mary Beth, "that's not all."

Mother looked anxiously at her three girls gathered around, taking it all in. "Perhaps we had better go upstairs and talk."

"No, no, It's okay, they know all about it anyway. Serves me right, doin' what I did."

"Anybody can make a mistake!" El said quickly, trying to ease the pain on the new bride's face.

This was Monday. Although Ben had left for Norfolk on Sunday, Mary Beth had spent another night in Pineville, unable to get a bus back to Coville until Monday morning. She had been married only two days. It seemed much longer. She dried her eyes and looked at Mother, Jane and El, one after the other. Quiet now, almost with dignity, she said, "Ben already knew. He told me he saw us. That's what he said."

Mother sat down quickly. "Well!"

"He married me to give my baby a name, not cause he thought it was his'n. He's shippin' out, don't know where to but he says it don't matter. Don't know if he'll get back, says that don't matter either. He said he thought Will was a skunk for running out on me, but he warn't much better because he tried the same thing, so if Will wouldn't give the baby his name, he would, and either way it would be a Gillespie, which was only right."

There was a moment of silence, then Mother sighed deeply. "Well, that Ben. He's a fine boy, Mary Beth. You're a lucky girl, lucky to have him. He'll stand by you."

Mary Beth dropped her hands between her knees and pulled her dress taunt; the skirt of her new going-away-and-back-again dress emphasized the slight bulge of her abdomen. Mother eyed her speculatively. "You're how far now?"

"Four and a half months, " she said. "Right, Jane?"

"End of March, April, May, June, July, half of August," Jane counted. "Nearly five" said Mother. "We've got to get you to Doc Steelman." She arose heavily and went to the railroad phone, placed a call through the Narrows power director to the clinic in Mullins, but Doc Steelman was at the Mayo Clinic with his wife, who was having surgery, and he wouldn't be back until next week. He would be in Coville next week anyway, Mother reported; it could wait until then.

August thirteenth was a Wednesday and the news seekers were reporting the President's yacht, with the President aboard, had vanished without a trace. Roosevelt was supposedly taking a vacation, and having always been a sea-going man he was taking it on his yacht, but with all the U-Boats known to be off the coast of the United States…

The Japanese Envoy had warned Japan that America was preparing for the worst, and Japan herself was now on full war footing. Only two steps remained to break with the Land of the Rising Sun: A complete embargo, and severance of consular relations. In another country, Marshall Phillippe Petain, at the age of eighty-five, realized that his plans for the regeneration and revitalization of France had failed and he aligned his country squarely behind the Nazis.

In Washington, the house passed a measure extending military training to eighteen months, and the measure removed all limitations on the number of men to be called.

Thursday's headlines screamed:

MAJOR U. S. MOVE IS BELIEVED NEAR
FDR— CHURCHILL MEETING SEEN

Whereabouts of Pres. Yacht Still Unknown
Churchill Missing

It was speculated that Franklin and Winston had met somewhere on the Atlantic, two old friends, two worried men. Nothing was known for certain.

Locally, the big news centered around the Lily Reunion, held annually on Flat Top Mountain. This year Jack Dempsey would attend! The main speaker was to be Dwight Green, Governor of Illinois, but there was more excitement over the famous prize fighter. Wouldn't Ben have gotten a kick out of seeing him? Like to have seen those two go at it, of course, now, if Jack was a lil bit younger…they fight jest alike, you know, same style exactly.

By Thursday night the temperature had dropped to fifty degrees and old timers predicted frost. Bluefield Chamber of Commerce promised free hot chocolate if it snowed and folks pulled more blankets out of the closets, chopped more kindlin' wood, walked a bit faster, whistled a bit more briskly.

Uncle Charlie and Aunt Bea came from Iaegar, planning to spend the night and then go on to the reunion, Uncle Charlie being a direct descendent from the Lily's who came to West Virginia from Maryland, back in the sixteen hundreds. The family was so numerous, they'd built their own Grand stand and Fair Grounds on top of the mountain and a hundred thousand people were expected to attend, according to "Cousin Abe" Lily, leader of the clan.

While Aunt Bea helped Mother and Jane in the kitchen, Uncle Charlie sat with Daddy in the big rockers on the front porch. El and Bun, wrapped cozily together in the swing under a granny-square crocheted Afghan, held old Marsha and Callie, the calico kitten, the only one of Marsha's babies to survive, the others having mysteriously disappeared during the hot days of

July. Now they sat close together to stay warm and listened to Uncle Charlie and Daddy talk.

"Where do you think he is?" asked Uncle Charlie.

"I figure halfway to England."

"You think so? You really think so?"

"Sure, don't you?"

"Naw, he wouldn't get out in those waters, not with all those Nazi subs nosing around."

"I figure he would. He's got to get with Churchill, plan out which way to go. Probably be quicker to meet at sea."

Uncle Charlie nodded thoughtfully. "You may be right, but that'd take a hell'ava lot a courage."

"Well, that's one thing he ain't short on. Any man could crawl out of that bed, knowing his legs was gone, and go on to be President of this country? Hell, that kinda man wouldn't mind a U-Boat or two!" Daddy stretched his feet out in front of him and contemplated his own sixteen inch boots. "You ever thought how it'd be, not to walk or run or climb a pole? Hell, I'd probably turn my face to the wall and never roll over again!"

"No you wouldn't old buddy, not you! The way you climb around those hot high-volt wires? And walk those bridges covered in ice—hell, man! You've got more courage than a bob-tailed cat when he's cornered!"

"No, that's just a job. You do what you have to do, whatever it takes to get the job done."

"That's what Roosevelt is doing, just what it takes to get the job done."

Silence, and Uncle Charlie's cigar smoke streaked across the light from the living room window; in the woods, back of the house and across the creek, came the sound of the night birds crying.

"Reckon he's still at sea?"

"I figure so."

"That's where he was when he come up with that Lease-Lend idea. Wonder what he'll come up with this time?"

"Hard to tell, but there's one thing for certain: Roosevelt will never let Churchill down!"

The blue cigar smoke lined out straight in the light and in the deep woods a dead limb fell with a crack that echoed in the quiet.

After supper, they gathered in the living room for singing. Bun stole the show. With a professional-looking bow, she clasped her hands together and sang her latest song, Jane at the piano playing for her:

Hut-Sut Rawlson on the rillerah and a brawla, brawla, soo-it.
Now the Rawlson is a Swedish town, the rillerah is a stream. The brawla is
the boy and girl, The Hut-Sut is their dream!

Uncle Charlie grabbed Bun and hugged her with a shout. "Honey Bun, there ain't nobody like you! You'll always be my best gal, no matter how many little brats come into this family!"

There was a sudden, deep silence. Aunt Bea said in disgust, "Now you've done it, you big galoote! They ain't told the girls yet!"

Mother and Daddy looked embarrassed; Jane looked pleased, a cat-in-the-cream-I -knew-it-all-the-time smile on her face; she laughed at El's reaction. Bun looked puzzled.

"Come on, Jane," said Aunt Bea, "Let's sing this one!" And she held up a piece of sheet music.

"You want to sing this?" said Jane and she laughed, taking the music from her Aunt.

"Aunt Bea, this is Rubinstein's 'Romance' and it's my recital piece, my lesson!"

Uncle Charlie was swinging Bun over his head and she squealed every time he tossed her up, but for El, it wasn't a time for laughter. Odd bits of information were flashing through her mind: Mother being sick in the mornings, Mother, letting Mr. Reeves take over the hoeing, buying diaper material, sewing baby gowns. It was true. Mother was going to have another baby. El turned and ran from the room, out to the porch swing and darkness. She could see the group in the living room through the window—Bun astraddle Uncle Charlie's neck, Daddy sitting in his chair with his pipe, Jane at the piano, Mother and Aunt Bea, harmonizing on a song they had grown up singing together: "K-K-K-Katie, Beautiful Katie, You're the only g-g-g-girl for me. When the m-m-m-moon shines, over the cow shed, I'll be waiting at the k-k-k-kitchen door."

Somehow, Mother looked younger, standing at the piano singing, and from her place in the swing El could inspect her without being observed. Mother had gotten much larger this summer, but El had thought it was just fat. As she looked closer, she suspected Mother was closer to delivery than Mary Beth. Why hadn't she noticed? She berated herself for being so dumb, so unobservant, so stupid! But how could she have known? Mother's weren't supposed to get pregnant! She tried to avoid thinking about how she had gotten this way, blocking out the image of Daddy's little squiggly sperm...she recalled the many times she had heard noise from their room, recalled clearly the first time they had awakened her, and the explanation she had been given the next morning, "Oh, we were just turning the mattress—you know how I hate it when the springs poke through!"

The next morning Mother sat down with the girls at breakfast and explained. "We wanted to wait a while, before we told you, because it takes so very long to have a baby—"

"How long?" asked El.

"Nine months, silly, don't you know anything?"

"And we wanted to be real sure—"

"A baby? For me?" squealed Bun, "A real baby?"

"Sure, Honey, a real baby," said Mother, "just for you!"

"A baby," Bun said again, beaming, obviously happy with the news. "A little baby sister and I can hold her!"

"Or brother," said Jane, "could be a boy, you know."

El knew they were waiting for her to say something, so said, weakly, "When?"

"Well," said Mother, hesitatingly, "we think about the first of November."

"What do you mean, "you think—" don't you know?"

"It's not always that easy," said Mother. "sometimes babies don't keep schedules."

El made no reply, but it went unnoticed as Uncle Charlie and Aunt Bea came downstairs, carrying their luggage. She and Bun went to the swing, watching as they prepared to leave for the Lily reunion. El pulled her little sister into her arms and pushed off the swing. No new little baby would ever take Bun's place with her, Bun was the only little sister she wanted. She couldn't give the idea that it might be a boy serious thought; boy babies were as foreign to her as— as kangaroos!

Uncle Charlie picked Bun up. "My little Bumpkin," he said. "Now, look here, you live up here"—he touched her forehead— "and I live down here"—he touched her chin, and "I'm coming up to see you"—and he brought his finger up, bumping her nose. Bun laughed and pulled Uncle Charlies nose in return. "Faith, no matter how hard you try, you won't have another to beat this one!"

He sat Bun down, picked up his luggage, looked over his shoulder to Jane and El. "Bye, girls! Take care!"

Aunt Bea patted Bun on her head and said, "Poor little thing, won't be the baby much longer." Then with tears in her eyes, hugged all three girls, hugged Mother again, and went to her car crying. "Why is Aunt Bea crying, Mother?" asked Bun. "Because she loves you," answered Mother.

Bun crawled back into the swing with El. "Ellie, why did Aunt Bea say 'poor little Bun' to me?"

"'Cause, when the new baby comes, you won't be the baby anymore."

"But, El," said Bun, wide-eyed and serious, "I don't want to be the baby anymore!"

El hugged her little sister. "You'll always be my little sister!" she said. "Let's play airplane!" She pushed the swing, getting it to go higher and higher, and she and Bun held on tight.

Mother came towards them, "Stop that! Rachel, you will jerk that swing right off the hooks! You know better than that! What's gotten into you!"

By Friday afternoon, El had accepted the idea of a new baby—accepted it, but didn't like it at all.

Sixteen

When Daddy came in from work, he brought all the answers to the questions about Roosevelt and Churchill; the Bluefield Daily Telegraph summed it up in one strong headline:

SWIFT MOVES TO AID FIGHT AGAINST AXIS FOLLOW SEA MEETING OF FDR, CHURCHILL

Parlay Brings United Stand. Parlay Rules Out Peace with 'Nazi Tyranny': sketches Framework of New World Order.

But the radio had preceded the newspaper with the news, and Congress had passed the bill extending Army duty from age nineteen to age thirty-seven. America had made three commitments:

-To support the British and Russians on every front,
-To aid in stripping the aggressor nations of their weapons, and
To help reconstruct post-war Europe.

The joint declaration of Roosevelt and Churchill expressed eight principles, and on these eight principles they based their hopes for a better future world:

-The U.S. and Britain seek no aggrandizement, territorial or otherwise.
-No territorial changes that do not accord with the freely expressed wishes of the people concerned.
-Self-government should be restored to those who have been forcibly deprived of it.

-All states, victor and vanquished, should have access on equal terms to trade and raw materials.
-After the final destruction of the "Nazi Tyranny", the United States and Great Britain hope for peace in which all men may live out their lives free from fear and want.
-All men should be able to traverse the seas and oceans without hindrance.

-All nations of the world must come to the abandonment of the use of force, and nations which threaten aggression must be disarmed pending a wider and more permanent system of general security.

"Boy! Who was minding the store!" Daddy read aloud the list of men who had attended the conference aboard ship, off the coast of Newfoundland: Gen. Marshall, Adm. Stark, Harry Hopkins, Averill Harriman, Adm. King, Adm. Pound, General Dill, followed by a long, low whistle. "Well, folks," he said, "we're in for it now! Wait until Germany gets this! Ol' Roosevelt and Churchill have joined forces and they sure are in for it now!"

And Mother, sitting with bowed head at the table. Said softly, "And so are we, dear God, so are we."

There was a picture of Franklin and Winston, standing together on board the *H.M.S. Prince of Wales*, in Saturday's paper. The picture was made after the joint declaration was signed, and the general feeling was that the United States had thrown down the gauntlet. While FDR and Winnie stood on the deck of the *Prince of Wales* singing "Onward Christian Soldiers," the world waited to see what Hitler would do.

Gasoline rationing had been established, and the amount available to stations in West Virginia and Virginia was cut by twenty percent. The call for September's draft went out, and the number to come from West Virginia was 1,441 whites, and 49 negroes.

"Remember Grandma Shrewsbury?" asked Daddy.

"Of course," said Mother. "What about her?"

"Saw her old neighbor down at the filling station; said the old place was loaded with blackberries this year, said we ought to pick 'em."

"Bud! Could we?"

"Don't see why not, if you've got any gas left after going to Mullins."

"We could go to Mullins by train!"

"And carry all the—"

"We don't need groceries, not a lot, and I'd sure like to go berry pickin'!"

"He said to tell you to locate the old garden, there's a fence around it, an old rail fence, covered up in blackberry canes." Daddy had known all along that Mother would figure out a way to go blackberry picking—she did it every year.

Saturday morning dawned bright and clear. Mother and the girls took the train to Mullins, leaving the gray car parked at the passenger station in Herndon. While they waited for the passenger train, El and Bun visited with Ol' Red Karrigan, covert objective, the lime-green suckers in the blue Mason jar. Before the prized suckers were obtained, Bun burst out with the news that they were going to have a baby at their house! El was so embarrassed she left the telegraph office without her sucker, but Mr. Kerrigan gave Bun two, which she promptly shared with El.

No. 3 pulled into the station right on time, eleven-fifty-eight, and Mother held the girls in the waiting room until the big PA popped off, avoiding the stream of hot steam coming between the big iron wheels—wheels higher than Ellie's head. The conductor raised the metal platform and uncovered the steps, placed a small iron stepstool on the pavement. El bounded up the steps, ignoring the portly conductor's outstretched hand. The conductor turned and swung Bun up, to her complete delight; next he handed Jane and Mother in, calling them by name and expressing pleasure at seeing them. El slid across the black leather seat to the window side.

"Rachel!" Mother, dismayed, shook her head. "You know better than to sit on that seat before I get it covered!" Obediently, El stood up, but it was too late; the back of her light blue skirt was already streaked with black coal dust; she sat down on the papers, knowing Mother had already seen the dirty skirt. She put her elbow on the window sill, cinders stuck to her skin and she hastily wiped the mahogany ledge, leaving soot and cinders on her hands.

The train paused at Herndon only long enough to pick up passengers and throw the mail bag into the wagon, and now it pulled out with a jerk and two long blasts of the whistle, the railroad signal for releasing the brakes. Hardly had it begun to move before the engineer gave a long, drawn-out pull on the signal cord, warning for an approaching station or crossing. They were already at Bud, but this was only a flag stop and they hardly slowed down.

The train rocked along the tracks, making a good thirty miles an hour, and El leaned out the window to see the engine as it rounded the curves. Mother reached out a restraining hand, pulling her back into the car. "We'll be at the tunnel soon," she said, and knowing the smoke would curl back into the car, she pulled down the window. Almost before she finished speaking, they entered the tunnel, the overhead lights came on, and the sound of the engine changed to a muffled, dulled, chu-chug, chu-chug.'

"Potty, El," said Bun, and Mother exclaimed," Bun! You just went!"

"That's all right, Mother," said El "I'll take her, I don't mind." She didn't explain that she, too, loved the tiny restroom with its stainless-steel fixtures. Bun lifted the lid to the toilet and watched the tracks below whiz by, fascinated by the sight. El flushed the tiny toilet repeatedly and they watched the water gush out over the tracks. They washed their hands at the tiny three-cornered sink in the corner, stopped for a drink at the stainless-steel fountain, and staggered back up the aisle, pretending to be drunk. They sat on the newspapers, Bun's short, fat legs sticking straight out, and watched as No. 4 passed on the eastbound track. Almost immediately the engineer pulled the whistle again, this time for Alpoca, a regular stopping place. As the whistle blew a long, uninterrupted h-o-o-o-o-, El thought she had never heard such a mournful sound.

"When I die," she said, "I want a train whistle to blow, 'stead of people singing."

"Ellie!" said Mother, sounding shocked, "Whatever—"

"Well, it's a much sadder sound," El insisted.

"What makes you think people will be sad when you die?" said Jane, sarcastically.

"Jane! That's enough!"

"And throw my ashes off the bridge!" continued El, pleased because Mother had called Jane down.

"And that's enough out of you, too!" Said Mother. But Bun slid her hand into El's and looked ready to cry. "I don't want you to die, Ellie! I'd miss you more than Shirley!"

"Don't be silly, Bun, I was just kidding. I'm not going to die, not ever!"

The train pulled into Mullins station at exactly thirty-six minutes after twelve. There were several passengers, and the girls waited their turn to step down to the wooden platform.

As they moved along the aisle, El looked out the windows at the people waiting to board. Almost directly facing her stood a man in a soft brown cap and a brown corduroy jacket; just as she recognized him, he raised his head and looked directly into the coach.

"Mother!" cried El, pulling at Faith's arm, "there's Emmett!" Faith bent down to look out the window, but the man had turned away and disappeared into the crowd. "Oh, I doubt it, honey," she said mildly.

"Mother, I know it was!"

"Well, so what! He's got a right to ride the train if he wants to!" said Jane.

"But Hollie said he was in the Army."

"Oh, for heaven's sake, Ellie, Hollie doesn't know where he is, hasn't heard from him in ages!"

"You just thought it was him because you were talking about Shirley," said Mother.

But El knew better. She thought back to the night on the bridge. Maybe they didn't think it mattered, but she knew Emmett had been in Coville on the night of her birthday. She was certain: Emmett had been the man on the bridge.

Franklin Roosevelt was safely back in the White House, joking with reporters, declaring that the United States was no nearer war after the meeting at sea than she was before. What he failed to say, said Daddy, shaking his head, was, how near we were before!

A three-power conference was to be called in the near future, to include Stalin, aimed at putting on the brakes. At this, it was Mother shaking her head. "Is there no way to stop this?" she asked, and Daddy silently indicated a sorrowful, "no".

Jack Dempsey had joined the circus! The old "Mauler" led the parade around the big top at the Lily reunion, first time he had been on a horse in twenty-five years, he said. When asked, "Wott-all did you want to jine up with a circus fer, Jack?" he answered, "Well, it's a helluva lot of fun!" And in Kentucky, twelve young men, ages 17 to 21, enlisted in the Army together. They had been to grade school together, high school together, and decided to see this thing through—together: it'd be a helluva lot of fun!

Mother tried to interest El in the coming baby more than once during the day, bringing out the small sacques and gowns which she and Jane had embroidered in secret, working on them at night when El and Bun were in bed. Another time she showed the girls the tiny booties she had crocheted, and while Bun was thrilled with the tiny pink and blue flowers on them, El could not be as enthusiastic. She was remembering all the nights she had to bathe Bun, all the trips to take her to potty, all the times she had to stay in the car with Bun while Mother and Jane went into the stores. For months now, she had looked forward to the time Jane would go to college and she could have the room at the top of the stairs as her own. Now she asked, "Where will the baby sleep?" and was told, the baby bed would be in Mother's room, for a while.

"Then where will it be?" she persisted.

"In my room", Jane put in quickly," there's no room in yours." El, somewhat relieved, kept silent. Let them think she wanted the new baby in her room! What did she care—long as she didn't have to take care of it. Still, she knew it would only be a matter of time until she'd have to help with it. Jane would be going to college in another year or two. Bitterly, she wished the new baby would not be born, but realized it was too late to make that wish. Anyone could tell by looking at Mother, it won't be long. Bun was happily putting the new booties on her favorite doll, completely unaware of the disaster to come.

Just before bedtime, Mother asked El to run down to Hollie's, ask her if she wanted to go berry picking with them in the morning. El was glad to get out of the house. She took her time walking down the hot, dusty road, enjoying the cooler twilight hour, past the Collins' house, dark except for Mr. Collins' reading lamp by the window, past grandma Gillespie's—where grandma had already gone to bed—to Hollie's, where the porch light shone brightly, moths already circling wildly under it, bent on self-destruction: in the morning they would be dead, lying on their backs in the window sill.

Hollie stood by her front gate, still dressed in the heaven-blue blouse and white skirt she had worn that morning to Sunday School, her hair floating out from her face in a golden halo, and in the road a man stood talking to her.

El's heart stopped: Emmett was back!

She heard Hollie's gay laughter—it must be all right— and she relaxed as the man turned to face her. It was Mr. Mitchell, and he was laughing too.

"Hey, Ellie! What'cha up to?"

"Mother wants to know if you want to go berry picking with us in the morning?"

"Sure do!" cried Hollie, "wouldn't miss it for the world!" And to Mr. Mitchell, she said, "I'll make you and the boys a cobbler tomorrow night."

"See ya in the morning," said El, starting back to her house.

It was blue-dusk, and over the company store the chimney sweeps were circling, dropping down into the old brick flue one at a time, filling the space between the roof of the store and the dark bridge looming high overhead, rising up, sweeping down, circling, round and round, elliptically, dropping one at a time into the chimney. She watched, standing still in the road, until they were gone. All of them. Swallowed by the chimney. Where did they go in the winter? When the fire heated the bricks and filled the flue with smoke, banked for a slow burn in the night, where did the birds go then? An uneasy feeling passed through her, and she hurried into the house, to the lights and music of her family. Yes, Hollie wanted to go berry picking, she reported and went upstairs to bed. The smell of fried bacon still filled the house, a breakfast smell, but Mother often fried fatback, potatoes, and eggs for Sunday night supper. A bacon smell and pitch-dark outside: everything was upside down.

Mother called them early. By the time Daddy left for work she had the car loaded with buckets, dish pans and baskets lined with newspapers. A thermos jug was filled with cold water and a brown paper bag contained wrapped sandwiches. She gathered up long-sleeved shirts of Daddy's to cover their arms, and her hoe was sticking out the back window, her twenty-two was in the trunk, just in case, and the girls were told to bring their galoshes as protection from snakes.

They climbed into the car wearing shorts and barefooted but brought along socks to wear in the boots. Hollie and Jane carried old pants, not about to get scratches on their legs.

They drove up Herndon Mountain, brown bags handy for the expected car sickness, but before the nausea started Mother turned off the paved highway and followed the crest of a hill, driving on a dirt road, the wheels deep in over-grown ruts. She pulled into the yard of the old Shrewsbury place and stopped the car.

The house, half of logs and half of weathered planks, nearly had collapsed; the porch had rotted out, the roof leaned down against the front wall, and vines—honeysuckle, poison oak, wild cucumber—covered the dilapidated building and ran into the yard. Mother pulled on her high-topped, black rubber boots, put on a long-sleeved shirt and instructed them to do the same, but to remain in the car until she looked around, picked up her hoe and disappeared from view.

In a few moments, she was back. "Come on! We've found a real bonanza! Put on your boots, watch for snakes!" She began to unload the car. They found an old low-branched apple tree and spread an old quilt beneath it, placed the sandwich bag and the water jug on it. "We'll pick while it's cool, then have a picnic. Stay close behind me, Bun, and the rest of you, watch for rattlers—they love blackberries!"

The old rail fence surrounded the original garden plot at the back of the house and it was covered with blackberry bushes, loaded with berries as large as a man's thumb, hanging in clusters of black and red berries, five to ten in a bunch, most of them so ripe they would fall into your hand when touched. The reddish canes arched over the fence row; their straight thorns ready to catch at everything. Mother, Hollie and Jane picked in five-gallon lard buckets; El and Bun carried Karo syrup buckets. El had nearly a half-gallon picked when Bun, straggling behind her, suddenly cried out. They all rushed to her, thinking rattlesnake. There stood Bun, blackberry juice all over her face and hands, being swarmed by small, yellow sweat bees.

"Make 'em go away!" she cried. "Make dose bees leave me alone!"

With great relief, they laughed at her—she had been picking and eating; her bucket was empty! El took her back to the quilt in the shade of the apple tree, wet her shirt-tail and washed her face, gave her a cool drink of water. The sweat bees stayed in the garden with Mother.

Looking for something to do, El climbed the old apple tree. She picked several of the little green apples, which she and Bun ate, even though they were sour. By noon all of the containers were full. They all sat down on the old quilt and ate the brown sugar and butter sandwiches and drank the cold water. The mountain-top breeze dried their hot faces, lifted their damp hair and cooled their perspiring necks. Jane and Hollie, like little girls, pulled the petals from big yellow and white daises that grew in the fields, playing the game "he loves me, he loves me not." El knew Jane was thinking of Ted, but who was Hollie thinking about? El thought she knew and suspected it wasn't Emmett at all when Hollie's daisy said she was loved.

Dry dust swirled in little puffs of air as they rested, enjoying the view. They could see the convoluted hills for miles, wave after wave of mountains, and the nearest of these were beginning to have touches of yellow and red marring the summer sea of green, a brown branch here, a bit of crimson there, the early signs of approaching fall becoming apparent in the heat of mid-summer.

A pileated woodpecker knocked on a short-leaf pine. Bun found a green salamander to play with, and Mother marveled at the trees, heavy with green-yellow apples: they would be coming back to grandma Shrewsberry's before winter.

Mother told them about the old lady, how she had died in Mother's arms, pneumonia developing when the old woman had wandered through the mountains searching for her dead husband in the dead of winter. El felt the elderly grandmother's presence in the hot summer air and shivered. She jumped up and began loading the berries into the car. "Time to go," she said, and Mother agreed. "Berries won't keep long!"

By the time Daddy came home from work there were thirty quarts of blackberries canned for cobbler, and twenty-four pints of blackberry jam sat cooling on the kitchen cabinet. The last few cups of berries had been turned into a cobbler, ready for supper, and Mother was lying on the living room sofa with a wet washcloth over her eyes, nearly dead with the heat.

"That does it!" exclaimed Daddy, looking at her, his hands on his hips. "No more canning 'til that electric stove gets here!"

But Mother replied mildly, "Berries won't wait, Bud."

Edgar was gone. He and Joe had been put on the bus to Logan by their father while El was picking blackberries, and she didn't even know they had planned to go. They had to visit their Grandma; she always bought their school clothes, and school was only two weeks away. They wouldn't be back until Labor Day weekend. And she didn't even get to tell him goodbye.

On Thursday, Doc Steelman came to Coville, making a house call. El met him at the door and took him into the living room to Mother. Mother talked to him for a few minutes, then sent El after Mary Beth. The doctor would see them both while he was here. Hollie and Jane were at the piano when the doctor came, and they stopped singing to greet him. Doc Steelman couldn't get over how well Hollie looked and said over and over how great it was to see her, and how was she getting along, and Hollie smiled and talked vivaciously, bringing the sunlight into the dark living room with her smile. Doc Steelman was extremely pleased to see her and could hardly take his eyes off of her, looking at Hollie even while he followed Mary Beth upstairs to Mother's room. Mother panted up the stairs behind them.

Mary Beth was the first one down. She grimaced when asked what the doctor said, shrugged her shoulders in reply. Jane and Hollie resumed their singing and Mary Beth joined them at the piano. In a short while Mother and Doc Steelman came down the stairs; he ducked his head into the room briefly, waved at the girls and was gone. When Mother came back from seeing him out, the music stopped. What did he say, Mother?

What did he tell you, Mary Beth? Mother smiled, waved her hand, like, nothing special, and went in the kitchen to start supper.

"I was scared," whispered Mary Beth. "He took a long time, and he really hurt me. And when he put that thing on his head and listened, and listened, I thought he'd never stop! I was beginning to think something was wrong, he took so long!"

"What did he tell you?"

"Nothin', didn't tell me nothin'!" She shook her head, then added, "Boy! He's got the biggest hands!"

El, sitting on the couch, took in every word.

The long days of summer stretched under a timeless sun, and El worked in the mornings, read in the afternoons, always staying close by for "fittings" now that Mother had started the school sewing. She alternated between *The Grizzly*, in which Bruce looked exactly like Edgar, and *The Trail of The Lonesome Pine*, in which she became the lovely mountain-grown June, and Edgar was, of course, Jack Hale.

It didn't surprise her when she got a letter from Edgar:

Dear El, I think I've found our Ma. They's a woman here looks just like Joe and she watches us all the time but Grandma won't let on and say she nos her. She looks pore and I want to talk to her if I can befor I come home. Don't you go nowhere without me because yo mite git hurt. Yor frind, Edgar Mitchell.

Jane teased her and Bun begged to see the letter, but El hid it under her mattress and only took it out when she stole a few minutes alone. It was her first love letter even if it was signed "Yor frind", and she knew how Edgar felt about her; it was the same as the way she felt about him.

A deep sadness filled her for the remainder of the day. She went to the living room book shelves and found the old, dog-eared copy of *Jane Eyre*; it suited her mood, and Edgar, of course, now became Edward and would remain so until he was home again.

Every afternoon the heavy thunder clouds rolled over the hills, but it did not rain. The air pressed down, intolerable without a breeze. El and Bun came in the house to avoid the sun, went out to seek moving air, came in, went out, in and out, until Mother screamed, "Shut that door!" They had let the house fill with small black houseflies, flies that crawled over the table, stuck to their arms, tangled in their hair. There was nothing to do but get out the can of Flit. Mother pushed the small pump attached to the can, sending out a stream of insecticide, a stream that ran down the windows and made oily splotches on the furniture. They sat on the porch, waiting for the fumes to evaporate. On the mountains, the clouds rolled together, separated, moved together again, tossed by some high unseen wind, but in the valley between the steep hills, the heat lay over everything, quiet, deathly still.

Shortly after four o'clock it began to rain; by the time Daddy got home it was a torrent, falling in silver sheets, blowing sideways, forcing the windows closed. The smell of Flit was strong; supper was not cooked when the lights went out. Mother, with a teasing smile, said, now, wouldn't I be up the creek if I had a new electric stove? And Daddy said, well, we'd soon wash down that creek if this keeps up. He stood at the dining room window and watched as the water began to rise. Within an hour the creek was running over the concrete wall, biggest flood since the terrible one in which Shirley had drowned—a thought they all tried to bury deep in their minds as they sat down to eat by lantern-light.

Aunt Maude called, biggest flood in the history of Galax, Chestnut Creek had near wiped out the town might near, maybe a million dollars in damage. Grandmother's house was flooded, she had to move in with Aunt Maude, they had a terrible mess to clean up. Could Daddy come? They missed Zane Gray— he would have helped so much; they were having a hard time without him. On the USS ARIZONA—THAT'S WHERE HE'S BEEN FOR A LONG TIME, ON THE ARIZONA OUT IN THE OCEAN, SOMEWHERE. Which ocean? They won't tell us, not things like that, just that he's eatin' good and he's well. He don't write much, but his ship is a real big one and would be important, if it came to war. Can you come, William? But Daddy said, "Hire some boys, Sister, I can't leave the railroad."

It had rained seven inches in Bluefield, and the same in Charleston. Bluefield, high in the mountains, had suffered little damage, but Charleston, on the banks of the great Kanawha, had suffered much. By nightfall the temperature had dropped into the sixties and Daddy was called out to work, first time in weeks, rock slides across the tracks, poles down, wire on the ground. "It's beginning," Mother said sadly, and when asked what was beginning, she answered, "the winter, the long, long winter, the bad weather, the night calls." With a deep sigh, she added, "summer has ended."

Like turning a page, summer moved into fall; although the calendar said August, the mountains knew. The dogwood's red berries were beginning to show as their green leaves developed yellow and rust splotches, chlorophyll retreating to the root system; the hickory and walnut trees were shedding their yellow, torpedo-shaped leaves and their nuts dropped noisily to the forest floor, exploding from their outer shells. The storm had put out the slow-burning slate piles in the coal camps, leaving the air fresh and clean. The sky had never looked bluer or the clouds whiter; the breeze had never felt fresher as it brisked through gaps in the early mornings and late evenings, but lying low during the heat of midday.

FDR had given a very brief report to Congress, reiterating his eight-point declaration of principles; he promised a Labor Day speech to the nation. Not to be outdone, Charles Lindbergh was preparing another speech also, this time to be given on Friday night in Oklahoma. Unlike Roosevelt, however, the "Lone Eagle" was having trouble finding a place to perch; the City Council had cancelled his permit to use the Municipal Auditorium. A spokesman for the America First Committee promised that he would speak, even if he had to use a cow pasture. Lindbergh, of course, was very familiar with cow pastures! Councilman A.P. VanMeter was quoted as saying: "We're not denying the right of free speech by refusing to rent a public building. Let him go elsewhere to speak, and when he gets tired of talking, he can go home!"

Mexico had closed the Nazi Consulate, and instructed her diplomats in German-occupied Europe to return home. Roosevelt had ordered the Navy to operate the New Jersey shipyards, on strike since the seventh of August. All gasoline stations were now closed on Sundays. British and Russian troops had invaded Iran in their first joint military move, racing to obtain the priceless oil wells in that country, while Japan charged that Churchill had lied about the British and United States efforts to keep peace with Japan: they had, in fact, disturbed the peace in Asia by giving aid to Chang Kai-Shek!

The new hosiery manufacturers had planned to use the lovely legs of Marlene Dietrich to popularize their substitution for silk stockings, but Miss Dietrich had tripped over a fire engine hose on a Hollywood set and fractured her ankle. Leg painting was tried by a group of artists who used an air brush to spray on color, followed by fine lines to simulate seams up the back. In Oregon, the girls shed their stockings in a "V for Victory" campaign, and artists painted "V's" up the back of their legs.

By Thursday, Colonel Lindbergh and Senator Wheeler had received numerous offers of a speaking site. The speech would be broadcast live to the nation at 9 p.m. CST.

"Oh, Mother! We'll really hear Charles Lindbergh's own voice!"

"Nine o'clock Central Time is 10:00 our time, past your bedtime, Ellie."

"But Mother, it's like hearing the President—or even better!"

Daddy put down his paper and explained gently, "El, I'm afraid that's not the main problem. He's talking over the Mutual Broadcasting Company. We can't pick that up, here in the mountains. All we get is NBC."

"You can try, can't you? Please?"

On Friday night, Daddy tuned the radio carefully, turning the dial slowly side to side, even switching to short wave channel; although he faintly picked up stations other than Bluefield's WHIS, he couldn't bring in the Mutual broadcast from Oklahoma.

"Why can't all stations carry a speech as important as this one?" she fussed, as she went to bed." Everybody doesn't like that ol' hillbilly music all the time!" Daddy, with a grin, turned the radio up louder—the Bluegrass Boys were playing one of his favorite songs.

Although El didn't get to hear Lindy's voice, she did get to read his speech in Saturday's paper. "It seems to me," the famous pilot had said, "that the quickest way for Germany to lose a war would be to attack America, and the quickest way for America to lose a war is to attack Germany!"

"He is on our side, isn't he, Mother?" asked El anxiously.

"Of course, he is, dear", replied Mother, but Daddy looked thoughtful and added slowly, "He may be on our side, but I'm not sure he's helping it."

B-25 Bomber Crashes on Test-Flight—built by North American Aviation Corporation, crashed four minutes after take-off, radio operator killed, pilot and co-pilot pulled out by bystanders. Cause of crash unknown. (Clipping saved for scrapbook)

Augustus F. Lindbergh, a cousin of Charles Lindbergh's and an Alabama attorney, delivered a speech over the Columbia Broadcasting System, under the sponsorship of a group called Fight For Freedom, said, "I haven't flown an airplane across the Atlantic; I haven't been elected to the U.S. Senate, but neither of these accomplishments have any particular qualities for brain-building." Daddy laughed out loud. "Listen to this," he said, and proceeded to read the article.

"Like most Americans, I don't hesitate to say what I think and so, just as an ordinary citizen, I am having my say, and as such, I have a right to say— that no man has the right to obstruct his government during a national crisis. And that is exactly what some of those on Capitol Hill and one member of the Lindbergh family are trying to do now..."

"Now, this Lindbergh is my kind of man!" exclaimed Daddy. "He thinks the way most Americans do!" Mother drew her lips into a straight line and said primly, "not ALL Americans, Bud." She would defend Charles Lindbergh to her dying day.

The Germans were drawing a close net around Leningrad. The Japanese sent FDR a conciliatory note to reopen negotiations, and in America, the first tanks rolled from three assembly lines, a white star painted on their sides.

Hitler and Mussolini continued their five-day secret conference, and Sunday's paper carried a picture of Adolf and Il Duce; the caption read,

They fashion 'harmony' for Europe. Their explanation was, a 'new Axis' was their purpose for war. Roosevelt worked on his Labor Day address, an address in which he would state, "...we do not covet one square inch of the territory of any other nation..."

Summer challenged fall for one more battle; the sun poured through the dining room windows, making lace patterns on the polished floor as the high-noon program was broadcast. Duke Ellington provided the music, assisted by the Jump for Joy Chorus from Hollywood, and the Golden Gate quartet from New York. William Green represented the AF of L while James Carey was there for the CIO. The President spoke eloquently, and all America listened intently:

On this day, this American holiday, we celebrate the rights of free laboring men and women. The preservation of those rights is now vitally important not only for us who enjoy them—but to the whole future of Christian civilization.

American labor now bears a tremendous responsibility...

We are not a warlike people. We have never sought glory as a nation of warriors...there has never been a moment in our history when Americans were not ready to stand up as free men and fight for their rights!

The cheering of the crowd could be heard in the background, and the group in the Phillips' dining room cheered also, settling quickly as the President continued:

The right of freedom of worship would mean nothing without the freedom of speech. And the rights of free labor as we know them today could not survive without the right of free enterprise...

...I give solemn warning to those who think Hitler has been blocked and halted, that they are making a very dangerous assumption. Where in any war your enemy seems to be making slower progress than he did the year before, that is the very moment to strike with redoubled force...

The Labor Day holiday resulted in five hundred and fifty deaths, up from the previous year's five hundred and fourteen, and nineteen of those were in West Virginia. On Monday night, forty-three of the nation's prettiest girls arrived in Atlantic City to compete for the Miss America Crown; it was ninety-six in New Jersey, in the shade—and there was very little shade.

School would start in the morning. Ten new dresses for school for each girl hung in their closets and one special one for Sunday's. El's favorite was the one specially made for Sunday. Mother had copied the Navy uniform, with a Middie blouse and a pleated skirt instead of pants. El's was navy blue with white piping and a white tie; Jane's was red and Bun's was light blue. Jane didn't appreciate hers, saying it was too 'little girlish' and she was too grown up. She managed to only wear hers when El and Bun were wearing something else. Mother had made Jane a gabardine suit with black buttons and a frilly blouse and Daddy said she looked twenty-five in it and that pleased Jane immensely. But El's excitement was not due to the new dresses! Edgar was coming home! He would be on the evening Greyhound Bus. She sat anxiously on the porch, and heard the air brakes of the bus as it stopped on the highway. He was coming!

"Rachel! Rachel?" Mother was calling from within the house—she'd just have to call!

Mother came to the door, opened the screen and stood with her hands on her hips. "Rachel, I know you heard me! I expect you to answer when I call. I need you this instant!"

There was nothing to do but follow Mother into the kitchen. Her chore was to take out the ashes from the big cook stove—mind you, clean it out good—I don't want ashes dribbling all over the floor when it's moved, and hurry, the men will be here with the new stove any minute now!

She knelt before the old cook stove and shoveled out the ashes, shaking the grate and scraping the few remaining coals through to the ashpan. It was a hard job, and a hot one, for the fire hadn't been out long and the cast iron sides retained the heat. She wiped her face with the back of her hand, unmindful of the soot that had settled there, and left a black streak across her nose. Picking up the pan of ashes, she pushed open the back door to empty them by the creek—and there stood Edgar.

He still wore his white cotton shirt and dark dress pants. He looked a head taller and a year older, and he was going into the seventh grade tomorrow.

El was embarrassed that he had caught her doing such a dirty chore, soot on her hands and ashes on her clothes, but she was unaware that she also had black streaks on her face. Edgar held the screen back and allowed her to carry the ashes through the back gate. Conscious of his new clothes, he remained in the yard as El threw the ashes over the creek bed to settle in the dried weeds along the bank. She sat the pan on the steps and ducked under the long-hanging wands of the willow tree where Edgar waited. They stood looking at each other.

Edgar's eyes looked a deeper blue in the shade of the willow, and his face was much browner than she remembered, but his smile was the same. He took a carefully folded white handkerchief from his hip pocket and wiped the soot from El's face, much like the way Daddy wiped her face, pushing hard with one finger.

"Grandma made me bring it, said I might need it—bet she'd be real surprised at what I need it for!"

They began to talk at once, in a rush, happy at being together. Did'cha get my letter? Did you talk to that woman? Was it your Ma? Went to the movies, got to see that one you saw with all the airplanes—*I Wanted Wings*—see the circus? Went to Virginia—You'll never guess, going to have a new baby at our house! Jane? No! Silly—Mother! Another little sister to sneak off from—could be a boy—no—hear the President's speech? No, I wouldn't go up there alone—tonight? Sure! Soon as Mr. Reeves makes his rounds! New dresses—six pairs of dress-up pants, nah Grandma don't spend on us, Pa gives her the money, El sure wish you were going to Herndon this year—don't want to go without you.

"Rachel! Rachel! You've got to get this job finished! Right now!"

"Gotta go—we're getting a new stove; I won't have to take ashes out ever again! Except from the furnace." As she went inside, the men from Montgomery Wards pulled up in a big truck and proceeded to unload the first electric range in the town of Coville, a white enameled stove with four electric burners, a big oven, and a clock on the front panel beside the dials. Faith declared it was the most beautiful thing she had ever seen. The men took the old coal stove away—a discount had been obtained with a trade in—and all that remained was for Daddy to install the pig-tail and plug it in. They had cold ham sandwiches for supper, leftovers from the Labor Day picnic ham.

After supper El took Bun upstairs early for her bath and scrubbed extra carefully herself." Tomorrow you get to go to school!" She told stories until the excited Bun went to sleep, then opened her book to read. When Mother came to tuck them in, she found everything ready for the morning. Clothes were spread out on the chest, new tablets, crayons and pencil boxes were stacked on a chair, hair ribbons and socks to match the dresses were on the dresser, shoes were lined up beside the bed. Mother observed the preparations and smiled. "You're glad to be going back to school, aren't you, honey?"

"Very glad, Mother," she replied. Her heart ached to add, "I'll miss Edgar," but she didn't dare. Mother wouldn't understand at all, and if she did, it would worry her. Best to say nothing. Mother turned off the light and pulled the door shut softly. Now all she had to do was wait for the gravel on the porch roof.

It wasn't long in coming; shortly after the train went by, it's lonesome whistle echoing down the valley, the rattle-tattle over the bridge diminishing as swiftly as it had come, she heard the rocks rolling down the roof, just loud enough to alert her. She sprang out of bed, dressed, crept out the window, slid down as easily as the rocks, down the post to the rail, dropped on the grass beside Edgar.

He looked more like himself now, with faded denim overalls and old shirt; she immediately felt comfortable with him. Which way? Through the woods, can't take a chance on being seen.

She told him about seeing Emmett in Mullins, and about Hollie receiving threatening letters. He confessed that he had recognized Emmett as being the man on the bridge. Can a man live in the woods and not starve? Hid from everybody? Sure, plenty of things to eat this time of the year, lots of squirrels, lots of nuts and berries—huckleberries are ripe now—but why would he? Lots of towns he can get lost in and nary a soul would know him; why would he stay in the woods? Made sense when she thought about it, but if that was the case, what was he doing on the bridge? And where did he go? They turned the problem over and over but there was no solution.

The new school year was much on their minds and in their conversation; neither wanted to be separated, neither could see how to change the situation. But I'll see you every evening and you can tell me what you are doing and I can tell you what I'm doing, and before long it'll be Christmas—but Christmas seemed light-years away for both of them. You know that B-25 that crashed in testing? Well, that radioman was from Logan; he graduated from Logan High School, took six weeks of schooling and went with that crew. Grandma knew him, knew his family real well. I've started a scrapbook, El confided, everything I find on airplanes; I'll show you. And what about that woman, Edgar, is she really your Mother? But all Edgar said was, best we be getting' back.

They were sitting on the town-side of the track, on the cold steel rail, right across from the wooden platform; in the distance, where the bridge ended and the hillside began, the tracks seemed to come together into a point, and while she was studying the optical illusion, Edgar leaned over and kissed her gently on the lips, like he'd been saving that for last. He grabbed her hand and pulled her to her feet, race ya', he said and started running on the crossties, hitting them square, easily, gracefully, as much at home on the high bridge as he was on the school basketball court, and just as confident. He reached the end of the bridge, turned and waited for El who was practicing running without looking at the spaces between the sleepers, but at a slower pace. They took the sloping road behind the houses, sneaking through the yard beside Edgar's house, across the road and into her yard. There he kissed her again, quickly, a gesture towards her, hardly more, and ran back to his house, disappearing into the shadows.

El climbed to her room, slipped on her gown and sat down by her window, too tense to sleep. She gazed at the high bridge, trying to realize she had actually been up there, looking down, only moments before; now she heard footsteps on the cindered road. She drew back from her window screen and watched, expecting to see Mr. Reeves, or even Emmett, but it was Mr. Mitchell who appeared, walking brisk and care-free, a glowing cigarette between his lips, glowing like the spring fireflies had glowed, on and off, on and off, regular as his breath. Edgar's had plenty of time to get to his own room, before his father came in, if he had gone directly there—but had he? Or had Mr. Mitchell caught him up and dressed when he'd said he was going to bed early, tired from his trip! She watched for several minutes but no light went on in the Mitchell house. Relieved, she slipped into bed beside the warm cuddlesome Bun and was soon asleep.

Seventeen

When the school bell rang on Wednesday morning, September 3, 1941, thirty million children stood with their hands over their hearts and recited the Pledge of Allegiance to the flag of America.

El and Bun stood in the black-dirt schoolyard beside the flagpole with Joe and Bob. Jane, Edgar, Billy and Judith had walked up the road to the highway and caught the school bus to the high school at Herndon. Mary Beth sat at home, waiting for her baby, Ben was on a ship somewhere in the Pacific Ocean.

Things sure were different this year.

El and Bun ran home at the end of that first day, and Mother had cake and milk waiting for them. Bun threw her arms around Mother and exclaimed, "We had fun! Look what I made you, Mama!" She held up a page from her tablet; she had traced her own hand and colored it bright purple. On each fingernail was printed the letter 'B'.

"It's lovely, Bun, but where is your hair ribbon?"

"Lost it," said Bun quickly as she reached for her milk, then added, "School is real fun, Mama. I should have gone last year!"

Daddy had completed the new line along Cub Creek, the new branch of the Virginian, and now coal could be hauled from Red Jacket mine. Logan field loadings had increased markedly over the previous year, in spite of a serious explosion that left one dead and one seriously burned; sparks from a compressor had ignited a pocket of gas. Three more miners were dead in a blast at a quarry. Miners should be accustomed to death, maybe should think, what's one more miner? But miners looked after their own: one hundred and fifty men—employees of the Atlantic Coal and Coke Company—closed their mine and began a search for one of their men who went into the hills looking for roots and herbs to make tea for an ailing stomach, and hadn't returned. It was reported that all he carried with him was a razor.

Two days later the miner turned up; he'd walked over the ridge, climbed to the top of a high peak in Wyoming County to find help, and sent word to a friend to come get him. He had found a ginseng root said to be seventy-five years old, said to weigh a full twelve ounces, a three-pronged stalk with one root as big as a walking cane, enough to heal a powerful lot of miner's stomachs. The miner said it would bring ten or twelve dollars, dried out, but most likely he'd keep it stead of selling. Ginseng grows easily in the rich mountain soil, and after hearing of the giant root, Daddy said he was going to quit railroadin' and go to farming ginseng for a living.

"Where would you plant it?" teased Mother, and Daddy said, "How about the Old Shrewsbury place?" Like he'd given it serious thought. Mother laughed; she had the only green thumb in this family.

"Seriously, Bud, when the girls and I went berry-picking, we found lots of yellow apples at Grandma Shrewsbury's. Why don't we pick some, maybe can a few for pies, or make applesauce—"

"Apple butter!" said Daddy quickly. "Can you make apple butter on that new stove?"

"Bud, I can cook anything that can be cooked on this stove!"

"We'll do it! Nothing better on a cold snowy day than a hot biscuit and apple butter!"

Three local men, two from Herndon and one from Alpoca, were included in the draft, and the Army announced that it would use the State's fire towers— all fifty-seven of them—for lookout posts, watching for more than forest fires now.

The Japanese press finally got around to commenting on the President's Labor Day speech:

The U.S. of late has unreasonably tightened economic pressure against Japan, and they have supplied materials to nations hostile to our Axis powers. Both of these American actions must be rejected by Japan. If the U.S. hides behind the name of freedom of the seas, and objects to Japan's justifiable road, Japan will not hesitate to break through whenever it is necessary.
When Roosevelt declared the Hitler Nazi Army should be wiped out, we believe he meant to say the Axis group should be wiped out as a whole. We

consider the U. S. went too far in declaring an intention to destroy the Axis without participating in the war, but merely by acting as a munitions factory.

With no further rain, the clay soil along the railroad tracks settled again and Daddy was home on time. As usual, after supper he and Mother sat in the dining room, waiting for the news broadcast. Not even something as simple as an apple-picking outing could be scheduled until they knew how things were going for the war.

"We can't trust those slant-eyed hypocrites," said Daddy. "I hope Roosevelt doesn't get blind-sided, concentrating on Hitler and his part in this fighting."

"Don't you think Roosevelt knows what he's doing, Bud?" asked Mother.

"Oh, I guess he does, but you know, a man can just get so much on his plate without it running over. I'm just telling you, there's more to this than what's going on right now—there's a reason Japan is a part of this Tri - - - tri—oh, you know what I mean! Birds of a feather, and so forth."

"You sound like Mr. Gillespie," said El. "He's always saying things like that."

"Speaking of the Gillespie's, anything new with his boys?"

"We know Ben's going to be shipped out, just don't know where he's going yet. Will, well, Mildred doesn't seem to know where he is, just that he's at sea."

"Which sea?"

"Pacific, I believe."

"Uh-oh," said Daddy, "That's not good—that's where those yellow bastards are running things."

"Bud! Your language!"

"Sorry, Faith. You know, sometimes it's difficult to separate my railroad language and my home language"

"Try, will you? For your daughters' sakes?"

"Maybe we'll have a boy baby, Daddy," said Jane, "then you'll have someone you can talk 'railroad' with."

"Yeah," said Daddy," and I can teach him all the railroad songs and jokes, and—"

"Bud! You wait just a minute—"

"Just kidding you, Faith, just kidding you!"

The first U.S. tanker carrying aviation gasoline for Vladivostok is due in the Sea of Japan this week and the Japanese have threatened to close the port as a safety zone around their country. The Russian Premier sends warnings to Japan. Friday's headlines were totally unexpected:

SUBMARINE ATTEMPTS TO SINK U.S. DESTROYER IN ATLANTIC

American Warship Counter-Attacks with Depth Bombs:
Results Unknown; Enroute To Iceland

It was the first hostile action against the U.S. since the war began, and the destroyer, the USS Greer, was carrying letters from home to the Army and Navy
operating out of the Icelandic base. Churchill chose this particular time to send out another appeal for help:

Britain without aid far greater than any yet received cannot win the war for freedom the world over.

Last spring Mr. Collins had left the world map tacked to the schoolroom wall; it showed England white against the ocean-blue background, while the countries across the channel were colored red. Now he extended that red color, spreading it across the borders of the USSR, to correspond with the spread of the German Army.

El, now in the sixth grade, sat in the last row, against the wall. The world map graced the space beside the blackboard, directly in front of her; she stared at that all day. If she sat with her back against the wall, sideways in her seat, she faced the other students, and beyond them, the windows. In this position she couldn't see the terrible map, seeing instead the great footers of the railroad bridge and the young maples that had sprung up along the fence almost directly below the bridge.

The maples were beginning to turn, faint red and yellow leaves among the green, and they stirred faintly in the downdraft below the bridge. She was glad when Joe rang the dismissal bell, inheriting that chore from his older brother, Edgar. For El, without Edgar in the room, it had been a long first week of school.

For the third day in a row, Bun had come home without her hair ribbons. Mother sat her down at the table. "We must have a serious talk, Naomi Louise," she said. El sat down too; it had been a long time since she had called Bun by her real name—it had to be important.

"Where is your ribbon?"

"Lost it."

"Look at me, Bun. Where did you lose it?"

"School."

"Inside?"

Bun looked thoughtful, then nodded.

"No, no you didn't. Someone took it out of your hair. Isn't that right?"

Bun hesitated. "Do you know what lying is, Bun?" asked Mother.

"Yes," said Bun, nodding her red-gold head.

"Tell me, who took your ribbon?"

"Katy Sue."

"Why?"

"She didn't have one."

"Did she take the one yesterday?"

"No."

"Who did?"

"Jo Anne."

"And the one you wore the first day of school?"

"Pansy."

Mother sat back, exasperated. "Bun, how many ribbons do you think I can buy? We can't supply every little girl in your room!"

"You don't have to!" exclaimed Bun, her face lighting up with a bright smile, "Clarissa has her own!"

In the early dawn morning the breeze was cool, moving downward from the woods through three shades of green, the light yellow-green of the sycamores and walnuts beginning to turn, the middle-green of great oaks not yet touched by frost, the deep dark green of hemlock and cedar. Later in the day, as the Earth moved and the mountains pointed to a slanted September sun, the heat would wave down the same light-path and push the cool air back into the night. On a southern slope high in an ancient oak, a rooster-raincrow cawed his pleasure in the soft cool dawn; his lonesome song traveled down the green-breeze path through the woods and spread over the town.

El lay still, feeling the morning. She heard Mr. Reeves leave the storage house and stumble his way home, his feet soft-crunching on the cindered road, slow-dragging over the footbridge, distant slam of the door. All night in the old house? Whatever for? In the air there was the faint smell of woods fire, reminiscent of the forest fires burning in the early summer, when they had suffered through sixteen hundred separate fires before the rains came, clean hardwood burning, without the sulfur smell of winter fires built with coal. The cool breeze and a wood fire: Barker's Creek camping-out sensations, but she had awakened in her own white bed. Why had she awakened so early? Then she remembered. It was Saturday! No school! They were going to pick apples and Mother had promised the Mitchell boys could come along! The whole day to play outside with Edgar and Joe!

Great crows flew over the narrow valley on their way to cornfields above Herndon, calling to each other in flight, their very gathering an early black omen of approaching fall. She heard Daddy and Mother talking, soft muffled sounds rising and falling like the waves of cool air, heard Daddy's feet hit the floor as he got out of bed to go to the bathroom; Mother would be close behind. The day had begun.

She jumped out of bed and dressed quickly, waking Bun with her movements. While Mother cooked a big Saturday breakfast of fried bacon— trimmed, unlike the way Grandma Gillespie left hers, with the thick rind on so it curled in the pan—potatoes, biscuits and eggs. Daddy drove down to Herndon to get the paper, taking Bun with him, returning just as Mother poured thick milk gravy out of a black iron skillet.

"Looks like we've planned th' apple-pickin' just in time," Daddy said.

"Why, what's the trouble, Bud?" asked Mother, looking over his shoulder to read the headlines as Daddy read aloud. "Railroad groups authorize strike for higher pay. Issue to go to President. Walkout set for September 11 by non-operating unions. Mediation Fails. A new major problem was dumped in FDR's lap when 1,250,000 railroad workers authorized a strike for higher wages. A strike of maintenance workers forced the closing of a New Jersey steel mill and some 20,000 Alabama coal miners remain out of their pits." Daddy folded the paper as they prepared to eat. As soon as the blessing ended, El asked, "If the railroad is on strike, will you be home like the miners were?"

"Ha!", said Daddy," If the railroad strikes, I'll be working day and night!"

"I don't think that's fair!" cried Bun, and El agreed.

"Fair or not, honey, that's the way it will be. You see, I'm on salary, and the strike is for those who get paid by the hour. When they lay off, I have three times as much to do—in fact, it's all I can do just to keep the lines hot so the trains can run!"

"But the strike won't start immediately, will it? Don't they have to appoint a fact-finding board and all of that?" asked Mother.

"Sure can tell you're an old railroader," said Daddy with a big laugh.

"What's going on?" asked Jane, coming to the table with a big yawn.

"Bout time you rolled out, sleepyhead!" Daddy said, then continued. "First a board, appointed by the President, then 30 days for a report, then 30 days more before they can strike. This vote was just to get the President's attention—like he don't have enough to worry about!"

"Says here, the crew of the USS Greer believe they sunk that Nazi sub," said Jane, picking up the paper.

"Oh, Wow! Then we are in the war!" cried El.

"Whoa, little girl! Not so fast! We're not quite in it—at least I hope not! We're nowhere near ready for it!"

"Well," interjected Mother, "I'm ready to pick apples! Anyone want to go with me?"

Edgar and Joe, dressed in old overalls and shirts, were sitting on the back steps, ready to go, when the family came out. They expected to do the climbing and tree-shaking for Mrs. Phillips and the girls to pick up. Having Mr. Phillips along was an added bonus— the boys didn't see much of him.

They drove up Herndon mountain, turned into the dirt road leading to the Old Shrewsbury place and parked beneath the gnarled trees. Mother spread her patchwork quilt as before but this time she had a picnic hamper and two thermos jugs of Kool-Aid: it took a heap more lunch when there were three men along.

Dress or no dress, El climbed the trees with the boys and shook the apples down for others to pick up; after all, climbing trees, getting as high up as possible, was the best part of the day!

Hours later, tired, happy, restored, they unloaded the small trailer which Daddy had pulled behind the car. They had picked sixteen bushels of golden delicious apples and Mother sent a good many to her neighbors. Daddy clamped the apple peeler on the edge of the kitchen table and as fast as El could wash them, he peeled them. Jane and Hollie sat with Mother, newspapers on their laps, and cored and sliced.

Shortly before six o'clock, Bun, who had been playing outside, came running into the kitchen.

"Quick! Quick! Come Quick! Come see the sky!"

She opened the back door, "Look, Look, Look!"

They put down their apples and hurried outside to see what had so excited her. The northern sky was glowing brightly, a deep golden hue with flashes of blue and green along the edges of the hills, a golden rainbow of colors, only it was all over the sky, not just a band, waves of gold, bronze and amber, streaks of red and orange, radiating above the hills like a halo.

"It's going to storm," said Daddy.

"That's superstition," said Mother.

"What is it?" asked El, "I've never seen anything like it," said Jane.

By this time the neighbors were out in their yard, talking, calling back and forth, greatly excited. "What do you make of it Tom?" Daddy called to Mr. Collins—as the most educated member of the community, it was his place to give an opinion, but he just shook his head in wonderment.

"It's the Aurora Borealis," said Mother calmly, "the Northern Lights."

Mr. Collins quickly agreed with her, but added, "I've never heard of them coming this far south before!"

"I saw them once," said Grandma Gillespie, "but I was a whole lot further north, and a whole lot younger, back in 1910, or was it 1908 "-she was lost in remembering."

Daddy shook his head and said again, "It's going to storm. Just wait and see. We're going to have a real gully-washer."

The next day they learned that Mother had been correct in her assessment of the spectacular show, but the weather remained warm and beautiful, with only whiffs of clouds drifting across an azure sky, not a sign of rain anywhere.

The U.S. and Nazi relations were entering an extremely critical stage. The Germans were blaming the USS Greer for the incident with the U-Boat, saying that the destroyer fired the first shot and that the submarine only used the torpedoes in self-defense. The Germans strongly denounced Franklin's policy and placed the entire incident at the President's feet. Roosevelt ignored the Nazi charge, but announced that he would address the nation again on Monday night—and arrangements were made to broadcast the speech in fourteen languages. The world awaited his message.

Greatest salvo in Naval history is heard as ten guns and 20,000 pounds of metal is fired from the USS North Carolina, a 35,000 ton battleship being tested. The ship gave a slight list as the shells screamed into the air. (Clipping saved for scrapbook)

"Let's see," said Mother, figuring on a brown paper bag with a stub of a pencil. "Jars, 80 cents a dozen, caps, 10 cents a box, sugar, five pounds for 20 cents, and apples for free. Comes to about twelve cents a quart. Not bad!"

"You forgot something," said Daddy.

"What?" demanded Mother.

"The gasoline—and my labor!"

"Oh, you!" and she threw her balled-up apron at him. "You'd better enjoy that apple butter! When this new baby comes, I'll not have much time for making apple butter and jam and such."

"Won't have the sugar, either," said Daddy," and probably not the gas to go after apples."

"We'll get by," Mother said softly, "now, I might have to take up squirrel-shooting again."

"You shot a squirrel?" demanded Bun.

"Best shot around," bragged Daddy, patting Mother on the shoulder. "Kept us in many a meal, back in the bad times, a fat squirrel and a little gravy—"

"What bad times, Mother?" asked El.

"Depression times, Ellie. I saw some terrible things; hope we never go through that again."

"Like what?" El insisted.

"Well, like a mother breast-feeding one baby and pregnant with another and her so thin, malnourished, poor as a whip-poor-will, but still milk for that baby because she didn't have anything else …"

"Here, now!" interrupted Daddy, "Mustn't be thinking about those times, you'll jinx our boy! You've got to think happy thoughts!"

They were immediately distracted. "You really think it'll be a boy, Daddy?"

"Of course it'll be a boy! My God! What would I do with another girl around here? Lord! Even the cats are female! I need somebody on my side!"

Bun, distressed as usual when Daddy pretended to feel sorry for himself, curled herself in his lap and put her white arms around his neck. "I'm on your side, Daddy" she said, hugging him hard, and Daddy hugged her back, grinning, the very picture of a satisfied man.

During the hot, torrid days of July and August events had seemed to move in slow-motion; now, with September, the pace accelerated: the Russian Army defeated eight Nazi Divisions near Smolensk in their greatest victory yet. The Railroad workers prepared to strike. Two hundred Keystone miners walked out in a dispute over a clause in their contract, and the population of Wyoming County rose, obtaining the greatest increase of any county in the state, a forty-two-point three percent increase over 1930.

Roosevelt's address for Monday night was anxiously awaited, but at noon on Monday, Mrs. Sara Delano Roosevelt, Franklin's beloved mother, passed away. The family retreated into privacy to mourn, and the speech was postponed. The funeral was held on Wednesday.

By Wednesday, the railroad had set their strike date for September fifteenth. Churchill was begging for more help from the U.S. Navy and a second U.S. freighter had been sunk in the Red Sea, again with no loss of life. The President's speech was rescheduled for Thursday night at nine o'clock.

Now that school was in session, the days settled into a routine. The two younger girls were dismissed at two-thirty, and when Joe rang the bell they raced home, El adjusting her long legs to Bun's short ones, threw their books and papers on the dining room table and attacked the milk and cookies ready for them. They ate and talked, telling Mother the news of their day, highlighting the events in response to her faithful attention. By three-thirty Jane was home from high school; while Mother listened to Jane, El and Bun could go out and play until suppertime. With cooler weather, ball games were resumed in the triangle, but sometimes jump rope, tag, or hide-n-seek were preferred.

When Daddy came home, at four or four-thirty, supper was ready, and they heard the news while they ate. After supper, while Jane helped Mother with the dishes, El helped Bun with her bath and bathed herself. After this they were expected to do assigned homework and review the day's lessons. If there was free time, they could read or listen to the radio until nine o'clock, which was bedtime, and that hour was changed only for very special events—like a Presidential speech.

On Thursday night, September 11, 1941, they sat at the dining room table in their nightgowns and listened while Franklin Roosevelt addressed the nation:

My fellow Americans:

The Navy Department of the United States has reported to me that on the morning of September 4th, the United States destroyer Greer, proceeding in full daylight towards Iceland had reached a point southeast of Greenland. She was carrying mail to Iceland. Her identity as an American ship was unmistakable. She was then and there attacked by a submarine. Germany admits that it was a German submarine…

Daddy placed the world globe in the center of the table, and as the President continued, he traced the ship's route on the globe for the girls to see.

"…I tell you the blunt fact that the German submarine fired upon this American destroyer without warning and with deliberate design to sink her…"

Mother sat by the good lamp, quietly stitching on a small flannel gown; now her needle was motionless, poised above the soft white material, as she listened intently.

…To be ultimately successful in world mastery, Hitler knows he must get control of the seas. He must first destroy the bridge of ships which we are building across the Atlantic, over which we shall continue to roll the implements of war to help destroy him and all his works in the end…

Bun had given up; curled on the floor beneath the dining room table, she was sound asleep. Daddy took his jacket from the back of a chair and covered her tenderly.

We have not sought a shooting war with Hitler, but neither do we want peace so much that we are willing to pay for it by permitting him to attack our naval and merchant ships while they are on legitimate business. Let this warning be clear. From now on, if German or Italian vessels of war enter the waters, the protection of which is necessary for American defense, they do so

*at their own peril. The Orders which I have given as Commander-in-Chief to
the United States Navy and Army are to carry out that policy at once!*

"We have just entered the war," said Daddy, and he bowed his head; it
wasn't clear if he was crying or praying, but tears ran down Mother's face and
she made no move to hide them. Jane quietly arose and went upstairs to her
room. El spun the globe on the table, blurring the outlines of the countries until
they ran together. Half-listening as the President continued, she made a
discovery which she would never forget: there was more ocean than land in
the world, for when the globe was spinning, there was more blue than green.
No wonder Hitler wanted to control the seas.

*...can only be regarded as a part of the general Nazi design to abolish the
freedom of the seas and to acquire absolute control and dominion of the seas
for themselves ...the next step would be domination of the United States...
You have now attacked our own safety. You shall go no further!*

"All that's needed now," said Daddy, "is the paper work—the formal
declaration of War. "He turned the radio off, picked up Bun, and over her
shoulder, said, "Coming, Mother?" El followed her Daddy up the stairs to her
own bed, and Mother was left alone, sitting with the baby gown in her lap,
quietly crying.

Charles Lindbergh responded to the President's speech with one of his
own, given in Des Moines, Iowa, prepared for the America First rally:

*"The three most important groups which have been pressing this country
toward war are the British, the Jewish, and the Roosevelt Administration."*

*They planned first to prepare the United States for foreign war under the
guise of American defense; second, to involve us in war, step by step,
without our realization; third, to create a series of incidents which would
force us into the actual conflict.*

In Tokyo, the Japanese were reviewing the whole question of war in the
Pacific, and changes were expected in their policy as the Japanese papers
indicated that Japan should depend on none but herself.

On Saturday it was learned that the Germans had launched a submarine attack on a British convoy and sunk twenty-two vessels. They responded to FDR's speech by saying his contentions were all lies, but the United States refused to draw "lines" in the ocean, repeating that attacks anywhere would hold the likelihood of retaliation.

Now the war colored every aspect of their lives: when the coal strike was discussed, it was in terms of what it would do to the war effort; when the rail strike was mentioned it was in respect to the tying-up of war goods, and when it was reported that the CCC boys on East River Mountain had killed three rattlesnakes, it was immediately recalled that Roosevelt had called the German subs the "rattlesnakes of the Atlantic". But, in the long run, Roosevelt's announcement was nothing more than a restatement of Hitler's warning after the Roosevelt-Chamberlain meeting in which Hitler had stated that the Axis would sink any ship that got in their way.

The British gave an account of the attack on their convoy on Sunday; three ships had been sunk by the German submarines, four by bombs from air, one was damaged by fire, for a total of eight; the Germans had claimed thirty-one ships were destroyed.

Even the preacher talked of war; his Sunday sermon was entitled, 'Victory Over Sin,' and Jane brought the 'redheaded peckerwood' home for dinner as usual, much to Daddy's dismay.

"They're getting too thick, Faith," he'd warn Mother every Sunday, as the young people walked down the road to Epworth League meetings and evening services. "We're asking for trouble."

Mother would smile and answer softly, "Trust your daughter, Bud. She's a good girl."

And every Sunday night El went out her window to join Edgar, waiting in the yard below her window. They slipped out regularly to climb the mountain and walk out on the high black bridge, considering the small wooden platform halfway out as their own special place, the one place where nobody would intrude as they discussed everything under the sun, or, rather, under the stars. They, too, talked about the war, thrilled with every report on the high-flying bombers which were spreading terror through the occupied territories with the constant pounding, the soundless flying in, the sudden release of bombs, the quick return to base.

Saturday night Mother had taken the girls to see *Dive Bomber* with Errol Flynn, Fred McMurray and Alexis Smith, while Daddy attended his meeting at the Masonic Lodge. She recounted every detail of the movie to Edgar while sitting high above the camp, overlooking the schoolyard.

When the subject of the movie was exhausted, they sat in silence for a few moments. Suddenly, El recalled what Mary Beth had said, about Ben seeing her with Will—and they had been behind the school! If *Ben had seen them, he must have been on the bridge!*

She sat still, looking down at the pine trees bordering the back of the schoolyard, visualizing the needle-strewn ground beneath their thick boughs, seeing the two young people straining together, primitive in their passion. She was seeing more than Mary Beth and Will. There were older generations now grown and gone, giving in to ancient rites, seeing young Indians rutting on the frost-covered ground, spawning in the flower-filled cove beside the small stream, raising their young beside the sweet-flowing waters of Gooney Otter creek, long before white lovers, before schools, leaving their song in the great-leafed trees, a song played every spring by the winds of time, playing now, for them, reaching across the centuries to stir their feelings. She became conscious of Edgar's warm arm beside her own, felt his breath as he looked at her, as he tried to read her thoughts watching the expressions playing over her face. *Ben would have been sitting where she and Edgar were sitting, a real bird's eye view. It pained her to realize that others came up on her bridge! Who else watched the goings and comings in the town from this high black aerie?*

Eighteen

Franklin Delano Roosevelt has requested another six million dollars under the Lease-Lend bill, making a total of twelve million dollars appropriated for the " foreign" war effort. Quick Congressional approval was expected. Yet, we were not "really" in the war. What do you think he'd ask for if we were "really in the war?" The discussion went on and on, everyone sitting on the edge of their seats, "waiting for the other shoe to drop," said Mr. Gillespie to anyone who would listen. He immediately followed that with, "I've got two boys in, you know, my only sons, both in the Navy, somewhere out in the ocean—which ocean? Hell, I don't know, they never tell us anything, you know."

Doc Steelman had examined Mary Beth and Mother during the early hours of the afternoon; when El and Bun came racing home from school, the doctor's car was parked in the road before the house and the big man was seated at the dining room table, enjoying a slice of lemon pie with his coffee. Mother quickly provided pie and milk for the girls and sent them to the front porch to eat; El suspected there was something wrong, but the windows were closed due to a slight chill in the air and it was impossible to hear their conversation. The question was, did Mother have a problem or was it Mary Beth?

Doc Steelman left, tossing Bun's red curls on his way out and patting El on the back, promising to see them next week.

That night as they gathered around the table to listen to the news, static crackled in the air and it was impossible to tune the radio. Suddenly, a weird red and yellow light filled the room, reflecting through the dining room windows in strange flaming shadows. They rushed outside to see a repeat of the northern lights, but this display was far more spectacular than the first: beams of red and violet light shot across the sky, licking upward like the forests were on fire, coming from the hills in radiant arms of red, green, blue, and violet, moving, flickering, grandly flaring above the hills. As neighbors gathered again, El shivered, possibly from excitement, but then she noticed that Mother had her apron wrapped around her arms for warmth, and Bun had crept into Daddy's arms. The temperature dropped suddenly, noticeably, and as the grand display ended, they felt the icy northern air sweep down from the mountains. It was impossible to listen to the radio, due to the magnetic storm, and they ate in near silence.

Near dusk, a flock of bluebirds settled on the front lawn for a few moments, gathering for a final chorus before flying south, bright pieces of blue-summer sky fallen on the drying grass. Across the creek crickets sang with a slower rhythm due to the cold, accompanying the wind whistling faintly in the trees.

Saturday morning saw the first frost on the mountain-tops, brightening the dogwoods to a fair red, sweetin' the fruit on the pawpaw trees, and putting a blush on the wild spicy-smelling grapes. Also on Saturday, the Nazis announced that the capitol of Kiev had been taken: four Russian armies were trapped and faced annihilation.

Fall arrived officially on September twenty-third, but by then the trees had burst into color like Abraham's burning bush, a brilliant sacrifice to the god of winter. On the twenty-third, another U.S. ship was sunk, the first one since Franklin Roosevelt had issued his, "You shall go no further" warning. The freighter carried a crew of thirty-four, and it was uncertain what had happened to them. The freighter, named "Pink Star", was a Danish steamship which had been taken over by the maritime commission. The next day the USS Massachusetts, a 35,000-ton battleship, was launched, and sixteen men from the Wyoming-Mercer County area joined the Navy.

September twenty-fifth: FDR requests the repeal of the Neutrality Act, and Charles Lindbergh has been accused of being anti-Semitic because of his speech in Des Moines. The policy-making body of the America First committee issue a statement which included, in part, the following: *There is but one real issue—the issue of war...*"

El and Bun raced home; this morning Mother had promised to make donuts for their snack, if she and Mary Beth got back from Mullins in time. In spite of the gasoline shortage, Mother had made two trips into town in one week, one on Monday, and again on Thursday. After the first trip she wouldn't say anything, and neither would Mary Beth. Even Hollie was mum about their reason for the second journey.

When they arrived home, the donuts were sizzling in the black Dutch oven, and Mother, Mary Beth and Hollie were sitting in the dining room laughing and joking, clearly excited about something, something they were calling a "grand surprise" but wouldn't share it until Jane got home, nearly another hour. El and Bun pestered and begged, but, no, it was Mary Beth's secret and she wanted to wait on Jane. A party-like atmosphere had taken over by the time Jane came in, dropped her books on the table and collapsed in her usual seat, held waiting for her. "Whose birthday?" she asked. "What's going on?"

"We're celebrating, all right," said Mother.

"Tell us! Tell us, Jane's here, you said you'd tell us."

"Well," said Mary Beth, her eyes shining, pleasure pinking her cheeks. "I know you'd never guess, so I'll just tell you! I'm going to have TWINS!"

In the shocked silence that followed only Bun spoke. "What's twins? Is that like Billy n Bob? You're going to have boys?"

Everyone talked at once; what did the doctor say? How does he know? Two heart beats, no, Bun, took a picture and there are two heads, no! not a baby with two heads, two babies! Ben doesn't know, he's on some ship on the sea—and Mary Beth burst out crying, long, hard sobs and drawn-out wails, "What am I going to do-o-o-o-o-?"

Finally, with a big gulp, she exclaimed, "I'm scared!"

Mother hugged the distraught girl to her, pulling her brown head against her own child-big belly. "Every woman who ever had a baby is scared, Mary Beth, wouldn't be natural, not to be afraid. But you'll forget all about that when you see the baby—babies! Forget the fear, the pain, you'll see! Now don't waste your time worrying, just take real good care of yourself and it'll be all right. You've got to eat good, walk every day, and think good thoughts. Everything else will take care of itself. Now, don't forget, you are eating for three!"

West Virginia farmers enjoyed nearly perfect weather in which to harvest their crops, as did most of the nation. Temperatures ranging upwards as high as ninety-four helped speed the gathering. Within the state one hundred and ten bushels of corn were produced per acre of hilltop land, and eight hundred pounds of tobacco per acre. Five million bushels of apples had been picked for marketing, milk production was up by three percent, and hens were laying an average of one hundred eggs each. Peaches, pears and grapes had exceeded last year's crop, while hay, oats and barley held the same.

Mr. Reeves spent most of his day cutting and shocking the corn around the old storage house, and late in the evenings he could be seen sitting on the old porch, shucking the long ears, dropping the outer shucks in a pile on the ground. He musta worked into the night, some said, 'cause way late the smoke poured out of the chimney, blue, hard-hickory smoke, filling the town with the brisk odor of wood-fires.

In Logan, two men were sent to jail for moonshining but released on five hundred-dollar bonds; a raid on Slate Creek produced two sixty-gallon stills plus four hundred gallons of mash. Those fellers, when caught, were given six months in jail.

Down in the Gulf of Mexico a great storm was brewing with seventy-five mile per hour winds, flooding Galveston and causing extensive damage, and in Washington, a different storm was raging as officials discussed methods of repaying the Lend-Lease funds. Some argued that the United States was receiving payments of sorts already, when the British passed on war secrets, and others said it was a mighty high price for an earful of gossip!

The Duke and Duchess of Windsor arrived for a visit to the White House. The Duke, dressed in a pin-striped double-breasted gray suit, and the Duchess—the former Wallis Warfield of the United States, for whom the Duke gave up the English throne—dressed in a black tailored suit and large turquoise earrings, appeared before a great crowd, and the crowd cheered and waved, declaring their eternal love for the romantic couple. Every woman in America wanted a black suit with turquoise earrings after their visit.

The Japanese quietly celebrated the first anniversary of their Axis Alliance on Saturday, it coming at a time when both Japan and America were trying hard to reconcile their differences. "The fundamental purpose of the Tripartite Pact is not the military alliance of the past," the Japanese declared, "but to restore peace." But on Sunday, the Japanese were wildly triumphant over the capture of Changsha, an important capitol of the Hunan province. Chaing Kai-Shek would be without important food supplies; American aid was on its way, arranged under the Lend-Lease program.

The radio was filled with reports that the Russians had captured thousands of German and Rumanian soldiers who had attempted to crack the defenses around Leningrad, and Winston Churchill announced that British shipping losses had diminished since Roosevelt's announcement that the U.S. would shoot back.

Lack of rain during September had hastened the turning of leaves and now reduced the fall pasture. Perhaps it was as the old timers said: the display of the northern lights was an omen of hard times to come. They recalled 916-1917 when the Aurora Borealis had been so bright that many thought the world had caught on fire, and during that winter it was so cold the cattle froze standing on their feet. Now the grass was so brown and dry that the livestock would be shipped to the packing houses early—cows don't fatten on roots alone.

Down in the coal fields all the talk of cows and farming seemed remote; it was hard to think of West Virginia as a farming state; all they saw was coal mining, railroading, and once in a while, a loggin' operation. Where were all those cows, anyway? In Coville, Old Bess was one of a kind, the only cow in town.

With October came the rain. Steady, soaking rain, falling from the gray cloud-mass that rested on the ridgetops like a lid on a kettle. The corn, oats and hay not already shocked lay sodden on soaked fields, left to rot or to feed the deer, wild boars and birds that roamed the hills through the winter.

The Russians lost Poltava, fifty-eight additional Czech hostages had been slain by the Nazis, and Roosevelt has asked Canada to admit U.S. ships to her ports: this would require reversing the Neutrality Act.

The rain didn't bother the Yankees and the Dodgers as they battled for the World Series championship. New York won the first game, three to two over Brocklyn. As they did every year, Mother and Daddy gambled, betting a quarter on their favorite team, Mother for the Dodgers, Daddy a firm Yankee fan.

Galax went dry, voting to reverse their stand on the sale of liquor, beer and wine, the ministers of the city having convinced the people that the great flood was God's punishment for their evil ways. Aunt Maude called to tell Daddy she had a great deal of expense, cleaning and repairing Grandmother's house, and since he couldn't come and "do his part" he could just send money, and yes, she had heard from Zane Gray and yes, he was on a really big ship, the Arizona, she thought, but she wasn't sure, they didn't get mail regular.

By Friday night both the Chinese and the Japanese were claiming victory in their battle, and the Dodgers won the second game of the series, three to two. It seemed that both battles were evenly matched.

With school now in session, Saturdays became shopping day; the girls went to Mullins with Mother while Daddy stayed by the phone. With all the rain, he expected slides on the railroad.

G.C. Murphy's had the new, sheer, crepe hose, advertised as 'silk crepe' by the manufacturers to confuse the ladies, and ease their pain at giving up 'real silk' stockings. The new product was on sale for a dollar, and Jane had saved her weekly allowance to buy a pair, declaring them to be a necessity, not a luxury, and as important as buying war stamps, which is where El and Bun put their dimes.

Faith bought a great roast, large enough for three meals, and fish and salmon, all at thirty-five cents a pound. As a special treat she bought grapes, both small green ones and large, purple ones, both for six cents a pound. With a bag of coffee, a pound of tea and bread, she could feed her family handsomely for two weeks or more, for everything else was canned, dried, or stored in sawdust under the house where it would keep all winter.

After a sustained silence, Hitler made a long, dramatic speech. He opened the Third Reich's Winter Charity Drive by declaring that Germany had unlimited war supplies, and their campaign was on schedule.

Roosevelt, speaking on behalf of the U. S. Community Chest, said,

The American people have given generously but this year we must give more...we must build up, not merely our army and our navy, but we must build up the well-being of our civilian population.

In Fort Wayne, Indiana, Charles Lindbergh also was speech-making, before a standing-room-only crowd in the Gospel Tabernacle:

...time has come when we must consider whether there will even be an election next year. Such a condition may not be many steps ahead on the road our President is taking us.

Puzzled, El asked, "Is Charles Lindbergh going to run for President, Mother?"

"Of course not, Ellie, it's just that he's so against getting involved with the war." But Lindbergh continued to plead for *a destiny for America that is independent of these European conflicts.*

Senator Pepper, (D. Fla.) took it upon himself to reply to Lindbergh's statements: "He is following the same path Hitler took—Hitler's highway

to power was by arousing the people against their government and making them believe he was their only savior, and by denunciation and persecution of the Jews, by stirring up class and race prejudices, and by drawing to his side the ambitious and misguided and deluded men of money!"

El was confused and questioned her parents. Was Lindbergh, right? Would the President get the country into war without anyone else having a say?

Daddy exploded. "For God's sake, Ellie, don't be ridiculous! This ain't Nazi Germany! And Franklin Delano Roosevelt ain't Hitler! Of course he'll go to Congress!"

But Mother quietly unfolded the newspaper, turned to the editorial page and handed it to El to read:

Lindbergh Unpopular Because He Refused To Join War Party

What a tragedy Colonel Lindbergh got off on the wrong foot and took the unpopular side of the foreign wars. Had the Lone Eagle espoused the cause of the war party and advocated this nation plunging into the embroglio, no doubt the drums would have rolled some time ago as our boys took their departure for the seat of conflict and as the U.S. Navy roared its guns into bloody battle.

"What's e-m-b-r-o-g-l-i-o?" asked El, spelling the word to Mother.

"Embroglio," said Mother, pronouncing the word easily. "Look it up."

El knew she would say that—she always did. She pulled the dog-eared Webster's out of the bookcase and turned to the "E's".

"It ain't in the dictionary!" she exclaimed.

"Don't say, 'ain't'," said Mother. "Look again. Spell it with an 'I'. Sometimes newspapers make mistakes."

"It means a fight, a big battle," said Daddy. "That's one of those fancy French words Hugh Ike Shot likes to use now and then." Mother looked at Daddy and smiled, nodding her head.

El continued to read: "Lindbergh would have been acclaimed our hero as of yore and have been placed at the head of the Air Force…"

El put down the paper, still confused. "Is he making fun of Lindbergh?"

"Not exactly, Ellie. He's making fun of the way we handled World War One."

"It's called sarcasm," said Mother, "saying the opposite of what you mean."

El still didn't understand. Was the paper supporting Lindbergh? Or Roosevelt? She gave up and returned to her book. It didn't matter; she, like Mother, would be on Lindy's side no matter what happened. She *was sure that Lindbergh would be one of the first to fight for his country if the Germans dared to come over here!*

"Look, Mother," Jane said, calling attention to an ad in the paper as Ellie laid it down. "New fashion trend—carpet all over the floor, instead of wood."

"Instead of rugs? Wouldn't that get awfully dirty? I like to take my rugs outside and beat them—I don't think I'd like them nailed down."

The third game of the World Series was rained out, first time in five years a game was not played due to rain. By Monday it was all over as the Yankees beat the Dodgers three to one for the world championship. "All right, now, "Daddy said, "Pay up! Where's my quarter?" She passed it to him, and he handed it right back. "Buy war stamps with it," he said, and El thought, "that wasn't really winning anything, why bet at all?"

The Nazis were pushing a long, hard, drive towards Moscow, determined to beat the winter snows, while in West Virginia it was anything but winter as the mercury climbed to an unprecedented ninety-four degrees, thirteen degrees above the norm for this time of the year. The leaves remained on the trees, turned by an early frost, but not yet falling, and the grass began to green up. Beside the house, Mother's rose bushes put out buds by the dozens, recovering from the severe cutting for the wedding with double the number of buds.

The Congressional committee approved the additional Lend-Lease funds, promising clouds of airplanes and acres of tanks to defeat Hitler. FDR asked for authority to mount guns on U.S. Merchant ships, and, at last, requested that Congress repeal the crippling provisions of the Neutrality Act. Our ships would bristle with guns like thorns on a rosebush before the winter snows.

For the last few weeks the relations between the United States and Japan had improved somewhat, but now the friction began to increase. Japanese leaders were telling their people that a break with the U. S. could be drawing near, but America was preoccupied with the terrible moves being made by Hitler as the German Army surrounds Moscow.

Now it is fall: frost settles into the valley as temperatures drop into the thirties; corn shuckin' and tater digging are resumed in earnest, and in the back yard the giant willow begins to shed its yellow leaves—miniature subs—covering the dried grass. A steady downpour begins, raining all night, Thursday, all day Friday, and into Friday night. By Saturday snow is reported in the mountains of Pennsylvania, but it failed to reach southern West Virginia.

Daddy went to work Thursday morning, as usual, worked through the night, all day Friday, and into Friday night, steady as the rain, replacing the poles he had put in during the summer along the new Cub Creek line. As the earth washed and settled, trying to stabilize into its newly made bed, the poles had dislodged.

El and Bun brought out their boots and waded the black mud to the schoolhouse, tracking it into the hall, bringing it home with them to the back porch floor.

The movie, *Sun Valley Serenade*, came to the Wyoming Theater and Jane started begging to see it. "It's Milton Berle, Daddy, and you like him!" When Daddy didn't respond, she added, "It's not the actors, Daddy, it's the music!"

"What's so special about the music?" he asked, too tired to even talk about going anywhere.

"Glen Miller and his orchestra are playing, and it's got a song about a train—" Daddy threw up his hands, "Good God! Why would I ever want to spend money to see a movie about a damn train!"

In spite of his protests, they talked him into going, and for the next few days the girls sang, "*Pardon me boys, Is that the Chattanooga Choo-choo? I've got my fare, and just a trifle to spare...*" Even Bun learned all the words and it became a family favorite in the sing-alongs around the piano. But the song Jane loved best, and practiced until she got it down perfectly, was called "In The Mood". When she played it everyone danced, or jiggled or tapped their feet.

The best thing about trips to town now was looking at the Halloween candy, and the girls begged Mother to buy it for Trick or Treat, but Mother repeatedly said, no, not yet, you would eat it all before Halloween. But Mother, it's only a couple of weeks...and I'll be going to town five times before Halloween, Mother would reply. Next to Christmas, Halloween was their favorite holiday.

Mother and Mary Beth were going to the clinic weekly now, and other days Mother was teaching Mary Beth to sew. They bought small squares of pastel gingham and percale and made little dresses and gowns by the dozens, tripling the number ordinarily needed for one baby. They made an equal number of pink and blue, stitched extras in green and lavender and yellow, until the dining room table looked like the baby department in a store. At night Mother sat with knitting needles and yarn, making booties and sweaters, for Mary Beth didn't know how to knit. It felt strange, Mother said, being a mother again, and at the same time feeling like a grandmother, because Mary Beth was one of her girls.

Although Hollie had gone to Mullins the first few trips, she was no longer going, saying only that she had things to do. Faith felt anxious about this and tried talking to Daddy about it, but all he said was hum, or un-hum. Nobody had seen or heard from Emmett in many weeks and he was never mentioned, like he had never been.

El slipped out on Sunday night as usual, to join Edgar on the bridge. She was now accustomed to walking the crossties and didn't even look at her feet, lifting her head instead to the brilliant heavens where the stars made an inspiring sight. Tonight, the moon was faintly silver, still too young to dim the beauty of the planets. Edgar identified the brighter ones. "that's Mars, there, just south of the Moon, and look—look there! That's Jupiter. Looks' like Venus, don't it?"

El agreed, not knowing one planet from another, wondered at his ability to pick out constellations as he named them. Edgar scolded, "Now, if you're going to be a pilot, you best git to learning the stars!"

"Maybe I'll be a nurse and fly as an airline hostess."

Edgar thought that over and nodded in agreement. El became angry when he accepted her change in plans so easily. Silently she resolved to learn all the planets, the dippers, the bears and everything—she'd show him! While he talked about basketball games at Herndon, and football at Mullins, she was quiet. Sensing that something was wrong, Edgar grew still also. It was peaceful on the bridge, only a faint, sweet breeze blowing, almost spring-like in its pleasantness. Gradually El's anger blew away and she wanted to talk. Edgar confided that he was one of the tallest boys at Herndon and would be on the basketball team. She looked at him proudly, admiration showing in her face. Embarrassed, she looked away quickly and asked, "Do you believe in ghosts?"

"No," said Edgar, laughing at her change in subject.

"Lindbergh did."

"No, what he saw was spirits. Not ghosts."

"Same thing, ghosts, spirits"

"No," said Edgar with a firm shake of his head. "Spirits, now, they're people you knew, and they're friendly, helpful-like. 'Member, they watched over Lindy, took care of him. Now, ghosts, they belong in their grave, except at Halloween or like Granny Hall, on the day she was killed, but they've got out, and they belong back in their grave. Now, spirits are good, but ghosts will chase you—"

"Lindbergh said he could see them without turning his head, said he was out of his body, floatin' with them—"

"Probably day dreaming, you've done that, ain't ya?"

El thought it over. That wasn't what Charles Lindbergh had written, and he should know. He was the one that had seen them. Aloud, she said, "You think Granny Hall is a mean ghost?"

"Sure, she's out to get you—all she's after is to scare you—Gr-rrr!"

Edgar lunged at her and El, screaming, rolled away from him. Edgar grabbed her, afraid she would fall between the sleepers, and holding her, his arms around her tight, he kissed her quickly. He read her well, saw her withdrawal, as she asked, "What are we going to do for Halloween?"

Releasing her, he said, "We'll think of something—maybe pull a good one on ole man Reeves—look, here he comes!" They lowered their heads and watched the man leave his house and go to the old storage building below them; minutes later he came out, walked up the road toward the highway, carrying his gun over his arm as always.

"Bet that gun don't even shoot," he said.

"Yes, it does. Mother saw him shoot the head off a rattler fifty foot away."

A car came up the highway from Herndon, turned beside Mr. Reeves, paused briefly and went back the way it had come. Mr. Reeves started back home.

"Old Coot. He's going to git caught one o' these days. They was lawmen in Herndon last week, smellin around."

"What do you mean, get caught?"

"Why, you do know what he'd doin', don't you? Why, he's moonshining, sure as shootin'! Right in the middle of camp, too! Ain't that nerve?"

"Hey, I've got an idea!" El suddenly cried, inspired. "On Halloween, let' tip over his still!"

Edgar leaned back and looked at her in amazement. "Why, Miss Phillips!! You do have the grandest ideas!" and they rolled with laughter, and El, afraid he'd fall off, grabbed for him. They rolled on the tracks together, like it was the grass in El's front yard. They'd get the whole gang and—

"Shush!"

Mr. Reeves was standing in the road, in front of the old storage house, a hundred and twenty-five feet directly below them!

"Do you think he heard us?" whispered El

"Don't know", Edgar said softly, "let's keep an eye on him."

They watched, staying low, knowing their heads would look like the ends of sleepers from below. Mr. Reeves appeared to be undecided, finally turned around and started down the road, his gun in his hands, stalking, turning back, like he was looking for something. He walked slowly, deliberately, until he reached the road leading up to the tracks, stopped again, turned and searched the camp, began climbing again: he was coming up on the tracks!

"He's coming up here! He heard us!"

"Quick! Before he reaches the tracks—let's go!"

They ran across the bridge, dived into the thick Laurel, plunged down the steep mountainside, and collapsed against the great bridge footers, well within the shadows "Did he see us?"

"Nope, but he may have heard us! We'd best git you home before he gits on the bridge and kin see us good!"

El took one quick look at the bridge before she climbed up to her porch roof. Mr. Reeves was not in sight. She slipped through her window, dropped to the floor and leaned on the sill, searching the quiet town. Edgar had reached the shadows of his porch. The moonlight was bright now, so bright she could see the clouds floating high above the black bridge, so light she could see— she could see a man standing at the far end of the bridge! It was Emmett! In her heart she knew it was him, even while logic told her it had to be Mr. Reeves! Deep inside she knew it was Emmett White, the way he stood, straight, taller than Mr. Reeves. She saw the man disappear, and waited, confused, bewildered, it makes no sense she told herself. Nothing moved but the wind, coming through the gap, stirring the leaves on the maples below the bridge.

Gradually her rapidly beating heart stilled; she crawled into bed beside the sleep-sweet Bun and closed her eyes.

Tomorrow was a holiday; she could talk to Edgar about her fears in the morning. Bless you, Christopher Columbus: Four hundred and forty-nine years ago you discovered America—and gave us a day off from school!

The time between Columbus Day and Halloween moved slowly. The grand glory of autumn lay upon the mountains as mother nature mixed the proper portions of sun and rain; the trees burst into red and gold, producing a flaming memorial wreath to lay upon summer's pyre.

Somebody died in Maryland and John Brown's vest turned up as a part of an estate settlement. Back in 1859, when John Brown was hung down at Charleston, on the banks of the Kanawha, he wore a brown vest with red polka dots to his hanging. The jailer saved that vest of the celebrated Harper's Ferry abolitionist, and it passed down to his heirs. Now the state of Maryland decreed that the famous vest be appraised and taxed. They located a historian who set the value at fifty dollars, about ten times what old John Brown paid for it, and that, Daddy allowed, was most likely the way it would be with the Lend-Lease, afore it was over.

The U.S. Government set out to prove that women could wear pants to work and still look feminine—not the women of leisure, or the "white collar" girls—just the factory workers. The Department of Agriculture released patterns for the pants, suggesting they be made at home in sturdy denim or chambray, an inexpensive fabric. Working out in a public place in pants? What next?

There was doubt that Russia would be able to save Moscow, and the women and children were being evacuated. A Portuguese steamer was sunk by a Nazi sub; the Germans towed the life boats filled with survivors to within twenty miles of the coast, even gave two women and two children a ride in the submarine itself.

Mary Beth was receiving letters from Ben regularly, and one day even got a package; it contained Ben's watch, his wedding ring, and his pocket knife; the Navy didn't permit the sailors to wear jewelry of any kind. Ben wrote that he and Will had applied for duty aboard the same ship, but didn't know if they would get it. Mary Beth wrote back about a man on the battleship Nevada; he had seven sons, all in the Navy. He joined up to be with his boys and the Navy waived a fifty-year age limit to accept him—he was fifty-two. They had a family reunion on board ship. Mother said she would hate being the wife left behind, and all her sons and her husband on the same ship? What if something happened to that ship? And Daddy said, well, maybe she had daughters at home.

By the end of the week the Russian officials were packing up to leave Moscow; the Germans were knocking on their eastern door, but withdrawal of the officials didn't mean they were giving up the city. Roosevelt had a long, secret talk with his top military people and his foreign advisors, as the Japanese Cabinet and Premier Konoye resigned. Lieutenant Eike Tojo assumed command as Premier.

The USS Kearney was hit by a torpedo, but limped into port under her own power; eleven men were killed. The U. S. House of Representatives approved, two to one, the bill allowing guns to be mounted on merchant ships.

Closer to home, the UMW decided to continue recognizing the Appalachian Conference as the bargaining agent for southern soft coal producers. The thirteen operators who withdrew from the Conference last spring, after the disagreement with the northern operators over the forty-cent wage differential, probably were going to send delegates to the conference, but the newly-formed Corporation of Southern producers would handle problems peculiar to the South, such as freight rates. The delegates would attend the Coal meeting in Cincinnati.

In Pineville, one hundred men registered with the draft board; thirty-five left for Huntington, and six left for the Navy, their names alone a roll-call of history: Gilbert Columbus Chester, Jesse James Cook, Woodrow Wilson Burcham, George Washington Smith, Roger Dale Clark, and Theodore Roosevelt McKinney.

Jane was devastated. "Why the Navy, Ted! Why? Your entire family served in the Army, why break tradition? You can be just as useful in the Army, maybe stay in Fort Meade, or someplace—some place—"

"Some place safe?" finished Ted quietly.

"No! Some place close!" and she cried unashamedly.

"It's hard to explain, Jane," Ted said, twisting his hat in his hands, "maybe it has something to do with Ben going in the Navy, or Will. I don't know. I'll likely be drafted anyway, and I don't want to be a foot soldier—heard my Dad talk about that, grew up on it! I want to serve my country—every McKinney whoever lived fought for his country—but I don't want the Army! Corny as it may sound, being a Chaplain in the Navy lets me combine service to my country and service to God." He finished with his voice almost a whisper. "That's what I really want to do."

Daddy looked at Ted in disbelief, said, "Well, I'll be damned—didn't know you had it in you, son."

As Jane continued to sob, Ted added with a little-boy grin, "Besides, with my red hair and freckles, I'll look better in the Navy blues!"

Tears rolled down Mother's cheeks as she bustled about, setting out cake and making fresh coffee. Jane fought for control and gradually stopped crying. After a few moments with the family, they walked out to the porch and sat in the swing; El and Bun, mesmerized by the tragedy, started to follow, but Mother reached out a prohibitive hand. They settled for peeking through the curtains from the living room sofa, where they could see but not hear; it didn't take hearing to see the kissing going on in the swing. This was on Sunday night. On Monday morning Ted left for the training center in Norfolk, and Jane, who had never missed a day of school in eleven years, stayed at home, and refused to leave her room all day.

At suppertime, when Jane didn't come down, Daddy went up to her room and closed the door behind him. Jane never would tell what Daddy had said to her but she came down to the table with him, a suffering, tragic figure in an old red chenille robe, remote, removed from the family circle, strangely come into her own. Supper was eaten in silence, the silence of pain anticipated; Jane was suddenly older—and more like Mother than ever.

Having a sister in high school had been an advantage before; now Jane was especially good to the younger girls. She managed to get her hands on the latest books in the library, and El read *Invitation To Live*, by Lloyd C. Douglas, three times before it was due back. Now she asked Jane to bring home Earnest Hemingway's *Farewell To Arms;* she had something she wanted Jane to read. She found the part about jaundice and suggested that Jane write to Ted, tell him how he could give it to himself and thus come home on leave, but Jane didn't appreciate the suggestion, saying Ted wouldn't touch a drop of alcohol and she loved him even more because he wasn't a coward, and Daddy looked at El from under his brows and asked what kind of books are you reading, young lady, and Faith, I think this girl best stick to books in her room, she's got a while before she needs to read high school books. Mother grinned. One thing Mother had never done: she'd never censored what books her girls read.

The next Sunday night, Jane accepted the nomination to be President of the Epworth League, first time a girl had been elected to that office in the entire history of the Herndon church.

Premier Eiki Tojo wasted no time in making a public statement of policy, once he took office as Premier: "I am fully convinced that speedy action and iron will under the aegis of the August virtues of His majesty, the Emperor, are the only way in which to overcome the present difficulties."

He then proceeded to outline his policy. He emphasized the determination of the Japanese to remain an active participant in the present crisis, stated that the world situation required that national affairs be entrusted to a military leader who had the support of the fighting forces, saying, "Internally we must consolidate a wartime structure while externally we strengthen our ties to the treaty nations."

Secretary Knox has declared that a clash with Japan is now inevitable; the United States is satisfied that Japan has no intention of giving up their expansion plans.

Roosevelt: ...*we do not covet one square inch of the territory of any other nation.*

And in America there were twenty-nine strikes, seven of which had a direct bearing on the production of war materials, among them the National Steel Corporation, Anaconda Wire and Cable Company, and the Bendix Corporation. The senate planned to call the labor leaders before an Investigating committee and force a showdown on policy, calling Stanley Hillman, William Green and John L. Lewis—who had ordered the captive mines to stop work on Saturday night. The railroad dispute moved to a showdown also, as fourteen non-operating unions rejected an offer to arbitrate.

The man in the moon has a patch on his chin, and Mother is making sauerkraut. The moon, nearly full, made it seem more and more like Halloween as the days inched forward. It was nearly dark by five o'clock now, and at dinner, the family exchanged news: Work was to start on the Mercer County side of Herndon mountain to pave Route 10 within the month. Wyoming County would be connected to the rest of the world by a paved road! No more rock slides and mud, no more eatin' dust on the trip to Galax. Daddy reported that the N&W had received their long-awaited passenger coaches, bright red, with gold trim, real streamlined, and on the inside there were pictures on the walls of each end of the cars, scenes of places along the N&W route, and he said, they were going to be used on "The Pocahontas."

One of the men on Daddy's line gang had ripe pears; if Mother wanted, he'd bring her some to can, since she couldn't drive any more.

"You can't drive?" A chorus of alarm went up from the girls.

"Doc Steelman says I must stay home, unless it's a real emergency," explained Mother. "Wouldn't want to have this baby on the side of the road!" She would miss Grand Chapter, Eastern Star, something she had really counted on this year, planning on going to Charleston with the other officers. Maybe next year, she added, somewhat wistfully, like she didn't really expect to go then either.

The Germans were within thirty-five miles of Moscow. The Senate approved the extra six million dollars for the Lend-Lease fund, but they restricted the food donated to only that grown in the United States.

The United Mine Workers demanded a union shop contract as 53,000 miners walked out of pits owned by steel companies, and John L. Lewis accused Sidney Hillman, the Co-Director of the Office of Production Management, of adopting a "vengeful and malignant" opposition to the UMW. The mines affected U.S. Steel, Bethlehem Steel, Republic, Weirton, Wheeling, Crucible, Youngstown Sheet and Tube, all together nearly eighty percent of the steel used in defense effort. The defense program would collapse with the closing of the mines. The sole issue remained: *The miners in the captive mines must join the UMW within thirty days of starting work.*

Mother's, don't name your sons John,
He'll sit by the window to see the faint dawn,
He'll lie awake nights o'er the trials of men,
A'singin' the troubles of a sad Union.

Can't blame the steel companies for objectin'—if'n th' mines unionized, it'd lead to th' same system in th' mills!

U.S. Steel turned the Kearney shipyards over to the Navy, rather than grant a union plan where employers would have to discharge a man if he didn't join the union.

The walkout hit District 17 hard; nine thousand men worked in mines that furnished coal to the steel mills, mines located at Logan, Gary, Springton—

over next to Matoaka—Kingston, and Pocahontas. William Blizzard journeyed to Welch to supervise the strike, and President Roosevelt worked on a speech for Monday night, calling it "Navy and Total Defense Day".

FDR denounced the German executions of French hostages, calling it the "acts of a desperate man", and Churchill called it, "butcheries", while Charles DeGaulle asked for a "Folded Arms" strike as a means of an outward and visible sign of protest, a movement that could be as insidious and effective as the "V" for Victory campaign started by the British—and that campaign had worked wonders on the German's nerves!

The Senate Foreign Relations Committee voted thirteen to ten in favor of arming all ships; senate debate would begin on Monday.

Monday, October twenty-seventh, almost Halloween. Mother had the trick or treat candy, she said, but it was well hidden. Doc Steelman had brought it on his last visit when he came to examine her and Mary Beth.

Begging never worked on Mother, but they decided to try. Tonight, it was Daddy who stopped the commotion: President Roosevelt was ready to begin his speech.

My Fellow Americans:
Five months ago tonight I proclaimed to the American people the existence of a state of emergency. Since then much has happened. Our Army and Navy are temporarily in Iceland in defense of the Western Hemisphere. Hitler has attacked shipping in areas close to the Americas in the North and South Atlantic. Many American-owned merchant ships have been sunk on the high seas. One American destroyer was attacked on September 4th. Another destroyer was attacked and hit on October 17th. Eleven brave and loyal men of our Navy were killed by the Nazis.
We have wished to avoid shooting. But the shooting has started. And History has recorded who fired the first shot.

"He's going to declare War!" Mother gasped, abruptly standing up, her knitting sliding to the floor. Daddy's pipe slipped to the table, spilling ashes. The girls sat paralyzed with fear. They knew it was coming, had been told it was coming, yet were surprised and unprepared.

...all that will matter is who fires the last shot. America has been attacked. The U.S.S. Kerney is not just a Navy ship. She belongs to every man, woman, and child in this nation.

Illinois, Alabama, California, North Carolina, Ohio, Louisiana, Texas, Pennsylvania, Georgia, Arkansas, New York, Virginia—those are the home states of the honored dead and wounded of the Kearny. Hitler's torpedo was directed at every American...

El sat on the floor, the globe of the world between her knees; she traced the states as the President somberly called them out in his deep, dramatic voice, slowly, lingering on each state named; she observed how he had crisscrossed the nation, east to west, north to south with his arrangement of the names, thus touching on nearly every state in the union. The word, map, caught her attention and she began to listen again:

...It is a map of South America and a part of Central America as Hitler proposes to reorganize it. Today in this area there are fourteen separate countries. The geographical experts of Berlin, however, have divided South America into five vassal states, bringing the whole continent under their domination. And they have also arranged it so that the territory of one of these new puppet states includes the Republic of Panama and our great lifeline—the Panama Canal...

El tilted the globe to look at South America; she found the tiny Gulf of Panama. There, clearly marked on the globe were the initials, U.S. She slowly turned the globe, keeping one finger on the Panama Canal, and placing a finger of the other hand on Germany; a third of the world apart!

Daddy, watching her, even as he listened, suddenly spoke aloud.

"That Hitler is an ambitious SOB ain't he?" and Mother, once again seated in her chair, chided gently, "Bud,"

. ...the clergy are to be forever silenced.

El could see somebody trying to shut up Ted McKinney, or Preacher Copeland! Nobody could hush that man!

...I say that we do not propose to take this lying down...

Here it comes: he is going to declare war.
*...the House of Representatives has already voted to amend part of the
Neutrality Act of 1937, today outmoded by violent circumstances...American
merchant ships must be armed to defend themselves against the rattlesnakes
of the sea...it can never be doubted that the goods will be delivered by this
nation, whose Navy believes in the tradition of "Damn the torpedoes;
full speed ahead!"*

*Yes; Our nation will and must speak from every assembly line, Yes; from
every coal mine—the all-inclusive whole of our vast industrial machine...
Our country was first populated, and it has been steadily developed by men
and women in whom burn the spirit of adventure and restlessness and
individual independence which will not tolerate oppression...'*
*Today, in the face of this newest and greatest challenge of them all, We
Americans have cleared our decks and taken our battle stations. We stand
ready in the defense of our nation and the faith of our fathers to do what God
has given us the power to see as our full duty.*

"Thank God," whispered Mother, "he stopped short of declaring war."

"He declared defense," said Daddy, "and it amounts to the same thing."

"No, Bud, not really," protested Mother, and Daddy, with a sarcastic bite
seldom heard in his voice, replied, "Yes, Faith, really!"

The radio interrupted the commentary following the President's speech:
Fifty-plus men were in a Kentucky mine when it suddenly exploded, knocking
out the men, ripping and twisting the mine car, the track and wiring, trapping
them twenty-four hundred feet from the opening. Those rescued had managed
to reach an old air shaft, had been hauled up in a barrel, one at a time.

Lewis turned a deaf ear to the President's third plea to keep the mines open,
and Roosevelt had written, "It is essential that the mining of coal should go on
without interruption." Lewis had replied that it was a fight between the labor
union, and 'a rich man named Morgan, referring to J.P. Morgan, a director of
U.S. Steel' which owned the mines. Roosevelt came back with, "Whatever the
issue between you and Mr. Morgan, the large question of adequate fuel is of

greater interest and import to the national welfare. There is no reason for stoppage of work!"

The brushy-browed Lewis replied: "If you would use the power of the state to restrain me, as an agent of Labor, then Sir, I submit that you should use that same power to restrain my adversary…"

John L. Lewis was named a "fourth member of the Axis party" by Senator Connally, a Democrat from Texas. Senator Byrd, another Senator from Virginia, served notice: I do not intend to consider voting one step closer to war, except in our own defense…"

Now eleven to twelve thousand miners sat at home in southern West Virginia, not even walkin' the picket lines, because the operators made no attempt to open in defiance of the walk-out. On the railroad long lines of coal cars sat empty, and on Capitol Hill, angry senators suggested the Army be called out as Lewis delayed his reply to the President's latest plea for reopening.

Germany reacted to the Navy Day speech by calling it libelous, full of suspicions, insults and slanders: a falsification. The South American countries responded cautiously, one Columbian newspaper stating that the speech had the "object of destroying Congressional resistance to a repeal of the Neutrality Act… we cannot contemplate without anguish the spread of universal war, heralded by this speech, and in which we will be involuntary participants."

To which Daddy growled," Aw, hell! Do they think we want to participate? Those idiots must have overlooked the fact that Hitler is running this show! To listen to them, you'd think we started this whole mess!"

Every time Franklin Roosevelt gave an important speech, Charles Lindbergh appeared at a rally to contravene. This time he spoke at the celebrated Madison Square Garden in New York. The great arena was packed, tiers of seats rising on all sides, row upon row on the main floor, where the great boxing and wrestling rings were placed, where ballgames and shows and circuses were held—long blocks of chairs with only narrow isles between, and every seat was occupied by a Lindbergh supporter: twenty thousand Americans waited to hear the famous man denounce the leaders of their country. Red, white and blue bunting draped the balcony railings and the speaker's stand. Overhead banners waved—dozens of banners, the thirteen red and white stripes, hanging horizontally, the forty-eight white stars on a blue field at the upper left-hand corner—the national emblem, symbol of a free land where any man could speak without fear of harm to person or property even if he advocated rebellion against the very system that protected that freedom.

Three hundred policemen strolled within the great hall, while another three hundred patrolled the outside; a crowd of thousands listened, some to cheer him, others wanting to silence him:

I appeal to all Americans, no matter what their viewpoint on war to be, to unite behind the demand for a leadership in Washington that stands squarely on American traditions—a leadership of integrity instead of subterfuge, of openness instead of secrecy; a leadership that demonstrates its Americanism by taking the American people into its confidence.

Lindbergh had to pause until the cheering subsided. Then he continued, his voice rising above the crowd:

In place of our traditional American idea of a government run by the people, President Roosevelt has substituted the new concept of a people run by the government.

Lindbergh again quoted Roosevelt's promise not to send American boys into a foreign war, and continued:

We are on the verge of a war that would require us to attack the strongest military power the world has ever known—a war that would probably force us into a fight in both the Atlantic and the Pacific, in both Europe and Asia, at the same time. To be successful we would have to transport mechanized armies of millions of men across the ocean, and land them on hostile coasts, defended by the best and most hardened armies of the eastern hemisphere. If we should be successful in such an enterprise it would involve the death and maiming of millions of American soldiers. Every family would have its wounded and dead. I say IF we should be successful.

Charles Lindbergh's speech was heard and taken to heart; those millions of Americans of which he spoke took his words deep inside themselves and weighed them well, mulling them over in the dark of night, studying them closely in the bright light of day, recalling them again and again when they looked at their boys, tow-headed blond of ancient Norwegians, dark-haired descendants of the French, blue-eyed sons of Ireland, brown-eyed daughters of Greece, all only a few generations removed from the lands now endangered by the Axis powers. Whether for him or against him, Americans listened to what Lindbergh had to say—recalling his brave, solo flight into the future when he flew alone to France—but NBC refused to broadcast the speech coast to coast as they had Roosevelt's, saying it was unreasonable to cancel programs already scheduled. The network finally allowed thirty minutes, from ten-thirty to eleven p.m., on sixty-three stations east of Chicago, but Wyoming County had to turn to the Bluefield *Daily Telegraph* for their hero's message: WHIS went off the air at ten o'clock.

In Bluefield there was a report of four brothers in the Army, named Smith; all four were over six feet tall, and their fifth brother was now in the draft. The four boys together had a combined total of thirty years in the Army, and one of them was a West Point Instructor. They were going to be stationed together, rumor said, and Mary Beth wrote to Ben, telling him about it; maybe his captain would let him and Will stay on the same ship, which was all Ben wrote about, except an occasional question about the baby.

"Mary Beth! You mean you haven't told him about the twins yet? Why in heaven's name not?"

"Superstitious, I reckon, 'fraid something will happen."

"Well, I'll tell you what's going to happen—he'll faint dead away when he gets that telegram! Best you tell him!"

So ran the advice to the huge mother-to-be, for in the last month she had grown so large she could hardly stand without assistance. Doc Steelman came every week and shook his head at the way her ankles puffed and said, "well, well," when he took her blood pressure. He listened long minutes to the two heart beats, one up high, the other down low, and smiled with satisfaction at what he heard, always ending with, now, if we can just hold off a few more weeks, even a few more days...

Compared to Mary Beth, Mother looked small, and they were taking bets on which one would deliver first. Papa Wooten, now one of the miner's on strike, walked his uncomfortable daughter up and down the road twice a day, holding her arm, protecting his grandbabies, something he had never done for Mama Wooten, not even when she had BillynBob.

There was a lot of walking in the evenings now, Mother, sometimes with Daddy, more often with El and Bun, Hollie walked with Mr. Mitchell, strolling around the triangle, not interfering with the ball game, avoiding the kids playing soldier in the road.

El thought about last Halloween. She, Edgar, Joe, Jane, Mary Beth, Ben, Will, Hollie and a dozen others, divided into two teams for a scavenger hunt that ended at their house for a real party, dunkin' apples, pin-the-tail, popcorn balls, apple cider—a real party. Now, only she, Edgar and Joe were left out of that group. Will and Ben were gone, Mary Beth was too big, Jane was too grown-up and Hollie was too sad.

That last was a real concern, and a puzzle, and she and Edgar talked about it. Hollie was growing thinner and thinner, like she never ate anything, her skin so white and translucent, and she never smiled, sad-looking even when others were laughing.

Finally, it was Halloween! The mine strike ended and the miners would go back to work while a mediation board tried to find a solution to the problems, returning to work on Saturday, November the first, to make up for lost production.

"Be lots of drinking going on, Bud, now that the strike is settled. Maybe the girls shouldn't go trick or treat?" But El and Bun raised such a howl that Mother made their costumes.

The week before Halloween, El swiped a black sweater of Jane's, one she thought wouldn't be missed, and over it she put a red vest. With black construction paper she made two large ears which she pinned into her hair. She came downstairs, and proclaimed," Mickey Mouse!" Mother burst out laughing; below her waist, El still had on the brown skirt, yellow knee-socks and brown shoes she had worn to school. "Please, Mother, make black pants for me, and a tail, and it will be perfect!" After a few mild objections, Mother had taken the idea and elaborated on it. She made Bun a polka-dotted dress, mouse ears and a long tail—Minnie Mouse. El kept her ulterior motive to herself as they dressed to go trick or treat. With a brown paper bag to hold the goodies, they waited until dark to make their rounds. El held Bun's hand tightly as they went up one side of the road and down the other, knocking on each door, threatening to "Soap yer windows, if you don't give us a treat!"

By the time they completed their rounds of all the houses, they had more candy than Santa Claus brought, plus pennies from Sarah Jo, who didn't believe in candy for kids, and a caramel apple from Mother who believed in extra effort for kids.

Happy with the evening's take, Bun willingly washed off her 'wide lipstick' mouth and tumbled into bed. Now the fun could begin!

El sat in her room and waited for Edgar's signal; when he came, she removed her mouse-ears cap and tail, left the red vest behind. She slid down the porch roof dressed all in black, and pants, just as she had planned, looking just like one of the boys. As they ran to the storage house, Edgar whispered, "We're going to knock out Ol' Reeves still, but I didn't tell them it was your idea." El didn't care who got the credit, as long as she could go with them!

There were about ten of them in the group and the leader was a high school boy by the name of Jock who had been one of Ben's best friends. El knew him, but not well, because Jane didn't like him, and never asked him to their house. Quietly, close together, they crept down the road to the old storage house, their shoes making a slight crunching on the cindered road, like cracking walnuts under your heel. Mr. Reeves was nowhere in sight, because, Edgar explained, Jock and his friends had led him a wild-goose-chase down through the camp, and then sneaked back. They'd have to be quick, ol' Reeves wouldn't be gone long! Jock and Edgar, as the biggest, slipped up to the front door. It was locked; it wouldn't budge. Next they tried to raise a window, but it was nailed shut.

"What'll we do?"

"Break a window!"

"No, he'd hear us—'sides, that's agin the law!"

It was never clear, later, just who's idea it was, but it didn't much matter, for once the idea was expressed, it was clear that it had been in everyone's mind: they could turn over the outhouse!

With one accord, they moved to the fenced yard, trod over the cut corn stobs, through the wild sweet potato vines and saw briars, and took their stance at the front and rear of the wooden two-holer. Jock, as commander-in-chief, counted: one, two, THREE! THE SOLIDLY BUILT JOHN WOBBLED, TILTED, AND FELL ON IT'S SIDE! Not a kid stepped in the pit!

As the outhouse crashed down, they let out a wild cheer—who cares if Reeves hears them now! Like wild Indians they scrambled back over the fence, fell to the ground, scrambled up and steaked up the back road toward the railroad—their first tactical error, because Mr. Reeves knew what they had done; he had no need to go to the house. He cut between the houses and came out on the back road right behind them—runnin,' shoutin,' and swearin'.

"Hyer! Hyer! outa here, you dang-nabbed sons of a cock-fightin' rooster! You bamboozlin' thieves, sons of Satan's daughters, you wicked, swoggle-eyed horse-thieving bandits you-you-"

Mr. Reeves stopped shouting, conserving his breath for the steep climb up to the railroad tracks. His physical condition was nearly as good as theirs for he was gaining on them, slowly but surely getting close enough to grab one of the younger ones who began dropping out, one at a time, rolling down the side of the hill, falling like green walnuts, one after the other, until only the larger boys and El were left. Jock, still in the lead, shouted, "Quick! The bridge! He won't get us there!"

"Jock! No! It's time for the train!" shouted Edgar, knowing the schedule to the minute, but it was too late. Jock led his troops out on the bridge, running with practiced steps in short, jerky motions, hitting each crosstie squarely in the center. The others kept pace as they could, and they gained the small wooden platform in the center of the bridge, crowding together to clear the rails just as the nine-thirty freight came roaring down the mountain on the westbound track. Coming square between them and Mr. Reeves, who was left standing at the end of the bridge.

El stood on the very edge of the wooden perch, Edgar's arms wrapped tight around her, the wind from the fast-moving train whipping her hair into her eyes, along with cinders from the empty coal cars interspersed between the box cars. The engine, an EL3A, was made up of three sections, three single units connected to increase power, and had a speed of thirty-eight miles per hour; combined as they were, and rolling down the incredible grade, the speed of the "square-heads" was closer to fifty miles per hour. The electric engines regenerate their power on the down-hill stretches and the engineer, old "Long-Haul Taylor" himself, said, the faster the run, the more the power, so let 'er rip, boys, let 'er rip, run 'er wide open!"

The iron bridge vibrated with the thunder, swayed in the wind from the four hundred thousand pound monster engines; the heavy-duty rails trembled with the fierce rush of cars, whined and cried with the flat gondolas, and when the motor passed, its whistle moaning loud and long as it blew for the Herndon crossing, the kids on the half-way deck were trembling and moaning as well: few, if any, had been on the bridge when a train went by.

They huddled together as the long train passed, not daring to move until the sound was well was out of sight, recalling the many stories they'd heard, about men who thought the way was clear, only to step out in front of a second train following close behind, its sound hidden in the noise of the one gone by.

The bridge settled again, and the boys pulled their bravado about their shoulders, shook themselves and straightened a bit taller. Old Man Reeves was forgotten with the coming of the train, and they assumed he had forgotten them until one of the younger boys, less occupied with screwing up his courage, spotted the "mean man" of the town: Mr. Reeves was walking out on the bridge, walking slowly, deliberately, just as he walked through the town, his shotgun braced over his arm, slowly, deliberately, inexorably. From somewhere above they became conscious of a low, mournful sound, beginning softly, increasing to a loud, vibrating pitch, a ghostly wail—Granny Hall! It was Granny Hall—making her regular Halloween night visit to the bridge!

For a fleeting instant the group faced their new foe disconcerted, then Edgar took charge.

"Quick! This way!" he shouted, and began running, to the end of the bridge, running to the steep side of the mountain, running, running, pulling El by the hand, the others following, running, running, hitting the sleepers awkwardly, stumbling, falling, running, clawing their way across the bridge with a new, more terrible monster after them, a combination of evils pursuing them, their breath caught in their throats, their mouth dry, their screams drowning out the wailing ghost and the cursing of Mr. Reeves, until, finally they tumbled headlong off the bridge into the laurel and rhododendron bushes, disappearing into the dark dead green of the night-forest, inhabited only by friendly, known ghosts, gentler, familiar spooks, softer hooting owls. Once on level ground, the group dispersed rapidly, each seeking the comfort and security of their own home.

El shimmed up the post and crept through her window without a thought to who might see her; all she wanted to do was get out of her mouse suit and into her own warm bed. She was shaking from head to toe, a combination of cold and excitement. If she had asked, Daddy would have said the ghost was electricity generated by the wide-open running of the nine-thirty freight, returning along the high wire, running up the mountain to Clark's Gap substation. But El knew better; she knew a ghost when she heard one! Frightened by Granny Hall, scared to death of Mr. Reeves—the excitement far outweighed the fear. She had satisfied one of her most-secret, most-cherished, life-long ambitions: **she had been on the bridge when a train went by!**

Nineteen

The worst thing about Halloween was, when you woke up the next morning it was November. The long, drab month lay smack dab between the glory of October, with its brilliant mountains of red and yellow, and December with its lacy hoarfrost and early snows making everything white and pure. November is the worst month of all, the mountains all wet-black and gray, heavy slate-gray skies, charcoal trees, mud-gray roads, and covered with drizzling, seeping-through, bone-chillin' gray rain. And gray spirits, the letdown almost as bad as the day after Christmas when you didn't get what you wanted.

The only holidays in November were Armistice Day—hardly a holiday at all, because you didn't get anything except a day out of school—and Thanksgiving, which was almost as bad, because all you got was plenty to eat, and they had that every day. 'Course, Thanksgiving was a little better—two days out of school—so thanking the Pilgrims was in order. Trouble was, there were twenty long gray days before turkey day came.

El lay in bed, trying to determine what had awakened her on such a gray, dismal day, then realized that Daddy was talking to someone at the front door; it was the knocking that had aroused her. When she recognized Mr. Reeves' voice, she knew it was going to be a bad month—it had already started.

Daddy called Mother to the door; there was further talking, but the voices remained low, making it impossible to hear what was being said. She slipped out of bed and hid her dirty Mickey Mouse suit in the back of her closet; she had slid halfway down the mountain, through the laurel and rhododendron and leaves, over the rain-soaked forest floor; there was mud on her black pants, on Jane's black sweater and caked on her boots. Mr. Reeves stopped talking and she expected to be summoned. Mother's voice came up the stairwell, raised in indignation, carrying clear and firm, like when she sang *The Old rugged Cross in* church.

"I appreciate your concern, Mr. Reeves, but I am certain, very certain, that MY girls were home in bed last night! Good day, Mr. Reeves!"

She couldn't believe her ears! She peeped out her window, careful not to move the lace curtains. Mr. Reeves was leaving! He's going out the gate! Home free!

"Rachel?"

She jerked around. Daddy was standing in the door of her room. Her surprise and guilt were sure to show on her face. She answered meekly, "Yes, Daddy?"

He came into her room and sat on her bed." Don't guess you have any idea at all what Mr. Reeves came about, do you?"

"No, Sir," she lied.

Daddy got up and walked to the window, lifted the curtain and looked out, clearly struggling with a decision. Was he thinking about paddling her— turning her over his knee like he had done in years past? Maybe considering how his hand might not be slapping on buttocks covered with muslin, but might be soft-thudding on the cotton pad of a girl-woman, changed from his child into her own being by the pubescent flow, that mighty river, once crossed, from which there was no return?

He dropped the curtain, having come to some conclusion, and sat again on the bed. Bun, half awake, crawled from beneath the heavy quilts to sit in his lap. Absent-mindedly, he caressed her coppery head.

"Rachel, I want to give you a bit of advice. Come here," he patted the bed beside him. "You're growing up now, almost a young lady. It's time to leave the tomboyin' behind."

He studied the floor a minute, struggling to get his thoughts in order.

"There's one thing you need to keep in mind, it'll serve you the rest of your life, no matter what the trouble." He moved her hair back from her face with a gentle touch. "When you're about to get into something, you stop and ask yourself, what would Mother say about this? Would she be happy? Or would she be hurt? Would she be proud of You? Or ashamed if she knew. Now, if you can learn to stop—just stop. Long enough to ask yourself that question, what would Mother think? You'll never go wrong in your whole life. Reckon you could try that?"

"Yes, Daddy," El said in a small voice.

He put Bun down, his duty as a good father satisfied. At the door he turned back. "And Rachel, one more thing. You'd better pray the rain washes that mud off the porch roof before your Mother sees it!"

El sat on her bed and thought about Daddy's advice. What would Mother say? She knew what Mother would say—and do! She had known even while she planned her all-black costume—but nobody had been hurt, it had been fun! Mother lived by the Golden Rule: Daddy lived by Mother's rule. No, she wouldn't want her two-holer turned over. She had made a mistake by participating. A mistake. The word triggered something in her mind: the white deer, the albino deer, killed by wild dogs, white and beautiful, lying on the pure white snow in its own crimson blood. The albino deer always reminded her of Hollie but it wasn't the albino deer this time, and it hadn't been Hollie who was making a mistake. It was the doe, she was remembering, the doe's eyes when she stepped off the truck ramp, wild and frightened, frozen. That was how she had felt, caught in the powerful beam of the train's headlight as it bore down on her—frozen and wild-eyed with fear—accidents happen, Mother had said, a mistake, Daddy had corrected her, "and we always pay for our mistakes." She thoughtfully considered last night's events. Daddy had said she was growing up. Well, growing up meant making her own decisions; uneasily she pushed away the knowledge that **it also meant paying for her own mistakes.**

TORPEDO SINKS U.S. WARSHIP; 44 CREW MEMBERS RESCUED

The first vessel sunk by a German U-Boat in the first World War was the *Jacob Jones*; it went down off the coast of England with 64 men lost. Now, the *Reuben James*, an American destroyer, had been sunk by a German U-Boat, and it was exactly the same kind of ship as *the Jacob Jones*. Sent to the bottom of the Atlantic off the coast of Iceland while on convoy duty. *The Jacob Jones* had lost 64 men; the *Reuben James* had 77 crewmen unaccounted for when sunk. In Congress, the debate over the Neutrality Act continued, brought to angry heights by the sinking of the ship. Crew members had written home, saying, "we're asking for it," and now their fears had materialized, come out of the sea-fog in the form of an enemy sub.

By Sunday, the Germans were formally charging the U.S. with aggression, saying the Reuben James had attacked their vessel, putting the blame on the

Greer and the Kearny, and Secretary Knox was crying that the United States was in the fight to the finish. In London, Churchill was battling with changes in his cabinet as unhappy Brits complained about the lack of aid to Russia.

When the local news came over the radio on Sunday evening it was learned that one of *the* missing *Reuben James'* crewmen was from Bluefield; another one, a torpedoman, was from Iaeger, the son of one of Aunt Bea's friends, two were from Charleston and even closer, one was from Beckley. Five hillbilly boys on the Reuben James, and none of the families knew whether their boy was among the forty-four saved, or the seventy-seven lost.

In the wake of the sinking of the *Reuben James*, the Japanese press said Tokyo would act with "independent judgement" on Berlin's charge that they had been attacked by the United States, and shortly thereafter they released a seven-point plan to ease the tension in the Pacific. The plan called for the United States to:

1. Stop military aid to Chungking, and to advise Chungking to make its peace with Japan.
2. Leave China free to deal with Japan and thus end hostilities.
3. Stop the encirclement of Japan with naval and air bases and by economic barriers.
4. Acknowledge Japan's co-prosperity sphere, her leadership in the western hemisphere, and leave other states and protectorates to establish their own political and economic relations with Japan without interference.
5. Recognize Manchukuo and the Emperor heading it.
6. Stop the freezing of Japanese assets in America, Britain and the Indies, and wherever that provocative measure is applied.
7. Restore all trade treaties, abolish all restrictions on shipping, undo everything wrongfully done in the name of peace but with the design for war.

Nowhere did it make mention of the steps Japan was willing to take toward peace, leaving it, instead, up to the United States to make amends.

In Russia, the German tanks were rolling ever steadily toward Rostov. The current joke making the rounds was, what does Mussolini call Vesuvius? The answer, of course, "his night light."

The railroad fact-finding board had suggested a pay increase of seven- and one-half percent for all operating personnel, nine cents an hour for non-operating groups; the head of the five railroad brotherhoods called the findings most disappointing and the threat of a railroad strike grew closer each day. The President warned labor, saying that no misguided labor leader shall delay preparations for defense of this nation! He then ordered a Lend-Lease credit of one billion dollars for the defense of Russia. Joseph Stalin thanked FDR for this "unusually substantial aid" in the "great struggle against our common enemy…"

Saturday morning Mother sent Rachel to the company store for bacon. Mr. Gillespie took pains to slice it thin, knowing Faith's preference.

"Going to have a nice Christmas this year, Rachel?"

"Hope so, Mr. Gillespie. I'd like to have a bike." El was standing before a counter in the back of the Company store; both the counter and a shelf across the back of the store already held toys.

"You'll probably have good weather to ride it. Woolly worms have a black collar on both ends this year." Interested, El returned to the meat counter.

"What does that mean?" she asked.

"Means we're going to have a hard spell early, then a mild spell, then another cold spell later—a split up winter." The big man was wrapping the bacon in brown paper as he talked.

"And the woolly worms know?" questioned El in awe, accepting the bacon and handing him her quarter.

"Sure they know! Your Daddy been huntin' yet?"

"No, Sir. All he does is work."

"He'll be gettin' a rest 'fore long, looks like the railroaders are about to strike."

"Daddy says it makes it harder on him—he's on salary, he won't be off."

"Why, come to think of it, I 'member, last time they went out, your Daddy was the only man working this side of Princeton! Guess it'll be right tough on him!"

"Bye, Mr. Gillespie!"

"You come back, Rachel!"

The railroad unions had decided to strike: three hundred and fifty thousand men would walk off on December fifth, at one-forty-five p.m., exactly thirty days to the minute from when the board had handed the report to A.F. Whitney,

355

President of the Brotherhood of Railroad Trainmen. Besides the trainmen, engineers, switchmen, the operating personnel the conductors, firemen and brakemen would also walkout. Four hundred general chairmen of these groups had totally rejected the recommended seven and a half cents pay boost recommended by the President's fact-finding board. Spokesmen for the non-operating Brotherhoods were remaining mum until after a meeting with their fifteen hundred general chairmen—and that meeting was scheduled for Wednesday.

The operating men were asking for a flat thirty percent increase in pay, the non-operating brothers were asking for thirty to thirty-four cents an hour, plus a week of paid vacation, like the miners were getting.

The report didn't say much for the "five wrong men" on the fact-finding board, as Daddy called them; he shook his head sorrowfully as he lit his Kaywoodie pipe. With winter coming on, and the defense needs, what a bad time was coming, enough to make a man old, old, old. And that was enough to bring three daughters around his neck with hugs and kisses, which was what he was after when he started talking!

The Senate had voted to arm the ships, to let them sail to any port, through any sea, including combat zones, the bill passing by a vote of fifty to thirty-seven. The House, confident that it had enough votes to pass the bill, planned to vote on Wednesday and send it directly to the White House. Roosevelt, anxiously awaiting the bill, confided he was considering withdrawal of the Marines from China, and reporters speculated that he was clearing the decks for a clash with Tokyo—in case the coming Peace talks failed.

Senator Chandler (D. Ky.) told the senate a long story about a mountaineer trying to use his powers of persuasion to urge passage of the ship-armament bill. It seems, he said, in his mountain-drawl, that a mountaineer down in the hills of Kentucky wanted to buy a gun. Now, mountain men like guns; he won't thieve, he won't lie, he won't harm his neighbors, but if you hurt him or one of his'n, he'll shoot you on the spot! Now this mountain man went into the country store to buy a gun; the store-keeper took down a rifle, a fine shootin' iron that cost twenty-nine dollars. The mountaineer stroked it, cradled it over his arm, cozied it agin his cheek, and finally opined: "That's an awfully lot of money, but I'll take her. I'll take her 'cause if I need her and don't have her, I'll never need her again!"

Saturday afternoon was cold and cloudy, maretails and mackerel clouds were scuddin' about in the upper layers, and Mother said Old Mother Goose would soon be picking geese, meaning it felt like snow.

El played ball with the boys, Edgar, Joe, BillynBob in the road, while Bun sat on her front steps picking Spanish needles out of her socks. Mr. Reeves came down the road, walking head down, holding a letter in his hand. They watched him, holding his letter in front of him and kept silent. They'd never admitted their guilt for the Halloween prank, much less apologized, and El wanted to speak to him. He walked on by, his cap pulled down over his eyes, his old Army coat buttoned to his chin, his gun in the crook of his arm, walked right past, unseeing, his hands holding the letter. El couldn't stand it, couldn't stand either being ignored, or her guilt. She called out, "You got a letter, Mr. Reeves?"

Mr. Reeves stopped, shook his head as if to clear his mind, and looked back at El. "Your Ma ta' home, Rachel?"

Surprised he knew her name, she answered, "Yes—" and added, "Sir." Something about the way he looked, solemn, different, sort of dignified. That was it: he had acquired dignity. The old coat was the same, the cap, put on sideways, but his manner, his stance—while she was puzzling over the change, Mr. Reeves opened the gate, went to her front door and knocked firmly. El followed, drawn by his suddenly changed persona, and Bun stopped picking her socks. The door opened and Mother drew the old man inside. El and Bun followed. Mother led Mr. Reeves into the dining room, where Daddy was sitting at the table. She poured him a cup of coffee as he took a chair across from Daddy, then sat down beside him. He handed the letter to Mother.

"It's from the Navy." Mr. Reeves nodded. "You want me to read it?"

"If you'd be so kind," he said. Mother adjusted her glasses, cleared her throat and read the letter aloud:

It is with deep regret that the Navy Department Notifies you from the latest available information that it appears your son, Charles Dawson Reeves, Jr., fireman First Class, lost his life in the line of duty in service to his country when the USS Reuben James was torpedoed and sunk.

There was silence in the room. Mr. Reeves bowed his head and so did Daddy. Mother touched his arm and said, "we are truly sorry."

In a moment the old man raised his head and said quietly," I figured it."
He stood up, turned his cap inside and outside, nodded at Daddy and went out
the door, leaving the letter on the table.

"Ellie, you run catch him, tell him to drop those overalls by, I'll put a patch
or two on them."

"I didn't know he had a son," El said. She turned and faced Daddy
squarely. She didn't say a word, but they both knew what she was feeling: she
was sorry for her part in the overturned two-holer.

El ran out the door and caught him at the footbridge over the creek.
"Mother says to drop those britches by and she'll put a patch on for you!"

Later in the week he did so, and Mother took out the side seams, put the
patches on, and resewed the seams, sewing them as carefully as she did
Daddy's, and El returned them, nearly good as new.

Hitler finally came up with a reply to the President's Navy Day speech,
saying, "As far as South America is concerned, it is as far away as the moon!"
and, "Berlin does not want to be a world capitol and Washington will never
be!" His comments only served to spur the passage of the bill allowing guns
on all American ships. Hattie Caraway, (D. Ark.), the Senate's only woman
member, herself a mother of two sons in uniform, said, "It is a strange theory
that our boys can be shot at without any means of defense."

FDR named Ickes to a "Coal-Czar" post, resembling that of the "Fuel
Administrator" post in the world war, now being referred to as "World War
One", as it becomes increasingly obvious that another war of global
proportions is pending. Closer to home, the good news is, another mine has
opened in Buchanan county, with a seam averaging fifty-eight inches high! A
coal miner's dream, a seam high enough 'til a man can almost stand up!

On Sunday night Mother missed the Second Sunday Singing at the church,
first time in many years, afraid to go because the baby might put in an
appearance. The number of young people walking to and from the services had
diminished markedly. Only a few months ago there had been a half dozen close
friends, Will, Ben, Mary Beth, Jane, Hollie and Emmett—now there was only
Jane, and those younger, more Ellie's age. Jane persuaded Mother to let her
drive to church, for practice just in case she was needed for an emergency
during Mother's three-week confinement. With Jane driving, there was no
need for El to walk—the fact that she wanted to walk carried no weight at all—
but her friends might be a distraction to Jane; they could not ride with her.

Thus, on Sunday night, only Jane and El attended the Sunday night singing, and El envied Bun who had been allowed to stay home with Mother and Daddy.

It was only ten o'clock, but it seemed as late as midnight to the tired girls. Fog lay over the road, drifting up from the creek bed and gathering between the steep mountains. Resenting the situation, El listened in stony silence as Jane talked about Ted, how she missed him, especially tonight, with the singing, how Ted enjoyed the singing—how much she enjoyed his letters, they were almost as inspiring as his sermons and much more personal, someday she might let Ellie read them, talking to El like a friend, like El was almost grown-up too, and when the war is over, we will get married, not that he had actually asked her, but she knew, and for her whole life she had known she would be a preacher's wife, someday, they'd have a little church, oh, not here, maybe in Virginia or she had heard that Ohio was nice, but in these steep mountains—

"Look out!" screamed El.

"A dog!" cried Jane, as something darted out of the heavy fog and ran in front of the car; she braked, skidded, narrowly missed the edge of the road. She hit the animal squarely, knocking it into the ditch on the other side. "It was a wolf!" cried El, gripping the dashboard with both hands.

Jane was shaking as she got the car under control; she had held it in the road but barely, actually feeling the shoulder crumble beneath the rear tires. "I've killed it, Ellie! Dear Lord, what should I do!"

"It's no crime to kill a wolf, hunters do it all the time." She tried to comfort her sister, realizing that Jane was still trembling. "Maybe you shouldn't tell Mother— she might not let you drive next week."

"I can't do that," protested Jane. "of course I'll tell her."

Of course you would, reflected El, realizing that she probably would not, if it had been her.

Once in the house, Jane immediately told Mother and Daddy what had happened. Daddy found his five-celled railroad light. "Let's see if you damaged the car. You're sure it was a wolf, El? Could be a neighbor's dog."

"It was a wolf," insisted El. "I saw its wild eyes."

"What color was it?" he asked as he checked his flashlight.

The girls answered simultaneously: "Black," said Jane, "Gray," said El.

"Bud, you'd better find out. Could be a child's pet," advised Mother. Daddy and the girls inspected the car but there was no damage. With him driving, they returned to the highway to find the animal, both concerned and curious, for, as Daddy explained, wolves ran in packs and it would be wise to know if they were in the area.

The white fog lay so thick it was difficult to find the exact place, but when they finally located it, Daddy turned the car around, with his headlights shining into the ditch where the dead animal lay. He examined it closely without touching it, moving his light over its face, body and extremities. It was gray with silver and black streaks in its coat, some tan on its face and feet; the animal was thin, emaciated. The fog was so heavy it looked like rain in the strong beam of the light and made their faces damp, glistening.

"Wild dog," Daddy said. "Probably wouldn't have lived through the winter. Probably did some farmer a favor by killing it, Jane, no need to cry over this one, he was probably a mean one."

Wild dog. Wild dog had killed the white doe: El was glad it was dead!

"How can you tell, Daddy? How do you know it isn't a wolf?"

"Study the markings, El. Look at those brown feet, that brown muzzle—got a lot of German shepherd in it, most likely, but he's a mixed-up son of a bitch, probably as wild as they come. Now, a real wolf is silver and black, gray, maybe, but not brown and wolves don't cross over, real wolves won't breed with dogs, no matter how wild they are. He likely needed killing."

El shivered.

"Here, now!" exclaimed Daddy, "let's get you back to the fire!"

El couldn't explain to Daddy that she wasn't cold, that it hadn't been from the damp, foggy air sweeping through the gap; she'd had a feeling, a premonition, a fear or dread, inexplicable, incomprehensible, even to herself—or, perhaps it was as Daddy said; perhaps she was simply cold.

President Roosevelt braved the cold and snow in Washington, standing bare-headed beside the Tomb of The Unknown Soldier, while an aide placed a wreath of snow-white chrysanthemums on the sepulcher. The Army bugler played Taps, and the President moved into the amphitheater to speak. NBC observed a full minute of silence before his speech began:

Among the great days of national remembrance, none is more deeply moving to the Americans of our generation as the eleventh of November, the anniversary of the armistice of 1918...

Our observation has a particular significance in the year 1941 ...Sargent York of Tennessee, on a recent day spoke to such a questioner: There are those in this country today who ask me and other Veterans of World War One, "What did it get you?" Today we know the answer—all of us...if our armies of 1917 and 1918 had lost there would not be a man, woman, or child who wondered why the war was fought. The reasons would have faced us everywhere...Sargent York spoke of these cynics and doubters: "The thing they forget is that liberty and freedom and democracy are so very precious that you do not fight once to defend them and stop. Liberty and freedom and Democracy are prizes awarded only those people who fight to win them and fight eternally to hold them."

The people of America agree with that. They believe liberty is worth fighting for, and if they are obliged to fight, they will fight eternally to hold it!

"Who is Sargent York?" asked El as the speech ended. "He was a World War One hero," said Jane.

"He wasn't a hero to start with," said Daddy, "he was a conscientious objector and he applied for exemption from the draft."

"A conscientious objector," repeated El thoughtfully, "like Lindbergh?"

"Well, not exactly", hedged Mother, as Daddy laughed.

"Come on, Faith, answer the kid's question!" he said, as it became clear that Mother was having trouble finding an explanation.

"Tell you what," Mother said, "I'll take you to see the movie when it comes around again, one night after this baby comes!"

"Now, if we can get Mother to get busy and have this baby—she's sure holding up things, isn't she!" said Daddy, letting Mother off the hook.

One more reason to resent the new baby—couldn't even go to the movies because Mother couldn't be left alone!

The Red Cross had taken over classrooms all over America for this one day, to expand their activities; they were organizing a "Jr. Red Cross" to give the youth an active part in formulating the defense of their country. After lunch the girls walked up the road to the schoolhouse to join. The theme for the national program was, "Citizenship Training for Internal Defense." Grade school children received a lapel pin to prove they were members but high school students only got a membership card to carry in their wallet. El and Bun proudly showed off their tiny Red Cross, and felt they came out much better than Jane.

On the evening news, Secretary Knox said that the decision was near on the Japanese question, saying that the United States should be prepared in the Pacific as well as the Atlantic, and over in Welch, West Virginia, a young man by the name of Harry Truman, a Senator from Missouri, addressed the Armistice Day crowd as guest speaker.

The state had escaped the snows of the more northernly areas, and the temperatures began to rise, but more than the weather heated up. The controversy between management and labor became hotter by the day. Franklin Roosevelt called a meeting to be held at the White House of all the men involved in the labor-steel dispute, requesting that they come to Washington on Friday. In London, Winston Churchill gave a speech, contributing some ideas for the consideration of the Japanese: An outbreak of hostilities between the United States and Japan would bring Britain in, within the hour. Further, he declared, American Naval patrol activities in the Atlantic already had made possible the transfer of British battleships to the Pacific if needed. Thirdly, British Air Power had now reached parity with Germany, and …British shipping losses had been cut to less than one third of that for the preceding four months.

"Good old Winnie!" Americans were smiling. Now, Japan, put that in your opium pipes and smoke it!

Friday. November fourteenth. Hard to believe the old gray month was half gone. The miners were on edge over the pending talk with FDR, in the White House, of all places! The railroaders were up in the air over the strike vote as the non-operating brotherhoods joined the operators. And now the news declared a fight pending between Lindbergh and Stassen, a fight to keep Lindbergh from winning nomination to the Senate.

"Mother", wailed El," now they are going to fight Lindbergh!"

"A political fight, honey, not a fist fight! And they are putting words into Lindy's mouth—he hasn't said he's running for the senate."

Stassen had brought up Lindy's remark that there might not be an election in 1942, replying in an interview, that he would fight the Lone Eagle in a battle to "set the political drums thumping from Times Square to where the creeks fork for the last time",

"Well," said El, "guess that would be right here in Coville!"

"Why do you say that?" asked Mother, eyes twinkling.

"Gooney Otter is the last fork on Barker's Creek, isn't it?"

"Seems the paper will print anything if it has to do with Lindbergh, whether it's true or not. Remember, honey, that's one reason he moved his family to England, all the publicity and attention. You just have faith in your hero, he won't let you down!"

El was confused as she read the long write-up about Lindbergh and Stassen; she wished she could talk to Edgar about it. She missed their time on the bridge, but, as Daddy had suggested, she was trying to do only those things of which Mother would approve—and she knew what Mother would think about the way she'd been crawling out her window at night and going up on the bridge—and with a boy!

Mother wouldn't understand. It wasn't defiance, or meaning to be bad, it was getting out at night, seeing the stars, the great mountains outlined in moon light, the town asleep below like a child's playhouse, all lined up in rows. It was being up so high, her feet off the ground, feeling the wind on her face, loving and cool, adventure, excitement, feeling— feeling free. Somehow she thought Charles Lindbergh would understand why she slipped out at night and stood in that high place; her spirit soared just as surely as Lindy's had when he flew across that ocean the first time, and, just as Lindy must have known fear, she knew it, lying like a cool satin ribbon beneath the excitement of tempting fate. She knew the danger on the high steel bridge but refused to acknowledge it, pushed it back into the dim regions of her mind, back into the box with the hardness of Shirley and the realness of death, with the pleasure and guilt of self-love, with the struggles and pain of growing up and living up to a man's creed: thou shalt not cry. With a little more effort, and a bit of luck, she could be a better boy than boys were!

A special envoy of Japanese officials reached California on their way to Washington to renew the peace talks, while in Japan, the Parliament met in special session to approve an extraordinary war fund. Blocked in the south by the United States and Great Britain, on the southwest by China, and on the north by the Russians, the Japanese might have to wait a while before attempting further expansion.

Daddy followed the story with special interest and then remarked, maybe she will and maybe she won't, never can tell with those Orientals, now when I was working on camp cars, back years ago, we had a Chinese cook—"

"Now, Bud, not another railroad story!"

"Tell us, Daddy! tell us!"

"We'd say, Lin-Lee, wot-all kinda soup's this? He'd say, chicken-coop soup, bossee, we'd say, Lin Lee, we don see no chicken in this soup, Lin Lee, he'd say, I open de coop, de chicken she fly, then how you make soup, Lin Lee? The soup she makes wi wot left, bossee, when de chicken flew de coop, make chicken coop soup!" And Mother, trying to stop the tale all through the telling, now laughed with the girls and added,

"That's as bad as Miz Tompkins's ducks!"

"What about Miz Tompkins ducks, Daddy?"

"Well, ole Miz Tompkins, she baked some pies, put 'em in the window to cool. Well, little' while later, the pies were gone. Now Farmer Brown, he stole the' pies, took them down to the pond to eat. About an hour went by, he come up the hill, saw Miz Tompkins standin' in her door, mad as an ole guinea-hen, her hands on her hips, and Old farmer Brown, he sez, "Miz Tompkins, yer ducks is sunk!"

El and Bun looked at each other. Was that all? Should they laugh? "We don't get it, Daddy!" but Daddy and Mother were laughing fit to kill.

Out of one hundred and forty-two officers and men aboard the *Reuben James*, forty-five were reported safe. Many letters were received in the area, in addition to the one in Coville. There was one in Jesse, one in Cabin Creek, and one in Logan. "Waiting was the hardest," said the families," and we've cried and cried, couldn't sleep, couldn't eat, and the Mister, said he don't want to work no more if'n our boy's gone."

El thought Mr. Reeves might be feeling like that; she noticed he no longer built a fire in the old storage house. He seldom sat on his front porch shelling corn now, but at nine o'clock, regular as the trains run, he would walk through the town, his old coat pulled up to his ears, his cap on sideways, his gun over his arm, like there was no change in anything. Where had his son been, before the Navy? Did he have a mother? How could he go on with his chores, knowing his son was buried at sea? She tried to show her sympathy by speaking kindly and with respect, but he seldom acknowledged her greetings, seemingly unaware that she had spoken to him at all. And thinner. He was shrinking right before her eyes, getting shorter, smaller, just like Hollie, both of them, shrinking and drawing in on themselves—anybody could see it, if they took the time to look.

Now people were talking about planes as big as boxcars, would carry a whole load of people across the ocean in one day's time. It is grand, of that she was sure, but wouldn't the world seem smaller? Just last week a four-engine Army bomber had made a trip around the world, first time ever, and when it got back to the United States it had thirty bullet holes in its wings, shot at by fighters who thought it was an enemy plane. Flew all the way from Honolulu to the coast, then on to Washington, bringing in people to work out the Lend-Lease to Russia.

Bet Lindy would have loved to fly that one—but no, he didn't have the nickname "Lone Eagle" for nothing, probably would prefer to fly alone. But to cross the Atlantic and the Pacific both? Some flight! She wondered what it would be like by the time she graduated from high school—if only she could talk to Edgar about it—she missed him. She had told him she wouldn't slip out any more and he had been mighty busy ever since, going hunting with Joe or BillynBob; she was no competition to a fat squirrel or a plump quail, and before long it would be deer season: girls never got to do anything!

Within the first two weeks of the month, the Virginian had two major wrecks; fortunately, no lives were lost, but Daddy spent more time on the railroad than he did at home. The rather vague due date for the baby was uppermost on everyone's mind, and they played the "What if" game constantly. What if Mother had the baby while they were in school? What if the baby came tonight, while Daddy was working? What if, what if… thus, when Aunt Bea suggested she come for a few days visit, Mother and Daddy were delighted. Not so, El.

For some reason, all Aunt Bea did was to hunt for something wrong with Rachel, while Bun could do no wrong. Jane spent most of her time in her room, homework, or writing long letters to Ted, but El and Bun were lost on these gray, rainy afternoons, now that they couldn't play outside. They turned to their paper dolls and playhouses, but everywhere they set up housekeeping seemed to be exactly where Aunt Bea wanted to sit, or talk, or something. Bun, good-natured as always, moved her dolls without a grumble, but El tried to defend herself and was promptly rebuked. "You should be ashamed of yourself! Aunt Bea takes the time to come to help Mother and all you do is fuss!" El bit her tongue, what she wanted to say, she couldn't, but truth was, she no more wanted this new baby than she did Aunt Bea!

On the night of the fourteenth, a Friday night, Daddy was at Maben; two coal cars had left the track and demolished the bridge over Slab Fork Creek. All traffic on the main line was stopped until the bridge could be repaired, the wire restrung, even if it took all night—or two or three nights! The front door opened and a cold draft swept across the wood floor; she expected it to be Daddy, and waited for him to call out as he always did, but why did he come in the front door? It wasn't Daddy! Uncle Charlie swept into the room, ruddy cheeked from the cold, slight wetness on his shoulders from the falling snow.

"It's snowing!" he shouted, gathering the girls into his arms, blowing kisses to Aunt Bea and Mother. "Couldn't spend the weekend alone, missed my gal!" and he hugged Aunt Bea.

Mother got up clumsily, put her yarn down and found her sweater. As she started for the door, Uncle Charlie stopped her. "Hey! Where do you think you're going!"

"If it's snowing, I'm going to cut my roses, they'll be black before morning, might as well cut them," said Mother.

"Now, Faith, you can't get out there. Those steps are already icy, it's dark—you could hurt yourself!"

"I'll cut them, Mother," cried El. "Please! Let me!"

"Well, if you're sure, if you know how, long stems—"

"I know, I've watched you! I can do it!" El ran for her coat, anxious to get out of the house, out in the first snow of the year—and it was early, just as Mr. Gillespie had said!

The air was crisp, arid-smelling as only snow could smell, filled with large fluffy flakes that were rapidly accumulating on the fence and the wooden steps. Best of all, Edgar and Joe were in their front yard, yelling and racing, shouting their pleasure in the first snow. El joined them and for several minutes they played tag, running up and down the dark road, screaming at each other in wild, ecstatic joy. The front door opened, and Mother was silhouetted in the light. El returned to the yard, and cut the long-stemmed American Beauty roses, late-blooming beside the house. She carried them to Mother, who waited on the porch, one at a time, prolonging her time outdoors as long as possible. When the last flower was collected, they went in and Aunt Bea found a vase for the flowers, while Mother returned to her chair, a queer look on her face.

"Did you get cold?" asked Uncle Charlie with concern.

Aunt Bea began to scold, "You shouldn't have stayed out so long, making your Mother have to come get you, now if she catches cold it'll be your fault, Rachel, anybody with half a brain would..."

El ran upstairs and shut the bathroom door on the fussing; she didn't know why her Mother let Aunt Bea get on her all the time, her Mother was a different person when her sister was here, she was so mean, so bossy! Someday she'd show her, when she was a pilot and became famous—maybe she'd fly a bomber, like the one that crashed in the Atlantic and disappeared without a trace—then Aunt Bea would be sorry she talked to her like that. She wished Daddy would come home, he'd make Aunt Bea leave her alone.

That bomber that crashed, that was on the same day Daddy's motor barn had caught fire, he's had to rush back to Herndon to replace the hot wires and the telephone lines, because the trains couldn't run until they were repaired. The Virginian had built a bigger barn for Daddy, got it done in a few days, a much nicer one, and Daddy said if he'd known they'd do that, he would have set fire to it himself, years ago.

Now that the weather was bad, Daddy was seldom home, the railroad always came first. She hated the old railroad! She hated Aunt Bea! And she hated the new baby that was ruining everything, making so many changes, and demands, without even being born! How will it be when it finally gets here?

Morning, and suddenly bears were everywhere. The great black bear of Russia roused herself, shook the first snows of winter from her shoulders and turned to face the Nazis scratching at her Moscow-den door. Madam Chang-Ki-Sheck arranged for a lovable Panda bear to be sent to the Bronx Zoo in exchange for aid to the China war effort. Down in Pineville, Phil Goodykoontz and John Paul Taylor dressed in corduroy britches and laced-up boots to go bear hunting in the mountains of Wyoming County, and in Coville, Hollie brought Bun a small brown and white teddy bear that had belonged to Shirley.

Hollie stood at the door, hesitating, uncertain of her welcome; it had been several weeks since she had visited. El swung wide the door and called out to Mother and Aunt Bea in the kitchen, "Hey! Look who's here!"

Mother came to the door and looked down the hall, "Well, don't just stand there!" and she held out her arms. Hollie came to her with a radiant smile—like coming home. "You know my sister, Bea," and Bea came to hug Hollie too. "I've brought this for Bun," she said, "Shirley used to sleep with it. And this is for Jane," she added, holding out a song book. "Come on in, honey, I know Bun will love the bear, and Jane always enjoys new songs. "With her arms around her, Mother eased Hollie into a chair and sat down beside her. "Now, tell me, what have you been doing with yourself? How have you been?"

Hollie was model-thin, almost gaunt; she removed a light jacket, one much too thin for a such a chilly day. Her white blouse was tucked in, bunched around the waist as if hurriedly put on; her blue skirt—one Mother had helped her make weeks ago—was lapped over and carelessly pinned. Both blouse and skirt looked two sizes too large for her. Her face was thinner too, pale, with high cheekbones suddenly looking aristocratic, with hollows and shadows that moved as she turned her head, and her eyes were darker, an older, deeper blue, no longer the morning-glory blue of early spring. El thought she was lovelier than anyone she had ever seen in real life, lovelier even than Veronica Lake on screen. She couldn't take her eyes off of her, staring and staring. Jane came in and exclaimed over the book, rewarded by a faint smile from Hollie, and Bun, awake from a nap, hugged the bear, and warm and smiling, climbed on Hollie's lap. Hollie, aware of El's staring, looked at her, then away, and back again. In the awkward silence, El blurted out, "Boy, Hollie! You sure are pretty! You get prettier and prettier all the time! Doesn't she Mother?"

Faith smiled, and agreed, "But you mustn't stare, Ellie, That's not polite."

"So, what have you been doing?" asked Jane, and Hollie fluttered one hand for a reply. Jane rushed on, school, ballgames, church, Ted, the Red Cross, chattering, more Ted, unlike her usual calm manner. El felt the uncomfortable words wash over her, lost in her gazing at Hollie, envying her long, gold hair so carelessly brushed back from her face, looking at her dark lashes lying so naturally curled on her ivory-silk cheeks. The pretty pink and gold Hollie had become a gold and white beauty, awesome in her loveliness. Mother again chided her softly, "Ellie, it's not polite to stare."

"She looks like Veronica Lake!"

"Oh, Ellie! How could I! I forgot to bring you something!" In confusion, she jumped up, "I've got to be going— come with me, Ellie, I have something I want you to have!"

She started for the door, Jane begged her to stay, El begged Mother to let her go with Hollie and in the middle of it, Bun started begging Aunt Bea to make hot cocoa, and Hollie and El slipped out the back door.

As they walked down the road, Hollie said, "Are you mad at me for not bringing you something?"

"Of course not!" said El.

"Then what's the matter?"

"You look so different, Hollie, I think there's something wrong, but I don't know what, and you seem different—older—or—"

"You can say that again! I feel older."

El repeated her remark, word for word, playing a game from happier days." That reminds me of your Daddy, you know, Pete and Repete," said Hollie. El gave a quick skip, "Oh, yeah! Pete and Repete were sitting on the fence, Pete fell off, who was left? Repeat, Pete and Repeat..."

Arm in arm, they skipped down the road, to Hollie's gate, and Hollie, now with a blush to her cheeks and a sparkle to her eyes, looked nearly as young as El. They fell against the fence at Hollie's house, shaking the blood-red berries from the tall polkweed that grew taller than their heads, its crimson stalk bare now that the leaves had fallen and only the berries, ripe and full, remained. El stepped on them as they fell to the ground, mashing out the deep red pulp from which the settlers made ink and the Indians made war paint.

Emmett never would have let the polk mature there, for the berries were poisonous, something El had learned before the age of five. Emmett would have cleaned out the fence row, mowed the straggly broomsage, picked up the trash blown into the yard. Sobered, they walked to the porch, thinking of Shirley and Emmett, each knowing the other's thoughts. "El, thanks for coming with me, don't know when I've had so much fun. Now, wait right here, I have something for you—"

But she spoke too slowly for El had followed her into the house and shut the door behind her, as of old.

The house was a "wreck, looking for a place to happen," as Daddy said when El let her room get disorderly; clothes were strewn over the bed and chairs in the front room and dishes sat on the kitchen table, clearly visible from the front door. As Hollie rummaged through a high chest drawer, El looked about. Most of the clothing seemed to belong to either Emmett or Shirley for Hollie's dresses were on hangers, neatly hung on the back of the kitchen door for lack of a closet. On a small table beside the bed a stack of letters lay open, and it was obvious that they had been handled many times. The one on top caught El's eye and, rude though she knew it to be, she read it at a glance: *I saw you with him agin an I will git you if I see it one mor time.*

Startled, she turned to face Hollie, and found Hollie looking straight at her.

"I-I'm sorry," sputtered El, bewildered. "I didn't mean to read it—Hollie, is this some sort of game?"

Hollie moved to the bed, sat down, and piled the notes in her lap. "My love letters," she said grimly, fingering them nervously. "All from my dear, dear husband!"

"From Emmett?" said El, puzzled. "Where is he?"

"Ha! I wish I knew!" said Hollie as she flung the letters away from her. The scraps of paper fluttered to the floor like leaves falling from the dark trees of November, and she let them lie where they fell. "You stay away from him or I'll…" read the one lying at her feet. "…nobody else can have you even if…" read another one close by.

"Are they all threats?" whispered El.

"Yep. And how he knows what I do, I'll never figure out. Remember your birthday party? That was the first one, when I got home, it was stuck in the door. I laughed at it. Then, they kept coming, almost every time I went out the door, there'd be one when I got back. It seemed like he was watching all the time. I got scared. Silly, I know, but sometimes it seemed he was looking in the window, seeing everything I did. Ellie, now, don't you tell nobody! Promise me you won't tell. People will think I've lost my mind, my baby gone, living alone and all, but honest, *I know he's still watching me!*"

"Who is he talking about in the letters? Mr. Mitchell?"

Hollie was silent for some time. El waited it out, quiet, like Mother did when she didn't want to tell. Finally, Hollie answered. "He'd been coming down once in a while, just to talk, mind you, that's all, just to talk. We both get so lonesome, seems like every time he was here, I'd get a note the next morning, so I asked him not to come any more."

El was distressed and sat down by the older girl. "Oh, no, Hollie! You mustn't do that! Mr. Mitchell is good for you!" El remembered the way they had walked about her yard, looking at the flowers, laughing, talking to each other, their happy looks and smiling eyes. "Can't you do something?"

"What?" asked Hollie, bitterly. "It's like chasing Granny Hall, you know she's up there, on the bridge, but when you look up, she's gone!"

"Why don't you talk to Mother?"

Hollie was thoughtful, considering how much she should confide.

"I did," she confessed, "and your Daddy did some checking for me. He said Emmett enlisted in the Army, about three weeks ago, and that must be so, because I haven't gotten any more notes on the door since then. They've all come in the mail."

She jumped up and started throwing clothes off the bed, "And I'm going to get rid of all this mess, and, starting first thing in the morning, I'm going to give every last one of these to Bun!"

"I'll help you!" El cried.

"Wait! I have something I want to give you, if you'll have it. It's solid gold. She handed El a tiny gold cross, on a fine, gold chain. "Emmett gave it to me, years ago. I don't want it now."

"But, Hollie—"

"Please. It's pure gold, I want you to have it, and please, don't say a word about how you found my house. Faith would have a fit!"

By the time El started home, going the back way along the creek, it was nearly dark; the birch trees along the far bank showed white, their honest bark peeled off, their few remaining leaves standing out starkly against the gray sky. She became aware of individual leaves left hanging on the tips of branches, left dangling alone, and she felt an affinity for each single leaf. A sense of impending winter filled her, and she thought the trees felt it too. Some had rushed to an early death, anticipating the dying so they might live again sooner, juveniles, rushing from one season to the next, already into winter before the fall was gone. Others held on, and on.

When she eased through the front door she was ignored; Daddy was home and he was getting all the attention. She slipped upstairs and placed the small cross under her pillow, unwilling to share it with anyone. She knew how Emmett was keeping up with Hollie, what she did, where she went, who she talked to, but the question was, what could she do about it. She decided her first move was to talk to Edgar—and that as soon as possible.

She wandered into the dining room nonchalantly, hoping to avoid questions, but she needn't have worried. Mother was sitting in her comfortable chair, her feet up on an ottoman, her hand on her abdomen. Daddy sat at the table, his watch lying face up on the white linen cloth. "Another false alarm", Aunt Bea was saying, as she moved about the room in agitation, " just another false alarm. Faith, if you don't have that baby soon, it's going to come out walking!"

Twenty

The Japanese envoy, Saburo Kurusu, arriving in Washington on Sunday night, stated that he had a difficult task, but, as long as there exists such sympathy on the part of the people of the United States, for Japan, he "still had a fighting chance to make a success of my mission."

The miners and steel owners were deadlocked. The cold coal-fields waited for word to walk out. Roosevelt talked to the Army, determined that the captive mines would continue to operate, but the UMW tentatively notified twelve thousand West Virginia miners to stay home on Monday.

Up on Stoney ridge, a hunter tried to smoke a squirrel out of a hickory tree; the tree caught fire and fell, setting two hundred acres of forest ablaze. Armistice Day was the opening date for hunting quail and rabbit, as well as squirrels, and most West Virginia boys spent the weekend in the woods. Edgar was no different, thus the days passed without a sign of him. El went to sleep Sunday night very disappointed, taking the thought of Hollie and her serious problems with her.

Something awakened her. She lay still, listening: there it was again, a low moan. Unsure whether it came from inside or outside, she sat up to listen, but the sound stopped. Bun was asleep beside her, curled up in a warm, red ball. The moon, opulently full, was sitting on top of the ridge and she could see the silver wires across the bridge, shining like they were wet. Under her door there was a thin light from the hall or bathroom. Now that she was awake, she had to go potty before she could go back to sleep. The wood floor was cold to her bare feet, and when she opened the door a cold blast from the stairwell made her shiver. The bathroom door was slightly ajar, and she could see the commode; it was unoccupied. She pushed the door open.

Aunt Bea was standing at the sink, running hot water into the basin. Steam covered the window, condensing on the inside, forming little rivulets that ran down the glass to drop on the window sill. A blanket was spread on the window seat, and on it lay the dirtiest, messiest, reddest little baby that El had ever seen. El looked at it, stunned. She had been prepared for a few wrinkles or squinched up eyes, but this? It looked awful! Ugly! Far worse than anything she ever imagined in all her speculations about the birth process.

"Rachel! What are you doing up! You get back in that bed!" Aunt Bea pulled a corner of the blanket over the baby, hiding her from view.

Rachel came closer, ignoring the command. "It's a girl?" she asked, knowing it before she asked.

"You mustn't see her like this—wait until I give her a bath! Go back to bed!"

"I have to go potty," said El moving towards the commode.

"Well, go, then! Then get out of here!"

"I've already seen her. Why is she so dirty?"

"Mother nature's way of protecting her skin," said Aunt Bea, testing the water with one elbow. She picked up the baby, cradled it in one arm and put water on its head. The baby gave a sudden piercing yell and Doc Steelman immediately appeared at the door.

"Everything under control here?" he asked, then, seeing El, he stopped short. "What are you doing here?"

"Peeing," said El, calmly.

"All the racket wake you?"

"Mother did."

"Your mother is just fine—just fine!" He turned to go back to Mother's room. "And so is your new baby sister!"

Aunt Bea had the new baby well soaped and rinsed with warm water by the time El was finished pretending she was using the potty, and she didn't object as El came to watch.

"What's that thing?"

"That's the cord, it fed her while she was in your Mommy's tummy."

"It looks yuk."

"It will come off in a few days, and she'll have a cute little belly button."

"And that's why I have a belly button?"

"Everyone has a belly button, unless they were hatched!" said Doc Steelman, coming to take the baby from Aunt Bea. "Scoot over, tyke," he said to El, "Let's have a good look at her!"

The baby lay happily on a dry towel, placidly looking at the lightbulb in the ceiling. Doc Steelman placed his stethoscope on her chest, looked into her eyes with a little light, tried to open her mouth, but the baby objected, sucking on his thumb instead. "Oh, ho, you're ready to eat, are you?"

The big man turned her over, listened to her back. "Dress her up, Auntie, and we'll take her in to see her Mommy!"

Aunt Bea took a small undershirt and a gown—which Mother had stitched so carefully—from the end of the window seat; she folded a diaper expertly, and El, watching, thought her aunt needed a baby of her own. "How did you learn to take care of babies?" she asked.

"Learned on you—and on Bun, and on Jane."

"You bathed me?"

"Yep!"

"Did I look like that?"

"No, you looked more like a prune!" said Aunt Bea.

El knew she was later than expected, she had no doubt she was uglier. Aunt Bea tied the small white ribbons under the baby's chin, straightened out her extra-long gown, and wrapped her in a pale pink blanket. She became—very suddenly—the most beautiful baby in the world, smooth, soft pink skin, large, wide awake dark eyes, and yes, she was almost smiling. Aunt Bea brushed her hair upward into a kewpie doll roll, and it curled, a dark, wet blond. Her miniature hands with perfect little fingers waved in the air, begging to curl around El's finger. She was so lovely El began to cry and didn't even think to hide it. "Oh, Aunt Bea, she's beautiful!"

"You might as well carry her into your mama" said Bea brusquely, hiding her feelings as best she could.

El took the new baby very carefully, gingerly walking across the hall. Mother was lying on high pillows, and Daddy sat on the edge of the bed beside her. Doc Steelman stood at the foot of the bed. El felt like she was carrying a very precious gift to a queen; she could almost hear the music, a grand march, like they played at graduation or in the movies when visitors were presented to royalty. Proudly she accomplished the long walk from the door to the bed, knowing all eyes were on the precious bundle she carried. She laid the infant between her parents and stepped back.

"Ellie! What are you doing up!"

Aunt Bea stepped behind her quickly. "She's been helping me!" she said, "couldn't have done it without her!" At that moment, Aunt Bea became her favorite aunt for life. The baby began to fuss, as if to remind them she was the center of attention.

"What's her name, Mother? What do we call her besides beautiful?" asked Daddy as he took her tiny hand in his.

Mother spoke softly, "I'd like to call her Shirley, if you've no objection."

"That's fine with me," said Daddy.

"And Ruth has always been one of my favorite Biblical figures."

"Shirley Ruth," said Aunt Bea. "That's lovely."

"Baby Ruth," said Daddy.

"Oh, now, Bud, don't start giving her nicknames already! Shirley Ruth is a perfectly good name." It was obvious that Mother had picked out the name some time ago.

"Sounds like a candy bar to me," said Aunt Bea, but they all knew the name would stay as Daddy had called it.

"You'll have to try again for that boy, William," said Doc Steelman, packing up his bag to leave.

"No Siree!" exclaimed Daddy. **"I've got four Queens now, and you can't beat a hand like that!"**

Although she had lost sleep, El was anxious to get up on Monday morning. She proudly broadcast the news of the new baby to the camp, stopping by the Belchers and the Company store before going to school, then visiting the other two rooms to make the announcement. After school, she raced Bun home, anxious to see what progress the infant had made during the day—progress toward being big enough to play with. In the girls' eyes, Baby Ruth had but one function in life, to entertain and amuse her sisters.

Gifts were arriving daily, a silver spoon from the Eastern Star ladies, flowers from the Masons, cards and letters from relatives El never knew she had. Neighbors sent pies and cakes, recalling the many favors Faith had done for them, and knowing she would be bed-bound for three weeks, the custom after child-birth. Baby Ruth's birth was second only to Christmas and Halloween, and a lot better than Thanksgiving.

In Morgantown, Undersecretary of War Patterson stated, "National defense is not a bargain—it's a duty!" And Roosevelt was tending his duty: he was meeting with Saburo Kurusu in their first efforts at peace talks. Japan had issued a clear warning that there was a "limit to our conciliatory attitude."

The President was meeting also with the railroad officials, both labor and management, trying to prevent the December seventh walkout. Out in the Midwest, two hundred and fifty thousand truck drivers, members of the AFL teamster's union, threatened to strike for higher pay and a new contract. Wednesday evening, fifteen hundred miners walked out of the mines in Logan, strictly a sympathy strike, for there were no captive mines in the area.

A troop train went through the coalfields and the local residents thought it was the Army moving in, but it turned out to be a transfer of men from Fort Benjamin Harrison in Indiana to Fort Bragg, North Carolina. By Wednesday night the state police had moved into Gary. Two miners were shot even though William Blizzard, District Vice President of the UMW, was predicting that all one hundred and five thousand West Virginia miners would strike in sympathy with the miners in the captive mines—and that strike would take place in forty-eight hours.

In Pittsburgh, the steel mills announced that it would be necessary to shut down the furnaces within forty-eight hours, if the coal was not brought in, and at Big Sandy, eleven thousand miners declared their intention to strike on Thursday morning.

John L. defied the Governor to use Army troops...

At Gary, the Independent Union announced, "Our men are anxious to work..."

Thus, when Thanksgiving Day arrived, more than forty thousand miners had joined the captive miners in a sympathy strike, and John L. Lewis had rejected the President's proposal for postponement of the closed shop issue until after the national emergency.

"Aw, Hell!" said Daddy, in response to the strike news, "those damn miners just want off work to go huntin'—ain't anything but a way to get a long Thanksgiving holiday!"

This Thanksgiving was unusual for many reasons. Jane had prepared the turkey—something she had never undertaken before—and there was much running up and down stairs for instructions. Aunt Bea was nearly as bad as she tried to bake pumpkin pies. Mother had made several fruit cakes, storing them in her stone crock, expecting to be confined over the holiday. The weather cooperated, permitting the children to play outside, and the railroad gave

Mother a special treat by allowing Daddy to take Thursday and Friday off, making it a four-day holiday for him—baring accidents, of course.

Although the railroad had given him the day off, his civic duty called him for several hours on Thursday morning. The Wyoming County Civil Defense had requested that each town paint markers on top of their highest buildings to direct fliers who might get lost in the area. The only two buildings in the county were the county court house in Pineville, and the Long-Wells Motor company in Mullins. Daddy was the only man in Coville with the experience—and the guts—to climb on top of the Company store, and when El suggested he let Mr. Gillespie do it, Daddy said, Ha! Old Rayford couldn't get his belly over the gutter—and he changed it immediately to, "couldn't get his gut over the gutter."

El went with him, watching as he painted a large orange arrow pointing to the north. El couldn't wait to get up on the high bridge to view his "art work". Keeping her mouth shut about it was painful.

By the time they finished the painting, Uncle Charlie was at the house, come to "see his girl," and to have Thanksgiving dinner with them. Mother wasn't allowed to come down stairs for dinner, but Jane fixed her a tray, complete with a small Fostoria vase holding a sprig of Holly with red berries, winter's traditional contribution to table decorations, replacing the rose of summer. El and Bun sat under the baby's crib, making room for chairs for the adults who came up to eat with Faith, and listened as the adults talked.

"Charlie's going to Virginia with me tomorrow, to take Old Bess home."

"Oh, no! Don't take her back to Ginnie!"

"Got to, she's almost dry," said Daddy. "Might be my only chance. If I wait, the weather might turn sour."

Daddy had brought the radio up to Mother's room until she was able to come downstairs. Now, he turned it on for the news, but there was not much different from what they had heard at noon.

"Ted says we will be in a shooting war before the first of the year. We need to be getting ready for that," said Jane.

"How is that red-headed peckerwood, anyway?" asked Daddy and El lost interest in the conversation; she knew from experience that Jane would still be talking about Ted an hour from now.

Baby Ruth was waking, and El jumped to be the first one to pick her up. She held her close, sniffing her powdered neck, thinking that Baby Ruth made it a special Thanksgiving for all of them. Gone were the ill feelings towards the new sister, forgotten the petulance and bad temper: Baby Ruth was as sweet, or sweeter than Bun had ever been.

Blue dark settled quickly between the hills, and it was night before five o'clock; a faint rim of light along the crest of the ridge distinguished west from east and El figured the sun was halfway around the world, or at least to California. She sat in the porch swing, not yet suspended from the ceiling because there were days in the fifties—and Mother hadn't been downstairs to do things as usual.

The quick flurry of snow on Sunday night had not remained on the ground. Surely Edgar would be home soon. Nobody could hunt after dark, unless they were running the dogs, red fox hunting, and Edgar didn't even own dogs.

The weather remained on hold, and the night birds sang like it was spring, the crickets rasped in the trees, a beat slower, but making themselves known. There was no sign of life around the Mitchell's house, but Mary Beth and Papa Wooten came slowly up the street, Mary Beth leaning on his arm, obviously needing his support.

"Want to see our new baby?" called El to the young mother-to-be and her supportive father. "Like to, Ellie, but I don't think I could make it up those steps."

"I can bring her down," said El

"Would yer Ma let you?" asked Mary Beth.

"Why, sure! I've picked her up, lots of times."

El could see their quick consultation, then Mary Beth entered the gate. She ran to open the door and Papa Wooten seated himself on the wooden steps to wait. El ran upstairs to ask permission to bring the baby down and was surprised by Mother's reaction.

"Now, just a minute! Little Shirley will just have to wait until I can come down too!"

"Oh, Mother, that will be three weeks and if Mary Beth has to wait three weeks to get about—Baby Ruth will be growed up before Mary Beth even sees her!"

"Grown, Ellie, not growed", said Mother automatically, studying the problem. Jane, hearing the discussion, came from her room. "I'll walk down in front of her, Mother, if that's the problem."

"Well, I guess I'm outnumbered. It's perfectly silly to have to lay here three weeks, I feel fine."

"Doctors orders," said Daddy from his side of the bed. New baby or no new baby, he took his siesta, as he called it, in his own place.

El lifted the baby carefully, and tucked the blanket around her, walked confidently down the stairs with Jane preceding her in case she stumbled.

Mary Beth sat in a straight chair; her knees wide apart to accommodate her huge abdomen. She reached for the infant, hesitated, uncertain about how to hold her, having no lap. El solved the problem by holding the baby herself, turning the blanket back so Mary Beth could see.

"How tiny!" Mary Beth exclaimed. "Makes me want to have mine!"

"She's not really small," said Jane, "weighed over seven pounds."

"So, this is our little Shirley," Mary Beth said gently.

"Daddy calls her, Baby Ruth," said El. "We like that best, don't we Jane?" To her surprise, Jane agreed.

"Sounds like a candy bar," said Mary Beth, " but it's real sweet!" They all laughed, and Bun, standing in the dining room door with jam all over her face, said, "Well if I can be 'Honey Bun' all my life, she can be 'Baby Ruth!'"

"Don't you like being called Honey Bun?" asked Jane, putting her arms around her.

"It's okay, but I don't want to call the baby Shirley."

El understood why Bun didn't want to be reminded of the first Shirley—she had been like a baby sister to Bun. "Let's just call her Baby Ruth and don't tell Mother!"

It was settled. The girls banded together and sided with Daddy. Baby Ruth it would be—for all of them.

"What do you hear from Ben?" Jane asked, taking the baby from El as she tired.

"Oh! Wait 'til I tell you! He's getting the same ship as Will! Just as soon as they dock, whenever that is, ain't that great?"

"Super!" the girls agreed. "Where is he now?"

"Beats me, some ocean," said Mary Beth. "Mrs. Gillespie might know, but she'd never tell me, you know how she is, wouldn't speak to me if her life depended on it."

"Ted is in Norfolk," said Jane, and was off and running on her favorite subject. El took the baby back upstairs and returned to the porch to watch for

Edgar, but the only one in sight was Papa Wooten, sitting patiently on the steps, waiting for his over-sized daughter to complete her visit.

High in the brown-leafed oaks, she spotted a ball of mistletoe, the first yuletide ornament, already hung, and well out of reach. Edgar came down the road, his gun over his shoulder, but emptyhanded. He turned in his gate with a casual wave at El and Papa Wooten, not waiting to talk to her at all. Dejected, she went in the house and found a book to read.

Daddy and Uncle Charlie left early Friday morning with Old Bess bawling in the small trailer pulled behind the gray car. Mother promised El and Bun they would bring the old cow back again, after she's had her new baby. Round-eyed, Bun asked, "Another baby?"

El answered, superior in her new knowledge. "Sure, Bun, cows have a baby every year!" Bun turned, silent, speculative, and looked at Mother.

Mrs. Gillespie came up the stairs, interrupting further questions. Quickly, El asked about Ben and Will, as if she hadn't heard news about them." They will be on the same ship, as soon as they made port, and the wonderful thing about it was, they were going to be on the West Virginia! Seeing as how they are brothers and from this state, and Will got into radio and he plans to go into television—you know what that is? Where you see pictures and hear radio at the same time, now Ben, he messed himself up by not finishing high school so he's just a fireman, says he don't do much…"

"Where are they? Which ship?"

"Why, Will, he's on the USS Maryland, said it was as close to the hills as he could get, and Ben, he didn't get a choice, not having no college and all, he's on the Tennessee, and it's just a bunch of hillbilly boys but he's happy, he don't write much, spends his time writing that girl I suppose…"

El, watching the neighbor, became more and more aggravated with her. She wasn't looking at Baby Ruth, holding her like a sack of flour on her lap; El took the baby away and Mrs. Gillespie didn't seem to know she was gone, just talked on about Will.

El thought about Zane Gray, somewhere out on the ocean, on the USS Arizona. The West Virginia was due back in Puget Sound, Mrs. Gillespie was saying.

Down in Newport, a new battleship was being launched, first one in twenty years. The 35,000-ton Indiana was ready to be christened, six months ahead of schedule. It would carry seventy-five officers and a thousand men. The USS

Indiana was built in the same shipyards that had made the 31,000-ton West Virginia, the last ship to be built in the Virginia docks, launched back in 1921, November 19th to be exact, twenty years ago nigh to the day! The North Carolina and the Washington were already in use, the South Dakota and Massachusetts were in the last spit and polish stage, and the Alabama would come out of dry dock in February or March of next year.

The President was going to Warm Springs, Georgia for a second Thanksgiving vacation because he got two Thanksgivings this year. Next year, Thanksgiving would be celebrated on the usual last Thursday of the month, but this year Roosevelt had moved it up one week, so folks could have an extra week to shop before Christmas—stimulate the economy, he said—and El had asked, How? Folks have got the same amount of money to spend, whether it's this week or next week—and Mother had said, are you running the government now Ellie? And Daddy said leave her alone she might do a better job than the ones are doing now. Thirty-six states were celebrating early, sixteen would celebrate next week, and Franklin would get in both of them.

Three pickets were wounded in Pennsylvania, but in West Virginia, most of the miners carried their guns into the woods to hunt. FDR prepared a bill to seize the mines, and the Army rallied the troops, ready to move.

A committee of three had been named to mediate the railway strike and to prepare a report for the President. The Carriers and the Brotherhoods got together *and the meeting lasted just five minutes.*

Those railroad men were operating on a short fuse, Daddy said, and Roosevelt orta do them like he done that dam out west, the one in Oklahoma, where the government took over to prevent interruption in the power for defense.

The Bluefield Daily Telegraph summarized the feelings of the people regarding the miner's strike and the railroader's threats in the editorial:

The force of public opinion is a strange phenomenon, and sometimes brings unusual results, some of them mysterious. At present there is an unfoldment of great interest. The coal miner's strike has aroused public opinion to the point where there is no distinction in the matter of labor disputes. The possible success of the Railroad men holding any considerable public sentiment favorable to their demands has gone a glimmering. The effect of the coal mine shut-down has made strikes unpopular, and while there is a radical difference between the coal miners and the railroad workers objectives, yet, in the public mind they are all in one category. In fact, the attitude of the mine workers has been very harmful to the Union labor cause generally and its outcome will probably be the basis for its settlement of all similar contentions at least during the endurance of the war threat and defense preparations. If the American people can trust their own senses, they know we are in the war…

Hitler, speaking in December of 1940 had stated: "Two worlds are in conflict…two philosophies of life…Our capital is our capacity for work and with it we will defeat the whole world."

That strange phenomena of public opinion produced fruit: on Sunday, November 23, the headlines proclaimed,

CAPTIVE MINE STRIKE ENDS

The miners and steelmen agreed to accept the decision made by arbitration board, led by Dr. John R. Steelman, a man with great experience in labor wrangling. The decision was a shock, for John L. had rejected FDR's offer, but it had been made in the best interests of the country. The miners returned to work on Monday, the children returned to school; best of all, Aunt Bea and Uncle Charlie went home. Everything returned to normal.

Baby Ruth was born after midnight, making her birthday on November 17, a Monday, and she was, as Monday's Child, fair of face. Within a week she had lost the redness in her face, and her fine gold hair had learned to cling around Mother's finger in the beginning of curls, much as the first Shirley's had curled, yet nobody spoke about that resemblance. She intruded lightly into the household, quiet and pleasant in disposition, eating on schedule, waking only once during the night to eat, allowing Mother to get her rest and recuperate rapidly. Her presence was most prominently noted in the upstairs hallway: a wooden rack stood over the register and was perpetually draped with wet diapers in one stage or another.

All the neighbors came, most of them daily, except for Mary Beth, for now she had been confined to her bed by Doc Steelman. Having pains, and now close to due date, the old Doc didn't want to take chances with the twins. The girl was so large, she was miserable sitting up. El waited anxiously for the delivery, figuring to herself: If they came before the seventh, they were Wills, if after the seventh, they belonged to Ben. She didn't dare talk about her speculations to anyone—she wasn't supposed to know that much about it. Doc Steelman had explained the number of weeks it took to have a full term baby, like Baby Ruth, but he had added, "give or take a week or two." And that she didn't understand. Why didn't he know exactly?

Mother, being Mother, had found a way to keep busy while Baby Ruth slept. She had started a new quilt top, piecing the squares together on her fingers because Doc Steelman had said no sitting at the sewing machine. None of Mother's quilts were patchwork now, or "quickies" as she called them. They all formed patterns, stars, flowers, diamonds, cabins, little pieces with blended colors and matched borders, backed with new bleached muslin or flour sacks, often sewing the matched flour sacks together for the lining. Her quilts went to 'Fairs', County or to State and the ribbons she won were kept in a red satin candy box hid in her bottom dresser drawer beside the secret medical book El wasn't supposed to know about.

Sometimes, on snowy days, she would allow El or Bun to take the box out and look at all the ribbons and they would lay them out on the bed, the red, blue, yellow and one big bright purple one, the grand prize at the West Virginia State Fair; here's the one she won at Lewisburg, this one at the coal exhibit, and loving the names of the quilts that won, Grandmother's Flower Garden, Rose of Sharon, Star of Bethlehem, and her own design, Iris in Spring.

This winter she had a new idea and as she explained it, El had a strange feeling of uneasiness, a feeling of dread or apprehension, a premonition, like thinking about saying goodbye when the party is not yet over. That was it. Mother was talking like she was leaving, but they weren't going anywhere— or were they?

The quilt for this year was to be the Little Dutch Girl pattern. The squares were to be a foot wide and a foot long, with a little girl in the center of each, with a long dress and a matching bonnet which hid her face—faces were hard to do—the bonnet and shoes were to be solid colors picking up one of the colors in the dress. The dresses would be scraps from their own dresses, and they picked up the scraps, naming whose dress it was, and where they had worn it. Each square would have a name on it," Mother explained, "the name of someone who had come to visit them this winter," and, she continued, "years later, I can look at the quilt and remember them."

"Me, too?" asked Bun.

"You too, Honey Bun, and you can pick the material for your Little Dutch Girl."

"Why won't they be quilted alike?" asked El

"Each one will be quilted with things that person likes. For instance, on your Daddy's I'll put lineman's pliers, a ladder, hammer, tools he uses every day. On Jane's I'll put music notes, something to do with singing."

"What will mine have?" asked El. "Oh, I don't know—you help me in the garden, how about flowers?" El thought quickly. "How about an airplane?"

"Make mine flowers," cried Bun.

"Birds," said El, "a red-tailed hawk, an owl. They were the first to fly."

"A crow," Jane said sarcastically, "or a bat, a ding-bat! El, I've told you not to wear my sweaters!" Jane was home from school.

"I ain't as batty as you, or as selfish!" cried El hotly. "And I ain't growed into an old grouch, either!"

"Mother, she's saying 'ain't' and 'growed'—you know better, El!"

"Why not! It's what I hear all the time!"

"Makes you sound like a hillbilly!"

"Well, I am a hillbilly, and proud of it!"

"Poor grammar doesn't make you a hillbilly, El" Mother said, "It just makes you sound ignorant." And she turned back to her quilt scraps.

"I knowed growed wasn't right," El said softly to Jane.

"Now she's saying 'knowed'."

"I heard her, Jane. She's just trying to irritate you."

"Well, make her stop, and tell her to leave my sweaters alone!"

"You should thank her, she did you a favor."

"What favor could she possibly do for me?"

"She brought the mail, and you have a letter from Ted."

"She'll be in a better mood now," said Mother, rearranging her squares. El went to her room, but she could still hear Mother explaining her squares to Bun, the neighbors would write their names on a square and she would quilt over it, preserving their names for all times. El had the feeling again—Mother's quilt was some over-sized autograph book, collecting signatures for some future time when all the people were gone, to be taken out when it was time to call the roll. Mother should have made her quilt sooner; there were already names that would never be inscribed: Shirley, Cliff Sanders, Emmett—

although he might come back someday. Ben, Will, Ted, Zane Gray—none of them will be coming to visit this winter, not now. Mrs. Gillespie had gotten another letter from Will. They wouldn't be putting into Puget Sound; they were headed out to sea. Mary Beth had gotten the same letter from Ben, although he might get to come home when the baby was born, maybe air-lifted off his ship by the Red Cross, but he didn't know for sure.

Mother cut out squares for her Little Dutch girl quilt and President Roosevelt sent troops to Dutch Guyana to stand guard over the mines.

"Why, Daddy, is West Virginia running out of coal?"

"Not coal mines, El. Bauxite. Makes aluminum. For Airplanes."

"But in South America? I thought the Dutch were in Holland!"

"Dutch Guyana, down near Venezuela. Get out your globe, El. Now you know why South America won't escape involvement in the war. It's only a jaunt across the water for the Germans—unless the Japs get there first!"

But the Germans were having a tough time of it; they had thrown their reserves against the British in a battle covering more than sixteen hundred square miles, and they were pushing hard at the Russian capital, Moscow, with somewhat more success.

During the supper hour, Jane shared parts of Ted's letter; now that he was in his sixth week of basic training, he would be commissioned a chaplain, and would ship out on the new, just christened, USS Indiana. But the best news of all was, he would be home for a week before reporting to his ship. He planned to see his family for a day or two, then he would be in Mullins. Preacher Copeland would put him up and he was coming to see her!

"When, Jane! When is he coming?"

His class finishes the second, ceremonies on the fourth, and his mother would be there, drive back to Ohio with her, be in Mullins on Sunday night in time for Epworth League. He wanted to see everyone before reporting back to Newport News on Thursday. He would have all of Monday and Tuesday with her. Jane paused and bit her lip, looking at Mother imploringly.

"Do you think I could take one day off from school? Ted wants to take me on a picnic."

Daddy snorted. "A picnic, in the dead of winter? What kind of tom-fool idea is that!"

"Now, I remember, one time, we went on a picnic and it was late September", Mother started, smiling strangely at Daddy.

"Aw, forget it," Daddy mumbled. "Do as you please, you're going to anyway."

In local news, West Virginians were upset over the placement of an Ohio plant, located to be "near" West Virginia coal. Why was it not in West Virginia, why treat our state like a red-headed step-child perhaps punishing the entire state for the antics of old John L.? And, another thing, why had the state received no defense appropriations? Billions had been handed out, but West Virginia hadn't been on the hand-out list; we paid taxes same as other states, supporting every program for defense. And what was this about the state being out of the Union?

Representative Johnson (D. W.Va.) said he was making every effort to bring the state back into the union, to see if something could be done. He complained to the Civil Aeronautics Administration about their failure to include the state in an airport improvement program, and the board replied that they were very sympathetic and as soon as they could find a defense objective that will permit consideration of any of West Virginia airports, we will certainly use it."

"Why can't they find a defense objective, Mother? It's not fair to leave us out."

"Think about it, Ellie. If we were invaded, where would you want to be?"

El considered. The pictures from the newsreels went through her head, enemy planes flying over, bombs dropping, boats coming ashore. The New England States. Virginia, the Carolina's, Georgia, Florida—all would be overrun; California's sloping coast would be easy. Maybe out West? Middle of the Country?

"No place to hide, El. Desert," said Daddy. "Right out in the open."

In the mountains there were tunnels, mine shafts, hidden trails, difficult terrain. *The same conditions that made the state difficult to settle would make it difficult to invade.*

She was in the best possible part of the country, right, Daddy? Right, El.

"Then how come they're linking all the fire towers for air raid warning stations, putting telephones in all seventy-five fire towers?"

"Forewarned is forearmed, El, same thing as putting a lookout tower at the fort. We're just watching for the Indians again, honey, just watching for the Indians."

387

The war in Europe surged forward on many fronts: Tobruk, Rostov, Libya—names unfamiliar only weeks ago now became household words. Von Ribbentrop was urging American people to disown their government, predicting that the steady stream of war materials flowing from the country would bring the nation to an economic catastrophe the likes of which no land has seen. He continued, "And with the new order marches the new order in East Asia under the leadership of Japan. No one can hold up this development permanently," But the uncertainty over Japan's intentions dominated the news.

On Thursday, November 27th, a day celebrated as Thanksgiving by sixteen of the forty-eight states, the head-lines read:

U.S. & JAPAN
FAIL TO FIND FORMULA FOR FAR EAST SETTLEMENT

Secretary of State Hull had given the Japanese Ambassador Nomura and Special Minister Kurusu a statement of policy which outlined the basic principles of the American Government. The document reiterated the policies stated by Hull in 1937, shortly after the Japanese began their invasion of China. *Same song, second verse, a whole lot louder and a whole lot worse.* Nevertheless, informed sources said that Japan was now faced with a showdown: she must negotiate on the basis of American policy—or take the consequences of her decision. The United States was pledged to help China in her struggle against Japan. The Ambassador and the Special Minister were expected to return to Tokyo to make a report and to receive further instructions. What would Japan do? *That was the question!*

By Friday there were signs that Japan was moving large masses of troops into Saigon and Haiphong, and the Japanese diplomatic representatives requested a meeting with Franklin Roosevelt. The strain in the Far East was forcing British troops to remain in the area when they were desperately needed in Europe, and was requiring an American build-up in the Pacific when more ships were needed in the Atlantic. When the two Japanese Diplomats were questioned by reporters, following their meeting with the President of the United States, they said only, there had been a friendly conversation.

In Japan the people waited for a report on the Washington talks, assuming that a decision was coming: many suggested that the talks were intended merely to keep Japan guessing while U.S. forces were moved into position.

The Americans were waiting on the Japanese to decide; the Japanese were waiting for the Americans. Nobody seemed certain what was happening. Saturday's paper stressed that Japan had the next move, and the only indication of what that move might be came from reports of continued troop buildup in Indochina.

President Roosevelt took the Saturday train to Warm Springs for a much-needed rest. The last time Secretary Hull tried peace talks, Japan had moved into Indochina. Like Hitler, Daddy said: Adolph Hitler always talked peace just before he made a major move into a country.

Mother was feeling much better; Baby Ruth was nearly two weeks old, and Saturday morning Mother got out of bed. While Daddy fussed and threatened, she directed the upstairs housecleaning, mildly promising she wouldn't go downstairs. El wished she would! She had them cleaning out their dresser drawers, and closets, sorting and separating clothes. In the midst of all the dragging out, Mother found the dirty Halloween costume and fussed unreasonably: it's been in your closet a whole month! And how did you get it so muddy! Now, you know, Rachel, you don't put dirty clothes in your closet—and the crushing blow—I've a good mind to keep you home with me tonight!

But Daddy came to the rescue, and after an early supper, Jane, El, and Bun went with him to see Betty Grable and Tyrone Power in *A Yank in the RAF*. When Mother allowed her to go, she knew she was forgiven. She never said how the suit got so muddy, nor did Mother press for an explanation. She came out of the movie dedicated to flying, now, more than ever. She had to tell Edgar about it, about the battle of Dunkirk and the Royal Air Force, even if she got caught slipping out! He was the only one who would understand.

On Sunday, November 30th, the "fat hit the fire," as Mr. Gillespie put it. He was knocking on the Phillips' front door before they finished breakfast. Daddy answered, still in his robe and slippers.

"What did he mean, Daddy? What does the fat hit the fire mean?" They were certain there was trouble, but what Mr. Gillespie was offering was a ride to church, since Faith couldn't be driving yet, and got to conserve gasoline, and with his boys gone, might as well go with him. El dressed quickly and ran to get Hollie, glad she was taking an active interest in church activities, determined to put her life in order again.

As they walked up the road together, El asked about the letters, but Hollie stopped her. "Oh, Ellie! It's such a glorious day! Almost like spring! Let's don't talk about Emmett, or anything bad!"

"Who's Emmett?" El took a quick skip. Hollie had her long, blonde hair turned under in a page-boy and it lay about her shoulders like gold silk, giving her face a light sheen. She was smiling and happy: El wouldn't change that for anything in the world.

With Ted gone, Preacher Copeland had come out of retirement and had been pressed into service. His sermon this morning was filled with references to war "a war to end all wars" and "a war the likes of which the world has never seen", known phrases fast becoming worn clichés. El lost interest when he started on Solomon's battles. Without Mother present to prohibit it, she had taken a seat on the next to last row, right in front of Edgar, Joe, BillynBob and Jimmy Jr. Plover. She managed to slip Edgar a note saying she had to talk to him, but the other boys saw it and he wouldn't acknowledge it.

After church, Mr. Gillespie was in a hurry to get home; El suggested that she, Judith, Hollie and Jane walk home, but Mr. Gillespie said, no. El pointed out that it felt almost like spring, the bees were buzzing around! Mr. Gillespie said, "No, I brought you, I'll take you home", and Jane said, "You must be crazy, think I want to walk in these shoes?" She held up her foot to show off her two and a half inch heels. El gave up, sighed with envy as she watched the boys walking up the road, yelling, playing, having fun. Boys had all the advantages.

Before church, Jane had put a large beef roast to cook for dinner; when she reached home, she immediately peeled potatoes and scraped carrots to cook on top, just as Mother would have done. El's duties were to set out plates and silver, but when she went to the dining room, she found the paper where Daddy had left it. One look at the headlines explained Mr. Gillespie's 'fat hit the fire' comment:

TOJO SAYS JAPS WILL PURGE U.S. INFLUENCE
FDR Asserts U.S. May Be Fighting Next Year.
Plans to Rush Back To Washington From Warm Springs
Because of New Turn In Japanese Situation
Cabinet Maps Reply To Note
Premier Hideki Tojo solemnly and publicly declared tonight the

Determination of Japan to purge British and American influence from East Asia "with a Vengeance—for the honor and pride of mankind."

El sat down and read the short paragraph. "The fact that Chang-Kai-Shek is dancing to the tune of Great Britain, America, and Communism, at the expense of able-bodied and promising young men in his resistance against Japan, is only due to the desire of Britain and the U.S. to fish in the troubled waters of East Asia by pitting East Asiatic people against one another and to grasp hegemony in East Asia..."

Daddy came into the dining room. "Thought you were supposed to be helping with dinner?"

"What does hegemony—h-e-g-e-m-o-n-y mean?"

From the kitchen came Jane's voice, "Look it up!"

"Hard to tell Mother is upstairs, ain't it?" Daddy grinned and shook his head.

El took the battered dictionary from the bookcase and tried to look it up, but the word wasn't listed. Exasperated, she carried the paper up to Mother. Mother moved Baby Ruth away from her breast and took the paper. "I'm not sure, Ellie, but it seems to mean that the United States wants to take over in East Asia. You're sure it's not in the dictionary?"

"I'm sure, Mother. We need a new dictionary. Couldn't we get one like they have at the high school? A bigger one?"

"I don't know, honey. They're right expensive, probably cost close to ten dollars. That would buy a lot of war stamps."

El sat on the bed, tapping Baby Ruth's tiny chin to bring a smile. The war! Everything depended on the war—everything they did and didn't do! And we aren't even in it!

"I don't see why we have to get into a fight between Japan and China!"

Mother smiled and picked up the baby." Reminds me of a story about Abe Lincoln. Want to hear it?"

El shrugged her shoulders; it was better than helping with dinner.

"Well, this tale is told for truth," Mother said. "Seems Abe Lincoln was on his way home one day and he passed a big mud hole. Now, out in the middle of that mud hole there was a pig. Abe stopped his horse and just sat there, watching. The pig was struggling and struggling, trying to get out, but he couldn't get his feet on anything solid. Now, Abe Lincoln had just bought a new suit and new suits were hard to come by. He studied the situation and decided there was no way he could help that pig without ruining his suit. So, he rode on by."

Daddy came in and sat on the other side of the bed, laughing as he recognized the story.

"What's that got to do with the war in China?" asked El

"It was a Poland China pig!' said Daddy, teasing Mother.

"Well, I'm not quite finished," she said. "Now Abe rode on for about two miles, thinking over what he had done. At first, he thought he'd just ignore it, but the sight of that poor struggling animal stayed with him until, finally, he turned around and went back. He tied his horse to a tree, found some rails from a fence, and walked out on them. He pulled that pig from the mud, but with a great deal of damage to his new suit. He saved the pig."

El thought about the story, and Mother waited for her comments. "China is the pig. Japan is the mud hole. Abe Lincoln is the United States." She reasoned.

"Right," said Mother. "Now, do you think Abe pulled the pig out because he was a kindly old man?"

"Yes, he really was," said El.

"That's not the way he told it," Mother said gently. "Abe Lincoln said later, when he told the story, that he saved the pig because he was selfish! You see, not saving the pig made an unbearable strain on him! It caused him pain. The only way he could ease his pain was to save the pig."

"Old Abe was suffering from a guilty conscience," added Daddy.

"A nation has a conscience too, El, just like a person. And right now, when we know what's going on in the world, we've got a terrible strain on it. I don't know how much longer we'll be able to keep our clothes clean, don't know how much longer we can bear the pain."

"I've got a mighty big pain in my belly right now," said Daddy, and the only thing that's goin' to cure it is a big slice of that roast beef I smell cooking!"

"I'm coming downstairs for dinner today, Bud," said Mother. "One more week, Faith, now you know what Doc said."

"But I feel so good!" said Mother.

"Yeah, and if you go down today, you will tomorrow, then the next day, and the next—no, we will bring a tray. You can take the stairs in one more week!"

El went to the big calendar on the wall. Next Sunday Mother could resume her normal activities. She found a pencil and drew a big circle around the date for next Sunday. "There, Mother, you can come down next Sunday, December the Seventh!"

"And for today, we'll bring your plate to you!" He put his arm around El's shoulders and they walked downstairs together. Jane was dishing up the roast and vegetables.

Four score and seven years ago our fathers brought forth upon this continent a new nation, conceived in liberty…

"What are you two up to?" Jane asked.

"Oh, not much," said El

"Listening to a tale about a pig in a mud hole," Said Daddy.

…and that Government of the people, by the people, and for the people, shall not perish from the earth.

The Railroad Fact Finding Board was trying to prevent the railroad strike, Daddy said, as they ate dinner. The carriers called the brotherhoods "blind and stubborn, while the railroaders said they were, "being frozen in an economic vacuum," with sub-standard wages. Mother made her contribution: yesterday, while they went to the movies, she had heard Verdi's "La Traviata." It had been carried live on WHIS for the first time, broadcast from the Metropolitan Opera House in New York. She had tuned in between the first and second acts, heard the tribute to the city of Boston.

"You mean, you listened to Opera after we left?" said Daddy, "Boy! We got out just in time!"

"That's right, and it's going to be a regular Saturday afternoon program, with a different city each time—you can hear it next week!"

Daddy's long face broke up the dinner.

After dishes, the girls joined the other young people in the triangle for a swift softball game. During one moment while exchanging bases, Edgar whispered to El, "See you tonight!" and the sunshine grew brighter for El. It was almost spring-like, birds singing, gentle breeze, didn't even need a coat!

After a cold supper of roast beef and fresh watercress—picked by Daddy on his walk by the creek, as a special treat for Mother—sandwiches, El spread the funny papers on the floor beside the radio and started on her regular winter-time chore of polishing shoes. While the shoes dried, she amused herself by drawing mustaches on Don Winslow, Dagwood, Major Hoople and others. When Mother spoke, El jumped guiltily, she knew she was wasting shoe polish.

"Would you see what Bun is doing? She's awfully quiet." El looked upstairs, then downstairs, finally finding her sitting in the floor of the kitchen pantry with a box of marshmallows between her legs and white powdered sugar from her nose to her chin. The box was nearly empty.

"Want a mush-meller, Ellie?" Bun handed the box to El.

"You're in trouble now!" El said. An idea flashed into El's mind. If she told, Bun could be sent to bed early and she could slip out to meet Edgar earlier. She hesitated, overcame the temptation as she realized Bun could as easily be spanked, instead of being sent to bed. "Come on," she said, "you can polish shoes with me."

By bedtime the temperature had dropped to forty degrees, but it was still pleasant outside for there was no wind at all. El volunteered to bring in the coal for Daddy, hoping to see Edgar, but he wasn't in sight. With Bun tucked in bed and asleep, she sat by the window and waited. Sounds came from Mother's room, the radio, turned down low, soft voices, an occasional cry from Baby Ruth as she was dressed for bed. Jane was in her own room, door shut as usual.

From up on the mountain came the mournful sound of the nine-thirty train, it's soft, round sound preceding it down the valley as it blew for the tunnel at Clark's Gap. In a few minutes it rattled across the bridge, trailing sound behind it, an uneven clack on the tracks where a single rail was loose, dropping cinders in a soft rain on the schoolyard and the road below. She counted the cars as they passed the mid-point catenary pole, easily reading the names on the side of the cars, Virginian, Norfolk & Western, New York Central, L&N, C&O, a long train, over forty box cars heading west to Logan, Huntington, and the great Ohio River, or turning north at Mullins to connect with the C&O or the NYC, and on to Charleston on the banks of the Kanawha. The train stirred a restlessness within her, a wanderlust for the world beyond the narrow valley, an impatience to grow up. Deep within her reverie, the gravel thrown on the porch roof startled her, followed by joy as she saw Edgar standing in the road below. She slipped out her window, closed it gently behind her; when her feet touched the grass, Edgar grabbed her in a quick hug.

"I've missed you!" he whispered, and taking her hand, they ran down the road, choosing the steep climb to the railroad tracks and the cherished bridge.

"One o' the men, works with Pa, said he saw a solid black deer down below Pineville, seen it real close. Said it came out of the woods right at him and then it ran off just as quick. Said it was as black as night. Me and Billy, we're going hunting tomorrow, season opens at th' break o' day."

"What about school?"

"Cuttin'."

"Your Pa know?"

"Said he did too, first day of deer season. His grades warn't near as good as mine."

As Ellie reflected again that boys have all the fun, Edgar asked, "What did you want to talk about?"

She told him about Hollie, about the notes and letters, about Emmett supposed to be in the Army, but she was positive she had seen him more than once. "And Hollie is scared. Real scared. What can we do?" she finished.

Edgar was quiet, his head down on his fist as they lay prone on the wooden overlook. El waited, trusting him to come up with an answer. She looked down at her school and thought about her teacher. Mr. Collins no longer stood so close to Mrs. Margaret, like he couldn't wait; they seemed older, more satisfied, content. That was it. Content. Like something that had caused a mighty struggle between them was settled now and the tension was gone. Yet there was no change in their arrangement. He still strolled up the road after dark, leaving his reading light on, light-stepped it back down the road to the creek, along the wall, in his back gate, stooping beneath the great willow, and in his back door; within minutes his reading light would go off, Mrs. Margaret's porch light would go off and the camp settled dark for sleep. Cliff Sanders was never mentioned and if he was missed, El never knew it; he had come and gone, leaving a hole like the one left when you took your hand out of a bucket of water.

Ending the long silence, Edgar asked, "Say your Dad checked and he's really in the Army?"

"That's what she said. I haven't asked Daddy—'fraid to. He'd fuss, say I was nosing around where I have no business."

"And you've seen him up here."

"I'm sure," she said with conviction. Edgar was quiet. In the silence she heard the wind, blowing faintly against the high wires, like a child trying to whistle.

"Been too cold fer him to stay hid in the woods Already two men froze to death this year. It was down to nineteen."

"I heard about the one those kids found. Sitting in his truck, froze stiff."

"There's another one, down at Tralee found him by the creek, drunk, they said."

"How could they tell if he was dead?"

"Smell it." Edgar explained. They thought about that, easy, quiet, like it had been only a few days since they had been together.

El studied the school, and the store. Could a man break in either, stay warm through the night? Not without buildin' a fire, Edgar said. The old storage house? Na, not without ol' Reeves knowing. And if he were AWOL Reeves would turn him in, him being in the army himself. He was in the Army? Told Pa so, when he was real young, first war. Edgar jerked upright beside her. "Got it!" he exclaimed. "Come on!"

He led her to the end of the bridge, stooping low, running lightly over the sleepers, making shadows on the shining rails. He stopped before the boarded-up mine entrance. "It'd be warm in there—never goes much below fifty, could even build a fire and nobody would see it. Wish we had a light!"

"We can't go in there!" gasped El. "It's been boarded up for years! It's restricted!"

"Huh, don't take long to pull a few boards loose. This is it, El, I know it! A man could live in there for years, hunt in the daytime—heck! I got two birds and a squirrel myself yesterday!" They tiptoed close to the weathered boards, listening, looking for a light, feeling for a loose corner. Nothing.

Edgar pulled her away. "We'd better get going. He could be watching us right now." They stole back down the road, whispering softly as they walked. Edgar decided to tell his Pa, and El agreed. Mr. Mitchell would be glad to know why Hollie had sent him away.

Edgar kissed her softly in the shadows of the porch, promising to tell her what his Pa said, first chance he got. There was a light frost on the porch roof, making it slippery as she climbed back to her window; she eased it open and crawled into the warm room. She'd never felt so cold—or been so worried. She went to sleep with Hollie's tiny gold cross in her hands.

"The High Trestle" Photographed by Alyssa B. Weisner

Twenty-One

According to Secretary Knox, there had been a fifteen percent decrease in enlistments since the *USS Kearny* and the *Reuben James* were hit; the nation took serious askance when one hundred and twelve American boys were killed. Parents became reluctant to allow those under the legal age of twenty-one to join the Navy. As a result, it was speculated that the two-ocean Navy might be operated by draftees, unless the 13,000 men needed each month began to volunteer. As it stood now, drafted men couldn't go outside of the western hemisphere, while volunteers could go anywhere; those regulations would have to change if boys were drafted into the Navy, and as Mr. Gillespie said, the standards would change too, which would be a shame. He shared Mildred's view: only the best boys were in the Navy. It was with great pride that she shared the letter received from her boys, written and signed jointly:

Dear Mama and Dad and Judith,
We want you to know we are together and that is what we want most of all, to be on the same ship. We are fine and sometimes we have chow together if Will comes to my part of the ship which he does real often. He can go anywhere. Mama, we hope you are feeling good and don't you worry. This is what we both want to do. We will be home soon when this mess is over and maybe before if we get leave. Judith it is beautiful here not like the mountains but different. I am a good swimmer and Will is learning some but he don't like it like I do. When we get a day off I am going to swim in the Pacific ocean like I did the Atlantic. Not bad for a kid raised on Gooney Otter right? Tell everybody hello for us and take care of each other.
Love from your sons,
Will and Ben
P.S. We all call our ship the WeeVEE and it is known for the good crew. We are proud to be on it.

Mother had tears in her eyes by the time Mildred finished the letter, reading it slowly, and Jane left the room to hide her tears, but El knew she was crying too. If Jane was so in love with Ted, why did a letter from Will and Ben make her cry? It didn't make sense to her, and besides, they sounded like they were having a real good time, plus seeing the world. What was there to cry about?

Japan had analyzed the situation, apparently, and had decided to continue negotiations towards a peaceful settlement, simultaneously emphasizing their wide difference in national policies. Having met again with Nomura, Sect. Hull had announced that talks would continue.

The railroad strike had been settled! More than three million dollars had been added to the operator's payroll, but other terms of the agreement were not disclosed.

The negotiations had gone on almost continuously for two nights and two days, and the strike threat had been removed. Faith heard the news over the radio and expected Bud to be in a good mood when he came in from work; she was surprised to see him clearly disturbed about something and questioned him to learn the reason. The strike news was good, he assured her, but two of his six men had given notice. They were quitting!

"Bud! Who?"

"Charlie and Dewey," he said, disheartened. "two of my best."

"But why? Not enough money?"

"No," and he shook his head sadly, "they are going to enlist in the Navy."

"But, Bud! Charlie has children!"

"I said the same thing. You know what he said? Said that was the reason! God, Faith! How am I going to keep this end of the railroad running with only four men?" He ate his supper and went to bed, didn't even listen to the news. Didn't tell Mother that the railroad wouldn't recognize her pass again until after the holidays, either. She learned that over the radio. It was because of the heavy traffic from the military and the schools, all the boys coming home for Christmas. And her trying to save gasoline, too.

December third dawned sunny and warm. The Russians were chasing the Germans toward the south, the Nazis were claiming progress toward Moscow. They were running out of Rostov and smashing through Tobruk. An Australian ship was sunk in a battle off the coast of Australia, and they sank a German vessel. Australia was having nightmares about Japan and had offered strategic bases to the United States, to which Japan responded by charging that the U.S. had instigated ill feelings for Japan among Australians.

In England, Churchill was asking that women between the ages of twenty and thirty be drafted. This news created a stir in the Phillips household as Jane declared she would volunteer if she were in England, and Daddy said, not as long as I'm alive! No daughter of mine will go in service! El took the article to school for her current events assignment, figuring it would create fireworks there also. She read aloud, quoting Churchill: "The crisis of equipment is largely over. The crisis of manpower and womanpower is at hand and will largely dominate 1942." He asked that the draft age be changed, advancing the upper limit from 41 to 50, and lowering it to 18 and one half. The discussion was heated in the classroom as the boys and girls divided.

"No American girls are going to fight in any war!" proclaimed the boys, "We'll do the fighting, let the women stay at home!"

The girls, led by El, declared, "We can fight too! Remember Mary Ingalls?"

"Well, that was here. We'll be fighting over there!"

"We can too!"

"No, you can't! How are you going to get there?"

"Same way you do! On ships!"

"Women ain't allowed on ships, it's bad luck, just like the mines!"

El came back quickly. "What about women passengers! They go on ships all the time!"

Mr. Collins held up his hand, stopping the argument with a wide grin. "Get out your geography books," he said, and El sat back, feeling like she had won. She wished she could go with the five congressmen who were going to visit Churchill as he celebrates his sixty-seventh birthday. Someday, she promised herself, some day she would see England—but she wouldn't go on some old slow-poke ship! She would fly!

By Thursday the war news from Europe was serious. Two divisions of Italian soldiers, thrown into the fight at Rostov, had surrendered to Russia but the threat to Moscow was very real. Billions of dollars were approved for defense as the United States added Turkey to the list of nations receiving aid under the Lend-Lease program. American supplies flowed through Great Britain to other countries as they tried to stop Hitler from reaching oil-rich Iran and Iraq. Turkey, FDR announced, was vital to the defense of the United States.

In Washington, the President announced at his press conference that inquiries were being made concerning the Japanese movement of troops into Indochina, and he sent word to the government in Tokyo that further talks depended upon an acceptable reply. The wide chasm between the United States and Japan remained.

Forty warships had been spotted, including an aircraft carrier, in Carnernah Bay, and five thousand natives had been drafted to build a new air base near the Gulf of Siam.

Forty-six American experts in mechanics and trucking had left for the Burma Road, assigned to keeping it open as a supply route to China. At the same time, workmen in Tokyo were using sledge hammers to knock down the ornamental iron fixtures and wrought iron fences, gathering scrap iron for the Japanese war industry

By Friday it was learned that Japan had rejected the document on American policy, saying that Hull's statement casts doubt on the sincerity of the U.S., and stressed the fact that Saburo Kurusu had been on his peace-seeking mission in Washington for seventeen long days. The diplomats were to give Franklin Roosevelt their reply to his demands for an explanation of troop movements.

In Mexico, the Japanese diplomats were making fast preparations to return to Japan, following a progress report received from Washington. They had applied for a visa for themselves and their families, planning to board a ship in Los Angeles. In the event of war, they knew Mexico would side with the United States.

The House of Representatives passed a bill to halt strikes, and it was sent speedily on to the Senate. Both the CIO and the AFL declared they would fight the bill, saying they had no intention of allowing such legislation to pass.

In Wyoming county, the Red Cross drive went well beyond expectations, with twenty-five hundred dollars earned and nearly every man, woman, and child enrolled as a member. The mines gave their support to Bluefield's yearly Community Christmas Tree program, and the slogan, "Not a Penny Profit, Not a Penny Overhead, Every Cent To Make A Child Happy," was adopted.

All over the county the harvest of mistletoe, holly, berries, ground pine and hemlock was being offered, and the Yule trees were everywhere for sale. Children collected baskets of pine cones and bundles of rhododendron branches and sold them door to door for extra gift money. El and Bun were already pestering Daddy to take them on their yearly jaunt up Gooney Otter Creek for the ceiling-high tree, promising to water it every day, when he used the excuse that it would dry out too soon. Next weekend, he promised, and that would still be two weeks before Christmas! Two weeks was long enough to rearrange and disorganize things for some old fat man in a red suit!

This brought Bun flying, fists doubled up, and ended in a tussle, which was what Daddy wanted anyway.

It had been cloudy all day, but the wind was light, stirring the trees along the ridge, moving gently through the narrow valley. El and Bun found chocolate cupcakes waiting for them when they got home from school, and brought them up to Mother's room.

"Mrs. Belcher baked those for you," said Mother. She seemed quiet, almost unhappy, not at all her usual cheerful self.

"Is our little baby Ruthie doing okay?" asked El, pulling the blanket back and peeping at the sleeping infant.

"She's fine," Mother replied absent-mindedly.

"You feeling okay?" she asked, probing for some reason behind the sadness.

"Yes, as a matter-of-fact, I am!" Mother said emphatically. "Too good to be cooped up here because of some old-fashioned rule!"

"You haven't been downstairs, have you?" asked El, knowing that Daddy and Doc Steelman would be upset if she had.

"No, not yet," said Mother. Bun had chocolate cupcake from one ear to the other and El went to the bathroom for a washcloth.

"El, do you think you could look after your two little sisters for a few minutes if I went out?"

El looked at her mother, apprehensively. "Are you supposed to go out?"

"I can't see why it would hurt me. After all, I can officially go out in another forty-eight hours. I really feel closed in."

El knew that feeling—she'd had it herself many times, like when she had pneumonia and had been in bed for two weeks, and sometimes, in school, near the end of the day— and that was just one day. Mother had been upstairs in her room for nearly twenty days—still, she knew Daddy would fuss—if he found out.

"Where are you going?" asked El.

"Down to the Wooten's," said Mother. "I've had Mary Beth on my mind all day. I'm afraid there's something wrong."

"Wouldn't they come for you if they needed you?" asked El. She thought about how Doc Steelman had always depended on Mother to keep check on the expectant mothers in Coville. She remembered, too, how he had told Mother, "you can't come down unless the house caught on fire!" Mr. Reeves had been tending the furnace until El got out of school; first one then another neighbor had cooked meals, or made stew, or a pot of beans, even though Jane could have managed without them. Now, El volunteered, "I could run down there, see if they need anything."

Mother thought about it, sighed deeply, and said, "That wouldn't get me out of the house, but it would relieve my mind."

El grabbed her coat, glad she didn't need boots; it had been so dry the black dirt road was packed and mud-free. She knocked on the Wooten's door, explained her mission, and stood by Mary Beth's bed. The large girl lay back against three pillows and still looked uncomfortably flat. Her eyes were puffy, her face and hands swollen. *Movie and True Confessions* magazines were scattered about the bed. A slice of gingerbread lay on a plate, half-eaten and dried out around the edges.

"Tell your Ma I'm fine," she said, "just can't roll over, can't hardly get up and down. The pains stopped when th' Doc put me to bed, but he says it could be any day now. Tell her I hope she can be here when I start gettin' serious. I'll be scared without her here."

"Mother said, ask you if they are both kicking good."

Mary Beth placed one hand up high under her breast. "I'm so sore, right in my ribs, I know it's a boy and he's playing football in there, and down low, I get such sharp jabs sometimes can't hardly stand it. That 'un can't wait to get out!"

El kept her visit short, having trouble finding things to talk about now that Mary Beth didn't go to school or to Church. They had covered the twins, told her about Baby Ruth, even Santa Claus had been discussed. There were several letters lying on the coverlet and El had looked at them repeatedly, wanting to ask about Ben and Will. Finally, Mary Beth volunteered information about the Gillespie boys. They were on the same ship, the *West Virginia*, and they were still at sea. She called the We-Vee, the State Ship, making it sound like the battleship belonged to West Virginia, and El didn't try to correct her.

El left, glad to be out of the cramped-up house and into the fresh air. In spite of the early hour there were pockets of dusk as the clouds moved over the tops of the mountains; the wind had picked up and came grieving through the trees, making it gloomy and lonesome-feeling. Her mind was on Mary Beth as she walked slowly up the road. Mary Beth was being punished for sinning, that was clear; God knew she had sinned twice, that was the reason for the twins. At first, when she heard about the twins, she thought it would be fun, like having two dolls to play with, but now, after seeing the grotesquely over-sized girl, it didn't look like pleasure; she felt sorry for her and strengthened her resolve: no boy would ever lay a hand on her! Not ever!

Edgar stepped out of the shadows and fell in beside her. "Well, I told Pa," he said.

"What did he say?" she asked.

"Said he'd check around, find out if Emmett had been seen in town. But I doubt if he'll do it, leastways, not any time soon."

"Why not?"

"Well, for one thing, he's working 'til long after dark now, with the mines going like they are. He has to go ahead of the crew, pin up the top. Makes him work 12-15 hours every day."

They stopped in front of Hollie's house and looked about carefully; Hollie was still at work. The house was dark and cold-looking; brown dried weeds lined the fence and the yard was bare dirt. No chairs were on the porch. It was the most deserted looking house in town. A deep feeling of uneasiness remained, and she could almost see through the dingy clapboards into the front room, almost see the stack of letters and notes, each one more threatening than the last. She didn't blame Hollie for feeling scared; she was frightened too. They moved on, turning at their own gates without further words. As an afterthought, Edgar shouted, "Hey! Sunday night?"

El raised her hand and waved, immediately cheered up. "Sure!"

By the time El got home, Jane was upstairs with Mother, talking about her school activities. Mother was brighter, and after El gave her report she was more cheerful. By the time Daddy came home she was her old self, giving the girls instructions regarding supper, listening to Bun read—Run Spot, run, see Spot run—and listening to Daddy discuss the news.

Japan had reported to the President as requested. The troop build-up in Indochina was in response to a heavy build-up by the Chinese across the border. Those in the know suspect that Japan planned an invasion into Thailand, and they stressed that the United States, as well as Great Britain and the Dutch East Indies, were ready to fight should this happen. One of the most encouraging bits of news that floated down to the local citizenry was the suggestion that a Japanese-American Commission be appointed to investigate the situation, acknowledging that both Japan and Washington would remain sincerely interested in finding a peaceful solution. The commission would search for some common ground on which to negotiate; such a commission, made up of respected and trust-worthy representatives would explore the economic, diplomatic, and political aspects of the disagreement while avoiding military measures.

While the Pacific unrest seemed improved, the battle in Europe worsened. Great Britain was about to proclaim a state of war against three countries— Finland, Hungary, and Rumania. Their goal was to place the three countries firmly on the Axis side of the table after the war ended. Britain had insisted they stop fighting Russia. So far there was no response from the demand.

And in the U.S. Congress, the House had approved further defense appropriations by a vote of 309 to 5.

Saturday, Mother decided her days of confinement were over; after all, she had started labor on Sunday, thus it had been three whole weeks. The girls cleaned house, anxious to make her first visit downstairs a pleasant one, waxing and shining and polishing until everything was in order. Daddy carried the Philco back to the dining room to its regular place; Baby Ruth's small crib— day crib—was placed in the corner beside Bun's card-table tent. Jane fried chicken, and El peeled potatoes for dinner. By the time the meal was ended and dishes washed, they felt back to normal. Clothes were ready for Church; Sunday School lessons were studied. Now that Mother could go, Baby Ruth would attend also, and she had a new bonnet and long dress to wear. Daddy, as usual, declined the invitation to join them, preferring his own routine.

On Saturday night they were allowed to stay up later, and listened to the Grand ole Opry on the radio, a happy family, almost a party-like atmosphere, so glad were they all to have Mother downstairs and back in charge again.

Although it was cold Sunday morning, the sun was shining and it was cloudless; the brief threat of rain the night before hadn't materialized and the wind played with the dry dead leaves along the fence, swayed the bare yellow willow branches, and swept the cinders from the bridge. It was a happy morning. Mother in her black hat with the real pheasant feathers, was in the driver's seat; Jane sat beside her and held Baby Ruth, wrapped in her brand new snow white blanket, sat beside her. El and Bun sat stiffly in the back seat, legs straight out, keeping the shoe polish off the gray upholstered seat. Mother backed the car down the road and blew the horn for Hollie. Hollie appeared promptly, dressed in the long violet coat given her by Mrs. Gillespie last spring, the one she had worn to Shirley's funeral. El tried to forget the last time she had seen the coat, but it did bring back memories of that awful time.

Hollie was hatless, and her hair had been brushed until it shined, flying about her face, static electricity making it crackle against the wool coat. El wanted to touch it, to see if it would shock her as Hollie got in the car beside her, but she was afraid Hollie would be shocked too. She contented herself with looking and telling Hollie how pretty she was. The short drive to the little white church had a holiday atmosphere like it was already Christmas.

Once they were in the church, Jane took her place at the piano, and the service began with carols, appropriate for the first Sunday of Advent. Preacher Copeland welcomed Mother back, asked her to stand and hold Baby Ruth up for the congregation to see their newest member, adding, we'll have a real baby to play Baby Jesus in our play this year. El decided immediately that if baby Ruth was to be the infant in the cradle, she would play the part of Mary. After all, it would be best to have someone the baby knew close by.

Preacher Copeland was making another announcement. "Now, I'm sure you all will be glad to know, our own Chaplain Ted McKinney will hold our evening service; Ted will be here in time for Epworth League, and there's one young lady in our congregation who's looking forward to it, I'm sure. Jane, I'm surprised you can play this morning! Now, we're teasing, Jane. You always do a fine job for us. Now, if you'll all turn to page 85 in your hymnal, we'll sing this song for Ted, and for all our young men who are gone from us, from out of our midst, gone to serve their country and their God, so that we here at home may remain a Christian nation, a nation who worships the Lord as the one true God. Now, rise and sing, all together now, *Onward Christian Soldiers, marching as to war, with the Cross of Jesus Going on before…*"

Preacher Copeland led the singing, and Jane played, smiling and lovely, and no one, looking at her would have thought it took her three hours to get ready for church: she looked as usual, neat dark hair shining, clear gray eyes wide open, skin without a blemish, and her remarkable smile.

The prayer followed and preacher Copeland asked for peace, and for each Herndon and Coville boy, calling them by name, as if calling their names out loud would keep them safe. The sermon was long and involved, and El wished the baby would cry, thinking that might end it. How lucky Daddy was, sitting at home, enjoying a beautiful morning, his coffee and his paper, peace and quiet. It might have been late summer or early fall instead of the seventh of December.

Dinner was delayed by the long service, and later still because baby Ruth had to be fed immediately on arriving home. "She was so good," cooed Mother, "best little lady in the world, my little Shirley Ruth."

"Jane, peel potatoes, Bud, get that ham out and slice a little, El, set the table," Mother directed from her chair.

"What can I do, Mother?" asked Bun, wanting to help.

"Honey, you can go upstairs and get my slippers—these shoes are killing me!"

Having the family back to normal was such a treat that El thought it called for special effort. She selected a white linen tablecloth, used the best china and silver, like it was Thanksgiving or Christmas. Mother watched her preparations with an approving smile, called her close and whispered, "Look in the nook behind the back porch." El did as instructed and came back in with shiny green holly, with bright red berries, an early festive touch for the lovely dinner table.

When they gathered around the table, Mother's blessing was only slightly shorter than Preacher Copeland's prayer, for Mother had much to be thankful for. The dinner was in danger of getting cold when Daddy cleared his throat and Mother hastily said, amen.

Dinner was a leisurely affair, with banana pudding for dessert, one of a few deserts Jane could make without Mother's assistance. When the dishes had been washed and everything back in order, the Sunday paper was divided and passed around. El quickly grabbed the comics, Daddy took the sports section and Jane took the advertising. Mother took the front page and immediately began reading aloud:

NEW NAZI DRIVE PUTS MOSCOW IN DIRE PERIL

Welders strike, Nationwide is ordered for Tuesday, Begins in Morgantown, W.Va.—Workers at Odds with AFL…

"Read the other column," said Daddy. El remembered, Daddy had already read the paper, while they were in church. Mother began reading: "President Roosevelt Sends Personal Note to Emperor; Jap Troops on Move. Note content Not Revealed Believed To Be Last Resort Avert Open Break."

"Roosevelt wouldn't contact the Emperor unless he thought there was a serious threat," said Daddy. "On down in there it says that the Japs have over a hundred and twenty-five thousand troops in Indochina."

"You remember, Bud," said Mother, "Roosevelt sent a direct message to the Japanese Emperor back in '37 when that gunboat was sunk."

"Yeh, and don't forget, he sent a letter to Hitler, too, just before the war broke out."

"That didn't change things one bit," said Mother. "Do you think the joint commission will help?"

"I doubt it," said Daddy, "we can always hope, but I seriously doubt it."

"Well, they can't keep on blaming each other forever!" said Jane." Something's got to give!"

The arbitration board was nearing a decision on the Union shop situation in the captive mines, and the new Norfolk and Western passenger station was ready for use, but, said Daddy, "it ain't any nicer than the one we have at Herndon, just bigger."

In Pineville, the Red Cross announced that there were one thousand, five hundred and ninety members of the Jr. Red Cross in Wyoming County schools, and one hundred and thirty-seven of them had completed their First Aid course in Mullins alone. Best news of all, Mullins was pronounced the State Football Champs!

Bun hadn't eaten well; when urged to finish her dinner, she had complained of a sore throat. Daddy tucked her in bed for a nap and came back to the table to finish his coffee. The radio was playing; Jane and El had finished the dishes. "Kaye's Melody" had just ended the Sammy Kaye Swing and Sway program; Ozzie Resch's last trombone wa-wah-wa-wah-wa-wah was fading away. El had just started to ask permission to go outside when the announcer interrupted:

WE INTERRUPT THIS PROGRAM TO BRING YOU A NEWS
BULLETIN...

He began to talk wildly, excitedly, in illogical sentences : hundreds of Japanese planes bombed Pearl Harbor, thousands killed, ships sunk, caught by surprise, heavy losses among Naval personnel, we are at war—war—war— war, the word echoed through the house, finding the empty corners of the rooms, lingering, driving out the happy sounds, the return-to-normal celebration, destroying the family dinner feeling of all's well with our world, unable to breathe, still, don't know who to look at, shocked faces, held in a moment of time that would never be forgotten within their lifetime. War.

El looked from her father to her mother and back again, seeking some valid reaction upon which to base her own response, but there was none. They sat in shocked silence as the few known details washed over them, given by a nearly hysterical reporter. Convoys had been sighted steaming towards the Gulf of Siam yesterday. Perhaps as many as eight or ten ships sunk. Surprise attack just after dawn, hundreds of planes coming in waves from an unexpected direction, no preparation for the attack. Many naval and civilian lives lost. Damage to Hawaii extensive. Most aircraft on Oahu either destroyed or damaged. It was a bright Sunday morning and most were blissfully asleep prior to the attack. They came in waves, dive-bombers, high-flying bombers, torpedo-planes, fighters, AIR RAID, PEARL HARBOR—THIS IS NO DRILL, THIS IS NO DRILL.

Mother and Daddy were stunned; now that it had come, they did not cry. Jane and El eased into chairs at the table; all four sat by the radio and listened. And listened. Finally, the announcer said, "Details are at a minimum, but we will continue to interrupt this broadcast as necessary..."

El put on her coat and walked outside; behind her the radio blared again with music. No one was in sight. She stood on the front porch, feeling the loneliness, thinking, I will never forget this. Old Marsha and Callie sat on the back steps catching the last rays of the afternoon sun, handily near whenever the back door opened to admit them. She went to the steps, sat between them, pulling them close against her.

"Well, Marsha, Callie," she said, "it's come. War."

Nothing was changed, but everything was different. The dark trees lined the ridge, outlined against the sky; the high black bridge loomed above her; starlings, black, ugly birds, lined the electric wires into the house, frightening away the smaller slate-colored juncos and the brown-speckled sparrows. She jumped up and ran at the big black birds, flapping her arms and screaming, "Go away! Go away! LEAVE US ALONE! LEAVE US ALONE!"

Twenty-Two

Old Marsha and Callie followed El into the back porch; she filled their bowls with scraps left from dinner. Daddy and Jane were sitting at the table, as she had left them. Mother, with Bun's assistance was changing Baby Ruth's diaper. Daddy crossed one knee over the other, tamped his pipe with his thumb, struck a match on the sole of his shoe and lit it, let it go out, and lit it again. All the while he listened. Jane wandered up and down the stairs, into the living room, fingered her music, but didn't play, and listened. Mother fed Baby Ruth, held her while she slept as if afraid to put her down, and listened. El and Bun sat on the floor and cut up the comics, making families out of the characters, and whispered, and listened. The atmosphere was funereal, and they were glad when it was time to prepare cold ham and potato salad for supper. Mother allowed them to have hot tea with milk in it, English style, as a special treat, making it herself in near-silence as they listened.

It was repetition. After the first few minutes, it was the same alarming news over and over. Nobody knew exactly how many battleships were sunk, or which ones. Nobody knew how many planes were destroyed or disabled; nobody knew how many men were killed or injured. Bits of news filtered through with the repetition of that first alarming cry. President Roosevelt had sent a letter to the Emperor, but it wasn't known whether or not he had received it prior to the attack. To fill the time, the announcer gave the history of the Emperor; the people considered him divine, a direct descendent of the Sun Goddess in a line unbroken since the beginning of time. The Emperor generally left the management of the country up to the ministers, the Army and the Navy, remaining aloof from material affairs.

The Japanese Embassy attaches had been recalled earlier; reasons were unknown at the time, to which Daddy said, "Aw, hell! Anybody can figure that out now!"

The Russian Ambassador was coming to the United States, bringing information on the Russian resistance to the German army which would have an important influence on the Japanese situation.

Finland sent word to the British that they intended to fight a "defensive" war only, but Canada declared war on Finland—and Rumania and Hungary—anyway.

The actual time of the attack was reported as seven-thirty-five, a.m. Hawaii time, which was five minutes after one p.m. eastern standard time. It was nearly two hours before the announcement was made to the American people.

All military personnel were recalled to their units immediately. Ted was to have been at the house by five. Now they knew. He wasn't coming. Jane remained dressed, waiting, checking her make-up in the hall mirror, combing her shining black hair, hope fading slowly, but they knew. Ted was an honorable boy. Wherever he had been when the announcement came, he would have reported to his ship as soon as possible.

After supper the house began to fill, neighbors arriving singly or in couples: Mr. and Mrs. Belcher, holding hands as they crossed the road; Mr. Collins, alone as usual on Sunday evenings until time to go to Mrs. Margaret's; Mr. Gillespie—Mildred had taken to her bed after the first report—Mr. Reeves, hat in his hands, wearing a clean white shirt under his dark suit coat, dressed for a wedding—or a funeral—looking odd out of his old Army coat; Grandma Gillespie, puffing a little as Mother offered her the rocking chair, refusing to take a chair in the kitchen; and Thelma and Jim Plover, Thelma setting a fresh-baked cake on the counter while her husband joined the men in the dining room. The men gathered around the Philco, holding a wake for the nation.

"They've called off evening worship," Thelma said, cutting the cake. " Preacher Copeland is in bed. Had a fainting spell when the news came. Ted didn't show up anyway." Jane stood up and quietly went upstairs and shut her door, closing out the questions and speculations about her Ted.

The women congregated in the kitchen; the men sat around the dining room table talking, their images reflected in the window. The window made a mirror against the dark outside, and the reflection reflected the window again, a box within a box and another one, smaller, and on and on, and the six men making twelve, then twenty four, and on and on, and El could see hundreds, thousands, millions of men in that one window, seeing past generations gathered around tables in large houses and small, around iron kettles in log cabins, around council fires in tents made of skins, around circles of rocks in rock-formed caves and the talk, no matter the circle, the talk was the same: war.

Their talk was of the battle across the sea, and the sound of their voices rose and fell, swelling, cresting, retreating, a tide of sound, rising in anger, slacking with sadness, rising and falling, rising, falling.

Mr. Gillespie looked at the economics behind the attack. "The country is industrial-minded but they don't have the raw materials to keep 'er going, and besides that, they need a bigger market. Now, you take Asia, they got the materials and China, now she's the best market any nation could hope for, no end to the goods that country needs. Now, if Japan can take control there, well—"

"Bastards. Caught us with our drawers down. Wouldn't be so bad if they hadn't been pussy-footin' around Washington making peace noises", said Daddy. "Treacherous. Bastards. No telling what they'll do next." Bitterness came through his words. Mr. Plover recounted the history of Japan, seeming extraordinarily well-read for an automobile mechanic until it was recalled that his wife was a school teacher. In a quiet voice, coming from deep in his chest, he growled. "Fought China, 1890's, Russia, 1904 and 05, Germany 1914, then China again, Indochina— sure did fool me."

Mr. Belcher meekly joined the conversation. "Where did you think they'd hit, Jim?"

"Thought it'd be south, all right, looked for them to hit the Malaya's, maybe even the Philippines." Sad shake of his head. "Never thought they'd make it all the way to the Hawaiian Islands."

"Well, when Japan joined up with Hitler, we knew we'd be in for it. Knowed it for over a year now. September, wasn't it, if I recollect?" said Mr. Reeves.

"Last September, 1940," agreed Mr. Collins.

"Played for a sucker," said Daddy, shaking his head. "Anybody would'a known better."

"Well, don't take it personal, Bud," said Jim Plover.

"How else we goin'a take it? We should have known!"

"Think Roosevelt knew it was coming?"

"Sure, he knew something was going to happen, sooner or later, but he's done all any man could do to get us ready, short of declaring war!"

"Might be he knew they were going to hit Hawaii," said Mr. Gillespie.

413

"Don't you even hint it!" said Daddy emphatically. "Roosevelt's too good a man—too good a Navy man—to let our fleet get caught in a rat trap if he could have prevented it! Hell, man, you think he'd give the country away? He's been trying to save the whole damn world—a million here, a million there—ships, tanks, guns, food—hell! The British would've been sunk long ago if it hadn't been for Roosevelt figurin' out how to help 'em, coming up with the Lend-lease!"

"He didn't figure it," said Mr. Collins quietly.

"Who the hell did!" exploded Daddy.

"Churchill," said Mr. Collins.

But Daddy didn't agree. "Naw, it was Roosevelt. He got out there on the ocean in his little boat and he got a different perspective. He saw how all the countries were joined by the seas, all on one round ball, and he saw it as one world. Now, some people don't get that view. You take Lindbergh, for example. He got out there, away from shore, out of the United States, and all he saw was the distance between countries, how the ocean separated us one from the other, thought it made us independent of each other, thought it made us safe."

"I'm not sure I follow you," said Mr. Belcher.

"Well. Look at it this way. One man climbs up Herndon Mountain and all he can see is forest, far as the eye can tell. If he climbs up a tree, or a pole, he can see Wyoming County on one side of the mountain, and Mercer County on the other side, two different counties separated by one hell of a pile of rock. But another man, he climbs the same tree and what he sees is two counties in the state of West Virginia. Both men looking at the same waves of forest, but it's all in how you look at it. "The men nodded in agreement, and Daddy added, "Anyway, the Japs looked at that ocean just like Roosevelt did, and what they saw was a way to move from their country to ours. They never once thought about it separating them. They didn't need Roosevelt's help—they had the Almighty!"

"Bud! How can you say such a thing!" Mother was coming through the door with slices of Thelma's cake and heard the remark.

Daddy laughed a bit sheepishly and added lamely, "Well, there's one thing for sure and certain—He didn't help us none!"

El had a sudden flash of thought: Daddy was deliberately taunting Mother about her religion!

The men joined Daddy, half-fearful of Faith's disapproval and only Mr. Reeves refused to laugh with them. He accepted his plate of cake with his odd little duck of his head and retreated to a seat in the corner, out of the circle of men. El wondered again about his dark dress suit, was he going on a trip? But the little man hadn't said a word about it.

"What got us into trouble was Tojo, when he went in as Prime Minister", said Mr. Plover. "He's the mechanic behind the wrench on this job!"

The men fell silent as the radio brought the news once again; they listened and concentrated on the cake and coffee.

"Well, might be down, but we ain't licked!" said Mr. Reeves, taking his plate and cup back to the kitchen. He thanked the women and left to make his rounds, a small, quiet figure, more used to being alone than in a gathering.

Daddy, watching him go, said, "He's already lost more than any of us."

"God forbid I should lose my sons," said Mr. Gillespie, and Mr. Plover put a hand on his shoulder, thinking of his own half-grown boy.

"Somebody's head will roll over this," said Mr. Collins, "wait and see."

"There's got to be an investigation," Daddy said, and the men agreed with him.

Before eight o'clock they were gone, leaving with silent hugs and wet faces, but feeling better for having been together. Mother, exhausted by her first full day downstairs without rest in the afternoon, took Baby Ruth upstairs and dressed her for bed, going to bed herself as soon as the baby was settled. El and Bun took their baths without being told; Bun felt feverish but when El told her, Mother didn't seem to hear, saying, sweet girls, go on to bed, and patting them before she turned her back to the light.

The nine-thirty freight went by, traveling fast over the bridge and El heard Daddy open the front door, walk out on the front porch to watch it pass. He'd left the radio on, saying, he wanted to hear any new developments and WHIS was going to broadcast all night for the first time in the history of the station. Said he couldn't help the boys in the Pacific. His job was to keep the trains running, only way he could help, and Mother had said that's a right big job, just doing that, and Monday morning would come too soon for all of them, but Daddy still didn't come up to bed right away. The whistle of the train echoed way down the valley before Daddy came back inside, and he hadn't hardly shut the door before the gravel hit the porch roof. Edgar had been anxiously waiting.

El slipped out her window and Edgar was so excited he was whispering, "Hurry, hurry up!" before she dropped to the ground beside him.

"I saw Emmett!" he said, pulling her around to the side of the house. "He went down the road to Hollie's house about dark!"

"You're sure?"

"Sure, I'm sure! It's him all right—and he's got on an Army uniform!"

"Come on—we can see from the coal house!" cried El, running toward the creek, staying below the concrete wall from habit.

They passed Mr. Collins house; his reading light was on, but his chair was empty. They knew where he had gone. Grandma Gillespie's house was dark and quiet. Hollie's kitchen light was on, but the shades were drawn; only a faint rim of light showed around them and there were no moving shadows. If Emmett was with Hollie, they were in the front room. They waited, becoming restless as the night-chill penetrated their coats. When Edgar suggested they go on the bridge to spy, El was quick to agree. They ran down the wall, following the creek bed until they passed the Wooten's.

"Mary Beth is still up," whispered El.

"Nah, she leaves that light on half the night," said Edgar, "but she won't see us—she don't git outa bed."

Once on the high bridge they flattened themselves against the sleepers; only their heads showed as they peered over the edge on the town side of the tracks. They lay silently beside each other, contemplating the town below. After a while, El said, "What do you think about today?"

"About the war?"

"Yes."

"I think those Japs will be sorry they ever tangled with the United States!"

"You really think so?"

"Sure, Ain't nobody beat us yet! It's like my Pa says, El. The USA ain't never tried to take the other guy's marbles, and that's why we ain't never been beat. That's why we're different!"

El reflected on what he'd said, shivering now that they were still again. Or was she shivering from the quiet thrill his words had given her, the first positive outlook after hours of solemnity from the adults? It was a relief to hear someone speak optimistically. Half the young men she knew were already in service; the back rows of the church were near empty. With Ted, Will, Ben, and Zane Gray fighting for their country, how could they fail?

"Ain't seen ole Reeves tonight," whispered Edgar. "he ain't made his rounds yet."

"He was at the house, earlier. Probably listening to the radio." El didn't give the old man much thought; her mind was once again on Hollie and Emmett. What if Emmett carried out his threat? She spoke her fears aloud. "If Hollie had trouble, we couldn't help her from here."

"You kiddin'? If she screamed once, we'd hear it, still as it is tonight. Sound would come right up here."

"She might not scream," said El, but Edgar had grabbed her arm. "Shush! Someone 's opened the door—it's Hollie!"

"She's running, Edgar! We've got to help her!"

"Wait! Don't let them see you!" Edgar grabbed her, pulled her back from the edge of the bridge out of sight. They could see Hollie, bright in the yellow dress Mother had made for Mary Beth's wedding, and close behind her was Emmett, wearing the Army uniform. Hollie was running towards the triangle, headed for Ellie's house and help. She reached the corner of the fence and Emmett caught her; they struggled, turning and twisting like dry leaves caught in a dust-devil in the middle of the road. Hollie broke free, but Emmett was blocking the way. She ran towards the lower end of the camp, turned up the road to the railroad tracks and Emmett was right behind her.

Edgar sprang to his feet, pulling El behind him, stumbling, gaining the entrance to the old mine shaft, pushing El into the shadows against the rough weathered boards. "Stay here!" he commanded," they can't see you. I'm going after Pa—Emmett's got a gun!"

El closed her eyes and drew into the corner against the rock-clay bank and the rough boards. She could hear water dripping inside the mine shaft, could smell the dankness, feel the cold air being drawn through the cracks between the boards; she could picture Hollie as she had seen her running up the road in her yellow dress, breaking free, running, the yellow dress pressed against her thighs, starlight sliding along her arms and legs, flowing over her long gold hair, white-faced, doe-eyed and frightened. She opened her eyes and gasped, alarmed by the sounds of a struggle close at hand. They had reached the railroad tracks, and Emmett was blocking the way. There was nowhere for Hollie to run except out on the bridge, and as she ran toward it, Emmett caught her, they struggled, and she fell. Emmett leaned above her.

Out of the dark came Mr. Reeves, swinging his old shotgun by the barrel, catching Emmett by surprise. Hollie broke free, sprang up and ran again for the bridge before Mr. Reeves brought his gun down, catching Emmett on the side of his head. When Emmett sank to the gravel, Mr. Reeves dropped the gun and ran for Hollie, his short legs pumping, his feet thumping loud on the creosoted crossties, shouting, "Wait! Wait! Wait!" His long wail of warning echoed along the cliff, wandered down the gorge with the night wind, but Hollie couldn't hear him, hearing only her own heart beating, her own wild sobbing, as she ran blindly, slipping, tripping over the sleepers, plunging onward, not daring to turn around, not knowing it was Mr. Reeves behind her, running and crying and around the curve of the mountain another sound, a special or a pusher—which track was it on!

Mr. Reeves heard it: squirrel-like, he flattened against the track, his ear to the rail. It was on the eastbound track! Hollie! Hollie! Lie down! Lie down Lie down, Hollie! Lie down! But she never looked back, never knew it was Mr. Reeves, not Emmett, Hollie, nearly to the wooden platform, reaching, stumbling, reaching, reaching...

El, on her knees beside the track, cut by the rock ballast, unfeeling, screaming, "Hollie! Hollie! Hollie!" Blinded by the great white light, the engine raced by followed by a whirlwind of sound.

The engine was gone. A pusher. Only a pusher. No cars. No cars at all. A single engine, unscheduled, returning to the roundhouse after pushing an above average load over the mountain, a pusher, only a pusher. She whispered, "Hollie, oh, Hollie, Hollie, Hollie."

If there had been a sound, any sound at all, when she fell it was lost in the wild roaring whine of the single squarehead engine. She had fallen, pitched forward, head first, gently, the yellow dress flowing along her slender hips, her arms outstretched, falling, and if she screamed it was lost in the groaning of the engine, the hurting of the wires, the crying of the wind. Just as there had been no sound from the rocks pitched to the road eons ago, there was no sound when she hit.

Mr. Reeves lay face down between the rails halfway to the platform. Idly, mindlessly, El wondered: did he lay on his hands, or were his fingers gone, dripping blood down between the sleepers, dripping into the bare red-maple trees below the bridge.

She stirred. Faintly, the sound of the pusher floated back; the electric wires hummed as the current returned to Clark's Gap substation—the voice of Granny Hall. Emmett lay on the westbound track, where Mr. Reeves had dropped him. He hadn't moved. Dead? She didn't know. She recalled his wild, glaring eyes: let the wild dog die!

Edgar. Edgar, where are you? She began to move, then faster, faster, help, help, help Mother, mother, help me helpmehelpme home. Home, home home, running, breath coming in gasps, sobbing, shaking, home, home, shaking, beside the schoolyard fence a patch of yellow, part of the moon pulled from the sky, running, running, a petal pulled from a yellow rose, a dandelion pulled from its stem, running, over the fence in one leap like long ago, breath short, pain, collapsing against the porch, Edgar, edgar edgar, shaking, hurting, red hot pain, clinging to the porch rail, unable to climb to the porch roof, strong arms picking her up, rough miner's coat, boosting her to the rail, cigarette smoke, clear blue eyes.

"Hollie," she gasped, "Hollie—on the bridge—Hollie—" bursts of searing pain—.

"Here, now, you git in that window before you're in serious trouble. I'll see about Hollie."

Shoes held in the dirty palms of his hands, a push, and she gained the porch roof, crept through her window. Her chest hurt, her side ached from the run down the mountain in the cold air. What should she do? Hollie was gone. Emmett could be dead as well. As for Mr. Reeves, she didn't know. She huddled beside her window, kneeling on the floor, shivering and sick, watching for Mr. Mitchell or Edgar, or perhaps Mr. Reeves. She should tell Daddy. She couldn't tell him. She should go up the road, find Hollie. She couldn't go up the road.

She tried to close her eyes, but the yellow dress, floating like a leaf on the wind, a yellow leaf, no,no,no, she squeezed her eyes together, shutting out the image of the high black bridge, the yellow dress glowing in the train's strong light, the white arms reaching, oh, God, no. Oh, God, why? Hollie, Hollie...

The house was cold. The floor was cold. Still she knelt there, bonded to the window. She heard footsteps on the road, muffled, tired, dragging steps, coming through her yard, up the front steps, loud on the porch, louder knock on the door. Now she didn't have to decide. She didn't have to do anything.

Daddy was answering the door, calling, Faith, can you come down? Mother, heavy on the stairs, listening, listening, crying out, Oh, God, No! Breaking the words into little pieces that fell into the cold silence of the house Oh, Bud, No, Oh, God, no. Then, clear and controlled as a crystal bell, "Come on in, Mr. Reeves. Bud will get dressed."

It was out of her hands. There was nothing she could do. Hollie was dead. She had failed her. Shivering, hurting, she crawled into bed fully dressed, too cold to think. She lay flat on her back, trying to stop the shaking, her eyes wide open, staring at the ceiling, seeing Hollie, bright, beautiful, golden Hollie. She heard Mr. Reeves leave, going out the door in spite of Mother's pleading, wait, wait, Bud will go with you, don't go alone. Mother in the kitchen, putting the coffee on, Hollie, running, running, a yellow leaf drifting down to the black dirt road, Oh God, make it go away, She jerked upright in bed, Mother, mother could help, blindly she ran down the stairs to the kitchen—and stopped short. Mother was kneeling in front of the oven door. Ill? No, praying. In the middle of the kitchen floor. She hesitated, uncertain. Lost. Mother wasn't there for her, Mother had gone to God. El shivered, waited, finally slipped to the floor, against the wall. She hadn't thought to pray.

Daddy came in the back door. Mother rose to meet him but he went straight to the sink and threw up. Mother wet a towel in cold water and wiped his face, led him to a chair at the dining room table, set a cup of strong coffee before him.

"Should I put in a call to Doc Steelman?" Mother asked.

"No hurry. Nothing to be done." He held on to her hand. "I'll need help."

"I'll help you."

"No."

"Bud, I'm use to things."

"You ain't used to this." He caught sight of El. "What are you doing out of bed?"

"She never sleeps," said Mother. He tried again to drink the coffee, but spilled it, shaking so hard. He was crying.

"I'll go with you," Mother said again.

"No."

"I've done things—"

"Give me a minute, let me think." Mother held his head against her breast, her arms supporting him.

"El, get your coat. Go over to Tom's. Tell him I need him."

El got her coat, went out the door and to Mr. Collins' fence, his light was still on—he wasn't home, she knew, and if she knocked it would wake Sarah Jo.

The Mitchell house was dark. Daddy had to have help. Mr. Gillespie—he was big and strong. She went to the other side of her house and climbed over the fence, knocked at the Gillespie door, banging as hard as she could. "Daddy sent me," she said, when Mr. Gillespie opened the door. "He needs help."

"Rachel! What's the trouble?" But El was already gone, over the fence and on her front porch. "Well, if he needs me—let me get dressed."

Daddy had the hall door off its hinges by the time Mr. Gillespie got there. Mother hung up the phone, saying Doc Steelman wasn't in but Mrs. Steelman would tell him when he got home. She would call the mortuary and send them on up. Baby Ruth was crying; Mother went upstairs, came down with the baby and a folded quilt, one of her best, a blue and white Star of Bethlehem pattern.

"You sure you want to use that?"

"I'm sure, Bud. She's one of my own." Daddy tucked the quilt under his arm, picked up the door and by the time he reached the gate, Mr. Gillespie was there. They went up the road together.

Mother absent-mindedly handed the baby to El. She sat in the kitchen, the baby in her lap, hollow-eyed and silent. Jane was up now, sitting in the dining room, crying like she'd never stop. Mother sat beside her, held her tight, patted, tears making her glasses slide down, she'd push them up, they'd slide down, pushed up, down, up... Mrs. Gillespie came, sat on the other side of Jane, locking her fingers together in her lap to hold them still. Mr. Collins came, said he saw the lights, left to go help Daddy and Mr. Gillespie. Mother took the baby, said go to bed, El, but El didn't move and Mother didn't tell her again. The coffee boiled over, El got up, moved it off the stove and turned the burner off. Shivering, she realized the house was cold, went out to the back porch and stoked up the fire.

The men were back. They left their burden on the front porch, wrapped in the blue and white Star of Bethlehem quilt; Mr. Collins and Mr. Gillespie stood beside it but Daddy came in the house, straight to the sink and was sick. He was so white Mother thought he was going to faint; she handed Baby Ruth to El and supported him while he retched, wiping his face with the cold cloth, holding him until he could sit down.

"Emmett, too. "he gasped, retching again. "don't understand it. When I went up there the first time there was only Hollie, but when we went back— Oh, God, Faith, he wasn't three feet away! Like they'd jumped together!"

"Oh, no! Bud, Dear God, No!" cried Mother. In the dining room Jane screamed, close to hysteria and Mother left Daddy to rush to her. Dazed, to no one in particular, he said, "We brought 'em both home."

Baby Ruth fussed, objecting to the way El was holding her, gripped so tightly, and Mother came, took the baby and put her back to her breast.

El walked into the dark living room, stared out the window at the high black bridge, the monster bridge, seeing the flutter of the yellow dress, seeing it drop down, down, down disappearing among the bare young maples, a yellow leaf, floating down, falling, falling—she closed her eyes, but it didn't help: she could see Hollie falling, her golden girl, her idol …far, far away she could hear Jane's sobbing, hear Mother's quiet talk, Daddy's broken answers, the sound flowing around her like water, deep, quiet water, moving her away from the sounds, a river, carrying her away from the blue and white quilt on the porch, away from the yellow leaf, away from the black iron bridge.

Papa Wooten had joined the men on the porch, standing over the bodies at the door. She could see his lips moving, but there was no sound, a silent movie, a puppet in a pantomime. He came into the hall, and Mother, with Baby Ruth in her arms, met him there.

Dimly the sound returned, terrible, terrible, he was saying, terrible, we won't forget this day, the words coming thickly through the water in her mind, flowing around her, please, Mrs. Phillips, call the Doc, my girl, it's her time, her water broke an hour ago.

Doc Steelman stopped his car in the road before the house, raised the quilt and dropped it, came into the hallway and put his arms around Mother." My God, Faith! What happened? Lord, Lord, Lord!"

"We're not real sure, not really. Mr. Reeves came, said Hollie had fallen from the bridge, then he left—disappeared. Before Bud could get dressed. We haven't seen him since. Then—then they found Emmett—"

Doc Steelman interrupted, moving on to something he could do, "You going to be up to helping me? Effie couldn't come, got another case down in Itman. I'm afraid Mary Beth's in for a rough time, the babies have gotten too big."

"Of course," said Mother, and seeing El in the living room, she handed Baby Ruth to her with instructions to put her to bed. El stood by the window, holding the baby, wooden and mute. The hearse came, and the men wrapped Hollie in the quilt. They discussed the situation, then put her on the carrier and picked up Emmett, placed him on the floor of the hearse beside her. Emmett's army jacket was split up the back, from the waist band to the neck, and when they picked him up his arm fell out of the jacket: his hand was turned backward. The hearse left, and Mr. Collins and Mr. Gillespie went home.

She willed her mind blank. Holding the baby in her arms, not feeling her weight at all, feeling only the red hot pain in her chest, burning, constant and deep, a searing that spread with each breath, like she was still running down the mountain in the clear, cold air, but each breath seemed to cry out, Hollie, Hollie. The pictures came back, Hollie falling, Emmett, wild-eyed and frightening. Mr. Reeves appearing out of the dark, the great engine passing over him, and Hollie falling, she had no sense of time passing, didn't know when Grandma Gillespie came, or when she took the sleeping baby from her arms, didn't remember lying on the sofa in the cold living room, didn't know when Daddy covered her with his coat.

What brought her back, wide awake and alert, was a sudden piercing scream from the dining room as Mildred Gillespie jumped straight up and went mad. She began tearing her clothes off, pulling her hair, and screaming, screaming, screaming.

Daddy took a hold of her, pushed her into a chair, held her there, telling Jane and Grandma to get some water. Grandma gave the baby to El again, gripped Mildred by the shoulders, shaking her. Jane brought water, and Daddy held the glass to the woman's mouth, forcing her to drink—or drown—but it stopped the screaming. As she quietened to hard, wrenching shudders, the radio droned on behind her:

USS West Virginia sunk. USS Oklahoma in flames.

A broadcast from Berlin had been picked up by CBS and relayed to other networks. The battle was still going on as the news was intercepted, and there were few details. Altogether, three ships were hit, but the third one was not identified, could be a transport. The announcer went on to give details about the ships, their weight and size, when they were commissioned, the number of men and officers, the type of guns, but no one was listening. After the immediate outburst Mildred sank into silence, her hands in her lap, her chest heaving, her muscles contracted and reeled into a shudder. They tried to calm her, but all their reassurances went unheard.

Will and Ben. Transferred to their State ship, so proud, writing that the crew of the West Virginia was sharp, talking about their "WeeVee" with pride and a feeling of belonging, of ownership, and now the ship was at the bottom of the ocean. Ben and Will. One or the other soon would become a father. Would they ever know?

Jane, her crying ended and functioning again, took Baby Ruth from El, went to her room, and tucked the tiny infant in bed with her, becoming little Mother, while Mother was gone.

Daddy put his jacket on and sat beside the radio, letting the fire die down.

El, shivering, aching, went upstairs and crawled into bed with Bun. So much had happened it seemed impossible, but as she pulled the covers tight, moving against Bun to get warm, she heard the twelve-thirty freight blowing for Clark's Gap tunnel. Fog had moved in around the base of the bridge, glowing white in the late moonlight; the great iron supports rose out of the mist like ladders reaching into a world beyond. Wearily she closed her eyes and slept, carrying the hot pain deep within her, half-conscious of it each time she moved, even in her sleep. At last, at long, long, last, December seventh had ended.

Twenty-Three

Most aircraft on the Island of Hawaii were destroyed or damaged beyond use, reported the radio, for the planes had been crowded together to prevent sabotage by Japanese natives living on the Islands. Black smoke filled the air and the ocean was burning around the ships as spilled oil caught fire.

In Washington, a crowd had assembled before the White House where Roosevelt and his staff had been meeting for hours. All reports of damage were being held now, no word about who had been killed or injured. The parents of every boy in service struggled with the fear and anxiety of not knowing. Every air raid warning device in the nation was activated, and along the California coast there was a total blackout as citizens expected to be attacked momentarily. Even the eastern seacoast took precautions, not knowing where the German subs could be lurking, perhaps waiting to coordinate an attack with the wily Japanese.

In New York, the police were posted around the Japanese consulate for their protection, and the emissaries were busily burning documents. Eleanor Roosevelt, speaking on her regular Sunday night program, had said, "You cannot escape anxiety. You cannot escape the clutch of fear at your heart, and yet, I hope that certainty of what we have to meet will make you rise above those fears."

Mildred Gillespie had been unable to rise above those fears, or anything else; she had huddled in her chair, shaking, silent, shrunken. Daddy and Grandma Gillespie had held her up, walked her to her own house and called Rayford to come get her. Grandma had gone in with Rayford to stay with her and Daddy had come back home.

"Mother! Mother-r-r-r-r-!"

"Don't holler, Bun! You'll wake little sister. Come down here if you need to talk to me."

"El won't get up!"

425

"Let her sleep, Honey Bun. She was up half the night. You can come on down."

El was awake. She hurt so badly she hated to move; she had pretended to be asleep to keep from moving. She heard the front door open, recognized Mrs. Belcher's voice.

"Faith? Faith—oh, there you are."

"Come on in, Mrs. Belcher, I'm making a cup of tea. Would you like one?" El wondered at Mother's calm voice. She sounded so—so normal.

"How is Mary Beth? I saw you come up the road, she have those babies?"

"She's still laboring. Slower than usual, even for a first time. I came home to feed Shirley Ruth, need to go back shortly."

"What about the girls? What can I do to help? Bud tell you about Mildred? I talked to Rayford a few minutes ago, Mildred's in a bad way."

"Jane is staying home. I don't think Ellie or Bun will go to school today, we had such a bad night. If you could look in on them? I've got to go to Pineville sometime today, make arrangements."

"When do you think the service will be?"

"Probably tomorrow. Bud is trying to locate family; someone thinks Emmett had a brother somewhere."

"I'd offer to help Doc Steelman, but I don't know a thing about having babies."

"Mother?" El stood in the kitchen door. "Hollie had some papers in her old Bible, they're in her top chest drawer."

Mother drew her close. "I thought I'd let you girls stay home today. Could you help Jane with your little sisters?"

"My throat hurts, and my side." Said El, leaning against her.

Mother felt her head, hugged her and suggested a cup of hot chocolate might make her throat feel better. Mrs. Belcher bustled around and cooked oatmeal, making extra for Jane when she got up. El tried to eat, but it burned her throat; she took her bowl into the dining room and turned on the radio. The Lonesome Pine Fiddlers were playing between news broadcasts and the energetic mountain music was more than she could tolerate. She turned it off, left the oatmeal in her bowl, and went back to bed.

Mother came upstairs before she left, felt her head again, said, rest, honey, I'll be back soon, and El went to sleep, the only way she knew how to ease the burning in her chest and side, the only way she knew to shut out the pictures running through her mind, pictures of Hollie and Emmett, and of Mr. Reeves, of the train with its bright light shining like a spot light on the yellow-gold dress, and Hollie, falling, falling oh, God, why, *why!*

A knock on the front door awakened her. She raised her head and looked out the window. A county Sheriff's car was parked beside the gate. Mrs. Belcher opened the door, said, "Yes?"

"Good morning, Mrs. Phillips?"

"No, I—"

"I'm Trooper Lewis. Hiram said I could get some information from You? Hiram Cobb, down at the mortuary in Pineville? He called us, said there was a double suicide up here last night, said I should do a little checking—"

"Mrs. Phillips is not at home," said Mrs. Belcher, drawing herself up like a banty hen. "She may be found at the last house on your left, right down the road."

The trooper retreated with mumbled apologies. "Sorry. I understood this was the house, wanted her to know, Hiram found Emmett White's orders in his jacket pocket. He was shippin' out, probably the reason fer it all. Thank you, Ma'am. I'll find Mrs. Phillips, I understand she's the next of kin."

"What do you mean—he had orders? He was in the service?"

"Yes ma'am, accordin' to Hiram, Army. And he was shippin' out. You can check with Hiram—"

"Oh, no, I just didn't know. Well, thank you, trooper. Thank you very much. You be sure to tell Mrs. Phillips about that. She's no kin, but you go on and talk to her."

El could see him as he opened the gate, hesitated, walked back to the porch. "By the way, Ma'am, do you know where I might find a Mr. Reeves? I understand he might know something about this?"

Mrs. Belcher walked out on the porch, pointed out Mr. Reeves' house, and the trooper left.

Would the police question everyone? Did Edgar go to school? Had he found Mr. Mitchell? She thought about Emmett, left lying on the tracks but found below the bridge, beside Hollie. She closed her eyes, willing herself back to sleep, feeling feverish, chilly, then hot again. She wished Mary Beth would have her babies so Mother could come home.

The radio was on downstairs, playing music again, then talking, then music, she drifted off, only faintly aware of the sounds, drifting into warm, gentle water, a sweet-flowing river, carrying her away from the breath-sharp pain, away from the bare maple trees, away from the high black bridge looming outside her window.

In Germany the report was that due to the "constantly increasing war-mongering of the American President Roosevelt in recent weeks, the first clashes between the Japanese and the United States armed forces occurred today." Honolulu had sustained heavy damage, and there were many deaths in the civilian population, the total as yet uncounted. At Hickman Field the first reports listed over a hundred dead and more than three hundred injured among the soldiers. They had been bombed twice, and attacks on Singapore, Malaya, Thailand, and the Philippines were reported now. There was little said regarding U.S. defensive action except that many American planes had been shot down trying to defend Honolulu and the ships. There were unconfirmed reports that the Americans had sunk a Japanese aircraft carrier off the coast of Hawaii, but no official word had been received. Submarines bearing torpedoes had struck an Army transport between Hawaii and San Francisco, and the people feared that same sub was lying off the coast, waiting to attack the mainland of the United States. San Francisco had called out her National Guard, and the troops, packs on their backs, had marched out of Fort Lewis and prepared for a national emergency.

On the civilian front, all private planes had been grounded by the Civil Aeronautics Board, and the Navy recruiting stations had stayed open all night. Bluefield had six men enlist within an hour of the attack.

President Roosevelt would address a joint session of Congress at twelve-thirty, for the purpose of declaring war on Japan, and the crowds around the White House were driving bumper to bumper on Pennsylvania Avenue, jamming the sidewalks, their noses stuck between the iron rail fence around the grounds. Extra Secret Service men were in place, augmented by the Washington police force.

Daddy was home, reading the special Extra edition put out by the *Bluefield Daily Telegraph* when El got up. He smiled briefly over the top of his paper when she entered the room, and continued reading: In Japan, Premier Tojo was telling the Japanese people they would have the "final victory", and that "the rise or fall of East Asia depends on the outcome of the fight." They had hit every major U. S. and British possession in the central and western Pacific, plus Thailand, in one fell swoop. "The claimed successes for this fell swoop included sinking the battleship *West Virginia*, and setting fire to the battleship *Oklahoma*. From that moment, each tense tick of the clock brought new and flaming accounts of Japanese aggression in her secretly launched war of conquest or death for the *Land of the Rising Sun*."

Mother sat in her rocking chair, eyes closed, looking tired, white, more physically exhausted than on the night Baby Ruth was born. She opened her eyes when El spoke. "Mother?"

"You're awake, honey! You've slept almost all day."

"Did Mary Beth have her babies?"

"Yes, Ellie, and they're fine. A boy and a girl. They're fine, healthy babies."

"How's Mary Beth?"

"She'll be fine in a few days. She had a hard time."

"Did she name them?"

"Hadn't when I left. She'd gone to sleep."

El eased into a chair at the table, moving carefully around the pain in her side. Daddy watched her over the edge of his paper. "Something wrong, El? Something hurtin' you?"

"My side, Daddy. My ribs."

"Did you fall?"

The question brought back the terrible pictures and the feelings of the night before. She closed her eyes, breathing cautiously, bracing herself for the pain before she answered. "No, I don't think so."

"Better eat something," Mother said, her eyes closed again. " See what's left of that stew Mrs. Belcher made. There may be cake, I'm not sure." The radio announcer began the evening news and their attention was held by his opening words:

"President Roosevelt appeared today before the Congress of the United States and asked for a declaration of war against Japan. Here are the key points of his address:

Yesterday, December 7, 1941—a date which will live in infamy—the United States of America was suddenly and deliberately attacked by the naval and air forces of the Empire of Japan."

"The United States was at peace with that nation, and at the solicitation of Japan, was still in conversation with its government and its Emperor looking toward the maintenance of peace in the Pacific. Indeed, one hour after Japanese air squadrons had commenced bombing in Oshu, the Japanese ambassador to the United States and his colleague delivered to the Secretary of State a formal reply to a recent American message. While this message stated that it seemed useless to continue the existing diplomatic negotiations, it contained no threat or hint of war or armed attack…"

"The President called the roll of those attacked: Hawaiian Islands, the Philippines, Guam, Wake island, Midway Island, Malaya, Hong Kong, and closed his speech by asking that Congress declare *a state of war has existed since yesterday, December seventh.* The President will address the nation by radio tomorrow night, and WHIS will bring you that broadcast."

El tried to pour a glass of milk but the gallon jug was nearly full and it was too heavy. She dipped up a bowl of nearly-cold soup from the pot on the stove, but as she looked at the thin film of grease on the top, she missed the old wood-burning range of last winter. The stew would've stayed hot on the back of that old stove. She missed a lot of things from last winter; warm stew was the least of them. She sat the bowl on the kitchen table and went back to bed.

Sometime in the night she awoke, aware that her gown and pillow were damp with perspiration; she tried to get out of bed but the pain was too severe. She tried to call mother but the effort was too great. Weak tears ran down her face but eventually she drifted to sleep again, sleeping restlessly until dawn.

She heard Daddy get up, heard the bathroom door close; moments later Baby Ruth cried and Mother got out of bed. This time, in the cold dawn, Mother heard her and came, feeding the baby as she walked. El began to cry when she saw her, weakly trying to tell her how much she hurt. In a matter of minutes, Mother had checked her temperature, called Jane to help, giving her aspirin, cough medicine and water. Bun, awake, and wanting attention, decided she had a pain too, placing her hand on her stomach. Daddy, dressed for work, took Bun downstairs with him, telling her that a biscuit would ease her pain, and they had to let Ellie rest. El went back to sleep, but only after fighting the dragons again, the monsters on the bridge, the bridge the most monstrous dragon of all.

She awoke feeling better—until she tried to move. Mother and Bun were in her room, tiptoeing around, talking in whispers. Bun was wearing her best Sunday dress; Mother was wearing a black felt hat.

"Where are you going?"

"You're awake, honey?"

"Where are you and Bun going?"

"We have to go to church, Ellie. Shirley's mother and daddy are in heaven with her," said Bun matter-of-factly. "You can't go 'cause you're sick."

Mother sat down beside her. "Mrs. Belcher is coming over to stay with you and Baby Ruth. I hate to leave you, but I feel like I've got to be there-" Mother's voice broke and she searched for an apron that wasn't there.

"I want to see Hollie," El whispered, holding her breath as much as possible.

"Honey, it's bitter cold outside," said Mother. "You could have pneumonia, I can't let you go, Ellie."

"I want to see her," El said, a little clearer.

"You couldn't see her if you went, El. It will be a closed-casket service. Nobody will see her. Or Emmett, either."

El was silent. Put in the ground without anyone seeing her again. She had been the last. She and Mr. Reeves. No, he hadn't seen her fall; the train was going over him. She had been the very last. A new image joined the specters going through her mind when she closed her eyes: two blue-steel coffins, placed side-by-side at the front of her church, where Shirley's had been, and there were others, brown ones, silver ones, dark blue ones, and she knew who was in each one but she couldn't recall, couldn't quite remember, the knowledge just below her consciousness; they were lined up, like the display caskets down at Sears Mortuary in Mullins, the ones she had seen when they went with Hollie to get Shirley's marker, rows of coffins, rows and rows. If she didn't go to the funeral, she would see those coffins forever. She had to go: Hollie deserved her best efforts.

El eased out of bed, one hand holding her side, pressed hard against her ribs. Her navy dress was clean and easy to get into. She tried to comb her hair but raising her arms hurt too much and she gave up. She found her blue toboggan, remembering what Mother had said about it being cold. Now combing her hair didn't matter.

By the time she came down the stairs, Mother, Bun and Jane were ready to go. Mrs. Belcher stood in the hall and Mother was giving her instructions for Baby Ruth's care. Mother looked up as El came down the stairs and their eyes met, Mother's concerned, worried, and El's determined, stubborn. She didn't say a word as El joined her sisters and went to the car.

There was a thin coating of ice on the steps, where water had dripped from the porch roof, and the windshield of the car had to be scraped. The dry, frozen ruts in the road were crusty and crumbled under her feet. Bun put her gloved hand in El's as they walked to the car, silently saying, I'm glad you are with me.

When they arrived at the church there were two vehicles from the mortuary parked beside the road; the caskets were already in place. El was surprised at the size of the crowd, considering that it was a work day, and considering how many of Hollie's real friends were unable to come, Mary Beth and Mama Wooten, Mildred and Grandma Gillespie, Ben, Will, Ted—in fact, she and her family were the only ones left who were really close to her.

Daddy joined them as they got out of the car, taking Mother's arm as they started in the church, and Bun, putting her hand in his, walked with them, Jane and El following. Even with the crowd, their seats were waiting for them—the front row, the row usually reserved for the family. The railroaders, members of Daddy's line gang, would be Hollie's pallbearers and the miners would carry Emmett. The men took the two front rows on the other side.

The coffins were blue, as El had pictured them, placed side by side beneath the pulpit. On each was a large spray of white chrysanthemums; there were no other flowers, but someone, Mrs. Collins, or perhaps Mrs. Plover, had put green pine branches along the alter railing, and the church was filled with its fresh, Christmas smell, like for the pageant, when the Holy family was placed where the caskets now stood.

Thelma Plover was at the piano, for nobody expected Jane to play. Preacher Copeland was waiting until his watch, held in his hand and set to railroad time, had exactly two o'clock. The choir was assembled and waiting.

It was warm in the church, but El was shivering, colder than she had been when she played out in the snow, colder than she had been on the bridge, and Mother, feeling her shivering, tucked her hand in hers to warm it. She wondered if Emmett's brother had been found, and looked about for strangers, but no strangers were seated on the front row. There was her family, the miners and the railroaders. Where had they all come from, these mourners? How had they known?

Preacher Copeland stood up, bowed his head to pray. His white hair was thinner now, more of the pink scalp showed. El tried to pray but couldn't close her eyes without seeing Hollie again. Hold on, she told herself, just hold on, it won't last long—but it did.

Preacher Copeland had been told that it was a double suicide, and that was a sin, making it necessary for him to pray them into heaven. He offered all the reasons they should be admitted to that promised land, the first one being, Jesus, Jesus, Jesus, Lord, saved both the Saints and Sinners, Jesus, Jesus, Jesus, quietly, at first, then the choir joined in, Jesus, Jesus, Jesus and Lord let some good come of this, Jesus, Jesus, Jesus, let these two lost souls into your promised land, Jesus, Jesus, Jesus, oh, Lord we implore, Jesus, Jesus, Jesus, take their sins away, yes, Lord, slowing it down, Jesus, Jesus, Jesus, and Preacher Copeland, speaking alone, again, Jesus, Jesus, Jesus, Amen. Amen, Amen.

The choir stood to lead the singing, but the song was unfamiliar, chosen for its words, and few had books:

> *In the hour of trial, Jesus plead for me,*
> *Lest by base denial I depart from thee…*
> *Should Thy mercy send me sorrow, toil and woe,*
> *Or should pain attend me on my path below…*

There it was again. God sent sorrow, toil and woe. If He sent it, He meant it, so why pray to take it away?

Jane was going to the piano. Mr. and Mrs. Plover were going to sing for special music. Thank God, the children weren't going to sing this time. The couple alternated verses, harmonizing on the chorus, and again El couldn't comprehend why the song was chosen:

> *I sing because I'm happy, I sing because I'm free,*
> *For his eye is on the sparrow, and I know He watches me.*

If God could see the sparrow fall, why didn't He see Hollie? Why didn't he catch her, or stop the train, or, better yet, *why didn't he change Emmett's heart?*

The service was over. The men gathered around the caskets, moved one in front of the other and they followed. As El went up the isle a hand reached out to her: Edgar. And he was crying. Dry-eyed, El walked by. Numb, she followed where she was led.

Once on the windy hill, Mother tried to persuade El to stay in the car, out of the cold. El didn't hear her. She watched as they placed the coffins over the yellow-clay holes, waited while the white flowers were laid just so, sat when the others sat, listened as Preacher Copeland, exhausted now, recited the Twenty-Third Psalm in a weak, tired voice:

The Lord is My Shepherd, I shall not want... El blanked it out. It was the same as when Shirley died. Preacher Copeland had a Bible in his hands, but he didn't read. He knew the verses by heart. He put his head back and looked right up into the steel-gray sky, talking directly to God in words nearly as old as the hills.

He came to the end of the Twenty-Third Psalm and kept on going, through the twenty-fourth, *The earth is the Lord's and the fullness there of; the world and they that dwell therein...*the Twenty-Fifth...

Yea, let none that wait on Thee be ashamed: Let them be ashamed which transgress without cause...remember not the sins of my youth, nor my transgressions...the troubles of my heart are enlarged: O Bring me out of my distresses. Look upon mine affliction and my pain; and forgive all my sins. Amen.

By the end of the scriptures, Preacher Copeland's voice was nearly a whisper, but El had heard, and for the first time, something she would remember forever: *The troubles of my heart are enlarged. This was gospel truth.*

The ride home was made in silent exhaustion. While the women gathered in the kitchen, as usual, the men congregated around the catholic radio. El crept up to bed. Mother brought warm milk, gave her aspirin, and rubbed her chest with Vicks salve even though she wasn't coughing, and in time, she slept.

It was dark when she awoke, and Daddy was sitting on the edge of her bed. "How are you feeling?" he asked.

"Better," she said, realizing that while that was true, she hadn't tried to move yet.

"President Roosevelt will be speaking soon. You want me to carry you downstairs?"

"I'm too big to carry."

"Nah, you'll never be too big for your Daddy to carry!"

"I'll come down, be there in a few minutes."

Daddy left and she eased out of bed. The pain was still there, under her ribs, but she set her chin in determination and made it down the stairs. Mother had spread a blanket over her rocking chair, and after El sat down, she tucked it around her. Jane brought a plate of food and a glass of milk. El realized she was hungry, and couldn't remember when she had eaten.

The President would speak shortly, but for now, the evening news was on:

All Class 1-A young men would leave immediately for training; this would amount to several hundred from each county. The Captive Mines would sign with the Union—Lewis had won!

Lewis was asked if the board reached its decision before the Japanese attack, and he replied that they had reached their decision yesterday and had spent today reviewing it.

"Why th'hell didn't he just say, No!" said Daddy.

Fairless also said, "…it violated a fundamental right of the American worker to a job regardless of membership or nonmembership in any organization."

"That decision will come back to haint us," said Daddy, and El's mind was triggered away from the news, away from the warmly lit room. She was back on the bridge, the electricity humming through the wires, the echo of a single engine still on the tracks—haint, spirit, ghost—all were the same, and she had her own now, one that would haunt her forever.

"I'm just glad the strike question is settled," said Mother. "We can't let the mines stop now of all times."

"Edgar came to see you while you were sleeping," said Jane.

435

"Came this morning, too," said Bun. "He didn't believe me when I told him you were sick."

She didn't want to think about Edgar now. It was easier to blame him instead of herself. If he hadn't suggested they go up on the bridge—if he hadn't left her to get help—he might have stopped Emmett himself—he could have caught Hollie— she forced her thoughts away from the events of that night, forced herself to concentrate on what the President was saying:

Powerful and resourceful gangsters have banded together to make war on the whole human race. Their challenge has now been flung at the United States of America. The Japanese have treacherously violated the long standing peace between us. Many American soldiers and sailors have been killed by enemy action. American planes have been destroyed...

She was trying to keep her mind on what the President was saying, but it wandered. Had Lindbergh made another speech? Was he in the Air Force again? Was he going to fight in this war? She wanted to ask Mother; Mother would know exactly what Charles was doing if it had been made public, but she knew better than to interrupt the President:

...are now in this war. We are all in it—all the way. Every single man, woman, and child is a partner in the most tremendous undertaking of our American history. We must share together the bad news and the good news, the defeats and the victories, the changing fortunes of war...

Were Ben and Will injured? They could be dead for all anyone knew! When would word come? It had been forty-eight hours since the attack.

...The casualty lists of these first few days will undoubtedly be large. I deeply feel the anxiety of all families...will give the facts to the public as soon as two conditions have been fulfilled : first, that all information has been definitely and officially confirmed; and second, that the release of the information at the time it is received will not prove valuable to the enemy...I tell you frankly that...not sufficient information to state the exact damage which has been done to our naval vessels at Pearl Harbor...

An Italian news service said it was the *Pennsylvania* and the *Oklahoma* which had been sunk; perhaps the *West Virginia* wasn't damaged at all. Guiltily she remembered that Zane Gray was on the *Arizona,* and she hadn't given him a thought. There was no need to worry about him: the *Arizona* hadn't even been mentioned.

...must be remembered by each and every one of us that our free and rapid communication must be greatly restricted in war time. It is not possible to receive full, speedy reports from distant areas of combat...for in these days of the marvels of radio ...this information...available to the enemy...

If Will had stayed on *the Maryland,* and if Ben had stayed on the *Tennessee,* neither would be in danger...if Emmett had reported for duty to his unit immediately, like Ted had done, Hollie...if...if the pain was back. How much longer would Roosevelt talk?

...Precious months were gained by sending vast quantities of war materials to the nations still able to resist Axis aggression. Our policy rested on the fundamental truth that the defense of any country resisting Hitler or Japan was in the long run the defense of our country...It has given us time...

Daddy laid his cold pipe on the table. Mother sat stiffly erect, her hands strangely empty and still, listening intently. Jane had her head on her arms, listening or sleeping, hard to tell, and Bun, as usual, was asleep in her 'tent'. She might as well have gone to bed right. The declaration of war, on top of the terrible funeral had left them all drained, emotionally and physically. As soon as Franklin ended his speech, they would all go to bed.

...it is not a sacrifice for any man, old or young, to be a part of the Army or Navy of the United States. Rather, it is a privilege...

The bus and train stations had been full of returning soldiers and sailors, and the women, the wives, mothers, sweethearts were crying. Once in a while singing would break out, *God Bless America*, or *You Are My Sunshine*, the singing sporadic; the crying was constant. There was one sailor, retired after twenty years, honorably discharged, when the attack came, looked at his wife and children, hesitated a few seconds, said, "I'm going." And the wife never said a word against it. This, they were saying, was the Spirit of '41, the spirit that would win.'

...In my message to Congress yesterday I said that we "will make very certain that this time of treachery shall never endanger us again. In order to achieve that certainty, we must begin the great task that is before us by abandoning once and for all the illusion that we can ever again isolate ourselves from the rest of humanity..."

Lindbergh. Charles Lindbergh. That is what he would have had us do. Where is he now? How did he feel about it now? Was he still saying, stay out of it? She had to know. Tomorrow. Tomorrow she'd ask Mother.

...The true goal we seek is far above and beyond the ugly field of battle...We Americans are not destroyers; we are builders...We are going to win this war, and we are going to win the peace that follows.

And in the dark hours of this day—and through the dark days that are to come—we will know that the vast majority of the members of the human race are on our side. Many of them are fighting with us. All of them are praying for us. For, in representing our cause, we represent theirs as well—our hope and their hope for liberty under God.

Twenty-Four

"Looks like Pleurisy. Probably pneumonia as well, got it because it hurts to take a deep breath. Any time the chest is kept still for a long time, whatever the reason, pneumonia sets in."

"But the pleurisy! How...?"

"Who knows, Faith. It's just one of those things, like measles or flu, who knows how it happens or why."

El, lying beneath a pile of quilts and still freezing, could have told Doc Steelman: you get pleurisy from running down a mountain road as hard as you can in below-freezing air, right after your heart has jumped into your throat and screaming has pulled your lungs loose. And all that lets the fluid in between the ribs and the lungs, which is what causes all the pain. She closed her eyes and listened while they talked; telling them wouldn't change a thing.

"If it gets any worse, might have to get her into the clinic down in Pineville, maybe draw that fluid off, keep her a few days."

"No." Flat statement from Mother.

"Well, anybody else, I might insist. Truth is, she'll get better care right here with you. Main thing, keep her warm, but fresh air. You know how. And fluids—when has she eaten? She's already dry. Is she drinking at all?"

"Why, I'm not really sure," replied Mother. "There's been so much going on—"

"Don't see how you're holding up yourself," said Doc.

"I'll make it," Mother said quietly. "I'll see that she drinks plenty. How are Mary Beth and the twins?"

"Doin' nicely, but Mama Wooten's got her hands full, with the three of them. Grandma helps some, but with Mildred like she is—now, there's a woman I find hard to understand. You take most, having twins for their first grandchildren—now, that's something—but she hasn't even seen them!"

439

"Mildred spends a lot of time dwelling in the past," said Mother, "can't seem to rise above it."

"Had a hard time, did she?"

"She was terribly mistreated. She told me about it, years ago."

"By who?"

"Her father, and some of his friends."

"Beat her?"

"No, not exactly—" El could hear the hesitancy in her Mother's voice, knew it was going against the grain to gossip, which Mother never allowed.

"He misused her," Mother said softly.

"Rape?"

"Well—"

"Worse?"

"Now, I know I can trust you never to repeat this," said Mother, hesitating again, and El could picture Mother looking at her carefully, making sure she was asleep, before she continued. She lay very still, holding her eyes closed without jerking, and Mother continued. "Will was born before Rayford married her. That's why they moved to Coville."

"Will is her father's boy?"

"Possibly."

Again, silence, then Doc cleared his throat. "Humph, now, there's something else I can't figure out, Faith."

Mother waited, and El hardly breathed, afraid they would figure out she was awake and listening.

"Those twins. One's got blue eyes, and real bright blue, too, just like Ben's. I'm almost certain the other will have brown."

"One's a girl and the other a boy, that wouldn't be unusual, they aren't identical twins!"

"No, no, they're fraternal, all right, but now Mildred, she's got pale eyes, blue or gray, never have figured out which, while Rayford, his are blue, like Ben's. Mary Beth, she's green, hazel, I guess you'd say, so where does the brown come in?"

"Well," said Mother, "that's little or nothing to worry about, probably an ancestor, or—"

"No, doesn't work that way. Brown is dominant. Be carried on before blue or green. I swear, Faith, I'm not saying for certain, but those babies have different fathers! Now, I'm not saying Mary Beth's not a good girl, and I'm sure it will work out all right now that she and Ben are married, but, well, couldn't help but notice."

"You see some strange things, don't you," said Mother.

"Well, let's just say, after practicing medicine as long as I have, there's mighty few surprises." Mother was silent. El wanted to open her eyes, to see how Mother was taking this, but she didn't dare let on she'd heard. She wondered if the doctor would tell Mary Beth what he had just told Mother. She heard the doctor close his bag, heard the scrape of his chair as he got up to leave." Be back tomorrow. Remember, if her fever goes up, use the tub. Keep her warm, push fluids every hour, round the clock."

By the time Mother came back from seeing the doctor out, she was asleep again, and faking wasn't necessary.

Mary Beth named her babies without a second thought, predestined, before conception, before the first groping beneath the trees, before the bedding on oak leaf and pine, before the awkward thrusts and inept fumbling, and named them as Ben would have wanted, including Will to be on the safe side. The boy was named first. Had there been two boys it wouldn't have mattered, but in the genetic cubicles of her mind the first one would be Will's and the second one Ben's. The boy was named Wilford Ben Gillespie, and Rayford couldn't be prouder, especially now when his boys could be dead or seriously wounded. The girl was named Sweet Alice, called "Sweets" right from the start, the mountain way of shortening names, unlike the Southern style of using two names when one would do. When asked about the odd name, Mary Beth would quote:

> *Don't you remember sweet Alice, Ben Bolt,*
> *Sweet Alice whose hair was so brown,*
> *Who wept with delight when you gave her a smile,*
> *And trembled with fear at your frown?*

Only to herself would she repeat the second stanza to the poem which gave Ben his nickname so long ago:

> *In the old churchyard in the valley, Ben Bolt,*
> *In a corner obscure and alone,*

They have fitted a slab of granite so gray,
And Alice lies under the stone.

True to the ballad, Sweet Alice had hair so brown, and from the first it looked like her eyes would be the blue of her Daddy's, while Ben, a sturdy, square-shouldered little boy-baby had black hair and dark eyes, so dark they were bound to be brown. Intuitively, Mary Beth knew that Ben would live and prosper; by the same intuition she knew Sweets would have to struggle. Thus, from the very beginning, the very earliest feedings, Sweet Alice was offered the big breast first, and Ben had to pull hard, his strong jaws working quickly to drain the last of her milk. Sweets, fed easily from over-flowing breasts, nursed gently, contented within minutes, and slept quickly, thus developing a gentle, easy nature; but Ben, fighting the half-drained ninny, working for his supper, lay awake wanting more, restless and fretful, creating an anxious reaction in his young, inexperienced mother, and an irritation to his older grandmother who had seen too many babies already. A good egg and a bad egg. Right from the start. A good seed and a bad seed. Pain and Pleasure. Right and Wrong. Sin and Salvation.

The Prince of Wales and *the Repulse*, both British ships, had been sunk. Guam had been invaded. Canada, the Netherlands, East indies, Batavia, Costa Rica—all had declared war on Japan.

Senator Wheeler, of the America First Committee, said, "The only thing now is to do our best to lick the hell out of them!"

Wendell Wilkie said, "I have not the slightest doubt as to what a United America can and will do!"

Former President Herbert Hoover called for an all-out fight, saying, "American soil has been treacherously attacked by Japan. Our decision is clear!" The Fight for Freedom Committee in New York said, "It's America First now!" They warned that the Japanese attack was Hitler's effort to turn America's attention away from the real war, the center of which was Berlin. But nobody heard a comment from Charles Lindbergh—Colonel Lindbergh was not talking in public.

Hot Lemonade. How she hated it. It burned the back of her throat almost as badly as the mustard plaster burned her chest, even though Mother rubbed on camphorated oil before laying the mustard plasters.

About fifteen hundred dead and an equal number wounded on Oahu, mostly Army and Navy personnel. Rayford said Mildred would be all right, once she knew: the uncertainty was killing them both, but he was holding up better.

The Office of Production Management (OPM) press release had a new slogan. Above the heading appeared these three words, in spaced capitals:

R E M E M B E R P E A R L H A R B O R

In one way, Daddy had been fortunate over the terrible days of the attack and the double funeral; the railroad hadn't made extra demands on his time. Now, they made up for it. A switching conductor at Elmore fell under the shifting cars and had his left arm cut off. Daddy and his men replaced the damage done by the cars; nobody could replace the arm. Reports of sabotage on the railroad flew wild and heavy, and the Virginian hired a hundred and fifty guards for the tunnels and bridges, the men working twelve-hour shifts. Two men were surprised while stuffing something in a drain pipe at Clark's Gap tunnel; after they ran off it was discovered that the 'something' was a bundle of rags and dynamite sticks, complete with fuse ready to light.

Hot tea, thick with extra sugar for nourishment, and honey in a spoon to follow terrible-tasting medicine and black tonic.

U.S. GOES TO WAR WITH AXIS POWERS;
ARMED FORCES DELIVER SMASHING BLOWS
TO JAPAN. HITLER DECLARES WAR,
MUSSOLINI PUTS NATION IN WAR, LINKS WITH JAPAN.

President Signs War Resolutions. Army Asks for Ten Thousand Nurses to Volunteer.

Bluefield Daily Telegraph: "Say what you please about Colonel Charles A. Lindbergh—you must give him credit for possessing vision—several years before the Second World War broke out, he predicted the next world war would be decided from the air."

The sheets stayed wet with perspiration; when she moved away from them, she chilled, feeling their dampness. Her skin would go cold, like a mountain breeze blowing on it after a swim in Barker's Creek.

Churchill. Five simple words: "We are all in this." The great English leader went on to say, "Our foes are bound by their ambitions and their crimes to seek implacably the destruction of the English-speaking world and all it stands for. It is the supreme barrier for all their kind. If this should be their resolve, we are prepared to meet it …there are quite a lot of us to be killed."

Claude Lefler, Principal of Herndon's grade school, gave each student a savings stamp book, and the children were bringing a dime a week for a stamp. Their club motto: "Whip Hitler."

She knew Edgar was coming over to see her, but she didn't want to see him. Jane brought new books from the high school library, *Random Harvest*, *Keys of The Kingdom*, but she couldn't stay awake to read.

DECEMBER THIRTEENTH: JAP NAVY CLAIMS USS ARIZONA SUNK.

Two hundred and sixty-three men enlisted last week. Newsboys are selling defense stamps and war bonds. Secretary Knox announced the losses at Pearl Harbor:

Destroyers—Cassin, Shaw, Downes
Target Ship—Utah
Mine Layer—Oglala
Battleship—U.S.S. Arizona

Dear Mr. and Mrs. Gillespie,

The Navy Department deeply regrets to inform you that your son, Wilford Ray Gillespie, Radioman, USN, is missing following action in performance of duty and in service to his country. The department appreciates your great anxiety and will furnish you further information promptly when received. To prevent possible aid to our enemies, please do not divulge the name of his ship or station.

There was a sharp pain in her side and back when she tried to move, but a rosy glow was reflected on the ceiling; she had to turn over to discover the source. A caboose stove sat in the corner of the room, brought by Daddy's line gang, a squat, iron two-eye stove like the one they had set up for Grandma Shrewsbury, with the pipe run out the window, and the windows opened top and bottom for fresh air. Wood was stacked beside the stove. Jane would be mad; it was against her piano. No, the piano was gone; she could see it through the French doors, in the dining room, where the radio usually sat.

Someone had pinned a newspaper over the lamp beside her bed, and the paper looked like a dunce cap, a three-cornered hat, casting a shadow like a pyramid, an Egyptian pyramid. Egyptian troops were on the move, U.S. tanks were in Libya, oh where have you been, Billy boy, Billy boy, oh where have you been Charlie Lindbergh? Across the sea, my bonnie lies over the ocean, oh bring back my song of sixpence, pocket full of rye, Oh Ellie, Ellie, give me your answer true, please wake up!

You mustn't be in here! You could catch pneumonia too upstairs, downstairs, stay with the baby, can't have all my girls sick, El, El, El along the banks of the Gooney Otter, mint grew all year round, crushed and rubbed on her skin to keep the mosquitoes away, smelled like Vicks salve, tea kettle whistling, steam in the air, so much promise, so much potential Will missing in action, gone away, gone away, so much promise, going to be an engineer, build bridges, bridges, bridges.

She's making progress, a class in illness or wellness, coming along, so hot, wrapped like a parcel ready to mail, how could he drown in a radio room, a whole room full of radios, Philcos sitting in a row, stained-glass window, the pain made her hands and feet disappear, only her body remained, a square chunk revolving, turning through the colors of pain, red, purple, blue fading into white, white clouds against a steel-gray sky and there were others with her, talking to her, all around her, she was no longer alone, she could see them without opening her eyes, she knew them, Lindbergh was right, she spoke to them without speaking, saw the ones behind her without turning around, heard them, absorbed their messages, knowing what they wanted to tell her, knowing, but it was growing dark and cold, blue-cold, deep-cold.

Carried, sheets wrapped around her, wait, wait, a warm well, water rising up, covering her, warm, warm, growing cool, cooler, folding around her, patting, it's all right, there-there, *Come Away, O human child...for the world's more full of weeping than you can understand...*

Hollie was with her and she slept.

When she awoke, Hollie was still there for the first fleeting moments, before the dawn intruded; the peace was remembered.

Throughout the day she lay in bed and experimented. She could select her thoughts of Hollie. Each time the falling form appeared in her mind she replaced it with a deliberate vision: Hollie, singing in the church choir, blue-robed and serious, golden light on her hair; Hollie, walking about the yard with Mr. Mitchell, a flower in her white hands; or pulling up daises, saying he loves me he loves me not; Hollie learning to sew with pins in her mouth like a porcupine; Hollie giving her the tiny gold cross. Hollie would be with her forever. She slept peacefully, and for the first time, the pain was gone.

Dear Mom and Dad and all,

I got burned when the Japs hit us and my buddy
Is writing this for me. When my hands get well I will
write but I am doing o.k. and I will be back in this
War as soon as the—Is my baby pretty?
Give my love to everyone and take care of each other.

Your son,
Ben

Grandpa Gillespie openly cried as he read the letter to the family; he still had one son, and that was more than a lot of folks had left. The boys' room was being fixed up. Mary Beth and the twins were coming to live with them. It would be good for Mildred, help her take her mind off Will; no, they hadn't heard any more. The Wootens didn't mind, they were being fine about it, after all, they still had two boys at home. Mary Beth had received an official card from the Navy, saying Ben was injured; he might even get to come home soon, but they weren't sure.

Now Mildred would have something to hold in her empty lap, something to do with her hands. Sweet Alice lay by the hour in her Grandma's lap, rocked slowly, methodically, mindlessly, while Ben lay in his crib, ignored until Grandpa came home from the company store. Mary Beth did what needed to be done, fed, changed, bathed the babies, and put them down. As soon as she got the letter from Ben saying he was alive, she changed the baby's name from Ben to Will, her first love, her true love. No one seemed to mind.

Roosevelt addressed the nation again on Monday, the fifteenth, reminding the citizens of the one hundred and fiftieth anniversary of the American Bill of Rights:

No date in the long history of freedom means more to the liberty loving countries than the fifteenth of December, 1791. On that day, one hundred and fifty years ago, a new nation, through an elected Congress, adopted a declaration of human rights which has influenced the thinking of all mankind from one end of the world to the other... We covenant with each other before all the world, that having taken up arms in the defense of liberty, we will not lay them down before liberty is once again secure in the world we live in. For that security we pray; for that security we act—now and evermore.

Somebody cut down the Japanese cherry trees in Washington during a black-out, and the Rose Bowl game between Duke and Oregon was moved to Durham, North Carolina because of the black-out in Pasadena and along the Pacific coast. Words like Luzon, blitz, Wake Island, and Borneo became household words, and on the nineteenth, school was dismissed for the holidays.

Congress celebrated by voting the draft registration of all men ages 18 through 64, expecting to call those age 20 to 44 immediately.

The letter from the War Department to Aunt Maude in Galax was not good news:

...regret to inform you, your son, Zane Gray...killed in action...line of duty and service to his country...

Aunt Maude called on the railroad telephone and Daddy stood barefooted in the hall while she cried, unable to talk. He hung up, sat on the living room couch beside El's bed, hands between his knees, staring at the floor, and to Mother's questioning, said only, "Zane. Gone."

El couldn't think about Zane Gray being dead. He was too energetic, too full of laughter and tease. Maybe God would have a special place in heaven for him and the other young men, where they could tinker with their cars without getting grease on the streets of gold. Zane Gray wouldn't be any good with a harp, but he sure could whistle with the choir.

El was sitting up for an hour at a time now, but her bed remained in the living room and Mother or Daddy slept on the couch beside her. Isolation had been removed and she could have company. Trouble was, she didn't want anyone to come except Bun, and she sat on the foot of the bed for hours, playing dolls or cut-outs while El did nothing at all.

Preacher Copeland came, sat with her, prayed, kneeling in the floor by her bed. As he prepared to leave, he said, "Now, Rachel, remember how much God loves you, and you'll be well real soon."

El answered, "God may love me, but I don't love Him!"

Mother exclaimed, severely, "Rachel! Being ill doesn't give you the right to speak like that!"

Preacher Copeland wasn't even shocked; he smiled and said, "Doesn't matter, Rachel, doesn't matter at all what you think of God, you are a child of His, whether you like it or not!"

He came back and sat beside her on the bed and took her hand. "You see, Ellie, that's what happened to Emmett. He shut God out, and he shut out God's messengers. That's what we are, just God's messengers, that's the only way he can speak, is through people, and when you shut out people you shut out God. Nobody makes it alone, Rachel. Nobody. Emmett tried and failed. Don't you make the same mistake."

"And Hollie? She didn't shut out anyone! Hollie didn't do anything wrong!"

Preacher Copeland smiled and shook his head. "When you're stronger we'll have a little talk about that. Right now, you just get well, young lady! I need you back in Sunday School!"

Mother walked to the door with the minister and came back to sit beside her on the bed. "It was an accident, Ellie. Mr. Reeves told your father all about it before he left. Hollie didn't take her own life. You must believe that." Mother didn't mention Emmett; it was as if he'd never been.

"Mr. Reeves is gone?" Pictures of the old man walking through the camp, wearing his old Army coat, gun over his arm, ran through her mind. She tried to see him behind narrow iron bars in some jail. Fearfully, she asked, "Where did he go?"

"Why, he joined the Army! Reenlisted, the day after Pearl Harbor! You didn't know?"

"The Army! But he's too old!"

"Rachel! You say the queerest things! Mr. Reeves isn't old—he's the same age as your father!"

El lay quiet, trying to adjust her picture of the old—of the man. Maybe being almost bald-headed made him look older, or maybe it was because he lived alone. Apparently, he hadn't told her parents she was on the bridge. Had he even known she was there?

"Daddy says there's not any such thing as an accident. We make a mistake, and we pay for it," El said softly.

"Well, he's entitled to his opinion, but I don't agree." Mother was looking at her thoughtfully. "Is there something you want to talk about, honey?"

"No."

Mother waited, then replied, **"God doesn't punish us, Ellie. We do that to ourselves."**

Twenty-Five

Mother went to the kitchen, and the rattle of pots and pans indicated she was starting supper.

El lay quietly, staring out the window, seeing only the corner of the Gillespie's house next door. Did accidents carry their own punishment, like mistakes? But every Sunday sermon, every Sunday School lesson, said God was to blame: "Should Thy mercy send me sorrow, toil and woe." Maybe Mother and Daddy did know and were waiting for her to get well. Maybe she wouldn't be punished as long as she was sick. There was a knock on the door. She scooted deep within the covers on her bed as she recognized Edgar's voice.

"Mrs. Phillips, can my Grandma come visit Ellie? She wants to meet her before we leave."

"Why, certainly, Edgar! Ellie could use some company. Might cheer her up!"

Mrs. Mitchell was less like a grandmother than anyone El had ever seen. She had red hair. Not auburn red, like Bun's, but a colored red, henna, out of a bottle: a sin, dyed hair. Her face was white and lined, and the lines had white powder in them. She wore a green knit suit with a gold chain for a belt, and around her neck was a long gold chain that held her gold-framed glasses.

She was no taller than Jane, and not nearly as filled out, bird-like, quick and bright, and her eyes were as blue and direct as Edgar's and his father's, making it obvious where they had gotten them. El could tell she wore perfume even before she got to her bedside; she looked nothing like the owner and manager of a railroader's boarding house.

Grandma Mitchell stood beside the bed, looking down on El, propped up on pillows, fresh-scrubbed for the Preacher's visit, her hair combed out straight, and her face as white as the pillowcase. The heavy quilts made her look flat, thinner than she really was.

"So, you are Ellie."

"Yes ma'am."

"I'll have a word with you. Move over. I want to sit down." El moved to the back of the bed. Mrs. Mitchell sat down.

"Edgar has told me about everything. He said you wouldn't talk to him."

"Is that why you've come—to get me to talk to Edgar?"

"No, I came to get my grandsons for the holidays. With their Pa working twelve, fifteen hours a day, seven days a week, he can't see after them proper. Besides, I was curious to see where it happened. Then, when I got here, Edgar said it wasn't at all like the paper had it."

They sat in silence, studying each other. "So, you are Edgar's friend." Finally, Mrs. Mitchell spoke. "He talks about you," the red-haired woman continued. El didn't know how to respond so said nothing.

The radiator gurgled, like it does when the water is turned on in the kitchen. Outside, in the triangle, Edgar, Joe, and BillynBob were shouting and running, playing ball.

"Look here, girl, you're going to have to pull yourself together if you're going to be good enough for my Edgar! He don't need a malingering ninny!"

El looked at her thoughtfully, "What's malingering?"

"Puttin' on an act, playing sick! Oh, I know you've had a rough time, pneumonia's no fun, but you are out of the woods now, time to get your spunk back!"

El looked at Edgar's grandmother, talking about her being Edgar's girl. Suddenly she recalled Betty Lusk, a bride at thirteen. Could have six or seven babies before she was twenty. Did Mrs. Mitchell think she was going to be like that? She closed her eyes and turned away. Mrs. Mitchell misunderstood.

"Now, none of that! The mistake was made! It's paid for, over and done! You've got years ahead of you, it'd be a sin to waste your life, child. You can't help them, you leave them up to the Almighty, he's the only one can help them now."

El wiped her face with the back of one hand while Mrs. Mitchell held firmly to the other. "Now, I know all about it. Edgar's told me everything, how he couldn't find his Pa, and how he thought he'd made a mistake leaving you alone and he run back up there but you was gone, it was too late. Now, listen, child, you had no business being there, but it didn't happen because you were there! It happened because they made a mistake and they paid, see, a mistake with their little girl, and they never learned to live with it." Mrs. Mitchell was

451

silent, twisting her glasses on the gold chain. El hoped she wouldn't cry, but she looked as if she might. Crying would wash all the powder out of the creases.

"I made a bad mistake once," she laughed shortly. "Well, I might of made more than one, but don't you see? The hardest thing is, no matter how you wish it, sometimes things can't be changed. You just pick yourself up, dust yourself off, and keep on trying. Ha! That's what the ole U.S. of A. has to do now, ain't it?"

She stood up, straightened her green knit skirt over her thin frame, adjusted the gold-chain belt. "And that's what you've got to do, Ellie. Now, you get well, get out'a this bed, and keep on going! I'm taking the boys back to Logan with me; they won't be back 'til after Christmas. You shape up by then, now. Edgar sets a mighty big store by you. Ain't no reason for you to hold it all against him."

"Mrs. Mitchell?"

"Yes, Ellie?"

"You know Edgar wants a bike real bad, don't you?"

"Ha! No wonder he thinks you're special! You're always looking out for him. Well, I might just see what I can do about that."

El lay quiet, looking out the window, seeing the white side of the Gillespie house. She could hear Mother talking to grandma Mitchell in the hall. She sat up, and found, to her surprise, she wasn't dizzy at all. She pushed the heavy quilts aside and swung her feet to the floor. It felt good to be out from under the heavy covers without chilling. She felt the slight draft from the front door on her feet, and the rug was cold. She stood up and walked to the front windows. The high black bridge loomed over the town, and the triangle was empty; only brown dried grass and black dirt road remained. The boys were gone. She could see Hollie as she had been, running to catch a fly ball, shouting, "I've got it! I've got it!" She could picture her walking up the road, going to work at the company store, the only woman in town to hold a job. She could picture her, slim and youthful, walking up the road in the cool of the morning, encouraging Mother in her weight-loss efforts. Hollie had joined Shirley in immortality. She didn't think about Emmett at all: there was no one left who had loved him.

"Ellie! You're up!"

Mother put her arms round her, hugging her close, crying with pleasure. "It's going to be all right, baby, it's going to be all right!"

But El knew. She was no longer Mother's baby. She patted Mother's arm, comforting her, forgiving her and herself: All that was left now was the forgetting.

Epilogue

Winston Churchill arrived in Washington in time for the Yuletide season; he joined forty thousand others as Franklin Roosevelt lit the thirty-foot spruce on the White House lawn. "Now, for the ninth time, I light the living Community Christmas Tree of the nation's capital."

Chimes rang, he pushed a button, and the tree blazed to light. Franklin, standing bareheaded and without a coat on the warmest Christmas Eve in the history of the U.S. Weather Bureau—fifty-eight degrees at two o'clock in the afternoon, the previous record being fifty-six degrees in 1900—and spoke to the nation by radio:

There are many men and women in America—sincere and faithful men and women—who ask themselves this Christmas: How can we light our tree. How can we meet and worship with love and uplifted hearts in a world at war, a world of fighting, suffering and death?

...Even as we ask these questions we know the answer. There is another preparation demanded of this nation beyond and beside the preparation of weapons and materials of war. There is demanded also the preparation of our hearts...

Winston stood bareheaded beside Franklin; he put on his horn-rimmed glasses and spoke:

Here in the midst of war, raging and roaring over all the lands and seas, creeping nearer to our hearts and our homes—here, amid all these tumults, we have tonight the peace of the spirit in each cottage home...

The family was gathered in the dining room, around the table as of old. The cathedral Philco stood in the corner, in its accustomed place. Jane's piano

454

was once again in the living room, and El was sleeping in her own bed. The Christmas tree occupied the corner where the bed had been, resplendent with colored lights, popcorn and cranberry strings, made for decorations but saved for the bluebirds wintering in the narrow valley. Beneath the tree were piles of red-wrapped gifts, waiting to be opened after the lighting of the national tree and a speech by the President. The room was warm, smelling of pine and turkey basting in the oven; the windows were fogged from the moisture, closing from view the outside world. They felt a part of the crowd around the tree on the White House lawn as Winston Churchill continued to speak:

Therefore we may cast aside for this night at least, the cares and dangers which beset us, and make for the children an evening of happiness in a world of storm. Here, then, for one night only, each home in the English-speaking world should be a brightly lighted island of happiness and peace. Let the children have their night of fun and laughter—let the gifts of Christmas delight their play...these same children shall not be robbed of their right to live in a free and peaceful world.

And so, in God's mercy, a happy Christmas to you all.

Bun squealed and exclaimed over her presents, books, new clothes and a tiny real-china tea set. Jane was pleased with her music and high-heeled shoes. The happiest, most excited one of all was El as she opened a new, hard-backed, fully indexed Webster's Collegiate Dictionary. She opened it carefully, reading the pages aloud. "All rights reserved under International and Pan-American copyright conventions by G. & C. Merriam Co". She couldn't have been more pleased.

On Christmas Day, the first B-25 bombers rolled off the assembly line, thirteen days ahead of schedule, and Mary Beth had a letter from Ben. He wouldn't be home after all, because his hands were better. It seems a sailor had seen an explosion and had ordered Away Fire and Rescue Party, to which Ben had responded, bringing him and hundreds of others topside, giving them a few moments notice before the ship was hit. Those few seconds had saved his life, but not his ship. He would be staying in...for some time, helping with repairs, and how wonderful it was that he was the father of twins; the Red Cross had reached him with the news. There was no word about Will, but he would continue to search for him until something was learned for sure. It was a cryin' out loud shame Will had transferred to the...because the...received the least damage of all. The biggest thing I want you to realize is...

Nobody could guess what had been deleted by the censors of the mail.

The Army, Navy and Air Force Commanders had been replaced in Hawaii, and General Delos Emmons, a West Virginia boy from Huntington, had replaced General Short as Army Commander and Military Governor of the Hawaiian department, and the investigation got under way.

Tuesday, December thirtieth. General Arnold announced over the radio that Charles Lindbergh had volunteered for the Air Corps, but Roosevelt had refused him. Mother looked at Daddy, nodding her head emphatically, and "I told You so" reverberated through the room although not a word had been spoken. El, like Mother, wasn't surprised. She couldn't keep still.

"I knew he'd want to fight!" she exclaimed. "He wouldn't stay out of it!"

"Someday we'll study Lindbergh's words, and give him the credit he deserves," said Mother.

"What has he said that is so great!" said Daddy sarcastically.

Mother got up, went to her desk in the living room, and returned with a metal box of newspaper clippings. Extracting one, she adjusted her glasses and began to read:

"Democracy is not a quality that can be imposed by war...The strength of a democracy lies in the satisfaction of its own people. Its influence lies in making others wish to copy it. If we cannot make other nations wish to copy our American system of government, we cannot force them to copy it by going to war."

El was no longer listening. Her faith in her hero restored, she walked into the dark living room and looked out the window. It had started snowing, great oval flakes drifting downward in straight lines, no wind at all; the snow would pile up fast. By morning they could build a snowman. She pictured Hollie, making Eenny, Meeny, Miney—they never had made Mo. Tomorrow she would make the fourth snowman. Edgar was due back in the morning; he would help her. She could talk to him about Hollie, tell him about Lindbergh. Edgar would understand.

The snow was falling hard now, thick and white. The high black bridge was almost obscured from view; the mountains were only dark shadows stretching upward into the snow-filled sky, but she knew they were there. The mountains would always be there for her, no matter how far or how high she flew, and she was going to fly. That she knew. Maybe not alone, like Lindy, maybe only as an airline stewardess, but she would fly: she knew it.

CPSIA information can be obtained
at www.ICGtesting.com
Printed in the USA
LVHW081220310523
748422LV00006B/58